100 wild little weird tales

100 wild little weird tales

Selected by Robert Weinberg,
Stefan Dziemianowicz,
and Martin H. Greenberg

BARNES & NOBLE

NEW YORK

1994 Barnes & Noble Books

ISBN 1-5661-9557-8

Printed and bound in the United States of America

05 06 07 08 09 MC 9 8 7 6 5 4 3

Acknowledgments

Grateful acknowledgment is made to the following for permission to reprint their copyright materials:

"Anton's Last Dream" by Edwin Baird; "The Archfiend's Fingers" by Kirk Mashburn; "The Black Madonna" by A. W. Wyville; "The Boat on the Beach" by Kadra Maysi; "Burnt Things" by Robert C. Sandison; "The Church Stove at Raebrudafisk" by G. Appleby Terrill; "The Closed Door" by Harold Ward; "The Cripple" by Maurice Level; "The Death Mist" by Captain George H. Daugherty, Jr.; "Dream Justice" by E. W. Mayo; "A Dream of Death" by Andrew Daw; "The Dream of Death" by Elwood F. Pierce; "Eric Martin's Nemesis" by Jay Wilmer Benjamin; "Escape" by Paul Ernst; "Fidel Bassin" by W. J. Stamper; "The Finishing Touches" by Renier Wyers; "The Girdle" by Joseph McCord; "The Gloves" by Garnett Radcliffe; "The Harbor of Ghosts" by M. J. Bardine; "The Hate" by Wilford Allen; "The Haunted Wood of Adoure" by Elliot O'Donnell; "The Hidden Talent of Artist Bates" by Snowden T. Herrick; "His Brother's Keeper" by George Fielding Eliot; "In the Dark" by Ronal Kayser; "The Justice of the Czar" by Captain George Fielding Eliot; "The Last of Mrs. Debrugh" by H. Sivia; "The Late Mourner" by Julius Long; "The Man in the Taxi" by Leslie Gordon Barnard; "The Man Who Was Saved" by B. W. Sliney; "Masquerade" by Mearle Prout; "Murder Mask" by Edgar Daniel Kramer; "Night and Silence" by Maurice Level; "The Nightmare Road" by Florence Crow; "Nude with a Dagger" by John Flanders; "The Ocean Ogre" by Dana Carroll; "On Top" by Ralph Allen Lang; "One Chance" by Ethel Helene Coen; "The Pale Man" by Julius Long; "The Phantom Bus" by W. Elwyn Backus; "Rendezvous" by Richard H. Hart; "The Ring" by J. M. Fry; "Soul-Catcher" by Robert S. Carr; "Swamp Horror" by Will Smith and R. J. Robbins; "The Teakwood Box" by Johns Harrington; "The Unveiling" by Alfred I. Tooke; "The Violet Death" by Gustav Meyrink; "A Visitor from Far Away" by Loretta Burrough; "Warning Wings" by Arlton Eadie; "What Waits in Darkness" by Loretta

Contents

Introduction   XVII

Across the Gulf   1
Henry S. Whitehead

Alice and the Allergy   9
Fritz Leiber

Anton's Last Dream   16
Edwin Baird

The Archfiend's Fingers   23
Kirk Mashburn

Berenice   27
Edgar Allan Poe

The Black Madonna   34
A. W. Wyville

The Black Monk   37
G. G. Pendarves

The Boat on the Beach   44
Kadra Maysi

Burnt Things   50
Robert C. Sandison

Cat's Cradle   58
E. W. Tomlinson

THE CAVERN   63
MANLY WADE WELLMAN

THE CHAIN   70
H. WARNER MUNN

THE CHURCH STOVE AT RAEBRUDAFISK   78
G. APPLEBY TERRILL

THE CLOSED DOOR   85
HAROLD WARD

COUNTRY HOUSE   92
EWEN WHYTE

THE CRACKS OF TIME   99
DOROTHY QUICK

THE CRIPPLE   108
MAURICE LEVEL

CROSS OF FIRE   112
LESTER DEL REY

DARK ROSALEEN   119
SEABURY QUINN

THE DEATH MIST   127
CAPTAIN GEORGE H. DAUGHERTY, JR.

THE DISINTERMENT OF VENUS   131
CLARK ASHTON SMITH

THE DOOM THAT CAME TO SARNATH   138
H. P. LOVECRAFT

DREAM JUSTICE   143
E. W. MAYO

A DREAM OF DEATH   145
ANDREW DAW

THE DREAM OF DEATH   150
ELWOOD F. PIERCE

ERIC MARTIN'S NEMESIS   154
JAY WILMER BENJAMIN

ESCAPE   161
PAUL ERNST

THE EXTRA PASSENGER   167
STEPHEN GRENDON

THE FEAST IN THE ABBEY   174
ROBERT BLOCH

FIDEL BASSIN   180
W. J. STAMPER

THE FIFTH CANDLE   187
CYRIL MAND

THE FINISHING TOUCHES   194
RENIER WYERS

A GIPSY PROPHECY   199
BRAM STOKER

THE GIRDLE   207
JOSEPH MCCORD

THE GLOVES   212
GARNETT RADCLIFFE

THE HARBOR OF GHOSTS   217
M. J. BARDINE

THE HATE   224
WILFORD ALLEN

THE HAUNTED WOOD OF ADOURE   226
ELLIOT O'DONNELL

THE HIDDEN TALENT OF ARTIST BATES   234
SNOWDEN T. HERRICK

THE HIGH PLACES   239
FRANCES GARFIELD

HIS BROTHER'S KEEPER   244
CAPTAIN GEORGE FIELDING ELIOT

THE HUNCH   247
GENE LYLE III

HYPNOS   251
H. P. LOVECRAFT

I CAN'T WEAR WHITE   257
SUZANNE PICKETT

IN THE DARK   264
RONAL KAYSER

THE IRON HANDS OF KATZAVEERE   269
DAVID EYNON

THE JAPANESE TEA SET   276
FRANCIS J. O'NEIL

THE JUSTICE OF THE CZAR   283
CAPTAIN GEORGE FIELDING ELIOT

THE LAST DRIVE   289
CARL JACOBI

THE LAST INCANTATION   293
CLARK ASHTON SMITH

THE LAST MAN   297
SEABURY QUINN

THE LAST OF MRS. DEBRUGH   306
H. SIVIA

THE LATE MOURNER   310
JULIUS LONG

THE MAN IN THE TAXI   313
LESLIE GORDON BARNARD

THE MAN WHO WAS SAVED   316
B. W. SLINEY

MASQUERADE   323
MEARLE PROUT

MR. BAUER AND THE ATOMS   328
FRITZ LEIBER

MUGGRIDGE'S AUNT   334
AUGUST W. DERLETH

MURDER MAN   340
EWEN WHYTE

MURDER MASK   348
EDGAR DANIEL KRAMER

THE MURDERER   355
MURRAY LEINSTER

NIGHT AND SILENCE   361
MAURICE LEVEL

THE NIGHTMARE ROAD   365
FLORENCE CROW

NO EYE-WITNESSES   370
HENRY S. WHITEHEAD

NUDE WITH A DAGGER   378
JOHN FLANDERS

THE OCEAN OGRE   381
DANA CARROLL

OFF THE MAP   389
REX DOLPHIN

ON TOP   397
RALPH ALLEN LANG

ONE CHANCE   400
ETHEL HELENE COEN

THE OTHER SANTA   401
THORP MCCLUSKY

A PAIR OF SWORDS   409
CARL JACOBI

THE PALE MAN   412
JULIUS LONG

PARTHENOPE   418
MANLY WADE WELLMAN

THE PHANTOM BUS   422
W. ELWYN BACKUS

RENDEZVOUS   427
RICHARD H. HART

THE RING   433
J. M. FRY

THE SEALED CASKET   440
RICHARD F. SEARIGHT

THE SEEDS FROM OUTSIDE   446
EDMOND HAMILTON

THE SIXTH GARGOYLE   450
DAVID EYNON

SOUL-CATCHER   457
ROBERT S. CARR

THE STATUE   464
JAMES CAUSEY

THE STRANGER FROM KURDISTAN   472
E. HOFFMAN PRICE

SWAMP HORROR   478
WILL SMITH AND R. J. ROBBINS

TAKE THE Z TRAIN   487
ALLISON V. HARDING

THE TEAKWOOD BOX   493
JOHNS HARRINGTON

THESE DOTH THE LORD HATE   498
MANLY WADE WELLMAN

THINKER   503
MALCOLM KENNETH MURCHIE

THRESHOLD OF ENDURANCE   510
BETSY EMMONS

TOP OF THE WORLD   512
TARLETON COLLIER

THE TREE OF LIFE   517
PAUL ERNST

THE TRYST IN THE TOMB   522
M. J. CAIN

UNDER THE EAVES   527
HELEN M. REID

THE UNVEILING   530
ALFRED I. TOOKE

THE VIOLET DEATH   534
GUSTAV MEYRINK

A VISITOR FROM FAR AWAY   539
LORETTA BURROUGH

WARNING WINGS   545
ARLTON EADIE

WHAT WAITS IN DARKNESS   551
LORETTA BURROUGH

WHEN THE SEA GIVES UP ITS DEAD   557
ROBERT PEERY

THE WITCH-BAITER   565
R. ANTHONY

THE WITCH-BALL   572
E. F. BENSON

INTRODUCTION

The term *weird tales* describes not only a type of fiction, but a special magazine that was created to showcase it. Published between 1923 and 1954, *Weird Tales* was the first publication of its kind, a magazine devoted exclusively to horror and fantasy fiction. Although one of numerous popular "pulp" fiction magazines that glutted newsstands during the first half of this century, it performed a function that set it apart from its few competitors and many imitators: in its pages, the weird tale was transformed from a type of story that followed the guidelines set down for gothic fiction over a century before into a fiction of thrills and chills that could accommodate an ever-expanding universe of themes or styles.

Weird Tales achieved this through its commitment and diversity. Over the course of its 279 issues it published several thousand stories by several hundred authors, each of whom tried to tell tales never told before in ways never tried before. With such a ferment of imagination in the magazine, it was inevitable that *Weird Tales* would attract the best and brightest writers of the several generations it served. So it was that *Weird Tales* became the home for H. P. Lovecraft's tales of extradimensional horror, Clark Ashton Smith's lyrical chronicles of nonexistent fantasy worlds, Robert Bloch's sardonic tales of just desserts, Seabury Quinn's blends of the detective and terror tales in his exploits of occult investigator Jules de Grandin, E. Hoffmann Price's retelling of Eastern myths and legends, Manly Wade Wellman's tales of southern folklore, Henry S. Whitehead's explorations of the mysteries of the West Indies, Edmond Hamilton's weird-science fantasies, and Fritz Leiber's modern updates of conventional gothic horrors, to name but a few of its more distinguished contributors.

Weird Tales encouraged diversity not only in the content of its fiction, but in its form as well. From its first issue, it established a policy of publishing tales varying in length from the short novel to what it dubbed the "five-minute" tale. Although it is most renowned today for its short stories and novellas, it also presented readers with many memorable short-short stories. Virtually all of the magazine's best-known contributors took respite from their usual duties to write at least one compact weird tale. They were joined by a multitude of other writers whose handful of stories or single sale in the short-short form are all they are remembered by today. In their representation of *Weird Tales* authors and the variety of themes they tackled, the short-short stories gathered into 100 *Wild Little Weird Tales* can be read as a good index to what *Weird Tales* was all about.

Virtually every theme synonymous with weird fiction was rendered in short-short form in *Weird Tales:* the vampire in traditional guise in Florence Crow's "The Nightmare Road" and in a more unconventional form in Richard F. Searight's "The Sealed Casket," the ghost in Henry S. Whitehead's "Across the Gulf" and G. G. Pendarve's "The Black Monk," witchcraft in R. Anthony's "The Witch-Baiter," the magic talisman in J. M. Fry's "The Ring" and Johns Harrington's "The Teakwood Box," the psychopath in Ewen Whyte's "Country House," the family curse in Cyril Mand's "The Fifth Candle," and the good old-fashioned monster in Will Smith and R. J. Robbins's "Swamp Horror." One of the most popular short-short story types was the *conte cruel,* a nonsupernatural tale concerned with the fundamental cruelty either of humanity or of fate, and typified by H. Warner Munn's "The Chain," G. Appleby Terrill's "The Church Stove at Raebrudafisk," and a pair by Captain George Fielding Eliot, "The Justice of the Czar" and "His Brother's Keeper."

Approaches to the short-short weird tale ranged widely. In one issue of the magazine readers might find a resurgence of the gothic in the purple prose of Kirk Mashburn's "The Archfiend's Fingers," and in another the contemporary American vernacular of Tarleton Collier's "Top of the World," which branded the story as the product of a specific place and time. Clark Ashton Smith's "The Last Incantation" and H. P. Lovecraft's "The Doom that Came to Sarnath" are examples of how authors intensified the atmosphere of their stories by cultivating a stylized prose form appropriate for their arcane horrors. There was even room for whimsy that softened the supernatural in the gentle fantasy of Thorp McClusky's "The Other Santa," or sharpened it in the outright comedy of Snowden T. Herrick's "The Hidden Talent of Artist Bates."

In addition to publishing the best of contemporary weird fiction, *Weird Tales* pursued an agenda of introducing readers to classics of weird fiction, many in the short-short story form. In this way, readers were able to trace the line of descent to pulp weird fiction from the work of Edgar Allan Poe ("Berenice"), translations of nineteenth-century Austrian fantasist Gustav Meyrink ("The Violet Death") and French realist Maurice Level ("The Cripple," "Night and Silence"), and even Edwardian ghost-story writer E. F. Benson ("The Witch-Ball"), several of whose stories received their first American publication in the magazine's pages.

But the short-short story in *Weird Tales* served primarily as the means by which hitherto unknown writers made their entry into the weird-fiction market and, in some cases, established themselves as leading practitioners. August W. Derleth sold his first short-short story to *Weird Tales* in 1926, and perfected the form through "Muggridge's Aunt," "The Extra Passenger" (written under his Stephen Grendon pseudonym), and scores of others that made him one of the magazine's most prolific contributors. Robert Bloch's "The Feast in the Abbey" is that rarest of short-short stories, a first professional appearance (published when he was only seventeen) so demonstrative of its author's talents that it has become a classic in its own right.

Although several of the stories collected here will be familiar to both devoted and occasional readers of weird fiction, most appear for the first time since their initial magazine publication. Their breadth of imagination demonstrates why *Weird Tales* had such a tremendous impact on the development of weird fiction in the twentieth century. It is nearly impossible to generalize about such a varied collection, except to say that all these stories prove that good things—which, in the case of weird fiction, is to say *bad* things— sometimes come in small packages.

—Stefan Dziemianowicz
New York, 1994

100
Wild Little
Weird Tales

Across the Gulf

Henry S. Whitehead

For the first year, or thereabouts, after his Scotch mother's death the successful lawyer Alan Carrington was conscious, among his other feelings, of a kind of vague dread that she might appear as a character in one of his dreams, as, she had often assured him, her mother had come to her. Being the man he was, he resented this feeling as an incongruity. Yet, there was a certain background for the feeling of dread. It had been one of his practical mother's convictions that such an appearance of her long-dead mother always preceded a disaster in the family.

Such aversions as he might possess against the maternal side of his ancestry were all included in his dislike for belief in this kind of thing. When he agreed that "the Scotch are a dour race," he always had reference, at least mentally, to this superstitious strain, associated with that race from time immemorial, concrete to his experience because of this belief of his mother's, against which he had always fought.

He carried out dutifully, and with a high degree of professional skill, all her various expressed desires, and continued, after her death, to live in their large, comfortable house. Perhaps because his mother never did appear in such dreams as he happened to remember, his dread became less and less poignant. At the end of two years or so, occupied with the thronging interests of a public man in the full power of his early maturity, it had almost ceased to be so much as a memory.

In the spring of his forty-fourth year, Carrington, who had long worked at high pressure and virtually without vacations, was apprized by certain mental and physical indications which his physician interpreted vigorously, that he must take at least the whole summer off and devote himself to recuperation. Rest, said the doctor, for his overworked mind and under-exercised body, was imperatively indicated.

Carrington was able to set his nearly innumerable interests and affairs in order in something like three weeks by means of highly concentrated efforts to that end. Then, exceedingly nervous, and not a little debilitated physically from this extra strain upon his depleted resources, he had to meet the problem of where he was to go and what he was to do. He was, of course, too deeply set in the rut of his routines to find such a decision easy. Fortunately, this problem was solved for him by a letter which he received unexpectedly from one of his cousins on his mother's side, the Reverend Fergus MacDonald, a gentleman with whom he had had only slight contacts.

Dr. MacDonald was a middle-aged, retired clergyman, whom an imminent decline had removed eight or ten years before from a brilliant, if underpaid, career in his own profession. After a few years sojourn in the Adirondacks he had emerged cured, and with an already growing reputation as a writer of that somewhat inelastic literary product emphasized by certain American magazines which seem to embalm a spinsterish austerity of the literary form under the label of distinction.

Dr. MacDonald had retained a developed pastoral instinct which he could no longer satisfy in the management of a parish. He was, besides, too little robust to risk assuming, at least for some time to come, the wearing burden of teaching. He compromised the matter by establishing a summer camp for boys in his still-desirable Adirondacks. Being devoid of experience in business matters he associated with himself a certain Thomas Starkey, a young man whom the ravages of the White Plague had snatched away from a sales-managership and driven into the quasi-exile of Saranac, where Dr. MacDonald had met him.

This association proved highly successful for the half-dozen years that it had lasted. Then Starkey, after a brave battle for his health, had succumbed, just at a period when his trained business intelligence would have been most helpful to the affairs of the camp.

Dazed at this blow, Dr. MacDonald had desisted from his labors after literary distinction long enough to write to his cousin Carrington, beseeching his legal and financial counsel. When Carrington had read the last of his cousin's finished periods, he decided at once, and dispatched a telegram announcing his immediate setting out for the camp, his intention to remain through the summer, and the promise to assume full charge of the business management. He started for the Adirondacks the next afternoon.

His presence brought immediate order out of confusion. Dr. MacDonald, on the evening of the second day of his cousin's administration of affairs, got down on his knees and returned thanks to his Maker for the undeserved beneficence which had sent this financial angel of light into the midst of his affairs, in this, his hour of dire need! Thereafter the reverend doctor immersed himself more and more deeply in his wonted task of producing the solid literature dear to the hearts of his editors.

But if Carrington's coming had improved matters at the camp, the balance of indebtedness was far from being one-sided. For the first week or so the reaction from his accustomed way of life had caused him to feel, if anything, even staler and more nerve-racked than before. But that first unpleasantness past, the invigorating air of the balsam-laden pine woods began to show its restorative effects rapidly. He found that he was sleeping like the dead. He could not get enough sleep, it appeared. His appetite increased, and he found that he was putting on needed weight. The business management of a boys' camp, absurdly simple after the complex matters of Big Business with which he had long been occupied, was only a spice to this new existence among the deep shadows and sunny spaces of the Adirondack country. At the end of a month of this, he confidently declared himself a new man. By the first of August, instead of the nervous wreck who had arrived, sharp-visaged and cadaverous, two months before, Carrington presented the appearance of a robust, hard-muscled athlete of thirty, twenty-two pounds heavier and "without a nerve in his body."

On the evening of the fourth day of August, healthily weary after a long day's hike, Carrington retired soon after 9 o'clock, and fell immediately into a deep and restful sleep. Toward morning he dreamed of his mother for the first time since her death more than six years before. His dream took the form that he was lying here, in his own bed, awake, — a not altogether uncommon form of dream, — and that he was very chilly in the region of the left shoulder. As is well-known to those skilled in the scientific phenomena of the dream-state, now a very prominent portion of the material used in psychological study, this kind of sensation in a dream virtually always is the result of an actual physical condition, and is reproduced in the dream because of that actual background as a stimulus. Carrington's cold shoulder was toward the left-hand, or outside of the bed, which stood against the wall of his large, airy room.

In his dream he thought that he reached out his hand to replace the bed clothes, and as he did so his hand was softly, though firmly, taken, and his mother's well-remembered voice said: "Lie still, laddie; I'll tuck you in." Then he thought his mother replaced the loosened covers and tucked them in about his shoulder with her competent touch. He wanted to thank her, and as he could not see her because of the position in which he was lying, he endeavored to open his eyes and turn over, being in that state commonly thought of as between sleep and waking. With some considerable effort he succeeded in forcing open his reluctant eyes; but turning over was a much more difficult matter, it appeared. He had to fight against an overpowering inclination to sink back comfortably into the deep sleep, from which, in his dream, he had awakened to find his shoulder disagreeably uncomfortable. The warmth of the replaced covers was an additional inducement to sleep.

At last, with a determined wrench he overcame his desire to go to sleep again and rolled over to his left side by dint of a strong effort of his will, smiling gratefully and about to express his thanks. But at the instant of accomplishing this victory of the will, he actually awakened, in precisely the position recorded in his mind in the dream-state.

Where he had expected to meet his mother's eyes, he saw nothing, but there remained with him a persistent impression that he had felt the withdrawal of her hand from where, on his shoulder, it had rested caressingly. The grateful warmth of the bedclothes in that cool morning remained, however, and he observed that they were well tucked in about that shoulder.

His dream had clearly been of the type which George Du Maurier speaks of in *Peter Ibbetson*. He had "dreamed true," and it required several minutes before he could rid himself of the impression that his mother, moved by some strange whimsicality, had stepped out of his sight, perhaps hidden herself behind the bed! He was actually about to look back of the bed before the utter absurdity of the idea became fully apparent to him. The back of the bed stood close against the wall of the room. His mother had been dead more than six years.

He jumped out of bed at the sound of reveillé, blown by the camp bugler, and this abrupt action dissipated his impressions. Their memory remained, however, very clear-cut in his mind for the next two days. The impression of his mother's nearness in the course of that vivid dream had recalled her to his mind with the greatest clarity. With this revived impression of her, too, there marched, almost of necessity he supposed, in his mind the old idea which he had dreaded,—the idea that she would come to him to warn him of some impending danger.

Curiously enough, as he analyzed his sensations, he found that there remained none of the old resentment connected with this speculation, such as had characterized it during the period immediately after his mother's death. His maturity, the preoccupations of an exceptionally full and active life, and the tenderness which marked all his memories of his mother had served to remove from his mind all traces of that idea. The possibility of a "warning" in his dream of his dear mother only caused him to smile during those days after the dream during which the revived impression of his mother slowly faded thin, but it was the indulgent, slightly melancholy smile of a revived nostalgia, a gentle, faint sense of "homesickness" for her, such as might affect any middle-aged man recently reminded of a beloved mother in some rather intense fashion.

On the evening of the second day after his dream he was walking toward the camp garage with some visitors, a man and woman, parents of one of the boys at the camp, intending to drive with them to the village to guide them in some minor purchases. Just beside the well-worn trail through the great pine trees, half-way up the hill to the garage, the woman noticed a clump of large, brownish mushrooms, and enquired if they were of an edible variety. Carrington picked one and examined it. To his limited knowledge it seemed to have several of the marks of an edible mushroom. While they were standing beside the place where the mushrooms grew, one of the younger boys passed them.

"Crocker," called Mr. Carrington.

"Yes, Mr. Carrington," replied young Crocker, pausing.

"Crocker, your cabin is the one farthest south, isn't it?"

"Yes, sir."

"Were you going there just now?"

"Yes, Mr. Carrington; can I do anything for you?"

"Well, if it isn't too much trouble, you might take this mushroom over to Professor Benjamin's—you know where his camp is, just the other side of the wire fence beyond your cabin,—and ask him to let us know whether or not this is an edible mushroom. I'm not quite sure myself."

"Certainly," replied the boy, pleased to be allowed "out of bounds" even to the extent of the few rods separating the camp property from that of the gentleman named by Carrington, a university teacher regarded locally as a great expert on mushrooms, fungi, and suchlike things.

Carrington called after the disappearing boy.

"Oh, Crocker!"

"Yes, Mr. Carrington?"

"Throw it away if Dr. Benjamin says it's no good; but if he says it's all right, bring it back, please, and leave it on the mantel-shelf in the big living room. Do you mind?"

"All right, sir," shouted Crocker over his shoulder, and trotted on.

* * *

Returning from the village an hour later, Carrington found the mushroom on the mantel-shelf in the living room.

He placed it in a large paper bag, left it in the kitchen in a safe place, and, the next morning before breakfast, walked up the trail toward the garage and filled his paper bag with mushrooms.

He liked mushrooms, and so, doubtless, did the people who had noticed these. He decided he would prepare the mushrooms himself. There would be just about enough for three generous portions. Mushrooms were not commonly eaten as a breakfast dish, but,— this was camp!

Exchanging a pleasant "good morning" with the young colored man who served as assistant cook, and who was engaged in getting breakfast ready, and smilingly declining his offer to prepare the mushrooms, he peeled them, warmed a generous lump of fresh, country butter in a large frying pan, and began cooking them.

A delightfully appetizing odor arising from the pan provoked respectful banter from the young cook, amused at the camp-director's efforts along the lines of his own profession, and the two chatted while Carrington turned his mushrooms over and over in the butter with a long fork. When they were done exactly to a turn, and duly peppered and salted, Carrington left them in the pan, which he took off the stove, and set about the preparation of three *canapés* of fried toast. He was going to serve his mushrooms in style, as the grinning young cook slyly remarked. He grinned back, and divided the mushrooms into three equal portions, each on its *canapé*, which he asked the under-cook to keep hot in the oven during the brief interval until mess call should bring everybody at camp in to breakfast.

Then with his long fork he speared several small pieces of mushroom which had got broken in the pan. After blowing these cool on the fork, Carrington, grinning like a boy, put them into his mouth and began to eat them.

"Good, suh?" enquired the assistant cook.

"Delicious," mumbled Carrington, enthusiastically, his mouth full of the succulent bits. After he had swallowed his mouthful, he remarked:

"But I must have left a bit of the hide on one of 'em. There's a little trace of bitter."

"Look out for 'em, suh," enjoined the under-cook, suddenly grave. "They're plumb wicked when they ain't jus' right, suh."

"These are all right," returned Carrington, reassuringly. "I had Professor Benjamin look them over."

He sauntered out on the veranda, waiting for the bugle call. From many directions the boys and a few visitors were straggling in toward the mess hall after a morning dip in the lake and cabin

6

inspection. From their room in the guest house the people with whom he had been the evening before came across the broad veranda toward him. He was just turning toward them with a smile of pleasant greeting when the very hand of death fell on him.

Without warning, a sudden terrible griping, accompanied by a deadly coldness, and this immediately followed by a pungent, burning heat, ran through his body. Great beads of sweat sprang out on his forehead. His knees began to give under him. Everything, all this pleasant world about him, of brilliant morning sunshine and deep, sharply-defined shadow, turned greenish and dim. His senses started to slip away from him in the numbness which closed down like a relentless hand, crushing out his consciousness.

With an effort which seemed to wrench his soul and tear him with unimagined pain, he gathered all his waning forces, and, sustained only by a mighty effort of his powerful will, he staggered through the open doorway of the mess hall into the kitchen. He nearly collapsed as he leaned against the nearest table, articulating between fast-paralyzing lips:

"Water,—and mustard! Quick. The mushrooms!"

The head-cook, that moment arrived in the kitchen, happened to be quick-minded. The under-cook, too, had had, of course, some preparation for this possibility.

One of the men seized a bowl just used for beating eggs and with shaking hands poured it half-full of warm water from a heating kettle on the stove. Into this the other emptied nearly half a tin of dry mustard which he stirred about frantically with his floury hand. This, his eyes rolling with terror, he held to Carrington's lips, and Carrington, concentrating afresh all his remaining faculties, forced the nauseous fluid through his blue lips, and swallowed, painfully, great saving gulps of the powerful emetic.

Again and yet again the two negroes renewed the dose.

One of the counselors, on dining room duty, coming into the kitchen sensed something terribly amiss, and ran to support Carrington.

Ten minutes later, vastly nauseated, trembling with weakness, but safe, Carrington, leaning heavily on the young counselor, walked up and down behind the mess hall. His first words, after he could speak coherently, were to order the assistant cook to burn the contents of the three hot plates in the oven. . . .

He had eaten a large mouthful of one of the most deadly varieties of poisonous mushroom, one containing the swiftly-acting vegetable alkaloids which spell certain death. His few moments' respite, as he reasoned the matter out afterward, had been undoubtedly due to his having cooked the mushrooms in butter, of which he had been lavish. This, thoroughly soaked up by the mushrooms, had, for a brief period, resisted digestion.

Very gradually, as he walked up and down, taking in deep breaths of the sweet, pine-scented air, his strength returned to him. After he had thoroughly walked off the faintness which had followed the violent treatment to which he had subjected himself, he went up to his room, and, still terribly shaken by his experience and narrow escape from death, went to bed to rest.

Crocker, it appeared, had duly carried out his instructions. Dr. Benjamin had looked at the specimen and told the boy that there were several varieties of this mushroom, not easily to be distinguished from one another, of which some were wholesome, and one contained a deadly alkaloid. Being otherwise occupied at the time, he would have to defer his opinion until he had had an opportunity for a more thorough examination. He had handed back the mushroom submitted to him and the lad had given it to a counselor, who had put it on the mantel-shelf intending to report to Mr. Carrington the following morning.

Weak still, and very drowsy, Carrington lay on his bed and silently thanked the Powers above for having preserved his life.

Abruptly he thought of his mother. The warning!

At once it was as though she stood in the room beside his bed; as though their long, close companionship had not been interrupted by death.

A wave of affectionate gratitude suffused him. Under its influence he rose, wearily, and sank to his knees beside the bed, his head on his arms, in the very spot where his mother had seemed to stand in his dream.

Tears welled into his eyes, and fell, unnoticed, as he communed silently with her who had brought him into the world, whose watchful love and care not even death could interrupt or vitiate.

Silently, fervently, he spoke across the gulf to his mother. . . .

He choked with silent sobs as understanding of her invincible love came to him and overwhelmed him. Then, to the accompaniment of a tremulous calmness which seemed to fall upon him abruptly, he had the sense of her, standing close beside him, as she had stood in his dream. He dared not raise his eyes, because now he knew that he was awake. It seemed to him as though she spoke, though there came to him no sensation of anything that could be compared to sound.

"Ye must be getting back into your bed, laddie."

And keeping his eyes tightly shut, lest he disturb this visitation, he awkwardly fumbled his way back into bed. He settled himself on

8

his back, and an overpowering drowziness, perhaps begotten of his recent shock and its attendant bodily weakness, ran through him like a benediction and a refreshing wind.

As he drifted down over the threshold of consciousness into the deep and prolonged sleep of physical exhaustion which completely restored him, his last remembrance was of the lingering caress of his mother's firm hand resting on his shoulder. ——

ALICE AND THE ALLERGY

FRITZ LEIBER

There was a knocking. The doctor put down his pen. Then he heard his wife hurrying down the stairs. He resumed his history of old Mrs. Easton's latest blood-clot.

The knocking was repeated. He reminded himself to get after Engstrand to fix the bell.

After a pause long enough for him to write a sentence and a half, there came a third and louder burst of knocking. He frowned and got up.

It was dark in the hall. Alice was standing on the third step from the bottom, making no move to answer the door. As he went past her he shot her an inquiring glance. He noted that her eyelids looked slightly puffy, as if she were having another attack—an impression which the hoarseness of her voice a moment later confirmed.

"*He* knocked that way," was what she whispered. She sounded frightened. He looked back at her with an expression of greater puzzlement—which almost immediately, however, changed to comprehension. He gave her a sympathetic, semi-professional nod, as if to say, "I understand now. Glad you mentioned it. We'll talk about it later." Then he opened the door.

It was Renshaw from the Allergy Lab. "Got the new kit for you, Howard," he remarked in an amiable Southern drawl. "Finished making it up this afternoon and thought I'd bring it around myself."

"A million thanks. Come on in."

Alice had retreated a few steps farther up the stairs. Renshaw did not appear to notice her in the gloom. He was talkative as he followed Howard into his office.

"An interestin' case turned up. Very unusual. A doctor we supply lost a patient by broncho-spasm. Nurse mistakenly injected the shot

9

into a vein. In ten seconds he was strangling. Edema of the glottis developed. Injected aminophylline and epinephrine—no dice. Tried to get a bronchoscope down his windpipe to give him air, but couldn't manage. Finally did a tracheotomy, but by that time it was too late."

"You always have to be damned careful," Howard remarked.

"Right," Renshaw agreed cheerfully. He set the kit on the desk and stepped back. "Well, if we don't identify the substance responsible for your wife's allergy this time, it won't be for lack of imagination. I added some notions of my own to your suggestions."

"Good."

"You know, she's well on her way to becoming the toughest case I ever made kits for. We've tested all the ordinary substances, and most of the extraordinary."

Howard nodded, his gaze following the dark woodwork toward the hall door. "Look," he said, "do many doctors tell you about allergy patients showing fits of acute depression during attacks, a tendency to rake up unpleasant memories—especially old fears?"

"Depression seems to be a pretty common symptom," said Renshaw cautiously. "Let's see, how long is it she's been bothered?"

"About two years—ever since six months after our marriage." Howard smiled. That arouses certain obvious suspicions, but you know how exhaustively we've tested myself, my clothes, my professional equipment."

"I should say so," Renshaw assured him. For a moment the men were silent. Then, "She suffers from depression and fear?"

Howard nodded.

"Fear of anything in particular?"

But Howard did not answer that question.

About ten minutes later, as the outside door closed on the man from the Allergy Lab, Alice came slowly down the stairs.

The puffiness around her eyes was more marked, emphasizing her paleness. Her eyes were still fixed on the door.

"You know Renshaw, of course," her husband said.

"Of course, dear," she answered huskily, with a little laugh. "It was just the knocking. It made me remember *him*."

"That so?" Howard inquired cheerily. "I don't think you've ever told me that detail. I'd always assumed—"

"No," she said, "the bell to Auntie's house was out of order that afternoon. So it was his knocking that drew me through the dark hallway and made me open the door, so that I saw his white avid face and long strong hands—with the big dusty couch just behind me, where . . . and my hand on the curtain sash, with which he—"

"Don't think about it." Howard reached up and caught hold of her cold hand. "That chap's been dead for two years now. He'll strangle no more women."

"Are you sure?" she asked.

"Of course. Look, dear, Renshaw's brought a new kit. We'll make the scratch tests right away."

She followed him obediently into the examination room across the hall from the office. He rejected the forearm she offered him—it still showed faint evidences of the last test. As he swabbed off the other, he studied her face.

"Another little siege, eh? Well, we'll ease that with a mild ephedrine spray."

"Oh it's nothing," she said. "I wouldn't mind it at all if it weren't for those stupid moods that go with it."

"I know," he said, blocking out the test areas.

"I always have that idiotic feeling," she continued hesitantly, "that *he's* trying to get at me."

Ignoring her remark, he picked up the needle. They were both silent as he worked with practiced speed and care. Finally he sat back, remarking with considerably more confidence than he felt, "There! I bet you this time we've nailed the elusive little demon who likes to choke you!"—and looked up at the face of the slim, desirable, but sometimes maddeningly irrational person he had made his wife.

"I wonder if you've considered it from my point of view," he said, smiling. "I know it was a horrible experience, just about the worst a woman can undergo. But if it hadn't happened, I'd never have been called in to take care of you—and we'd never have got married."

"That's true," she said, putting her hand on his.

"It was completely understandable that you should have spells of fear afterwards," he continued. "Anyone would. Though I do think your background made a difference. After all, your Aunt kept you so shut away from people—men especially. Told you they were all sadistic, evil-minded brutes. You know, sometimes when I think of that woman deliberately trying to infect you with all her rotten fears, I find myself on the verge of forgetting that she was no more responsible for her actions than any other miseducated neurotic."

She smiled at him gratefully.

"At any rate," he went on, "it was perfectly natural that you should be frightened, especially when you learned that he was a murderer with a record, who had killed other women and had even, in two cases where he'd been interrupted, made daring efforts to come back and complete the job. Knowing that about him, it was plain realism on your part to be scared—at least intelligently apprehensive—as long as he was on the loose. Even after we were married.

"But then, when you got incontrovertible proof—" He fished in his pocket. "Of course, he didn't formally pay the law's penalty, but he's just as dead as if he had." He smoothed out a worn old newspaper clipping. "You can't have forgotten this," he said gently, and began to read:

MYSTERY STRANGLER
UNMASKED BY DEATH

Lansing, Dec. 22. (Universal Press)—A mysterious boarder who died two days ago at a Kinsey Street rooming house has been conclusively identified as the uncaught rapist and strangler who in recent years terrified three Midwestern cities. Police Lieutenant Jim Galeto, interviewed by reporters in the death room at 1555 Kinsey Street . . .

She covered the clipping with her hand. "Please."

"Sorry," he said, "but an idea had occurred to me—one that would explain your continuing fear. I don't think you've ever hinted at it, but are you really completely satisfied that this was the man? Or is there a part of your mind that still doubts, that believes the police mistaken, that pictures the killer still at large? I know you identified the photographs, but sometimes, Alice, I think it was a mistake that you didn't go to Lansing like they wanted you to and see with your own eyes—"

"I wouldn't want to go near that city, ever." Her lips had thinned.

"But when your peace of mind was at stake. . . ."

"No, Howard," she said. "And besides, you're absolutely wrong. From the first moment I never had the slightest doubt that *he* was the man who died—"

"But in that case—"

"And furthermore, it was only then, when my allergy started, that I really began to be afraid of him."

"But surely, Alice—" Calm substituted for anger in his manner. "Oh, I know you can't believe any of that occult rot your aunt was always falling for."

"No, I don't," she said. "It's something very different."

"What?"

But that question was not answered. Alice was looking down at the inside of her arm. He followed her gaze to where a white welt was rapidly filling one of the squares.

"What's it mean?" she asked nervously.

"Mean?" he almost yelled. "Why, you little dope, it means we've licked the thing at last! It means we've found the substance that causes your allergy. I'll call Renshaw right away and have him make up the shots."

He picked up one of the vials, frowned, checked it against the area. "That's odd," he said. "HOUSEHOLD DUST. We've tried that a half dozen times. But then, of course, it's always different. . . ."

"Howard," she said, "I don't like it. I'm frightened."

He looked at her lovingly. "The little dope," he said to her softly. "She's about to be cured—and she's frightened." And he hugged her. She was cold in his arms.

But by the time they sat down to dinner, things were more like normal. The puffiness had gone out of her eyelids and he was briskly smiling.

"Got hold of Renshaw. He was very 'interested.' HOUSEHOLD DUST was one of his ideas. He's going down to the Lab tonight and will have the shots over early tomorrow. The sooner we start, the better. I also took the opportunity to phone Engstrand. He'll try to get over to fix the bell, this evening. Heard from Mrs. Easton's nurse too. Things aren't so well there. I'm pretty sure there'll be bad news by tomorrow morning at latest. I may have to rush over any minute. I hope it doesn't happen tonight, though."

It didn't and they spent a quiet evening—not even Engstrand showed up—which could have been very pleasant had Alice been a bit less pre-occupied.

But about three o'clock he was shaken out of sleep by her trembling. She was holding him tight.

"He's coming." Her whisper was whistly, laryngitic.

"What?" He sat up, half pulling her with him. "I'd better give you another eph—"

"Sh! What's that? Listen."

He rubbed his face. "Look Alice," after a moment, he said, "I'll go downstairs and make sure there's nothing there."

"No, don't!" she clung to him. For a minute or two they huddled there without speaking. Gradually his ears became attuned to the night sounds—the drone and mumble of the city, the house's faint, closer creakings. Something had happened to the street lamp and incongruous unmixed moonlight streamed through the window beyond the foot of the bed.

He was about to say something, when she let go of him and said, in a more normal voice, "There. It's gone."

She slipped out of bed, went to the window, opened it wider, and stood there, breathing deeply.

"You'll get cold, come back to bed," he told her.

"In a while."

The moonlight was in key with her flimsy nightgown. He got up, rummaged around for her quilted bathrobe and, in draping it around her, tried an embrace. She didn't respond.

He got back in bed and watched her. She had found a chair-arm and was looking out the window. The bathrobe had fallen back from her shoulders. He felt wide awake, his mind crawlingly active.

"You know, Alice," he said, "there may be a psychoanalytic angle to your fear."

"Yes?" She did not turn her head.

"Maybe, in a sense, your libido is still tied to the past. Unconsciously, you may still have that distorted conception of sex your aunt drilled into you, something sadistic and murderous. And it's possible your unconscious mind had tied your allergy in with it — you said it was a dusty couch. See what I'm getting at?"

She still looked out the window.

"It's an ugly idea and of course your conscious mind wouldn't entertain it for a moment, but your aunt's influence set the stage and, when all's said and done, *he* was your first experience of men. Maybe in some small way, your libido is still linked to . . . him."

She didn't say anything.

Rather late next morning he awoke feeling sluggish and irritable. He got out of the room quietly, leaving her still asleep, breathing easily. As he was getting a second cup of coffee, a jarringly loud knocking summoned him to the door. It was a messenger with the shots from the Allergy Lab. On his way to the examination room he phoned Engstrand again, heard him promise he'd be over in a half hour sure, cut short a long-winded explanation as to what had tied up the electrician last night.

He started to phone Mrs. Easton's place, decided against it.

He heard Alice in the kitchen.

In the examination room he set some water to boil in the sterilizing pan, got out instruments. He opened the package from the Allergy Lab, frowned at the inscription HOUSEHOLD DUST, set down the container, walked over to the window, came back and frowned again, went to his office and dialed the Lab.

"Renshaw?"

"Uh huh. Get the shots?"

"Yes, many thanks. But I was just wondering . . . you know, it's rather odd we should hit it with household dust after so many misses."

"Not so odd, when you consider . . ."

"Yes, but I was wondering exactly where the stuff came from."

"Just a minute."

He shifted around in his swivel chair. In the kitchen Alice was humming a tune.

"Say, Howard, look. I'm awfully sorry, but Johnson seems to have gone off with the records. I'm afraid I won't be able to get hold of them 'til afternoon."

"Oh, that's all right. Just curiosity. You don't have to bother."

"No, I'll let you know. Well, I suppose you'll be making the first injection this morning?"

"Right away. You know we're both grateful to you for having hit on the substance responsible."

"No credit due me. Just a . . ." Renshaw chuckled ". . . shot in the dark."

Some twenty minutes later, when Alice came into the examination room, Howard was struck, to a degree that quite startled him, with how pretty and desirable she looked. She had put on a white dress and her smiling face showed no signs of last night's attack. For a moment he had the impulse to take her in his arms, but then he remembered last night and decided against it.

As he prepared to make the injection, she eyed the hypodermics, bronchoscope, and scalpels laid out on the sterile towel.

"What are those for?" she asked lightly.

"Just routine stuff, never use them."

"You know," she said laughingly, "I was an awful ninny last night. Maybe you're right about my libido. At any rate, I've put *him* out of my life forever. He can't ever get at me again. From now on, you're the only one."

He grinned, very happily. Then his eyes grew serious and observant as he made the injection, first withdrawing the needle repeatedly to make sure there were no signs of venous blood. He watched her closely.

The phone jangled.

"Damn," he said. "That'll be Mrs. Easton's nurse. Come along with me."

He hurried through the swinging door. She started after him.

But it wasn't Mrs. Easton's nurse. It was Renshaw.

"Found the records. Johnson didn't have them after all. Just misplaced. And there *is* something out of the way. That dust didn't come from there at all. It came from . . ."

There came a knocking. He strained to hear what Renshaw was saying.

"What?" He whipped out a pencil. "Say that again. Don't mind the noise. It's just our electrician coming to fix the bell. What was that city?"

The knocking was repeated.

"Yes, I've got that. And the exact address of the place the dust came from?"

There came a third and louder burst of knocking, which grew to a violent tattoo.

Finishing his scribbling, he hung up with a bare "Thanks," to Renshaw, and hurried to the door just as the knocking died.

There was no one there.

Then he realized. He hardly dared push open the door to the examination room, yet no one could have gone more quickly.

Alice's agonizingly arched, suffocated body was lying on the rug. Her heels, which just reached the hardwood flooring, made a final, weak knock-knock. Her throat was swollen like a toad's.

Before he made another movement he could not stop himself from glaring around, window and door, as if for an escaping intruder.

As he snatched for his instruments, knowing for an absolute certainty that it would be too late, a slip of paper floated down from his hand.

On it was scribbled, "LANSING, 1555 Kinsey Street." ——+——

ANTON'S LAST DREAM

EDWIN BAIRD

Anything that man can dream, man can do. So believed Anton Slezak, the chemist.

Man had dreamed of flying, Anton would argue, and now he flies across the seven seas. He had dreamed of annihilating distance, and today he sends his voice round the world with the speed of light. He had dreamed of penetrating the mysteries of the universe, and now he sees trillions of miles into space.

So argued Anton, the chemist.

Anton had dreamed many dreams, and some had vanished mistily and some had become reality. But none was too fantastic for Anton's laboratory tests.

Upon the chemist in his laboratory, Anton often said, rested the future development of mankind. And the future, Anton promised, would outshine the present as the present outshines the past.

No poor dreamer was Anton. His dreams had brought him great riches. For he had turned his genius to practical matters, and, working miracles in his laboratory, had discovered ways of converting waste into things of commercial value—cornstalks into cloth, weeds into paper, coal soot into lacquer—and from these and other such discoveries Anton had derived much wealth.

He had bought a magnificent home. He had married a young and lovely woman. He had a nephew who idolized him; and he had many friends and admirers and loyal assistants, and a truly beautiful wife, who, as anybody could plainly see, loved him devotedly. He had, indeed, one might have said, everything worth living for.

And now, at the age of fifty-two, he seemed on the threshold of still greater achievements.

At the moment, however, Anton was employed in developing a dream, the fulfilment of which could have no practical value whatever.

He knew that others had dreamed the same thing. They had put it in motion pictures, in pseudo-scientific writing, in extravagant fiction. But it remained, as yet, merely a dream that nobody would believe.

Anton was determined to make this dream come true.

He brought to bear upon the task all the resources of his scientific mind, all his knowledge of physics and chemistry. He concentrated upon it day and night, experimenting, testing, trying first this, then that, and then discarding everything and starting all over again. He worked in secrecy, in his private laboratory. He told none of his corps of assistants about it; nor his wife; nor his nephew. He wanted nobody to know of this dream—until he was through with it. Then, if he succeeded, the whole world should know about it.

And at last the day came when he knew he *had* succeeded.

He was in his laboratory, that day, when his young and beautiful wife entered. She was an exquisite creature, vibrant with youth, aglow with health, athrob with the joy and zest of life.

"Anton," she said, "you ought to get outdoors for a change of air. You've locked yourself in here for weeks, and you're looking ghastly." She anxiously regarded his scholarly face. Against his black Vandyke beard, his skin was startlingly pale. Yet his eyes glowed with intellectual fire.

"I know, my dear," he said, patting her shoulder; "but I've nearly finished now, and presently we shall celebrate—you and Robin and I—the triumph of my greatest experiment."

Her long blue eyes surveyed the litter of test-tubes and retorts.

"What is this experiment, Anton?"

"You will soon know, my dear. And it will astonish you. I promise you that. Now run along, like a good little girl, and enjoy yourself." His tone was paternal, and as they stood together they might well have been mistaken for father and daughter—he, tall and dark and somehow elderly; she, small and blond and gloriously youthful.

"I wish, Anton," she protested, "you wouldn't always treat me like a child. After all, you know, I *am* your wife. . . . And I am proud of you, Anton. I like to be seen with you, and watch people point you out as a great celebrity, and let them know that you're my husband. So suppose you drop everything for this afternoon and go places with me. We could drive through the park, stop somewhere for a cocktail, go somewhere else for dinner, and then to a theater if you like, or to a night club. . . ."

"No, my dear. But you and Robin go."

She moved a disdainful shoulder. "Robin! It's only a bore, going places with Robin. He's such a—"

She bit her lips, for at this moment Robin entered—an athletic young chap of sparkling eye, of sun-tanned skin and exuberant spirits.

" 'Lo, Uncle Anton! How comes the Great Experiment?"

"Most satisfactorily, my boy. It will soon be finished, and it will amaze you and Zora—and all the world."

"Well, Anton," said Zora, "if I can't coax you outdoors, I'll be running along. I've some letters to write."

"Wait, my dear."

She paused at the door, her hand on the knob, and looked back at him. She ignored the younger man as she might have ignored a small boy.

"Since you and Robin are to share in the success of my experiment"—Anton beamed upon them—"it is only fitting that you should also share in its consummation."

He walked to a cabinet, from which he took two pairs of white gauntlets.

"First," he said, "you must put these on. . . . And now," he added, when their hands were gloved, "take this material and dip it in here."

From a shelf of the cabinet he had taken a large roll of white cloth, wrapped in cellophane, and from a white-enameled vat he removed the lid, disclosing a milky fluid.

He stood between them at the round vessel, giving instructions, while they immersed the cloth in the chalky liquid—"Be careful," he warned, "not to let it touch your clothing"—and, with his pointed black beard and in his long white apron, he might have been some high priest standing beside a cauldron, instructing novices in a pagan ceremony.

"That will do," he said, and covered the vat. "Now, your gloves."

He removed their gauntlets and cast them into a metal container.

"And is that all there is to it?" asked Zora.

"That is all, my dear—until the three of us meet again. Then we shall commemorate what I am sure you will agree is the most astounding discovery in the history of chemistry."

"Meanwhile," she said, "I'll get at my letter-writing."

She kissed him fondly, spoke to the young man—in the condescending tone of one addressing a small child—and left the laboratory.

As the door closed behind her, Anton turned to his nephew. A sudden change had come over him.

"My boy," he said gravely, "there is something I must speak to you about." He paused, passing his long fingers across his wide brow, as if uncertain how to continue. "I wish, Robin," he said finally, in a hesitant voice, "you would try to be a little more considerate of Zora. You scarcely speak to her."

The young man flushed beneath his tan, "But, Uncle Anton! I *do* try to be considerate of her. And you see how she treats me. As if I were a school kid! . . . But she adores *you,* Uncle Anton. She thinks you're the greatest man in the world."

"Does she, indeed?" murmured Anton, and a soft light shone in his deep-set eyes. "Well, it's pleasant to hear that."

"And now, Uncle Anton—if you don't mind—I think I'll run out to the Broadmoor Club and play a set or two of tennis."

"Run right along, my boy—and play a set or two for me."

Anton closed the door behind him, and locked and bolted it. Then he walked to the vat and lifted the cover.

The entire contents of the vat had vanished!

He gazed into the empty vessel, his fingers caressing his pointed beard, his eyes glowing with satisfaction.

And now he did a number of strange things. First, he went to an alcove and wheeled out a full-length, triple mirror, which he adjusted in the center of the room. Then he removed all his clothing. And then he walked to the vat and began a weird pantomime. He reached inside as if drawing forth various garments, and, standing before the triple mirror, he went through the motions of putting them on. And as he made these motions he gradually disappeared: first, his legs; then his feet; then the upper part of his body, and finally, as he seemed to pull an elastic cap over his head and ears, only his hands and face were visible; and these had the eery appearance of floating in space.

Presently these, too, vanished as he brought forth a bowl of the milky fluid and bathed his face and hands in it, and soaked his eyeglasses and put them on.

With that, *Anton Slezak became completely invisible!*

His experiment was a success. His dream had come true. He had proved his belief that there are certain colors, or combinations of colors, that are invisible to human eyes; and he had also proved that by juggling and interchanging the molecules of certain dyes he could produce this invisible coloring.

Careful to make no sound, he unlatched the door and walked through the outer laboratory, where his assistants were employed. He tested his invisibility on them—though he knew it needed no testing—and passed on to the street and started briskly downtown.

Anton might have called upon his friends and, like a disembodied spirit, joined in their conversation and created who knows what havoc among them. But he did not visit the haunts of his friends. He visited the city's largest hotel.

Here, again, he might have been an unseen spectator of loves and hates, and intrigues and jealousies and exotic adventures—rich human drama on a cosmopolitan stage—had he so desired. But Anton had no such desire.

He threaded his way through the hotel lobby, weaving in and out through the crowd, and went to one of the tower elevators and thence to the forty-ninth floor. The elevator boy, answering a signal, opened the door, and Anton slipped ghostily out.

Down the hall he went, straight to Room 4901. He knocked on the door. A peculiar knock: two taps, a pause, then three taps.

And almost instantly the door was opened.

It was opened by his nephew, Robin.

As Robin opened the door, his young face was alight with an eager expression—an expression that quickly changed to one of blank surprise. Puzzled, he stepped outside the door and looked up and down the corridor. And, since he left the door standing open, Anton crossed the threshold and walked inside the room. He moved to a corner near a deep-cushioned couch and stood there watching Robin.

He watched him step back inside and close the door and look nervously about the room, his handsome features half comical with perplexity.

Then he heard another knock at the door. It was the same knock that he had given: two taps, pause, three taps.

He saw Robin open the door again and heard his low joyous cry: *"Sweetheart!"*

And then Anton saw his young and beautiful wife.

He saw her in Robin's arms. He saw her arms around Robin. And he saw their lips and bodies meet and cling in rapturous embrace.

Robin had closed and locked the door when she entered, and they stood there, now, for a long minute, kissing each other passionately.

"Well, *darling!*" she breathed.

"A queer thing just happened, sweetheart—just before you came. Rather uncanny, too. I heard somebody knock, and when I opened the door nobody was there."

She removed her hat and fluffed her pale-gold hair. "Somebody had the wrong door, of course. Kiss me again, darling."

He kissed her again. "But it was *your* knock, dearest."

"Pure coincidence, my lamb." She tossed the hat on a table.

"And not only that," said Robin, "but while I stood there, with the door open, I thought I heard, or felt, somebody move past me. It was like a ghost."

She laughed throatily. "You *are* getting jittery, aren't you, darling?"

"Just the same," he persisted, "I still have the feeling that somebody came inside this room."

She looked about her happily, her long blue eyes humid with love. "Well, there's nobody here now, my precious—nobody except you and me. And that's all that matters—ever!"

She slipped his arm around her supple young body, and together they moved toward the couch.

And as Anton watched them sink down upon it—and also sink, in mad abandon, into the purple abyss of passion—there visited his deep-set eyes the same soft expression they had known a while ago, when Robin had said to him: "But she adores *you,* Uncle Anton."

He heard her say now, a disturbing note in her throaty voice:

"Oh, Robin, I love you so! So much, my darling, it almost frightens me!"

"It frightens me, too, sometimes," said Robin, "when I think what might happen if Uncle Anton—d'you know, Zora, I sometimes wonder if he doesn't suspect . . ."

She smiled dreamily into his eyes and kissed him lingeringly on the lips. "You funny boy! Why, he even thinks we hate each other!"

Robin also smiled, somewhat quizzically. "Only this afternoon he told me to be more considerate of you! . . . But seriously, Zora, we can't go on this way indefinitely. He'll *have* to know, sometime. We—you'll have to get a divorce, or—or something."

She closed his mouth with her kisses. For a space he was silent. Then: "I wonder what this new experiment of his is."

"I don't care what it is," breathed Zora, her arms around his neck. "All I care about, darling, is you."

"This afternoon," Robin went on, "he seemed to imply—"

"That all three of us," smiled Zora, "might celebrate tonight."

And now Anton stood before them. He spoke purringly.

"And so we shall, my dear," he said.

Had the hotel walls caved in, the two lovers could have suffered no greater consternation. They sprang to their feet. They looked wildly about. They stared at each other in bewilderment.

And all the while, Anton's voice purred softly on from his invisibility:

"It is no use, my dear. You cannot see me. Nor will you ever see me again. Nor you, either, Robin, my boy. The experiment was a perfect success. Did I not say it would astound you?"

Frantic with fear—fear of they knew not what—both rushed for the door. But Anton got there first.

And now they saw, suspended in midair, a revolver menacing them.

Robin lunged for it desperately—but too late. The revolver spoke, once, and he sank to the floor. Zora screamed, her eyes widening with horror upon his twitching body. She clutched at her throat. She screamed again, insanely, and reached out for the door. Then the revolver spoke a second time, and she collapsed beside her lover.

Anton knelt beside them and watched them die. They were an unconscionably long time about it, he thought.

The telephone began ringing. That would be the management. Somebody, of course, had heard the shots and Zora's piercing screams.

Anton, still kneeling beside their bodies, watched their blood flow together and stain the rug with a grotesque pattern.

The telephone continued to ring. Suddenly there came a sharp knock at the door. That would be the house detective.

Anton made sure they were both quite dead; and then he rose and crossed the room and sat down upon the couch.

He had one shot left in his revolver. And—just as the door burst violently open—he sent it neatly through his heart. —+—

The Archfiend's Fingers

Kirk Mashburn

What place this was into which he had stumbled, John Power neither knew nor cared. It was some shady cabaret; some dimly lighted dive of sinister shadows, perhaps near to the waterfront.

Slumped at a small table, he sensed little of what went on around him, remembered nothing of how he had become separated from his friends. It was carnival time, Mardi Gras Day in New Orleans. Vaguely, Power knew that he had celebrated too enthusiastically, had drunk too freely. There was a blank in his memory, and everything was rather more than hazy. He had no knowledge, even, that the thinning backwash of the carnival crowds no longer eddied in the street outside, had wearily dissolved in the early night.

Something of his surroundings obscurely troubled the bemused man. But it was too weighty and painful an effort to think. His head throbbed dully; nausea reached slyly, touched him with a tentative finger. It seemed that some one spoke, from across the table—

"Your pardon, sir. I have no wish to intrude, but you appear in need of something to lower your stomach, and raise your spirits."

In blurred, indistinct outline, Power saw that there was indeed another person seated opposite him. The stranger laughed dryly, as though his indulgence might be tinged with faintly contemptuous amusement. He beckoned, spoke succinctly to a none too clean waiter who answered the gesture.

A drink was brought, a palely green drink that shimmered in its glass, as if with flecks of gold in its depths. The stranger pressed the greenish drink upon the younger man with obdurate, if kindly guised insistence. Power groaned weakly, swallowed the virescent potion and nausea together; knowing he was shortly to be ill; hoping, with feeble malice, that he would be very unpleasantly ill. Then, perhaps, they would let him alone.

The draft stung his palate, seared his throat, struck his stomach like flowing fire. Amazingly, almost before he could gasp for breath, nausea vanished; the throbbing at his temples began to still, the fog to lift from his wits.

"Ah, that is better! Is it not?" The stranger nodded, smiled easily. Power looked across at him with mixed emotions, in which some trace of resentment lingered.

He took in the dark, saturnine countenance, about which there was something familiar—vaguely and disturbingly familiar. Somewhere, he thought, he had seen that high forehead; the whisper of memory strove to identify that arrogant, narrow-bridged nose, the oddly arched brows and the thin-lipped mouth that presently wore a smile of tolerant amusement.

Only the eyes were unfamiliar. John Power felt that he had seen the face without having looked into the dark, glittering eyes: his memory could not otherwise have escaped some record of their chill fascination. It was as if he remembered a picture of the face, rather than the living countenance.

"I feel better," Power belatedly acknowledged. "That is—I don't feel ill, nor stupid, as I did. But"—he brushed a hand uncertainly across his eyes—"I don't know—"

The stranger—he made no move to identify himself; nor, strangely, did the thought occur to Power—the stranger laughed again. His was an enfolding laugh, a laugh of comprehension. It was as if he knew and understood all the insidious perplexities of mankind—and was glad of mankind's human frailty.

The waiter brought more of the green drinks. The stranger talked to Power while they were coming, and the latter listened. They drank often, always the green drinks; but Power had never felt more alive, his mind had never before seemed quite so active. Occasionally the stranger passed him cigarettes, apparently of tobacco in which the blending gave a peculiar distinctive taste that was not, however, displeasing at the moment.

At length the bracing effect Power had experienced with the first draft of the green liquor began to wear off. His head was resuming its throbbing, and thinking was again an effort. A feeling of uneasiness assailed him with recurring insistence. He sensed something disturbing in his surroundings; something that included his unknown yet oddly familiar table companion.

He decided to go while the effort was still possible—wondered that he had not taken his leave after that revitalizing first drink. With difficulty, he gained his feet, hastened by a sudden, rising impulse of dread: instinctive, insinuating dread, that came unsummoned and unexplained.

"Surely you will not leave so early?"

It was the stranger who spoke; but the simple question seemed, to Power's tortured fancy, fraught with irony and all the weight of a command. Giddily he sought to focus his thoughts. Thickly he repeated his intention of departing; thinking that, despite himself, he spoke so low that his words were almost whispered. Then he wondered whether, instead, he had shouted: every one in the place appeared to have centered attention suddenly in his direction.

As Power peered about him, each face among those present flared into startling distinctness—and what faces they were! There were nightmare visages of horror; grotesque, distorted faces that worked with slavering malice as they approached. . . . *(God! What place was this into which he had blundered?)* There were other faces, pale with the pallor of death, set masks of woe and utter, horrible despair.

One fantastic shape detached itself and came forward, apart from its fellows. It wore a Spanish helmet and breastplate of antique design, and was shod in high Spanish boots. The shadowing helmet blurred the face beneath, and that but intensified an impression of hideous fearsomeness. As the monster came beneath a ceiling light— *or was there a light there? was there even a ceiling?*—Power observed that its armor, its garments even to the high boots, looked to be splotched and smeared with red—bloody splotches that spread and merged until they wholly enveloped the sinister figure.

"Who are *you?*" Power snarled in uneasy anger. There was no answer. It was an easy and natural transition, in Power's irrational condition, from disturbed peevishness to sudden, flaring rage.

Still snarling, he staggered up, seized his chair and raised it to hurl at the motionless figure in ancient Spanish armor. But his table companion, who had sat motionless until the moment, sprang forward with outstretched hands.

Suddenly it seemed to Power that he saw the Stranger with blinding clearness, as if a veil had been torn aside—saw him, and knew him for what he was! At the sight of those reaching talons, fear snapped the last shreds of his control. He screamed aloud in panic—

"Help!" and again, "Help!"

From a door in the rear of the place leaped a figure, and Power shouted with joy upon recognizing the waiter who had served his table. But no!— Before his eyes, an awful metamorphosis occurred . . . . The attendant was but another demon come to join the grim, silently encircling throng.

"Away, fiends!" Power shrieked, again raising the chair he held. Before he could fling it, the Stranger had seized his wrist. To Power, it felt as if those taloned fingers seared through his flesh to the bone.

"Back! All of you stand back!" cried he of the clutching hands. "Let me deal with him alone!"

The words seared Power's brain: He was claimed by *the Archfiend himself!*

The thought gave final impetus to his madness. Wrenching violently from the grasp that pained his wrist, and swinging the chair before him, Power swept a path of havoc to a door.

The door opened. Power gained the street with a bound, fled over ancient flagstones down dim, narrow, cobbled streets. What course he covered in twisted flight, he never afterward knew. At the moment, he cared only that it was away from the clamorous pursuit upon his heels. At length, looking up, the fugitive recognized an enclosure within a high iron fence — a fence in which gaped an open gate.

Clanging shut and latching the gate in the faces of the foremost of the racing figures at his back, Power bounded across Jackson Square, where the hero of Chalmette sat his charger in bronze disdain of the turmoil boiling in his shadow.

The gate stopped pursuit for a precious moment. Power made for the opposite side of the square, where Saint Louis' Cathedral loomed out of the shadows, across a narrow street. He was spent; a myriad aches racked his heaving chest, but he knew that he *must* cross that street, gain the cathedral. *They* could never enter there!

He staggered into the open vestibule as the chimes pealed on the stroke of midnight. The period of carnival was over; Ash Wednesday and Lenten penitence were ushered in, while Power beat against the inner doors. The patter of pursuing feet sounded without, as their spent quarry sagged and crumpled to the floor.

"Sanctuary!" he sobbed. "Sanctuary!"

A sound as of rushing waters filled his ear-drums almost to bursting; darkness crowded in, encompassed him. The gasping figure in the cathedral vestibule sank into merciful oblivion.

Power recovered his senses in what seemed a few seconds. Triphammers pounded inside his head, and he was conscious of acute and consuming thirst. Still dominating every other thought was the urge to crawl farther into the cathedral.

It had been so much darker a moment ago, he thought with vague wonder as he strove to drag himself forward. Something interfered with his effort; he peered dazedly to see what it was. Then Power sat up with a jerk that nearly burst his head, filling him with giddiness. He groaned aloud.

He was in a small white bed, in a white-walled room with other small, white beds . . . a hospital ward! At his movement, a white-uniformed nurse came briskly forward.

"What happened?" Power croaked, ignoring the nurse's injunction to lie down and be quiet. "How long have I been here?"

"Since last night, when you were found collapsed at the doors of Saint Louis' Cathedral," the nurse replied. Her voice was brittle with disapproval.

"Why was I brought here?" Power demanded, gropingly insistent.

"Because you were suffering from the effects of acute alcoholism," tartly returned the nurse. "And also"—her tone was definitely accusing—"you were raving as the result of smoking *marijuana.*"

"*Marijuana?*" Power stupidly repeated.

"Sisal—hasheesh," crisply affirmed the nurse, turning away. "Will you please lie down?"

But Power had become aware of a dull pain that was apart from the bursting of his head. Lifting a hand, he stared at the bandage swathing his wrist. He would never be able to forget the Stranger who had shared his table, uninvited, in a shadowed, unknown place; hazily, he remembered smoking cigarettes of a peculiar, acrid taste.

But premonition whispered that drink nor drug would ever explain the reason for the gauze wrapped about his wrist. Slowly, Power removed the bandage.

Except that they were burned like a brand into the flesh, the marks upon his wrist were the livid imprint of a thumb and four long, pointed fingers. ——

BERENICE

EDGAR ALLAN POE

Misery is manifold. The wretchedness of earth is multiform. Overreaching the wide horizon as the rainbow, its hues are as various as the hues of that arch—as distinct too, yet as intimately blended. Overreaching the wide horizon as the rainbow! How is it that from beauty I have derived a type of unloveliness?—from the covenant of peace, a smile of sorrow? But, as in ethics, evil is a consequence of good, so, in fact, out of joy is sorrow born. Either the memory of past bliss is the anguish of today, or the agonies which *are*, have their origin in the ecstasies which *might have been.*

My baptismal name is Egæus; that of my family I will not mention. Yet there are no towers in the land more time-honored than my gloomy, gray, hereditary halls. Our line has been called a race of visionaries; and in many striking particulars—in the character of the family mansion—in the frescoes of the chief saloon—in the tapestries of the dormitories—in the chiselling of some buttresses in the armory—but more especially in the gallery of antique paintings—in the fashion of the library chamber—and, lastly, in the very peculiar nature of the library's contents—there is more than sufficient evidence to warrant the belief.

The recollections of my earliest years are connected with that chamber, and with its volumes—of which latter I will say no more. Here died my mother. Herein I was born. But it is mere idleness to say that I had not lived before—that the soul has no previous existence. You deny it?—let us not argue the matter. Convinced myself, I seek not to convince. There is, however, a remembrance of aërial forms—of spiritual and meaning eyes—of sounds, musical yet sad; a remembrance which will not be excluded; a memory like a shadow —vague, variable, indefinite, unsteady; and like a shadow, too, in the impossibility of my getting rid of it while the sunlight of my reason shall exist.

In that chamber was I born. Thus awaking from the long night of what seemed, but was not, non-entity, at once into the very regions of fairyland—into a palace of imagination—into the wild dominions of monastic thought and erudition—it is not singular that I gazed around me with a startled and ardent eye—that I loitered away my boyhood in books, and dissipated my youth in revery; but it *is* singular, that as years rolled away, and the noon of manhood found me still in the mansion of my fathers—it *is* wonderful what a stagnation there fell upon the springs of my life—wonderful how total an inversion took place in the character of my commonest thought. The realities of the world affected me as visions, and as visions only, while the wild ideas of the land of dreams became, in turn, not the material of my everyday existence, but in very deed that existence utterly and solely in itself.

Berenice and I were cousins, and we grew up together in my paternal halls. Yet differently we grew—I, ill of health, and buried in gloom—she, agile, graceful, and overflowing with energy; hers the ramble on the hillside—mine, the studies of the cloister; I, living within my own heart, and addicted, body and soul, to the most intense and painful meditation—she, roaming carelessly through life, with no thought of the shadows in her path, or the silent flight of the raven-winged hours. Berenice!—I call upon her name—Berenice!—and from the gray ruins of memory a thousand tumultuous recollections are startled at the sound! Ah, vividly is her image before me now, as in the early days of her light-heartedness and joy! Oh, gorgeous yet fantastic beauty! Oh, sylph amid the shrubberies of Arnheim! Oh, naiad among its fountains! And then—then all is mystery and terror, and a tale which should not be told. Disease—a fatal disease, fell like the simoom upon her frame; and even while I gazed upon her, the spirit of change swept over her, pervading her mind, her habits, and her character, and, in a manner the most subtle and terrible, disturbing even the identity of her person! Alas! the destroyer came and went!—and the victim—where is she? I knew her not—or knew her no longer as Berenice!

Among the numerous train of maladies superinduced by that fatal and primary one which effected a revolution of so horrible a kind·in the moral and physical being of my cousin, may be mentioned as the most distressing and obstinate in its nature, a species of epilepsy not unfrequently terminating in *trance* itself—trance very nearly resembling positive dissolution, and from which her manner of recovery was, in most instances, startlingly abrupt. In the meantime, my own disease—for I have been told that I should call it by no other appellation—my own disease, then, grew rapidly upon me, and assumed finally a monomaniac character of a novel and extraordinary form—hourly and momently gaining vigor—and at length obtaining over me the most incomprehensible ascendency. This monomania, if I must so term it, consisted in a morbid irritability of those properties of the mind in metaphysical science termed the *attentive*. It is more than probable that I am not understood; but I fear, indeed, that it is in no manner possible to convey to the mind of the merely general reader an adequate idea of that nervous *intensity of interest* with which, in my case, the powers of meditation (not to speak technically) busied and buried themselves, in the contemplation of even the most ordinary objects of the universe.

To muse for long unwearied hours, with my attention riveted to some frivolous device on the margin or in the typography of a book; to become absorbed, for the better part of a summer's day, in a quaint shadow falling aslant upon the tapestry or upon the floor; to lose myself, for an entire night, in watching the steady flame of a lamp, or the embers of a fire; to dream away whole days over the perfume of a flower; to repeat, monotonously, some common word, until the sound, by dint of frequent repetition, ceased to convey any idea whatever to the mind; to lose all sense of motion or physical existence, by means of absolute bodily quiescence long and obstinately persevered in: such were a few of the most common and least pernicious vagaries induced by a condition of the mental faculties, not, indeed, altogether unparalleled, but certainly bidding defiance to anything like analysis or explanation.

Yet let me not be misapprehended. The undue, earnest, and morbid attention thus excited by objects in their own nature frivolous, must not be confounded in character with that ruminating propensity common to all mankind, and more especially indulged in by persons of ardent imagination. It was not even, as might be at first supposed, an extreme condition, or exaggeration of such propensity, but primarily and essentially distinct and different. In the one instance, the dreamer, or enthusiast, being interested by an object usually *not* frivolous, imperceptibly loses sight of this object in a wilderness of deductions and suggestions issuing therefrom, until, at the conclusion of a day-dream *often replete with luxury,* he finds the *incitamentum,* or first cause of his musings, entirely vanished and forgotten. In my case, the primary object was *invariably frivolous,* although assuming, through the medium of my distempered vision, a refracted and unreal importance. Few deductions, if any, were made; and those few pertinaciously returning in upon the original object as a center. The meditations were *never* pleasurable; and, at the termination of the revery, the first cause, so far from being out of sight, had attained that supernaturally exaggerated interest which was the prevailing feature of the disease. In a word, the powers of mind more particularly exercised were, with me, as I have said before, the *attentive,* and are, with the day-dreamer, the *speculative.*

My books, at this epoch, if they did not actually serve to irritate the disorder, partook, it will be perceived, largely, in their imaginative and inconsequential nature, of the characteristic qualities of the disorder itself. I well remember, among others, the treatise of the noble Italian, Coelius Secundus Curio, *"De Amplitudine Beati Regni Dei";* St. Augustin's great work, "The City of God"; and Tertullian's *"De Carne Christi,"* in which the paradoxical sentence, *"Mortuus est Dei filius; credibile est quia ineptum est; et sepultus resurrexit; certum est quia impossibile est,"* occupied my undivided time, for many weeks of laborious and fruitless investigation.

Thus it will appear that, shaken from its balance only by trivial things, my reason bore resemblance to that ocean-crag spoken of by Ptolemy Hephestion, which steadily resisting the attacks of human violence, and the fiercer fury of the waters and the winds, trembled only to the touch of the flower called Asphodel. And although, to a careless thinker, it might appear a matter beyond doubt, that the alteration produced by her unhappy malady, in the *moral* condition of Berenice, would afford me many objects for the exercise of that intense and abnormal meditation whose nature I have been at some trouble in explaining, yet such was not in any degree the case. In the lucid intervals of my infirmity, her calamity, indeed, gave me pain, and, taking deeply to heart that total wreck of her fair and gentle life, I did not fail to ponder, frequently and bitterly, upon the wonder-working means by which so strange a revolution had been so suddenly brought to pass. But these reflections partook not of the idiosyncrasy of my disease, and were such as would have occurred, under similar circumstances, to the ordinary mass of mankind. True to its own character, my disorder revelled in the less important but more startling changes wrought in the *physical* frame of Berenice—in the singular and most appalling distortion of her personal identity.

During the brightest days of her unparalleled beauty, most surely I had never loved her. In the strange anomaly of my existence, feeling with me *had never been* of the heart, and my passions *always were* of the mind. Through the gray of the early morning—among the trellised shadows of the forest at noonday—and in the silence of my library at night—she had flitted by my eyes, and I had seen her— not as the living and breathing Berenice, but as the Berenice of a dream; not as a being of the earth, earthly; but as the abstraction of such a being; not as a thing to admire, but to analyze; not as an object of love, but as the theme of the most abstruse although desultory speculation. And *now*—now I shuddered in her presence, and grew pale at her approach; yet, bitterly lamenting her fallen and desolate condition, I called to mind that she had loved me long, and, in an evil moment, I spoke to her of marriage.

And at length the period of our nuptials was approaching, when, upon an afternoon in the winter of the year—one of those unseasonably warm, calm, and misty days which are the nurse of the beautiful Halcyon—I sat (and sat, as I thought, alone) in the inner apartment of the library. But uplifting my eyes, I saw that Berenice stood before me.

Was it my own excited imagination—or the misty influence of the atmosphere—or the uncertain twilight of the chamber—or the gray draperies which fell around her figure—that caused in it so vacillating and indistinct an outline? I could not tell. She spoke no word; and I—not for worlds could I have uttered a syllable. An icy chill ran through my frame; a sense of insufferable anxiety oppressed me; a consuming curiosity pervaded my soul; and, sinking back upon the chair, I remained for some time breathless and motionless, with my eyes riveted upon her person. Alas! its emaciation was excessive, and not one vestige of the former being lurked in any single line of the contour. My burning glances at length fell upon the face.

The forehead was high, and very pale, and singularly placid; and the once jetty hair fell partially over it, and overshadowed the hollow temples with innumerable ringlets, now of a vivid yellow, and jarring discordantly, in their fantastic character, with the reigning melancholy of the countenance. The eyes were lifeless, and lusterless, and seemingly pupilless, and I shrank involuntarily from their glassy stare to the contemplation of the thin and shrunken lips. They parted; and in a smile of peculiar meaning, *the teeth* of the changed Berenice disclosed themselves slowly to my view. Would to God that I had never beheld them, or that, having done so, I had died!

***

The shutting of a door disturbed me, and looking up, I found that my cousin had departed from the chamber. But from the disordered chamber of my brain had not, alas! departed, and would not be driven away, the white and ghastly *spectrum* of the teeth. Not a speck on their surface—not a shade on their enamel—not an indenture in their edges—but what the brief period of her smile had sufficed to brand in upon my memory. I saw them *now* even more unequivocally than I beheld them *then*. The teeth!—the teeth!—they were here, and there, and everywhere, and visibly and palpably before me; long, narrow, and excessively white, with the pale lips writhing about them, as in the very moment of their first terrible development. Then came the full fury of my *monomania*, and I struggled in vain against its strange and irresistible influence. In the multiplied objects of the external world I had no thoughts but for the teeth. For these I longed with a frenzied desire. All other matters and all different interests became absorbed in their single contemplation. They— they alone were present to the mental eye, and they, in their sole individuality, became the essence of my mental life. I held them in every light. I turned them in every attitude. I surveyed their characteristics. I dwelt upon their peculiarities. I pondered upon their conformation. I mused upon the alteration in their nature. I shuddered as I assigned to them, in imagination, a sensitive and sentient power, and even when unassisted by the lips, a capability of moral expression. Of Mademoiselle Salle it has been well said: *"Que tous ses pas étaient des sentiments,"* and of Berenice I more seriously believed *que tous ses dents étaient des idées! Des idées!*—ah, here was the idiotic thought that destroyed me! *Des idées!*—ah, *therefore* it was that I coveted them so madly! I felt that their possession could alone ever restore me to peace, in giving me back to reason.

And the evening closed in upon me thus—and then the darkness came, and tarried, and went—and the day again dawned—and the mists of a second night were now gathering around—and still I sat motionless in that solitary room—and still I sat buried in meditation —and still the *phantasma* of the teeth maintained its terrible ascendency, as, with the most vivid and hideous distinctness, it floated about amid the changing lights and shadows of the chamber. At length there broke in upon my dreams a cry as of horror and dismay; and thereunto, after a pause, succeeded the sound of troubled voices, intermingled with many low moanings of sorrow or of pain. I arose from my seat, and throwing open one of the doors of the library, saw standing out in the antechamber a servant maiden, all in tears, who told me that Berenice was—no more! She had been seized with epilepsy in the early morning, and now, at the closing in of the night, the grave was ready for its tenant, and all the preparations for the burial were completed.

I found myself sitting in the library, and again sitting there alone. It seemed to me that I had newly awakened from a confused and exciting dream. I knew that it was now midnight, and I was well aware, that since the setting of the sun, Berenice had been interred. But of that dreary period which intervened I had no positive, at least no definite, comprehension. Yet its memory was replete with horror —horror more horrible from being vague, and terror more terrible from ambiguity. It was a fearful page in the record of my existence, written all over with dim, and hideous, and unintelligible recollections. I strived to decipher them, but in vain; while ever and anon, like the spirit of a departed sound, the shrill and piercing shriek of a female voice seemed to be ringing in my ears. I had done a deed— what was it? I asked myself the question aloud, and the whispering echoes of the chamber answered me—*"What was it?"*

On the table beside me burned a lamp, and near it lay a little box. It was of no remarkable character, and I had seen it frequently before, for it was the property of the family physician; but how came it *there,* upon my table, and why did I shudder in regarding it? These things were in no manner to be accounted for, and my eyes at length dropped to the open pages of a book, and to a sentence underscored therein. The words were the singular but simple ones of the poet Ebn Zaiat:—*"Dicebant mihi sodales si sepulchrum amicae visitarem, curas aliquantulum fore levatas."* Why, then, as I perused them, did the hairs of my head erect themselves on end, and the blood of my body become congealed within my veins?

There came a light tap at the library door—and, pale as the tenant of a tomb, a menial entered upon tiptoe. His looks were wild with terror, and he spoke to me in a voice tremulous, husky, and very low. What said he?—some broken sentences I heard. He told of a wild cry disturbing the silence of the night—of the gathering together of the household—of a search in the direction of the sound; and then his tones grew thrillingly distinct as he whispered me of a violated grave—of a disfigured body shrouded, yet still breathing— still palpitating—*still alive!*

He pointed to my garments; they were muddy and clotted with gore. I spoke not, and he took me gently by the hand: it was indented with the impress of human nails. He directed my attention to some object against the wall. I looked at it for some minutes: it was a spade. With a shriek I bounded to the table, and grasped the box that lay upon it. But I could not force it open; and, in my tremor, it slipped from my hands, and fell heavily, and burst into pieces; and from it, with a rattling sound, there rolled out some instruments of dental surgery, intermingled with thirty-two small, white, and ivory-looking substances that were scattered to and fro about the floor.

THE BLACK MADONNA

A. W. WYVILLE

Houses with shuttered windows, houses with a hangdog air, going to ruin. Houses about which strange tales are told. Tales of strange happenings. Such will always fire the imaginative. Of such a house I tell.

It was situated on the outskirts of a small village, a village famed in the Revolutionary War. I lingered and gathered its history, bit by bit. A story that will draw smiles from the unbelieving, yet cause thoughtful men to pause, as I paused, pondering over the strange ways in which fate sometimes evens scores.

The house had been vacant several years. Shunned by the villagers. They did not claim that it was haunted. Its gruesome story forbade tenants.

The last occupants had been two brothers. One a tall, hawk-nosed, surly character, the younger a pleasant chap with dark brown eyes and a small mustache. Slight of build. Chemists they were; brilliant chemists, we heard. They hired no one, doing their own cooking and general work. Partitions had been torn out and an expensive laboratory installed. Bottles upon bottles. Retorts and electric furnaces of the most elaborate description. Word went around that they were working on a great chemical problem, the solution of which would revolutionize a major industry.

Although the elder brother was seldom seen on the village streets, the younger would often pass through on his way to the city, driving an expensive car. Sometimes he would stop and talk. He talked on many subjects but never of his work. All such questions he skilfully parried. While his main interests were centered on his work, he also spent some time on a hobby, zoology. He would often be seen in the fields on a summer day, equipped with a long-handled net. A strange combination of interests.

Lights glowed in their house until far into the night. A tall figure could be seen moving behind the shades. Not long after the brothers had moved in, there came to the village one night the sound of a muffled explosion. Lurid flames shot from the house of mystery. The village fire department soon had the flames under control, however. To do so they had been obliged to enter the laboratory, from whence the explosion took place. What they saw was the talk of the town, although the occupants had got them out as soon as they could, seeming to fear that they would see too much. Some people wondered if perhaps they were not counterfeiters.

The brothers repaired the damage and the talk died down. The next happening of interest came from a different quarter.

It came in a bunch of bananas. The local grocer found it. A hairy spider, with a bright red spot on its back. It was then the middle of winter and the repulsive thing was in a torpid state from the cold. Instead of killing it, the grocer, perhaps with an eye for advertising, placed it in a small wire cage with a lighted electric lamp for warmth.

He had not misjudged its potential attraction qualities. Revived by the warmth, it was soon crawling around its cage seeking an opening. The whole town had seen it and speculated about it, when it was drawn to the attention of the young chemist, he being "interested in bugs and sich," as they put it.

One look at the spider, and the young man drew in his breath sharply.

"A Black Madonna," he whispered.

Of course that meant nothing to the villagers. He explained. It seems that the Black Madonna is the most poisonous spider known to science. Death almost invariably follows its bite.

This information put the grocer into a cold sweat, for he remembered how free he had been in handling it. He was for immediately destroying it. The young chemist offered to buy it, alive. The grocer dubiously assented. After all, it was clear profit. We never saw it again.

Spring came in cold, severe snowstorms following on one another's heels. The two brothers were more or less isolated. Late wayfarers reported that the lights burned as brightly as ever in the house.

From this point my story will have to be partly guesswork and deductions from what came to light later.

Upon arriving at the house with his prisoner, the young man took it to his room to examine at his leisure. Kept it warm and fed it gnats. It seemed to thrive. However, he did not let it interfere with his research work.

The two brothers were working independently toward the same goal. The elder worked at night, while his brother utilized the daylight hours. Each kept his progress to himself. An odd arrangement.

The younger man won. When his brother rose from his bed one afternoon, having worked through the night, he found the other with shining eyes. Yes, it had been by accident. Just stumbled on it. Meant international fame!

Just stumbled on it! Just by accident! The words repeated themselves in the elder brother's brain. He almost hated his kinsman. All his work for nothing. More than life itself he craved the fame that would come with success.

His brother heeded it not. Honor was reaching for him, and he was blind to the other's expression. An expression not good to look upon. He locked his notes in the cabinet and went to his room. Here he made a discovery that sobered him for a minute. The Black Madonna had escaped!

Carefully and thoroughly he searched the room. The spider was nowhere to be found. The window was partly open, and he finally decided that it must have departed through this opening. Well, it would soon perish in the cold.

Long into the evening his brother stayed in the laboratory. After the first questioning he did not seem curious regarding the achievement. The other wondered. Oh, well, he would feel better and congratulate him tomorrow. He was sometimes like that. Sometimes a poor sport.

The elder slowly went over his notes. Sometimes he stared out of the window and fought a hideous temptation. His brother came in and worked at his desk. The other's eyes rested upon his back. It would be so easy! To hide and explain it. No, he must not think of such a thing. His hands clenched until the knuckles showed white.

Some time later the younger arose, said good-night, and went to his room. Could he do it? A madness came upon him. He bided his time.

Several hours later the door to the brother's room opened and a tall dark figure entered. A knife makes no sound, and it was soon over.

The dirt basement provided a good burial ground. He washed his hands, a maniacal gleam of satisfaction in his eyes. Better go up to the room again and make sure that there were no blood-spots. People that make sudden trips to the city and disappear do not leave blood-spots on their beds. Oh, he would be clever! . . .

The room was soon put in order. As he was leaving he felt a sudden chill. His brother's old sweater was hanging on the bedpost. Callously he put it on. Mustn't catch cold. Now for those notes.

Carefully, methodically, he transcribed them into his own hand-writing. His scientific training triumphed over his madness for the time being. He was again the chemist.

As he worked, life stirred. Life in the pocket of the old sweater. A hairy leg reached for the edge of the pocket. Perhaps it was the heat of the man's body. Slowly the revolting creature worked its way up the sweater. The man wrote on. Inch by inch the hairy legs reached toward the collar, unnoticed. Then, for some reason, the spider turned. On the under side of his arm it worked, swaying with the motion of the writing. It continued testing its way. On the edge of the cuff it paused, then lowered itself onto the moving hand. The man dropped the pencil with an oath. The next second a long shiver ran over him, the blood drained from his face, the pupils of his eyes become pinpricks. . . .

Days later the villagers found him. Dead, staring, two tiny red spots on his hand, the evidence of his attempted theft in front of him. ⟶⊢

THE BLACK MONK

G. G. PENDARVES

Yes. It's true that I'm dictating this, but don't picture to yourself a famous author, a luxurious study, and a highly paid secretary. No! I'm dictating this for publication because I promised the Abbot of Chaard that I would. I can't go against his wishes. Not again.

"All lies and rubbish! Don't you believe a word of it, sir. It suits them," the gamekeeper jerked a thumb in the direction of the monastery behind him, "to keep such fairy-tales alive. Gives them a hold on the people. Everyone on this island believes in the Black Monk, swears they've caught sight of him on the prowl. I never have—and why? Because I'm not afraid. It's all rubbish, so I tell you straight, damned rubbish."

I looked at Morton. His brown deep-set eyes, his wrinkled face, his long lean body in its ancient brown tweeds, even his old leggings and the way he carried his gun and wore his cap expressed contempt. He'd no use for the monks or for anyone else on the island.

Stayed because he'd no chance of work elsewhere. Owed everything to the Abbot and hated him in proportion to his debt.

"They give chapter and verse for it at the monastery," I ventured. "Got old documents. Supposed to be treasure buried here in the Fifth Century when Britain was conquered by the English. Brought by a faithful monk who came up the Thames from Kent. Got across here, buried his treasure, and died on the island, keeping guard to the end. And he's still on duty, it appears."

"Treasure and guardian! Tale for children and the bloody fools that spend their days gabbling prayers when they'd be a sight better digging and planting and weeding on this blamed island of theirs. I'm the only man does a decent day's work here. And what do I get for it? A damp cottage, wages that don't even run to a twist of baccy, and a lecture from his reverence when the monastery kitchen isn't stocked with game to suit him."

"And so you've never caught a glimpse of the Black Monk?" I persisted. "Never seen him by the old fish pond, or pacing the cliffs, or going down the Long Lane after sundown?"

"No, nor never will! The only Black Monk on the island is up at the monastery—that colored fellow from the West Indies. They don't want anyone blacker than Brother Ignatius. Looks a proper crow with his black habit and black face and all. Not but what I think he's a deal better in black than in white like these here Benedictines on Chaard."

"Of course," I suggested, "you've got to remember that some people aren't able to see things like—well, like the Black Monk. Just as some people don't take certain diseases."

"No one's ever seen the Black Monk and no one's ever going to see him. Why? Because he don't happen to be on Chaard Island! The monks keep the old tale going to frighten the people into going regular to mass and confession. And visitors like it. They go round with eyes popping out of their silly heads. They talk and write things to the papers—see! That's all advertisement and helps to bring money in. It's a put-up game and a pack of damned nonsense, I says."

I left him glooming at his gate and turned down the Long Lane. Morton versus the monks amused me. An idea struck me, result of the recent talk and a most perfect night. A big golden harvest moon was rising. No wind. Mild, almost warm for late October. I'd stay out, all night if necessary, and follow the legendary track of the Black Monk from Pirates' Bay, where he was said to have landed, to a certain wood where he was popularly supposed to have buried his treasure. No one seemed to have tried to stalk him with any method. No one wanted to follow him. His cowled figure had been glimpsed at various points of his route—dark on the pale sands of the landing-beach—melting into shadows cast by Long Lane's steep hedges—a hurrying figure on the skyline of high plowed fields—a tall sentinel by the old neglected green-scummed fish pond—or vanishing into the fir wood.

My brief holiday was almost over. I'd got what I came for—an account of the annual Passion Play the monks gave. It would pay my expenses here. A night's ramble over the romantic island might inspire another article. I lighted a cigarette and made for the beach.

Chaard was settling down for sleep already. The revolving brilliance of its lighthouse grew brighter as lamps went out in cottage windows. Down the Long Lane where nut-trees rustled withered leaves, down past the postoffice *cum* store that served the island's needs, down under the walls of the big white monastery with its towers and turrets, its balconies and chime of bells, its red roofs and steep gables, down to the sand-dunes where tall rushes dipped and whispered in the moonlight, down to the crescent of Pirates' Bay— its fine pale sand ground by thundering surf that now was a mere murmurous line of white edging distant sea.

There I go . . . there I go! I apologize. I'll restrain myself. You'll understand later why the enchanted background of the island on a supremely lovely night is so difficult for me to keep out of this account. You may forgive a poor devil then for looking back on a lost paradise.

I sat on an upturned boat, smoked and dreamed, let the long strange history of Chaard Island float across my mind like weed on a shallow pool. An hour—two hours—I don't know how long I sat there. My lighter ran dry at last, I had no matches, and the search for them shook me out of dreams. I felt stiff and rather cold.

"Well, you're late if you mean to land tonight, old man!"

I spoke aloud, and glanced back across broken rocks that formed one curving horn of my crescent shore. For a moment, actual funk paralyzed me. For a moment I really believed the absurd legend was true. A dark cowled figure was skirting the rocks—moving toward me.

I confess that I didn't move because literally I couldn't. When I saw at last who it was, relief was so overwhelming that I fairly went off like a rocket.

"Brother Ignatius! Upon my word, d'you know I took you for the Black Monk himself! You loomed up there in the moonlight as big and black as a nursery bogy."

The West Indian's gentle liquid speech was the friendliest sound I'd ever heard.

"You ought not to be here," he reproved. "The Father-Abbot would not like it. You are, in a sense, a guest of the monastery since it governs the whole island and its affairs."

"I'm only a heretic." I laughed over-loudly. The sound jarred on that quiet lonely shore. "My soul's more or less lost anyhow in the Abbot's eyes, I expect."

"Yes," agreed Brother Ignatius.

I was irrationally annoyed. "Oh, well, live and let live!" I babbled. My nerves still quivered. My tongue clacked like a toy bell.

"It is difficult, sometimes, to know what that means. It is difficult, sometimes, to say what is life and what is—death."

I'd never realized what a bore the fellow was. I'd rather liked the gentle simple creature before. Now I was irritated. His prosings had broken the magic spell of the night for me.

"On your way to the monastery, I suppose? I'm going to dawdle about another hour, or so. Good-night."

"Not alone! No, really, it is not safe for you alone here. The Black Monk—"

"That's why I'm here," I interrupted the serious quiet voice. "I'm waiting for him. When and if he shows up I'm going to follow him, discover the long-lost secret of his treasure."

"You don't understand." Brother Ignatius was now genuinely perturbed. "It is very dangerous for you."

I made an impatient movement, and half turned to leave him.

"If you wish it so much," his words came slow and hesitant, "if you have made up your mind—perhaps—it would be better that I should—"

"Well?"

I looked up and caught the faint glimmer of white teeth as his lips parted in a smile under his cowl's dark shadow.

"I think the Father-Abbot would forgive me, since you are, in a sense, his guest. Yes, I will show you. I will lead you to the place where the treasure lies buried."

"*What?*"

"Yes. I will take you," murmured the monk.

"But—there isn't any treasure! It's only a wild old tale. What d'you mean?"

"There *is* treasure—golden glorious treasure," softly affirmed the other. "And rather than leave you here, alone, I will show you."

I began to doubt my companion's sanity. I'd no idea what he was talking about. My journalist's imagination began to weave a new story. Well, why not go with him? My mood for solitude and a night's wandering under the moon was gone. I'd humor Brother

Ignatius. He was stooping toward me, apparently very keen on his idea.

"Have it your own way," I agreed. "It may save me from a chill, if not from your friend the Black Monk. By the way, suppose you find him on his job—guarding the treasure!"

"No. You won't see him there. Not if you are with me."

The grave reply and the air with which he turned to cross the sandhills rather took my fancy. Long cloak swaying and billowing in the rising wind, Brother Ignatius strode a few paces ahead. Given the right clothes, I thought, the colored man does redeem movement from the commonplace.

I could see myself, in plus-fours and cap, a discord, an alien figure on that lonely, lovely silvered shore. I could see the monk as a tree whose dark boughs swept the ground or as a wave rising—falling. Part of the earth, possessed by it and possessing it.

"Must be getting a temperature," I told myself. "If I work any little stunt of that sort into my article they'll give me the comic-strip to do."

A new idea struck me.

"I've never met any of you before at this hour. Aren't there rules? I thought the monastery bolted and barred you in your cells long before this."

We'd reached the high heathery cliffs above Pirates' Bay. Brother Ignatius kept the lead. His answer came back on the wind, his cowled head turned to me, and again I caught a flashing glimpse of his gentle smile.

"You forget the weeks for retreat."

He gestured toward a solitary wooden building not a hundred yards distant.

"Of course. I had forgotten. But—if you're in retreat—surely you're breaking your rule now in being here with me."

"The Father-Abbot would put your safety before a rule of this sort. It means, of course, that the month's solitude must begin again. It was necessary. Nothing else would have taken you from that dangerous shore—nothing except my promise to take you to the treasure."

I felt uncomfortable. The Abbot had been extremely courteous to me, given me a good many little privileges, allowed me to go where most visitors are forbidden. To interfere with the religious observance of his order was a poor way of acknowledging his consideration.

Then I shrugged off my qualms. I didn't believe the legend. I didn't think the Abbot believed it. Brother Ignatius had broken his retreat to save me from a non-existent danger, had insisted on this fantastic expedition, and was, in fact, a little mad. I absolved myself from blame and followed on.

At last we came to a small dense wood in a fissure between Hawk's Point and Shark's Fin—two cruel masses of rock jutting out to sea where many ships had piled up in old days. The monk waited.

"Take hold of my cloak," he advised. "The path is narrow, but I know every inch of the way. You won't fall if you follow my lead exactly."

His cloak, between my fingers, was rough and dry as bark. We plunged into the wood. Dark as a shaft here. Fairly smooth underfoot but an endless, endless way. I protested at last.

"We must be going in circles. The wood's small enough to cross in five minutes."

Brother Ignatius stopped as I spoke.

"We are here now. Sit down. Sit down on the soft mossy earth and rest."

I sank down, feeling as if I'd walked to the other end of the earth. Something, immensely heavy, cold, and round was put into my hands.

"What's this? Feels like a crown. What a weight! But I can't see a thing. How do I know if this is gold or lead?"

"Gold, pure gold." Brother Ignatius spoke with awe. "And here are plates and goblets and scepters. Here are candlesticks. This is a great jeweled cross that took a lifetime to fashion. This, too, is set with jewels, a little altar lamp, a most precious relic though so small."

One after another, these things were put into my hands while the monk's quiet voice expatiated on their beauty. I fingered the small heavy lamp. Exasperation seized me.

"But what's the use!" I burst out. "It's absurd to be fumbling away in the dark like this. I want to see them!"

I stood up suddenly, felt the ground slippery underfoot, reached out for support. I called sharply. The monk's cloak brushed my outstretched hands. I tried to grasp it, slipped again, plunged forward, hit my forehead a smashing blow against a tree-trunk and fell heavily.

My senses returned slowly. Darkness, like walls of black velvet, shut me in—darkness and warmth. The wood had seemed damp and cold before. I felt horribly confused. On all sides my hands encountered brush and thorn. Impossible to take any direction in such complete darkness.

"Where are you?" I shouted. "Where are you? Hello! Hello! *Helloooo!* Brother Ignatius, where are you?"

I went on shouting. Anger and increasing warmth in the dark wood served at least to heat my stiff chilled body. I grew more and more furious. The monk must be mad as a hatter. Why hadn't anyone warned me about him? Perhaps they hadn't wanted to discredit their precious monastery.

Exhausted, hungry and thirsty, pricked and scratched with thorns, I sat still and yelled until I was hoarse. When a voice hailed me at last I was in pretty bad shape. I felt like bursting into tears instead of answering. It was the gamekeeper, Morton.

"Have you hurt yourself, sir?"

His strong wiry arm was about my shoulders, raising me to my feet.

"Get me out of this confounded wood, Morton!" I demanded. "I've been hours here. That crazy monk, Brother Ignatius, brought me. I was a fool to follow him, of course, but I'd no idea he was mad."

Morton made no response save by a sudden stiffening of his arm about me.

"Get me out of this wood, d'you hear!" The darkness was becoming a torture now. "Get me out and I'll explain afterward. I don't want to spend the rest of the night here."

"You're not in any wood." Morton's voice seemed choked and indistinct. "You're in a gorse-patch on a headland right over at the back of the island. I came after rabbits and heard you yelling."

"But it's dark! You're drunk, man, you're drunk! It's dark. It's the middle of the night."

"It's eight o'clock in the morning, sir. And the sun's shining full and early."

"You're drunk. You're lying. It's perfectly dark. Pitch-black night."

Then I heard the larks, chimes from the monastery tower for eight o'clock service, chirrup of insects in the grass, lowing of cattle. I knew the truth at last.

I was blind.

"Sir!" Morton's voice came to me from some remote distance. "It couldn't ha' been Brother Ignatius you saw last night. He left the island day before yesterday along with Brother Stephen and the Prior. I rowed 'em all three to the mainland. No one comes or goes from here without I takes 'em. They won't none of them be back for a month."

"You *are* drunk, after all, disgracefully drunk!" I talked now to fight back my thoughts. "No other monk here wears a black habit except Brother Ignatius. How could I possibly mistake a Benedictine's white habit for a black one? I tell you I was with Brother Ignatius for hours. I recognized him—his voice, his smile! It was Brother Ignatius."

Morton didn't argue. He took me to the monastery. The Abbot heard me out.

"Treasure is buried on this island, I believe." His slow solemn tone chilled me. "But it was not Brother Ignatius whom you met on Pirates' Beach."

"But—but—" I stuttered, "I tell you I saw him, talked, walked with him for an hour at least."

"The monk you met was one who has guarded the treasure through centuries. An ancient and cunning guardian."

"No! No! No!" I heard myself; whispering. "There is no such one! I met a man—an ordinary man."

"You met the Black Monk of Chaard Island, for whose tormented weary soul I pray. And for you in darkness and despair, for you, too, I ask deliverance, my son." ——

THE BOAT ON THE BEACH

KADRA MAYSI

The life-guards watched her, every night, come down the boardwalk from the beach hotel, cross the dunes obliquely, and go to sit in the boat.

They talked about her—idly, but speculatively, as lonely men talk about the smallest thing which crosses their horizon—and they agreed that "she wasn't bad-looking."

She was a slim woman—probably somewhere in the thirties—a slim woman, dressed all in white, with a lot of wavy, blue-black hair. They noticed that her hair was unusually beautiful and most unusually abundant. They noticed that she had narrow feet in the low-heeled, one-strap white kid pumps, and slender ankles above them. They noticed that she wore no color on her clothes, her cheeks, or lips.

One day she turned and looked directly up when the boy in the observation room had the glass trained upon her. The boy fell back a step and said, "Good God!" When the others asked him what the matter was, he said, "I saw her eyes." They asked him what color her eyes were and what was the trouble with them. He said,

"They're big, and I think they're black as her hair, but they look—they look—well, they look like you'd expect the eyes of somebody nailed on a cross to look!"

She did not look up again, but every evening, before dark, she came down and crossed the dunes and sat in the life-guards' boat for several hours. And the life-guards talked about her—idly, when they were not discussing the far more important topic of the latest maritime disaster.

For this was just three weeks after the passenger steamer *Astarte* had sprung a leak and foundered—in foul weather—just a few hundred miles off the coast. For some reason, which the surviving members of her crew could not satisfactorily explain, her S.O.S. had not been sent out in what her surviving passengers and the public considered time enough to bring her aid. More than fifty per cent of those on board had perished either in the launching of the lifeboats or in the stormy, bitter cold of the days before that pitiful flotilla was picked up by the rescue ships.

Shipping boards and owners, passengers and reading public, investigated, questioned, promised explanations, threatened suits, wrote to the papers. And when they were through nobody knew any more than they had known at first. For the only man who had that secret locked under the breast of his blue uniform had done his best —whether right or wrong—and had gone down on the bridge of his ship.

It was a far more important topic than idle discussion of a slim woman in white who sat alone in a boat on the beach from sunset until the three-quarter moon had passed high overhead toward the west.

The life-guards were discussing it gravely, humbly, understandingly, as beseemed men who know that the sea has crises too great for any man to meet.

The boarders at the beach hotel—most of whom had never taken a longer sea voyage than that afforded by the six-mile ferry from the mainland to the island—were discussing it shrilly, assertively, not hesitating to censure and to state what should or should not have been done.

But everybody was discussing it—even the eight-year-old small boy who came every day from the nearest cottage to inspect the life-guard station, to mount the lookout ladders, to climb into the boats, to help the sunburned men in white wash, paint, scrub brass, and oil the heavy two-wheel carriages so that they might be, momentarily, ready to be launched upon their runway to the sea.

The small boy knew that a boat had sunk—a big boat, full of men and women and little boys and girls. His daddy had said they were drowned because the captain had not sent a wireless off in time. But the oldest life-guard—the little one with the bow-legs and the grizzled hair that stood up straight—had said: "Sonny, all a man can do is do his best." The small boy understood, too, and, privately, he agreed with the life-guard rather than with his daddy. He was in the third grade—would be when school opened again—and he practised writing on the beach "A-S-T-A-R-T-E."

One morning while he was laboriously tracing it the lady in the sleeveless white silk dress came up behind him. She said:

"You, too?"

And, not understanding but liking her voice, he looked up and smiled at her with his wide "governor's gates" of missing teeth.

She said: "Will you come down to the drug store and eat an ice cream cone with me?"

At the counter she said: "What do you want?"

He chose a strawberry one and asked politely: "What do *you* want?"

She looked at him with her wide black eyes, and the soda jerker heard her say: "A little boy like you—for a sea anchor!"

But she ordered another strawberry cone and then, for some reason, did not eat it and asked him if he would be kind enough to eat it for her.

That evening she came down, as usual, along the walk, across the sandhills. Looking up over the dunes from the boat she saw the sea-oats etched in golden grain and sheaf against the sky. Sunset, out on the back beaches, had set the marsh aflame. Up to the zenith its wastrel opals spattered the western clouds. East, the giant copper disk of the moon came out of the sea.

She sat there so long—so long—with her arms clasped around her knees. The wind was whipping her thin white dress and loosening strands of her long black hair. But her body did not move. To the life-guard up in the observation tower she looked a woman carved in stone. She saw the moon go higher and cut, in the sea's green jungle, a silver road. It stretched from the climbing planet straight to the boat on the beach. Her brain was grasping at scattered thoughts as a drowning person grasps drifting straws. She was half-remembering queer old lines—things that nobody reads nowadays. Who wrote

> "—wished that the ebbing tide
> Would bear me away on its bosom
> To the ocean far and wide?"

The life-guard up in his conning-place remembered that next night would be the full moon and the flood tide. He looked again to see that the boat, on its heavy carriage, was well above the high tide mark. It was well above it, there in the moonlight, with that lonely figure sitting in the stern.

The small boy, lying on his stomach on a sand dune just a hundred yards away, was watching too. He had seen the red moon rise and throw that path across the sea to the boat. Being a child and nearer to God, his vision was clearer than theirs. He saw what the life-guard did not see—what the slim woman in the boat did not see although she looked for it with eyes which bore witness to her crucifixion every night. He had been watching every night—the small boy on the dune. It had happened every night—and it was happening again. But the woman in the boat sat, marble-still. The wind moved only her dress and her hair. She seemed to think that she was alone at the end of that long moon-sequined path.

Flood tide foamed on the beach next night—brimmed the gutters and shallow pools—washed the sides of the outpost dunes into new, concave, wave-carved shapes.

Just before sunrise the lookout saw that the boat on the beach was gone. The man who had had the night watch reported having seen it shortly before midnight. Tide had turned three hours before that time and it was then well above the water. Anyway, it was an eight-man boat and it took two husky ones to launch it. Yes; he was sure he had seen it at eleven-fifty P.M. He was absolutely sure—for the woman in white had been sitting in it then.

The two life-guards who went down to investigate found the heavy carriage with its two broad-tired wheels, its chassis, pole, and ropes, well out in the surf of the now incoming tide. That in itself proved that someone had taken the boat. Had the flood tide, coming higher than usual, washed it out, it would have taken the boat alone and not the carriage with its sand-imbedded wheels. Some persons —for the strongest life-guard could not alone roll that carriage down the shingle—had rolled it out into the surf deep enough to launch it.

With one man hauling on its rope and one pushing on the pole, they got it back to its place high on the beach. Starting up the boardwalk, they met a group of men from the hotel. The manager himself was one of them and he was speaker.

"We've just been to the station to report a woman missing. One of the ladies didn't come in last night. Can you help us?"

"What did she look like? We'll send a man out on the beach and send a boat out, too, right away."

"She was a slim woman, with a lot of dark hair. And she was dressed all in white."

"That's the woman who sits in the boat," said the grizzled life-guard. And the younger one added:

"She was in it last night. Sawyer said he saw her there just before midnight."

"What boat? Where's the boat?" demanded the manager.

"The station boat that sits on its carriage just across the dunes. She's been coming down and sitting in it for hours every night."

"Where is it now?"

"We'd like you to tell us that. Somebody rolled the carriage down the beach and launched it sometime between midnight and day-break."

"And you say a slim woman—a woman in white—was sitting in it last night?"

"Sawyer saw her in it at eleven-fifty."

"But, great God," said the manager, "that was Mrs. Card!"

"What Mrs. Card? You don't mean—"

"Yes; I do mean," said the manager. "That was *the* Mrs. Card— wife (I should say widow) of Captain Card of the steamship *Astarte*."

"I hadn't heard she was here," one of the coast-guards said.

"She registered under a different name," answered the manager. "She wanted to be quiet, and that was the only way. But she told me who she was and why she was doing it. Do you think we'll find her on the island or do you think—?"

Nobody said what he thought, but they all were thinking hard. Not one of them failed to wonder whether the theft of a seaworthy boat, by parties unknown, and the suicide of a woman beside herself with grief might not be unrelated incidents occurring only by coincidence on the same night.

Within thirty minutes there were half a dozen volunteer boats, as well as the station boats, out past the breakers, and posses were patrolling the beach and every foot of the island.

But midday came without a trace of lost woman or lost lifeboat.

The oldest guard was in the lookout room when the little boy climbed the ladder. He usually came earlier, but he had been follow-ing the search. The station was quiet, for all the men except the lookout and the wireless operator were engaged in that search.

He climbed the ladder—the little boy did—and stuck a tow-head in a cap much too large for it into the door of the lookout room. And the grizzled lookout dropped the glasses in his hand and stared as if he saw a ghost.

"Godamighty! Where'd you get it? Where'd you get that cap, Buddy?"

The little boy took it off and, proudly, held it out to him. And the man set it on one gnarled fist and turned it slowly, unbelievingly, around with the other hand.

It was the regulation blue and white cap of a passenger steamship's officer. Its gold braid and insignia told those who knew the sea that it was a master's cap. And the lettering above its vizor told anyone who read that it was property of the *"S.S. Astarte."*

The lifeguard was still turning it, slowly, unbelievingly.

"Where'd you get it, Buddy?"

"On the beach—where the man dropped it while he was shoving the boat last night."

"What man, Buddy?"

"The man who came and took the boat and the lady away with him, the same man who used to come and sit, every night, in your boat with her."

Landsmen have always called sailormen a superstitious folk. This is as it should be, for superstition—like everything else—lends itself to the individual interpretation. And those who go down to the sea in ships know well enough that there occur phenomena which are outside landsmen's experience.

So the old life-guard turned the cap in his rope-gnarled, salt-scarred fingers.

"Tell me about it, Buddy. Sure you didn't dream it?"

"No, sir. I was wide awake, sitting out on the sandhill there. Nights that mother and daddy go to the hotel dances I stay out until the music stops, then run back home before they get there."

"Tell me what you saw. You say you've seen him before?"

"Oh, yes; he's come every night since the lady came. I don't know which side he comes from. I never see him until he's on the beach, at the edge of the waves, right where the end of the road of moonlight is. He goes and sits in the boat with her. But she never seemed to see him before. Perhaps she saw him last night because the moon was so bright and big."

"She saw him?"

"Yes, she saw him. She held out her arms to him, and he came across the beach and put his arms around her. I watched him launch the boat and, when it was afloat, jump in it with her. I thought he had a right to do it because he was dressed like an officer."

"He was dressed like an officer?"

"Yes; like the captain of the ferry that brought us over here. He had a blue uniform with gold braid on his cuffs. And he had this cap. He dropped it on the beach. Can I keep it?"

The telephone bell. It was the hotel manager asking whether there was yet any news of boat or woman.

"No; not yet," said the grizzled guard; and, after he shut the telephone, he handed the blue cap back to the little boy.

"Yes; you can keep it, Buddy," he said, "because—there won't be any news!" ——

Burnt Things

Robert C. Sandison

De next town am Como, sah!" said the porter, lugubriously. He said it in much the same tone that he might have used in announcing that my coffin awaited.

I swore under my breath, impatiently. This confounded mystery was getting on my nerves. First the ticket agent at Ralston.

"Como?" he had said blankly. "You want a ticket for *Como?*" The inference plainly was that no human being in his right mind could ever wish to go to Como. "Oh—uh—ticket for Como, yessir."

And then the conductor. The way he had stared at my ticket and at me, and finally asked, as if doubting the evidence of his eyes: "You're going to Como, are you?"

"For heaven's sake," I answered, "why shouldn't I be going there?"

He had looked at me oddly and shook his head without answering.

And then at the junction where the train had changed crews, the new conductor had repeated the performance.

"Been there since the fire?" he asked, when he was finally assured of my destination.

I shook my head. I remembered reading in the papers that a month or so before, the sugar factory at Como had burned under queer circumstances, and the death list had been appalling. It had taken half the town with it, and I thought the mystery was explained. When half a town of two hundred population burns, the remnant is scarcely visible to the naked eye, and certainly could hold little attraction for the visitor.

"You know there ain't any—ain't many people there now," the conductor persisted.

I hate making explanations, but he was plainly awaiting one.

"I'm visiting friends on a ranch near there."

"Oh, that's different." His voice indicated positive relief. "They'll be waiting to meet you, I suppose."

"Why, no, they won't. It's a surprize visit. I'll stop in the village over night, and hire someone to drive me out next morning."

"Stop there over night?" The conductor spoke so sharply that I jumped. "Say, if there's no one to meet you—say, it's only ten miles into San Benito. Why don't you ride on down there and catch Number One back in the morning. Then you'll get there in daylight."

"I'm not scared of the dark," I said, with what I hoped was withering sarcasm. "Please have the porter make up my berth. I'll knock off a little sleep before we get there."

The conductor opened his mouth two or three times, but finally went his way without speaking. He was back in a few minutes with the porter, to whom he spoke heavily:

"Take good care of this gentleman, Sam. He's going to Como."

"Fo' de Lawd's sake!" The negro's eyes and mouth both popped wide.

"I am!" I said irritably. "And please make up my berth!"

The conductor passed on down the aisle, and the porter, after a moment of goggle-eyed amazement, began to prepare the berth.

"You'll be sure and wake me in time?" I added.

"Yessuh, yessuh!" The negro spoke abstractedly; then turning to face me: "Boss, does yo' know yo'll git in there at one o'clock in the mo'nin'?"

"What about it?" I asked.

"Ever'body done moved away from there, boss, 'scusin' one old geezer, what'd make good food fo' the squirrels."

"What's wrong with him?"

"Sorta weak in the haid. An' then there's—there's—say, boss, you been there since the fire?"

"No."

"Funny things goin' on there, boss—funny things. Lots o' men died in that fire, an' they do say as how it was set."

"An incendiary fire? Yes, I read of it. And I suppose the ghosts of the burned come back for vengeance?"

"All right! All right, boss! Laugh as much as yo' want to. But she's a mighty queer place fo' to spend a night in!"

I turned away impatiently, and as soon as the blankets were spread, turned in. I was half tempted to ride on into San Benito, as the conductor had suggested. But after all I had said, that might be construed into a confession that I *was* afraid of the dark! So I remained silent, and presently dropped asleep.

"De next town am Como, sah!" the porter had said, and I sat up sleepily and began drawing on my clothes.

"Listen, boss. Be a lot safer if yo' was to ride on to San Benito with us."

I had been thinking the same thing myself, but this only stiffened my determination to leave the train there, if I died for it. But of late I've been valuing my life more highly.

I had scarcely finished dressing when the train began to slow down, and I hurried out to the vestibule. The porter dropped the steps, his eyes rolling uneasily over his shoulder. I was scarcely on the ground when he hurled the steps back into the car, and followed them so fast that his white coat fairly blurred, in the darkness.

"De Lawd take keer o' yo', boss," he said as the train chugged out. It gathered speed so rapidly, it almost seemed the engineer was anxious to leave Como behind—far behind.

"Nice, cheerful cuss," I murmured, as I picked up my suitcase and stared doubtfully around me.

It had been more than a year since I had been in the village, and the fire had changed the face of things vastly. The gutted factory still dominated the town, however, as of yore. Its broken, fire-blackened walls still towered jaggedly, out there across the tracks.

The depot was a mere heap of ashes, as were all the near-by houses, but up where Main Street had been some brick buildings had partly withstood the flames. Apparently they had also acted as a fire-stop, for other houses beyond there seemed to be untouched. I wondered why people should abandon perfectly good homes in that fashion.

I picked up my suitcase and set out. There were no lights showing, but knowing that the old man at least still lived in the village, it shouldn't take long to locate him. And after all, Jim's ranch was only six or eight miles away, if walk I must.

There was something horribly depressing about the deserted street—as if I were walking in a village of the dead. I found myself thinking of the entire families who had perished in the fire—of the two score men trapped in the factory and incinerated.

It was no sort of thing to ponder on at one o'clock in the morning —even though the fresh, clean smell of western prairies swept in out of the darkness. For it had been raining that day and heavier and nearer at hand was the smell of wet ashes and dead embers.

I gained the main street and stood looking helplessly about. I had no idea in which house the old man might live, and it looked as if I might shift for myself in one of the unburned buildings.

"Good evening," said a voice, pleasantly.

I had not heard the man approach. I must have broken all records for a standing high jump. He stood close behind me, dressed in the greasy clothes of a factory laborer, with a cap pulled far down over his face.

"You startled me," I said with a laugh. "I was beginning to think I was the only person in the village."

"Old John Barry's still here," said the stranger. "You'll find him over yonder. He never comes over here where the fire was."

"I'd like to find him," I admitted. "I'll have to stay in town over night, until I can get transportation out to Jim Donnelly's ranch."

"He sleeps all day and prowls around all night, so you'll find him all right—over yonder."

I thanked him and turned away, when he took two quick steps forward and rubbed both hands violently along my overcoat. Then he vanished among the ruins, so quickly it seemed as if he had vaporized into air.

Perhaps he was the lunatic the porter had described, I thought as I crossed the street. Certainly he had been dabbling among the wet ashes, for he smelt abominably of burning, and some of the smell had transferred itself to my coat.

Finding old Barry proved no difficult task. I had gone scarcely a block beyond Main Street when I saw him, coming toward me.

He was no inspiring sight. An old, old man, with scraggly, grizzled hair; a mouth that held only the stumps of teeth; a face netted with a thousand wrinkles. No dignity of age was here; rather, a maniacal glitter in the sunken eyes, a lunatic leer in the twisted face. It made me no easier in mind to see that he leaned on a shotgun in lieu of a cane.

He stopped as I approached, and stood eyeing me warily.

"Mr. Barry, I suppose?" I began.

He made no answer.

"The town's rather deserted since I was here last." And I paused, feeling the remark was scarcely tactful.

"Where'd you come from?" he asked gruffly.

"Ralston," I said, taking a step or two forward. "I'm here to visit friends on a ranch south of here. And now I'm—"

I stopped again. Undoubtedly the old man was shrinking away from me. I got the idea he was *smelling* me: certainly he was sniffing at something—that unpleasant smell of scorching on my overcoat, I supposed.

And then he screamed. A wild, goblin wail, it was.

"You're one of them! Don't tell me! You're one of them. With the smell of burnin' on your clothes. An' you come from across the street! I knowed it! I knowed it! Knowed sometime you'd come across after me!"

"Listen," I said, "I've no idea what you're talking about!" (Though I had an uneasy feeling I knew all too well!) "All I want is a night's lodging, for which I'll pay—"

He screamed again, disregarding me.

"Put you in my house? So it has to be in a house, does it?" His face writhed in stark madness. He threw up the shotgun. "Get back where you belong! You don't belong over here! Get back! I'll shoot!"

I tried to speak but he refused to listen. And the twin muzzles were pointing directly at my belt buckle. I backed away. He followed me.

I remembered that lunatic fellow with the smell of ashes on him had said Barry never crossed Main Street into the ruins. Then here was an easy way to rid myself of him.

I increased my backward pace a little and he pressed after me—and burst into cackling laughter.

"Afraid of me! Yessir, afraid of me! An' for weeks I been afraid of you! Ho! ho! ho! Get back there!"

We reached Main Street and I started across, backward. At the curb, the old man hesitated a moment, looking from me to the blackened ruins beyond. Then, half fearfully, he put one foot off the curb, then the other. Slowly, as a man wades into deep water, he followed.

Not so good. Being marched through a village of the dead by a maniac at one-thirty in the morning is no experience to be envied. I looked around for the other lunatic but he was nowhere in sight.

We crossed the street and I plodded slowly backward toward the depot. And the old man followed me. We were already half the distance, when I saw a shadowy figure creep from behind a broken wall.

The old man was still babbling insanely.

"I killed you before! And I can kill you again. Kill you so you'll stay dead! Afraid of me! Ho! ho! ho!"

And then the figure leaped. The old man screamed shrilly as the gun was twisted from his grasp; as he was swung aloft in a fireman's carry to the other's shoulders.

"Much obliged!" I said with heartfelt relief. "They shouldn't let a lunatic like that run loose—"

The man had made no answer. He was plodding methodically down the street, with old Barry still swung across his shoulders.

"Where are you taking him?" I asked curiously.

"To the factory," said the man shortly. I recognized the voice as that of the man who smelt of ashes.

And then old Barry recommenced his screaming. God! such rending screams, like a lost soul in endless anguish.

"Don't! Don't let them take me! Don't—oh Jesus, help me!"

"What are you going to do with him?" I insisted.

"Come along and see!" And the man gave a little, throaty chuckle.

I thought then it was the wind whistling, for the chuckle seemed to be echoed and re-echoed through the ruins, as if each separate brick and fallen timber were enjoying some ghoulish joke.

I hesitated a moment, and followed. Even though old Barry were a lunatic, so, unquestionably, was his captor. And knowing something of the strength of madmen, I thoughtfully retrieved the shotgun.

Straight down the street, past the depot, across the tracks, up the driveway to the factory, I followed. Once, I remembered, that driveway had been lined with cottonwoods. Now only their charred and blackened trunks towered, lifeless, to the sky. And though I looked about a score of times and could see nothing, I could have sworn a host accompanied us. There was the rustle of many feet through the ashes, the plod of them in the dusty road, and always a subdued, ghoulish chuckling—a chuckling almost drowned in the ceaseless screaming of Old Barry.

The great driveway door was nearly choked with debris, but we threaded our way through it, and inside the door Barry was lifted high in the air and dashed violently to the floor.

I leaped forward. Lunatic or not, I wouldn't see him killed. I caught his captor by the shoulder and swung him violently about. His cap, loosened by the jerk, slipped back on his head.

And what had once been a face leered up into mine. No nose, no lips, no eyes; only fragments of charred flesh clinging to blackened bones. And the smell of scorching meat—

I screamed as I leaped back and turned to run. And the subdued chuckle rose to a mighty roar of horrible laughter. And I stopped. For something was forming between me and the doorway—something that made the heaps of blackened rubbish look hazy and misty. It was as if a gauze curtain had been pulled down.

And the curtain was moving, swaying, as if in some unfelt breeze. It was knotting and twisting—separating into distinct forms.

The old man was moaning faintly, yet he still lay motionless on the floor, where he had been hurled.

I looked again at the curtain. It had melted into separate units now. They seemed to be drifting toward us. And then again, I screamed my loudest.

Forms of men, they were—or had been. But men with arms—with legs—burned away; with twisted, seared, blackened faces; with great patches of charred skin clinging to burned, black flesh. And skeletons with only bits of flesh still hanging on the incinerated bones. And the smell—oh God!

Did you ever smell meat burning and charring in the oven? Imagine that smell multiplied a thousand times—the reek of searing human flesh, of red-hot, crumbling bones. And there were the contorted faces of men cooked alive—fire-blackened faces still twisted and set in the last fierce agony of death.

I screamed as I threw up the shotgun. Its double report shook the tottering walls. The shot sprayed through that curtain and harmlessly into the rubbish beyond. And still the things came on, with ghastly arms outstretched.

My recent rescuer gave a loud shout. His clothing fell away, revealing his fire-racked body. He joined the slowly drifting throng.

Old Barry was on his feet now, backing slowly away, his eyes fixed on those burned things with the horrible fascination of a bird charmed by a snake. With all my heart I wanted to turn, to run, but to turn my back on those horrors—I could not.

Slowly we backed away together among the heaps of rubbish, of wrecked machinery, from the fallen roof and second floor. Past the beet-slicers, past the big cookers, down through the beet-end, we crept backward, with the bodies of the dead drifting slowly after us.

Past the Oliver presses, past the centrifugals. We couldn't go much farther. The rear wall towered above us. The doorway to the old warehouse was choked with the wreckage of vacuum pans. I threw an arm across my face. I couldn't bear the sight of those shapeless, fire-racked bodies.

I found the darkness even more unbearable. In fancy, I could feel those bony hands with their scraps of charred, crumbling flesh fastening on me. I screamed again, and pressed tightly against the wall.

There was a chant in the air. Surely it never came from those fleshless, lipless mouths.

"Come with us! Into the fire! The nice, warm fire, John! Come with us!"

"No, no!" The old man was on his knees. "I never meant—I didn't know—don't hurt me! Oh, don't hurt me!"

And still the chant went on:

"The fire! The nice, warm fire!"

They were very close now. I whirled about desperately.

Almost five years before I had worked in the factory. I knew there should be another door—the door to the boilerhouse. Could I find it in the darkness and litter? In a maniac rush, I sprang over the piled wreckage. A wave of devastating heat scorched my face as the dead men swept up. There was a crackling of flames among that burned-out rubbish. The old man screamed horribly.

I pressed my hands over my ears as I stumbled and staggered onward. Still I could hear him scream. God, I can hear him yet!

"Jesus! Oh, Lord Jesus! It burns. They're burning me—"

Thank God the little doorway was open and partly clear. I pushed, squeezed, tore my way through the rubbish. I was out in the areaway east of the boiler-house. Those things were behind me—and the old man was still screaming. More faintly, now. And a babble.

"Oh, Jesus! Oh, Jesus! Oh, Jesus! It burns—it burns—"

With my hands still over my ears, I raced away from that place of madness.

How I reached Jim's ranch I never knew. I don't even remember getting there. It is eight miles from Como. Only, when I opened my eyes, Jim was leaning over me, alternately pouring something raw and fiery down my throat, and shaking me, while shouting:

"Bob! Bob! For God's sake, what's the matter?"

Hallucinations—nightmare—the doctor from San Benito said. And I think Jim believed him, at first. Probably I would have believed him myself, if it hadn't been for my scorched hair and burned face; relic of that searing wave of awful heat.

And Jim believes now, too. For today he handed me a clipping from the San Benito paper:

> ANOTHER BODY FOUND AT COMO
>
> Further mystery is added to the great fire at Como by the discovery of the remains of John Barry, former watchman at the factory of the Como Sugar Company.
>
> Readers will recall that Barry was suspected of starting the fire in revenge for what he considered an unjust discharge. No proof could be offered, however.
>
> Yesterday his charred body was found in the ruins of the factory, identification being possible by means of an old-fashioned watch he always carried. It is surprizing the body has not been discovered sooner, for it lay in plain sight, near the warehouse wall.
>
> The mystery is heightened by the fact that several reputable people claim to have seen Barry prowling among the ruins of Como as recently as last Sunday. That this is impossible is evidenced by the watch, the

hands of which stopped at two-fifteen. This is the approximate time the factory's night-shift discovered they were trapped by the flames. ——✦——

CAT'S CRADLE

E. W. TOMLINSON

It has been a long time since I have seen children playing at cat's-cradle. It was a popular pastime when I was a boy and I can remember how children were set to playing the game as an engagement for long Sabbath afternoons when custom and parents required quiet and repose. On such occasions my sister and I faced each other from hassocks placed in the large parlor bow-window and for several hours were occupied with a long loop of cord and a printed chart which showed us how to begin and how to progress, alternately lifting a continuously more intricate complex of cord from each other's hands.

I have often wondered how the game ever came to this country — what strange group of immigrants brought the cat's-cradle with them from over the sea. But more I wonder how it ever came to assume the rank of a game for children, whose nearest approach to evil was an occasional raid on cookie-jar or jam-pot. Even in the mild form it assumed there remained a taint of an old evil, especially since some of the figures were called by such names as "Hang the Witch," "Flying Goblin" and the like. I can now see more clearly this truth because of what happened to a friend of mine. I trust his veracity completely for reasons which need no explanation here. And I know that his powers of observation are remarkable.

My friend is a man only a little older than myself and we were brought up together. The houses of our parents were so placed that their alley-entrances were exactly opposite and the children of both establishments were constantly back and forth. My sister and I were as much at home in my friend's house as we were in our own and I am happy to remember that the reverse was also true. Our father was the minister of a local church while my friend's father was the director of a bank. So it was that my friend inherited a sizeable and well-invested fortune which has left him free to do as he liked. He has always used his money well, never squandering it as so many wealthy sons of wealthy parents have done. His tastes were always serious and his money only enabled him to indulge his predilection for travel and education. Late in life he married and became himself a father, but the incident which I am about to relate occurred to him when he was a young man. He had been pursuing his studies at the Sorbonne toward a graduate degree. It was near the turn of the century. Science was in the air and superstition had been (it was supposed) thrown upon time's scrap-heap of outmoded things — along with revealed religion, public morality and the divine right of kings. My friend was a child of those times, deeply infected with an aversion to immaterial things which cannot be examined under a microscope or contained in a test-tube.

The summer had been fine and my friend had long looked forward to a holiday in the Pyrenees after a protracted season of seminars. He had gone by train to Lourdes, examined the records and watched the pilgrims with a preconceived disbelief which no amount of visual proof could touch. Beyond Lourdes he had traveled by voiture up the lower slopes of the chain of rough mountains which separates France from Spain. He had spent some time in the tiny mountain state of Andorra, looking into its strange dualistic government. But when the life in Andorra began to pall he hired a donkey and set out to travel on foot into the Spanish country beyond.

The road soon became little more than a track across barren stones and earth and my friend had begun to feel a little shut in by the towering peaks and looming sun-baked cliffs. Night was approaching and my friend had seen no sight of human habitation since early afternoon. He was beginning to wonder if he would not be forced to sleep cold upon the ground when he saw with distinct relief a well-constructed house facing him as he rounded a turn among the boulders. For a moment he wondered how anyone could scratch a living from the bare earth and rock about the house but quickly put aside a problem which concerned him less immediately than a warm supper and a comfortable bed.

The lower story of the house was of roughly dressed stone and the upper half-story was of planed timber surmounted by a tiled roof. A few thin chickens scratched dispiritedly in the dooryard and a sleek black cat sat warming itself in the dying rays of the sun. A stout girl was cooking something on an outdoor brazier behind the building, but it required more than one hail to bring her to the roadside. My friend had some difficulty in making her understand his wants, for he spoke the best of French and Spanish while the girl spoke only the bastard Pyrenean patois — so it was more by gesture than word of mouth that my friend finally conveyed the idea of his wishing a meal and a night's rest. It was the pesetas which he displayed which appeared to illumine his meaning best of all.

The dull-eyed girl surveyed my friend and his money, then turned and called raucously toward the house. The door was opened and another woman appeared, a stout woman who from resemblance appeared to be the girl's mother. But while the girl was roughly clothed, wearing a cloth about her head and rope sandals on her feet, the mother was well dressed in heavy black silk. Her graying hair was pulled tautly back with combs and she wore black patent-leather buttoned shoes over the high tops of which bulged her fat ankles. Her fingers were so loaded with broad gold rings set with bright stones, and such a large gold brooch was set in the black silk at her throat that my friend thought suddenly of the border smugglers of whose activities he had lately heard. Somehow he wished he had not so definitely requested his night's lodging. Perhaps the stones of the roadside would have been preferable. However, the deed was done. After an unintelligible conversation with her daughter the old woman took my friend's money, dropped it into a capacious bosom and ushered him into the house.

My friend hardly recalls the supper which was served him because during the meal his attention was so riveted upon a large stuffed crocodile which hung from the ceiling of a recess in a wall. He does recall that the meal was plentiful and good and that the girl ate greedily, leaning over her plate, while the mother ate daintily as a duchess, pausing at intervals to survey her visitor and to direct unanswered remarks to the girl. The sun had set by now and a lamp had been lighted. Its rays were oddly reflected from the teeth and shiny glass eyes of the crocodile, as well as from the highly polished surfaces of a few tall old chairs and a heavily carved armoire which were the room's only furnishings. The ceiling overhead was composed of wooden beams, overlaid by the flooring of the upper attic story. The floor was of stones cut in such a way that a design of a six-pointed star enclosed in a hexagon stood out against regular horizontal lines.

So much my friend observed of the main room of the house. Then, the meal being finished, he was led down a short hall. At its end was a ladder leading upward through a hole in the ceiling to the attic. It was indicated that his room was above, and when he had climbed the ladder a lighted candle was passed up to him. By its light he saw that a low bed was situated at the end of the attic under a window and that at the other end were several very old chests, carved and bound with brass. He was very tired after his long day of walking and climbing and without delay pulled off his shoes and outer garments, blew out the candle and was soon asleep.

He relates that he could not have been asleep long when he was awakened by a high, thin sound which reminded him of the distant howling of a dog, but infinitely higher in pitch and more prolonged. Sitting up in bed he placed the sound as coming from the room below and suddenly the short hair on the back of his neck stood erect as a cold chill swept over him.

Quietly getting out of bed he peered down the trap-door of the garret but could see only a flickering light on the floor beneath it, a reddish light reflected from the parlor. His curiosity infinitely aroused and his inexplicable fear overcome he peered about him in the darkness, his eye finally encountering a red gleam among the chests at the far end of the attic. It came from a small knothole in the floor boards, upon which he lay down at full length in order to peer through into the parlor. He saw something which to this day his mind will not accept—and about which he has spoken to no one other than myself.

The view which his vantage-point disclosed was broad enough to include the parlor below nearly from wall to wall. Directly beneath him was the six-pointed star. He could see that at each point of the star had been set a low dish containing some material which was burning redly with a great deal of pungent smoke. The two women were seated cross-legged upon the floor within the star and between them lay a square of carpeting. Upon this carpeting rested the black cat which my friend had observed in the dooryard. It crouched, and its tail twitched as if it were thinking of pleasant things. Over its back and in the air between the women stretched a long loop of cord upon which were strung many bright beads. The women appeared to be playing cat's cradle and my friend was intensely puzzled as to what might be their purpose in playing such a game at such an hour under such strange circumstances.

The high, thin noise he had heard appeared to come from the women, but by now it had been completely sustained, without break or pause. The red light had become more intense and the room below was becoming partially obscured by smoke. The loop of cord whipped and flashed, evolving patterns more and more complex, the affixed beads seeming to slip into strange planes and angles, from one design into another like the bright patterns in a kaleidoscope. Its effects were hypnotic and my friend now believes that he slipped into a semi-comatose state as he watched the changing shapes through the obscuring smoke in which all outlines were growing dimmed, so that the whole scene below him took on the aspect of a scene under water—objects moving into focus and slipping out of focus in a celeritous rhythm of strange value.

The square of carpeting appeared to roll and twist upon itself in a slow and doubtful fashion while the cat appeared to have rolled on its back with its legs stretched as if being pulled asunder. The loop of cord moved at dizzying speed, the women's hands dipping and twisting like evening birds as they passed the cord back and forth to each other. The old woman's tightly confined hair fell from its combs and over her shoulders in a great cascade and she bent backward and forward to the rising and falling of the thin wail which now seemed to come out of the very walls. The girl appeared to grow larger, to impose herself on the scene as it were, and her hands moved with lightning rapidity in opposition to those of the older woman.

Suddenly the noise ceased. The intense activity stopped. The red light flared once more and quickly died away, the smoke seeming to dissipate itself. And my friend saw—but what he saw was impossible for him to accept and oppose. So his senses left him; but not before he saw the girl pick up the cat—if cat it still was—and, opening the bosom of her dress, appear to nurse it as a woman would nurse an infant. The old woman slumped forward like a half-empty meal sack.

This much my friend saw before he fainted. When he came to himself it was dawn and the pale light in the garret enabled him to see well enough to get into his clothing. He slipped down the ladder and crossed the empty parlor. As he opened the door the glassy eyes of the crocodile seemed to gleam with mockery. But the sharp, cool air of the mountain morning heartened him as he untied his burro and hastened away from the house and up the valley.

A few hours later he made his breakfast at a small settlement which clung to a hillside like barnacles to a ship's hull. At the inn a few guarded queries elicited responses which showed that the villagers detested the old house down the valley—because, Señor, those women are witches. Oh surely, Señor, we go there sometimes to obtain a love-potion or a medicine against the murrain, but no, Señor, we hold no frequent business at that house. It is better, Señor, not to tempt the Devil!

This then is the story told me by my friend when we were both young men and he just returned from Europe. He did not know what to think of his experience, since it fell into no category with which he was familiar—for his mind does not allow for the possibility of witchcraft. But I, being somewhat better versed in these matters, believe that what he saw was nothing less than a sacrament of sorcery, a feeding of the familiar.

Of course, I do not *know*, but that is what I believe. At any rate, my friend says that the simulacrum which the girl lifted from the

square of carpeting was alive, for he saw it move. He says guard-
edly, however, that the object was obviously neither animal nor
human. ——+

THE CAVERN

MANLY WADE WELLMAN

*We tread the steps appointed for us; and he whose steps are
appointed must tread them.*
— *The Arabian Nights*

The old fortune-teller had done with her prattle about crossing
water and receiving letters full of money. She gathered up her
grimy deck of cards and shuffled away, leaving Stoll and me to
finish our dinner under soft lights, accompanied by soft music. I
sighed and wondered aloud why the hag had singled us out of all the
patrons in the crowded restaurant.

"Because she knew I believe," replied Stoll as he poured wine.

I was amazed and a bit shocked. "You believe in fortune-tellers?
Nobody of education and intelligence can possibly—"

"Granted that I have no education and intelligence, but I believe." He was quite solemn. "I've seen one come true."

I dared hope for one of Stoll's rare stories. Why do men like Stoll,
who have seen so much and behaved so well in far places, keep their
mouths shut? I waited, and eventually he added:

"It wasn't my fortune, but Swithin Quade's."

"Swithin Quade," I repeated eagerly. "The African Quade? The
one in the Sunday feature sections?"

"Right. I met him on his first day in Africa."

Swithin Quade was the sort of budding empire-builder Kipling
used to write about (began Stoll). You know what I mean—broad
shoulders, long legs, golden-brown curls, eyes like the April sky,
close-clipped young mustache, close-clipped young attitudes, and
adventure hunger enough for all the explorers since the launching of
the Argo. His people had no money, but they had managed to edu-
cate him well, and through influential friends he'd been signed up to
cut his teeth on the tomb of a priest-noble of the Hyksos, up Nile a
way. I was camp and digging chief on that job, under Thomson, the
big Egyptology pot.

Alexandria was even more garish then than now—there was considerable tourist money, and no war scare. As soon as Quade hit the dock he wanted to see dancers, snake-charmers, mosques and all the rest of it. I took him 'round, because Thomson was busier than I and didn't know so many places. Quade and I wound up late the first afternoon in a loudish spot, with striped awnings, and mutton stew, and hashish in the coffee. A bunch of vicious-looking blacks were belting away at drums and wailing on pipes, and a very dirty and ragged old Arab sidled up to whine for *"Bakshish!"*

I warned him off with the traditional *"Mafish!"* and tried to ignore him. But the old duffer—bent he was, and dried up like a bunch of raisins—began to plead for a chance to tell fortunes. Quade asked what it was about, and I explained.

"Good egg," said Quade at once, his face as bright and happy as a child's behind that trim mustache. "Have him tell mine."

The walking mummy understood Quade's enthusiastic manner, if not his English, and right away set down his little tray of polished wood on the edge of our table. Then he poured sand on the tray, from an old tobacco pouch. He began to fiddle with his scrawny fingers, making little rifts and ridges and hills.

"Good egg," Quade repeated. "This blighter is just what I hoped to run into. Picturesque and all that—hurry up, old fellow!" And his smile grew wider.

But the sand diviner did not smile back. He only paddled in the sand, and stared out of ancient eyes that looked dim and foul, like pools with scum on them. Finally he mumbled something.

"What's he saying?" asked Quade, and I translated:

"Death sits waiting in a cavern. . . ."

The old bat had waited for me to pass this along. And now he added something on his own hook. "This other *effendi*," he said, turning his dim gaze on me, "shall be witness, and will know that I have not lied."

Quade's grin faded into a frown of intense interest, and he leaned forward to look at the sand on the tray. It was all smoothed out, under those dirty claws, and in the middle was a little hole. Funny that it should look so deep and dark, that hole; there wasn't more than a handful of sand, yet you'd think the diviner had made a pit miles deep.

I saw that Quade was suddenly repelled, and I gave the old vulture a piece of silver, a shilling I think. He bowed and blessed us, and gathered up his tray of sand and scrabbled out. Quade drank some coffee.

"I say, that was nasty," he mumbled to me. "Let's go back to the hotel, eh?"

So we went. But he found it was close and hot there, and stepped out to take a bit of a stroll by himself. Back he came in half an hour, and he looked quite drawn and stuffy.

"These swine are pulling my leg," he said angrily, and then he told me what had happened. Down in some narrow alley full of shops and booths, he had come upon another fortune-teller, a baggy old woman who spoke English. Probably he hoped to hear something conventional about a blond wife and a journey across deep water, to take the taste of the other prophecy out of his mouth. So he stuck out his palm for her to read.

"And I swear, Stoll," he told me, "that she gave one look and then screwed up her face, and said the same thing."

"What same thing?" I asked him.

"What that filthy old Johnny with the sand said. 'Look out for the cavern,' or 'Death waits in the cavern,' or the like. See here, I jolly well don't like it."

I advised him to keep his chin up and not bother about natives. Finally he managed to make light of the business, but not very convincingly. And when we got to Cairo—Thompson had to stop there for a big row with the officials—he gave the business a third try.

It was in a cool, conventional little tea garden—run by a smart Scotswoman, who knew how a place like that would catch homesick English travelers. She had native waiters dressed like Europeans, and crumpets and all that, and a very lovely girl in a stagy gipsy costume to read the leaves in the cups. Quade wanted to test fate again.

The girl came to our table when he beckoned, and she was plainly intrigued by his grin and his curls and his youth. I think she intended to give him such a reading as would fetch him back later—maybe not for tea alone. But as she turned the cup and squinted at the tangle inside, her handsome face grew grave, and its olive faded to a parchment tint.

"You must take care," she said huskily, in accented English. "Take care of the cave—the cavern." Her eyes grew wider, and she looked at me with them. "You, sir, will see a terrible fate that is his. . . ."

That night Quade packed his bags, and told Thomson and me that he was chucking his job.

"I'm not having any of that cavern," he said. "Three warnings are quite enough."

"What cavern?" I demanded, smiling a little.

"Cavern or underground tomb, what's the difference?"

"You can't take such prophecies seriously," put in Thomson.

Quade replied, very tritely, that there were more things in heaven and earth, and so on. "I know you chaps think I'm afraid," he added.

"Neither of us said anything like that," I replied at once.

"And no more am I afraid," he almost snapped back. "I'll stay in Africa—but in the open. Call me idiotic, or superstitious, or what you will. Better safe than sorry, is my motto."

He was as good as his word for ten years, and he thrived enormously on African danger.

Today he is a tradition, a legend even. Everybody has heard about how, in Jo'burg, he walked up on a mad Kaffir with a gun, who had even those tough Transvaal police buffaloed for the moment; the Kaffir fired twice, stirring Quade's curls with both shots, and then Quade knocked him loose from the gun with one straight dunt on the mouth. Some sort of foundation wanted to give him a medal, but he wouldn't accept. He went instead with some romantic Frenchmen who tried to find the Dying-place of the Elephants— sure, people still look for it; I, for one, believe it exists. But all Quade got was a terrible dose of black-water fever. He recovered from that and complications, though eleven men out of twelve would have died.

Next he got up into West Central, and visited the Lavalli-valli. Instead of thinking that he was a missionary and eating him, they thought he was a god and worshipped him. I understand that Quade had to fight one skeptic, a big brute about seven feet tall, very skilful with the stabbing-spear. But Quade dodged the first thrust, got in close and took the spear away, and gave it back right through the fellow's lungs. That made him solider than teak with the Lavalli-valli, who love a fighter better than anything else in all the cosmos. Quade might have ruled there forever, but all he wanted was to trade for the native rubber they had. He got a whole caravan-load, and lost it to Portuguese gamblers in Benguela. Broke, he accepted an offer to help the inland Boer settlers fight off a Gangella uprising. He had more escapes than Bonnie Prince Charlie.

Then he went to Ethiopia, just as the Italians pushed in. Quade took up for Haile Selassie, who dubbed him "Ras Quedu" and put him in command of a kind of a suicide division. His men—Africa's tallest and finest, as I hear—were slaughtered almost to the last one, in the fighting around Jijiga. But Quade was captured by some of Mussolini's Moslem auxiliaries. While the chiefs were arguing whether he should die as an infidel or live as a prisoner of war,

Quade throttled a sentry and escaped. He fled clear through the interior, safe into British territory.

That and a thousand other things made him news. Lowell Thomas began talking about him on the radio, and W. B. Seabrook or somebody of that sort wrote a biography, *Quade the Incredible.* I daresay he'll be a solar myth before the century is out.

I cut his trail just about a year ago, on the fringe of a rain-forest somewhere in the 'tween-mountain country of Portuguese West. If we had a map I'd show you where. His boys and mine entered a little village from opposite sides. I, following in, heard, "Hullo there, Stoll! This *is* a lark!", and there was Quade. Not the curly golden boy any more, but a tough-tempered, lean-cheeked hunter. He had grown a short beard, into which the toothbrush mustache had lengthened and blended. His rosy face had been baked brown, and his was the ready way of moving and standing that comes from harsh life gladly met. The one thing that made me remember the old Swithin Quade—or, rather, the young Swithin Quade—was his bright blue eye, as happy and honest under his worn slouch hat as it had been that first afternoon in Alexandria.

When we had crushed each other's hands and slapped each other's backs almost purple, we quartered our outfits side by side, just at the gate of the village stockade. Then we went together to buy beans and manioc, and he invited me to supper at his fire. After eating we swapped yarns, and of course Quade's yarns were by far the best.

"You still remember those Alexandrian fortunes?" I asked at length.

He smiled, but nodded, and said that he had more than remembered. He had asked fortunes from varied seers—Kaffir witch-doctors, Moslem marabouts, and ordinary crystal-gazers in Cape Town and Durban. "And they've been strangely unanimous," he summed up. "I give you my word, that again and again there's been something about a cave, or a cavern, or just a hole. And I'm always told that I'd best stay out."

"And have you stayed out?" I prompted.

"I have that," he chuckled. "I must say that, if death waits for me in a cavern, it has remained there. Mine's the traditional charmed life."

"Don't forget," I reminded, "that I'm supposed to witness your fate in a cavern."

"I haven't forgotten, Stoll. But I'm here to hunt—hippopotami just now, I've been too busy all these years to get one—and if you come along tomorrow, we'll take care to stay clear of holes. Then, when we separate in a day or so, I'll be safe again, what?"

I joined in chuckling over the conceit.

But he was dead serious on one point—staying in the open. That night he slept in a tent, not the snug hut that the solicitious villagers had built especially for him. His gun-bearer told my head-man that Quade always slept that way; that, when in the settlements, he, Quade, never sat in a house without the windows open, and had twice refused to take a job in the diamond country for dislike of entering a mine. I heard all this at breakfast in the morning, and made bold to ask Quade about it when he came over to renew his invitation to the hunt.

"My bearer's a gossipy chap, but he's telling the truth," Quade confessed cheerfully. "I go into precious few houses except when it's necessary, and into no cellars whatever. Now then, what heavy rifles have you? . . . Oh, I see, Dutch guns. Two nice weapons, those. Well, shall we start?"

Away we went, with our gun-bearers and a leash of villagers for guides. Down valley from the camp we approached a great tangled belt of the forest, and one of the local hunters pointed to a tunnel-like opening among the trees and bushes, the "hole in the jungle" made by nothing but a hippo.

"I say, that looks as if it might be the cavern you and I heard about once," said Quade, and not in a joking manner. He hesitated, but only for a moment, and then led the way in.

We traversed the leafy passage, and I felt as jumpy as Quade. But the closest approach to danger along the entire way was an ineffably beautiful little snake, that struck at a village boy and missed. My bearer killed it with a stick he carried.

At the other end of the tunnel we came out on the banks of one of those African rivers unknown and uncharted—deep, swift, tree-walled, as dark and exotic as the one in the poem about Kubla Khan. As a matter of fact, Quade muttered a phrase from that very poem about "Alph, the sacred river," but I refrained from adding the bit about "caverns measureless to man." Meanwhile, the villagers poked into a clump of sappy-leaved bushes, and drew into view a brace of dugouts, very nicely finished and perfectly balanced. Quade and his bearer got into one of them, and I with my bearer took the other. Each of us had a pair of villagers to paddle. Together we dropped downstream.

It was I, a little ahead of Quade, who saw the hippo first.

He was floating like a water-soaked log in a little bay where the current slowed down considerably. His nostril bumps were in sight, and his ears pricked up to show that they heard us, but he kept perfectly still, hoping we'd pass him by.

My bearer snapped his fingers backward to attract Quade's attention in the rear boat, and I, sitting in the bow, set my elbow on my knee and aimed for what I could see of the hippo's narrow, flat cranium. He was no farther away than the door yonder — I couldn't miss. And I was using a three-ounce explosive slug, big and heavy enough to go through a brick wall.

I couldn't miss, I say. But I did miss. No, not quite; I must have nicked an ear or grazed an eyebrow. For next instant the hippo, stung and furious, swung round in the water like a trout, and charged.

He didn't charge me. He didn't even notice me, then or later. He tore past me in the water — perhaps it was shallow enough for him to run on the bottom — straight at Quade's boat.

I heard Quade curse in Umbundu, and his express rifle roared. Whatever the bullet did, it was not enough to stop the hippo. I, snatching my second rifle from my bearer, saw the great lump of a head dip down under the keel of Quade's boat. The hippo tossed, as a bull might toss, and the canoe with its four passengers whirled lightly upward in the air. I've seen an empty bottle tossed like that, by a careless drunkard.

The three natives, shrieking horribly, flew in all directions and splashed into the water. Quade must have been braced or otherwise held in position at the bow, for when the boat came down he was still in it. There was a great upward torrent of water, and through it I saw the bottom of the stricken canoe. The hippo, close in, bit a piece out of one thwart, as a boy nibbles ginger-cake. I had my second gun and was aiming. This time I wouldn't miss; but before I could touch trigger, Quade came to the surface, right in the way of my shot.

"Down! Down!" I yelled at him, and he turned his face toward me, as if mildly curious at my agitation. And then the hippo had him, in a single champing clutch of those great steam-shovel jaws. Quade screamed once, and I saw him shaken like an old glove by a bulldog.

I fired, and the hippo sank on the instant. He took Quade with him. The ripples were purple with blood — Quade's or the beast's. And we got for shore and safety. Later we tried to recover Quade's body, but we never did.

Stoll was silent, and sipped wine to show that his story was finished.

"But the cavern," I protested. "What about the cavern, where death was waiting for him?"

Stoll lifted his eyebrows, as a Frenchman might shrug his shoulders.

"Did you ever see a hippopotamus open its mouth—wide?"

THE CHAIN

H. WARNER MUNN

Through a circle that ever returneth
To the selfsame spot,
And much of Madness, and more of Sin,
And Horror the soul of the plot.

—POE: *The Conqueror Worm*

His first sensation, when he groaned back to consciousness, was that of bitter and intense cold. Then, becoming fully awake, he was aware of grinding pains in his body, as though each bone and muscle owned a separate ache. He shivered convulsively and opened his eyes.

It was very dark and he could see nothing around him, but high above there gleamed for a second a lurid, ruddy glare, which flickered like leaping flames, then vanished—accompanied by a clang of metal, as though a furnace door had been opened and closed.

Puzzled, he listened, but could hear no sounds except a far, faint crackling like hemlock boughs snapping in a fire. His eyes ached with the strain of watching, and he closed them, too weary to move.

Where was he? Surely he must be dreaming in his bed at the castle of Rutzau, owned by his cousin Franz, and yet he seemed to be awake.

Ah, Franz the blockhead, Franz the cuckold; yet Franz the lucky, for he was fortunate—Franz with the beautiful wife!

What a joke it was on Franz, to be sure, that he should thus entertain his wife's lover so unsuspectingly! Perhaps his wits had been addled as well as his body smashed when Franz had fallen from the cliff two years before. And the cream of the jest was that Franz had never known how the accident had come about, but still believed that the edge of the cliff had crumbled away beneath him!

How could a man be such a fool and live? No wonder that Olga despised her husband now!

The man chuckled at the thought, and sneezed violently. He must be taking cold; how came it that the bed was so damp and—hard?

He rolled over, and his hands came in contact with rock—bare, icy, and wet. He was shocked wide awake at once. Where in God's name could he be?

Abruptly, horror surged around in the dark and left him trembling.

Rock! Wet stone! Half-forgotten tales from the black history of Rutzau swarmed through his head.

If ever a castle were haunted by ghosts, it should be Rutzau, if even a third of the stories that had been whispered about its torture-chambers were true. Rumour spoke, with hushed breath and backward-roving eye, of deep pits and rooms cut out in the solid rock that formed the castle's foundations; murmured, too, of men that had entered the castle and never returned—as men; told also of others who were not seen again, and guessed darkly at the reason; mentioned tortures under which men prayed to be placed upon the rack instead, regarding it as a pleasant couch in comparison to the bed of pain they lay upon.

Also there were whispers regarding rooms where dwelt the Iron Maiden, ever ready with insatiable crushing embrace for any victim; other rooms where the strappado, thumb-screws, and the boot wrung truth or anything that the master of Rutzau wished to know from lying tongues that would not reply to minor tortures, but answered eagerly, hoping their reward would be quick death, as they underwent the Greater Question.

Too, he had heard of the oubliette, a pit with walls of sheer stone, peopled by rats, fierce with hunger, to which men were flung living.

Could he be in the dungeons of Rutzau? Did Franz *know?*

He staggered to his feet, swaying with faintness. Again that lurid flare overhead, followed by the ominous clang, as though someone stoked a furnace in the air.

He began to run in the dark, drunkenly weaving from side to side. Almost at once he felt the impact of a tremendous blow upon his entire body, and he was hurled backwards, striking his head cruelly upon the ground.

Like a dog which has received an unexpected kick, he yelped with the pain and, upon hands and knees, scuttled crabwise backward. Soon he encountered another obstacle with his heels, which resisted further progress, and he stood up, reaching as high as possible with his hands. Nothing projected from the wall, which was smooth and slippery to the touch as his exploring fingers passed over its damp surface.

The wall was gently curved, and, keeping his left hand upon it, he set out to follow whither it might lead him. He had taken nine steps when his hand plunged into vacancy and he stumbled.

The recess in the wall was not deep, but it was already occupied by a furry body that squealed and writhed under his hand and squirmed when he gripped it, setting sharp teeth into his thumb. He jerked his hand out of the hole, with the creature hanging from his thumb, holding tight with teeth and claws and a prehensile tail that wound snakily about his wrist.

With his other hand he loosened the claws one at a time, which fastened elsewhere, while the teeth went on gnawing hungrily. Half crazed, he fought the thing that seemed bent on eating him in small mouthfuls, snarling while it chewed. He screeched like a beast when the teeth met through the fleshy portion of his hand and tore a bit away.

With his free hand he clutched the thing by the back and ripped it loose, battering it on the floor until it wriggled no longer; but his furious rage was not satisfied until he had torn it into ragged halves and hurled them, wet and flapping, from him.

He stood, breathing hard in great gasps, and something began to fight with another something not far away in the dark, squealing little wicked cries.

Something ran across his bare feet and he kicked at it, but struck the wall instead. He cursed vehemently and, limping, resumed his journey along the wall. The wall was at his left, the clamour of a bloody quarrel at his right. Yet, as he advanced, the row did not lessen with distance, but continued undiminished, so that an ugly worm of fear began to crawl in his brain—a thought which he dared not allow himself to dwell upon.

When his hand again entered an opening in the wall, and the squabbling over the dead beast was no farther away, he could no longer deny the fearful fact. He was in the oubliette!

For a third time the heights glowed red from an unseen fire, and again followed that solemn boom like a funeral bell tolling dismally one—a long pause—two and three—and from above a shower of small glittering particles rained down—a sparkling hail.

Many went dark before they reached the floor, but others, larger than the rest, shone like fireflies as they fell; and stretching out his hand he caught one in his palm.

With a cry of pain he dropped it. It was a hot coal, a red ember that stuck to his hand and hissed.

Then through the darkness of the pit, from high in air, floated down a sardonic chuckle. Instantly, without a second's warning, the pit was flooded with light from invisible sources, which revealed to the man, after the first blinding glare had passed, the horror of his prison.

For a hundred feet the walls of the pit rose sheer and smooth, with neither crack nor cranny for a foothold. About four feet from the floor, several openings pierced the rock, and into them were tumbling in a headlong scramble grey shapes as large as cats, round-eared and gaunt, their pointed snouts blood-dabbled from the cannibal feast, and in the centre of the floor lay in fragments what had been a huge rat.

High above, a cripple stumped about the edge of the oubliette, and the man below knew it for his cousin, his heart saying gloomily: "Franz knows!"

Franz lay down and swung an arm over the pit's edge—an arm that, curiously short, seemed to have been broken in several places and clumsily reset.

Was he shaking his fist? And then the man below saw that Franz was beckoning to him. Faintly fell a word: "Climb," then again: "Climb up the chain," and he saw that from the hidden mysteries above a long beam was swinging out until its end was directly over him.

Upon the metal beam there was fixed a pulley, over which ran continuously joined links of iron which now were moving and falling —down.

Slow-dropping, the end of the chain came nearer until his hands could grip it, and still descended. It touched the floor and stopped, swaying there. As he held to the cold links, he could feel the vibration of the engine that had lowered it.

The links were large and heavy, their openings large enough to insert a hand or foot. He fixed himself comfortably as might be and waited to be lifted from the pit.

How Franz would suffer for this when he got out! Let him taste a little of his own pit, perhaps! And then again from above fell the word "Climb," interrupting his pleasant, vindictive thoughts.

Perceiving that the cripple did not intend to lift him out, he set his teeth and began to climb the hundred feet of chain. Franz would have his little joke, he thought, but when he got out—an ugly grin— someone else might laugh.

Still, he might have to beg for help after all: only half-way up now, and he did not feel strong.

Why, he had been climbing for hours, it seemed! Strange he was not already at the top towards which he strained!

He glanced below, and nearly fell in horror. The floor of the pit, nearly forty feet across, was carpeted with the masses of the fallen chain. The chain was being lowered at the same speed at which he was climbing! While he looked below he dropped ten feet nearer the bottom of the pit.

Furiously he began again to climb, regained his ten feet, five feet more, and the chain at an increased rate dropped down.

Above, Franz laughed, but it was more nearly a cackle, and the man below felt hope die within him, for he knew that Franz the cuckold was fully aware, and mad.

"Climb!" he shouted down. "Climb!"

But the man no longer climbed; holding tight instead, he watched the floor come near.

Fifteen feet from the bottom, the chain was loosened suddenly, then caught, and he fell from it. Before he could rise, a heavy length of metal lay across his body, pinning him down. His flimsy night-garments tore as he struggled loose.

While he was freeing himself, the chain hung steady without dropping, but when he moved away the swaying thing followed, guided by the patient cunning of the crazed man above.

The rough metal cut his feet as he walked over it, and he wished for shoes. He kneeled down close by the wall, took off his jacket, and tore it into strips, which he bound about his feet. While he was doing this the chain was coming slowly down, building heaps of metal which overbalanced and fell dangerously near, but not touching him.

Then as he anxiously sought for some retreat from the growing menace, he saw a slight depression in the wall; he *might* fit himself into this and be safe from a direct blow.

He dived for it, and as closely as might be he flattened himself into the niche and, scarcely breathing, waited. Perhaps Franz had not seen!

The hope was vain, for the chain swung from him and a broad mound of metal links rose, like a titanic mushroom lifting its head before the niche. With the squeal of a trapped animal, he darted from his lair, clawed the chain aside, sprang through the narrowing aperture that was left, and sprawled upon his face.

Before he could scramble erect, something struck his shoulder. The chain was at his side. Already a tremulous pile shook uncertainly above him, about to topple.

He rolled aside as it fell, but not far enough to escape, for an arm was caught. Desperately he pried and struggled to get away, finally pulling loose at the expense of a torn hand.

While he fought, the chain had withdrawn to the other side of the pit and had filled it high, a terrace like tangled, petrified, disjointed snakes. Now, when he stood up, it swung towards him again.

He sprang away; the chain followed as he backed towards the

wall. He ran; and then began a strange pursuit, for, ever as he fled, at his heels marched like a sentient thing—the Chain!

It poured into the pit, link after link piling upon the others to form vast heaps of metal which would topple and fall. The man wandered helplessly among these metal tentacles that were thrown out, all but crushed by the heavy coils and mounds that swayed erratically all about him.

Again he slunk behind a heap of metal and mouthed and mowed, gibbering at the chain as it sought him out.

To his tortured mind and feverish imagination the chain, while it swung and created a hill of metal in the centre of the pit, took on a new and monstrous shape. It seemed like a metal giant, its blind head above the clouds, swaying rhythmically from side to side and searching for him in the oubliette. Fumbling about with a hundred clanking arms, it stalked him with a dreadful ghastly patience, for the end was sure. And towering mightily before his hiding-place, it drove him forth again and struck him down with a hundredweight of iron links.

He struggled up once more, clinging to life, bruised and hurt, whining and whimpering now, all pride forgotten. Bitterly he cursed the name of the woman whose fair face had brought him here to walk with Death.

From high overhead came down a malignant sound—the low, quiet tittering of the madman, watching, planning, carefully goading his victim round about the pit. The man below looked up, a curse upon his lips in which the name of Franz was mingled—a curse which gave place to a scream of abysmal terror as he realized the inconceivable frightfulness of the approaching doom.

For several yards from the lip of the pit the chain glowed red with heat, and as he watched, the links that now came following shone yellow, then white, flaked with black patches of soot on which ran and twinkled tiny racing crowds of sparks in endless chase.

The chain was passing through the roaring furnace above; white-hot and coming down. . . .

It touched the colder links and made a pile which he avoided. It swung around the pit and laid a circle around him; swinging still, it formed a narrowing spiral at whose centre he stood shivering with the agony of anticipation. It neared him, hung steady, then swung quickly at him like the leap of a python. He shrieked and darted aside.

His feet came down on the glowing links, and the rags around his feet smoked and burst into flame. Weeping, he tore them away and trod the flaming path with naked feet.

That which followed was a matter of moments, but to him it seemed a foretaste of eternity spent in punishment.

The chain came slowly down, livid with heat and leprously scaled with oxydized metal, pulsating in ripples along its length from the throbbing engine that lowered it to the floor, building shimmering heaps for his tortured climbing.

Stumbling over scorching ridges, he rounded the pit, limping feebly along over the hideous surface that drove him to his doom. Rest impossible, he tottered on his way, hope as dead within him as in any poor lost soul that crosses with treadmill trot some smoking, horizonless plain of hell.

From the walls, cracking with heat, jetted out white puffs of steam, but above their piping whistle there rumbled in the man's crazed brain strange roaring voices, and sometimes he vacuously smiled as he listened to the ravings of a mind in dissolution—and plodded on his way. And, though his eyes were clouded and dim, he began to see a vision, and to him the livid swaying chain appeared hazily to be the dancing white body of the woman he had loved.

He turned to follow instead of fleeing as before, but she tripped away lightly, mocking, and he could come no nearer, for the maniac above managed the chain so that his prisoner should not be touched by it, thinking perhaps that he had not yet paid fully and would find Death too dear a friend.

The man below was growing unconscious of his pain, mercifully believing, with his shattered mind, that he dwelt in happier days, and once he muttered as he stumbled on: "Oh, Olga, Olga! How your kisses burn!"

He thought he had whispered, but the words burst out in a rasping croak and a gush of blood from a half-cooked lung followed and hissed upon the chain.

Nerves have their limits. They can be strained to a certain point, but beyond that they refuse to function, which in a way is merciful. So it was with the man. The breaking-point had been reached and passed, and his suffering was no longer so intense.

Dying on his charred stumps of feet, he hobbled amid the coils of clanking metal that flowed relentlessly down like a slow thread of lava trickling over the lip of the pit. Occasionally the chain swung in an unexpected direction and laid a fiery tentacle across his shoulders, searing anew an earlier burn; or again he heard, through the drumming stutter of the heated blood in his pounding head, the hiss and sharp puff of steam as a white-hot link accidentally pressed against his naked side.

But though he winced and cried out at every motion he was compelled to take, it was more because the cringing seemed by then to be the proper thing, necessary, and a part of the torment, than because of any new agony that he experienced.

He had nearly ceased to think. Now and then, while he reeled and staggered over the loosely shifting heaps that illuminated the pit with a ruddy light, a groan of relief hissed through his baked lips as the dull brain told the cracking body that the end must be very near.

Once he thought he heard a cry far away, and not repeated. The voice seemed familiar; it was, in fact, the yell of the maniac who was dancing around the rim of the pit, perilously near but wary of his own trap and shrieking down curses at his enemy.

Only the one sound had pierced to the seat of memory, but it was enough to cause the man to hope again. Perhaps Franz, the merciless, had relented!

He summoned his lagging energies and tried to speak, but the sound that issued from the throat was only a gurgle. Again he tried; it was agony even to breathe; a harsh, inarticulate croak, in which were only fragments of words, was the only result, and his deafened ears refused to carry the answer.

Hope died and a more bitter despair took its place. The reaction produced an even keener torture, if such were possible. It was almost as though a lost soul, who knew himself to be in the deepest chamber of hell, felt the floor drop from beneath him and precipitate him still farther down.

He struggled on beneath the iron flails, through a misty haze of smoke, a fog of sooty vapour from his own smouldering body, a stench hanging around him not merely of burned flesh but, even more repulsive, the repugnant odour of charred bone; and the demon above forgot to yell in his wonder that life could linger so long in such a mutilated being.

And still the dead man walked and stumbled, mechanically complaining in inhuman, querulous moans, glaring straight ahead, though his eyeballs were seared over with the heat.

The horror could not long continue. Inevitably the moment came when he could not avoid the moving pillar of shining metal.

Blind, hands stretched before him, feeling his way forward, one hand and arm passed by the chain and the other arm upon its other side. Just before his face touched the glowing link he realized his mistake, but not in time to dodge the blow, and the link covered his face like a brand.

For a second he was conscious of a terrible withering heat, an intolerable piercing glare that beat into his brain like jagged arrows —and then reason fled. With it passed any sense of pain, and a numbness that felt chill in that place of fire stole around his heart like a caress.

He crept aimlessly for a few feet on hands and knees, stiffened, rolled upon his side, and placed his bleeding head upon his charred arm quite naturally as though he had laid him down to sleep upon soft grasses instead of a bed of fire. Yet so indomitable is the will to live that still one fingerless hand dabbed feebly at the chain for a space, although his brain was dead within him.

And, no longer swaying, but descending evenly, the chain dropped upon him and buried him from sight.

Up through the interstices of the glowing heap of metal thick smoke seeped, black and heavy, drifting lazily in the currents of heat that danced in the pit.

The chain cooled and shrank, contracting with now and then a jangle of links slipping into new positions, and a hollow commenced to take place upon its surface.

And as the smoke diminished from this trough, coffin-like in shape, gorgeous colours shimmered along the hollow, melting into new forms and shades like the rainbow hues of oil on water—crimson and green and blue.

High overhead—beside the roaring furnace—the low, nervous tittering of a madman!

Then in the myriad cells of water-soaked rock the steam expanded until the pressure was irresistible. A rending shock, and a crack, jagged and growing wider, crept on the walls. The castle quivered to its highest spire.

Still the madman tittered his mechanical laugh.

Then the walls caved in, the furnace dropped into the abyss like a live coal falling from a grate, and the ceiling fell.

The Castle of Rutzau would no longer menace the peasants in the valley. It and the pit of torment were no more. ——✠

THE CHURCH STOVE AT RAEBRUDAFISK

G. APPLEBY TERRILL

I threw a piece of string into the grate, where presently it began to smolder.

Kobyssu stopped talking and sniffed. Although in appearance he is ferocious, with his little simian forehead, his black bushes of eyebrows, and his big, bristling mustache, he is in reality a fellow of most pleasant, even temperament. But it was plain that the string had disturbed him greatly. His cheek had paled, and I got a glimpse of his eyes as he bent forward swiftly in his chair and leveled them at the hearth. The expression in them was twofold. There was deep anger; there was equally deep horror.

He saw the string, snatched at it, and cast it into the heart of the fire, so that it flamed instantly.

"Pouf!" he said, waving his hands in front of his nose, and now exceedingly white.

I was amazed, but all I said was: "Sorry, I didn't think the smell would worry you."

Kobyssu looked round his café, deserted at this hour of the afternoon. He looked at the neat tables, at the walls, at his desk, rather with the air of a man who wished to assure himself that he was indeed in Wardour Street, London, and nowhere else. Then he faced the fire again, his eyes more normal but very somber.

"That smell of slow-burning hemp—it reminded me of something in Czergona."

"But," said I, "you often tell me that every memory of your native country is dear to you. Only yesterday you quoted some absurd proverb—"

" 'To a Czerg the howl of a wolf in his homeland is more comforting than the lowing of his cattle in a foreign land.' It is a true proverb. My country may be merely what your newspapers say, 'a barren mountain range in mid-Europe,' but I love every memory of it—except one. That is a memory of dreadful things."

There was a table with coffee between our chairs. He filled my cup.

"From any country, however great and refined, one may get a memory of dreadful things," he said, defending Czergona.

I nodded.

"Yet these were strangely dreadful." He drew in his breath with a long hiss, staring broodingly at the sugar-bowl. "The odor of that string recalled to me the church stove at Raebrudafisk—so suddenly, so without warning, that I believed I was back in the past, and I felt the feelings of twelve years ago. Ah-h, I had a shock."

"What about this stove? But pardon, Kobyssu; perhaps it would pain you to tell me? Perhaps the matter is personal?"

He shook his head.

"I was not directly concerned, I am thankful to say. But the story is too fearful a thing to relate idly over coffee. And you would be sorry if I put it in your mind. You would strive to forget it, and never forget it—no, no, I do not want to tell it."

But my curiosity had risen high. I urged Kobyssu and he yielded. I am punished. I wish I had not heard a word of the tale of the church stove at Raebrudafisk, which Kobyssu narrated in the fluent English that he has acquired so praiseworthily during recent years.

"Raebrudafisk," he said, "is the village I was born in. It is on a hillside, in a fir wood. The church, which is of stone, is a quarter of a mile from it, up the hill. When, as a little boy, I was taken to church by my parents, the stove used to interest me very much. It was not far from where we sat, near the north wall. It was an upright iron cylinder about three feet high and two feet in diameter, having a flat top, with a flap at the edge of this, which opened so that coal and wood could be poured in. A stout pipe went from the stove right up to the roof and through it.

"In summer, of course, the stove was not lit. In winter it was attended to by old Uflio Vaang. He would start the fire some two hours before the morning service—and why the stove interested me was this: by the time I entered the church the flat top would be a glowing red, with dazzling sparks appearing suddenly on it when specks of stuff fell there from the ceiling; and the pipe would be red, half-way to the roof, brilliant red at the base, duller the higher you looked—yet hot, you can imagine.

"I was extremely fond of that stove, especially at evening service, when snow and darkness and wolves were outside the church. I yearned to spend the night by it, and thought pastor and people would be much more sensible to do so instead of faring down the hill, all in a bunch for fear of the wolves.

"And I was a young rascal! I got into the habit of flicking bits of string on to the stove, to see them smoke and burst into flame. But a thrashing from my father and another from the pastor cured me of that.

"There was a good draft to that stove—it had some bars low down in front. And old Uflio, though everybody warned him not to, drenched the fuel with oil before lighting it. Stove and pipe were red long before church-time."

Kobyssu drank some coffee, and made a considerable pause. I knew he was hoping that some customer would arrive and give him a pretext for breaking off altogether. None came, however, so he shrugged his shoulders and proceeded.

"Old Uflio Vaang was wonderful. He was completely blind. He had been blind since early manhood. With no difficulty he would find his own way to the church, place his hand on anything he required, and set the stove going. Dangerous work for a blind man, you will think, eh? Yet he was known to be so careful that, despite the matter of oil, people did not fear an accident. Uflio's perception was uncanny. I have noticed the stove fail a trifle toward the end of morning service, the top go from yellow-scarlet to crimson; and Uflio, sensing the change, has risen from his chair and tiptoed down the church, and picked up a small tongs and opened the flap, gripping it at the first attempt; and, lump by lump, not to make a loud noise, he has dropped coal into the red-hot thing, running no more peril of burning himself than would a man with two healthy eyes.

"Well, twelve years ago, when I was a swineherd of twenty, and had not commenced to think of London or even of Warsaw, old Uflio was still tending the stove. Naturally, I had lost my boyish interest in it. I never supposed that I should be interested in it again."

Kobyssu paused once more. When he resumed, such a note of sadness was in his voice that I experienced a chill—a dread, and the first of my regrets at having importuned him for the story. I had not reckoned on a tragedy to a young girl, which I perceived looming.

"Uflio Vaang had a daughter," said he; "Djira. She was sixteen, pretty, bright-natured—oh, delightful. She was the old man's only child, and, as his wife was dead, all in the world he had to care for. I was not in love with Djira. I was thinking of a girl in the next village. But the other young men of Raebrudafisk were in love with her, as, unhappily, was a man not young. That was Olk Sturl, whose age was forty, and who was often in prison for stealing or violence. He was a sullen blackguard ordinarily; when enraged he was the evilest of brutes.

"Of course, his chance to win Djira, the sweet, fresh bud, was hopeless. But I suppose he did not believe this until he waylaid her one afternoon far from our village. Then she must have convinced him. Would she had not, poor child! poor little innocent! The truth infuriated him. He cut her throat—there and then."

"Kobyssu!"

"He did—there and then," said Kobyssu, the deep anger in his eyes again, and his teeth glinting under his mustache. He clenched his fist, and shook it at the floor. "He did," he repeated, "and he did more. That the scent of much blood might bring the wolves, who would hide his crime, he stabbed, he hacked her little pure body— ah-h!" Kobyssu blew out his breath and drummed his fingers agitatedly on his knees.

So this was what the stove, that Djira's father tended, reminded Kobyssu of. As it was fact, not fiction, I did not want to hear anything further. And yet I felt I must know what happened to the villain Sturl. I said so, and added in dismay: "Kobyssu! you don't have capital punishment in Czergona, do you!"

"No," he answered, with a peculiar inflection of his voice. "The wolves did not get Djira," he went on. "We young men of

Raebrudafisk reached her first. For a boy saw what Sturl did and ran to tell us. He ran for his life, since Sturl had caught sight of him and was chasing him. Sturl could not overtake him, and turned in another direction when he perceived the lad would gain the village.

"Yes, we went to Djira; and then we and the men of the whole countryside sought Sturl. Many among us vowed to slay him when we came upon him, but the pastor and Schoolmaster Wiec, who was the magistrate of the district, sternly forbade this.

"For over two weeks, in wild weather of sleet and bitter winds, we hunted vainly, scouring woods, climbing to the niches in the mountaintops, and even searching our coal mine, to which we thought the piercing cold might have driven Sturl. We wondered how he obtained food, and at every step we took amid the trees or up the rocks we expected to discover him dead from exposure.

"You can conceive and pity Uflio this while. I consider that his lot was worse than Djira's. She, the one earthly gladness of his blind life; she, the bright, the gentle, whose lips and hands caressed him so lovingly, whose greeting woke him in the morning, whose voice told him the hues of the sky and the promise of the garden; she—held by a foul hand, and slaughtered! That is what he had to think of. Small wonder that for days the torment made him almost insane, and that our womenfolk could give him no consolation.

"The Sunday after the murder he did not go to the church, being too ill and weak. On the following Thursday, however, when there was an evening service, he took up his routine, and the stove was glowing when we entered the church. It was sad indeed to look at Uflio, in his usual seat, but bent and tremulous, with his cheeks so sunken and ghastly that he was scarcely to be recognized. Perhaps it was saddest to notice the coal smears and a tiny gleam of oil on his hands when he raised them. Little Djira had always been most careful to wipe them for him ere service began.

"As I said, for over two weeks we searched for Sturl; and we found not a trace of him. Then, at dawn one morning, our village was roused by a new alarm. The village of Phyamu, four miles away, where they find and store oil, was on fire. Schoolmaster Wiec wanted every man of us to hurry across and aid the Phyamu people. I had broken my arm two days previously—seeking Sturl. To witness the blaze, however, I set out with the rest. My chum, Vavik Rista, I, and a dozen others, took a path which went by the church. Although it rose steeply we began to cover it at a trot. We had gone a hundred yards past the church when a man, his clothes fluttering in rags, sprang out into the way in front of us, sprang as if from his sleep; and, trying to run before either of his feet was well back on the ground, he seemed to wrench one, and fell.

"He was Sturl. Vavik and several more, darting forward instantly, reached him as he came to his knees, and held him.

" 'Lend me a knife,' said Vavik, whom Djira had shown many indications of loving.

"But two or three cried, 'No, no; what will the pastor and Schoolmaster Wiec say?'

"Yet there were others who agreed with Vavik, and it was a long time before we could quiet them.

" 'And all this while Phyamu is burning, and we are needed!' cried someone. He pointed to the thin, strong ropes many were carrying to the scene of the fire. 'Tie the beast to a tree until we come back.'

" 'Wolves,' objected someone else.

" 'So much the better!' shouted Vavik.

"But a voice suggested leaving Sturl in the church, and thither we dragged him.

"We bound him, meaning to let him lie on the floor. Seeing him gnash with his teeth at the ropes about him, and knowing him to be so supple that he might stretch to, and gnaw through, some, we gagged him very firmly; so that, though he was raging at us, the sounds he made were but as the hiss of the wind about the church. Then he began to roll and to knock his head against the floor.

" 'We must make him fast to something,' said one of us.

"We stared around the church. There were no pillars, there seemed nothing to lash Sturl to. And then Hrok Nalti, the chairmaker, pointed to the stove.

" 'Stand him on that. Tie him to the pipe.'

"We did so, fetching a ladder and a high bench from the vestry. We pressed Sturl against the pipe and bound him tightly to it; and, in a hard spirit, for which we might be forgiven, we bound him more than was necessary. We swathed and swathed him with rope until nearly all was used. With the last length, since he made an attempt to beat his head against the pipe, we bound that also, passing the rope thrice across his brow and round the pipe, thus forcing the back of his skull immovably against the iron.

"Then we hastened to Phyamu.

"You will have observed that I have said 'we' in all this. It is right that I should, as I was of the party. But the work was not the sort for a man with a fractured arm, so that throughout I was an onlooker. Justifiably or not, I find relief in the knowledge of this.

"We hastened, I said, to Phyamu.

"Keeping together, for no particular reason except that we arrived together late, and telling none that we had captured Sturl, because we were jeered at for our tardiness, we started to roll casks of oil into safety. I helped with one hand, and time was passing, when suddenly Hrok straightened his back and flung out his arms stiffly, uttering a queer, gurgling groan.

" 'It is Sunday morning!' he said.

"It took us not a second to realize his meaning. We saw Sturl, a figure of rope, stiff and upright like some strange soldier, on the stove in the church at Raebrudafisk—Sturl incapable of movement, incapable of sound save such as the wind was making. We saw the church door slowly open and Uflio, stone-blind Uflio, appear. We saw him go to the vestry, and emerge with fagots, paper, and coal. We saw him arrange the fuel in the stove, utterly unconscious of Sturl, although his fingers would approach to within a few inches of the wretch's feet whenever he manipulated the flap at the top. We saw him bring a bottle of oil from his pocket, soak the fuel, and light it.

"And then we felt the sensations of Sturl, the terror which seized him as soon as he perceived what was to come, the leap of hope which his heart would give when Uflio's hand came near him, the frenzy of awful despair which beset him as he strained and strained to loosen a limb or to shift the gag with his tongue. We felt the first slight warmth to the soles of the feet. We felt the pipe against the back of the head, and the slow, sure heating of the pipe. . . . We saw and felt all these things instantaneously, as it were; and, far faster than we had run to Phyamu, we ran from it toward our church, all except Vavik, who continued his work."

"No more!" I said, standing up. But Kobyssu really was in the past now. He did not hear me; and, instead of walking out of earshot, I remained, dazed.

"I was speedy of leg," said Kobyssu, "and, though I could swing only one arm, I led the way with Hrok. We were not certain what time it was; we believed there was no chance of saving Sturl; yet, in case there might be, we tore along. Our earliest glimpse of the church showed us smoke blowing from the chimney. As to Sturl having been discovered—well, presently we made out Uflio sitting quietly by Djira's grave, and the pastor and some of the womenfolk coming up through the firs from the village with no sign of excitement. Still we ran, ran through the churchyard, ran to the church door. Hrok opened it, and the hot air from inside met me. There was a reek of smoldering hemp, just like that of the string you allowed to smolder, only much more powerful; and following it was another reek—"

"Stop!" I yelled; and I shook Kobyssu roughly by the shoulder.

Then I sat down, feeling indubitably faint. "You'd better give me a drink, Kobyssu," I said. "I might have stood it in print, but to hear you tell it, you who were a witness—

"And yet," I said, when I was recovering, "I can't help referring to the matter once—once only, though. Something strikes me as curious. You said that Uflio's perception was uncanny. In that case I consider it strange that a palpitating human being should have been within six inches and he have no inkling of the fact."

Kobyssu, who had gone white again toward the finish of the tale, had brought a measure of brandy for himself, and this he drained before replying.

"I will tell you," he said, "a detail that was seen only by Hrok and another, who cut down the—the remains, and by me; for Hrok wiped the face very quickly. . . . For a number of years Sturl had borne on his left cheek a scar, a large, puckered scar that stood out from the rest of the flesh. Sturl's face, when Hrok lowered him, was wrought on by the heat, yet some peculiar marks were still visible on the left cheek. They were little stripes, apparently a mingling of oil and coal dust, such as might have been made by the fingers of, let us say, a blind person, who sought, by feeling for the scar, to satisfy himself as to the identity of the man he had discovered on the stove." ⸻

THE CLOSED DOOR

HAROLD WARD

Dying, Obie Marsh cursed his wife as he had cursed her every day of their wedded life.

"You've poisoned me!" he gasped, writhing in agony. "Yes, you've poisoned me, you she-devil!"

Lucinda, his wife, nodded dully.

"Yes, I poisoned you," she answered without emotion. "You are going to die, anyway; the doctor said so. It's just a matter of time— maybe years, maybe months. And I can't stand this fightin' any longer. Fifteen years of it! Fifteen years of hell!"

"Damn you!" Marsh snarled through his clenched teeth, his bearded face twitching as a spasm of pain shot through his vitals.

"We should have never got married," the woman went on quietly. "I never loved you and you never loved me. 'T was a case of your folks and my folks stickin' in between us and the ones we loved. You've always hated me 'cause of Lizzie Roper, an' God knows I wanted t' marry Al Sides. Just 'cause they wanted the farms joined, they made us get married, me an' you. Now we can't get a divorce 'cause of the church and I've just got sick of it all, Obie—sick of it all."

"You hellion!" he gasped, his body twitching spasmodically.

"I got the idee of poisoning you when you first took sick," she went on in the same even tone. "Old Doc Plummer said that you might linger along for years. And I just couldn't stand it, Obie—I just couldn't stand it any longer, your constant bullyin' an' runnin' over me."

"You'll hang for it," Marsh said huskily. "I hope they torture you in hell—"

"Probably they will," Lucinda Marsh answered without emotion. "But it's worth it t' have a little peace here on earth. It hasn't been any heaven livin' with you."

Marsh twisted convulsively, his gnarled fingers closing and unclosing, his thick lips drooling. He pulled himself together with a mighty effort. He was a hard man and strong; hard men are difficult to kill.

"I'll come back . . . from th' grave, you hussy!" he gasped.

" 'T would be like you," his wife answered.

". . . Waitin' for . . . you—" he went on, trying to shake his fist in the woman's face.

The effort was too great. He dropped back upon the pillow again, the sweat standing out on his forehead in beads, his body shaking with spasms.

"God, it hurts!" he whispered. "Just like a . . . knife."

The woman suddenly lifted her head. She was listening.

"Somebody coming," she muttered, moving swiftly to the window.

A roadster was entering the lane.

"It's old Doc Plummer," she said, half to herself, half to the dying man. "Th' old fool's earlier'n usual. An' you c'n still talk."

The man on the bed quivered. His fists clenched and his muscles tensed as he tried to drag himself back from the yawning pit that awaited him.

". . . Getting . . . dark—"

"Doc's liable to rec'nize th' symptoms," the woman went on as she heard the car come to a stop in the front yard. A sheet had been thrown carelessly across the foot of the bed. Seizing it, she wadded it into a bundle and pressed it against the face of the dying man. He fought against the stoppage of his breath with a feeble effort. She threw her whole strength against him. Suddenly his limbs straightened jerkily. She knew that he was dead. She sat up with a sigh of relief.

The outside screen door slammed shut. Leaping to her feet, she threw the sheet across the back of a chair and turned to meet the doctor.

"He just passed away in one of those spells," she said without emotion. "Come on him all of a sudden. Both th' kids are at school and I didn't have nobody to send for you. 'Tain't no use to say I'm sorry, for I'm not. I'm glad he's dead."

The physician shook his head sympathetically. Like all country practitioners, he was conversant with the family affairs of his patients. For a moment he stood looking down at the still form of Obie Marsh. Then he pulled a sheet over it and turned to the woman.

"Better sit down and take things easy, Mrs. Marsh," he said, following her into the other room. "I'll notify the undertaker and stop at the school and have the teacher send Mary and Jimmy home. Anybody else you want?"

She shook her head negatively.

"Tell Bill Reynolds to come prepared t' take th' body back with him," she said slowly. "This is my house, now—mine. That's th' way my pap and his pap fixed up th' deeds. An' the quicker I get him outen my sight, th' better it'll suit me. I never want t' see him again 'till th' day of th' funeral, an' I wouldn't 'tend that if it wasn't that people'd talk.

"He made life hell for me," she went on bitterly. "I've hated him from th' day I married him. It's my house now and I'm goin' t' lock that room as soon's they take him away. I never want t' see th' inside of it again. There's too many mem'ries hovering around it. I'd burn it to th' ground if it wasn't for burnin' th' rest of th' house."

She dropped into a rocking-chair and gazed at the doctor, her gaunt body quivering with unshed tears. The physician patted her on the shoulder sympathetically.

"You're overwrought, Lucinda," he said kindly, "overwrought and nervous. I'll fix up a tonic and bring it over tonight."

"I don't need no tonic," she responded. "Knowin' he's dead'll be tonic enough for me."

The physician wagged his head solemnly.

"Let's not speak ill of the dead," he said. "Everybody knows how he treated you. If there's nothing else I can do, I'll be getting along."

In due time the undertaker and his assistant came with their narrow wicker basket. Lucinda Marsh stood beside the door and waited for them as they carried their burden out. They looked at her queerly as she turned the key in the lock, then, removing it, placed it in her pocket.

"I hope t' God I never see th' inside of that room till my dyin' day," she said.

Bill Reynolds, the undertaker, shook his head in agreement. He, too, knew the life that she had led with Obie Marsh.

The passing years brought little change in the outward appearance of Lucinda Marsh. Gaunt, hard-featured, tight-lipped and unemotional, she moved about the farm as of yore, doing a man's work in the field, adding to the dollars that were already in the bank, conducting her business along the lines to which she had been trained. She had never had friends; Obie Marsh had seen to that. She made none now.

Her children grew to manhood and womanhood. Little Mary married and moved to the adjoining township. Lucinda made no complaint and no comment. Jimmy took the place of the hired man, lifting a bit of the burden of labor from his mother's shoulders. But she still held the reins of management. Then he, too, married and brought his wife to the big, gloomy old house at the end of the lane. Children came, six in quick succession. If their happy laughter wrought any change in the heart of the grim, silent old woman, she never showed it. Emma, Jimmy's wife, busy rearing her brood, was content to remain in the background; Lucinda Marsh was still mistress of the house.

Through all the years that one room just off from the parlor—Father's room, they called it—remained closed, the key hidden away in Lucinda's bureau drawer. It was never mentioned in the family circle. The children knew that there was something—some horrible taboo—that kept it from being talked about. Their childish imaginations did the rest. They passed it with baited breath; when darkness fell and shadows hovered outside the circle made by the big kerosene lamp on the center table, they always played on the other side of the room, casting furtive glances toward the dark panels behind which lurked they knew not what.

Then, with the passing of the years, came the hard times. First the grasshoppers destroyed the crops. Then came the drought. Prices went up; wages dropped. Factories closed.

Mary was the first to feel the blow. The bank foreclosed on her husband's farm. Then came illness and another baby. Finally she was forced to come home with her sick husband and her little brood. Lucinda Marsh, as unemotional as ever, made room for them. Jimmy's wife's brother lost his place in the city. Destitute, he appealed to his sister. She told her troubles to Lucinda Marsh.

"Four more won't make no difference at th' table," the old woman said grimly. "Write an' tell 'em we'll make room for 'em somehow. Goodness knows, though, where we'll sleep 'em."

They were sitting at the supper table when this conversation took place. It was Mary who, with a quick glance at her brother, ventured to speak that which was in all of their minds.

"Father's room," she said timidly. "Couldn't we open that up and air it before they come and let 'em sleep in there?"

For a moment there was an awed silence. Lucinda Marsh turned her sunken eyes on her daughter, then glanced at the faces of the others.

"I vowed that I'd never set foot in that room 'till my dyin' day," she said finally.

"But they—they wouldn't be you, Mother," Mary argued. "And we're cramped for room right now. Where else can we sleep 'em?"

Lucinda Marsh quietly laid down her knife and fork, her thin lips set in a straight, grim line.

"If anybody sleeps in that room, 't will be me," she said finally. "I lived with your father for fifteen years, hatin' him every day more'n more. And he hated me worse'n I hated him—if such a thing is possible. The room's filled with our hatred—it's locked up in there smolderin' an' ready t' be fanned into flame again."

"But, Mother—"

Lucinda Marsh straightened her bent old shoulders with a gesture of finality.

"I'll move into it," she said grimly.

"I wish that I hadn't mentioned it," Mary said regretfully. "I knew that there was some sort of sentiment attached to it, but—"

The old woman cut her off.

"Sentiment! Hate, you mean," she snapped. "But maybe it's for th' best. I'm an old woman—'way past seventy. I'm about due to die, anyway."

She stopped, her aged eyes taking on a far-away look.

"Maybe it's foreordained," she said, half to herself. "He said that he'd be . . . waitin' for me. Maybe he is. Who knows?"

She rose from the table and took a step toward the door.

"I'll open it up in the mornin' and let it air out," she said.

She moved up the stairway to the upper floor, her lips straight and tight.

For a long time Lucinda Marsh sat in the straight-backed chair beside her bed, her weary eyes gazing into vacancy while the panorama of the years unfolded itself. To her had come a great urge, a desire which she had kept in leash for close to half a century—the longing that comes to all murderers—a yearning to visit the scene of her crime.

A thousand times before, the same desire had swept over her and she had always fought it off. Now, however, with the fulfillment of her wish only a few hours away there had come to her a seeming need for haste. The closed room was calling to her. Within her brain a voice was shrieking: *"Now! Now!"* To her aged mind it was the voice of the man she hated—the man she had killed.

Getting up, she went to the bureau and, opening the drawer, found the key where she had hidden it so many years before. She held it in her gnarled fingers, fondling it, crooning over it.

Her room was at the head of the stairs. One by one, she heard the members of the household go to their rooms. Finally the gloomy old house was filled with an indescribable quietness.

Rising, she opened the door a tiny crack and peered out into the dark hallway. Satisfied that all were asleep, she picked up the small hand-lamp and tiptoed furtively down the creaking stairs.

A storm was in the air. She could hear the wind rising and shrieking through the branches of the trees. There was something reminiscent about the mournful wail. She stopped a moment, her head bent forward. Then remembrance swept over her.

" 'T was like this th' night before—before he died," she muttered to herself.

Her heart was beating a trifle faster as she reached the dark, grim door. She hesitated an instant. Then, transferring the lamp to her left hand, she inserted the key in the lock. It turned hard, as if reluctant to reveal the mysteries it hid. Then the tumbler shot back. For a moment she waited, her fingers on the knob. She was trembling now—shaking with an emotion she did not understand.

"He said that . . . he'd be . . . waitin' for me," she murmured. "I wonder . . . if he is."

She turned the knob and pushed against the panel. The aged hinges squeaked protestingly. Then the door swung open. A wave of malignancy and hatred surged over her.

She stepped inside, her lips closed in a tight, grim line. Just inside the door she waited, the lamp held high above her head, her eyes taking in every detail. There was the bed, unmade, where he had died. The thought came to her that Bill Reynolds, the undertaker, the last person to step foot in the room, was gone, too. At the head of the bed was the little stand; on top of it was the glass in which she had administered the poison. Beside it was a bottle of medicine, half empty; the label, covered with old Doc Plummer's crabbed hieroglyphics, was yellow and faded. Doc Plummer . . . he, too, had been festering in his grave for years. There was the pillow where

Obie's head had rested when he died; one corner was twisted where he had held it when the last spasm of agony had knifed its way through his vitals. Nothing was changed.

"He said that he'd . . . be waitin' for me," she said again.

The room was musty and mildewed, the dust of years over everything. She closed the door and set the lamp upon the little stand. Going to the window, she pushed it up to its full length. The wind swept in, howling and shrieking.

The lamp sputtered, causing queer, grotesque shadows to dance in the distant corners. Across the back of the chair where she had thrown it years before was the yellowed sheet with which she had smothered the dying breath out of her husband. There was a darker spot upon its mildewed surface; she knew it for the spittle that had drooled from his mouth.

She moved to the center of the room, still peering furtively into the shadows.

"He said that he'd come . . . back from th' grave an' be . . . waitin' for me," she said again and again.

A fresh gust of wind howled through the window. The lamp sputtered, smoked, flared up, then went out.

With the sudden darkness came a feeling of dread. For the first time in her life Lucinda Marsh was afraid.

Out of the darkness came a thing—a shapeless thing of white. For a moment it hung suspended in midair. It hovered over her, its long, shapeless arms reaching out for her. The wind shrieked with merry gusto.

". . . said that he'd be waitin'—" she murmured.

It swept over her, holding her in its folds, twisting about her, smothering her. . . .

"God!" she shrieked, clawing at the enveloping tentacles. "He kept his word! He was . . . waitin'—"

In the morning they found her. Twisted about her head and throat was a yellowed sheet—the sheet with which she had smothered her husband. ——

COUNTRY HOUSE

EWEN WHYTE

It was a task that women everywhere, all over the world, do thousands upon thousands of times. Nothing to mark it from those others except that this was herself, Patricia Eldridge, and she thought, and chided herself for the thinking:

"I don't really like to go up there alone! But that's silly, isn't it? Someone has to do it, and I'm the only someone!"

They'd looked so hard for a place in the country, and the house in Bellemore had been discovered by one of those accidents when the quest for just such a coincidence fitted in perfectly with its availability.

Ray, of course, couldn't get away from the office. Their old car had made the trip to Bellemore a week ago for the final decision and the signing of the lease but had sputtered home in poor shape and was now laid up in the repair shop.

Never mind, she could get somebody from the next-door apartment to stay with their three-year-old son, she told her husband. She'd take the train.

The house was tucked away on a ridge some miles outside of Bellemore Village. It was all weather-beaten shingled with a stone chimney, ivy-covered. For companions the house had a forest that closed closely around it. The gurgling trace of a brook ran not far away from the back stone terrace. It was, as Ray Eldridge had said, a "find," and if the price they'd finally been able to compromise on was a bit above what they'd wanted to pay, the sacrifice would certainly be worth while.

It was afternoon before Patricia had time to think. The sun had fallen off to the west, but its rays coming through the bare February limbs of the trees that stood near the eaves sent lengthening shadows across the barren floors. She'd arrived soon after eleven, taxied out to their house—and my, didn't that have a fine sound!—from the Bellemore station.

The day had been taken up with those innumerable little things. The measuring and sizing-up of rooms; where she and Ray would be and then where they'd put Robbie. She had some curtain samples she'd brought up from the city and she tried to decide which would look the nicest in the room that would become their parlor. For her, it was happy indecision.

She sat for a moment now, perched on a packing box in one of the upstairs rooms, still in her fur coat, for there was no heat in the house, and for the first time, she felt the chilliness. Her ears were ringing, something she'd noticed when she'd been up here with Ray a week ago. It was the silence of the country, an unaccustomed change for a city-dweller who lives amidst the scenery and sounds of constant activity. A plane flying far above the Bellemore Valley filled the winter air with its drone. And then there was a sound from outside.

Pat got up. Mrs. Brown, the real-estate agent, had said she'd drop out sometime during the day just to see how things were coming along, what with the telephone not connected yet.

As Patricia passed the mirror at the head landing, she shook her dark curls and thought that her fur coat looked just a bit shabby for folks who were buying such a scrumptious country house. But then, after all, you have to make certain sacrifices.

The front door opened—you don't think of locking them in the country—and she took the first step of going down. The stairs crooked away and she could see nothing but a pattern of yellow light against the turn of the stairwell.

"Missus Brown?" she called. "Hello, Missus Brown!"

Of course it was Mrs. Brown. Or had the taxi man come early? It was a bit past four.

"Is that the taxi man?"

For an answer the front door—and it was a heavy one—closed with a thud, and that was punctuated by a scuffling sound that faded almost instantly, but inside the house. Patricia Eldridge felt herself tighten.

"Who is it! Who's down there!!"

Nothing. She stood poised, one foot down on the first step, her hand gripping the bannister, and the wind touching the weather-vane on the top of the house counted the long seconds off by squeaking the painted metal rooster and swiveling it with an airy cold breath.

Pat very carefully withdrew her descending foot and stood at the top of the landing, afraid now to call out again, afraid to move beyond the sudden and terrible pounding of her heart. The fears of womankind came to her then. The thing she'd chided herself about.

Don't be silly, Ray! Nothing ever happens in the country! *Darling*, it's the only way to get the place fixed up.

A train in the distance whistled with far-away detachment. Its remoteness made her think of the city and of Ray. Oh Ray, honey, do you know how frightened I am now? Where *was* Mrs. Brown! She'd called down enough, of that she was certain, with the kind of true intuition that only a woman can have. Whoever it was, whatever it was downstairs knew of her presence as much as she knew of its.

There was a step. In its texture and quality it was heavy, and that put new thunder to her heart. The taxi man was smallish; Mrs. Brown's steps wouldn't scuff and clump so that the very house shook!

Slowly, slowly, Pat inched backward. She chose the west room because, frighteningly, deepening shadows had claimed everywhere else now from the pale setting winter sun. A board under her high heels creaked, and she held her breath.

The first step on the stairs was not a surprise. She had expected it and had been listening for it so hard. Whoever it was was coming up. If she had wanted to call out now, she would not have been able to. Her mouth was dry and her throat constricted.

There was a dressing room off the west chamber. It connected with the other upstairs bedroom, and that had its own door onto the hall. By the time the steps reached the top of the stairs, she had vacated the room nearest their approach. She still tiptoed, but the time for cat-and-mouse was nearly over. The steps quickened, echoing hollowly as they crossed the bare wooden floors.

Patricia slipped through the dressing room, through the next room and out into the hall. The tempo of the steps behind her quickened even more. She gained the hall while whatever it was, like in a child's game of hide-and-seek, circled noisily through the rooms she had just left. She ran for the stairs now, all attempts at quiet gone. She ran clattering down like a frightened schoolgirl.

She made the great front door, pulled it open with desperate hands and stumbled outside into the sudden gloom of early evening. Her heels turned on the rough stone of the driveway, hurting her ankles cruelly as she ran on. Despite herself and her fear at what she would see, she turned and looked back. But only the top of the house had brightness left upon it. The lower floor was shrouded in shadow. Somebody, or something, came through the door. Of that she was sure, and as she plunged on the road into the forest that lined it, she knew that whoever, whatever it was, was after her!

Patricia Eldridge ran as any hunted creature does, without direction, for she did not know the woods or the terrain they covered, but her instinct made her seek the darker places in the already blackening woods, and she ran agilely with all the dexterity of her slim, strong young body as though she were back thousands of years in time and in some primitive race of long ago.

The terror in her was a thing of civilization, though. The fears that crowded down upon her mind forced her heart rate even more than the strenuous activity of running. Behind, in the darkness—though now she turned not once to look as if afraid of confirming her worst fears—the crashing sounds of her pursuer were unmistakable. An outflung branch caught her across the face, cutting her cheek and her mouth but she ran on barely slackening stride, feeling the moistness of blood on her face.

Somewhere inside of her was the strong logic that if she could run far enough and fast enough, she would come out of this nightmare, come to another house, a road with cars, somewhere, anywhere, with people.

She fell then, tripped by an unseen root or rock, and sprawled heavily, full-length, the wind wooshing out of her. She scrambled to all fours, regained her feet and went on, but there was faintness in her now and lightheadedness that played tricks with whatever sense of direction she might have had. From the sounds behind, her pursuer was closer.

She thought of Ray and three-year-old Robbie and how much they needed her and loved her and of what pathetic uselessness all that was now. She came into a little clearing, and thankfully, oh God, thankfully, there was a rude building of sorts ahead, a shack or cottage.

She breathed a prayer and threw the rest of her strength into a forward lunge, but she had overestimated her failing powers. Again she tripped and fell very heavily. Her chest was crushed. Her breath became fire, put out finally as the dark ground and the silent black trees came together beneath and over her.

When Pat came to, it was to feel with relief a hard wooden floor beneath her, and the man bending over her was . . . why, he was some sort of policeman, off duty perhaps, but the midnight blue serge of his dress was unmistakable. She struggled to get up, and he helped her, his strong hands gentle despite their size.

Profound relief battled with the awful terror and panic she felt so recently. For a while, Pat could say nothing and then—because prosaic things came so much more easily than the myriad questions in her mind—she asked,

"Can I sit on your tool box here?"

He nodded, and she sat there fighting to regain composure, seeing that her hands were still trembling and then finding the self-control to say,

"Somebody . . . something was chasing me out there. I don't know who or what. I guess I fell and fainted."

He nodded.

"You're all right now," he said.

His voice was gruff and large as the man himself, and in the largeness she felt a warm security. Here, but a few moments ago, there had been nothing in her but terror and desperation as the result of that horror and a terrible cold reconciliation when there seemed there was no escape.

Pat fluttered her hands and tried to stand up.

"Thank you so much! I wonder if you could help me. Show me how to get back to the house. I don't even know what time it is! The taxi man's coming and—" She started to rise, and weakness almost took her legs from under her. Patricia sank back on the box.

He nodded his head as though in agreement with her decision.

"You'll feel better after a bit, I dare say."

He turned to something he was brewing on a small stove, and she saw gratefully that a coffee pot percolated there. After a while, he brought a cup over to her.

"Milk's all I've got," he said apologetically.

He watched her drink the coffee, and she noticed what kind, sky-blue eyes he had. She set the cup down, thanked him again.

"You're a policeman. Is this your home, or . . . ?"

"Outpost," he supplied laconically.

She wondered if he had a pretty wife and a three-year-old like Robbie.

Patricia had enough interest now to look around the cottage. It was filled with man stuff. There were a couple of animal traps in the corner, tools, a lantern, and on the wall a rifle and a policeman's cartridge belt with what looked to be a holster. She asked him about the house, her house, theirs, Ray's and Robbie's.

Sure, he knew it, knew it well. In fact, did you know, he'd lived there once for a short piece himself. He smiled wryly. He'd lost his wife there. She was contrite even as he answered. There had been a couple of tenants since then. Families? No, no, two single folks. One a policeman. What, another policeman? She didn't think of the Law as having enough money to own a place like that. Well, you know, in some periods when houses stood untenanted. . . . Skip it.

And Mrs. LeClerc, an older woman. He became a little more loquacious. Always thought it was better to have that place empty. She could understand that and she dropped the issue, after his wife and all. Poor man, poor lonely man, with those sky-blue eyes that were wide, almost like a child's!

Irrelevantly, it made her think of that line from Gilbert and Sullivan: "A policeman's lot is not a happy one."

Patricia was feeling better. The coffee was strong and good, and its heat had spread strength through her veins and limbs.

"I think I could try getting back now," she said dutifully. "Could you show me?"

"I'd have to," the man replied.

"Gracious, it certainly *is* lonely around here! What do you suppose—?" The question had been nagging at her. "What do you suppose . . . who do you suppose it was after me out there? I shouldn't think . . ." she gave a small laugh, ". . . that Bellemore would have much of a crime problem!"

"Hard to tell," was his only reply.

She guessed he knew his job. For all she knew, he'd routed her pursuer when he'd come upon her outside this cottage.

The dial on her wristwatch nagged her. It was getting late. In fact, the taxi man would have come and gone, or come and be waiting at the house. She'd already missed the train she'd planned on taking, and Mrs. Brown might have visited and would be worried that she wasn't there.

You can't take somebody like this off his beat or duty or whatever they call it in the country, she reasoned, and it was important to her as it would be to Ray to get off on the right foot in this community. Country people aren't the same as their urban cousins. They did things, well, pretty much when they got around to them, foregoing the feverish tempo of the city dweller.

She thought it over carefully and finally said, almost tentatively, "If you'd give me a lantern, show me the way and just start me off; I'm sure I could. . . ."

He was silent for a moment as though he mulled it over and then he shook his head determinedly.

"No," he said, "no, that wouldn't do."

She waited, thinking that chivalry was warring with duty in his case. When he said nothing more, after a reasonable length of time she put in again, "Really, I do have to start back! How far are we from the house or a road?"

He was tinkering in the corner, and she rose from the tool box, almost impatiently now. He was humming to himself, and it irritated her a bit even through the gratitude she'd felt for his help earlier. It was as though her time, her appointments, and responsibilities were as nothing to him!

Oh, these country people! There was, she supposed, nothing to do but to humor them and let them take their own time. Did he think she was ungrateful or did he, like so many rural characters, resent her because she was from the city? She realized the news gets around in a small place and that by now everybody in Bellemore would know about the Eldridges—city folks—who'd bought the empty house out in the valley.

But still, this was hardly fair—he was, well, quite maddening!

"Please!" she said, with an edge of sharpness in her voice.

He left the corner and whatever small, irrelevant task he'd been doing there. He shrugged his massive shoulders and said, "Well, guess I've got to go to work!"

So he was going on duty perhaps and had wanted to take her at the same time. Despite herself, the toe of her highheeled shoe tapped impatiently against the oversized tool box she'd been sitting on.

He crossed leisurely to the wall and took down the cartridge belt, hooked it carefully around his great girth. She saw then that the cartridge loops were empty and what she'd supposed was a gun holster was, instead, a knife sheath from which protruded the bone handle of a hunting blade.

He turned and walked toward her slowly, one hand hooked casually under the belt where the sheath hung.

How blue his eyes were, she thought, and then he said almost apologetically before he reached her,

"You see, ma'am, I'm really *not* a policeman and that . . ." he'd reached her side then and kicked at the large tool box with his big shoe, ". . . that isn't really a tool box!"

He grasped her wrist in one huge hand and raised the lid of the box even as she murmured almost stupidly, for it seemed so trivial, "You're not a policeman?"

He raised the lid more and pushed her ever so gently forward to look within the chest.

"He's in there, ma'am, along with Missus LeClerc!"

He let the cover of the box fall with a thud and stepped closer to Patricia Eldridge. She didn't even have time to be frightened. ——

THE CRACKS OF TIME

DOROTHY QUICK

It was when the cocktail party I was giving for Myra was at its height that I first saw the face.

I had been listening to the one hundred and fourth "But my dear, your engagement was such a surprise—You know you have all my best wishes—Now I want to congratulate the lucky man," and wondering how Myra ever found the right words to reply. Marveling, too, at the ease with which she did so, and passed the people on to Henley, who managed them equally well. They were a good pair, my younger sister Myra and Henley Bradford. They'd have a happy marriage.

It was to hide the rush of tears to my eyes that I looked down, and saw the face. The sun room's floor was done with tiles Jason and I had brought from Spain while on our honeymoon—when we had been happy. They were a sea green-blue, some with geometric designs, some perfectly plain, their only ornamentation the patina of the glazing and the dark lines, or cracks, which time had given them. In this particular tile that caught my eyes the cracks had patterned a face. It was only a vague outline, the profile of a man with full, thick lips—sensuous lips, slanted eyes, and a forehead from which the hair rose up into a point that looked like a horn. There was nothing more that was definite. The rest was blurred and vague, like some modern, impressionistic picture, of the shadowy school which suggests its subject, rather than portrays it.

I was about to call out and tell the crowd what I'd discovered. I thought I'd make a game of it, because, in a way, it was like "statues," or finding shapes in clouds. The words "See what I've found!" were actually on my lips when the eye of the face looked a warning from under its slanting lid, and then the lid came down, covering the eye.

It was a trick of lighting, of course. The face was in profile and the eye was open. The shadow of someone's foot in passing must have made the effect of the lid closing. The eye looking at me in warning was imagination plus several cocktails. But what I had been going to say was still-born. I didn't mention the profile but kept looking at it as the afternoon progressed, and it seemed to me that the face became clearer and more sharply etched. I began thinking it resembled the ancient sculptures of Pan.

By the time the guests had drunk themselves into a state of hilarity I had forgotten the face. I didn't notice it again until Jason came over to me and, in a rare mood of affection, put his arm around my shoulder. "Sheila," he whispered in a voice liquor had thickened, "you're the best-looking girl here. Why don't we kiss and make up?"

I knew he wouldn't have said that, sober. I also knew that our quarreling had gone beyond the point where we could follow his suggestion. Jason's charms were legion but so was his drinking and the other women that went with it. I had out-forgiven myself—there just wasn't any more of that virtue left in me. Still, perhaps I should try once more. Maybe it wouldn't be right to reject this offer.

It was then I looked down and the face was moving from side to side, obviously saying "no" to my charitable inclinations. "No, no, no!" I caught myself up sharp. This was ridiculous; I was letting my imagination run away with me. The afternoon shadows were tricky things and I certainly couldn't let shifting light betray by better impulses.

So, when Jason repeated his question, kissing the place behind my ear that he called his, I said "Yes, Jason."

It seemed to me then that the one eye of the face completely closed and that I saw a tear trickle down the high-boned cheek. It was ridiculous but that's the impression I received.

"Hi, folks," Jason was calling, as he swirled me around in a wild dance. "Let's have another round. I'm celebrating the fact I've got the loveliest wife in the world, the kindest, the sweetest—"

I didn't hear the rest of the adjectives. My handkerchief had dropped during the turns we'd made. As Jason talked I bent down for it. The tiny square of white had fallen over the face. When I picked it up, it was wet. Liquor? Something spilled from a cocktail? That's what I thought, but when I lifted it to my nose there was no alcoholic odor. I touched it to my lips, the tip end of my tongue, and there was the bitter salt taste of tears.

And I had seen a tear roll down the face! Incredible, but in my mouth was the tang of a man's tears. I looked down. The face *was* much clearer; the back of the head was completely filled in, with the hair clustered on it dark and curly. The eye was open now and it had acquired depth and perspective. It looked down at me with admiration and a kind of pathetic appeal. The full lips trembled. It was as though they were calling out for me to lean over and touch them.

So strong was the illusion that in another moment I might have done so, but Jason came back just then with two cocktails. "Here you are, darling." He handed one to me.

I took it, and he encircled me with his arm. "Sweet, let's drink to us!" He was very tight, but his charm was in the ascendancy. I drank with him and forgot about the face.

The reconciliation proved very absorbing. Not since our honeymoon and the first year of our married life had Jason been so completely devoted. It was as though the five miserable years through which we had quarreled had not existed. We were suddenly back, continuing the first twelve months of our felicity. I had fully intended to examine the tile with the face most carefully, the next day, when there would be no feet to cast shadows, no liquor to give ideas. But as it happened it was over a week before I went in the sun porch.

To begin with, there was the new devoted Jason, a round of parties for Myra, and several days of rainy weather, which always put the desirability of the sun porch at low ebb.

The cocktail party had been on a Saturday. It was exactly ten days later—Tuesday, to be definite—that the sun shone so brightly I said I'd have my lunch in the sun room. I had completely forgotten the face by then.

But once seated on the red bamboo chair with my lunch tray on a matching table before me, the face obtruded itself into my vision. It was slightly to my right and not as much *en profile* as I'd thought. It was more three-quarter; there was a glimpse of the other cheek, more than a suggestion of the other eye. The original one looked at me reproachfully.

I caught my breath. The effect was really amazing. Since I'd seen it the face had gained dimensions too. There was depth and thickness to it now, and it was larger—the hair had spread over to the next tile. I leaned over and examined the lines—the cracks of time. They were deep, almost fissure-like, quite outstanding against the blue-green glaze. It was almost as though some artist had made a sketch freehand of Pan, before the tiles went to the kiln, and it had lain under the glaze for years until time and wear had brought it back to the surface. I had no hesitancy about knowing it was meant to be Pan; the little forehead horns were very clear now, and the full, sensuous lips could have belonged to none other. Pan in the deep wood, admiring a dryad, with all the connotations of a satyr.

I wasn't particularly interested in my lunch but I went on eating it automatically, watching the face as I did so, surprised to see the reproach melt away to admiration, then longing, and finally desire undisguised.

At that point I caught myself up sharply. "Sheila, you're being ridiculous," I said aloud.

Johnson, the maid, appeared in the doorway. "Did you call?" she asked.

"No." I was amused. She'd heard me talking to myself. "But now you're here, you can take the tray. I'll just keep my tea."

When she came over I pointed down to the tile. "Look, Johnson. Don't you think it's funny the way those lines on that tile make a face?"

She peered down and then drew back. "It is, indeed, Madame, a strange face—not quite human, although it's not very clear, is it?"

The outlines weren't vague to me now but they had been when I had first seen them. Suddenly there was a voice in my ear. "You have tasted the salt of my tears; that is why you see more clearly."

The tea cup I had been holding crashed to the floor, the china ringing hard against the tiles as it shattered into bits. I found control of myself quickly. "Oh, Johnson, I am sorry. It just slipped out of my hands."

"And your good china, too," she sighed. "I'll clean up, Madame, and give that tile a bit of an extra rub, too. Maybe we'll be able to wipe that ugly face out."

But I knew she'd never be able to erase it from my mind.

Or the floor, either!

In fact, her efforts only made it more distinct to me, although she seemed to think she had obliterated some of it.

When she had finished and gone, I sat there trying to figure it out. There *was* an outline of a face on the tile. Johnson saw it, so it wasn't entirely imagination. She wasn't educated enough to know about Pan; if she had been, she too would have seen the resemblance. So I wasn't completely off track. There was a face. It was inhuman, but there actuality stopped. The rest had to be imagination. The cracks of time could make a face but they couldn't make it weep or speak. That had been my own mind, and yet what it had said made sense in a way: "You have tasted the salt of my tears; that is why you see more clearly."

There was a fairy tale I remembered from my youth and Andrew Lang's colored fairy books. It was called "Elves' Ointment" as I recollect, and it was the story of a midwife brought to attend the birth of an elf. Given ointment to put on the new baby's eyes she had inadvertently gotten some on her own, and had seen everything differently thereafter—that is, until the elves caught on and took her new sight away from her, with quite tragic results, as I remembered.

But the analogy held. I looked at the face again. The full lips were parted. I could almost feel the hot quickened breath on my nearby ankle.

This was getting beyond sense. I was making myself see things that couldn't be, hear a voice, feel emotions that should be kept under cover. It was incredible, yet it was so real! It was uncanny. It made me a little afraid.

I decided I would go up to the attic and see if there were any left over tiles and if there were, I'd have this one, with its cracks of time, removed as quickly as possible.

"Of course," I told myself sternly, "it's only because you've been emotionally stirred up these past days. What with Myra's engagement and Jason, no wonder you're full of imaginings."

Then I heard the voice again, an ageless voice, thin and reedy, yet with a curious appeal. "Don't fight me. Just listen to my music."

The music was soft at first, fleeting into my brain with gently vibrating notes. From its first sound I didn't think any more. I couldn't. I could only listen to something indefinably lovely—music that soothed and made me know that nothing apart from it really mattered. It held the essence of life.

Suddenly it changed and became little tongues of flame licking around me, touching me here and there like caressing winds. Then there were waves of sound that vibrated through my entire being. And it seemed as though all the magic there had ever been was in them, weaving itself around me until I was a part of it, and I knew that nothing so lovely had ever happened to me before. I was suddenly a part of nature. Soon all its secrets would be known to me, and—

Jason's voice: "Hi, Shelley, where are you?" came from the living room, driving the music away. I didn't answer. I didn't want Jason to find me. I wanted the music back again. I wanted to lose myself in it.

"Shelley." Jason was calling. "Shelley." His pet name for me, part nickname for Sheila and partly made up from my admiration for the poet.

I looked down at the face. There was a finger touching the lips, as though to enjoin silence. Another crack of time, but it looked like a finger and its meaning was plain: the music was to be our secret, there was no mistaking that. And I wasn't imagining it. There *was* a finger on the thick lips.

For a minute I thought of them touching mine, and I knew that was what I wanted most in the world—that, and the music.

"Soon. It will be soon." The thin, reedy voice was like the notes of a pipe, coming from far-off enchanted places. A pipe, Pan's pipe.

Then Jason was in the room, exclaiming: "What the—! Why didn't you answer me? Didn't you hear me call?"

"No. I—I guess I was half asleep."

He leaned over and kissed me. There was warmth in his kiss but it left me cold. The wonderful music had deadened my senses to everything but its own magnificence, and Pan's, the god who had called it to being.

I looked down at the tile. The finger was no longer against the full lips. Instead, they were forming a word, "Wait." It was as plain to see as though I had studied lip-reading.

Jason's eyes followed mine. "Hello! Look at that cracked tile. We'll have to change that. You know, those cracks make a face, a horrible, repulsive face that gives me the shivers. I'll go to the attic tomorrow and fish out another tile and get rid of that face on the bar room floor."

Against my will I laughed. Against the hurt look in Pan's eyes. But suddenly the expression changed to one of cunning, combined with determination.

Words came to my lips. Without any volition of my own I found myself saying, "There's a piece of broken china still there. I broke a cup."

Jason bent down, picked up the piece of the tea cup the maid had overlooked, which I hadn't even know was there. He swore softly and shook a few drops of blood from his finger. Aghast, I watched the full lips catch them, suck them in.

"Jason," I cried. "You're hurt!"

He laughed. "Don't look so horrified; it's only a small cut." Again he shook off a few drops of blood, which the mouth on the floor caught.

I shivered. There was something so horrible about the mouth and the blood that I forgot the music.

"Come on." Jason caught me up. "I'll let you put a band-aid on it and then we're stepping out. The Crawleys are waiting for us at Agello's."

Agello's was our local "21." Going there was always an event. I was quite excited. There in the bright lights, with the gay music, I could forget the face and the silly things it provoked me into imagining.

I thought that, and I was happy, looking forward to fun at Agello's with Jason and the Crawleys, a couple we both liked tremendously. I was quite elated. Jason had his arm around me and it felt fine—warm and vibrant.

But as we left the porch I saw the face again. The lips had color, and they formed a word, "Soon." And as we left, an echo of the thin, fluting pipes sounded in my ear.

At Agello's I managed to forget. I had to forget, otherwise I would begin to think I was going mad. The face on the floor was genuine enough; Jason and the maid had both seen it. They had sensed evil. The maid had said it was inhuman, Jason that it was repulsive. So the face was all actuality. The rest had to be an over-worked imagination, and I didn't like the implications of that. I made up my mind there on the crowded floor dancing with Jason that I'd help him find another tile and get rid of the one with the cracks of time as quickly as possible. After that, I proceeded to enjoy the evening.

It was late when we left Agello's. Once we were home, Jason didn't give me time to think. It was like our honeymoon all over again, and I was glad of that.

The next day was Sunday. Sunday was the day we usually had breakfast on the sun porch in our pajamas. In the light of day I wasn't worried about the face, but it was comfortable in our room. "Let's be sissies," I said, "and have breakfast in bed."

"Lazy." Jason laughed. "But it's too nice a day to be on the north side of the house. No, Shelley, we're going to bask in the sunlight. And just to pamper you, I'm going to carry you thither." He leaned over the bed and gathered me into his arms.

"This is fun," I grinned, "but in the interests of modesty you'd better let me have a negligee."

He held me down so I could retrieve my blue crepe housecoat from the foot of the bed. I clutched it to me, and we were ready.

On our way, Jason paused a minute before the mirror set into my closet door. "See what a pretty picture you make," he whispered in my ear. "You're like a slim dryad of the woods, and I—" he squared his massive shoulders and I felt the muscles of his chest hard against me—"am Pan."

There wasn't any music—no thin fluting or wondrous tones; only a resentment and a feeling of instinctive recoil—as though anyone could be Pan but the face. I made myself look in the mirror. Just as we were we might have posed for a calendar picture of a dryad being abducted by a satyr—not Pan. Jason's face was lascivious enough but there was no suggestion of the god in him. He was of the earth.

I, in my white satin nightie had a classic look, for the satin moulded my form and was a startling contrast to my red-gold hair.

Jason, in blue foulard pajamas, looked like an advertisement straight out of "Esquire." Direct physiological appeal. But I knew instinctively that within him there were no nuances, none of the subtle approach that is so dear to a woman's heart. His was not the knowledge that Pan possessed.

It was at that moment I heard the music—the faint, thin piping that shivered against my nerves and made them vibrate to its tune, music that grew louder even as I listened.

Jason started towards the door.

The music was calling to me. Calling to me to come, to give myself up to it completely.

Suddenly I was afraid. Jason was very dear, human and near. I clung to him. "Don't go downstairs," I begged. "Let's stay here." I tried to put allure into my voice. Anything to keep him here where it was safe, where I could shut the door and drown out the music that attracted me, as something evil that is yet beautiful can always do.

Jason's mind was one track. "Breakfast first, darling." He walked on, and the music swelled in tone. It was making me forget everything but my desire for it—and Pan, for the two were inescapably one.

Still I tried to hold to reality. "Do you hear music?" I asked Jason, as he descended the stairway.

"Music? Lord, no! But I do hear a vibration like the jangling note of a wire that's off-key. After breakfast we'll look for it."

"There may not be time." The words said themselves.

"We've got all day, darling." He was at the bottom of the steps, advancing to the living room. The music was becoming more and more pronounced. Like Wagner's fire music, little tongues of flame licking about me, growing larger and stronger.

I knew they were waiting to envelope me. I made a last effort. "Jason, we mustn't go to the sun room. There's something there—something—" "Evil" was what I'd meant to say but the word was still-born on my lips. The music had taken possession of me. I was encased in it as surely as Brunehilde ever was on her fire-ringed mountain. Little flames of music were licking about me.

Then we were in the sun room and Jason put me down.

My wrapping the negligee around me was mechanical, and wasted, for Pan's eyes looked through the material, yes, through the skin, into my very soul. He was complete now, a full-grown figure, and even as I watched he rose from the blue-green tiles, wholly dimensional. His boring eyes held mine and the music was like a flowing river of fire, touching me, everywhere.

"So, you have answered my pipings?" It was as though we were singing.

"Yes," I replied, "And now that I am here?"

"Shelley, what are you talking about?" Jason's voice was impatient.

The music diminished. "Didn't you hear?" I began.

"Wait." Pan's voice was thunder-clear.

Suddenly arrested, I stood still. But my gaze betrayed me.

"What is it?" Jason asked. Then, when I made no reply he became insistent. *"What is it?* What do you hear?"

That caught me up short with surprise. It didn't seem possible that he didn't hear that glorious, engrossing, enveloping music. I found words. "But you *must* hear the music. It's so wonderful. And you must see —"

I looked at Pan. He was regarding me strangely and shaking his head.

I stopped short. Jason followed my gaze. "It's that darn tile. You've been acting peculiarly ever since you saw those cracks. I'm going to dig it out."

"No," I cried. "No, Jason, let it alone. There's danger!" I don't know how I knew there was danger for Jason, perhaps it was the expression in Pan's eyes. But how, or why I knew Jason went in peril? And at that moment the urgency was upon me to save him.

"Don't be foolish, Shelley. How could there be danger in a tile — a cracked tile, at that?"

"But he's larger than you." I was struggling against Pan and the music now, trying to save Jason from something intangible, some danger I sensed but couldn't rightly name. I was afraid, and yet, what did Jason — anything — matter, against the vibrant music that was swelling around me?

"Sheila!" Jason exclaimed. "I think you must have a hangover — seeing things. A hangover, or be mad. That tile has bewitched you. I'm getting rid of it now — this second."

He went to an old sea chest where he kept tools and things. He opened it and took out a hunting knife.

I could see Pan's triumphant smile.

"No, Jason, no!" I shrieked, and then the music was so loud, so beautiful that I couldn't think of anything else. I was completely lost to the music, hypnotized as any snake by a master piper, enveloped by melody which was part of Pan.

As in a dream I saw Jason advance toward the tile, knife in hand. I saw Pan moving towards him.

The music accelerated. For one desperate moment I came to my senses. "Jason, come away!" I screamed, and rushed to him.

Pan was before me. With one hand he thrust me back; with the other he turned Jason's arm with the knife inward, so that the knife was toward Jason's body. I saw the blue tile gleaming, crackless and pure, just like the others. Pan had left it. He had materialized. Just as I realized this, Pan pushed Jason. My husband fell, and as he did so, impaled himself on his own knife as surely as any ancient Roman running himself through with his sword.

There was a funny gurgling noise. Then Jason rolled over on his back. I knew the danger had struck. Jason was dead.

But Pan was alive!

Alive and wholly man, and the music too was a living, throbbing thing, marvelous beyond human knowing, enveloping me until I was part of it.

The wonder of the music was completely mine now. It swept me forward, into Pan's arms.

I don't mind being in prison, or the fact that I am on trial for my life, charged with the murder of my husband. I don't even care that they are saying I am mad, perhaps because I know that if I told them the truth they would be certain of it.

I don't mind being confined in this horrible cell, or any of the rest of it. I don't mind, because the cracks of time opened for me, and now the wonderful music is always in my ears, and the remembrance of Pan's kisses on my lips.

And the certainty that at the end I shall feel them again! ⚔

THE CRIPPLE

MAURICE LEVEL

Because he knew good manners, and although there was no one present but Farmer Galot, Trache said on entering:

"Good day, gentlemen!"

"You again!" growled Galot, without turning round.

"To be sure," replied Trache.

He raised his two maimed hands, as if explaining, by their very appearance, his instructions.

Two years ago, in harvest-time, a threshing-machine had caught him up and, by a miracle, dashed him to the ground again instead of crushing him to death. They had borne him off, covered with blood, shrieking, with arms mangled, a rib smashed in, and spitting out his teeth. There remained from the accident a certain dullness of intellect, short breath, a whistling sound which seemed to grope for words at the bottom of his chest, scrape them out of his throat and jumble them up as they passed his bare gums, and a pair of crooked hands which he held out before him in an awkward and apprehensive manner.

"Well, what is it you want?" snapped Galot.

"My compensation money," answered Trache with a weak smile.

"Compensation money! I haven't owed you anything for a long time. There's nothing the matter with you now but laziness and a bad disposition. To begin with, you were drunk when the thing happened. I needn't have given you anything."

"I was *not* drunk," said Trache quietly.

The farmer lost all patience.

"At this moment you can use your hands as well as anybody. You keep up the sham before people, but when you are alone you do what you like with them."

"I don't move them then; I can't," mumbled Trache.

"I tell you, you are an impostor, a trickster, a rascal; I say that you are fleecing me because I have not been firmer with you, that you are making a little fortune out of my money, but that you shall not have another cent. There, that's final. Do you understand?"

"Yes, from your point of view," assented Trache without moving.

Galot flung his cap on the table and began to pace the room with long strides.

Trache shook his head and hunched up his shoulders. At last Galot squared up before him.

"How much do you want to settle for good and all? Suppose we say five hundred francs and make an end of it?"

"I want what is due to me according to the judgment of the court."

Galot became transported with rage:

"Ne'er-do-well, lazy-bones, good-for-nothing; I know what you told the court through the mouth of your doctor, and why you would not let mine examine you."

"It was upon the sworn evidence of the doctors that the case was decided," observed the cripple.

"Ah, it isn't they who have to pay!" sneered Galot. "Let me see your hands. . . . Let me look, I say: I know something about injuries."

Trache stretched out his arms and presented the wrists. Galot took them between his heavy hands, turned them over, turned them back, feeling the bones and the fleshy parts, as he would have done with cattle at a fair. Now and then Trache made a wry face and drew back his shoulder. At last Galot pushed him away with brutal force.

"You are artful, cunning. But look out for yourself: I am keeping my eye on you, and when I have found you out, look out for your-self! You will end by laughing on the other side of your face, and to get your living you will have to work—you hear what I say?—to work."

"I should like nothing better," sighed the cripple.

Pale with wrath, Galot emptied a purse of silver money on the table, counted it and pushed it toward him.

"There's your money; now be off."

"If you would be so good as to put it in my blouse," suggested Trache, "seeing that I can't do it myself. . . ."

Then he said, as on entering: "Good day, gentlemen," and with stuffed pocket, shaking head and unsteady step, he took his departure.

To return to his lodging he had to pass along the riverside. In the fields the patient oxen trudged on their way. Laborers were binding the sheaves amid the shocks of corn; and across the flickering haze of the sultry air the barking of dogs came with softened intonation.

Near a bend of the river, where it deepened into a little pool, a woman was washing linen. The water ran at her feet, flecked with foam and in places clouded with a pearly tint.

"Well, are things going as you wish, Françoise?" asked Trache.

"Oh, well enough," said she. "And you?"

"The same as usual . . . with my miserable hands."

He sighed, and the coins jingled under his blouse. Françoise winked at him.

"All the same it isn't so bad—what the threshing-machine has done for you, eh? . . . And then, to be sure, it's only right; Galot can well afford to pay."

"If I wasn't crippled for life, I wouldn't ask for anything."

Thereupon she began to laugh, with shoulders raised and mallet held aloft. She was a handsome girl, and even a good girl, and more than once he had talked to her in the meadow, but now he reddened with anger.

"What is the matter with you all—dropping hints and poking your fun at me?"

She shrugged her shoulders.

"If I gossip it's only for the fun of gossiping."

He sat down near her, mollified, and listened as she beat her linen. Then, wanting to smoke, and unable to use his helpless hands, he asked her:

"Would you mind getting my pouch out of my pocket and filling my pipe for me?"

She wiped her hands on her apron, searched in his blouse, filled his pipe, struck a match and, shielding it with her hand, said jokingly:

"You're lucky in meeting me."

He bent forward to light his pipe. At the same moment she slipped on the bank, lost a sabot, threw up her arms and fell backward into the water.

Seeing her fall, Trache sprang up. She had sunk immediately, dragging her wash-tub after her, in a place where the water was deep and encumbered with weeds. Then her head reappeared, stretched out into the air, and she cried, already half choking:

"Your hand! Your hand!"

Trache stopped short, his pipe shaking in the corner of his mouth. Shriller, more despairingly came the cry:

"Your hand; I'm drowning. . . . Help! . . ."

Some men in a neighboring field were running. But they were at a great distance, and could only be seen as shadows moving over the corn.

Françoise sank again, rose, sank, rose once more. No sound came from her lips now; her face was terrible in its agony of supplication. Then she sank finally; the weeds, scattered in all directions, closed up again; their tangled network lay placid as before under the current. And that was all.

It was only after an hour's search that the body was found, enmeshed in the river growth, the clothes floating over the head. Trache stamped on the ground.

"I, a man, and powerless to do anything! . . . Curses, curses on my miserable hands!"

They tried to calm him as they condoled with him on his wretched lot, accompanying him to his cottage in their desire to soothe. Seeing him approach in this way, his wife uttered a piercing cry. What new disaster had befallen her husband? . . . They told her of the catastrophe, and of his anguish at not being able to save Françoise, whereupon she joined her lamentations to his.

But when they were alone behind closed doors, taking off his hat with a brisk movement, Trache rubbed his benumbed hands, stretched out his fingers, worked his joints, drew forth his pouch full of coins, flung it on the table and said:

"No, damn it. A fine business if I had given her my hand and she had gone and chattered to Galot! . . . No! damn it. . . ." ⸺

CROSS OF FIRE

LESTER DEL REY

That rain! Will it never stop? My clothes are soaked, my body frozen. But at least the lightning is gone. Strange; I haven't seen it since I awoke. There was lightning, I think. I can't seem to remember anything clearly, yet I am sure there was a fork of light in the sky; no, not a fork; it was like a cross.

That's silly, of course. Lightning can't form a cross. It must have been a dream while I was lying there in the mud. I don't recall how I came there, either. Perhaps I was ambushed and robbed, then left lying there until the rain brought me to. But my head doesn't hurt; the pain is in my shoulder, a sharp, jabbing ache. No, I couldn't have been robbed; I still have my ring, and there is money in my pocket.

I wish I could remember what happened. When I try to think, my brain refuses. There is some part of it that doesn't want to remember. Now why should that be? There. . . . No, it's gone again. It must have been another dream; it had to be. Horrible!

Now I must find shelter from the rain. I'll make a fire when I get home and stop trying to think until my mind is rested. Ah, I know where home is. This can't be so terrible if I know that. . . .

There, I have made a fire and my clothes are drying before it. I was right; this is my home. And I'm Karl Hahrhöffer. Tomorrow I'll ask in the village how I came here. The people in Altdorf are my friends. Altdorf! When I am not trying to think, things come back a little. Yes, I'll go to the village tomorrow. I'll need food, anyway, and there are no provisions in the house.

But that is not strange. When I arrived here, it was boarded and nailed shut, and I spent nearly an hour trying to get in. Then my feet guided me to the cellar, and it was not locked. My muscles sometimes know better than my brain. And sometimes they trick me. They would have led me deeper into the cellar instead of up the steps to this room.

Dust and dirt are everywhere, and the furniture seems about to fall apart. One might think no one had lived here for a century. Perhaps I have been away from Altdorf a long time, but surely I can't have lived away while all this happened. I find a mirror. There should be one over there, but it's gone; no matter, a tin pan of water will serve.

Not a mirror in the house. I used to like my reflection, and found my face fine and aristocratic. I've changed. My face is but little older, but the eyes are hard, the lips thin and red, and there is something unpleasant about my expression. When I smile, the muscles twist crookedly before they attempt my old cockiness. Sister Flämchen used to love my smile.

There is a bright red wound on my shoulder, like a burn. It must have been the lightning, after all. Perhaps it was that cross of fire in the sky I seem to remember. It shocked my brain badly, then left me on the soggy earth until the cold revived me.

But that does not explain the condition of the house, nor where old Fritz has gone. Flämchen may have married and gone away, but Fritz would have stayed with me. I may have taken him to America with me, but what became of him then? Yes, I was going to America before . . . before something happened. I must have gone and been away longer than I look to have been. In ten years much might happen to a deserted house. And Fritz was old. Did I bury him in America?

They may know in Altdorf. The rain has stopped and there is a flush of dawn in the sky. I'll go down soon. But now I am growing sleepy. Small wonder, with all I have been through. I'll go upstairs and sleep for a little while before going to the village. The sun will be up in a few minutes.

No, fool legs, to the left! The right leads back to the cellar, not the bedroom. Up! The bed may not be the best now, but the linens should keep well, and I should be able to sleep there. I can hardly keep my eyes open long enough to reach it.

I must have been more tired than I thought, since it's dark again. Extreme fatigue always brings nightmares, too. They've faded out, as dreams do, but they must have been rather gruesome, from the impression left behind. And I woke up ravenously hungry.

It is good that my pockets are well filled with money. It would take a long time to go to Edeldorf where the bank is. Now it won't be necessary for some time. This money seems odd, but I suppose the coinage has changed while I was gone. How long have I been away?

The air is cool and sweet after yesterday's rain, but the moon is hidden. I've picked up an aversion to cloudy nights. And something seems wrong with the road to the village. Of course it would change, but it seems to have been an unusually great change for ten years or so.

Ah, Altdorf! Where the Burgermeister's house was, there is now some shop with a queer pump in front of it—gasoline. Much that I cannot recall ever seeing before, my mind seems to recognize, even to expect. Changes all around me, yet Altdorf has not changed as greatly as I feared. There is the tavern, beyond is the food store, and down the street is the wine shop. Excellent!

No, I was wrong; Altdorf has not changed, but the people have. I don't recognize any of them, and they stare at me most unpleasantly. They should be my friends; the children should run after me for sweets. Why should they fear me? Why should that old woman cry out and draw her children into the house as I pass? Why are the lights turned out as I approach and the streets deserted? Could I have become a criminal in America? I had no leaning toward crime. They must mistake me for someone else; I do look greatly different.

The storekeeper seems familiar, but younger and altered in subtle ways from the one I remember. A brother, perhaps. "Don't run away, you fool! I won't hurt you. I only wish to purchase some vegetables and provisions. Let me see—no, no beef. I am no robber, I will pay you. See, I have money."

His face is white, his hands tremble. Why does he stare at me when I order such common things? "For myself, of course. For whom else should I buy these? My larder is empty. Yes, that will do nicely."

If he would stop shaking; must he look back to that door so furtively? Now his back is turned, and his hands grope up as if he were crossing himself. Does he think one sells one's soul to the devil by going to America?

"No, not that, storekeeper. Its color is the most nauseous red I've seen. And some coffee and cream, some sugar, some—yes, some liverwurst and some of that brown sausage. I'd like some bacon, but cut out the lean—I want only the fat. Blutwurst? No, never. What a thought! Yes, I'll take it myself, if your boy is sick. It *is* a long walk to my place. If you'll lend me that wagon, I'll return it tomorrow. . . . All right, I'll buy it.

"How much? No, of course I'll pay. This should cover it, if you won't name a price. Do I have to throw it at you? Here, I'll leave it on the counter. Yes, you can go."

Now why should the fool scuttle off as if I had the plague?

That might be it. They would avoid me, of course, if I had had some contagious disease. Yet surely I couldn't have returned here alone, if I had been sick. No, that doesn't explain it.

Now the wine-dealer. He is a young man, very self-satisfied. Perhaps he will act sensibly. At least he doesn't run, though his skin blanches. "Yes, some wine."

He isn't surprised as much as the storekeeper; wine seems a more normal request then groceries. "No, white port, not the red. Don't look so surprised, man. White port and light tokay. Yes, that brand will do if you haven't the other. And a little cognac. These evenings are so cool. Your money. . . . Very well."

He doesn't refuse the money, nor hesitate to charge double for his goods. But he picks it up with a hesitant gesture and then dumps the change into my hand without counting it out. There must be something in my looks that the water did not reveal last night. He stands staring at me so fixedly as I draw my wagon away. Next time I shall buy a good mirror, but I have had enough of this village for the time.

Night again. This morning I lay down before sunrise, expecting to catch a little sleep before exploring the house, but again it was dark before I awoke. Well, I have candles enough; it makes little difference whether I explore the place by day or night.

Hungry as I am, it seems an effort to swallow the food, and the taste is odd and unfamiliar, as if I had eaten none of it for a long time. But then, naturally the foods in America would not be the same. I am beginning to believe that I was away longer than I thought. The wine is good, though. It courses through my veins like new life.

And the wine dispels the lurking queerness of the nightmares. I had hoped that my sleep would be dreamless, but they came again, this time stronger. Some I half remember. Flämchen was in one, Fritz in several.

That is due to my being back in the old house. And because the house has changed so unpleasantly, Fritz and Flämchen have altered into the horrible travesties I see in my dreams.

Now to look over the house. First the attic, then the cellar. The rest of it I have seen, and it is little different except for its anachronistic appearance of age. Probably the attic will be the same, though curiosity and idleness urge me to see.

These stairs must be fixed; the ladder looks too shaky to risk. It seems solid enough, though. Now the trap-door—ah, it opens easily. But what is that odor? Garlic—or the age-worn ghost of garlic. The place reeks of it; there are little withered bunches of it tied everywhere.

Someone must have lived up here once. There is a bed and a table, with a few soiled dishes. That refuse might have been food once. And that old hat was one that Fritz always wore. The cross on the wall and the Bible on the table were Flämchen's. My sister and Fritz must have shut themselves up here after I was gone. More mysteries. If that is true, they may have died here. The villagers must know of them. Perhaps there is one who will tell me. That wine-dealer might, for a price.

There is little to hold me here, unless the table drawer has secrets it will surrender. Stuck! The rust and rotten wood cannot be wrong. I must have been away more years than I thought. Ah, there it comes. Yes, there is something here, a book of some sort. *Diary of Fritz August Schmidt.* This should give me a clue, if I can break the clasp. There should be tools in the work-room.

But first I must explore the cellar. It seems strange that the door should have been open there when all the rest were so carefully nailed shut. If I could only remember how long I've been gone!

How easily my feet lead me down into the cellar! Well, let them have their way this once. Perhaps they know more than my memory tells. They guided me here well enough before. Tracks in the dust! A man's shoe-print. Wait. . . . Yes, they match perfectly; they are mine. Then I came down here before the shock. Ah, that explains the door. I came here, opened that, and walked about. Probably I was on my way to the village when the storm came up. Yes, that must be it. And that explains why my legs moved so surely to the cellar entrance. Muscular habits are hard to break.

But why should I have stayed here so long? The tracks go in all directions, and they cover the floor. Surely there is nothing to hold my interest here. The walls are bare, the shelves crumbling to pieces, and not a sign of anything unusual anywhere. No, there is something; that board shouldn't be loose, where the tracks all meet again. How easily it comes away in my hand!

Now why should there be a pit dug out behind the wall, when the cellar is still empty? Perhaps something is hidden here. The air is moldy and sickening inside. Somewhere I've smelled it before, and the association is not pleasant. Ah, now I can see. There's a box there, a large one, and heavy. Inside. . . . A coffin, open and empty!

Someone buried here? But that is senseless; it is empty. Too, the earth would have been filled in. No, there is something wrong here. Strange things have gone on in this house while I have been away. The house is too old, the villagers fear me, Fritz shut himself up in the attic, this coffin is hidden here; somehow they must be connected. And I must find that connection.

This was an unusually fine coffin once; the satin lining is still scarcely soiled, except for those odd brown blotches. Mold, perhaps, though I've never seen it harden the cloth before; it looks more like blood. Evidently I'll not find my connection here. But there still remains the diary. Somewhere there has to be an answer. I'll break that clasp at once, and see if my questions are settled there.

* * *

This time, reading and work have given me no chance to sleep through the day as before. It is almost night again, and I am still awake.

Yes, the diary held the answer. I have burned it now, but I could recite it from memory. Memory! How I hate that word! Mercifully, some things are still only half clear; my hope now is that I may never remember fully. How I have remained sane this long is a miracle beyond comprehension. If I had not found the diary, things might . . . but better this way.

The story is complete now. At first as I read Fritz's scrawl it was all strange and unbelievable; but the names and events jogged my memory until I was living again the nightmare I read. I should have guessed before. The sleeping by day, the age of the house, the lack of mirrors, the action of the villagers, my appearance—a hundred things—all should have told me what I had been. The story is told all too clearly by the words Fritz wrote before he left the attic.

My plans had been made, and I was to leave for America in three days when I met a stranger the villagers called the "Night Lady." Evil things had been whispered of her, and they feared and despised her, but I would have none of their superstition. For me she had an uncanny fascination. My journey was forgotten, and I was seen with her at night until even my priest turned against me. Only Fritz and Flämchen stayed with me.

When I "died," the doctors called it anemia, but the villagers knew better. They banded together and hunted until they found the body of the woman. On her they used a hartshorn stake and fire. But my coffin had been moved; though they knew I had become a monster, they could not find my body.

Fritz knew what would happen. The old servant sealed himself and Flämchen in the attic away from me. He could not give up hopes for me, though. He had a theory of his own about the Undead. "It is not death," he wrote, "but a possession. The true soul sleeps, while the demon who has entered the body rules instead. There must be some way to drive out the fiend without killing the real person, as our Lord did to the man possessed. Somehow, I must find that method."

That was before I returned and lured Flämchen to me. Why is it that we—such as I was—must prey always on those whom we loved? Is it not enough to lie writhing in the hell the usurper has made of our body without the added agonies of seeing one's friends its victims?

When Flämchen joined me in Undeath, Fritz came down from his retreat. He came willingly if not happily to join us. Such loyalty deserved a better reward. Wretched Flämchen, miserable Fritz!

They came here last night, but it was almost dawn, and they had to go back. Poor, lustful faces, pressed against the broken windows, calling me to them! Since they have found me, they will surely be back. It is night again, and they should be here any moment now. Let them come. My preparations are made, and I am ready. We have stayed together before, and will vanish together tonight.

A torch is lit and within reach, and the dry old floor is covered with rags and oil to fire the place. On the table I have a gun loaded with three bullets. Two of them are of silver, and on each a cross is cut deeply. If Fritz were right, only such bullets may kill a vampire, and in all other things he has proved correct.

Once I, too, should have needed the argent metal, but now this simple bit of lead will serve as well. Fritz's theory was correct.

That cross of lightning, which drove away the demon possessing my body, brought my real soul back to life; once a vampire, again I became a man. But almost I should prefer the curse to the memories it has left.

Ah, they have returned. They are tapping at the door I have unfastened, moaning their blood-lust as of old.

"Come in, come in. It is not locked. See, I am ready for you. No, don't draw back from the gun. Fritz, Flämchen, you should welcome this. . . ."

How peaceful they look now! Real death is so clean. But I'll drop the torch on the tinder, to make doubly sure. Fire is cleanest of all things. Then I shall join them. . . . This gun against my heart seems like an old friend; the pull of the trigger is like a soft caress.

Strange. The pistol flame looks like a cross. . . . Flämchen . . . the cross . . . so clean! ⎯✚⎯

Dark Rosaleen

Seabury Quinn

Marcia

Marcia hummed a snatch of tune as she let the long, swirl-skirted dinner dress slip down her sleek hips to form a circle on the floor about her feet. The old song had been ringing in her head all afternoon since they had picked it up on the radio as they left Maplewood, fitting its rhythm to the rhythm of the tires as the car sped like the shuttle of a loom across the Jersey highways, over Pennsylvania's brick roads, and up and down the rolling contours of the Maryland turnpikes: In thine arms enfold me, my beloved . . . For thy loss a world could not atone . . .

She stood for a moment before the long mirror, looking at the slim perfection of herself reflected in the glass. "I *am* pretty!" she whispered, as if she had just discovered what she'd known for at least twenty of her twenty-three years.

The pleased exclamation was no overstatement. In her wisp of nylon garment and her gold-kid sandals she was as bewitching as a dryad; azure-eyed, with short hair yellow as new honey, pink-cheeked, slim of hands and feet and ankles, lissome, beautifully shaped, radiating health and happiness and eagerness.

She turned from her reflection, took the filmsy *robe de nuit* from her new pigskin bag and slipped into it, paused to study herself for another moment in the glass, then snapped the light off and crept into the big four-poster bed with its percale sheets and lace-trimmed pillows and the "wedding ring" design patchwork quilt. "Rex!" she called softly, and in the darkness she could feel the not entirely unpleasant warmth of a blush on her cheeks and brow and throat. "Rex!"

They had been married just at noon in Saint Justin's, and afterwards there was the ordeal by reception at the Blenheim Towers, then the frantic dash for escape in the new convertible that was her father's wedding present, shaking off pursuit somewhere between Coytsville and Bordentown, followed by the long drive to the cottage at Catoctin which Aunt Martha had lent them for their honeymoon.

The little house, less than a rifle's reach from the locale of George

A. Townsend's novel, was ideally suited to their purpose as if it had been built for them. Stone walls a foot thick held the July heat at a respectful distance, the floors were odd-width planks of polished oak held to their joists with wooden pegs, in all directions there were vistas of the Blue Ridge as entrancing as a picture, the brick-walled garden was a fenced-in bit of paradise, with phlox and zinnias in riotous bloom and roses climbing over an old arbor.

They had dinner in the open air with Aunt Martha's maid Susannah in attendance, stepping softly as a cat for all her wrestler's bulk, and with a tender hand for food and china. Only in Maryland—and not often there—are such dinners to be had: Potomac bass fried saddle-brown in country butter, crackling-hot fried chicken breasts with creamy white gravy, served with stewed celery tops and quince-mint jelly, potatoes whipped in milk, tossed salad, beaten biscuit, and for dessert a deep-dish apple pie. Too, with the meal there was the true "wine of the country"—dandelion wine as white and well-nigh tart as Chablis with the fish, elderberry wine as red and fine as any vintage out of Burgundy with the chicken, and apple brandy of amazing potency with dessert.

They had dined late and lingered long after coffee, content to be alone at last, and, as children might deliberately prolong the ecstasy of anticipation by delaying to eat a sweet, putting off the time of going in until long after the midnight express thundered through the valley on its way to Washington. Now, as Marcia snuggled down between the cool, clove-scented sheets, there came the distant hooting of a diesel locomotive as it dragged a train westward, and the distant, eerie baying of a dog that found an echo somewhere farther off in the hills, then thinned out to a long drawn, wavering howl that echoed mournfully as the lament of a lost and wind-vexed ghost.

"Rex!" she called a little louder, just a little frightened by the grieving ululation. "Rex, dear!"

She knew the room reserved for him lay just beyond the bath. She had helped him unpack, hanging his tweeds in the closet and laying out his fishing gear for the next morning. "Get ready to eat fish till you grow scales!" he had warned her. "You're married to old Izaak W. Walton himself, young lady!" As she undressed she had heard him come upstairs and heard the latch of his door click. "Rex, dear!"

From his room came a sound, the sort of sound that had no business in a bridegroom's chamber; a low-pitched, controlled laugh that held a note of triumph, a woman's laugh that bore a freight of victory; of jubilant, exultant conquest. Then Rex's pleading, panic-stricken "No! No!" and that slow, soft, vaunting laugh once more.

"Rex!"

There was no answer.

The pitter-pat of her feet on the cool boards of the floor was panic made audible. "Rex!"

The door of his room swung a little open, and a single lamp upon the bedside shed a meager, honey-pale light. By the dim illumination she saw him sitting on the bed, stripped to his underwear, one shoe and sock removed. He leaned slightly forward, as if listening, but when she called he gave no answer. Then she saw his face, and her scream rose like the sudden flaring of a flame. It mounted in a thin, sharp spiral, piercing, poignant, shriller and more shrill until it seemed no human throat could stand the strain of it. When it was over it began again, or, rather, it never quite finished, but grew lower by gradations of agonized modulations, prolonging itself in a rhythm of monotonous despair.

The mask—it could not properly be called a face—into which she looked was lifeless as a plaque of molded clay. His features sagged as if they had been formed of wax and had slipped in the mold, or softened with the heat. His cheeks hung pendulously and his mouth was slack, his chin had dropped, and on the rim of his teeth his tongue lolled, almost as if he made a grimace. But it was his eyes that appalled her. Glaucous, expressionless, yet somehow deep as fathomless twin openings into hell they were; the eyes of one who lived without a soul or spirit or intelligence—the eyes of a breathing dead man, a zombie.

She made no effort to arouse, to waken him; she knew intuitively the soul of him was gone, that here was nothing but a physical residuum, as hopelessly devoid of life and future as a body lying in its casket.

So she stood there till Susannah, wakened by her screams, came to her with soft words of meaningless comfort: honey-chil'; po' lamb; Susannah's po' li'l baby-gal.

REX

A journey of a thousand miles begins with a single step, the Manchu proverb says. Rex Moynahan's descent into Avernus began when his plane was forced down on its way from St. John's to Croydon. Officials of the Irish government were courteous, the airline's officers did everything for his comfort, but there could not be another flight that evening; he would have to spend the night in Limerick, or Luimneach, as they insisted on calling it.

He dined excellently at the airline's expense, mutton cutlet, potatoes, green salad and an apple tart that was the last word in perfection of the baker's art, with perhaps just a mug or two too many

Guinnesses and possibly too many samples of John Jameson's product, but he was far from drunk—just comfortably fuddled—when he set out to explore the town.

The sweet, long Irish twilight lent an air of unreality to everything as he strolled through the streets, the cut of his clothes proclaiming him American and his air of tolerant sophistication tabulating him as a New Yorker.

He did not note the street's name, or even notice if it bore a sign, but as he turned from a wide throughfare he found himself in a small semilunar byway where trees seemed gossiping leafily, where red-brick houses stood side by side like guardsmen on parade. Here and there among the residences with their window boxes bright with nodding geraniums was a little shop with bow-front windows of small panes set in neat wooden frames; a fruiterer's, a green grocer's, a chemist's, finally an art store. Its window held but one exhibit, an unframed oil painting some eighteen inches wide by twenty-four in height, but as he looked at it he felt a dazed, almost enraptured sensation; his heart beat faster and there was an ache in his throat. The subject was a woman, young, perhaps; perhaps mature; he could not say, he knew only that she was like a sudden close-up view of something he had known vaguely in dreams, the concrete realization of a hazy ideal he had cherished almost since infancy.

She stood in an arched doorway, the ruined entrance to some long-dilapidated castle or abbey, perhaps, and the background shaded by gradations from the green, green grass of Erin at her feet to the young, tender, yellow-green of early leafage behind her. Her costume was the simplest, just a gown of white stuff flowing from her throat to insteps, belted at the waist with a black sash. One hand was raised to rest against the stone jamb of the archway, and where the long sleeve fell away it showed a wrist and arm as white as milk and moulded with a perfection that would have sent Praxiteles into mute rapture. All black and white she was: black, misty hair drawn back from a high, snowy brow and gathered in a loose knot at the nape of her neck, black, brooding eyes between long, curving lashes, eyes that somehow seemed to express sensuousness and humility at once; white cheeks, white throat, white hands, white feet—even the nails of her long, tapering fingers and delicately shaped toes were vivid black, as if enameled with jet lacquer. Her lips, too, seemed black at first glance, but as he looked again he saw their black was underlaid with red, like garnets smeared with soot, or rubies dipped in ink.

The fascination of his wonder grew as he looked at the picture.

Who was she? Flesh and blood? An artist's concrete conception of something vague and abstract, tenuous and allegorical?

The gallery's proprietor came from an inner room and greeted him with a smile. "Yis, sir?" His Irish accent was no brogue, but just the merest differentiation from the speech a cultured Londoner or New Yorker would use. He was a small man, rather old, Rex judged, for his hair, what there was of it, was as gray as pewter and his small, neat beard and mustache were almost white, while about his bright black eyes and on his brow and cheeks was a network of small wrinkles. "Yis, sir?"

"I—" somehow Rex found it embarrassing to state the question— "I'd like to know about that picture—the one in your window, you know."

The little man looked at him under lowered lids. "And what is it you'd like to know?"

"Why—er—what's it represent? Is it supposed to be a portrait, one of those neo-classic things like the French did in the Directoire and First Empire periods, or—"

The shopkeeper's small eyes burned with sudden intensity, perhaps with anger, possibly with ardor. "It's supposed to be an allegory, sir. Shawn Kennedy did it just before he went mad. He called it Róisín Dubh, and but for one thing it's a damnable libel."

"A libel—?"

"Yis, sir. Róisín Dubh, Dark Rosaleen, the Anglo-Irish call it, means the Little Black Rose, and symbolizes Ireland. She ought to be presented as a cold, chaste being, as lovely as an angel, and as sexless. He made her Circe o' the Isles, a seductress, a vampire-woman."

"Oh?" Rex sparred for an opening. How the devil could he come right out and ask about the artist's model? "You say the artist went mad?"

"Mad as a hatter, sir. He was one of our most promising young painters, exhibited in Dublin, London, Paris, New York—on his way to real fame when he came up with that picture." Abruptly, irrelevantly, it seemed to Rex, he asked, "D'ye know Mangan's poem, Dark Rosaleen?"

Rex shook his head.

"You wouldn't. Few foreigners do. Young Kennedy claimed he took his inspiration from that song, but I'm after thinkin' it came from a darker source. She who posed for that picture was no mortal woman, I'll be bound."

"How do you mean?"

* * *

The dealer shook his head. "It's hard to put it into words, sir, and practically impossible to make a foreigner believe, especially an Englishman or American. Shawn Kennedy did that picture two–three years ago, and raised as much tumult with it as the Devil amongst the tailors. Next we heard it was a thing that he was marryin' Lady Frances Holahan O'Toole, an' married they were in the Cathedral, with the Archbishop's self celebratin' the nuptial Mass. *A mhuire!* on his weddin' night, afore he'd let his bride's hair down or loosed her girdle, he was stricken. In a moment, in the twinkling of an eye, his brain went soft like mush and he became a helpless, hopeless imbecile, just a livin', breathin' *thing*, without a mind or soul or spirit in him.

"So that's the end o' Mister Shawn Kennedy, one o' Ireland's foremost young painters, livin' out the wretched remnant of his life in a nursin' home, with her that was the Lady Frances Holahan O'Toole bewailin' her virginity like Jephtha's daughter, for it's a maid-wife she is, held to him by the bonds o' holy matrimony, and held from him by his hopeless idiocy. He might 'a' known as much afore he set his brush to canvas for that picture!"

Rex had an eerie feeling, as if small red ants were racing up and down his spine. "I don't think I quite understand. What connection—"

"Musha, man," the art dealer leaned toward him confidentially. "I'm after tellin' you it was no mortal woman sat for that picture! 'Twas the very Leanhaun Shee herself."

"The Leanhaun Shee—"

"Precisely. The Leanhaun Shee's a fairy wife who comes out from the Sliábh-na-mban, the Hill o' Women, that is, to seek the love o' mortal men, and if they give in to her blandishments she binds 'em to her till the end o' time, when she and they and all the fairy folk and their changelings will vanish in the brightness of God's face like dewdrops in the risin' sun. 'Tis said that in the old days she was Princess Edáin, daughter o' the High King, who was stolen on her weddin' night and taken to Tir-na-n-Og, the Country o' the Young where age and death are unknown and there are neither tears nor loud laughter. I wouldn't know about that, sir; but this I know: It is an evil thing to see the Leanhaun Shee and hear the softness of her voice and feel the softness of her arms, for he who can resist her is a better man nor Saint Anthony, and he who succumbs to her is doomed to lose his soul—"

Rex could not hold his laugh back. "Well, all I've got to say," he chuckled, "is that it would be worth it. To be accepted as a lover by the Lean—whatever you call her—would be worth the price of 'most any man's soul, certainly I'd gladly give mine—"

"Ochone!" The little man stared at him aghast. "Out o' my shop! Out, I say!" He crossed himself and came from behind the counter. "Off with ye, an' quick! Sayin' things like that beneath this roof! It is an evil thing ye've done, so 'tis. The Leanhaun Shee's but waitin' to hear mortals talk like that—"

Still laughing, Rex went out into the soft, sweet twilight of the Irish evening.

DARK ROSALEEN

The tower clock of Saint Bridget's had sounded midnight, then a quarter past, finally one o'clock, but still Rex fought for sleep. Since his return to the hotel he'd had a feeling of malaise, not quite amounting to the jitters, but not far from it. The flight was scheduled for five-thirty in the morning, and he'd be a complete wreck if he did not get some sleep—confound this Irish hospitality! He knew he should have eaten less at dinner, and that Guinness, and the whiskey! He'd be glad to get back to New York where the martinis made you comfortably drowsy instead of tauting your nerves like fiddle strings.

Before he went up to his room he'd found a book of Irish poems in the hotel library, and read James Clarence Mangan's *Dark Rosaleen* for the first time. Now its cadences ran through his mind with an insistence not to be denied:

> "Red lightning lightened through my
>   blood,
>   My Dark Rosaleen!"

> "I'd give my life and soul anew,
>   A second life and soul anew,
>   My Dark Rosaleen!"

The four-barred chime that told the hour trembled on the air. It hung and clung and vibrated till he did not know if he still heard it or only imagined it, and would go on hearing it in his imagination till the end of time.

The sound stopped as abruptly as a cymbal's tintinnabulations cease when a hand is laid upon the quivering brass, and with the sudden, almost deafening, silence she came.

He'd locked the door of his room, and the key lay on the dresser, but the latch snapped back with a sharp click, the door swung open, and she entered, softly, soundlessly as a zephyr. The long silken gown that flowed back against her figure was white, dead white, and so were her slim throat and face and brow. Her hair, her eyes, were black as rain clouds, and the nails of her slim hands and narrow, high-arched feet shone with the blackness of cut jet. Beneath the slumberous, brooding eyes, set in their ambuscades of curving lashes, her lips showed blackly, with an underlie of red, and back of the black lips was the white line of little, milk-white teeth. "*Ocuisle*— O pulse of my heart!" she whispered, and held out slim white hands to him. He rose to meet her, drawn as to a magnet.

Her warm, soft arms twined round him like the tendrils of a vine —the ivy vine that strangles the oak—and her lips were on his, soft and tender, mercilessly, avidly hungry. Heady perfume, laden with the scent of clover blossoms and spring roses, was in his nostrils like a drug, and he felt himself go weak to sickness with desire as the blackly-red lips moved against his own. . . .

After a time came satiety, a feeling such as he'd known when coming out of anesthesia after an appendectomy; a subdued feeling, strangely calm, as if he were at rest after an ordeal. An immense weariness was on him, marrow-deep, exhausting, paralyzing.

She laughed softly as she rose and drew the black sash tight about her waist. Softly and triumphantly. "Thou art mine, Rex *omuirnin*—Rex my love—" she told him as she held her white feet out for him to lace the tiny black sandals on them. "Mine alone."

"Thine alone!" he answered in a voice more sob than whisper. "Thine alone, Edáin *mo muirnin!*"

"Another night I'll come for thee and take thee with me to Tir-na-n-Og, the land where no one grows old, where worldly wisdom has no place, nor prayer nor preaching; where bitter words and tears are unknown."

"Come soon, O pulse of my heart, breath of my life!"

"It may be sooner than thou thinkest, Rex *omuirnin*."

"Boy, what a dream you had last night!" he had told himself next morning as he shaved. "You're getting out of Ireland none too soon, young feller. If you stayed here you'd be takin' dope to keep asleep and dreamin' twenty-four hours a day."

He was tireder than he'd realized. The drive down from New York had taken more out of him than he'd bargained for. Slowly, almost reluctantly, he took his tweeds off, reached for the crisp, new pajamas he'd bought just two days ago, dropped down on the bed and began unlacing his shoes. Marcia was in her room; Marcia, his bride—

"*Omuirnin!*" The whisper came as softly as the echo of an echo, laden with a load of longing not to be gainsaid. "Rex *omuirnin!*"

Like the shadow of a wind-blown cloud she came toward him, slim, white hands outstretched, blackly-red lips smiling. "I've come to take thee, lover, pulse of my heart. The time is come for us to go to Tir-na-n-Og."

The perfume of her wafted toward him like an anesthetic, a paralyzing drug that stole his strength away, and in a moment he felt soft hands on his cheeks, soft lips on his lips.

"No! No!" he gasped. "Not now, not yet, Edáin! I've just been married—"

A slow laugh crept from between her black lips. "Since the days when the Five Kings ruled Ireland no mortal woman has stood between me and my desire, *ocuisle*. Dost thou not remember what was said when first we met? 'Thou'rt mine!' I told thee, and, 'Thine alone!' thou answered. 'Twas then we made our compact, Rex my love, a compact that cannot be broken. Come." Her lips were on his lips, her arms were round him, tenderly, resistly. Her warm, perfume-laden breath was in his mouth.

For just a moment he fought, futilely as a man fallen in deep water fights drowning. Remembered words rang in his brain, "—afore he'd let his bride's hair down or loosed her girdle . . ."

"Rex!" he heard Marcia's frantic cry. "Rex!"

And then he heard no more. —+—

The Death Mist

Captain George H. Daugherty, Jr.

Through the jagged stumps of the Argonne forest swirled the mist of a November evening. Lieutenant John Blackmer, U.S. Infantry, blundered into a clearing and stopped. To his bewildered gaze the trees assumed fantastic shapes, seemed to close around him, then to retreat far off in the eddying fog. The muffled popping of rifle fire he had heard faintly some moments before was silent. The war and all the world had vanished, leaving him alone in a universe of grayness. The heavy vapor lifted a trifle so that he could see that he stood on the edge of a shell hole. Beyond it was the dim outline of a big tree broken off near the ground. As the cloud lifted again, the white wood of the broken trunk showed in livid streaks. On the other side of the shell hole sprawled a dead man, with arms and legs extended woodenly, like some broken puppet.

Not so much weary as unutterably depressed in spirits, Lieutenant Blackmer sank down upon a log. For a time he stared idly, his mind as much a blank as the grayness around him, but always with a terrible sense of despair clutching him. Little by little his thoughts took definite shape. This was the end. Tonight, or tomorrow at the latest, he would stumble on his outfit, or, failing that, be arrested as a straggler. Then would come the inevitable questioning. Why had he become lost from his command? Why had he not carried out his orders?

For a moment a gleam of hope flashed through his mind as the thought struck him: perhaps Captain Racker, his company commander, had been killed or wounded. Might not his defection from duty pass unnoticed? Then realization rushed over him again like the icy waves of the fog. Even if Racker were dead, the three majors knew his story, and the lieutenant-colonel, and the colonel. At this moment, the regiment, or what was left of it, would be digging in for the night. He was missed, was being asked for, no doubt, at this moment. He groaned, or at least he thought he did; although no sound disturbed the silence of the clearing. They would think he was dead, no doubt, and so would forget him, *until he turned up.* For a minute he considered the possibility of desertion, then decided it was of no use. The military police would only pick him up, and he would have no defense. As matters stood, he could at least claim that he had been temporarily separated from his men, or stunned by a shell-burst. If this were only the first time, that might do. But it wasn't the first time.

As he stared into the shifting eddies of the mist he recalled vividly the colonel's headquarters, the grave face of the C.O., grizzled, stern; Captain Racker, with heavy eyebrows knit into a ferocious scowl; the solemn majors, even the rubicund Lieutenant-Colonel MacNamee with an expression of pain on his round and usually jovial countenance. He heard again the colonel:

"Lieutenant Blackmer, it plainly appears that you have failed in your duty. For the second time you have become separated from the men in your command, leaving them in a perilous situation in the face of the enemy. I have heard that the first time this happened there *seemed* to be some extenuating circumstances; but this time we can not admit them. The only thing that saves you from a general court-martial is the fact that Corporal Jason of your command, by extraordinary presence of mind, managed to lead your patrol safely back to our lines. I tell you that if a man of your patrol had been killed I would have no choice but to order you under arrest. I would do it now were it not for the disgrace that would attach to the entire regiment. Therefore I will give you one more chance. Go back to your company, sir, and try to remember at least what you owe to this regiment, if not to yourself, your men, and your country. One more such failure to do your duty, and I will see that you go to Fort Leavenworth."

Lieutenant Blackmer remembered, with shame, the episodes to which the colonel referred. Not that he had meant to be a coward. Nor was he entirely sure that he was a coward. Twice he had been ordered to lead a night-patrol. The first time, all went well until suddenly guttural voices sounded in front. Machine-guns clattered. A German grappled with him. When he got free of the fellow by a stab with his trench-knife and three shots from his automatic, the platoon was gone; nor did he find them until they blundered into the American trench ten minutes after he had wormed his way there. None of them had seen him struggling with the German, so that his story was incredulously received by Captain Racker. The captain, however, said nothing about it, *that time.*

The second episode was worse. Blackmer writhed mentally as he thought of that night—the sudden star shells, the bursting grenades, his dive into the shell hole, the paralyzing fear that prevented him from leaving until it was too late to rejoin the patrol. This time, Captain Racker reported both episodes to the colonel. Blackmer shuddered again.

The fog had now lifted until it seemed to hang in the limbs of the trees of the clearing. The light being stronger, the lieutenant noticed the dead body again. It lay on its back with its arms flung wide, and its face turned away so that only a gray cheek was visible. For a moment the lieutenant had an impulse to go over and make sure that the man was dead. Then he noticed, even at that distance, the red splotch on the tunic and the heavy grotesque posture of the corpse. No living body, even in the soundest sleep, assumes the stuffed-doll attitudes of death.

Again he took up the thread of his recollections. Why had he failed again today? He had led his platoon out of their fox-holes at the time of the jump-off with the fixed determination to keep the men together and gain the objective. Nor had he felt any especial fear, even when they went through the enemy barrage just as they entered the wood. There he had seen two of his men blown to atoms, and three others wounded, one horribly, so that he screamed; and his screams followed the platoon for a long time through the trees. There were snipers and machine-gunners in the woods. Twice the platoon had to drop flat, and worm their way cautiously to flank the positions from which came those deadly streams of lead. Both times they lost heavily, and both times it was the lieutenant who led the final rush and hurled the grenades which put the machine-guns out of business, with the gunners sprawled across them. Recalling these things Blackmer again asked himself, Was he a coward? Yet, as he did so, he marvelled both at the thrill of combat he had felt in the morning, and at his present desperate and hopeless depression.

Again he resumed his recollections of the battle. So far, all was clear and even to his credit. After the capture of the second machine-gun he had reorganized the platoon, now reduced nearly half, and had sent runners to right and left. These returned in good time with reports of contact established. One of them carried a message from Captain Racker to move forward at once. He did so, though the undergrowth was very thick and a gray mist had already begun to form. What then? Another furious barrage. Shell bursts flaming red in the murk. Thunderclaps of sound. The shriek and hiss of fragments. It was just after this, he recalled, that they must have run into a German company. Brown and gray figures had grappled. Shouts, screams, the clatter of rifle fire, the booming of grenades: all seemed to mingle as in an endless nightmare. At first he was with his men; then they had evaporated. He had gone in frantic search of them. Once he was suddenly among a group of the enemy. He remembered, in a flash, their bucket-helmets and bearded faces all about him; again he was almost atop of a machine-gun that spat directly at him, yet never touched him. . . . Once more the mist swirled over all, until suddenly he realized that the battle was far away, and he was alone, he knew not how or why.

Looking up, he saw that the fog was nearly gone, but that the forest would soon be dark. Faint shots and the faraway clatter of a machine-gun in front of him showed in which direction the front lay.

He rose to go, with the leaden feeling that it was to his own execution. At the same time, he wondered why he seemed not to notice the weariness, hunger, and faintness that usually tortured him after such a day. Instead, he felt only a horrible despair.

All at once, with intense amazement, he looked again about him. . . . That broken tree—had he not seen it topple and fall, leaving that bunch of splinters on the stump like some fantastic, clutching hand? Then he recognized the clearing. The platoon had passed that way in the afternoon. Was it not here that the second rain of shells had caught them, just as the fog closed down? And the dead man—he must have been one of Blackmer's own outfit.

Feeling his own despair lighten in a sudden wave of pity for the poor devil, Lieutenant Blackmer went toward the body. In this lonely place, he thought, the corpse might easily escape notice, and so remain unburied, while the man would be listed for ever among the missing. The lieutenant could at least take one of the neck-tags and give directions for the location and proper burial of the body. It would be the last service he could render any one of his men, and that but a poor return for his desertion of them in the thick of the battle.

So thinking, and again in the grip of the deathly chill at the thought of his own past and future, Lieutenant Blackmer approached the dead man. But what was this—an officer? Could it be Captain Racker? Blackmer bent over the corpse. Then, as the icy waves of the fog rolled over him for the last time, he realized the cause of his despair. *The convulsed and blood-stained features which stared at him were his own!* ⚔

THE DISINTERMENT OF VENUS

CLARK ASHTON SMITH

I

Prior to certain highly deplorable and scandalous events in the year 1550, the vegetable garden of Perigon was situated on the southeast side of the abbey. After these events, it was removed to the northwest side, where it has remained ever since; and the former garden-site was given to weeds and briars which, by strict order of the successive abbots, no one has ever tried to eradicate or curb.

The happenings which compelled this removal of the Benedictine's turnip and carrot patches became a popular tale in Averoigne. It is hard to say how much or how little of the legend is apocryphal.

One April morning, three monks were spading lustily in the garden. Their names were Paul, Pierre and Hughes. The first was a man of ripe years, hale and robust; the second was in his early prime; the third was little more than a boy, and had but recently taken his final vows.

Being moved with an especial ardor, in which the vernal stirring of youthful sap may have played its part, Hughes proceeded to dig the loamy soil even more diligently than his comrades. The ground was almost free of stones, owing to the careful tillage of many generations of monks; but anon, through the muscular zeal with which it was wielded, the spade of Hughes encountered a hard and well-buried object of indeterminate size.

Hughes felt that this obstruction, which in all likelihood was a small boulder, should be removed for the honor of the monastery and the glory of God. Bending busily, he shoveled away the moist, blackish loam in an effort to uncover it. The task was more arduous than he had expected; and the supposed boulder began to reveal an amazing length and a quite singular formation as he bared it by degrees. Leaving their own toil, Pierre and Paul came to his assistance. Soon, through the zealous endeavors of the three, the nature of the buried object became all too manifest.

In the large pit they had now dug, the monks beheld the grimy head and torso of what was plainly a marble woman or goddess from antique years. The pale stone of shoulders and arms, tinged faintly as if with a living rose, had been scraped clean in places by their shovels; but the face and breasts were still black with heavily caked loam.

The figure stood erect, as if on a hidden pedestal. One arm was raised, caressing with a shapely hand the ripe contour of shoulder and bosom; the other, hanging idly, was still plunged in the earth. Digging deeplier, the monks uncovered the full hips and rounded thighs; and finally, taking turns in the pit, whose rim was now higher than their heads, they came to the sunken pedestal, which stood on a pavement of granite.

During the course of their excavations, the Brothers had felt a strange, powerful excitement whose cause they could hardly have explained, but which seemed to arise, like some obscure contagion, from the long-buried arms and bosom of the image. Mingled with a pious horror due to the infamous paganry and nudity of the statue, there was an unacknowledged pleasure which the three would have rebuked in themselves as vile and shameful if they had recognized it.

Fearful of chipping or scratching the marble, they wielded their spades with much chariness; and when the digging was completed and the comely feet were uncovered on their pedestal, Paul, the oldest, standing beside the image in the pit, began to wipe away with a handful of weeds and grass the maculations of dark loam that still clung to its lovely body. This task he performed with great thoroughness; and he ended by polishing the marble with the hem and sleeves of his black robe.

He and his fellows, who were not without classic learning, now saw that the figure was evidently a statue of Venus, dating no doubt from the Roman occupation of Averoigne, when certain altars to this divinity had been established by the invaders.

The vicissitudes of half-legendary time, the long dark years of inhumation, had harmed the Venus little if at all. The slight mutilation of an ear-tip half hidden by rippling curls, and the partial fracture of a shapely middle toe, merely served to add, if possible, a keener seduction to her languorous beauty.

She was exquisite as the succubi of youthful dreams, but her perfection was touched with inenarrable evil. The lines of the mature figure were fraught with a maddening luxuriousness; the lips of the full, Circean face were half pouting, half smiling with ambiguous allure. It was the masterpiece of an unknown, decadent sculptor; not the noble maternal Venus of heroic times, but the sly and cruelly voluptuous Cytherean of dark orgies, ready for her descent into the Hollow Hill.

A forbidden enchantment, an unhallowed thralldom, seemed to flow from the flesh-pale marble and to weave itself like invisible hair about the hearts of the Brothers. With a sudden, mutual feeling of shame, they recalled their monkhood, and began to debate what should be done with the Venus, which, in a monastery garden, was somewhat misplaced. After brief discussion, Hughes went to report their find to the abbot and await his decision regarding its disposal. In the meanwhile, Paul and Pierre resumed with their garden labors, stealing, perhaps, occasional covert glances at the pagan goddess.

2

Augustin the abbot came presently into the garden, accompanied by those monks who were not, at that hour, engaged in some special task. With a severe mien, in silence, he proceeded to inspect the statue; and those with him waited reverently, not venturing to speak before their abbot had spoken.

Even the saintly Augustin, however, in spite of his age and rigorous temper, was somewhat discomfited by the peculiar witchery which seemed to emanate from the marble. Of this he gave no sign, and the natural austerity of his demeanor deepened. Curtly he ordered the bringing of ropes, and directed the raising of the Venus from her loamy bed to a standing position on the garden ground beside the hole. In this task, Paul, Pierre and Hughes were assisted by two others.

Many of the monks now pressed forward to examine the figure closely; and several were even prompted to touch it, till rebuked for this unseemly action by their superior. Certain of the elder and more austere Benedictines urged its immediate destruction, arguing that the image was a heathen abomination that defiled the abbey garden by its presence. Others, the most practical, pointed out that the Venus, being a rare and beautiful example of Roman sculpture, might well be sold at a goodly price to some rich and impious art-lover.

Augustin, though he felt that the Venus should be destroyed as an impure pagan idol, was filled with a queer and peculiar hesitation which led him to defer the necessary orders for her demolishment. It was as if the subtly wanton loveliness of the marble were pleading for clemency like a living form, with a voice half human, half divine. Averting his eyes from the white bosom, he spoke harshly, bidding the Brothers to return to their labors and devotions, and saying that the Venus could remain in the garden till arrangements were made for her ultimate disposition and removal. Pending this, he instructed one of the Brothers to bring sackcloth and drape therewith the unseemly nudity of the goddess.

The disinterment of this antique image became a source of much discussion and some perturbation and dissension amid the quiet Brotherhood at Perigon. Because of the curiosity shown by many monks, the abbot issued an injunction that no one should approach the statue, other than those whose labors might compel an involuntary proximity. He himself, at that time, was criticized by some of the deans for his laxness in not destroying the Venus immediately. During the few years that remained to him, he was to regret bitterly the remissness he had shown in this matter.

No one, however, dreamt of the grave scandals that were to ensue shortly. But, on the day following the discovery of the statue, it became manifest that some evil and disturbing influence was abroad. Heretofore, breaches of discipline had been rare among the Brothers; and cardinal offenses were quite unknown; but now it seemed that a spirit of unruliness, impiety, ribaldry and wrong-doing had entered Perigon.

Paul, Pierre and Hughes were the first to undergo penance for their peccancies. A shocked dean had overheard them discussing with impure levity, certain matters that were more suitable for the conversation of worldly gallants than of monks. By way of extenuation, the three Brothers pleaded that they had been obsessed with carnal thoughts and images ever since their exhumation of the Venus; and for this they blamed the statue, saying that a pagan witchcraft had come upon them from its flesh-white marble.

On that same day, others of the monks were charged with similar offenses; and still others made confession of lubric desires and visions such as had tormented Anthony during his desert vigil. Those, too, were prone to blame the Venus. Before evensong, many infractions of monastic rule were reported; and some of them were of such nature as to call for the severest rebuke and penance. Brothers whose conduct had heretofore been exemplary in all ways were found guilty of transgressions such as could be accounted for only by the direct influence of Satan or some powerful demon.

Worst of all, on that very night, it was found that Hughes and Paul were absent from their beds in the dormitory; and no one could say whither they had gone. They did not return on the day following. Inquiries were made by the abbot's order in the neighboring village of Sainte Zenobie, and it was learned that Paul and Hughes had spent the night at a tavern of unsavory repute, drinking and wenching; and they had taken the road to Vyones, chief city of the province, at early dawn. Later, they were apprehended and brought back to the monastery, protesting that their downfall was wholly due to some evil contagion which they had incurred by touching the statue.

In view of the unexampled demoralization which prevailed at Perigon, no one doubted that a diabolic pagan charm was at work. The source of the charm was all too obvious. Moreover, queer tales were told by monks who had labored in the garden or had passed within sight of the image. They swore that the Venus was no mere sculptured idol but a living woman or she-devil who had changed her position repeatedly and had rearranged the folds of the sackcloth in such manner as to lay bare one shapely shoulder and a part of her bosom. Others avowed that the Venus walked in the garden by night; and some even affirmed that she had entered the monastery and appeared before them like a succubus.

Much fright and horror was created by these tales, and no one dared to approach the image closely. Though the situation was supremely scandalous, the abbot still forbore to issue orders for the statue's demolition, fearing that any monk who touched it, even with a motive so pious, would court the baleful sorcery that had brought Hughes and Paul to disaster and disgrace, and had led others into impurity of speech or actual impiety.

It was suggested, however, that some laymen should be hired to shatter the idol and remove and bury its fragments. This, no doubt, would have been accomplished in good time, if it had not been for the hasty and fanatic zeal of Brother Louis.

3

This Brother, a youth of good family, was conspicuous among the Benedictines both for his comely face and his austere piety. Handsome as Adonis, he was given to ascetic vigils and prolonged devotions, outdoing in this regard the abbot and the deans.

At the hour of the statue's disinterment, he was busily engaged in copying a Latin testament; and neither then nor at any later time had he cared to inspect a find which he considered more than dubious. He had expressed disapprobation on hearing from his fellows the details of the discovery; and feeling that the abbey garden was polluted by the presence of an obscene image, he had purposely avoided all windows through which the marble might have been visible to his chaste eyes.

When the influence of heathen evil and corruption became manifest amid the Brothers, he had shown great indignation, deeming it a most insufferable thing that virtuous, God-fearing monks should be brought to shame through the operation of some hellish pagan spell. He had reprobated openly the hesitation of Augustin and his delay in destroying the maleficent idol. More mischief, he said, would ensue if it were left intact.

In view of all this, extreme surprize and alarm were felt at Perigon when, on the fourth day after the exhumation of the statue, Brother Louis was discovered missing. His bed had not been occupied on the previous night; but it seemed impossible that he could have fled the monastery, yielding to such desires and impulsions as had caused the ruin of Paul and Hughes.

The monks were strictly interrogated by their abbot, and it was revealed that Brother Louis, when last seen, had been loitering about the abbey workshop. Since, formerly, he had shown small interest in tools or manual labor, this was deemed a peculiar thing. Forthwith a visit was made to the workshop; and the monk in charge of the smithy soon found that one of his heaviest hammers had been removed.

The conclusion was obvious to all: Louis, impelled by virtuous ardor and holy wrath, had gone forth during the night to demolish the baleful image of Venus.

Augustin and the Brothers who were with him repaired immediately to the garden. There they were met by the gardeners, who, noticing from afar that the image no longer occupied its position beside the pit, were hurrying to report this matter to the abbot. They had not dared to investigate the mystery of its disappearance, believing firmly that the statue had come to life and was lurking somewhere about the garden.

Made bold by their number and by the leadership of Augustin, the assembled monks approached the pit. Beside its rim they beheld the missing hammer, lying on the clodded loam as if Louis had cast it aside. Near by was the sacking that had clothed the image; but there were no fragments of broken marble such as they had thought to see. The footprints of Louis were clearly imprinted upon the pit's margin, and were discernible in strangely close proximity to the mark left by the pedestal of the statue.

All this was very peculiar, and the monks felt that the mystery had begun to assume a more than sinister tinge. Then, peering into the hole itself, they beheld a thing that was explicable only through the machinations of Satan—or one of Satan's most pernicious and seductive she-demons.

Somehow, the Venus had been overturned and had fallen back into the broad deep pit. The body of Brother Louis, with a shattered skull and lips bruised to a sanguine pulp, was lying crushed beneath her marble breasts. His arms were clasped about her in a desperate, lover-like embrace, to which death had now added its own rigidity. Even more horrible and inexplicable, however, was the fact that the stone arms of the Venus had changed their posture and were now folded closely about the dead monk as if she had been sculptured in the attitude of an amorous enlacement!

The horror and consternation felt by the Benedictines were inexpressible. Some would have fled from the spot in panic, after viewing this frightful and most abominable prodigy; but Augustin restrained them, his features stern with the religious ire of one who beholds the fresh handiwork of the Adversary. He commanded the bringing of a cross, an aspergillus and holy water, together with a ladder for use in descending into the pit; saying that the body of Louis must be redeemed from the baleful and dolorous plight into which it had fallen. The iron hammer, lying beside the hole, was proof of the righteous intention with which Louis had gone forth; but it was all too plain that he had succumbed to the hellish charms of the statue. Nevertheless, the Church could not abandon its erring servant to the powers of Evil.

When the ladder was brought, Augustin himself led the descent, followed by three of the stoutest and most courageous Brothers, who were willing to risk their own spiritual safety for the redemption of Louis. Regarding that which ensued, the legends vary slightly. Some say that the aspersions of holy water, made by Augustin on the statue and its victim, were without palpable effect; while others relate that the drops turned to infernal steam when they struck the recumbent Venus, and blackened the flesh of Louis like that of a month-old cadaver, thus proving him wholly claimed by perdition. But the tales agree in this, that the strength of the three stout Brothers, laboring in unison at their abbot's direction, was impotent to loosen the marble clasp of the goddess from about her prey.

So, by the order of Augustin, the pit was filled hastily to its rim with earth and stones; and the very spot where it had been, being left without mound or other mark, was quickly overgrown by grass and weeds along with the rest of the abandoned garden. ⚓

THE DOOM THAT CAME TO SARNATH

H. P. LOVECRAFT

There is in the land of Mnar a vast still lake that is fed by no stream and out of which no stream flows. Ten thousand years ago there stood by its shore the mighty city of Sarnath, but Sarnath stands there no more.

It is told that in the immemorial years when the world was young, before ever the men of Sarnath came to the land of Mnar, another city stood beside the lake; the grey stone city of Ib, which was old as the lake itself, and peopled with beings not pleasing to behold. Very odd and ugly were these beings, as indeed are most beings of a world yet inchoate and rudely fashioned. It is written on the brick cylinders of Kadatheron that the beings of Ib were in hue as green as the lake and the mists that rise above it; that they had bulging eyes, pouting, flabby lips, and curious ears, and were without voice. It is also written that they descended one night from the moon in a mist; they and the vast still lake and grey stone city Ib. However this may be, it is certain that they worshipped a sea-green stone idol chiselled in the likeness of Bokrug, the great water-lizard; before which they danced horribly when the moon was gibbous. And it is written in the papyrus of Ilarnek, that they one day discovered fire, and thereafter kindled flames on many ceremonial occasions. But not much is written of these beings, because they lived in very ancient times, and man is young, and knows but little of the very ancient living things.

After many aeons men came to the land of Mnar; dark shepherd folk with their fleecy flocks, who built Thraa, Ilarnek, and Kadatheron on the winding river Ai. And certain tribes, more hardy than the rest, pushed on to the border of the lake and built Sarnath at a spot where precious metals were found in the earth.

Not far from the grey city of Ib did the wandering tribes lay the first stones of Sarnath, and at the beings of Ib they marvelled greatly. But with their marvelling was mixed hate, for they thought it not meet that beings of such aspect should walk about the world of men at dusk. Nor did they like the strange sculptures upon the grey monoliths of Ib, for those sculptures were terrible with great antiquity. Why the beings and the sculptures lingered so late in the world, even until the coming men, none can tell; unless it was because the land of Mnar is very still, and remote from most other lands both of waking and of dream.

As the men of Sarnath beheld more of the beings of Ib their hate grew, and it·was not less because they found the beings weak, and soft as jelly to the touch of stones and spears and arrows. So one day the young warriors, the slingers and the spearmen and the bowmen, marched against Ib and slew all the inhabitants thereof, pushing the queer bodies into the lake with long spears, because they did not wish to touch them. And because they did not like the grey sculptured monoliths of Ib they cast these also into the lake; wondering from the greatness of the labour how ever the stones were brought from afar, as they must have been, since there is naught like them in all the land of Mnar or in the lands adjacent.

Thus of the very ancient city of Ib was nothing spared save the sea-green stone idol chiselled in the likeness of Bokrug, the water-lizard. This the young warriors took back with them to Sarnath as a symbol of conquest over the old gods and beings of Ib, and a sign of leadership in Mnar. But on the night after it was set up in the temple a terrible thing must have happened, for weird lights were seen over the lake, and in the morning the people found the idol gone, and the high-priest Taran-Ish lying dead, as from some fear unspeakable. And before he died, Taran-Ish had scrawled upon the altar of chrysolite with coarse shaky strokes the sign of DOOM.

After Taran-Ish there were many high-priests in Sarnath, but never was the sea-green stone idol found. And many centuries came and went, wherein Sarnath prospered exceedingly, so that only priests and old women remembered what Taran-Ish had scrawled upon the altar of chrysolite. Betwixt Sarnath and the city of Ilarnek arose a caravan route, and the precious metals from the earth were exchanged for other metals and rare cloths and jewels and books and tools for artificers and all things of luxury that are known to the people who dwell along the winding river Ai and beyond. So Sarnath waxed mighty and learned and beautiful, and sent forth conquering armies to subdue the neighbouring cities; and in time there sate upon a throne in Sarnath the kings of all the land of Mnar and of many lands adjacent.

The wonder of the world and the pride of all mankind was Sarnath the magnificent. Of polished desert-quarried marble were its walls, in height 300 cubits and in breadth 75, so that chariots might pass each other as men drave them along the top. For full 500 stadia did they run, being open only on the side toward the lake; where a green stone sea-wall kept back the waves that rose oddly once a year at the festival of the destroying of Ib. In Sarnath were fifty streets from the lake to the gates of the caravans, and fifty more intersecting them. With onyx were they paved, save those whereon the horses and camels and elephants trod, which were paved with granite. And the gates of Sarnath were as many as the landward ends of the streets, each of bronze, and flanked by the figures of lions and elephants carven from some stone no longer known among men. The houses of Sarnath were of glazed brick and chalcedony, each having its walled garden and crystal lakelet. With strange art were they builded, for no other city had houses like them; and travellers from Thraa and Ilarnek and Kadatheron marvelled at the shining domes wherewith they were surmounted.

But more marvellous still were the palaces and the temples, and the gardens made by Zokkar the olden king. There were many palaces, the least of which were mightier than any in Thraa or Ilarnek or Kadatheron. So high were they that one within might sometimes fancy himself beneath only the sky; yet when lighted with torches dipt in the oil of Dothur their walls shewed vast paintings of kings and armies, of a splendour at once inspiring and stupefying to the beholder. Many were the pillars of the palaces, all of tinted marble, and carven into designs of surpassing beauty. And in most of the palaces the floors were mosaics of beryl and lapis-lazuli and sardonyx and carbuncle and other choice materials, so disposed that the beholder might fancy himself walking over beds of the rarest flowers. And there were likewise fountains, which cast scented waters about in pleasing jets arranged with cunning art. Outshining all others was the palace of the kings of Mnar and of the lands adjacent. On a pair of golden crouching lions rested the throne, many steps above the gleaming floor. And it was wrought of one piece of ivory, though no man lives who knows whence so vast a piece could have come. In that palace there were also many galleries, and many amphitheatres where lions and men and elephants battled at the pleasure of the kings. Sometimes the amphitheatres were flooded with water conveyed from the lake in mighty aqueducts, and then were enacted stirring sea-fights, or combats betwixt swimmers and deadly marine things.

Lofty and amazing were the seventeen tower-like temples of Sarnath, fashioned of a bright multi-coloured stone not known elsewhere. A full thousand cubits high stood the greatest among them, wherein the high-priests dwelt with a magnificence scarce less than that of the kings. On the ground were halls as vast and splendid as those of the palaces; where gathered throngs in worship of Zo-Kalar and Tamash and Lobon, the chief gods of Sarnath, whose incense-enveloped shrines were as the thrones of monarchs. Not like the eikons of other gods were those of Zo-Kalar and Tamash and Lobon, for so close to life were they that one might swear the graceful bearded gods themselves sate on the ivory thrones. And up unending steps of shining zircon was the tower-chamber, wherefrom the high-priests looked out over the city and the plains and the lake by day; and at the cryptic moon and significant stars and planets, and their reflections in the lake, by night. Here was done the very secret and ancient rite in detestation of Bokrug, the water-lizard, and here rested the altar of chrysolite which bore the DOOM-scrawl of Taran-Ish.

Wonderful likewise were the gardens made by Zokkar the olden king. In the centre of Sarnath they lay, covering a great space and encircled by a high wall. And they were surmounted by a mighty dome of glass, through which shone the sun and moon and stars and planets when it was clear, and from which were hung fulgent images of the sun and moon and stars and planets when it was not clear. In summer the gardens were cooled with fresh odorous breezes skilfully wafted by fans, and in winter they were heated with concealed fires, so that in those gardens it was always spring. There ran little streams over bright pebbles, dividing meads of green and gardens of many hues, and spanned by a multitude of bridges. Many were the waterfalls in their courses, and many were the lilied lakelets into which they expanded. Over the streams and lakelets rode white swans, whilst the music of rare birds chimed in with the melody of the waters. In ordered terraces rose the green banks, adorned here and there with bowers of vines and sweet blossoms, and seats and benches of marble and porphyry. And there were many small shrines and temples where one might rest or pray to small gods.

Each year there was celebrated in Sarnath the feast of the destroying of Ib, at which time wine, song, dancing, and merriment of every kind abounded. Great honours were then paid to the shades of those who had annihilated the odd ancient beings, and the memory of those beings and of their elder gods was derided by dancers and lutanists crowned with roses from the gardens of Zokkar. And the kings would look out over the lake and curse the bones of the dead that lay beneath it. At first the high-priests liked not these festivals, for there had descended amongst them queer tales of how the seagreen eikon had vanished, and how Taran-Ish had died from fear and left a warning. And they said that from their high tower they sometimes saw lights beneath the waters of the lake. But as many years passed without calamity even the priests laughed and cursed and joined in the orgies of the feasters. Indeed, had they not themselves, in their high tower, often performed the very ancient and secret rite in detestation of Bokrug, the water-lizard? And a thousand years of riches and delight passed over Sarnath, wonder of the world and pride of all mankind.

Gorgeous beyond thought was the feast of the thousandth year of the destroying of Ib. For a decade had it been talked of in the land of Mnar, and as it drew nigh there came to Sarnath on horses and camels and elephants men from Thraa, Ilarnek, and Kadatheron, and all the cities of Mnar and the lands beyond. Before the marble walls on the appointed night were pitched the pavilions of princes and the tents of travellers, and all the shore resounded with the songs of happy revellers. Within his banquet-hall reclined Nargis-Hei, the king, drunken with ancient wine from the vaults of conquered Pnath, and surrounded by feasting nobles and hurrying slaves. There were eaten many strange delicacies at that feast; peacocks from the isles of Nariel in the Middle Ocean, young goats from the distant hills of Implan, heels of camels from the Bnazic desert, nuts and spices from Cydathrian groves, and pearls from wave-washed Mtal dissolved in the vinegar of Thraa. Of sauces there were an untold number, prepared by the subtlest cooks in all Mnar, and suited to the palate of every feaster. But most prized of all the viands were the great fishes from the lake, each of vast size, and served up on golden platters set with rubies and diamonds.

Whilst the king and his nobles feasted within the palace, and viewed the crowning dish as it awaited them on golden platters, others feasted elsewhere. In the tower of the great temple the priests held revels, and in pavilions without the walls the princes of neighbouring lands made merry. And it was the high-priest Gnai-Kah who first saw the shadows that descended from the gibbous moon into the lake, and the damnable green mists that arose from the lake to meet the moon and to shroud in a sinister haze the towers and the domes of fated Sarnath. Thereafter those in the towers and without the walls beheld strange lights on the water, and saw that the grey rock Akurion, which was wont to rear high above it near the shore, was almost submerged. And fear grew vaguely yet swiftly, so that the princes of Ilarnek and of far Rokol took down and folded their tents and pavilions and departed for the river Ai, though they scarce knew the reason for their departing.

Then, close to the hour of midnight, all the bronze gates of Sarnath burst open and emptied forth a frenzied throng that blackened the plain, so that all the visiting princes and travellers fled away in fright. For on the faces of this throng was writ a madness born of horror unendurable, and on their tongues were words so terrible that no hearer paused for proof. Men whose eyes were wild with fear shrieked aloud of the sight within the king's banquet-hall, where through the windows were seen no longer the forms of Nargis-Hei and his nobles and slaves, but a horde of indescribable green voiceless things with bulging eyes, pouting, flabby lips, and curious ears; things which danced horribly, bearing in their paws golden platters set with rubies and diamonds containing uncouth flames. And the princes and travellers, as they fled from the doomed city of Sarnath on horses and camels and elephants, looked again upon the mist-begetting lake and saw the grey rock Akurion was quite submerged.

Through all the land of Mnar and the lands adjacent spread the tales of those who had fled from Sarnath, and caravans sought that accursed city and its precious metals no more. It was long ere any traveller went thither, and even then only the brave and adventurous young men of distant Falona dared make the journey; adventurous young men of yellow hair and blue eyes, who are no kin to the men of Mnar. These men indeed went to the lake to view Sarnath; but though they found the vast still lake itself, and the grey rock Akurion which rears high above it near the shore, they beheld not the wonder of the world and pride of all mankind. Where once had risen walls of 300 cubits and towers yet higher, now stretched only the marshy shore, and where once had dwelt fifty millions of men now crawled only the detestable green water-lizard. Not even the mines of precious metal remained, for DOOM had come to Sarnath.

But half buried in the rushes was spied a curious green idol of stone; an exceedingly ancient idol coated with seaweed and chiselled in the likeness of Bokrug, the great water-lizard. That idol, enshrined in the high temple at Ilarnek, was subsequently worshipped beneath the gibbous moon throughout the land of Mnar. ———

DREAM JUSTICE

E. W. MAYO

The strange circumstances surrounding the death of Edward Martin were never fully revealed to the public. It was thought by most people that he died of causes unknown, even to the doctors.

But the following I found in his diary; and although there is no way of proving the truth or untruth of it, I nevertheless am inclined to think it explains his death more satisfactorily than any other reason given:

Feb. 7—Last night I had a dream—a dream that was only too true. I dreamed that a murder I had committed three years ago, which I thought had been successfully covered up, had been brought to light. The evidence against me was so forceful that I confessed. I was then taken to the county jail, where I was charged with murder in the first degree. At this point I awoke and found myself wet with perspiration. Why, although the facts concerning the murder are true, I should have a dream of this sort, I can't explain.

Feb. 8—My dream was continued last night. This time it seemed to cover a period of some weeks. I was convicted and sentenced to die in the electric chair August 20. After my sentence was passed I again awoke to find myself in a cold sweat. I was extremely nervous today and am hoping I won't have another of these foolish dreams. The murder is completely covered up, I'm sure, and I was never suspected, so there is no need to be afraid or worried even if I do dream of it. But still I would like an explanation for it.

Feb. 9—It was awful last night. Time passed quickly and it was only three days before the day set for my electrocution when I awoke. It really seemed as if I had spent those long weeks in my cell, waiting and waiting. Today I was really worried, and my friends wanted to know what was wrong with me.

Feb. 10—Two more days—and then—? I can't get away from it, I dream and dream—it is terrible. I even plotted an escape from prison last night—but failed. The thing preys on my mind all the time now—day and night. I can't eat, I can't do anything—I look and act insane; my friends demand to know what the trouble is—but I don't dare tell them—they couldn't help me. No one can help me—if only I could get away from those cursed, those infernal dreams!

Feb. 11—One more day. Last night was a repetition of the one before. I didn't go out today—I was afraid my friends might hear me talking and muttering to myself. I seem to be out of my head—I feel weak and can hardly think at all. I only dread what tonight will bring.

Feb. 12—Tonight at 12—I'm doomed to go then. But I think I have a way to fool them—I won't go to sleep—I'll stay up and awake until after 12—maybe that will end it all—maybe the spell will be broken then and I shall be saved. I'll drink coffee—black coffee—lots of it—that will keep me awake.

10 P.M. — So far I've been able to keep awake — but I'm getting a little drowsy — I guess I need more black coffee.

11 P.M. — I'm so tired and sleepy I can hardly hold my head up — maybe I need a little fresh air — going to open a window. Just another hour or more and then — if I can only hold out till then!

11:55 P.M. — I can barely write — I almost went under that time — a few more minutes — I can't — I can't — my eyes — I can't hold them open — I'm going — I'm going —

Such were the contents of the late Edward Martin's diary.

And what was found when his bedroom door was forced?

His dead body, slumped down in a big armchair, with peculiar marks on his wrists and ankles — marks that weren't explained at that time — or ever. —————

A Dream of Death

Andrew Daw

A piercing flow of light which caused fantastic shadows to dance grotesquely within his slumber-burdened mind roused Blaine from his sleep. The reading-lamp beside his bed had been switched on and in the outer rim of its glow he saw the pale, haggard face of his nephew.

"What is it, Raymond?" he asked. "Is anything wrong?"

At the sound of Blaine's voice Raymond's lips moved nervously.

"I didn't know you were awake," he mumbled. "I was thinking, trying to decide . . . that is, perhaps I should tell you."

Raymond ceased speaking for a moment. He was sitting in a chair near the bed, making nervous, clawing motions with his hands. His strained face showed clearly how strenuously he was trying to become calm. Gradually he gained control over his agitation. At last he said quite composedly, "I want to tell you about a dream I had."

"So that's your reason for awakening me in the middle of the night!" exclaimed Blaine irately. "Get back to your bed. You can tell me about your dream in the morning."

"But I can't wait until tomorrow," insisted Raymond as he leaned forward and thrust his pale face closer to Blaine's. "This dream," he said. "I have dreamt it often lately. It is hideous. Always the same. I am looking at a room, in the center of which I see a man and woman seated at a table. On the table stands a burning oil lamp. Frequently the man and woman look toward me, and whenever that happens the woman's eyes are filled with a soft and glorious light. She smiles at the man; he at her. Behind the man is a curtained window. The curtain moves slightly as if blown by a breeze. Evidently the window is open. It is upon this curtained window that I am compelled to focus my attention. I say 'compelled' because somehow I am horribly afraid of that window. I feel—I know—that something ghastly, something gruesome is about to happen and that the window is connected with the horror to come.

"While I stare at the wavering curtain, I am aware that the woman has left the room. My terror increases. Then something black and slender stealthily thrusts the curtain aside. It is a rifle. I want to shout a warning to the man at the table, but before I can do so the gun is fired.

"Slowly the man gets up from his chair. There is a surprized expression on his face, and he paws with blood-spattered hands at the wound the bullet has ripped in his neck. A second shot is fired, and this time the man sinks to the floor beneath the window. There he lies writhing in a spreading pool of blood.

"Now a man's head appears in the window. The murderer is making sure that his victim is dead. He is looking down, and I can't see his face. In fact, not once during the events that follow directly do I see his face. At this point the woman returns to the room. When she sees the corpse, her face becomes a mask of heart-rending despair. The killer has not noticed her entrance and continues to look down upon the dead.

"Cautiously the woman moves toward the window. Fury and deathly hatred contort her beautiful face. She crouches as she steals forward, holding in her right hand a heavy glass bowl. At last only a few feet separate her from the murderer. She tenses herself, raises the bowl, at the same time taking a quick step forward to get within reach of the killer. But her foot loses its grip on the slippery floor and she falls across the dead man she was trying to avenge. She looks up toward the face of the killer, screams, and makes a vain attempt to get up from the bloody floor before the killer can lunge through the window. But before she can get to her feet, the killer has entered the room. He stands with his back toward me, staring down at the woman, who is kneeling on the floor, looking at him with a pitiful expression on her madonna-like face. Tears glisten on her cheeks as she pleads, making futile gestures toward him with her hands. The killer stretches his hands toward her white throat as if to choke her, is hesitant, and finally allows his hands to drop, while he stands irresolute. Then as the woman again begins to scream, a frenzy grips the killer. He reaches for a chair, swings it savagely down upon her head and shoulders, and stands back looking at her.

"Apparently the chair has not struck her squarely on the head, for slowly, with stiff, mechanical movements, the woman rises from the floor. One of her shoulders sags. Down the left side of her anguish-twisted face, blood is streaming. Her eyes stare fixedly into space as she fumbles about for something to support herself with. Once she stumbles and almost falls. While moving about unsteadily, trying to regain her balance, she strikes against the table. For a moment she steadies herself against it, all the while staring with distended, unseeing eyes into the flickering flame of the lamp upon the table. From her lips come guttural, moaning sounds.

"Once more the murderer strikes. Uttering a hoarse cry, he leaps forward and grasps the woman by the throat. I seem to hear him screaming, 'Die, damn you! Die!' The force of his attack drags the woman to the floor. As they fall, her arm is flung against the lamp, which topples and crashes on the floor. There is a flash of flames. Swirls of smoke eddy about the room, and while I am trying to see through the haze, I awaken."

Not once while speaking had Raymond taken his eyes off Blaine. And now, as silence cast its spell over the room, Blaine found it difficult to endure the youth's unwavering stare. He shuddered faintly as he seemed to sense that while Raymond was speaking the shadows from the distant corners of the room had crept nearer to his bed. Presently, unable to endure the stillness, he asked lamely: "Well, is that all?"

There was a catch in Raymond's voice when he answered. "The man and woman who were killed were my father and mother."

"Nonsense!" exclaimed Blaine. "You were barely more than three years old when your parents died. At that age it would hardly be possible for you to form a concept of what they looked like which would serve you to identify them years later."

"But I know," persisted Raymond. "Listen. When I first experienced the dream, I could not identify the characters in it, although they seemed familiar to me. One day I happened to look at a picture of my father and mother. The instant I saw it, I recognized my parents as the people in the dream. You do know my parents were murdered. That much the police did find out when they examined their charred bodies. And somebody—a somebody cruel enough to kill them but not a baby—carried me out of the burning house, away from danger. You yourself have told me that."

"Yes, you are right about that," assented Blaine.

He felt strangely weak. With his hands he wiped away the perspiration that had gathered on his forehead—a pale, blanched forehead whose only trace of color was a dark red birthmark the size of a quarter.

Blaine looked at his hands and silently cursed his weakness when he saw how his fingers trembled. He clenched his jaw, tried to say something, but failed to speak. Raymond's precise description of that crimson nightmare of long ago had ripped asunder time's veil of forgetfulness and upset his nerves. Blaine felt as he had that night when, upon returning to his home after the killing, he had washed his gory hands, and, while looking down into the basin where ripples of bloody water formed shifting patterns, he had glimpsed the blood-smeared, pain-racked face of Raymond's mother surrounded by leaping flames. He had screamed then, as for an insane moment his mind had wavered perilously on the brink of that horror-infested chasm in which dwells madness. Ever since he had been trying to forget. At times it was not difficult. During the day the affairs of a prosperous business held his attention. The life insurance for which he had killed Raymond's father had been the foundation of his fortune. The pleasures of power which his wealth gave him usually sufficed to overcome any feeling of regret concerning the means by which the power had been acquired. Even the fact that Raymond's father had been his own brother did not bother him. It was only when the image of Raymond's mother obtruded itself before his eyes that remorse touched him. There was that about killing a woman . . . too bad his gun had jammed . . . it was easier just to shoot . . . he had been forced to choke her . . . there had been blood on her neck and her flesh had seemed to squirm between his hands . . . at least he had spared Raymond. But what was Raymond staying for? He had told his dream. Odd fellow, Raymond. Just like his father. The emotional type. No head for business. But he was not sorry he had taken care of him. That was one of the things which had made it easier to forget.

Blaine had carried his chain of thoughts to that point when he was interrupted as Raymond began to talk.

"I would have forgotten about the dream," said Raymond, "if it hadn't been for the fact that it kept on repeating itself. Night after night during the last month it has haunted me. Always I woke up possessed with a feeling of abysmal horror. Episodes of the dream persecuted me daily. I became nervous, and lost interest in my studies. Finally, just before returning here for vacation from college, I asked a professor of psychology what might be the cause of the dream. It was his opinion that the dream represents an actual experience, long ago forgotten, which has lain dormant in the recesses of my subconscious mind. Some chance thought or event has caused a reflex to function. As a result, the forgotten experience is asserting itself upon my conscious mind. This, he pointed out, would naturally occur during the period of sleep, as only at that time, or when the conscious mind is in a hypnotic state, does the subconscious mind have a chance to assert itself. He told me of persons who, while under the influence of hypnotism, were able to recognize their kindergarten teacher, whom they had not seen since childhood, although previous to their being hypnotized they had failed to recognize the same person. The professor's reason for stating that the dream represents an actual experience was that it recurred. This, he pointed out, is true only of dreams representing actual incidents from the dreamer's life. Does that sound logical to you?"

"Yes, I don't doubt that such is the case," assented Blaine.

"I am glad you understand," said Raymond. He stood up, raised his right hand.

Blaine noticed the movement. The next moment his eyes bulged with fear, and a gasp of terror escaped him as he looked at the revolver in Raymond's hand. Hoarsely he muttered, "No. No. Don't. Don't shoot."

Raymond's hand did not falter. The revolver drew closer to Blaine, pointed directly at his heart. In the eyes behind the gun there was no sign of mercy; only hatred—and irrevocable doom.

Fear spurred Blaine's tongue. "Are you crazy?" he shouted. "What are you pointing that gun at me for?"

"You killed my father and mother!"

"I didn't. I swear it." Blaine's eyes narrowed. He felt certain he was confronted by a madman. There was no other way of explaining the situation. Raymond had no proof. His voice became coaxing.

"Put the gun down, Raymond. I don't see why you should want to kill me. You can't prove I killed your father and mother. You didn't see the face of the killer in your dream. You said so yourself."

For a while Raymond said nothing. During the pause Blaine again wiped the perspiration from his forehead—that pale forehead with its ugly crimson stain.

Raymond eyed the mark, and a crafty look came into his burning eyes. He bent forward and hissed softly at Blaine:

"But I didn't tell you all about what happened tonight. Tonight the dream was different. You see, tonight I didn't wake up so soon— the dream lasted longer. I saw a face. A pale face. It hovered over me as I felt myself being carried out of a burning house. I shall never forget that face. Those haunted eyes! Such ghastly pallor! Ah, but the forehead was different. The whiteness of the forehead was marred by a dark red blotch. . . . Why are you so pale? . . . it will be over in a second . . . you should be glad I am not choking you to death. . . ." ——▎

THE DREAM OF DEATH

ELWOOD F. PIERCE

The queer figure of a man sat deep in the chair in full repose. His eyes, usually sharp, were now listless and just a little sleepy as he watched the crackling fire. He felt a chilly draft at his back, and immediately there was the click of a door closing softly, after which feet shuffled across the floor. Unconsciously Anderson Brenton, psychologist, sucked at his empty pipe. The intruder moved to the log fire, holding his shaking hands to the blaze, and shiveringly seated himself on a stool Professor Brenton had been using as a foot-rest.

The man who thus for a moment had startled Brenton was the half-witted brother of his landlady. Two nights before, the little psychologist had rented the room on the third floor front, and as he bargained with Mrs. Thompson he noticed the actions of the demented one. The landlady had said her brother was harmless, and Brenton did not give him thought.

"What are you doing here?" the lodger asked sharply, now that the brief sensation of fright had passed. "I thought it was understood that I was not to be disturbed. What do you want?"

The psychologist's brows were shaggy, and so was his beard. He was a shaggy person, and being small, impressed one as a weakling physically. But his eyes were penetrating, combative, and he eyed his visitor fiercely. There was something utterly repulsive about the man who trembled in front of the fire.

"Cold," the half-wit murmured. He shivered and turned anew to the blaze. "Cold!" His body was shaking.

Professor Brenton, contributor to the cause of science, might have found it hard to explain why he was occupying the third floor front room. Perhaps it was because once in a while he liked to get away from Daly College and to pursue certain of his studies uninterrupted. The room on the third floor had been advertised for rent and he had taken it—that was all. Almost immediately he recognized in Gus Acre an interesting subject, but until the moment the old man shuffled into his room and complained of the cold it had not occurred to the psychologist to attempt a mental investigation. But this was the beginning.

Brenton noted the apparent harmlessness of the man and was interested. Then, casting into the half-wit's mind with questions that served as primary experiments, he became fascinated. Later, his tests were tedious and delicate and afforded him an opportunity of determining the worth of certain theories he recently had developed, theories which were disputed by his scientific associates. Perhaps from a humane standpoint Brenton was a bit cruel, but his examinations at least were in the spirit of the botanist who studies a rare flower.

The psychologist learned that the man's intellect, unable to hold anything of itself, was keenly awake to the workings of the minds of others. He found that virtually without effort he could transfer his thoughts to the witless creature and the man would respond in a manner all but normal and as if the thought were his own. But no thought was retained. Gus Acre's mind reached out and fed on the intelligence of others, but the moment the thought had been transformed into action, he again became an imbecile, with blankness of mind equal to that of a cleanly wiped slate.

Of one thing Professor Brenton was certain: this was not hypnotism. Nor did his power over the half-wit have any relation to hypnotism.

For many nights Acre was subjected to examination and new tests. Brenton dug deep and without mercy, in the hope that he might unearth the reason for the hidden phenomena.

At first there was no explanation. But he found out much during his hours of research, and finally came to the most important discovery of all.

It was a cold night in December, and Professor Brenton was seated in his easy chair. That was two weeks after Gus Acre first appeared in his room. Suddenly Brenton perceived that his fire was out, all that remained in the grate being some dying embers. Grumbling, he arose and slipped on his great coat, reflecting, almost unconsciously: *"I wish Gus Acre would bring up some wood!"*

Shivering, he resumed his reading. A few minutes later there was a scraping outside his door and Acre entered with an armload of fuel. He dropped the sticks by the fireplace and stared vacantly at the little professor. There was the usual look of dumb terror, after which his eyes grew listless and he seemed to wonder at his surroundings.

"Who told you to bring up the wood?" Brenton asked.

Acre mumbled, rolled his eyes and left the room without attempting reply. Apparently he did not understand the question. Brenton listened to the man's retreating steps, shrugged his shoulders, and kneeling, built a new fire. He was disturbed by this new and uncanny power, but it opened a curiously marvelous field for him. He might, after all, be able to prove his theory that the mind is never a free agent.

An hour later, still deep in thought, he turned to his window overlooking a plot of ground that in summer was a rose garden. Now there was snow on the ground, the bushes that abounded being slightly tinctured with white. The professor noticed a shifty figure emerge from the shadow of the house and move aimlessly among the sleeping bushes with their ghostly shrouds. It was Gus Acre—poor, hopeless, demented Gus Acre.

Curious to give his power farther trial, the psychologist permitted himself to wish for the presence of Gus Acre in the room with him. Almost instantly the figure below straightened and a startled face was raised to the window before which Brenton stood. Then the man went indoors.

He did not move hastily, but in his slow shuffling manner, as if he had finished his walk in the garden and was returning to the house under a natural impulse. Brenton still stood at the window marveling. Then the door opened, and he knew what that meant. The imbecile would do whatever the professor willed that he should do. Without the practise of hypnotism the psychologist was able to unite his mind with the mind of Gus Acre and control his actions. All that was necessary to bring this about was the barest thought.

"Why don't you knock when you come in?" Brenton demanded.

Acre did not reply but shuffled his weight from one foot to the other, then turned and left the room. But the professor had done no more than wish for his presence, and any desire that he may have had for the man to remain was only negative in value. The reaction of Gus Acre was merely positive, and very naturally so.

After that Brenton was to experience a sensation of fear. He wanted to halt the experiments, and indeed did make an attempt to do so, but found, just as he had feared, that he rapidly was coming under the influence of a mind that, one almost could say, did not exist. Yet it weakened him, sapped his energy day by day, did this mental intercourse with a vacant brain. There even were times when Brenton found it difficult to breathe. And thinking was not always easy.

He began, when it was too late, to realize that he was to be penalized for his unnatural experiments. The little professor was suffering from "nerves." Perhaps it was old age creeping on, he told himself, casting about for an excuse.

Could it be that the imbecile was making demands upon him — eating into his brain? And then there was his vitality, now at ebb. His capacity for work had decreased, and it was difficult for him to concentrate even on his reading.

"It's time I was ending this vacation," Brenton decided. "I must get back to the old routine. Enough of this foolishness."

But he could not leave. Very rapidly indeed his own mind and the mind of Gus Acre were merging, and his own mind slowly was being sucked away.

All but helpless, Brenton began to be concerned for his own sanity.

At last he came to fear Acre, to dread the sight of him, and yet a dozen times a day he found it necessary to call the imbecile to his room, much to the discomfort of the landlady, who was unable to understand anything that would suggest a friendship between the queer little scientist in the front room on the third floor and her witless brother. It wasn't reasonable, she interpreted.

The end came at last. Brenton, suddenly aroused, sat up in the old-fashioned bed that formed no mean part of the furnishings of the room. His body was clammy and he was gripped by a fear of the unknown. Brenton, a brave man as shown by his experiments covering many years, seemed to sense that mighty fingers were at his throat.

He had been dreaming. And what a dream!

He had seen Gus Acre creeping up the stairs, a long kitchen knife in his hand. The half-witted creature had stood over him, and then —

It had been at this point that the psychologist awoke — just as the knife was descending.

A few minutes later he was calmer and did succeed, to a degree, in putting aside his fears. He pulled the covers over his shoulders, for it was cold and the log fire was now only so much ashes.

Footsteps outside his room. Boards creaking. A hand fumbling at the door. The door swinging open. A shaft of moonlight penetrating the room and falling upon the figure that crouched in the doorway just as it had been seen to do in the dream a few minutes before.

Brenton screamed.

The thought whirled through his mind that he was helpless. The action of his dream was such that the witless man would carry it out. He was trembling, too, and his eyes burned into his head like torches that flamed in white heat.

The figure crossed the floor, still crouching. There was the glitter of the long kitchen knife.

Brenton's effort to gain control of the mind of Gus Acre was futile. He knew what he must do to save himself, but the mental effort that would control the man was impossible of accomplishment. He struggled like one seeking to arouse himself from a nightmare.

The figure crept upon him, slowly and with a great show of stealth. The scientist could hear the man's short breathing, see the very gleam of his eyes as the moonbeams shot into his face. The boards of the floor creaked and creaked, and the sound was not like anything Brenton had ever heard before. It made him think of a bat beating its wings against the walls of a tomb.

A single thought, a moment of mental action, would change the course of the half-wit's movements. But the psychologist knew that his mind had been sucked dry and that the man creeping upon him was the one who now held the scepter of power.

Anderson Brenton was as one paralyzed. And he could only watch Gus Acre approach with the long knife in his hand, the moonbeams falling upon his purple face. Just as in the dream.

One last scream!

The next morning the witless man was found by his sister, asleep on the floor of the front room on the third floor. There was a kitchen knife in his hand, a long knife stained with blood.

And Brenton, who had not been able to will that Gus Acre should not carry out his unfortunate dream, was dead. ✦

Eric Martin's Nemesis

Jay Wilmer Benjamin

Eric Martin fingered the sharp knife he had fashioned from a piece of heavy tin broken from the dangling spout by the jail's upper window and planned for the time when he would use it to gain his freedom.

He didn't intend to spend the next ten years of his life in the state penitentiary. He had stolen the money, of course—who wouldn't have if given the chance? The county prosecutor had spoken of him as weak-willed, a coward who had taken advantage of his position in the bank to steal the savings of widows and orphans. The bonding company had made good, hadn't it? Anyway, he had meant to pay it back, just as soon as he doubled or trebled it on the races. He could have, too. But they hadn't given him a chance. And now he faced ten long years in the penitentiary.

He rubbed his thumb against the knife, under his shirt, and wet his lips nervously. Not while he had his strength, he wouldn't. . . .

It seemed to Martin that things were breaking just right for him. The usual crowd of Kingstown's Saturday drunk-and-disorderly prisoners had been released. Three negroes were in the back cage, a half-dozen white men were idling the time away in the front cage. Those two big rooms were where the common run of prisoners were kept. But he was in a solitary cell—just a small room with a wide-barred door—just off the top of the stairs, outside of the main rooms. As a prisoner booked for a trip to the state penitentiary the next morning, old Tom Brenner, the jailer, had felt it would be safer to have him there. Old Tom hadn't known about that broken spout just outside of his window. That was old Tom's tough luck.

Maybe Brenner had thought he would rather be alone. A great one for preaching sermons, Brenner was. Martin had known the jailer all his life. He drew his face into a scowl. Trying to tell him to be good, and let this be a lesson to him! Sunday School tripe! It wouldn't be any lesson to him—except to teach him to be more careful. He was going to be a big shot when he got out. . . .

It was almost time. Lights were out. Probably a majority of the other prisoners were seeking freedom in sleep. He had asked Brenner to bring him some ice-cream about eleven o'clock, and the jailer had promised to get it from the one café which kept open till midnight. Kingstown wasn't an all-night town. The rest would be easy, if he used his head—and the knife.

He heard Brenner coming upstairs. The door to the inner room was closed. Not that it mattered, for there was a barred door inside of the wooden one. But it would be better, by far, to be unseen.

He held the crude, sharp piece of tin in his right hand, kept it out of sight inside his shirt. Brenner wheezed into view. He carried a cardboard container of ice-cream.

"Here it is, Eric," he said, and held it out before him.

"Bring it closer," demanded Martin.

Old Brenner complied. Martin stuck his left arm through the bars, suddenly grabbed Brenner by the neck. His right hand came up, holding the knife. He poised the sharp point against old Brenner's Adam's apple.

"Will you open up?" he demanded tensely.

155

Brenner clenched his teeth, shook his head carefully left and right.

Martin meant to hit him with the heavy end of the improvised weapon, to pound him into unconsciousness. But Brenner struggled, and all of Martin's rage boiled over. He struck swiftly, blindly. Red spouted from Brenner's severed jugular.

The jailer opened his mouth as if to scream, but no sound came. He sprawled to the floor. It seemed to Martin that everyone must hear him. But there was no noise from the inner room. The jailer lay there wide-eyed. A pool of crimson grew larger on the floor beside his body.

Brenner tugged at the body through the wide-apart bars of the door. He obtained the keys from Brenner's pocket, unlocked his cell, went into the passage.

The jail prisoners wore no uniforms, of course. In the darkness, it would be a simple matter for him to walk out and away. He stopped downstairs, took Brenner's gun from its holster slung over a chair in the dead man's cluttered living-room, pocketed a double handful of cartridges. Not that he expected to need them, but he had gone too far to take chances now.

Even as he worked, the horror of his position came to him. For the first time he realized that he had gone farther than he had planned, that he had killed a man in cold blood. If he were caught, that would not be a jail sentence. It would mean the gallows. . . .

He found a topcoat in the closet, together with a battered felt. He put on the coat, turned up the collar, pulled the hat low over his eyes. Martin peered cautiously through a window. He knew there should be no visitors to see Brenner at this hour, but he meant to take no unnecessary risks. He wanted to go it alone. The county prosecutor had been right, he realized. He *was* a coward. He shivered as he thought of Brenner lying dead upstairs, shook physically as he visualized the trap, his own body falling, falling—the neck breaking. . . . He forced the pictures from his mind. He must think of other things. Once away from town, out of the state, he could get clear all right. He walked quietly out of the door to freedom. . . .

It was when he turned the corner into the alley a block from the jail that he first had the feeling that he was being followed. He waited there in the darkness, not daring to run, his heart pounding madly in his breast, steeling himself to club his pursuer with the gun butt. His nerve wasn't as taut as it had been when he had used that improvised knife. The idea of clubbing someone didn't appeal to him. Suppose he missed!

But no one came along. In the half-light shining through the trees from the arc on the corner, he saw no one moving away from the jail. He decided it had been his imagination.

Martin skirted the one-block business section, going through a cross-alley. He came out by the creek near the railroad station. It occurred to him that they might use bloodhounds when they found Brenner's body in the morning. He entered the creek, waded about fifty yards up the shallow stream. At the foot-bridge which led across to the station, he pulled himself up onto the wooden floor, crossed toward the railroad.

No one was on duty at the station. Probably a coal drag would be along soon. They ran all the time, especially at night.

Martin walked the ties toward the water tank. Occasionally, he tried to balance himself on a rail, with a vague idea that it might help throw off the hounds if they ever got that far, keep the officers from being sure where he had gone. Of course, in the morning word would go out everywhere to pick him up, but if he could catch a freight and be in the city by that time it shouldn't be impossible to lose himself. It had been done. . . .

Again he had that strange feeling that someone was following him. When he sat in the shadow of the water tank, he peered back over the route he had followed. The moon was riding low in the sky. No one was to be seen.

A whistle wailed in the distance, the rails began to hum. Soon the long, thick finger of light from a locomotive's single eye touched the side of the tank, sent him scurrying behind it.

The freight stopped for water. He had counted on that. When the empties started clicking past again, Martin swung himself up and over, climbed carefully into a car. He stayed there for a good five minutes, until the scattered lights of the county seat were lost around a bend, then found a more comfortable place under the slanting end, between two cars. He had seen hobos riding there. All he had to worry about now was the brakeman, and it was unlikely that a brakeman would come climbing over the empties on the night run.

Suddenly he was quite sure that there was someone near him. His heart seemed to miss a few beats, then to pound ahead with renewed fury. He tried to get hold of himself, fingered the gun in his top-coat pocket. But the feeling persisted. He told himself there was no reason for his belief. Nevertheless, he *knew* that someone had followed him from the jail.

He stood up cautiously, holding tightly to the rods on the car, bracing himself to keep from falling between the whirling wheels. No one was in sight, but the fear inside of him did not abate. It grew. His heart wouldn't behave. He felt smothered, and opened his collar for air.

He decided on action. He was a good thirty cars from the engine. Clutching the hand bars with grim resolve, he climbed over the unaccustomed surfaces of the car ends and interiors. As he made his way toward the front of the train, he continually stole glances back toward the distant caboose. Only on an occasional long straightaway could he discern the tiny point of light which marked the rear end of the freight.

They were traveling fast. Once he thought he saw a vague shape outlined against the sky, but he told himself it was a brake wheel, suddenly caught by his eyes just as the cars lurched around a curve and outlined it against a gray cloud. But he was not sure.

He put the space of eight cars between himself and his former position. And all the time that fear grew. The faster he tried to run away from his imaginary pursuer, the more frightened he became, and the more certain he was that a pursuer really existed.

He was safely braced in his new place when he saw it. It was the shadowy form of a man, and it sat on the end of the next car down from him. It had not been there when he passed. It *was* following him!

Martin ducked out of sight, peered over the car top. It sat there, motionless, looking at him.

He thought perhaps it was a hobo. Well, he had a gun. He wanted to travel alone. Setting his jaws, he started back through the car. The man on the other end started back too. When he reached the place where the other had sat, he saw the figure perched quietly at the far end of the car. Again he started toward it. Again the figure retreated. He turned, came back. The figure followed. Like a shadow, it hounded him. He was afraid to relax, to sit down quietly out of sight. He pulled his gun, threatened to shoot. The man ignored his gestures, just sat there.

Martin was afraid to fire the gun. He didn't want to murder anyone else. Besides, he feared his shot might draw the train crew. No telling who might hear the sound.

He decided to leave the train at the first opportunity and go it alone, on foot. Whoever this fool was, whether it was some railroad detective or a crazy hobo, he wanted no part of the stranger. He could catch another freight.

His chance came when the freight slowed down just after passing Ranside. It was a long haul up the hill, and even a string of empties had to lose speed. Martin, in his inexperience, misjudged the speed of the train, landed running but fell flat on his face and rolled over and over down the cinder bank of the right of way. He lay there in a heap in the shadow until the train passed, and the clatter of the wheels became a low rumble in the distance.

The moon was high now. He stood up, brushed some of the cinders from his clothes, limped experimentally. He was not badly hurt; only scratched and bruised. He looked around, moved away from the railroad.

He was about a hundred feet from the embankment when he had that feeling again, stronger than ever. He turned swiftly. The half-familiar figure was coming down the bank, sliding along after him determinedly.

Martin ran then. He didn't stop to reason. He just found himself running. He glimpsed a road paralleling the right of way, and streaked for it as fast as his bruises would allow him to travel. He glanced back over his shoulder. Without sound, seemingly without effort, the figure followed after.

Martin reached the dusty road, turned right, ran on. The other followed his trail. He ran until he gasped for breath, stumbled a few steps more, fell to the ground exhausted. He was afraid to look back. He had completely forgotten Brenner's gun by now. He cowered there, waiting for he knew not what. He fought desperately to keep his reason, tried to conquer this fear which was driving him mad.

For what seemed an eternity, but must have been but seconds, he lay there in the dust of the road. Finally he jerked himself to his knees, turned to meet the figure. It sat in the road, about a hundred feet away.

Martin had the feeling that the thing was a nightmare. It couldn't be real. It must be something he was dreaming—it had to be. . . .

His elbow hit the hard object in his topcoat pocket. He drew the gun with a little sob of thanks, aimed at the man on the ground.

"Stand up!" he ordered. Nothing happened.

Martin himself stood up then. So did the other. Martin took a few steps toward his pursuer. The other walked away as he approached.

Suddenly Martin's taut nerves broke, and a red mist came over his eyes, and he was cursing and sobbing wildly—broken meaningless curses, directed at the figure which stood so quietly watching him.

He squeezed the trigger fast. A jet of flame shot from the gun, and the crash echoed back from the embankment. The figure stood there unmoved.

Eric Martin fired five more bullets. Then, screaming like a maniac, he hurled the gun at the silent creature, ran again. He knew now what was pursuing him. He had known all along. But he hadn't wanted to admit it. It was old Tom Brenner, come back from the dead! He was being followed by a murdered man's ghost. . . .

The idea wasn't fantastic any longer. It was not just an idea. It was reality. He staggered, screaming and sobbing, up the road toward Ranside, looking for someone, anyone, who would take away that impossible figure that followed him so ominously, whose pursuit he could not shake off.

He found the night policeman. Rather, the night policeman found him, when that gentleman came out to see what drunk was disturbing the peace and quiet of the night.

"Take him away!" screamed Eric Martin, reeling blindly into the policeman's arms. "It's old Tom Brenner—I killed him! I killed him! Do you hear me—I killed him! There he is—there he is—take him away!"

The policeman looked down the road. "I see nobody," he said, jerking Martin by the coat collar to make him quiet. "You're crazy drunk!"

"He's there—right there!" insisted Martin, pointing a shaking finger at the figure which stood about a hundred feet away.

The policeman had heard of old Tom Brenner, Kingstown jailer. He was sure this fellow had a good case of the blind staggers. But he locked Martin in a cell for safe keeping until morning, and hurried to a long-distance telephone.

It was when Martin, tossed into a corner of the cell, heard the key turn in the lock and came dizzily to his feet that he saw the figure again. It was closer now—it was in the cell with him!

And then he really knew the truth. Then he recognized his pursuer. Tom Brenner, come back from the dead, would have been bad enough, beyond all sense, enough to drive him mad. But it wasn't Tom Brenner. It was Eric Martin. . . .

Eric Martin knew, then, that he had killed himself, that he had lost his soul. The other Eric Martin stood there, just looking at him. Its eyes were the saddest things he had ever seen. There was no fire in them—only an utter hopelessness. They had lost all hope in life and death, all belief in a here or a hereafter. Somehow, Eric Martin felt that this other self he had killed would haunt him always, here and in eternity.

At first he tried to grapple with it. He had a desperate notion that if he managed to lock the figure in his arms he could merge it into himself again, regain his soul. But when he approached the other Eric Martin, it moved away. He walked faster, chased it around the little cell. He could not catch up with it. He screamed and cursed, until the other inhabitants of the jail cursed him in turn, and finally he fell unconscious on the cell floor.

They found him there after the telephone call confirmed his babbling.

He was judged to be crazy beyond a reasonable doubt. A kindhearted lawyer appointed by the judge sought to comfort him.

"They aren't going to hang you, Martin," he explained. "You're just going to be sent to the insane asylum, where you can be cared for and live quietly, alone—"

Alone! Eric Martin went berserk at that. He tried to tell them that he didn't want to live, that he wasn't crazy, that the self he had murdered would stay with him always, would make his life a hell on earth, that he wanted to die. But he only gibbered meaninglessly in a shrill cracked voice, and tried to crash his head against the wall, so that they had to strap him in a straitjacket. And all the while the other Eric Martin stood silently beside him, looking at him with its hopeless eyes . . . stood as he knew it would stand through endless days and nights. . . . ——+——

Escape

Paul Ernst

He had the craziest form of craziness I've ever seen.

Of course, I hasten to add, I hadn't seen much. I'd been through an asylum once before, as now, to get a story for my paper on treatment and conditions of State inmates, and that was all. On that former trip I'd witnessed nothing like this; nor had I, till now, on this trip.

The man didn't look crazy. So often they don't. He was a medium-sized chap with gray in his hair and a look of sadness on his thin, mild face. A look of sadness—and determination. Neatly dressed, precise of movement, he was very busy in his cell. He paid no attention for a while as the guard and I stood at the barred door and watched him.

He was building something. He would pick up a tool, adjust it carefully, work with all the delicacy of a watchmaker for a moment. Then he would lay the tool down and pick up a gage and check his work. All very accurate and careful.

The only thing was that you couldn't see what he was building. And you couldn't see any tools, nor gages nor work-bench. There was nothing in the cell but the man, and a bolted-down cot and chair.

Nevertheless, the fellow was extraordinarily industrious. He would seize a nonexistent tool, examine it with a frown, and then use it on thin air, after which would come the inevitable measuring movements.

"It certainly looks," I said in a low tone to the attendant, "as though there should be something there."

The attendant grinned and nodded. And I continued to watch, fascinated.

You could follow the man through his whole box of tools, from his rational movements. Now he was boring a hole, obviously a very small hole, with a tiny metal-drill equipped with an egg-beater handle. Now he was just touching a surface with a file. Now he was sawing something else, after which he took the sawed part from an imaginary work-bench and tried it in its place—whatever and wherever that was.

I got still another glimpse of unity of effort as I watched him. Each little period of accurate workmanship ended with a trip four steps to his left, to a corner of his cell which was bright with sunlight. There, his motions said, was the thing he was working on. There was the object, slowly growing bit by accurate bit, which he was making and assembling.

It was uncanny. There simply ought to have been something there—a cabinet, chair, whatnot—and there wasn't.

The man slowly screwed an imaginary part to an imaginary whole, then laid down his imaginary screw-driver and walked to the door, for the first time acknowledging our presence there.

"Hello, Nick," he said to the attendant. His voice was as mild and as sad and as oddly determined as the rest of him.

"Hello," said the attendant affably. His good-natured, broad face turned from the man in the cell toward me.

"Meet Mr. Freer, Mr. Gannet. Mr. Freer's with a newspaper."

"Oh?" said Gannet, politely. He put out his hand so that I could shake it if I reached through the bars of his door a little. I hesitated, then grasped it. He didn't look dangerous.

"How're you doing with your what-is-it, Gannet?" the attendant said, nodding solemnly toward the bright corner where lay the object of the man's attentions.

"Pretty well," said Gannet. "This damned floor isn't quite level. It's three thirty-seconds of an inch to the foot off. I have to allow for that in every line and angle, and it makes it needlessly difficult."

"*What* is it you're building?" asked Nick wheedlingly. "You won't tell any of us, but won't you tell Mr. Freer, for his newspaper story?"

"There it is," shrugged Gannet, pointing to the corner. "See for yourself."

I stared involuntarily at the corner, then, feeling like a fool, back at his mild, sad face. Was there a ghost of a twinkle in his gray eyes? Or was it my imagination? I couldn't tell. I was beginning to feel a little crazy myself.

We walked away. The big library and lounging-room where the almost-cured could sit and read was left for me to see. But I looked around without much interest as we passed through. I kept thinking of Gannet.

"Has he been going through that set of motions very long?" I asked the attendant.

"He started right after he got here," said Nick. "That was a year ago. He came here raving, trying to fight free and get back to the house where he'd lived with his son and daughter-in-law. There was something in his room he had to get, he said. Then he calmed down, and next day began going through the routine you saw. Some days he 'works' only a few hours, sometimes all day long and up until lights-out at night."

"The way he puttered around that corner made me think I was off myself, for not seeing something there," I said. "It was amazingly realistic. As though you could surely *feel* what he was working on, even if you couldn't see it. Has anybody ever felt around that corner where he spends his time?"

"Hey, boy," said Nick, "easy, now. Pretty soon we'll be sending a wagon for you."

"But has anybody?" I persisted, smiling.

"No. That's the one thing that brings out Gannet's kink: If anyone gets too close to that corner he gets quite violent. So we don't even clean there. We're trying to cure these folks, not upset 'em needlessly."

We went out the massive door of the main building, where a stalwart attendant eyed us sharply. There were nicely kept grounds, and then a high fence with inward-slanting barbs on its top.

"You don't want anybody to escape from here, do you?" I said, nodding toward the heavy door and the high fence.

Nick grinned. "Nope. And nobody ever has. Or ever will, I reckon. See you in church."

But he saw me sooner than that.

I kept thinking of the spare, mild-mannered man with the sad, determined eyes all evening, after I'd handed my story in to the paper. I kept thinking about him next morning. And next afternoon saw me at the asylum again, standing in front of Gannet's barred door.

He was as busy as he had been yesterday. But his activity seemed more mental than physical today. He would stand in the center of his cell, hand rubbing jaw, while he stared at the sunny corner. Then he would walk to the corner and touch a spot in midair with an inquisitive fore-finger. Then he would step back and survey the atmosphere again, eyes running slowly up and down as though over the lines of a quite tangible thing.

Finally he took something out of his pocket and walked with a more decisive air to the corner. I saw his hands move close together, for all the world as though he were adjusting a micrometer or other delicate measuring-device. He applied his hands to the questionable point in nothingness.

As he had done yesterday, he paid no attention to observers at his door, at first. But finally he spoke, without looking up from his task.

"Hello, Freer."

"Hello," I said. Gannet had an unimpaired memory, at any rate.

"Come for another story?"

"In a way," I evaded.

He shook his head, meanwhile stepping a foot to the right and staring critically at nothing.

"I don't see how you stand it."

"Stand what?"

"Your work. The madness and despair of humanity—that's your stock in trade. You deal in war and famine and flood, in social injustice and political and civil brutalities. They're the intimate facts of your life. I don't see how you can live among such things. I can't even read about them."

I stared at him. I'd never met a man who seemed less crazy.

"Whether you face the facts intimately or detachedly," I said, "they are still facts and they're still there. You can't avoid them."

"But you can. At least *I* can. And I'm going to. I'm getting out of all this."

He squatted on his haunches, and began running his hands slowly over space, up and down, then horizontally. He straightened and repeated the process. I'll swear I could make out what he had in his mind. It was a sort of chair, with a very high back and unusually high arms.

Just as I had decided this—he sat in it.

You've seen stage tricksters sit in chairs with arms folded, when there are no chairs there to sit in? Well, this was the same. I gaped at Gannet, sitting in thin air. Not an impossible stunt, but always an arresting one.

He got up and came to the door.

"I can't take life as it's lived today, Gannet. A weakness, no doubt, but there you are."

"So you're getting out of it," I nodded.

"So I'm getting out of it. It's not for nothing that I am a mathematician and an inventor."

What a shame! I almost said it aloud, but didn't. I'd conceived a positive fancy for the sad-faced Mr. Gannet.

He stared at me quizzically.

"You needn't hunt up Nick," he said. "I'm not hinting at suicide. It's a more literal escape, I mean."

"Escape? With these barred doors, the high wall outside?"

"Oh, walls! Bars!" He waved his hand, dismissing them.

He walked back to his sunny corner and resumed his critical ocular and manual examinations of—nothing.

"You may have another story tomorrow, Freer," he said mildly. And then he turned his back, thereby dismissing me as he had the walls and bolts of his confinement.

I hunted up Nick on the way out. I felt like a traitor, but I knew it was for my new friend's own good.

"Gannet's talking of an escape," I said.

Nick's customary grin appeared on his broad face.

"Forget it. He's handed out that line before. Nobody could get out of here."

He walked to the high gate in the fence with me, and waved as I got into my car.

I wasn't coming back any more. I didn't want to see Gannet again. He was such a nice little guy. But next noon saw me knocking for admittance a third time, summoned by a call from Nick.

"Got an exclusive for you, if you want it," he said. "An escape. I don't know that it's very important to you, but we've never had one before. That might make it worth a couple of inches."

"Escape?" I said.

"Yeah. Your man, Gannet."

"So he did it! But how?"

Nick grunted. "Suppose you tell me."

"In the night?" I asked.

He shook his head. "A little while ago, in broad daylight. He was seen in his cell at ten. An hour later the room was empty. He was gone."

"But he couldn't have simply walked out of the place in broad daylight."

"No," said Nick, "he couldn't."

"Was his door unlocked?"

"It was not. It was locked, from the outside, when we came to investigate the report that he was gone. His window bars are all right, too."

"You've searched the grounds?"

"Of course. He isn't in them. He isn't in any of the buildings. Nobody saw him after eleven o'clock. He's just gone, with his cell still locked so even a monkey couldn't slip out."

"You must have some idea how he got away."

"No idea. Because it can't be done. Only, it was."

"How am I going to get a story out of that?" I asked.

"How in thunder would I know? That's *your* worry."

I put a cigarette between my lips unlit because smoking wasn't permitted here.

"What in the world do you suppose he . . . thought he was building?" I mused.

Nick snorted. "I don't suppose anything about it. If I did, I'd be as crazy as he was. Well, there's your exclusive, if you know what to do with it."

I didn't know what to do with it, so I finally handed it in as it stands now. This very story, in fact. And the little man with the big vizor at the editor's desk promptly handed it back. Not that I blame him.

Nobody ever saw Gannet again. Nobody ever thought of him again, I guess. Except me. I had a rush of curiosity to the head a few days later, and went to his cell armed with a level and a steel rule.

The floor of the barred cubicle Gannet once occupied *is* three thirty-seconds of an inch off level. Now how do you suppose he could have determined that without tools of any kind to aid the naked eye? ——✦

THE EXTRA PASSENGER

STEPHEN GRENDON

Mr. Arodias had worked a long time on his plan to kill his eccentric uncle, and he was very proud of it. But then, Mr. Arodias was a very clever man; he had lived by his wits for so many years that it had never been necessary for him to kill Uncle Thaddeus before. Only, now that Mr. Arodias was getting along toward middle age, and his fingers were no longer so nimble as they had once been, the time came. He began by thinking that he ought not to be deprived of his inheritance any longer, and ended up by working out the perfect crime which he defied Scotland Yard to solve.

Like all such plans, it was almost absurdly simple, and Mr. Arodias indulged in many a self-congratulatory chuckle when he contemplated the bumbling efforts of the C.I.D. to solve it. Uncle Thaddeus, who was a recluse, lived on the edge of Sudbury, which was on the Aberdeen line from London. Three squares from his tree-girt house lived another solitary who owned a fast car and kept it carelessly in an unlocked shed some distance from his house. Sixty miles from Sudbury, where the night train to Aberdeen stopped, lay the hamlet of East Chelmly, the next stop, rather in a curving line from Sudbury, so that it was farther by rail than by highway. It would be a simple matter to take off for Aberdeen from London on the slow night train, slip out of his compartment at Sudbury, "take care" of Uncle Thaddeus, then appropriate his neighbor's fast car, and arrive in East Chelmly in adequate time to slip back on to his train, with none the wiser. A perfect alibi! Ah, what chuckle-heads he would make of the laddies from the Yard!

Moreover, it worked like a charm. True, the old man had recognized him and had muttered something about coming after him before the light in his crafty eyes went out and his battered head fell forward—but it was just a matter of moments; the whole thing had been rehearsed in Mr. Arodias' mind so often that he knew just what to do, and flattered himself by thinking that he could have done it blindfolded. The old dodderer nearby had left his car plentifully supplied with petrol, too, as if he had been an accomplice, and it took Mr. Arodias to East Chelmly in the dead of night, never meeting anyone on the long road, never seeing anyone in the little hamlets through which he passed. He arrived in East Chelmly in excellent time, and like a shadow he slipped around to the station and into his compartment with no one seeing.

No one, that is, except the extra passenger.

For at this point in his perfect crime, Mr. Arodias came face to face with a factor for which he had made no provision. He had left his compartment empty, save for his bags and golf-clubs; he came back to it to find huddled in the opposite seat, with his hat well down over his face, an extra passenger. It was possible that the fellow had not marked Mr. Arodias' entrance, but, much to his annoyance, Mr. Arodias could not be sure.

"Sorry to disturb you," he said genially. "I have been in the lavatory."

No answer.

Mr. Arodias hawked once or twice.

No sign of life.

Mr. Arodias settled back, relieved, feeling very comfortable and secure. This pleasant feeling of security did not last, however. In a few moments he was asking himself where in the devil the extra passenger had come from? There had been no stop between Sudbury and East Chelmly. The compartment was in one of the through coaches, not a local. It was barely possible that a passenger from one of the other compartments had mistaken Mr. Arodias' for his own in the dark, and now occupied it by mistake. For it was still dark, being somewhat past midnight, and the lights in the corridor were dim.

But this explanation did not satisfy Mr. Arodias, and he was possessed of a normal dislike of unsatisfactory matters. This was all the more true when the matter in question represented a potential flaw in what he felt was a very perfect plan. His fellow-traveler, however, was apparently oblivious of his growing perturbation; he continued to huddle there without movement other than that of the train rushing through the night. This troubled Mr. Arodias; he expected nothing less than a full account explaining the extra passenger's presence.

Failing this, he began to imagine all kinds of things, and he took every opportunity to examine his companion in the light of passing stations. He wore heavy, almost loutish shoes. Obviously a countryman. His hands, which did not seem clean, were those of an old man. His hat had seen much roughing. Of his face, Mr. Arodias saw nothing. How long, he wondered, had he been sleeping? If he had just simply blundered into the compartment and settled down and dozed right off, all would be well. But if he had not done so, he might well be in a position to ask annoying questions about what kept Mr. Arodias in the lavatory for time enough to enable the train to put close to sixty or seventy miles behind from the time he had entered the lavatory—which was, of course, presumably at the same hour the extra passenger had entered Mr. Arodias' compartment.

This thought needled Mr. Arodias with desperation. Already he had visions of some officious bumpkin plodding to the police station in Aberdeen and solemnly deposing that Mr. Arodias' late entrance was a suspicious circumstance. He could see it in cold print. *"Sudbury Victim's Heir Questioned,"* the headline would read. And this unwelcome stranger, huddled there like a tangible threat to his security, would have put all his suspicions down. " 'E come late into 'is seat, an' I could na' 'elp wonderin' where the zur kep' 'imself all that time. A good hour, 't was. Nor did 'e 'ave the look of a sick man about 'im."

Mr. Arodias could hardly contain himself. He coughed loudly. Fancying that he saw a movement about his fellow traveler not inspired by the train, he said hastily, "Forgive me. I didn't mean to awaken you."

But there was no answer.

Mr. Arodias bit his lip. "I say," he said firmly.

Silence.

The sounds of the train filled the compartment—the whistle up ahead, the rush of steam, the clicking of the drivers—filled the room and rolled around in it, swelling and growing. It was grotesque. It made such a sound that it would have awakened the dead, thought Mr. Arodias. Yet the extra passenger slept calmly through it, huddled there like someone lost in the deepest dream.

He leaned forward and tapped the fellow on the knee.

"Look here, this is my compartment, you know."

No answer.

Oh, it was maddening! Especially so for a man of Mr. Arodias' temperament, and most particularly since this was happening just after he had brought off what was certain to come out in the end as his most successful coup in a career of successes. This confounded extra passenger, by his very presence, however innocuous he might be, was taking the edge of enjoyment off his pleasure in his accomplishment of that night.

Mr. Arodias considered shaking the fellow.

But this he dismissed from his mind within a few moments. There was, after all, no good in antagonizing him. There was no reason to believe that he had seen a single thing which might make him suspicious. Indeed, he might leave the compartment at any place along the line without once realizing that he sat in the same train with the heir to the Sudbury recluse. No, there was absolutely no good in unnecessarily attracting attention to himself.

He felt frustrated, and he redoubled his efforts to examine his fellow traveler. He took the trouble, finally, to take out his pipe, fill it, and strike a match, rather more for the purpose of examining the extra passenger in its flickering light than for that of lighting his pipe. Then for the first time he observed that the fellow had no baggage of any kind. Manifestly then, he had stumbled into the wrong compartment. The shoes were country shoes, all right. Clod-hopperish. Mud on them, too. And on his hands. Uncouth fellow.

Or was it mud? The match went out.

Mr. Arodias was afraid to light another. For one cataclysmic moment, the stuff on his fellow traveler's hands and shoes had looked like blood! Mr. Arodias swallowed and told himself that he was having hallucinations stemming from some rudimentary conscience which had not died with the rest of it in that long ago time when he had entered upon his life of dubious practices and crime.

He sat for a long moment in silence. The hour was now past two in the morning. He busied himself for a little while peering out of the window, trying to ascertain just where the train was at the moment. Approaching the Scottish border, he decided. He closed his eyes and tried to think how he must act when they found him in Aberdeen and told him his Uncle Thaddeus was dead, slain by an unknown assailant in the night, while he was on his way to Scotland under the protection of such a perfect alibi. But there was nothing to be gained in thinking about this; he had decided upon his course of action right up to the moment he actually took possession of his inheritance—he had decided upon that long ago; it was all an integral part of his plan. Indeed, the only incident which was not integral to his plan was this extra passenger.

He turned to him again, hawked once more, coughed loudly, knocked his pipe out on the window-sill, and looked hopefully over through the darkness of the compartment at that huddled old fellow in the corner of his seat.

No movement.

"This has gone far enough," he said aloud, becoming vexed.

Silence.

He leaned over once more and tapped his companion on the knee, with some persistence. "Look here, you're in the wrong compartment, sir."

This time he got an answer. It was a muttered, sleepy, "No."

The voice was guttural, broken. Mr. Arodias was slightly disconcerted, but in one way relieved.

"I'm sorry," he said, in a more pleasant tone, "but I believe you got into my compartment by mistake."

"No," said his companion again.

Instantly annoyed once more, Mr. Arodias wondered why the fellow insisted on talking from beneath his hat.

"Where did you get on the train?" he asked with some asperity.

"In Sudbury."

Sudbury! Of course! That could have been. Why had he not thought of that? He had been in such a hurry to get off the train he had not thought that someone might get on. He was about to speak again when his companion added a catastrophic afterthought.

"Where you got off," he said.

After but a moment of cold shock, Mr. Arodias rallied. "Yes, I stepped out for a breath of air, and then went to the lavatory when I got back."

"I thought," the old man went on with a burr of dialect in his voice, just as Mr. Arodias had imagined, "you might have gone to see your uncle."

Mr. Arodias sat quite still. Faced with this challenge, his mind worked with the speed of lightning. Within ten seconds Mr. Arodias decided that, whoever he was, the extra passenger must never leave the night train alive. He might know nothing at all of the crime, but he nevertheless knew enough to hang Mr. Arodias. He knew enough, indeed; he knew Mr. Arodias, he knew he had got off at Sudbury, and no doubt he knew he had reappeared in his compartment in the vicinity of East Chelmly. That was enough to doom one of them, and Mr. Arodias, having got this far, had no intention of being doomed.

Mr. Arodias needed time, and he was now quite willing to spar for it until he had evolved some plan for eliminating this menacing old fellow and dumping his body somewhere along the right-of-way.

"You know my uncle?" he asked in a strained voice.

"Ay, quite well."

"I don't know him too well myself. I'm a Londoner, and he keeps to his own place in the country."

"Ay. He has reasons, you might say."

Mr. Arodias pricked up his ears. "What reasons?" he asked bluntly.

"A pity you don't know."

"I don't," said Mr. Arodias, irritated.

"A pity you didn't know a bit more."

"If there's something about my uncle I ought to know, I would like to hear it."

"Ay, you shall. Your uncle's a mage."

"A mage?" Mr. Arodias was mystified.

"A warlock, then, if you like that better."

Mr. Arodias was amazed. He was also touched with a kind of macabre amusement. He did not know why the fact that the old man's fellow villagers regarded him as a warlock should amuse him; yet it did. Even in his amusement he did not lose sight of his decision that this prying oldster must die, and he was contemplating whether he should dispatch him with a quick blow or two or whether he should stifle his outcries and strangle him. The important thing, of course, was to prevent the guard from hearing anything suspicious. Meanwhile, he must carry on. Best to humor the extra passenger.

"Warlock, eh? And no doubt he had some special talents?" He caught himself just in time to prevent his saying "had"; it would never do to refer to Uncle Thaddeus in the past tense—just in case something went wrong and his curious fellow-traveler got away after all.

"Ay, that he had."

"Foretold the weather, no doubt."

"That any gibbering fool could do."

"Told fortunes, then?"

"A gypsy's trade! Not he! But then, you always did underrate him."

"Did I, now?"

"Ay."

"What was so wonderful about his being a warlock—if he was."

"Oh, he was. Never a doubt about that. He had his familiar, too —on wings."

"Wings?"

"Ay. He brought me to the train."

Mr. Arodias looked askance. A kind of premonitory tingle crept up his spine. He blinked and wished the light were a little stronger. There was beginning to be something uncomfortably challenging about his chosen victim; Mr. Arodias did not like it.

"And he could send about a lich or two, if he had a *mind to.*"

"A lich?" said Mr. Arodias in a dry voice. "What the devil's that?"

"You don't know?"

"I wouldn't ask you if I did."

"It's a corpse, that's what."

"Send it about? What are you talking about?" demanded Mr. Arodias, feeling a chill along his arms.

"Ay—for a special purpose. Oh, your uncle was a great one for things like that."

"Special purpose," repeated Mr. Arodias, and at that moment his foot touched upon a sturdy weight which had the feel of a sash-weight, and he bent to take it in his hand.

"A special purpose," said the extra passenger. "Like this one."

Mr. Arodias was suddenly aware that his traveling companion had been speaking of his uncle for the past few minutes in the past tense. A kind of constriction seized upon his throat; but his fingers tightened upon the weight in his hand. The extra passenger knew or guessed far too much; whatever the risk, he must die now—quickly. He leaned forward, stealthily, as if he thought that the old fellow could see him despite the darkness and the hat over his face.

Then he snatched the hat away, and aimed his first blow.

It did not fall.

The head under that was hardly half a head—smashed in, and with the blood run down all over the face—the head of his Uncle Thaddeus! A scream rose and died in Mr. Arodias' throat.

The eyes in that battered head were looking at him, and they were shining as if lit by the fires of hell.

No word, no sound passed Mr. Arodias' lips; he was incapable of speech, of movement. A power, a force beyond Mr. Arodias' comprehension emanated from the thing on the seat opposite. The eyes held him, the eyes encompassed him, the eyes drew him. Mr. Arodias shrank together and slipped from the seat to his knees on the floor of the compartment. As in a dream he heard the sounds of the train, coming as if from very far away.

"Come to me, Simon," said the thing that had been his Uncle Thaddeus.

And Simon Arodias crept across the floor and groveled.

"Bring your face closer, Simon."

And Simon Arodias raised his head, with a harsh whimpering sound struggling for utterance in his throat. Powerless to move, he watched one of the thick bloody hands of the extra passenger come down like a vise upon his face. Then he saw nothing more.

The guard who found Mr. Arodias collapsed from shock.

The medical examiner at Aberdeen was upset for a week. Nevertheless, despite the condition of Mr. Arodias' face—what was left of it—it was ascertained that he had been suffocated—"by person or persons unknown." Circumstances notwithstanding, Mr. Arodias could not have committed suicide.

As for those fumbling chuckle-heads at Scotland Yard—they had already found the gloves which Mr. Arodias had discarded on his way from the stolen car abandoned in East Chelmly to the station, the gloves which were to lead them all in good time to the little plot of ground where Mr. Arodias was enjoying, not his Uncle Thaddeus' money, but his own just due. ——

THE FEAST IN THE ABBEY

ROBERT BLOCH

I

A clap of thunder in the sullen west heralded the approach of night and storm together, and the sky deepened to a sorcerous black. Rain fell, the wind droned dolefully, and the forest pathway through which I rode became a muddy, treacherous bog that threatened momentarily to ensnare both my steed and myself in its unwelcome embrace. A journey under such conditions is most inauspicious; in consequence I was greatly heartened when shortly through the storm-tossed branches I discerned a flicker of hospitable light glimmering through mists of rain.

Five minutes later I drew rein before the massive doors of a goodly-sized, venerable building of gray, moss-covered stone, which, from its extreme size and sanctified aspect, I rightly took to be a monastery. Even as I gazed thus perfunctorily upon it, I could see that it was a place of some importance, for it loomed most imposingly above the crumbled foundations of many smaller buildings which had evidently once surrounded it.

The force of the elements, however, was such as to preclude all further inspection or speculation, and I was only too pleased when, in reply to my continued knocking, the great oaken door was thrown open and I stood face to face with a cowled man who courteously ushered me past the rain-swept portals into a well-lighted and spacious hallway.

My benefactor was short and fat, garbed in voluminous gabardine, and from his ruddy, beaming aspect, seemed a very pleasant and affable host. He introduced himself as the abbot Henricus, head of the monkish fraternity in whose headquarters I now found myself, and begged me to accept the hospitality of the brethren until the inclemencies of the weather had somewhat abated.

In reply I informed him of my name and station, and told him that I was journeying to keep tryst with my brother in Vironne, beyond the forest, but had been arrested in my journey by the storm.

These civilities having been concluded, he ushered me past the paneled antechamber to the foot of a great staircase set in stone, that seemed hewn out of the very wall itself. Here he called out sharply in an uncomprehended tongue, and in a moment I was startled by the sudden appearance of two blackamoors, who seemed to have materialized out of nowhere, so swiftly silent had been their coming. Their stern ebony faces, kinky hair and rolling eyes, set off by a most outlandish garb—great, baggy trousers of red velvet and waists of cloth-of-gold, in Eastern fashion—intrigued me greatly, though they seemed curiously out of place in a Christian monastery.

The abbot Henricus addressed them now in fluent Latin, bidding one to go without and care for my horse, and ordering the other to show me to an apartment above, where, he informed me, I could change my rain-bedraggled garments for a more suitable raiment, while awaiting the evening meal.

I thanked my courteous host and followed the silent black automaton up the great stone staircase. The flickering torch of the giant servitor cast arabesque shadows upon bare stone walls of great age and advanced decrepitude; clearly the structure was very old. Indeed, the massive walls that rose outside must have been constructed in a bygone day, for the other buildings that presumably were contemporaneously erected beside this had long since fallen into irremediable, unrecognizable decay.

Upon reaching the landing, my guide led me along a richly carpeted expanse of tessellated floor, between lofty walls tapestried and bedizened with draperies of black. Such velvet finery was most unseemly for a place of worship, to my mind.

Nor was my opinion shaken by the sight of the chamber which was indicated as my own. It was fully as large as my father's study at Nîmes—its walls hung in Spanish velvets of maroon, of an elegance surpassed only by their bad taste in such a place. There was a bed such as would grace the palace of a king; furniture and other appurtenances were of truly regal magnificence. The blackamoor lighted a dozen mammoth candles in the silver candelabra that stood about the room, and then bowed and withdrew.

Upon inspecting the bed I found thereupon the garments the abbot had designated for my use during the evening meal. These consisted of a suit of black velveteen with satin breeches and hose of a corresponding hue, and a sable surplice. Upon doffing my travel-worn apparel I found that they fitted perfectly, albeit most somberly.

During this time I engaged myself in observing the room more closely. I wondered greatly at the lavishness, display and ostentation, and more greatly still at the complete absence of any religious paraphernalia—not even a simple crucifix was visible. Surely this order must be a rich and powerful one; albeit a trifle worldly; perchance akin to those societies of Malta and Cyprus whose licentiousness and extravagance is the scandal of the world.

As I thus mused there fell upon my ears the sounds of sonorous chanting that swelled symphonically from somewhere far below. Its measured cadence rose and fell solemnly as if it were borne from a distance incredible to human ears. It was subtly disturbing; I could distinguish neither words nor phrases that I knew, but the potent rhythm bewildered me. It welled, a malefic rune, fraught with insidious strange suggestion. Abruptly it ceased, and I breathed unconsciously a sigh of relief. But not an instant during the remainder of my sojourn was I wholly free from the spark of unease generated by the far-distant sound of that nameless, measured chanting from below.

2

Never have I eaten a stranger meal than that which I partook of at the monastery of the abbot Henricus. The banquet hall was a triumph of ostentatious adornment. The meal took place in a vast chamber whose lofty eminence rose the entire height of the building to the arched and vaulted roof. The walls were hung with tapestries of purple and blood-royal, emblazoned with devices and escutcheons of noble, albeit to me unknown, significance. The banquet table itself extended the length of the chamber—at one end unto the double doors through which I had entered from the stairs; the other end was beneath a hanging balcony under which was the scullery entrance. About this vast festal board were seated some two-score churchmen in cowls and gabardines of black, who were already eagerly assailing the multitudinous array of foodstuffs with which the table was weighted. They scarcely ceased their gorging to nod a greeting when the abbot and I entered to take our place at the head of the table, but continued to devour rapaciously the wonderful array of victuals set before them, accomplishing this task in a most unseemly fashion. The abbot neither paused to motion me to my seat nor to intone a blessing, but immediately followed the example of his flock and proceeded directly to stuff his belly with choice titbits before my astounded eyes. It was certain that these Flemish barbarians were far from fastidious in their table habits. The meal was accompanied by uncouth noises from the mouths of the feasters; the food was taken up in the fingers and the untasted remains cast upon the floor; the common decencies were often ignored. For a moment I was dumfounded, but natural politeness came to my rescue, so that I fell to without further ado.

Half a dozen of the black servants glided silently about the board, replenishing the dishes or bearing platters filled with new and still more exotic viands. My eyes beheld marvels of cuisine upon golden platters—verily, but pearls were cast before swine! For these cowled and hooded brethren, monks though they were, behaved like abominable boors. They wallowed in every kind of fruit—great luscious cherries, honeyed melons, pomegranates and grapes, huge plums, exotic apricots, rare figs and dates. There were huge cheeses, fragrant and mellow; tempting soups; raisins, nuts, vegetables, and great smoking trays of fish, all served with ales and cordials that were as potent as the nectar of nepenthes.

During the meal we were regaled with music from unseen lutes, wafted from the balconies above; music that triumphantly swelled in an ultimate crescendo as six servitors marched solemnly in, bearing an enormous platter of massy, beaten gold, in which reposed a single haunch of some smoking meat, garnished with and redolent of aromatic spices. In profound silence they advanced and set down their burden in the center of the board, clearing away the giant candelabra and smaller dishes. Then the abbot rose, knife in hand, and carved the roast, the while muttering a sonorous invocation in an alien tongue. Slices of meat were apportioned to the monks of the assemblage on silver plates. A marked and definite interest was apparent in this ceremony; only politeness restrained me from questioning the abbot as to the significance of the company's behavior. I ate a portion of my meat and said nothing.

To find such barbaric dalliance and kingly pomp in a monastic order was indeed curious, but my curiosity was regrettably dulled by copious imbibing of the potent wines set before me at the table, in beaker, bumper, flask, flagon, and bejeweled cup. There were vintages of every age and distillation; curious fragrant potions of marvelous headiness and giddy sweetness that affected me strangely.

The meat was peculiarly rich and sweet. I washed it down with great drafts from the wine-vessels that were now freely circulating about the table. The music ceased and the candle-glow dimmed imperceptibly into softer luminance. The storm still crashed against the walls without. The liquor sent fire through my veins, and queer fancies ran riot through my addled head.

I sat almost stupefied when, the company's trenchermannish appetites being at last satisfied, they proceeded, under influence of the wine, to break the silence observed during the meal by bursting into the chorus of a ribald song. Their mirth grew, and broad jests and tales were told, adding to the merriment. Lean faces were convulsed in lascivious laughter, fat paunches quivered with jollity. Some gave way to unseemly noise and gross gesture, and several collapsed beneath the table and were carried out by the silent blacks. I could not help but contrast the scene with that in which I would have figured had I reached Vironne to take my meal at the board of my brother, the good curé. There would be no such noisome ribaldry there; I wondered vaguely if he was aware of this monastic order so close to his quiet parish.

Then, abruptly, my thoughts returned to the company before me. The mirth and song had given place to less savory things as the candles dimmed and deepening shadows wove their webs of darkness about the banquet board. Talk turned to vaguely alarming channels, and cowled faces took on a sinister aspect in the wan and flickering light. As I gazed bemused about the board, I was struck by the peculiar pallor of the assembled faces; they shone whitely in the dying light as with a distorted mockery of death. Even the atmosphere of the room seemed changed; the rustling draperies seemed moved by unseen hands; shadows marched along the walls; hobgoblin shapes pranced in weird processional over the groined arches of the ceiling. The festal board looked bare and denuded—dregs of wine besmirched the linen; half-eaten viands covered the table's expanse; the gnawed bones on the plates seemed grim reminders of mortal fate.

The conversation was ill-suited to further my peace of mind—it was far from the pious exhortations expected of such a company. Talk turned to ghosts and enchantments; old tales were told and infused with newer horror; legends recounted in broken whispers; hints of eldritch potency passed from wine-smeared lips in tones sepulchrally muted.

I sat somnolent no longer; I was nervous with an increasing apprehension greater than I had ever known. It was almost as if I *knew* what was about to happen when at last, with a curious smile, the abbot began his tale and the monkish presences hushed their whispers and turned in their places to listen.

At the same time a black entered and deposited a small covered platter before his master, who regarded the dish for a moment before continuing his introductory remarks.

It was fortunate (he began, addressing me) that I had ventured here to stay the evening, for there had been other travelers whose nocturnal sojournings in these woods had not reached so fortunate a termination. There was, for example, the legendary "Devil's Monastery." (Here he paused and coughed abstractedly before continuing.)

According to the accepted folk-lore of the region, this curious place of which he spoke was an abandoned priory, deep in the heart of the woods, in which dwelt a strange company of the Undead, devoted to the service of Asmodeus. Often, upon the coming of darkness, the old ruins took on a preternatural semblance of their vanished glory, and the old walls were reconstructed by demon artistry to beguile the passing traveler. It was indeed fortunate that my brother had not sought me in the woods upon a night like this, for he might have blundered upon this accursed place and been bewitched into entrance; whereupon, according to the ancient chronicles, he would be seized, and his body devoured in triumph by the ghoulish acolytes that they might preserve their unnatural lives with mortal sustenance.

All this was recounted in a whisper of unspeakable dread, as if it were somehow meant to convey a message to my bewildered senses. It did. As I gazed into the leering faces all about me I realized the import of those jesting words, the ghastly mockery that lay behind the abbot's bland and cryptic smile.

The Devil's Monastery . . . subterrene chanting of the rites to Lucifer . . . blasphemous magnificence, but never the sign of the cross . . . an abandoned priory in the deep woods . . . wolfish faces glaring into my own . . .

Then, three things happened simultaneously. The abbot slowly lifted the lid of the small tray before him. ("Let us finish the meat," I think he said.) Then I screamed. Lastly came the merciful thunderclap that precipitated me, the laughing monks, the abbot, the platter and the monastery into chaotic oblivion.

When I awoke I lay rain-drenched in a ditch beside the mired pathway, in wet garments of black. My horse grazed in the forest ways near by, but of the abbey I could see no sign.

I staggered into Vironne a half-day later, and already I was quite delirious, and when I reached my brother's home I cursed aloud beneath the windows. But my delirium lapsed into raving madness when he who found me there told me where my brother had gone, and his probable fate, and I swooned away upon the ground.

I can never forget that place, nor the chanting, nor the dreadful brethren, but I pray to God that I can forget one thing before I die: that which I saw before the thunderbolt; the thing that maddens me and torments me all the more in view of what I have since learned in Vironne. I know it is all true, now, and I can bear the knowledge, but I can never bear the menace nor the memory of what I saw when the abbot Henricus lifted up the lid of the small silver platter to disclose the rest of the meat. . . .

It was the head of my brother. ———

FIDEL BASSIN

W. J. STAMPER

It cannot be done. It would be the most dastardly deed in the annals of Haiti. Send all prisoners to Port au Prince with the utmost celerity. The general orders. The general be damned!"

Thus spoke Captain Vilnord of the Haitian army as he finished reading the latest despatch from headquarters. He was the most gentle and by far the most humane officer yet sent to Hinche to combat the ravages of the Cacos, the small banditry that continually terrorised the interior. Although he realised that many a brave comrade had lost his head for words not half so strong as those he had just uttered, he did not care, for he had almost reached the breaking point. For months he had observed the rottenness and cruelty with which the government at the capital dealt with the ignorant and half-clothed peasantry of the Department of the North. His considerate nature revolted at the execution of the despicable commands of General La Falais, the favourite general of the administration at Port au Prince. Hardly a day came but brought an order directing the imprisonment of some citizen, the ravage of some section with fire and sword, the wanton slaughtering of cattle or the burning of peaceful homes. He was a servant of the people and he had obeyed orders; but this last was too much.

"Any news of my captaincy?" inquired the rotund negro lieutenant, Fidel Bassin, as his chief finished the despatch.

For answer Vilnord crumpled the message in his hand, threw it in the face of his subordinate and strode angrily out of the office. He went straight to the prison and entered without even returning the salute of the sentinel on duty.

Here was a sight that would turn the most hardened beast to tears. He had viewed that noisome scene every day for weeks, powerless to aid or ameliorate the terrible suffering. No food, no clothing, no medicine had arrived from Port au Prince, despite his urgent and repeated appeals. As he passed through the gloomy portal, a purpose, a firm resolve was taking root in his bosom, and another sight of the cowering victims would steel him and launch him upon the hazardous course he had seen opening for months.

The prison was a long, low adobe structure with three small grated windows but a foot from the roof. These furnished little ventilation, for the heat was stifling and the foul odours sickened him. Two hundred helpless men and women were crammed into this pesthouse of vermin and disease, and all under the pretext of their being friendly to the Cacos. Old men lay writhing on the floor with dirty rags bound tightly about their shrivelled black skulls, and as Vilnord passed they held up their skinny arms and pleaded for food. Withered old women sat hunched against the walls and rocked back and forth like maniacs. The younger men who yet had strength to stand, paced restlessly up and down with sullen and haggard faces. From every dusky corner shone eyes staring with horror. Ineffable despair overhung them all.

Vilnord stooped over an emaciated old man, who seemed striving to speak through his swollen lips, and asked:

"What is it, papa?"

"It is the dread scourge, *Capitaine*," he rasped, "the black dysentery; and I must have medicine or I go like my poor brother, Oreste."

He pointed to a mass of rags beside him.

Without fear of the dread disease whose vicious odour pervaded the whole room, Vilnord gently lifted the remains of a filthy shirt under which Oreste had crept to die.

No man who has never looked upon a victim of tropical dysentery after life has fled can imagine the deadly horror of the thing. The lips were so charred with the accompanying fever that they had turned inside out, and from the corners of the gaping mouth there oozed a thick and greenish fluid. The skin was drawn tightly over the bony cheeks, and the eyes had entirely disappeared, leaving but dark and ghastly holes. He had been dead for hours. With a scream like a wounded animal, Vilnord rushed from the charnel-house and to his office, where Fidel was still waiting.

He opened the drawer of his desk, pulled out a parchment neatly bound with ribbon, and to the amazement of his subordinate tore it in pieces. It was his commission in the army, just such a paper as Fidel had desired for many years.

"Fidel, I am through," he roared. "I will stand this wanton murder no longer. Do as you like about those orders, for you are in command. I leave for Pignon to-night to join Benoit, the Caco chief."

"But, *Capitaine,*" remonstrated Fidel, "you must not do such a thing. La Falais will send all his regiments to seek you out. He will camp in Hinche for ten years or capture you."

"I defy La Falais and his black murderers! Let him camp in Hinche for ten years. I will stay in the deep mountains of Baie Terrible for ten years. With Benoit I will fight to the death."

With these words Vilnord strode to the door, Krag-Jorgensen in hand, and mounted his waiting horse.

Fidel followed him out, and as he was adjusting his saddle bags, inquired, "Would La Falais promote me if I failed to carry out those orders? Would he not stand me up before a firing squad?"

"You may pursue the same course which I have chosen, the only honourable course," answered Vilnord.

"But I am due for promotion."

Vilnord tore the captain's insignia from his collar and hurled them into the dust.

"You will never be a captain. *Au revoir,*" he cried back to Fidel as he fled toward the bald mountains of Pignon.

A blazing sun beat down upon the grief-stricken village of Hinche. There was bustle and commotion outside the prison. Fidel was preparing to execute the orders of his superior. There in the dusty road was forming as sorry and pitiable a cavalcade as ever formed under the skies of Africa in the darkest days of slavery.

Men and women filed out of the door between two rows of sentinels whose bayonets flashed and sparkled in the sunlight. There were curses and heavy blows as some reeling prisoner staggered toward his place in line. The prisoners formed in two lines facing each other. Handcuffs were brought out and fastened above the elbows, for their hands and wrists were so bony that the cuffs would slip over. Two prisoners were thus bound together with each set, one link above the elbow of each. A long rope, extending the full length of the line, was securely lashed to each pair of handcuffs so that no two prisoners could escape without dragging the whole line. Many were so weak with hunger and disease that they could not stand without great difficulty. None of them had shoes, and they must walk over many miles of sharp stones and thorns before arriving at Port au Prince. The trip would require many days, and no food was taken except that which was carried in the pouches of the sentries who were to act as guards.

Suddenly there arose a hoarse and mournful cry from the assembled relatives, as two soldiers emerged from the barracks, each with a pick and shovel. Fidel knew that most of the prisoners would never see the gates of Port au Prince, and he had made provision.

"Corporal," he said, as he passed down the line inspecting each handcuff, "you will bury them where they fall. If they tire out, do not leave them by the roadside."

Weeping friends and relatives surged up to the points of the bayonets begging that they might be allowed to give bread and bananas to the prisoners, for they well knew there was no food between Hinche and the capital, except a few sparse fields of wild sugar cane.

"Back, vermin! Forward, march!" commanded the corporal.

His voice could scarcely be heard for the screams and moans of the relatives as they shrieked:

"Good-bye, papa! Good-bye, brother!"

Down the yellow banks of the Guyamouc wound the cavalcade, into the clear waters many of them would never see again.

Hinche mourned that day, and when the shades of night descended upon the plains there was nought to be heard save the measured beat of the tom-tom and the eerie bray of the burros.

Sleek, well-fed Fidel sat calmly smoking with his feet propped upon the very desk vacated by his chief the day before and mused upon the prospect of his captaincy, which he felt confident would be forthcoming. He had carried out the orders of La Falais and he knew that crafty general would not be slow to reward him when news of the desertion of Vilnord reached the capital. He muttered half aloud: "A captain within a month. Not so bad for a man of thirty."

But his black face twisted with a frown as he recalled the solemn, almost prophetic words of Vilnord: "You will never be a captain."

There came a voice from the darkness outside.

"May I enter, *Capitaine*?"

He liked the title, "Captain." It sounded so appropriate.

"Come in," he commanded.

It was the aged and withered old magistrate of Hinche, who had seen his people maltreated for years and who, no doubt, would have joined the Cacos long before had his age permitted.

"I have come to make a request of you in the name of the citizens," he said, and there was a strange light in his eyes.

"In the name of the citizens!" Fidel repeated sneeringly, and added: "Anything you ask in that august name, no man could refuse. What is it?"

"We beg that you release the remaining prisoners, those who are unable to walk because of hunger and disease, and allow them to return to their homes where they can be cared for. They are dying like hogs in that pesthouse. Will you let them out?"

"Never," was the firm reply. "I will bury every festering Caco-breeder back of the prison with the rest of his kind."

The magistrate folded his arms and with shrill but steady voice cried out: "La Falais, and you too, Fidel, shall render an account before history for this foul action, this heartless torture, this wanton murder of your own people. We, who are left, have arms, and we shall oppose you to the last drop. This very night has settled upon the fresh graves of our best people. Along the trail to Ennery and Maissade they have died, and over the graves your vicious troopers have put up forked sticks and placed on them a skirt, a shoe or a hat in derision of the dead. To what purpose did the immortal Dessalines and Pétion fight and wrest our liberty from the foreigner when it is snatched from us by our own bloody government?"

"Be careful of your words, old man," replied Fidel. "I have but to command and my soldiers will shoot down every living thing and lay this Caco nest in ashes."

"I have been very busy to-day, *mon capitaine*. Your soldiers at this very moment have scattered among the bereaved families of those who lie dead by your hand. You have no troops—they have become the troops of Haiti."

With a curse Fidel snatched his pistol from the holster. But before he could use it, a half dozen burly blacks leapt from the darkness outside where they had been waiting, and bore him to the floor. His hands were bound behind his back, and two of his own soldiers stood over him with drawn revolvers.

"I'll have the last man of you court-martialled and shot!" he stormed. "Release me immediately."

"Small fear of that," answered the soldier. "We go to join Benoit, the Caco chief, when we have finished with you."

The magistrate walked to the door and spoke a few whispered words to one of the blacks, who hurried away into the darkness.

Every shack sent forth its avenger. Torches flared up, and soon the house was surrounded by a writhing, howling mob, eager for the blood of the man who had sent their loved ones to die on the blistering plains of Maissade, and all because he wanted to be a captain. The soldiers had cast away their uniforms, but their glittering bayonets could be seen flashing in the red torchlight. Wild screams rent the night as the brutishness of the mob-will gained ascendency.

"Let us skin him alive and cover our tom-toms with his hide!" shrieked an old hag as she squirmed through the crowd.

"Let us burn him or bury him alive!" yelled another.

By what magic the old magistrate gained control of that wild multitude who may say? Standing in the doorway facing the mob, he lifted his withered hand and began: "Countrymen, for ten years I have meted out justice among you. Have I not always done the proper thing?"

"Always," they answered with one voice.

"Then," he continued, "will you not trust me in this hour when the future of Hinche hangs in the balance?"

"Leave it to the magistrate!" someone yelled, and the whole mass took up the cry.

"Norde, do you and Pilar bring along the prisoner. Follow me."

The two blacks designated seized Fidel roughly, lifted him to his feet and, preceded by the magistrate, hurried him across the road toward the prison. The mob followed, and the pale light of the torches shone on horrible faces, twisting with anger and deep hatred.

What could the magistrate have in mind? He knew the right thing, the course that would best satisfy the mob.

The procession moved up to the prison door, and as the vile and sickening odours struck Fidel in the face, he drew back with a shudder, his eyes wild and rolling with terror. One torch was thrust inside the door, and its red light threw fantastic shadows over the yellow walls. All the prisoners had been removed, and there was nothing in sight save a mass of rags in a corner at the far end.

"Yonder," said the magistrate, "is Mamon. He died last night. But before we leave you, you must see the face of your bedfellow." As the mob grasped the intent of the speaker, loud cheers filled the night: "Leave it to the magistrate! He will do the right thing."

Fidel shivered with fear, not so much the fear of the dead as of the terrible malady which had burned out the life.

Norde pushed the shaking Fidel through the door, and the mob, forgetting the dread disease in their desire to see him suffer, followed him up to the pile of rags.

"Now," said the magistrate, when Fidel's hands were loosed, "uncover the face of your victim."

With trembling fingers Fidel lifted a filthy rag from the face of the corpse. Did human ever look on sight so horrible? The eyes were gone, sunken back into their sockets, leaving but dark and ghastly holes. The tongue was lolling out, black and parched, furrowed as if it had been hacked. Out of the corners of the gaping mouth there oozed a thick and greenish fluid.

The skin was drawn tightly over the cheeks, and the bones had cut through. There was a sparse and needlelike growth of beard standing up straight on the pointed and bony chin.

Fidel dropped the rag and screamed with terror. Norde picked it up, and, with the aid of Pilar, smothered his screams by wrapping it around his head. He hushed presently and when, at length, the rag was removed, the magistrate commanded: "Uncover that!" and he pointed to the stomach of the corpse. Fidel obeyed.

The stomach was black and flabby like a tyre, and the skin had pulled loose from the supporting ribs.

"Here, *mon capitaine*," said the magistrate, "you will live with this dead man until the black dysentery has claimed you."

With a wild shriek Fidel fell fainting across the festering body of Mamon.

The magistrate barked out his commands quickly and sharply.

"Norde, bind him fast where he lies!"

In a moment Fidel was lashed to the fast decomposing body, his hair tied to that of the corpse; and cheek to cheek they left him with the dead.

It was high noon when a strange cavalcade headed toward Pignon, the lair of the Cacos. The old magistrate was leading. Men, women and children carried their few belongings on their heads. Hinche was deserted.

At the same time there entered Hinche by another trail two horsemen, who, after stopping at the office of Fidel, moved on to the prison. They were Vilnord and Benoit, the Caco chief. The prison door was ajar.

They entered, and what they saw was this—*the dead, cheek to cheek*, slowly sinking into each other.

Outside, Vilnord whispered to his companion as they mounted their horses: "I told him he would never be a captain"; and they rode away toward the bald mountains of Pignon. ——

THE FIFTH CANDLE

CYRIL MAND

I fled, and cried out Death;
Hell trembled at the hideous name, and sighed
From all her caves, and back resounded Death.
                              —MILTON: *Paradise Lost*

Laughable—isn't it?—that one so cynical and unbelieving as I should sit here, quivering and shaking in fear of a specter; that I should cower in dread, listening to the inexorable ticking of the remorseless clock. Amusing, indeed, that I should know terror.

And yet five years ago when we sat at this table, we five Brunof brothers, the way we laughed! The pall of stale, blue cigarette smoke that hung over us was an exotic mask for the strident laughter that echoed and re-echoed through it. The dim electric light filtered through its mistiness, centering upon the figure of the Old Man at the head of the table, frothing in fury. We were taunting him —perhaps a little too much, for of a sudden he calmed. His face became grim, almost imposing in spite of the tracks of illness and age. His thin falsetto voice took on tone.

"So be it then! You, my evil sons—you who instead of filial love and respect have given me affront and irreverence—you who have repeatedly brought disgrace upon my name—you who have been profligates, who through your squandering have nearly ruined me— you who have brought me to death's door—you shall now pay for your flagrancy.

"I was born in Russia—not the gay, carefree Russia of Moscow or Saint Petersburg but the silent, frigid Russia of the Kirghiz levels. The knowledge that for centuries has been the lore of these steppes was born into me. Jeer if you want to. My years of study in the occult have not caused you alarm thus far. Let them not trouble you now.

"Look at that candelabrum with its five candles. I die tonight. But every year on this day, March 21, at this hour, eight o'clock, I shall return to this room to light a candle in that candelabrum. And as each candle burns itself down and flickers and dies, so shall one of you weaken and die. May this be my legacy to you, my evil sons!"

He retired beyond the scope of the haze-diffused light into the black yawn of the hallway, leaving us laughing and hurling gibes at his retreating figure. Later, we did not laugh so much, when we went into his somber walnut-paneled room and found his shriveled body at the desk, his lifeless head with beady eyes glazed in death, pillowed on the crumpled pages of one of his evil Russian volumes.

The Old Man left the house to all of us, together. Because of this, and also of our lack of money, March 21 of the next year found us all, but one, Sergei, seated at the table at dinner. The odors and harsh clatter of dinnertime jarred against the calm placidity of approaching spring. We were laughing again. Ivan, who always did seem like a younger and more droll edition of myself, had remembered the anniversary of the curse. With mock ceremony he had abstained from lighting one of the candles in the candelabrum and had made us leave the chair at the head of the table vacant. Now we sat listening to his ribald jests at the Old Man's expense.

"Be patient, brothers. But four and one-half minutes more," he said, glancing at the huge, gold-handed Peter the First clock at the side of the room, "and we shall be again honored by the presence of our esteemed father. And who shall be the first he takes back with him? Certainly not me—the youngest. Probably you, Alexei," he grinned at me. "He always did hate you most. Ever fleering him in your nice quiet way. Sneering. Laughing up your sleeve at him and his distemper. And then, too, you are the oldest of us. You're first in line. Boris, why don't you pray for him a bit? A religious cove like you ought to be able to really go to town on his black soul.

"Ah, it's time for our phantom. It's eight o'clock. Hello, Old Man." He rose, bowing to an imaginary figure at the door. "How are you? How's it back there in Hades? You *did* go there. Sit right dow—" His speech died off.

The chamber darkened. A queer, spectral haze filled the room. It swished and swirled, yet ever contracted toward a single point—the chair at the head of the table. We gazed, stupefied. It became a shape. The shape became—a man. There could be no mistake. The shriveled figure; the wolfish head with its piercing, beady eyes, hawk-like nose, bulging forehead, and parchment cheeks—it was the Old Man!

We stared aghast. Ivan staggered back. Boris crossed himself. Dmitri and I just sat, unnerved, frozen into impotency. The Old Man stood up. He slowly extended his fleshless hand toward the malefically scintillating candelabrum on the table. The unlit candle flared into life! His well-remembered falsetto came as of old, seeming strangely melancholy.

"Even as this candle burns down and flickers and dies, so shall you weaken and die, Ivan."

Ivan gasped. Dmitri's oath shattered the silence as he leaped up and reached for the fowling-piece over the mantel. He grasped it and fired blindly as he turned. The detonation echoed back and forth in the narrow confines of the room. The air was polluted by gun smoke and the bitter tang of exploded powder. The candle sputtered, undulated, and flamed on. The smoke cleared slowly. The misty figure of the Old Man was gone. And on the floor, thrashing frantically, lay Ivan, blood spurting from a wound in his chest.

We rushed to him, all except Boris, who stood, devoutly blind eyes fixed on the ceiling, muttering monotonous prayer. Dmitri cursed himself violently. It was a mortal wound. We bandaged him in vain. His life ebbed out with his blood. And as he breathed out his last, the lone candle flickered and went out.

The trial was a nightmare. Of course, we three brothers stood firmly behind Dmitri. Sergei was the real mainstay, though. He saw to the selecting and the hiring of the lawyers, and the various other matters of Dmitri's defense. As a prosperous business man his influence and money aided us immeasurably. Throughout Dmitri's successive convictions for first degree murder, it was always Sergei who secured another appeal and carried the case to a still higher court while the months dragged along. But it was all futile. Dmitri and Ivan had always been utter opposites in character. As a result, they had had violent and frequent quarrels. It was these clashes of opposing wills—in reality unimportant, but to the world highly significant—that were now continually flaunted before the jury. At each trial we repeated the story of the Old Man's curse and the part it had played in Ivan's death—and were laughed down as liars, lunatics, or both. We only succeeded in making our case ridiculous and in tying tighter the noose around Dmitri's neck. We fought on in vain.

In the heat of litigation we almost forgot the shadow that hung over us too. And yet the sands were running low.

Finally, the inevitable occurred. On January 30, the highest court of the state set the date of execution by hanging for the week of March 17. The governor refused a reprieve. We could do no more. We gave up the fight and went home.

On the night of March 21, a few minutes after eight o'clock, at the same time that three brothers sitting at dinner watched a lone candle flicker and burn out, Dmitri Brunof at the state penitentiary was executed for murder in the first degree.

Boris was really frightened now. According to age he was next to go after Dmitri. He lived in a mortal funk of terror. For a time he turned to religion as a means of escape. The pageantry and ceremonies of the Church imparted to him an illusion of power and protection. However, religion was not the thing for him now. It had an undue influence on his mind, battered as it was by repeated shock and terror; and his inherent mysticism was intensified by it to a stark fanaticism.

His superstitions, too, were magnified and stimulated. He grew into an unreasoning dread of the dark. He became the victim of charlatans and fakes. He spent his money on occult remedies and charms. Any exhibition of seemingly supernatural power awed and frightened him.

And then at a stage show of Edward Rentmore, the English wizard, he went into hysterics. This and the notoriety we had achieved through our evidence at Dmitri's trial were enough to gain us Rentmore's attention. Besides being an illusionist, he had gained quite a degree of fame as a medium. To Boris, whom he now befriended, he was another bulwark against the power of the Old Man. Under his influence Boris became an adherent of spiritualism. He developed into an actual disciple of Rentmore. And finally Rentmore brought his mind to bear upon his underling's problem. As was natural to him, considering his vocation, he decided that the best protection against the Old Man would be to fight him with his own weapon—the occult. And so, during the time remaining till March 21 Boris and Rentmore were engaged in preparing for the destruction of the Old Man on the night of his appearance. They sat up far into the night poring over the Old Man's malefic Russian volumes. It was in that dimly-lit library that they learned to develop their innate mind-forces. Sergei and I just waited, watching skeptically, grimly amused.

On March 21 at dinner, Rentmore, Boris, Sergei and I were seated at the table. It was almost eight o'clock. The dim, inadequate light illuminated us feebly: Sergei, white face twisted into a cynical smile; Boris, nervously confident; and Rentmore, his sallow, yellow face frozen into a featureless impenetrability.

We were hardly surprised when that unearthly mist came and condensed, forming the shape of the Old Man. Sergei and I sat as if drugged, detachedly curious as spectators, conscious of the seething ferment of battle around us. We *felt* that struggle—mind against mind, will against will, knowledge against knowledge.

Then, as the beat of the hostile wills fell upon it, the form of the Old Man seemed to blur, diffuse, go queerly out of focus. We were winning! My detachedness vanished. I felt jubilant. The shadow that hung over us was lifting. But no! The figure of the Old Man once more took on its sharp, well-defined lines. Inexorably his arm reached out. Slowly, almost as if reluctantly, the candle in the candelabrum flamed up in response to that outstretched, withered hand. That thin statement of doom once more shrilled through the air.

"Even as this candle burns down and flickers and dies, so shall you weaken and die, Boris."

We stared at the candle, fascinated—not even noticing in what manner the Old Man went. The Peter the First clock ticked on, its golden hands slicing time and life, slowly and deliberately. The candle burned with a steady, even flame. Minutes passed. Rentmore lay in an exhausted stupor. The flame flickered, danced wildly as some slight current of air twisted it askew. It steadied, then flickered again. For a moment it writhed fitfully, sputtering.

Boris screamed—a long, agonized shriek. He started up, with one hand sweeping the candelabrum from the table, with the other fumbling at the insecurely mounted light-button. Then, suddenly, he choked, gasped, as if suffocating. The candelabrum seemed to cling to his hand. His twisted face mimicked our horror.

He slumped to the floor, breaking that lethal current of electricity, a grotesque heap of death. The candelabrum slipped from his hand, its clatter muffled by the exotic thickness of the Khivan rug.

Sergei had always been the cleverest one of us. He was practical, and besides his native cunning he possessed a good amount of real intelligence. Therefore, to him, of all the brothers, had passed the administration of our affairs. And certainly he had always done well in this capacity.

Whenever he had a problem, either personal or of business, he sat down alone in a half-dark room and there analyzed, speculated, and made and discarded schemes until he was sure he had the correct solution. It was this that he did now. The day after Boris' death he sat for a long time in the huge, half-lit dining-room, staring with perplexed eyes and knit brows at the candelabrum. It was long after I had gone to a sleepless bed that I heard him tread heavily up to his room.

The next morning he gave me his solution as I knew he would. "It seems that just two things are menacing us—the Old Man and the candelabrum. It is these two things that we must fight against if we want to survive. The Old Man is, of course, beyond our reach. However, the candelabrum—" His hand had knocked over a glass of water. He regarded the weaving track of the spilled liquid. "It is of solid gold and valuable. This afternoon when I go to the city I shall take it with me. At the Government mint I shall sell it as old gold. Within a week, probably, it will be melted down and stamped into coins. The coins will circulate and by March 21 the candelabrum will be scattered all over the country. Then let us see how our esteemed father will take the loss of his precious candelabrum. In his present state he can hardly curse another of the things. Yes, I think we are safe. . . ."

I rather agreed with him. I rejoiced now as in the old days Ivan, Dmitri, Boris and I had rejoiced together in having a brother gifted with that elusive thing—common sense. I was confident that Sergei's canniness had saved us. The candelabrum was duly sold and, as our inquiries a few months later proved, melted down. Thus with the material threat of the curse removed, our fears vanished. We joked again, if rather grimly, of the Old Man. We mocked once more—mimicking the Old Man's falsetto voice. We speculated endlessly as to what the Old Man would do when he failed to find the candelabrum when he came to light it—or did he know already? We laughed again. . . . The days and weeks and months passed quickly, unclouded.

March 21 found me at a friend's house. Sergei was traveling again on one of his business trips, and I had no desire to be present alone when the Old Man came to light the candle in the vanished candelabrum. The day, the evening, and even the eighth hour passed easily. My friend and I chatted, supped, and played chess. Finally we went to bed.

I dropped off to sleep almost immediately. And then—out of the forefront of oblivion, as if he had been waiting for me, came the Old Man. The black nothingness behind him became a swirling mist that advanced and settled down around us. I was seated at the table. I looked wildly about me. There at the side the Peter the First clock marked eight o'clock. The candelabrum occupied the center of the table. And as the candle in it flared into life, the Old Man's words came to me.

"Even as this candle burns down and flickers out, so shall you weaken and die, Sergei."

I awoke shrieking at the gray dawn.

I dressed hurriedly, rushed downstairs, and seized the newspaper. The front page was smeared with a flamboyantly written and detailed account of a railway wreck. I read it through carefully. Among the killed was—Sergei Brunof. I looked for the time of the crash, strangely calm now. Yes, it had happened just after eight.

For two weeks I could not bring myself to go to the mansion. Not only was it the fear of that lonely old building with its charnel atmosphere, but also melancholy that kept me away. I knew how sad it would be to live there with the shades of vanished lives and muted laughter. The phantoms of my four brothers and the Old Man still peopled those silent rooms and empty halls.

Finally I did again venture into the dark oppressiveness of the house. And then in the dining-room I received another shock. There on the table where it had always stood before, and where I had seen it in the dream, was the candelabrum. Ridiculous, fantastic, impossible! And yet there it was, its dull golden glitter mocking me! I was stricken, bemazed—and yet really I knew that I had expected some such thing. So I just left it there.

And so it stood there throughout the year. Every day I sat at the table and ate my lonely meals, watching it cautiously, as if it were a live, malevolent being. I think I went a little mad watching it. It seemed to hypnotize me, too. It possessed an eery power over my mind. It drew me from whatever I was doing at times. I sat and gazed at it for hours. I mused endlessly as to what strange hands had hammered it again to its old shape, what weird tools had again formed its graceful branches. And all the time it seemed to be possessed of that same unearthly sentience. I could hardly bear even to dust it. I tried a few times to escape its evil spell. I went away—only to leave abruptly wherever I was, lured back to the dank old house and the glittering candelabrum. I lost contact with all humans. My supplies were sent out from the city by a boy who seemed to fear me as if I were the devil himself. I hardly ate. I just watched it. It seemed the only real thing in a house of mist and indistinctness. Vague and unrelated thoughts crept into my mind. I felt strangely confused and bewildered. It inspired me with an irrational and insatiable longing for something—I don't know what. I took to stalking the long, gloomy corridors in a frenzied search for the non-existent.

Today, cold fear jelled my panic into a sort of blunt insensibility when I realized that it was March 21. I sat all day at the table in a dull stupor, staring with dead, vacant eyes at the golden candelabrum.

Suddenly the desire to set this tale on paper came to me. The reaction to my apathy set in. Of a sudden I was full of a nervous, driving energy. For the past hour I have been sitting here writing. I am glad that I have been able to finish in time. The hour for the fifth candle draws near.

Ivan, Dmitri, Sergei, Boris—they are all gone. The Old Man took them. And certainly he will take me, too. Perhaps it will be just as well if I join them. I'll be back among my own. Dust to dust. . . .

It is after eight already. The candelabrum is empty of candles. I wonder, will he bring one. . . . ——+——

THE FINISHING TOUCHES

RENIER WYERS

andriv said that he had come to borrow money. Blake gave it to him willingly. Had they not formerly been good friends? Of course that was long ago and Tandriv obviously had degenerated since then. Yet — Blake wanted to aid him in some way — just for "auld lang syne."

And for "auld lang syne" Blake tried to stir up conversation. "Is there anything else I can do?" he asked as his visitor pocketed the money.

"No!" replied Tandriv gruffly; then added with an attempt at courtesy, "I've been working hard. I'm nervous. Don't want to seem ungracious. Thanks."

Blake nodded. He found it difficult to realize that this wreck of a man was the Tandriv who had been his classmate but a few years before. The once thick, glossy black hair now hung in dead, graying strands over the tall wrinkled brow that had been fair and smooth. Deep grooves of bitterness were plowed in the pasty cheeks. The Tandriv eyes which had always been a bit too bright, now gleamed as two yellow-green orbs that were danger signals of approaching madness.

"Are you working on a painting?" Blake inquired tentatively.

"Yes."

"I'd like to see it sometime, Tandriv."

A cold smile that came dangerously close to being a sneer crept over the other's features. "You wouldn't like it, Blake. Our ideas of art differ. You've become famous for your flattering portraits, idealizing commonplace people, while I have — well, I'm here borrowing money tonight, from *you*."

His expression grew hateful. Springing to his feet he began pacing back and forth.

"But my time will come!" he cried, gesticulating wildly. "Too long the world has been blinded by illusions of piety and goodness — lies. You and everyone else striving for 'beauty' will be forgotten when I'm worshipped. There is no 'beauty' in real life or real art. There's only pain, and cruelty, and horror — that's what I'm painting."

Blake's curiosity was aroused. He remembered their art student days and how untractable Tandriv had been. No one could teach *him* anything about art! He refused to follow the classic standards of composition or color. Then, too, the recalcitrant Tandriv's choice of models had been the talk of the art colony. He would frequent the lowest dives in Paris and haunt the slums, looking for subjects to portray on canvas. Aged, drunken women; garbage-grubbing old men who had lived too long; idiots; misshapen cripples; lascivious-faced vixens; murderous Apaches; rat-like sneak-thieves—all were limned by the Tandriv brush in those early student years.

"If I remember correctly," said Blake, "what you are saying now is quite consistent with some of the ideas—and subjects—you entertained in Paris."

"Bah! That was only the beginning," snorted Tandriv. "I've made great strides since then."

"Toward what?"

"Toward what? Immortality! I'll prove it to you. Come to my place, Blake, and I'll show you a creation, the like of which no man has ever seen before—on canvas."

There was a fanatical enthusiasm in his manner and a hint of forbidden revelation in his tone that resulted in Blake's accompanying him.

A brisk twelve-minute walk brought them to a bleak, treeless district of poverty-tainted tenements and ugly factory buildings.

"Here's an atmosphere you 'nice' artists avoid," said Tandriv as they strode along through the deserted streets. Save for the widely spaced street-lamps there was no light on the thoroughfare. Even the dwelling buildings were darkened, for people who must live in tenements must rise early and light bills drain the pennies from kitchen shelves.

"Here's where life is raw and unveneered," he added. "Here the *real* man comes to the surface, selfish, cowardly, and treacherous. Dog eat dog, you know. Beauty? Ha! In spots like this, in every big city on the globe, glorious man, made in His image and likeness, spawns the future criminals of the world. Don't think that this slum is but a phase of life with no relation to the rest of the city. It's the rotten heart of it; the enslavement of men, women and children behind those factory walls makes it possible for 'refined' ladies to pay you big prices for their portraits."

He tapped Blake's arm and turned down a side street, meaner than the rest. "We'll be there in a minute," he said.

Passing through an areaway between two tenement houses they came upon a refuse-littered yard. A white, full moon broke clear of the clouds and mercifully camouflaged the scene with white splashes of light and black shadow. Carefully stepping over and around heaps of rubbish and tin cans which prowling rats could not believe were quite empty, the two men came to Tandriv's door, at the side of a long, flat, brick house.

Once inside, Tandriv turned the switch on an unshaded light bulb. "What a depressing workshop!" thought Blake as he blinked his eyes and looked about. The light revealed the interior of the house as being one long, narrow room, its brick walls unpainted. No ceiling hid the cross-beam that supported the roof. Dirt and disorder were everywhere. Paints, canvases, clothing, and cooking-utensils were strewn about, indicative of the slovenliness of the man who ate, slept, and painted here.

Blake's attention, however, was soon drawn to a huge painting leaning against the rear wall of the studio. It reached from the floor to the roof and from one side wall to the other, fitting snugly between. It was fully fifteen feet high and at least three times as wide.

"Good Lord! Tandriv!" gasped Blake hoarsely. "What is it? What does it mean?"

Revolted, yet fascinated by the very hideousness of the painting, he stared at it for a long time. It was like looking into an immense window of hell, against which swarmed a myriad of things with distorted faces and ectoplasmic bodies, seeking to enter this world from a terrible dimension outside human ken.

Now Blake knew what Tandriv had meant when he said his earlier works had been "only the beginning." These things were the development. The painting was a decadent exaggeration of all evil with all trace of anything redeeming omitted. It was an array of bestial, libidinous thoughts given a semblance of ugly, ante-human form by a brush that had been dipped in oils of primordial ooze. So crowded with the Things was the canvas that no background or perspective was shown.

One figure in particular, near the center of the picture, seemed to reveal the motif of the work to Blake's startled eyes. It had a sinister, elongated, ocher-colored face, surmounted by a gnarled forehead from which protruded two horns. Its upper torso was of human proportions but covered with bluish-green scales. Rearing up on two furry goat-like legs that terminated in cloven hooves, it appeared the most menacing of all because of its likeness to man and because of the malignant intelligence in its features.

"That shall be my masterpiece," Blake heard Tandriv hiss. "I'm putting my very *soul* into it. I've been planning it, sketching it for years—gathering material for its execution and seeking atmosphere for it in all parts of the world.

"You know that I started my search while we were studying together," he went on, "but you did not know what became of me after that. I've been everywhere. I've witnessed black masses presided over by apostates from every creed. I went eastward and southward to the cradle of the human race and human sin. I went farther eastward and lived among the outcasts from Lhassa who crouch in wind-swept caves of the Tibetan Himalayas. For more than a year, with my skin dyed black as coal, I officiated at voodoo rites in the West Indian jungle.

"Who is better qualified to paint that picture than I?" he concluded boastfully.

"But Tandriv, it's horrible—obscene. What are you striving for?"

"What difference does it make to you?" Tandriv retorted. "I tell you I've had a 'call' to make that painting—a commission from the powers that ruled before man and his gods and will rule again." Then, observing Blake's fixed stare, he added, "That central figure, which apparently interests you, is my guide and inspiration. Call him Lucifer, Ahrimanes, Belial, Satan, or what you will—names and words mean nothing. But my portrait will awaken the world to what and who he really is."

All vestige of sanity was wiped from his face as he raised his clenched fists and cried deliriously:

"Only a few more finishing touches and my work will be done. I must finish—I must paint what I see—the only things I see! Night and day, for years they have burned themselves into my brain. The real things of life, Blake—real! Real!"

"Then you and I see life differently," said Blake with an uneasy little laugh. He regretted having come to view this diabolic daub. Although he tried to look at it objectively, it had started a mental maelstrom in which his critical faculties and primal fears whirled about confusedly, making technical shop-talk impossible. Well, he didn't have to stand here gazing at the accursed picture. Besides, Tandriv, somewhat calmer now, was still decidedly unsociable. Apparently he wanted to get back to work at his evil miscreation. There was no use trying to reason with him. Blake left. . . .

Returning to his own apartment, he tried to forget what he had seen. But the pageant of foulness persistently intruded upon his consciousness. He dozed in fitful slumber. Every time he closed his eyes the painted horrors danced before him. After an interminable period of restless tossing he arose. Gray day was breaking.

Mechanically donning his clothing he left the house. For some reason not quite clear to himself he followed the route he and Tandriv had taken some hours before. As in a dream, he trudged through the morning fog and turned into the cold, damp areaway.

Stepping into the disordered little yard, he pulled himself up out of his somnambulistic state with a start. Something had happened!

People were standing about. Poorly clad working-people from the neighborhood were standing in a huddled group, talking with subdued excitement; a note of superstitious awe ran through their murmuring. Two uniformed policemen stood guard before the door to Tandriv's studio.

" 'Tis the devil," Blake heard one pugnacious little old woman say, "that got Mister Tandriv. Didn't I hear him a-talkin' with the devil many a night? An' didn't I see the red fire of hell a-gleamin' through the cracks in his door and window shades?"

"Yes, yes, I heard him, too," said another woman, fumbling with a shawl about her head.

"He was after callin' to the devil ag'in last night," went on the first woman. "Then all of a sudden there's a rumblin' like thunder only there's no storm in the sky and the rumblin' comes from underground; and there's terrible wailin' like a thousand banshees and the red gleam lights up the whole alley so that you can see the rats run for cover."

" 'Twas the wailin' and screamin' that woke me," said a third woman. "I told my John to find out who's makin' the awful racket in Mister Tandriv's place. But John wouldn't get up, him sayin' it's none of our business what a crazy artist is doin' in the middle o' the night."

Waiting to hear no more, Blake shouldered his way through the crowd to the policemen, the elder of whom, after satisfying himself that Blake was not of the neighborhood or an idle curiosity-seeker, agreed to let him enter the studio.

"It's O.K., Cassidy," the officer remarked to his younger partner. "Maybe this man can throw some light on the case—he says he knew Tandriv. But mind you, don't either of you touch anything 'til the coroner comes."

Blake, escorted by the young patrolman, went inside. The place was a shambles. It was as though titanic forces had struggled here. Every piece of furniture was smashed. In the center of the debris was the mangled body of Tandriv.

"There's been hell to pay here," observed Cassidy as he and Blake stood over the corpse. Prepared as he was for the worst, Blake could not restrain a gasp of horror at what he saw. The body, grotesquely twisted, was heaped on the floor as though it had fallen from a great height or been violently hurled to the bare boards. From its twisted position it was apparent that both legs and arms were broken. The eyes of the victim were rolled upward, their pupils half hidden under the upper lids. As a final touch to the terrible deed, there was stamped on the dead man's brow the impression of a *cloven hoof.*

"We couldn't figure out what kind of a weapon made *that* mark," said Cassidy. "What do you think? What do you believe killed him?"

"They did—those Things," cried Blake impulsively, at the same time swinging about to point at the huge canvas that leaned against the rear wall. "They—"

He stopped short, his mouth agape, and stared with amazement. The broad expanse of gray-white canvas was blank!

"What were you saying, Mr. Blake?"

"Nothing, officer," he managed to reply weakly; "I don't—know. Let's go outside." ——

A Gipsy Prophecy

Bram Stoker

I really think," said the doctor, "that, at any rate, one of us should go and try whether or not the thing is an imposture."

"Good!" said Considine. "After dinner we will take our cigars and stroll over to the camp."

Accordingly, when the dinner was over, and the *La Tour* finished, Joshua Considine and his friend, Doctor Burleigh, went over to the east side of the moor, where the gipsy encampment lay. As they were leaving, Mary Considine, who had walked as far as the end of the garden where it opened into the laneway, called after her husband:

"Mind, Joshua, you are to give them a fair chance, but don't give them any clue to a fortune—and don't you get flirting with any of the gipsy maidens—and take care to keep Gerald out of harm."

For answer Considine held up his hand, as if taking a stage oath, and whistled the air of the old song, *The Gipsy Countess*. Gerald joined in the strain, and then, breaking into merry laughter, the two men passed along the laneway to the common, turning now and then to wave their hands to Mary, who leaned over the gate looking after them.

It was a lovely evening in the summer; the very air was full of rest and quiet happiness, as though an outward type of the peacefulness and joy which made a heaven of the home of the young married folk. Considine's life had not been an eventful one. The only disturbing element which he had ever known was in his wooing of Mary Winston, and the long-continued objection of her ambitious parents, who expected a brilliant match for their only daughter. When Mr. and Mrs. Winston had discovered the attachment of the young barrister, they had tried to keep the young people apart by sending their daughter away for a long round of visits, having made her promise not to correspond with her lover during her absence. Love, however, had stood the test. Neither absence nor neglect seemed to cool the passion of the young man, and jealousy seemed a thing unknown to his sanguine nature; so, after a long period of waiting, the parents had given in, and the young folks were married.

They had been living in the cottage a few months, and were just beginning to feel at home. Gerald Burleigh, Joshua's old college chum, and himself a sometime victim of Mary's beauty, had arrived a week before, to stay with them for as long a time as he could tear himself away from his work in London.

When her husband had quite disappeared, Mary went into the house, and, sitting down at the piano, gave an hour to Mendelssohn.

It was but a short walk across the common, and before the cigars required renewing the two men had reached the gipsy camp. The place was as picturesque as gipsy camps—when in villages and when business is good—usually are. There were some few persons round the fire, investing their money in prophecy, and a large number of others, poorer or more parsimonious, who stayed just outside the bounds but near enough to see all that went on.

As the two gentlemen approached, the villagers, who knew Joshua, made way a little, and a pretty, keen-eyed gipsy girl tripped up and asked to tell their fortunes. Joshua held out his hand, but the girl, without seeming to see it, stared at his face in a very odd manner. Gerald nudged him:

"You must cross her hand with silver," he said. "It is one of the most important parts of the mystery."

Joshua took from his pocket a half-crown and held it out to her, but, without looking at it, she answered:

"You must cross the gipsy's hand with gold."

Gerald laughed. "You are at a premium as a subject," he said.

Joshua was of the kind of man—the universal kind—who can tolerate being stared at by a pretty girl; so, with some little deliberation, he answered:

"All right; here you are, my pretty girl; but you must give me a real good fortune for it," and he handed her a half-sovereign, which she took, saying:

"It is not for me to give good fortune or bad, but only to read what the stars have said."

She took his right hand and turned it palm upward; but the instant her eyes met it she dropped it as though it had been red hot, and, with a startled look, glided swiftly away. Lifting the curtain of the large tent, which occupied the center of the camp, she disappeared within.

"Sold again!" said the cynical Gerald.

Joshua stood a little amazed, and not altogether satisfied. They both watched the large tent. In a few moments there emerged from the opening not the young girl, but a stately-looking woman of middle age and commanding presence.

The instant she appeared the whole camp seemed to stand still. The clamor of tongues, the laughter and noise of the work were, for a second or two, arrested, and every man or woman who sat, or crouched, or lay, stood up and faced the imperial-looking gipsy.

"The queen, of course," murmured Gerald. "We are in luck tonight."

The gipsy queen threw a searching glance around the camp, and then, without hesitating an instant, came straight over and stood before Joshua.

"Hold out your hand," she ordered.

Again Gerald spoke, *sotto voce:* "I have not been spoken to in that way since I was at school."

"My hand must be crossed with gold."

"A hundred per cent at this game," whispered Gerald, as Joshua laid another half-sovereign on his upturned palm.

The gipsy looked at the hand with knitted brows; then suddenly looking up into his face, said:

"Have you a strong will—have you a true heart that can be brave for one you love?"

"I hope so; but I am afraid I have not vanity enough to say 'yes.'"

"Then I will answer for you; for I read resolution in your face—resolution desperate and determined if need be. You have a wife you love?"

"Yes," emphatically.

"Then leave her at once—never see her face again. Go from her now, while love is fresh and your heart is free from wicked intent. Go quick, go far, and never see her face again!"

Joshua drew away his hand quickly, and said: "Thank you!" stiffly but sarcastically, as he began to move away.

"I say!" said Gerald, "you're not going like that, old man; no use in being indignant with the stars or their prophet—and, moreover, your sovereign—what of it? At least, hear the matter out."

"Silence, ribald!" commanded the queen, "you know not what you do. Let him go—and go ignorant, if he will not be warned."

Joshua immediately turned back. "At all events, we will see this thing out," he said. "Now, madam, you have given me advice, but I paid for a fortune."

"Be warned!" said the gipsy. "The stars have been silent for long; let the mystery still wrap them round."

"My dear madam, I do not get within touch of a mystery every day, and I prefer for my money knowledge rather than ignorance. I can get the latter commodity for nothing when I want any of it."

Gerald echoed the sentiment. "As for me I have a large and unsalable stock on hand."

The gipsy queen eyed the two men sternly, and then said:

"As you wish. You have chosen for yourself, and have met warning with scorn, and appeal with levity. On your own heads be the doom!"

"Amen!" said Gerald.

With an imperious gesture the queen took Joshua's hand again, and began to tell his fortune.

"I see here the flowing of blood; it will flow before long; it is running in my sight. It flows through the broken circle of a severed ring."

"Go on!" said Joshua, smiling. Gerald was silent.

"Must I speak plainer?"

"Certainly; we commonplace mortals want something definite. The stars are a long way off, and their words get somewhat dulled in the message."

The gipsy shuddered, and then spoke impressively:

"This is the hand of a murderer—the murderer of his wife!" She dropped the hand and turned away.

Joshua laughed. "Do you know," said he, "I think if I were you I should prophesy some jurisprudence into my system. For instance, you say 'this hand is the hand of a murderer.' Well, whatever it may be in the future—or potentially—it is at present not one. You ought to give your prophecy in such terms as 'the hand which will be a murderer's,' or, rather, 'the hand of one who will be the murderer of his wife.' The stars are really not good on technical questions."

The gipsy made no reply of any kind, but, with drooping head and despondent mien, walked slowly to her tent, and, lifting the curtain, disappeared.

Without speaking, the two men turned homeward and walked across the moor. Presently, after some little hesitation, Gerald spoke.

"Of course, old man, this is all a joke; a ghastly one, but still a joke. But would it not be well to keep it to ourselves?"

"How do you mean?"

"Well, not to tell your wife. It might alarm her."

"Alarm her! My dear Gerald, what are you thinking of? Why, she would not be alarmed or afraid of me if all the gipsies that ever didn't come from Bohemia agreed that I was to murder her, or even to have a hard thought of her, whilst so long as she was saying, 'Jack Robinson.' "

Gerald remonstrated. "Old fellow, women are superstitious—far more than we men are; and, also, they are blessed—or cursed—with a nervous system to which we are strangers. I see too much of it in my work not to realize it. Take my advice and do not let her know, or you will frighten her."

Joshua's lips unconsciously hardened as he answered: "My dear fellow, I would not have a secret from my wife. Why, it would be the beginning of a new order of things between us. We have no secrets from each other. If we ever have, then you may begin to look out for something odd between us."

"Still," said Gerald, "at the risk of unwelcome interference, I say again: be warned in time."

"The gipsy's very words," said Joshua. "You and she seem quite of one accord. Tell me, old man, is this a put-up thing? You told me of the gipsy camp—did you arrange it all with Her Majesty?" This was said with an air of bantering earnestness.

Gerald assured him that he only heard of the camp that morning; but he made fun of every answer of his friend, and, in the process of this raillery, the time passed, and they entered the cottage.

Mary was sitting by the piano but not playing. The dim twilight had waked some very tender feelings in her breast, and her eyes were full of gentle tears. When the men came in she stole over to her husband's side and kissed him. Joshua struck a tragic attitude.

"Mary," he said in a deep voice, "before you approach me, listen to the words of Fate. The stars have spoken and the doom is sealed."

"What is it, dear? Tell me the fortune, but do not frighten me."

"Not at all, my dear; but there is a truth which it is well that you should know. Nay, it is necessary so that all your arrangements can be made beforehand, and everything be decently done and in order."

"Go on, dear; I am listening."

"Mary Considine, your effigy may yet be seen at Madame Tussaud's. The jurisimprudent stars have announced their fell tidings that this hand is red with blood—your blood. Mary! Mary! my God!"

He sprang forward, but too late to catch her as she fell fainting on the floor.

"I told you," said Gerald. "You don't know them as well as I do."

After a little while Mary recovered from her swoon, but only to fall into strong hysterics, in which she laughed and wept and raved and cried, "Keep him from me—from me, Joshua, my husband," and many other words of entreaty and of fear.

Joshua Considine was in a state of mind bordering on agony, and when at last Mary became calm he knelt by her and kissed her feet and hands and hair and called her all the sweet names and said all the tender things his lips could frame. All that night he sat by her bedside and held her hand. Far through the night and up to the early morning she kept waking from sleep and crying out as if in fear, till she was comforted by the consciousness that her husband was watching beside her.

Breakfast was late the next morning, but during it Joshua received a telegram which required him to drive over to Withering, nearly twenty miles. He was loth to go; but Mary would not hear of his remaining, and so before noon he drove off in his dog-cart alone.

When he was gone Mary retired to her room. She did not appear at lunch, but when afternoon tea was served on the lawn, under the great weeping willow, she came to join her guest. She was looking quite recovered from her illness of the evening before. After some casual remarks, she said to Gerald: "Of course it was very silly about last night, but I could not help feeling frightened. Indeed I would feel so still if I let myself think of it. But, after all, these people may only imagine things, and I have a test that can hardly fail to show that the prediction is false—if indeed it be false," she added sadly.

"What is your plan?" asked Gerald.

"I shall go myself to the gipsy camp, and have my fortune told by the queen."

"Capital. May I go with you?"

"Oh, no! That would spoil it. She might know you and guess at me, and suit her utterance accordingly. I shall go alone this afternoon."

When the afternoon was gone Mary Considine took her way to the gipsy encampment. Gerald went with her as far as the near edge of the common, and returned home.

Half an hour had hardly elapsed when Mary entered the drawing-room, where he lay on a sofa reading. She was ghastly pale and was in a state of extreme excitement. Hardly had she passed over the threshold when she collapsed and sank moaning on the carpet. Gerald rushed to aid her, but by a great effort she controlled herself and motioned him to be silent. He waited, and his ready attention to her wish seemed to be her best help, for, in a few minutes, she had somewhat recovered, and was able to tell him what had passed.

"When I got to the camp," she said, "there did not seem to be a soul about. I went into the center and stood there. Suddenly a tall woman stood beside me. 'Something told me I was wanted!' she said. I held out my hand and laid a piece of silver on it. She took from her neck a small golden trinket and laid it there also; and then, seizing the two, threw them into the stream that ran by. Then she took my hand in hers and spoke: 'Naught but blood in this guilty place,' and turned away. I caught hold of her and asked her to tell me more. After some hesitation, she said: 'Alas! alas! I see you lying at your husband's feet, and his hands are red with blood.'"

Gerald did not feel at all at ease, and tried to laugh it off. "Surely," he said, "this woman has a craze about murder."

"Do not laugh," said Mary, "I cannot bear it," and then, as if with a sudden impulse, she left the room.

Not long after, Joshua returned, bright and cheery, and as hungry as a hunter after his long drive. His presence cheered his wife, who seemed much brighter, but she did not mention the episode of the visit to the gipsy camp, so Gerald did not mention it either. As if by tacit consent the subject was not alluded to during the evening. But there was a strange, settled look on Mary's face, which Gerald could not but observe.

In the morning Joshua came down to breakfast later than usual. Mary had been up and about the house from an early hour; but as the time drew on she seemed to get a little nervous, and now and again threw around an anxious look.

Gerald could not help noticing that none of those at breakfast could get on satisfactorily with their food. It was not altogether that the chops were tough, but that the knives were all so blunt. Being a guest, he, of course, made no sign; but presently saw Joshua draw his thumb across the edge of his knife in an unconscious sort of way. At the action Mary turned pale and almost fainted.

After breakfast they all went out on the lawn. Mary was making up a bouquet, and said to her husband, "Get me a few of the tea-roses, dear."

Joshua pulled down a cluster from the front of the house. The stem bent, but was too tough to break. He put his hand in his pocket to get his knife; but in vain. "Lend me your knife, Gerald," he said. But Gerald did not have one, so he went into the breakfast room and took one from the table. He came out feeling its edge and grumbling. "What on earth has happened to all the knives—the edges seem all ground off?"

Mary turned away hurriedly and entered the house.

Joshua tried to sever the stalk with the blunt knife as country cooks sever the necks of fowl—as schoolboys cut twine. With a little effort he finished the task. The cluster of roses grew thick, so he determined to gather a great bunch.

He could not find a single sharp knife in the sideboard where the cutlery was kept, so he called Mary, and when she came, told her the state of things. She looked so agitated and so miserable that he could not help knowing the truth, and, as if astounded and hurt, asked her:

"Do you mean to say that *you* have done it?"

She broke in, "Oh, Joshua, I was so afraid!"

He paused, and a set, white look came over his face. "Mary!" said he, "is this all the trust you have in me? I would not have believed it."

"Oh, Joshua! Joshua!" she cried entreatingly, "forgive me," and wept bitterly.

Joshua thought a moment and then said: "I see how it is. We shall better end this or we shall all go mad."

He ran into the drawing-room.

"Where are you going?" almost screamed Mary.

Gerald saw what he meant—that he would not be tied to blunt instruments by the force of a superstition, and was not surprized when he saw him come out through the French window, bearing in his hand a large Ghurka knife, which usually lay on the center table, and which his brother had sent him from Northern India. It was one of those great hunting-knives which worked such havoc at close quarters with the enemies of the loyal Ghurkas during the mutiny, of great weight but so evenly balanced in the hand as to seem light, and with an edge like a razor. With one of these knives a Ghurka can cut a sheep in two.

When Mary saw him come out of the room with the weapon in his hand she screamed in an agony of fright, and the hysterics of last night were promptly renewed.

Joshua ran toward her, and, seeing her falling, threw down the knife and tried to catch her. However, he was just a second too late, and the two men cried out in horror simultaneously as they saw her fall upon the naked blade.

When Gerald rushed over he found that, in falling, her left hand had struck the blade, which lay partly upward on the grass. Some of the small veins were cut through, and the blood gushed freely from the wound. As he was tying it up he pointed out to Joshua that the wedding ring was severed by the steel.

They carried her fainting to the house. When, after a while, she came out, with her arm in a sling, she was peaceful in her mind and happy. She said to her husband:

"The gipsy was wonderfully near the truth; too near for the real thing ever to occur now, dear."

Joshua bent over and kissed the wounded hand. ——<del>—</del>—

THE GIRDLE

JOSEPH MCCORD

The pool of mottled light on the table-top had drifted over to where Sir John's clawlike fingers, emerging from the silk sleeve of his dressing robe, drummed slowly on the black oak.

Carson, erect on the hearth rug, had ignored the chair indicated by the fingers and was filled with a sudden resentment as he sensed the indifferent weariness of their tapping. And this old man was Pelham's father! It was all so different than he had pictured. There was no fathoming the expression of that masklike face with its impenetrable stare, settled in the cushioned depths of the wheel chair.

The heels of Carson's boots came together with a suggestion of military stiffness, and he spoke curtly: "I confess I don't understand."

And his host replied, in a curiously dry voice: "Perhaps it is not altogether necessary that you should."

The words carried a studied courtesy, but their veiled irony was not lost on the officer.

"Granted. But Pelham was my friend—if he was your son—and I am here only because he asked—"

"Of course," interrupted Sir John. "Spare me the formula, if you will. He's dead. It was arranged you should come and tell me how well he died. He was to perform the same service for you, no doubt, had the circumstances been reversed. The Pelhams always die well. It's in the breed. If you insist, however—"

Carson choked back his resentment.

"There were circumstances that make it seem necessary—and yet—"

"Pray get on."

"Then I'll make it short." Carson advanced a little nearer the table. "It was in a little hut I last saw him—alive. Enemy ground, newly occupied it was, and here was this hut in a small clearing. It might have been a woodcutter's and it was empty, save for some heavier furniture.

"Several of us were poking about its one room, then Pel started up a crazy ladder at one end leading to a small loft. I heard him moving around and scratching matches, then he was quiet. I walked over near the ladder and hailed him.

" 'Nothing up here but an old chest,' he came back, 'and empty at that.' Then I heard him laugh. 'Somebody left me a Dutch Sam Browne—thought the cursed thing was a snake—felt cold!'

"I heard the lid of the chest fall, then Pel started down into the room. Part-way, he turned and faced me. He had the end of a belt in each hand, holding it behind him as if he were going to wear it. I didn't notice that, though. All I saw was his face—the way he looked."

"The way he looked," prompted Sir John, as the younger man stared at him soberly. "And, pray how did he look?"

Carson seemed to pull himself together with an effort. "That's exactly what I have to tell you. I'll try to." He seated himself on the edge of the table, one booted foot swinging nervously. "Why, it was his eyes, I think—yes, that's what it was. There was something in them that shouldn't ever be in a man's eyes. You've seen a dog that was vicious and a coward—all at the same time. He wants to go at your throat and something holds him for the moment." He drew a long breath. "It was like that," he decided.

Sir John was watching one of his visitor's hands; it had gripped the edge of the table and the knuckles were white. The boot was motionless, tense.

"As you say, like a dog. Well?"

At the quiet words, the younger man relaxed. "Yes, sir," he agreed gratefully. Then: "I spoke to him, and he never answered. He came on down the ladder, slowly—still facing us. The others were drawing up behind me—I could feel them. We all watched Pel. It wasn't that he just moved slowly either—it was something different. Slinking! I think that's the way to say it. And he watched us—never blinked. No one said a word.

"When Pel's feet hit the floor, he began moving toward the door —it had come shut. He backed to it and began feeling for the latch with one hand, holding the belt all the time. He kicked the door open with his heel.

"Then I knew we were losing him—if you can understand what I mean—knew he'd got to be saved—from something!"

Carson's voice was curiously strained.

"I wanted to stop him—I tell you I did want to! I tried. I started for him."

"And the belt?" interposed Sir John quietly.

"The belt," echoed the other man dully. "Oh, yes. He held it all the while—I just told you that."

"But he escaped."

"He did. I had scarcely moved. He gave a dreadful sort of cry and leaped out of the doorway—backward. We rushed it then. But he had made the trees and we could hear him crashing through the undergrowth, as though there hadn't been a boche within a hundred miles of us. That's how he went."

The heavy silence that followed was broken only by a coal falling in the grate. With a long sigh, Carson raised his head. He fumbled a pack of cigarettes, thrust one between his lips, but made no move to light it.

"I am waiting," came the voice from the chair.

"Waiting?"

"Come, come! You tell me my son is dead. If I recollect, you mentioned gallantry. So far, you have suggested desertion. The details."

"Oh, yes. The details. But you won't believe them. One would have to have seen."

"Have the kindness." Sir John leaned back wearily among his cushions and closed his eyes.

"Well. It was the third evening after that—I think it was the third. There had been an advance, a lot of machine-gun work. It was growing dark, I remember. Harvey, my sergeant, came up and asked if he could speak to me. 'I've seen Lieutenant Pelham,' he whispered queerly.

" 'He's dead?' I said. I knew he was dead.

" 'Yes, he's dead, sir,' says Harvey, 'but there's something queer about him. Will you have a look?'

"He led the way and I followed."

Carson's voice was becoming strained again. Sir John leaned forward and stared steadily into his eyes.

"We came to a little open place. There was some light there— enough to see the dreadfullest group God ever bunched in one place!

"First of all, I saw Pel—sitting with his back against a little tree, chin on his knees. He was staring straight to the front—dead. But around him! Five German infantrymen—dead too. Dragged into a sort of semicircle. And they weren't shot and they weren't gassed— nothing like that. Everyone had his throat torn! Torn!"

Carson leaned close to the old man; his voice shrilled as he demanded, almost piteously, "You hear me, can't you?"

"They would be—torn," said Sir John Pelham very quietly. "Finish your story."

The officer pulled himself together with an effort. "It makes it easier, having you understand. I've seen men—"

He thrust the fingers of one hand into the collar of his tunic, as though it choked him. "I've seen men, sir, meet death in a thousand ways—but not, not that way! And Pel wasn't marked at all—I looked."

The father leaned forward in his chair, but the gesture of interest was not reflected in his impassive face.

"What of the belt?"

"He wasn't wearing it, but the thing was there—lying at his feet. And it was coiled!"

"Show it to me."

"Why I—yes, I took it. I don't know why. I dropped it in my kit bag—next day I got mine. I'm just out of the hospital by a month. Otherwise I'd have been here sooner."

With an unexpected clutch at the wheels of his chair, Sir John was close to the table, one white hand extended.

"Give it me."

An instant's hesitation, then Carson slowly pulled a paper-wrapped object from his pocket, laid it easily on the table.

"It's in there," he muttered. "I don't like the damned thing."

With deft fingers, the baronet loosened the paper, shook the contents on the table.

There lay the leathern belt, coiled compactly. In the waning light it was of a pale brown color, thin and very flexible. On the other end was a metal clasp, its surface cut with marks that might or might not have been characters. There was a reading lens lying near and Sir John used it to study the coiled strap. He examined it grimly, from many angles, without once touching it. Finished, he leaned back in his chair and thoughtfully tapped the palm of his hand with the lens.

"Captain Carson."

"Sir."

"Attend most carefully to what I say—follow my instructions exactly. Take that belt in one hand only. Carry it to the hearth—lay it directly on the coals. When it is burned, quite burned, you may tell me."

Carson got slowly to his feet. With a hand that hesitated and was none too steady, he reached for the coiled belt, lifted it a few inches from the table. At his touch, seemingly, the coil loosened; it started to unroll. He caught at it with both hands.

For a fraction of a second his body seemed caught in a strained tension. Then he began backing away from the table, noiselessly, furtively. With an end of the belt in each hand, he shifted his eyes to Sir John and they glowed with a strange, sinister light. From his sagging jaw came his tongue, licking.

Screaming an oath, Sir John Pelham flung the reading lens with all his frail strength full into that distorted face.

"Drop it!" he bawled savagely. "Jarvis!"

At the call an elderly man-servant came hurrying. He saw his master supporting himself on the arms of the chair, trembling with the exertion, and staring curiously at the uniformed visitor. Carson was swaying unsteadily, one hand pressed against his face, blood trickling from between his fingers. At his feet lay the belt and the shattered lens. Jarvis saw all this and took his post near Sir John, waiting his orders.

"Jarvis."

"Yes, sir," said the man-servant evenly.

Sir John sank back wearily.

"The tongs, Jarvis. Fetch the tongs. Pick up that strap. Only the tongs, mind you—don't touch it with your hands. So. Now lay it on the coals—hold it down hard."

The three watched the burning in deep silence, watched the belt writhe and twist in the heat, scorch with flame, fall in charred fragments.

"Jarvis."

"Yes, sir."

"Lights, then brandy for our guest. You may bring things and patch that cut for him." To Carson: "Sit down, man, and pull yourself together. I regret I was obliged to strike you, but, under the circumstances, you will agree it was quite necessary, I think."

"I don't understand," muttered Carson dully. He slumped weakly into a near-by chair. "I'm—I felt—I don't know." His voice trailed off; his chin sagged on his breast.

"You don't wish to eat, by any chance?"

"What made you ask that? God, no! I couldn't eat—I only—"

But Jarvis was offering him the brandy.

"None for me," said Sir John shortly. "But you may help me over to the far case—I am looking for a book."

In a few moments, Jarvis had wheeled him back to the table and he was leafing the pages of a small book he had found. It was bound in parchment and bore evidence of great age. Carson shiveringly helped himself to another drink, as his host turned the crackling pages until he found what he sought. Tracing the lines with a lean forefinger, he read silently for a moment, then looked shrewdly at his guest.

"This may interest you, Captain. Read here," and he indicated the place.

Carson slowly deciphered the strange script of the hand-printed page:

> Another means wherethrough men have become were-wolves is that they in som mannere getten a belt or girdel maked of human skin. By an autentyke cronicle a yoman hadde such a girdel which he kept locken in a cheste secrely. It so felle on a day that he let the cheste unlocken and his litel sone getteth the girdel and girteth his midel with it. In a minute the childe was transmewed into a mervilously wilde beste but the yoman fortuned to enter the house and with spede he remewed the girdel and so cured his sone who, sayde he remembered naught save a ravissing apepetyt.

The book slipped from Carson's nerveless fingers. Wide-eyed he stared into Sir John's impassive face.

When he could find the words: "God! You never mean—you couldn't mean—"

"I was in hopes," mused the old man, "you know I was quite in hopes you would feel hungry." ———

THE GLOVES

GARNETT RADCLIFFE

I hadn't gone into Mr. Robinson's shop to buy gloves. I had gone in hoping to find among the miscellany of junk that filled the place literally from floor to ceiling a bracket for a shaving cabinet, and I was poking about when the gloves caught my eye. They were on a chair near the door, and I did not at once realize that they were for sale.

"One of your customers has left his gloves behind," I told Mr. Robinson. "You'd better put them somewhere safe for he may come back for them."

Mr. Robinson, who is middle-aged and worried looking, clicked his tongue—a sign of annoyance.

"I'd have sworn I put 'em away," he said. "Gettin' absent-minded in my old age, that's what I am. No, they haven't been left behind. I gave that ferrity-faced loafer Joe Larkin ten bob for them the other day. 'Spect he pinched 'em, but that's not my business. . . . You feel the quality. . . . Real hogskin, those gloves are."

I examined them. They were genuine hogskin with a wool lining, and they had been very little worn.

"How much?" I asked.

"Twelve and six to you." Mr. Robinson said. "They're a bargain. Last you a lifetime those will!"

As it happened I needed a pair of gloves, having left my own much inferior ones on a bus a few days before. When I'd tried them on and found they fitted perfectly the chance of obtaining a first-class article at a very moderate price overcame my dislike of second-hand goods.

"Twelve and six it is," I said.

When I'd returned to the bachelor flat I was renting in that bee-hive called Harbinger Mansions I examined my purchase again. Yes, they were excellent gloves and practically unsoiled except just inside each wrist where both wool linings had a ring of faint, brown-ish stains. I told myself no one would ever notice that and put them away in the top left-hand drawer of my chest of drawers.

I don't keep a diary, nor have I a very retentive memory. When I say it was about a week later that the first incident in connection with those gloves occurred I am merely hazarding a guess.

It was such a trivial incident that at the time it hardly registered itself on my mind. It was only when subsequent happenings induced me to look back that I recalled it as being the first of a chain of rather curious events.

All that happened was that the gloves seemed to have moved themselves inside the drawer. When I went to take them out—it was a cold, wet morning most appropriate for the wearing of wool-lined, hogskin gloves—they were not stretched on a collar-box as I distinctly remembered having left them. They were on top of some socks in the front portion of the drawer, and the fingers were curled into the palms so that they looked like a pair of clenched fists.

Of course there was an obvious explanation. Mrs. Hubbard, the amiable lady who "did out" my flat during my absence must have been doing a bit of prying. She'd noticed the gloves, had taken them out to try them on her own fat hands and had omitted to replace them as she'd found them.

I decided I'd say nothing to Mrs. Hubbard. She was a good old soul whose services I wouldn't have risked losing for half-a-dozen pairs of gloves.

I wore the gloves that day with satisfaction. They were warm and comfortable and they looked good. A gentleman's gloves, I flattered myself. Gloves are great conveyors of personality, and I could picture their previous owner—their real owner I mean, not the ferrity-faced Mr. Larkin who had sold them to Mr. Robinson—as having been the old-fashioned country squire type who appreciated good leather, sound horses and vintage port. It may seem ridiculous to deduce all that from a pair of gloves, but when I looked at these with their hallmark of quality and faint indentations on the palms as if they had once gripped reins, that was the very vivid impression I got.

When I got back that night they were too wet to be replaced in the drawer, so I put them on the back of a chair within reasonable distance of the radiator.

And so came incident No. 2. which can be just as easily explained away as the first. Presumably, I hadn't balanced them very well on the chair, or they were disturbed by a draught, for in the morning I found they had fallen to the floor and rolled several feet away from the chair towards the window. Somehow when I saw them lying on the carpet, backs uppermost and fingers spread out and slightly curved, I was put in mind of a man crawling on his face.

The impression was so strong I disliked picking them up. They still felt a little damp and—presumably because of the radiator—warm as if they had recently been worn.

After that there was a spell of fine weather during which I had no occasion to wear or to think of gloves. I'd quite forgotten them when one evening when I was asking for my letters the hall porter gave me a message.

"Mrs. Hubbard, the lady who does your flat, thinks you've got mice, sir," he said. "If you've no objection I'll arrange for a trap to be left in the bedroom."

Mice are not to be tolerated in a hive for humans such as Harbinger Mansions. I told the porter I thought a trap would be an excellent idea. That evening it was the first thing I saw when I entered my bedroom. Probably on the advice of Mrs. Hubbard it had been placed close to the chest of drawers.

That night I heard the mice myself. From the sounds they made they were robust mice. Lying awake and furious, I could picture a couple of large rats romping about inside the chest of drawers. A rat hunt in pyjamas and bare feet didn't appeal to me, so I pulled the sheets round my head and eventually, despite the scrabbling, scratching sounds. I fell asleep.

Next morning the trap was empty. I looked in the chest of drawers. Only the top left-hand drawer had been disturbed. In there the rats had worked havoc. Handkerchiefs, socks and collars had been flung about and mixed as if by a rake, and the paper which lined the bottom of the drawer had been scraped up and torn. I found the gloves almost hidden beneath the paper. I put the drawer to rights and went out cursing all rats.

The following night was very similar, except that the rats were even more frisky. After listening to the scrabbling, bumping sounds for a couple of hours, I sprang out of bed in desperation and yanked open the drawer whence the sounds seemed to come.

The contents had been disturbed and flung about, but no sign of a rat. I returned to bed leaving the drawer open. I must have scared the rats for silence followed. As I was dropping off to sleep I thought I heard a soft flop, flop, as if the intruders had hopped from the drawer on the carpet, but I was too weary to get up again.

"Git, you brutes!" I hissed, and I turned deeper into the pillow.

I didn't sleep as well that night as I usually do. Several times I half-woke to hear the rats scampering about the room, and once I'd an unpleasant nightmare in which a pair of soft, flabby hands seemed to be groping round my face and neck. My last recollection is of a sound of drumming at the window as if someone were tapping on the glass with his fingers.

In the morning I found the rats had pulled the gloves out of the drawer. After a search I found them beneath the chest of drawers whence I had to retrieve them with the crook of my umbrella. They were dusty and crumpled, so that they looked like a couple of dead crabs. Somehow I disliked handling them.

I wasn't going to suffer another such night. After I'd put my drawer straight I went down and spoke my mind to the hall porter.

If he could not get rid of the rats, I threatened I would leave Harbinger Mansions.

He promised strong measures. In the evening I found a second trap had been installed and poisoned bait had been left in strategic points. Hoping for the best I went to bed early.

I slept badly and had a dream in which I saw a finger beckoning to me from the top of the chest of drawers. Then I dropped off only to be woken a little later by the sound of my door opening as if someone had given it a violent jerk. I sat up. Sure enough the door opening on the corridor was open. I could see the dim blue light which always burns in the corridor and I could feel a cold draught.

Cursing and rather scared I got out of bed, trying to assure myself I hadn't closed the door firmly and the draught had blown it open. As I was about to close it I heard a frightened yell from the direction of the main stairway.

I hurried down the dim corridor fearful of seeing I knew not what. On the landing a figure cowered against the wall. It was one of the night-porters, an elderly individual with a bibulous countenance and a ragged white mustacthe. As he pointed down the stairs his hand shook, and his face was ashen.

"Spiders!" he gasped. "A couple of whopping great brown spiders! Gawd, am I seein' things?"

I told him that what he'd imagined to be spiders were in all probability the rats that had been haunting my bedroom. After a bit I persuaded him to accompany me down the main stairway to the entrance hall where we turned on lights and peered under chairs and sofas. There were no rats to be seen. I told the porter that what Harbinger Mansions needed was a good fox-terrier.

"They *were* spiders," he insisted. "Rats don't run like this," and he illustrated what he meant by making his hands dart along the counter at the inquiry desk, the fingers moving very quickly so that they looked like the legs of running spiders. I wish he hadn't done that, for later on I had yet another creepy dream in which I was following a pair of hands that scuttled like crabs along wet streets and roads until they reached a dirty little house with no lights where they groped up the wall and vanished through a broken window into a dark room. I seemed to hear then a scream like the hoot of a railway engine and I woke up sweating and trembling.

But at least the rats had left my room, never to return again. Apparently they'd either eaten the gloves or dragged them off with them for nesting purposes, for although I searched high and low they were nowhere to be found.

And is that the end of the story? Well, on that point I'd rather not offer an opinion. But I will relate something that some readers may think casts a light on what happened in my flat.

The facts came to me through the mouth of Mr. Robinson. I was poking about in his shop after my wont when he asked me if I still had the gloves I'd bought.

"They've vanished," I said, which was nearer the truth than if I'd just said I'd lost them.

"Vanished, eh?" said Mr. Robinson. "Well, the fellow who sold them to me, that ferrity wastrel Joe Larken, has vanished too! Leastways, he's dead. He's been found strangled in his bed in that old condemned house of his by the Minchley railway line."

"*Strangled?*" I repeated.

"Yes, strangled," said Mr. Robinson. "And the police haven't a clue who did it. The murderer wore gloves and he didn't leave a trace. What beats the police is how he got into the house with all the doors and windows fastened. They say he didn't leave so much as a footprint in the dust. . . . Anyway Joe Larkin was no loss. . . . Do you know where I believe he got the gloves I sold you?"

"Where?" I asked.

"You remember the crash on the Minchley line when the London express collided with a goods train? It happened in the cutting just below Joe's house. He was there all right, but I bet he didn't waste time helping people out of the wreckage. Loot—that would be Joe's game. . . .

"I could just see him creeping round the burning coaches like the human rat he was. . . . He'd have pinched the wallet off a dying man . . . or the shoes off a dead baby! I bet that's where he found those gloves."

That was what Mr. Robinson told me. Later, curiosity caused me to go to a public library where I could read the back numbers of the papers reporting the Minchley crash. Among the list of the killed I remarked the name of a certain Colonel Belcher-Price, an ex-Hussar and M.F.H. of the Minchley Hunt. It stated in the paper that he'd had both hands severed at the wrist when his first-class carriage was telescoped by a goods truck.

I'll leave the reader to draw his or her own conclusions. . . .

THE HARBOR OF GHOSTS

M. J. BARDINE

It always came to me just at the edge of twilight, that strange figure. Never was there spoken word, yet I knew there was a message for me could I but find the key. That was when I was very young and could not put into words the idea which so dimly presented itself. The figure never came to me except in the old attic of my grandfather's house where I loved to go in the afternoons after school hours, there to dream over the many strange things he had brought with him from the fascinating countries he had voyaged to in his ship, *The Golden Girl*, the ship that had disappeared that last fatal trip the year in which I was born.

I was never afraid, for it seemed to be a natural thing, and the figure, vague and gossamer, not unfriendly. These excursions into the attic lapsed during my term of apprenticeship in my father's shipbuilding yards. My family were all more or less seafaring; it was in the blood, and my father carried on the traditions of the family by building the more modern carriers of our flag in the merchant trade, and I was destined for the service.

Thus it was that when I had finished my poring over maps, plans and instruments, my father found a berth for me on the *Joseph B.,* which followed in the paths of the long-gone *Golden Girl* in the China trade.

I was soon ready for sea; my sea-chest was aboard, and then before the ship sailed the next morning, I journeyed the short distance down to the old house where I had spent so many of my childhood days with the old aunt who still lived there.

Once more I was drawn to the attic to say good-bye to the strange weapons—the feathered head-dresses, the sandalwood boxes and embroidered shawls that had journeyed with my grandfather through wind and rain, salt spume and torrid sun. And then once more the veiled figure came to me from the shadow of the carved screen whence it had always appeared. The eery sensation of my youngster days came back to me as I felt its presence. The lips moved, and in the recesses of my brain echoed the whisper, "Go back! Go back!" What I was to go back from I did not know. Now, too late, I know. The figure faded and melted into the shadows as I pretended a bravery I did not feel. I left the attic telling myself it was all imagination built up from some remembrance of my childhood days.

The *Joseph B.* sailed next day with me at the rail. I felt very important and part of the great world as I stood there gazing back at the little group of relatives and family friends whom I now seem fated never to see again.

I am writing this by the fitful gleam of a lantern hung at the taffrail on the *Golden Girl*—my God, yes! the *Golden Girl!* But wait, after I have set down a story so strange, so unbelievable, I will place what I have written in a bottle, cork it and set it adrift, hoping that even should there be no escape for me from this ghastly place, some strange tide may carry word of my fate back to the world of living men.

The first half of the voyage in the *Joseph B.* was uneventful to my shipmates, who had gone over the way so many times. But for me, who for the first time gazed upon the colorful ports, it was all strange and wonderful, the jargon of unfamiliar tongues, the noisome odors of the oriental waterfront making it all an epic of adventure. In Ceylon we took on a load of teas and spices; silks and Chinese merchandize in Hong Kong, and so after loading turned to the long journey home. Then in the straits the glass started to fall, ominous clouds gathered and the wind blew until it seemed we were caught in a maelstrom of fury. The wheel refused to respond to human intelligence, and we were whirled hither and thither in the vortex of a sea seemingly gone mad with hatred of the puny thing which was our ship, now tossed like a cork, with straining seams and laboring engines. We had been taking turns at the pumps; for by now the ship was leaking badly, and after my period of duty I went to my cabin and, utterly exhausted, threw myself on my bunk. I was asleep before my head touched the pillow.

I must have slept quite some time; for I had dream after dream, or I should say nightmares, wherein the veiled figure was trying to hold me back from something. I was awakened by a terrific crash, the impact of which hurled me from my bunk against the door opposite. I shook myself together and gradually came back to the reality of what was going on. I could dimly hear the shouted orders of the captain on the deck outside, while the ship quivered in every timber and listed sharply.

I managed to get the door open and staggered onto the sea-swept deck. A terrific flare of lightning showed our position. We were hard fast on a jutting rock thrust up in the midst of the boiling sea—a rock which must have been the result of some submarine upheaval. We had struck almost amidships, or else the rock had been forced up under us; for the deck was splintered, telling me we were broken in two. Giant waves dashing against the rock drenched our bows, and the ship was being rapidly pounded to pieces.

Drenched and shivering, I held onto a stanchion until I could steady myself in a slight measure. A wave tore loose my hold, and sliding, gasping for breath, I slid down against the rail, which I grasped with desperate strength and held while fresh seas poured over me.

The captain, clinging to the splintered rail on the foredeck, stood shouting his orders, his stentorian voice heard even above the roar of the elements. "Man the boats" was the order now given, though how a boat could live in that seething pit of hell I could not guess. As rapidly as possible the crews responded and the boats were swung out. One was smashed against the side of the ship and the other capsized as it struck the water, spilling its human freight into the sea. And now I think our captain must suddenly have gone mad, for, with uplifted fists and screaming an imprecation to the heavens above, he dived into the black depths that had claimed his crew.

I was left alone, clinging as best I could to whatever had not been washed overboard. How long I struggled against being swept into the sea I do not know, but at length the wind died down; but the first faint streaks of dawn told me as I gazed at the sharp tongue of rock which pierced our vitals, that I could not long remain aboard and live; for at any moment the ship might break. There was still one boat in the davits; so I hurriedly provisioned it from the cook's galley. The food and a plentiful supply of water I placed in the boat, and then set about getting over the side. This was not so difficult, as the side of the ship on which the boat was swung had listed until it was almost at the water line. I cast off and slowly moved away, wallowing in the trough of the sea.

I had gone only a short distance when there occurred a boiling of the water; a geyser shot up, and ship and rock sank from sight. I was now in very truth alone. I had no compass or sextant; I could only trust that I would drift to land or the path of some ship left alive by the storm.

I am going to keep a log. As near as I can determine I have now been adrift ten days. Our ship struck September thirteenth, on a Friday. This must be then September twenty-third. It has been a period of sleeping and awakening, the sun has burned steadily down upon me, and I have sheltered myself as best I could under the canvas boat covering.

Sept. 24th — I have seen no sail of any kind. I seem to be caught in some current carrying me steadily forward in the same direction.

Sept. 26th — I did not enter any happening in the log yesterday. Was it my imagination, born of my loneliness and despair, or did my fancy conjure up the veiled figure of my childhood? It seemed to sit there in the bow of the boat last night. Perhaps I am going mad.

Sept. 27th — Still drifting. It is getting colder.

Sept. 28th — Still colder. I cannot understand this. Could I be drifting toward the Antarctic circle? I must be traveling faster than I am aware of.

Later — I cannot date this for I have been very ill, and unconscious, and do not know how many days have elapsed. It is now very cold and I have had to wrap myself in the canvas covering my stores. I hope I am not deluding myself, but I seem to see the vague outlines of mountainous land. I am too weak to row. I can only let the sea carry me; perhaps it will cast me upon some strange shore.

Later — I am still steadily drifting. The land — for it is land — is nearer. It is too dark now to write further in this undated log.

That was the last entry I was fated to make in my log; for during the night I entered what seemed to be a subterranean passage. I had a feeling of being closed in, and the water seemed to be lapping against walls. I had given up hope of ever seeing the sky again, when suddenly I came out into a bay or harbor surrounded by towering cliffs of ice. I could only gaze in amazement and wonder if in some bygone age this could be the crater of a volcano which the sea entered during the forming of the ice age, and so it has stood unchanged through countless centuries. High above the cliffs the moon, pale and full of distant mystery, shone down upon the icy water. And then, as I grew accustomed to the half-light, I made out the outlines of many ships all vague and silent, the shapes strange and different from any I had ever seen except in pictures of the old sailing-ships of my grandfather's day.

For the first time in weeks I pulled upon my oars. The ice seemed to draw away and make a lane of clear water, which I followed to the nearest ship, and as I drew closer a hope formed in my heart that I would find someone to share the now almost insupportable loneliness.

"Ahoy!" I called, as my boat touched the side of the ship, but only an echo came back to me, thrown from the towering cliffs. With numb fingers I made my boat fast to the rusted chain hanging from the ship's side, and then as I started to climb aboard I looked up at the almost obliterated name and with a feeling of astonishment made out the lettering. The *Golden Girl!* My own grandfather's ship, and I of all the world knew now where that ship rested.

A chill ran down my spine, yet I crawled over the rail. The moonlight threw into relief the coiled ropes on the deck as I slowly made my way to the chartroom. I entered, and there seated at his table with the log-book open before him was a man. I spoke to him but received no answer. I laid my hand upon his shoulder but he did not move. Bending down, I peered into the bearded face, and it was the face I had seen in pictures in my childhood home. It was the face of my own grandfather, cold and immovable in death. The figure sat stony and rigid, the quill pen still held in the stiff fingers. I peered over his shoulder and read the last entry in the log before him; it was in the cramped handwriting I had seen in old letters and documents penned by my grandfather. I turned with tears coursing down my cheeks, and looked again at that kindly dead face, and then once more read the log's entry:

"*Dec. 8th, 1888*—I put over the side today all that was mortal of Leatherbreeches, otherwise James Coggswell the ship's carpenter. This freezing cold has done its work well. I will have to carry on as best I can, hoping that I may be delivered from this haunted harbor of lost souls. If only the storm had left us one boat I might find a way out. If I can endure this cold I will build a boat or raft and try to find—"

The entry stopped, broken off as though he had been interrupted. I left the chartroom and made an inspection of the deck; everything was shipshape and the deck as clean as though it had been holystoned that day. I returned to the chartroom and in the captain's quarters adjoining found his bunk neatly made up.

Somehow I was not made nervous by that dead presence outside. I felt almost as if he protected me from some evil which seemed to be all about me. I lay down and drew the covers up about my face and fell asleep almost at once. I was awakened by the ghostly sound of a ship's bell. It was one o'clock. And then my hair rose on my head, for I heard in that graveyard of dead ships the words: "All's well!" And then the culminating horror, for the chair was pushed back in the chartroom and I heard the measured tread of footsteps. I raised up my head and looked through the door and saw my dead grandfather come back to seeming life. My senses reeled and I fell back upon the pillow.

When next I opened my eyes it was daylight. I again looked through the door into the chartroom; once more that rigid figure sat there, the glassy eyes staring down at the log. I arose, wondering if it had all been hallucination born of the terrible experiences I had passed through. Quickly I left the captain's quarters and went on deck and looked over the harbor. The ships lay silent, wrapped in mystery, no sign of life or sound.

From the stores in my boat I made a frugal breakfast, after which I decided to investigate the nearest ship. I slid down the chain into my boat. The ice in the harbor moved restlessly, showing here and there lanes of clear water. I took the chance of being crushed between the ice cakes rather than remain on the *Golden Girl* with its silent watcher. After a long time, during which I stood in my boat poling with one oar through the icy lanes, I reached the other ship, made fast and clambered aboard. I looked about me. Oh, that I could erase from my memory the sight of what met my eyes! Sprawled about the deck were the dead members of what I now know to be that ship's unholy crew; one with a knife in his breast, another with his head crushed and half his face torn away, while a third, whom I took to be the captain, stood with a marlin-spike in his hand, snarling down at the mutilated face, all frozen and immovable.

I ran, stumbling, to the side and half fell into my boat. The *Golden Girl* with its dead master seemed a friendly place, and glad I was when I once more stood upon its deck. I took the lantern from the taffrail, and going below found a few pieces of old lumber, with which I made a fire in the cook's galley. The awful cold has settled in my very marrow and I will try to warm myself as long as fuel lasts. Tonight I am resolved to stay awake and learn what I can of this strange harbor of ghosts. I must have dozed off despite my resolution; for the fire was out and there was a deadly chill in the air when I awoke.

Just then the ship's bell sounded one, and "All's well!" echoed over the harbor. I looked out, and lights flickered from the silent ships about me. I heard again the measured tread of footsteps from the chartroom and watched the figure of my grandfather come out.

He stood near me for a moment, looking across at the ship I had visited that day, and I heard the dead lips mutter: "How long, O Lord, how long?" Then he moved to the rail, where he stood as though listening to the terrible oaths and bloodthirsty yells which came from that other strange ship. Frozen with horror I too looked as lurid flames sprang up and revealed the fighting on that deck. All night long I watched the awful scenes repeated over and over until they died with the coming of dawn, as I have watched every night since, until now, when I feel that I too am doomed to become one of this ghastly company in the harbor of dead ships.

I have watched the dead man in the chartroom, in my loneliness have tried to talk to him, but he never turns his head to listen. I watch him go to the rail, stooping for something which he casts over the rail, perhaps the phantom form of Leatherbreeches the ship's carpenter; then that unholy ship whereon men go through the form of murder nightly. Oh, that I could not see the happenings there! but something impels me to look and listen.

It is bitter cold and I feel the chill reaching to my heart, and I have just enough life left to place what I have written in this bottle and cast it over the side, with the hope it will drift out of this ice-locked harbor and fare to the pathway of ships on the bosom of some sunny sea. After I have done this I will go to the chartroom and sit down by my dead grandfather and remain with him in his silent vigil, believing that when the chill which is nearing my heart reaches my brain, I too will become one of this ghostly company in this graveyard of lost ships, and when one o'clock comes I also will rise and walk again. ———

THE HATE

WILFORD ALLEN

The thing began far back in time, while the great Frank, Charles, claimed dominion over the rude western world. Deep in the mountain mass of northern Spain, a pair of youths loitered laughingly up a rocky path under the spotted shade of scrubby trees. A clatter and rattle of stones came suddenly from above, and they looked up to see a burly figure, accoutered in the skins and half-armor of the time, striding down the trail. Automatically, both lads stepped aside to let the petty noble pass; for who were they, common peasants and unarmed, to crowd such as he?

And then it happened, without reason or excuse. As he came abreast of the two, the stocky stranger suddenly whipped his short sword out, and in one quick motion ran it through the body of the nearer youth.

The other could have turned and run; indeed it was the expectation of the Killer that he would. If he had done so, the Killer would have roared and howled at his terrified flight, then have gone on his way, well pleased. But the other's reaction to the situation was not what the Killer's would have been, had the situation been reversed. Instead, he sprang full at the Killer's throat, unarmed though he was, but his frail strength was no match for the stouter man, who with a single hand brought the youngster into submission.

For a long moment the Killer looked gloatingly into the horrified eyes of the helpless boy; then, deliberately and shaking with fiendish laughter, he began to press the blade into the slender boy. Not quickly, as he had with the other, but slowly, pausing after each advancement of the stinging point to feast on the anguish of the dying lad, and, when that anguish did not seem of the ultimate degree, to twist the blade in the squirming body.

Whole minutes it lasted, and the end did not come until another Thing was born to take the place of the life which was ebbing into oblivion—a thing of which the Killer was unconscious then, but which was to live a thousand years; a Thing so contrary to the experience of human senses that it can not be described as one can describe a picture; a Hate too great ever to die until it had brought its maker and an adequate vengeance together. This hate can not be pictured: it was composed of that act which gave it birth, caught and frozen into invisible existence as if it were a four-dimensional thing, and also of its mission of Vengeance. Together they made up the Hate and gave it life and being, if not existence in time and space as we know them.

The day had been nasty. A thunderstorm of unparalleled violence had lasted from 3 o'clock until after dark, and the ground was still littered with the melting hailstones. A bedraggled figure in horizon-blue slogged from the trench into the officers' dugout and jerked painfully to a salute as it faced the lieutenant.

"Corporal," the officer said after a perfunctory acknowledgment of the salute, "it is not often that I beg a man's pardon, but I do for sending you out into this night of hell. But it must be done, for the colonel orders that we obtain information from in front of our sector. So it is you I am sending, for it is you who can do well what must be done well. Take two men, and tonight at fifteen minutes after 11 make patrol into the front and get the necessary information."

A night of hell it was. Caught by a flare, his two men were riddled at the very outset, leaving the corporal alone in his hole a bare stone's toss from the hostile trench. Ahead of him a machine-gun at the apex of a salient swept the ground about him with its humming death at each stir upon his part. The pain from his knee, which had been torn by a bullet that had mushroomed and cut the flesh into strips, throbbed in rhythm with the ever-pounding pulse. Pain was soon reinforced by fever and thirst, but, although the ground in the depression was yet moist from the recent deluge, no water had collected there, for it drained deeper into some dank cavern below, and he licked the steaming earth in the futile effort to stop the maddening thirst.

At last, in desperation, he drew himself chokingly over the edge of the hole. A burst of fire spurted toward him at the movement, and he tumbled back with blood streaming from a face marked with three parallel furrows. Another hour of torment passed; then, knowing that death was only a matter of time, the bullet-riddled Frenchman again stumbled over the edge of the shell-hole, but toward, not from, the enemy.

At the first appearance of his head over the earthen parapet the machinegun began to stutter, and the impact of heavy blows told the half-delirious man that he was being struck, though there was no sensation of pain from the fresh wounds. Grimly he staggered on, while the thud of bullets against his flesh kept time with the rapid put-put of the gun.

As the man still moved doggedly ahead, the stocky gunner in the salient began to wonder, and then to fear. Surely he could not be missing, but with equal certainty no human being could come on against that hail of death. Yet on the dimly visioned figure came. On, and on, and at last it was so close that in the weird light of the flares the gunner could see the shots shake their target. A leg was dragging awfully, but still the figure advanced in a series of hops.

A change came over the gunner. Fear vanished, and puzzlement, and there remained only a gloating joy as each tearing bullet struck. The gunner counted each burst of shots with a brutish grunt of satisfaction, as it tore through the approaching figure. But on the other came, a musket which it had picked up held out stiffly with bayonet fixed. Right up to the brink of the trench it came out of reach of the gun at last, and the gunner saw that the man was cut to pieces.

And then the gloating died and turned to fear. Fear and visions. Before him there lived the vision which had flamed in the consciousness of the other during that terrible march up to the spitting muzzle of the gun. In a distant twilight he saw the skin-clad figure of a lad, whom he was piercing with a stubby two-edged sword, his gloating smile met by a look of horror which gradually became transformed into one of unutterable hatred. The young figure sank lifeless, but on its face the hate still lived.

Outside, in the darkness following the death of a flare, the dead man lowered the point of the bayonet till it was level with the throat of the Killer; then he sprang. There was a burst of many-colored flame which lighted the world in the consciousness of both. Then they were gone. Only the sulfurous odor of the lines hung over the ground, which steamed in the darkness like a fetid thing. ⚔

THE HAUNTED WOOD OF ADOURE

ELLIOT O'DONNELL

There were three of us, Alphonse Duroque, literary editor of the Lyons *Gazette*, Gus Lawrence, sub-editor of the Chicago *Saturn*, and myself, and we were seated in the parlor of the only inn in Gretagne, discussing ghosts.

Presently Lawrence exclaimed, "Did you ever hear of an executioner being haunted? I have met quite a number in my time — Pete Barrow of St. Louis, Ed Gover of Saratoga, and a host of others, but when I have asked them if they have ever seen a ghost — and who more likely than a man who has sent so many people into the next world?—they have only laughed."

"That's in America," Duroque remarked quietly. "There seems to be some antagonism in that country of yours, either in the soil, or the atmosphere, or the people, that keeps ghosts away. In France it is different. I know an executioner in Lyons who once had a very startling experience with a ghost."

"Tell us about it," I chimed in.

"Eh bien," Duroque observed, "and remember it is true. I guarantee it. Vibert, who narrated it to me, never lies. He is—what do you call it?—the very incarnation, embodiment of veracity, and it happened to him, himself. At the time it occurred he had only recently been appointed to the post of assistant executioner in the Province of Bayenne, which, you doubtless know, lies about fifty miles to the southwest of the Cevennes. Well, one afternoon—to be correct it was the last afternoon in 1900—he left Ravignon, the town where he resided, and set off on his bicycle, one of the old-fashioned sort— push-bikes I think you call them—for Delapour, to make arrangements for an execution which was to take place there in a week or so's time. His knowledge of Bayenne was, at that period, very limited, and as he had forgotten to bring his road map with him, he had to stop frequently to ask the way. This, added to the roughness of the roads, which, for a considerable distance were undergoing repair, delayed him very considerably, and it was almost dusk when he reached Blanchepard, a tiny town lying barely half-way on the road to Delapour. Feeling hot and tired and badly in need of refreshment, he stopped at an inn and ordered refreshments."

"Wise man!" Lawrence remarked. "For a Frenchman, extremely sensible."

"Bayenne red wine and chicken," Duroque observed, ignoring the interruption, "are excellent things when one is tired, and Vibert did justice to them both. Indeed, he dallied so long over his meal that the dusk had given place to darkness and the shadows of night were already conspicuous by the roadside when he finally got up from the table and asked mine host the nearest way to his destination.

" 'The nearest way to Delapour,' mine host replied, his eyebrows contracting in a slight frown, 'is through the wood of Adoure, but I do not advise you to go that way tonight.'

" 'And why not, pray?' Vibert asked. 'Is the track very bad?'

"Mine host shook his head.

" 'No,' he said, 'the track is not bad. It isn't good—none of the roads in this part of Bayenne are good just at present, but it is passable. It is the wood itself, *monsieur;* it has not a good reputation.'

" 'Not a good reputation!' Vibert ejaculated. 'Bears, or robbers? Which?'

" 'No, *monsieur*, neither one nor the other. The wood is haunted; and tonight, remember, is New Year's Eve.'

" 'Surely it is only on Midsummer's Eve and All Hallow's E'en that the spirits of the dead wander,' Vibert laughed.

" 'That is so, *monsieur*,' mine host said gravely. 'It is the spirits of the living that are seen tonight and they sometimes rehearse deeds and scenes that are none too pleasant. If *monsieur* is wise he will shun the wood and get to Delapour by way of Baptiste and St. Gabrielle.'

" 'Is that a much longer way?' Vibert asked.

" 'It is longer by about five miles,' mine host replied.

" 'That settles it, then,' Vibert answered lightly. 'Ghosts or no ghosts I go through the wood,' and after settling his account with mine host, he once again mounted his machine and set off in the direction of the Wood of Adoure. Pedalling quickly through the main street of the little town that looked bright and festive, as it should do on New Year's Eve, he soon gained the high road, stretching as far as he could see into the gloomy countryside ahead of him. A few farm teams returning from their labor in the fields passed him, and an Old World, slow-going wagon, with its tinkling bells, swinging lamp, and quaintly clad driver; and these were the only cheery sights and sounds he was destined to encounter for some time.

"For many a mile after this the road led up a gradual ascent and Vibert was exposed to the full fury of a sudden windstorm that howled and moaned piteously. Having at last gained the summit of the hill he found himself on a seemingly interminable plateau. Overhead ragged clouds drifted over a wild, lowering sky, and all around him no living thing was visible, except a few rooks, whose croaking voices blended well with the soughing of the wind.

"Anxious to escape from this inhospitable spot, Vibert rode on as quickly as possible and eventually came to some crossroads, where a signpost pointed down a very steep descent to the Wood of Adoure. Some half-hour's careful riding, for the ground was very rocky and full of ruts, at length brought him to the confines of a forest of seemingly vast extent. He guessed at once it was the Wood of Adoure. He got off his bicycle to relight his lamp, which had suddenly gone out, and then, remounting his machine, pushed along a narrow track bordered on either side by tall trees, whose knotted and gnarled trunks gleamed a ghostly white wherever the moonbeams fell on them.

"The valley in which this wood was situated was far below the level of the road he had recently been traversing, and the wind, which had swept with great force across it, was here scarcely noticeable, and no sound save the faintest rustling of the tree tops far overhead and the occasional crackling of brushwood under the feet of some wild animal of the night was to be heard.

"Having arrived at a comparatively smooth piece of ground, albeit the descent was into a slight hollow, he was pedalling rather fast down it, when either a hare or a rabbit shot across his path, and in swerving to avoid it, he crashed into a boulder and was pitched over the handlebar of his machine. After a few seconds he got up, feeling rather dizzy and shaken, to find the front of his bicycle practically crumpled up. He was deploring the prospect of being obliged to perform the rest of his journey on foot, trundling the two wheels along with him as best he could, when through the naked branches of the trees, away in the distance, he espied a light.

"He at once made for it and found, to his joy, it proceeded from a small house on the banks of a swift-flowing and very swollen stream. In answer to his repeated raps, the weather-beaten door was at length very cautiously opened, and a girl appeared on the threshold, with a lamp. By its sickly light he saw she had black hair, very dark and rather obliquely set eyes, high cheek bones and perfectly even teeth that gleamed like pearls. She was good-looking, but it was in rather a strange way, and there was a curious glitter in her eyes as she stared at him that reminded him of the glitter he had seen in the eyes of leopards and other big animals of the cat tribe. Like so many French women, even of the poorer classes, she had very shapely hands, with long, tapering fingers and almond-shaped nails that shone like agates.

"In response to his request for a night's lodging she demurred, but, on his pleading inability to go any farther, owing to his complete state of exhaustion, she told him he could wait in the hall while she went to consult her husband.

"Apparently the house was very old. The hall was low-ceilinged, and stone-flagged, and on one side of it was an ingle, and on the other a broad oak staircase leading to a gallery. Several oil paintings in tarnished frames hung on the oak-paneled walls and in one corner stood a great grandfather clock, a fishing-rod and blunderbus.

"Vibert had no time to take in further details, for the girl now suddenly appeared in the gallery and telling him to come up stairs, bade him, before he did so, carefully to latch and lock the front door.

"On entering the room into which she ushered him, he received a surprize that almost amounted to a shock, for seated in an armchair by the fire was a feeble old man, who rose to greet him with difficulty.

" 'My husband,' the girl said shortly, avoiding Vibert's wondering gaze as she spoke. 'He is an invalid.' And she pointed to an array of medicine bottles on the mantelshelf. 'Henri!' and she raised her voice almost to a shout, 'this is the gentleman who wants a bed.'

" 'He can have one,' the old man croaked. 'Six francs bed and breakfast, and you pay me, not her. Money is not safe with women, they are too addicted to spending it.' And he gave a feeble laugh which ended in a wheeze.

" 'Asthma is one of his complaints,' the girl explained. 'He is seldom free from it. You would like some supper?'

" 'If it is not giving you too much trouble,' Vibert said, gallantly. 'I am famished.'

" 'Give him some ham and milk,' the old man chimed in. 'That is all we can do for you, *monsieur*, and it will be two francs extra. Food in these parts and at this time of the year is dear, very dear.' And leaning forward in his chair, he waved his skinny hands over the crackling pine logs—the only cheerful sound, Vibert thought, in the house.

"Supper over—he consumed it, conscious all the time that the dark, sloe-like eyes of the girl-wife were fixed on him with a strangely intent expression—he asked to be shown to his room. It was in a long corridor, lighted at the farthest end by an oriel window. The room, in keeping with the rest of the house, was low-ceilinged and oak-paneled and had many curious nooks and corners, besides several cupboards inset in the walls. In the center of the room stood a great, grim-looking four-poster bed, with the usual ponderous canopy, and over this and everything hung an atmosphere of gloom.

"Directly the girl was gone, Vibert scrambled into bed. He put his lighted candle on a little table close to the head of the bed, but well out of the way of the curtains, and for some minutes read an evening paper he had bought during his journey. Tired after his long ride, however, he gradually dozed off, leaving the candle still burning.

"He awoke suddenly and completely, with a vivid sense of being no longer alone. Opening his eyes he stared round, without lifting his head from his pillow, and reassured no one was in the room, he was about to close them again, when he suddenly heard the tap, tap of high-heeled shoes on the polished oak floor of the corridor, faint but distant, and growing nearer and nearer. All his faculties at once on the alert, he sat up in bed and listened. Saving for those sounds all was silent, with a death-like oppressive silence such as one never experiences save in lonely country places.

"There was not even a breath of wind stirring the leaves on the branches of the great elm trees outside, and inside not even the friendly scratching of a mouse to be heard behind the wainscotting. Nearer and nearer drew those footsteps, cautious, rather hesitating, but all the same persistent. They came right up to the door of Vibert's room and halted. Vibert could feel someone was there listening, intent on catching the sound of his breathing in order to tell if he were asleep or awake. Recollections of stories he had heard about murders in wayside inns came crowding into his mind and filled him with cold terror. It was so hopeless to be trapped here in this remote wood, miles away from any village or town and, in all probability, far away from any other dwelling, and he was unarmed, too. Like a fool he had forgotten to bring his revolver.

"He had a knife, a small pocket dagger, it was true, but of what use would that be against bludgeons or firearms? Would it not be better, he thought, to take the plotters by surprise and either burst through or attack them, than to have them suddenly burst into the room and attack him? Besides, the suspense was intolerable. Naturally brave and impulsive, he decided to adopt the former course.

"Getting out of bed without making a sound, and tiptoeing noiselessly across the room, he turned the key quickly in the door and tore it open, expecting to see, if not several, at least one person; namely, the wearer of the high-heeled shoes. To his utter amazement, however, the corridor was absolutely empty. Nothing was to be seen there saving the moon, shining clear and bright through the oriel window, and on the walls, looking out from their gilt frames, the calm, immovable faces of men and women, ancestors, presumably, of the old man who occupied the house.

"Vibert stood for some time straining his ears, but he could catch no sound, not even the ticking of the clock in the hall beneath. Thinking it very odd, but persuading himself that he must have been mistaken and that the sounds he had heard were due to rats, he shut the door softly and locking it, got back into bed.

"Once more he fell asleep, but only to awake, as before, very abruptly, and with a sensation of intense horror. The moonbeams poured in through the window and illuminating the curtains on either side of it, made them appear like tall specters. They gleamed, too, with an unearthly whiteness across the bed, and Vibert, constrained somehow to follow their course, observed that they shone with a peculiar intensity upon the door, and he could not remove his eyes from it. The handle of the door, especially, had a horrible fascination for him, and he kept watching it. He strove with all his might to look elsewhere, but he could not. All his senses seemed to be forcibly centered on it. Then, suddenly, he gave a great start. God in heaven, was it fancy or reality? The door-handle was turning.

"Slowly, very slowly, it turned and the door began equally slowly to open. He tried to move, to do something, but he could not. His limbs refused to act, he was paralyzed, paralyzed and tongue-tied. Still the door kept on opening, while the moonbeams seemed to get whiter and colder and the room fuller and fuller of them. Then, round the door there suddenly appeared a head and face, a bullet-shaped, close-cropped head, with very projecting ears and dark, gleaming eyes that wandered round the room and at last settled on the bed with ferocious glee.

"Vibert now became conscious of someone lying on the bed by his side. He saw nothing, for he was unable to remove his gaze from the face in the doorway, but he could hear the person beside him breathing, the deep, heavy inhalations of a person wrapped in profound slumber. Meanwhile the door kept on opening, and at last, into the room with soft, cat-like motion stepped a broad-shouldered, muscular man, holding in one hand a large horn-handled knife, the sharp blade of which gleamed hideously in the moonlight. Behind him, holding a basin in her hands, was the girlwife, a look of horrible cruelty in her sloe-like eyes. They approached the bed noiselessly, apparently too intent on the object by Vibert's side to notice Vibert himself. In a large mirror, i.e., a cheval glass that stood facing the foot of the bed, Vibert now saw, reflected with frightful clarity, everything that happened. He saw the man seize hold of the head of the recumbent person by his side, whom he now recognized with a thrill as the old husband of the girl. He saw the girl place her basin under her husband's neck and he watched her face light up with unholy glee as the cruel knife, flashing through the moonbeams, was drawn ruthlessly across the old man's throat. There was one awful gurgling groan and then silence, broken only by the ghastly sounds of rushing, dripping blood. For some minutes neither of the murderers stirred, but stood by their victim, alternately gazing at him and at each other. Then suddenly Vibert caught them in the mirror looking at him. His candle had long since gone out, and the moon being at this moment suddenly obscured behind clouds, the room was now plunged in utter darkness.

"Vibert made a colossal effort to move and free himself from the fearful terror which rendered him powerless. It was in vain.

"After what seemed an eternity the bed creaked and a big, coarse hand gripped him by the throat. At this juncture human nature succumbed and he fainted.

"When he recovered consciousness and opened his eyes, the early morning sun was pouring in through the window-panes and some-one was rapping loudly at the door. It was the young wife with his breakfast of coffee and a roll and fresh country butter. He looked round, in fearful expectancy of seeing some signs of the terrible drama he had witnessed in the night. There were none, and when he tried the door it was still locked on the inside.

"Much puzzled, for his experience seemed far too real and vivid for a dream, he took in his breakfast, and after consuming it, dressed and went downstairs.

"To add to his bewilderment the old husband who had played such a ghastly role in the midnight tragedy was sitting in front of the log fire in the parlor smoking serenely and occasionally wheezing.

" 'I hope *monsieur* slept well,' the girl wife said, as Vibert, having settled his account, prepared to depart.

" 'I had some rather queer dreams,' Vibert replied, looking with no little admiration at her teeth, which, as I have already remarked, glistened like pearls.

" 'Ah, *monsieur*, it was New Year's Eve,' the girl laughed. 'If they were unpleasant, I hope they won't come true.'

" 'I hope not, too,' Vibert said dryly, and bidding her good-bye, he picked up his broken bicycle and resumed his journey.

"Ten months later he was at Baptiste, this time in the capacity of executioner. It was a sudden call. Emile Guilgant, his chief, had been taken ill and he was called upon to act in his stead. Hitherto he had merely been Guilgant's understudy. He knew little about the case, saving that a man named Bonivon was to be guillotined for the murder of Gaspard Latour, a well-to-do, retired wine merchant of Marseilles. The murder had been committed in the Cevennes district and Latour's wife had assisted in it. Although she was probably the instigator of the crime, the judge who tried her, having regard to the verdict of the jury (French juries are noted for their leniency where women are concerned), merely sentenced her to a term of imprison-ment. That was all Vibert knew; he was ignorant of the exact spot where the crime had been committed and of the details of the case which had shocked all Bayenne.

"He did not see the condemned man till a few minutes before the execution, when, in company with two warders, he entered his cell to pinion him. He then received a shock. The man was the exact counterpart of the murderer in his dream or vision or whatever else it was that he had had on New Year's Eve in the Wood of Adoure.

This man that he was about to execute had the same bullet-shaped head, the same projecting ears, the same dark eyes and the same short, broad figure. Also, he had the same huge, coarse hands. Vibert would have known them anywhere; he had felt their grip, and a shudder ran through him as he looked at them.

"As their eyes met, an expression of bewilderment came into those of the murderer, which expression suddenly gave way to a look of recognition, mingled with diabolical hatred. Vibert said nothing; he simply pinioned the man, and walked with him to the scaffold.

"When it was over and he was lunching with several of the officials of the prison, he asked them where the murder had taken place and how it was done.

" 'Why, don't you know?' one of them replied. 'What curious chaps you executioners are! In the Wood of Adoure, of course. Bonivon cut poor old Latour's throat, while Madame Latour held a basin to catch the blood.' " ——

THE HIDDEN TALENT OF ARTIST BATES

SNOWDEN T. HERRICK

When Mr. John Haslet Bates was 20 and a student at the New York Art Student's League, he dreamed of Monet, Manet and Millet, and *la vie de Boheme de* Greenwich Village. At the age of 33 he had achieved a wife, three kids, the left half of a two-family house in semi-suburban Queens Village, and a career with Waxman, Flaxman, Carmichael and Oglethorpe, Inc., an advertising agency specializing in menswear, womenswear, sportswear and infantswear.

The particular task of artist Bates was to add to sketches drawn by other artists of men, women and children clad in garments of varying degrees of intimacy appropriate backgrounds. For instance, the man at the next desk in the W. F. C. & O. art department would draw a picture of a luscious damsel clad in a Beautiform Foundation ("builds you up without a letdown"). Bates would create around this gorgeous item a Chippendale boudoir and a feeling of frustration.

Because Bates' soul still harbored an ambition: to draw the figures as well as the backgrounds. Unfortunately, in common with many artists. Bates was unable to draw a human being that looked like anything but a self-portrait. What's more, he was always the only one who couldn't see the resemblance. Since he was personally distinguished by an Adam's apple that protruded beyond his chin, his involuntary self-portraits were scarcely of commercial value. In landscapes he was the Cezanne of the ad world; in figures he should have stuck to finger painting.

The man who was aware of this crippling weakness in Bates' artistic armory was thereby responsible in Bates' mind for dooming the poor draftsman to a life of inanimate objects, and he hated him with a hatred as intense as his Adam's apple was prominent. The target of this consuming feeling was his art director, Mr. Clifton Oglethorpe, vice-president of W. F. C. & O. in charge of the art department. Oglethorpe was a man who wore sincere neckties until the publication of "The Hucksters" sent sincere neckties out of fashion in the advertising business. He was as unaware that the drab little artist hated him as he was convinced that "Advertising Is the Life Blood of the American Way of Life."

The great day of John Bates came in the summer of 1948—but he did not realize it at the time. New Yorkers remember it well, because that was the day the tower fell off the Empire State Building. An unsuspected structural fault, the investigators said, weakened by the incessant swaying of the world's tallest building.

On that day Bates was handed a picture of two implausibly handsome men wearing Heart o' Hollywood LEEsure jackets. His job was to place them in a New York skyline setting, to indicate, perhaps, the coast-to-coast stylishness of the jackets. He quickly penciled in the skyline, with windows suggested here and there, and sent it on its way through the channels of W. F. C. & O.

In about 30 minutes Clifton Oglethorpe bounded out of his office, furnished with blond-wood desk, bar and bookcase, and lined with proofs of prize-winning ads. Carrying the skyline and jacket drawing between his fingers, he fluttered it in front of Bates' Adam's apple.

"For God's sake," he snapped. "Are you blind, Bates?"

"Yessir," said Bates, out of habit.

"Can't you see that this space is reserved for the copy? We've got enough trouble trying to fit in the trade mark, the slogan, the store name, the firm name, the fabric name, the address and the price without your sticking the Empire State Building up there."

"Yessir," said Bates.

"Dammit all, you fix that right up. We've got to get it approved in fifteen minutes."

"Yessir," said Bates.

The artist bared his teeth at the receding figure of the art director, picked up his art gum eraser, and savagely erased the tower of the Empire State Building. At that precise instant, the great collapse occurred which was to leave the Chrysler building without peer.

Bates, working in an office in the East Fifties, didn't learn about the disaster on 34th Street until he was reading his evening paper on the subway to Queens. By then it was too late to put two and two together.

A few days later a similar incident took place. Bates was, as usual, doing a background job, this time in Radio City. The ad would show a group of youngsters wearing Kiddiekins Snosuits peering over the edge of the sunken plaza at the foot of the RCA Building. Bates was sketching the sprawling statue of Prometheus surrounded by the circle of the zodiac (or escaping the wedding ring, as local mythology has it).

In drawing the gilded Titan he was having trouble with the rock upon which Prometheus is precariously balanced. Reflecting that this was probably the closest he would ever get to drawing a figure, he rubbed out the rock. The famous Greek promptly dove into the fountain.

Bates was happy to be present at this interesting event, but he still didn't catch on. The great revelation of his hidden talent was scheduled for that very night, when he was working late and alone at the office.

Bent over his sloping drawing board, Bates was afflicted simultaneously by the stifling darkness of the night, by his secret yearning and by his hatred of Oglethorpe. His model was an elaborately embroidered peacock tapestry draped on an easel. Before him was a sheet of paper bearing a menswear masterpiece Bates had had no part in—a picture of a pipe-smoking, supercilious young man wearing a gaudy necktie. Forming a border around the ad-to-be were many more gaudy ties ("Tw-w-w-ist them, pul-l-l them, thr-r-r-ow them in the furnace"). Roughed-out lettering said: "Be a peacock . . . attract the female of the species," followed by an idiot row of exclamation points.

It was up to Bates to copy laboriously the peacock in the white space reserved for it alongside the young man. He found it very discouraging. He didn't like working late, anyway, because it interfered with his efforts to keep the left side of his two-family garden more productive than the rival right side. Furthermore, he considered it rank unjustice for Oglethorpe to put a landscape man to work on a silly fowl when the art staff included a perfectly good bird, beast and baby man. Finally, the drawing wasn't going well at all. The tail was way out of proportion.

With a quick, peevish swipe, he drew his art gum across the offending tail feathers. As he did so, he heard a tearing noise. It wasn't the paper, thank God, and then he looked up at the embroidered peacock and trembled. Matching perfectly the erasure mark was a rip through the peacock's tail. Bates nervously dropped the art gum and sat back in his chair. He stared at the mutilated cloth and at his drawing. He fumbled with his pencil. He picked up the rubber square and looked at it. He very lightly brushed the peacock's head on the paper. The embroidered head dimmed. He rubbed harder. A hole appeared in the cloth. He stopped to think.

In his not especially perceptive mind, John Haslett Bates lined up the peacock and the diving statue. Then he reached back and added the Empire State incident. There was no getting away from it: this nonentity of an advertising artist, slave to a huckster, was not as other men. With a flick of his wrist he could literally erase buildings.

Other men might have had other thoughts, but Bates' first reaction on discovering his new talent was not an exalted one: how was he to explain the damage to the peacock? An idea came. He hastily completed his drawing, hoping it would be acceptable. Then, on another piece of paper, he copied the peacock and the cloth it was on, faithfully imitating every fold. With the eraser he obliterated the drawing of the fabric. When he was through the easel was bare. As he swept up the dust, he thought, "they can ask me where it is. The last I saw of it was tonight, when I went home."

For the sake of his explanation he went down the elevator empty-handed. On the ride home he paid little attention to his paper (which carried a picture of Prometheus on his belly) and on his arrival he neglected children, wife and garden. His wife remarked that he was working too hard. He laughed, the first time he had ever laughed at that suggestion.

The laughter continued, in secret, and in secret the mousy Bates became a practical joker. On the subway in the morning a woman's hat with three pomegranates and two pheasant's feathers tickled his nose. He sketched it on the margin of his paper, erased it, and it crumbled around her ears—to her consternation and loud cries.

One evening his neighbor made an unfortunate comparison of the two gardens. From behind a curtain Bates drew and erased the neighbor's highest hollyhocks and biggest roses. He derived considerable satisfaction from the determined war on Japanese beetles which followed.

But this was petty stuff for Bates. He wanted to draw figures and he wanted retaliation for the indignities he had suffered from Ogle-thorpe. And then one day he had his answer.

He would draw two pictures. One would be a fashion drawing for the new College-Tex Fruit of the Lamb Clothing account ("climb out of that barrel and get into a College-Tex—the *Class* of the Year"). This he would present to Oglethorpe to prove his ability. The concept of the other picture was a triumph of the Batesian imagination. This drawing would be a carefully done portrait of Clifton Oglethorpe himself—complete to the cutaway collar and sunlamp tan. If Oglethorpe should reject his request for advancement, woe to Oglethorpe. An eraser operation on his picture would be much more enjoyable than sticking pins in a wax image.

Bates worked late all week on his project and both drawings were finished by Monday morning. The clothing drawing looked very handsome to him; considering the subject, he couldn't say the same for the Oglethorpe portrait. Clearing his throat and adjusting his tie, he picked up the fashion art and went in to see the vice president in charge of the art department.

"Mr. Oglethorpe," he began.

"Yes," said Oglethorpe.

"Mr. Oglethorpe, I'd like you to look at this picture for the College-Tex account. I'm sure I can do figures now, and I wish you would give me another chance to draw something besides backgrounds."

Oglethorpe took the picture, examined it, and smirked.

"Bates, you've still got your old trouble. Look at that Adam's apple; a customer for College-Tex Fruit of the Lamb doesn't want to think he looks like *that*. Until you can stop drawing pictures of yourself, you'd better stick to furniture and landscapes."

Bates felt the top of his head grow warm, and with a mouse's fury he scampered out of the office. He sat down at his desk and mumbled, "I'll show him, I'll show him."

He picked up the drawing of Oglethorpe and said to himself: "Doesn't like Adam's apples, eh? I'll fix *his* Adam's apple."

Fiercely he drew his eraser across Oglethorpe's penciled throat— and slumped over his drawing board, the blood streaming from his own neck. He hadn't been able to draw anyone but himself. His portrait of the art director looked exactly like John Haslet Bates.

THE HIGH PLACES

FRANCES GARFIELD

*. . . the high places of our air are swarming full of those
wicked spirits, whose temptations trouble us.*
— COTTON MATHER: *The Devil Discovered*

We were still arguing as Swithin parked his car in the gloom at
the edge of the airport—arguing gently. Everything about
Swithin was gentle, even his arguments. For a moment we sat
together in the snug dim light of the car's interior. Swithin's lean
gloved hands rested slackly on the wheel, and his soft gray eyes
regarded me thoughtfully, studiously.

"Here we are, Katharine," he said, "but I still have that premonition about the danger of your flying. For the last time, please let me
take you to the railroad station."

"And for the last time," I said firmly, "I've got to budget my
hours. I want to spend the week with my brother, not on trains."

It was true. I could spare only a week from my job, and my
brother Bill was getting married, a thousand miles away in Chicago.
A plane was the only answer, and Swithin at last bowed his brown
head in token of defeat. We got out together, went through a gate,
and across the wide, flat field.

The long hangar was dimly illuminated at one end, with only
three or four men in sight—mechanics, I supposed. Floodlights illumined a cemented patch, with strange shadows clustered around.
No other passengers; I would be alone on the spur hop to Wichita,
where we met the TWA.

Swithin put his arm around me.

"Wire me at once when you land," he whispered, and kissed me.
It soothed, that kiss, if it did not galvanize. "And now I'll go. I hate
to see a loved one sail away from me."

We parted, and I turned to meet an attendant who took from me
my two suitcases. The plane was already buzzing, like a huge
dragon-fly ready to skim off above oceanic ponds and immense
reeds and lily pads. And now I thought, as I tried not to think, of
Enic Graf, who had done things to my heart I had never thought
possible, who had hurt and dazzled me, whom I was to have married
when, a year ago, he fell out of the sky, aflame in a flaming ship.

Dead now, his body ashes where other bodies were dust, he could

239

still make my heart stop, my feet falter, my lips grow dry. Even now I had not wholly escaped his compelling, crude grasp; not even though Swithin and I had found each other, had settled into a tender and peaceable relationship of understanding happiness.

The pilot was before me, saluting as though I were a superior officer.

"You're the passenger for Wichita, lady?" he asked in a high, cheerful voice. "We're ready if you are."

"Thank you," I said. Who had said that all pilots resembled each other, with piercing, narrow eyes and square jaws? This was a thin-faced young man, stooped in the shoulders and as anxious to please as a waiter. Not much about him of Rickenbacker, Lindbergh, Corrigan, nothing at all of Enic Graf. "What sort of a journey will we have?"

He shook his head dubiously. "Lots of clouds off there," he said, and for the first time I realized that the moon should be shining.

He helped me into the cabin of the plane. It was all of brown paneling and wide glass panes, like the inside of a station wagon, and had room for only three passengers. I took the seat behind his, and he drew a safety belt of strong webbing across in front.

"Maybe we'll have bumpy weather," he explained.

And then we were off, off and up. A glance sidewise showed me the lights and the hangar dropping and dwindling. Dew seemed forming on the pane beside me, and the upward slope of the ship made me slide down into the angle of the seat.

I had never flown before—strange, since I had known and loved Enic. I would not be flying now, if Swithin had had his way. I sought for novel impressions, but it all seemed as if I had done it before. Perhaps too many friends had talked to me of the joys and thrills of flying.

The light in the cabin was too dim to read by, and in any case a humming vibration of the craft would make reading uncomfortable. I leaned back and closed my eyes, thinking of Bill and his approaching happiness, of the gift I had brought for the Mrs. Bill to be—a Zorinos cape, one I would have loved to keep. It was stowed behind me, in one of the suitcases, all of brown skins sewed together in little bands that displayed in a succession of patterns, like the graining of fine wood, the pelt-markings. She would like it, no matter what type of woman she might be. The thought came, and I dismissed it, of the day when my own wedding had been at hand, and the news of Enic's crash came like a heavy door slamming against my face. And then I was asleep. I dreamed the plane was falling.

I awakened with a sickening jerk. I may have screamed. The pilot turned halfway around.

"What's the matter, lady?" he called above the growl of the motor.

"I had a bad dream," I called back.

"Don't be scared. No danger. Just bumpy weather—clouds. I'm going to get above them."

There was evidently rain, and the windows were thickly misted. The pilot did things with his controls, and again the nose of the craft lifed itself, as though it climbed steep stairs. I could see the hands of the pilot on his instruments. They, at least, were typical, comfortingly so—big, blunt, capable. Enic's hands had been long and sensitive, like a surgeon's or a violinist's, and across the back of his right hand had sprawled a jagged Z of a scar. Again I drove the thought of him from my mind, and lay back for another snatch of the sleep that seemed determined to possess me.

My awakening was calm. The plane flew on a smooth level, and light filled the abyss outside my window. I mopped with one gloved hand at the glass, and peered out into a sky filled with the light of the great cream-colored moon. Far below were the clouds, or what must be the clouds, a drab continent without visible rent or lump in it. I gasped with the beauty of it, then with the terror of thinking how high we must be.

"What's our altitude, pilot?" I cried out, trying to be gay.

His head began to turn on his stooped shoulders—to turn slowly, slowly. And of a sudden I thought I was going mad.

It was not his lean face that came around, but the face of another, a face that I knew. Square jaw, wide lips with bracket-like lines at their corners, proud broken nose, eyes as deep and dark and shining as two pools by lanternlight—so pale, so stiff, so utterly without the flavor of Enic Graf, yet so unmistakably Enic.

Frost-cold nails of fear dug into my backbone. I reasoned with myself, flatly and a little stupidly, as one reasons with a panicky child. This wasn't Enic—Enic's handful of remains had gone to the grave twelve months before. It was a mask. That was it, a false face, cunningly made but not cunningly enough.

I leaned forward.

"This is a very poor joke," I said, too loudly for dignity. "And it's a cruel one."

And I heard his soft chuckle, as plainly as though the engine had shut off—his soft, deep chuckle, the chuckle with which Enic once maddened and conquered me. The face came all the way around, and, for all its stiffness and dead pallor, the eyes were bright and alive.

"Joke?" he repeated, in Enic's deep voice, and chuckled again. "I don't joke with you, Katharine."

His left hand only remained on the controls. His right elbow hooked over the back of his seat, and its hand came into view—a slender, delicate hand, a hand I knew, and upon its back, shining in the dimness like touchwood, a jagged Z-scar.

All these details wavered before my eyes, like a very old motion picture, but I could not deny that they were definite. The pilot had changed, had melted and run into a travesty of Enic. Reason tried to hold command, frantically and inadequately, like a leader against whom tried old troops had rebelled.

Something dawned in my head, a saving thought: ectoplasm . . . what was it? I had heard of ectoplasm, had read of it in Swithin's books, had laughed over a comedy film about it. The name of the film was *Topper*—but that was hardly important now. Ectoplasm, the spirit-commanded aura that could flow forth, become solid and take shape, to form upon a living body the strange semblance of a dead person—this must be the answer.

"Who are you?" I asked, knowing all the time who it was, and Enic chuckled yet again, with almost honest mirth.

"Why do you ask, Katharine?" he mocked me, in that soft deep voice that I could hear above the roar of the motor. "There's no reason to ask."

"What do you want?" I cried, and marveled at the hysterical ring of my voice in my own ears.

"You," he answered. "You, of course." Dead hand lifted to dead face, long fingers tapped line-bracketed cheek. "Did you think you would ever be quit of me? I died up here, Katharine. And I waited. You came up, and we're together again."

I shrank back, as though he had moved to seize me. "But you're dead," I protested wildly. "And I'm—I'm alive!"

"Yes," he nodded, as one who concedes an unimportant item of a discussion. "Anyway, you aren't bringing Swithin into this." His lips widened in a tigerish grin. "You don't love him as much as you think."

"Enic," I said, and paused to govern my voice. I must keep steady, in word and in heart and in mind. "Enic, you're wrong. I love Swithin."

"And you don't love me?" His voice was suddenly plaintive, offering the note that had so often melted my resolve in the past.

"I can't love you, Enic. Not now. You're dead," I cried at him again. "The dead can't love—"

"Can't they, though?" His left hand crawled over his controls, doing something I did not recognize. "I'm dead, but I love you. I'll have you, Katharine. You'll see."

The ship bucked and leaped around us. Suddenly I slid forward in my seat, almost fell out of it but for the safety belt.

"What's happening?" I screamed.

The motor's roar rose high, cracked, and became a terrifying whine.

"We're falling," said Enic, and still his voice could dominate the din. "I'm letting us crash, Katharine."

"No! No!" I begged.

"You'll never feel it," he told me, as though to comfort me. "We're going faster, Katharine—faster—you'll lose your wits, go to sleep—to sleep—and when you awaken—"

That whining wail was the air that tore at the struts, I knew. It was quieter now, or my ears were growing numb. And the pale, stiff face of Enic Graf was growing dim, distant. Fog shadowed it.

"We'll be together up here in the heights," he was promising me, not loudly, but from worlds away. "Together, Katharine—"

I was hanging limp against my safety belt. It was the only solid thing in the universe. And I went deaf, blind. I was swallowed by black silence.

Then a roar, a prickling sensation in my toes, and lurid light in my eyes; it sounded as though the motor was going. And a high, anxious voice was dinning at me: "Lady! Lady, are you all right?"

I pawed at my face, sat up straight. The plane was traveling on a level once more. And the pilot, his heavy hands on the controls, was sitting with his thin face half over his shoulder.

"That was a close call," he told me, striving hard to sound cheerful.

"Was it?" I mumbled idiotically. I knew that I looked unkempt, that my hat must be askew, my rouge smeared. For the moment I did not care. "What happened to us?" I demanded.

"Well, I don't rightly know," he said, slowly and embarrassedly, like a schoolboy unable to recite. "I got up above the clouds, 'way up there, and tried to level her out—and she kept going up."

He shook his head and thrust out his thin jaw. "Nothing jammed or anything, because it's all right now. But she kept going up, up, as if a big hand had grabbed us and was lifting us."

"Yes," I prompted. "And then?"

"Then I seemed to pass out. Maybe the air was thin . . . but I didn't have any sense of danger. It was more like leaning back while the relief pilot takes the controls. Does that sound crazy?"

"Not very crazy," I assured him. "But you don't remember what happened?"

"Not a thing," he confessed. "Not until we were falling, and I shook it off and pulled us out of the dive."

I gazed at him searchingly. "What's your name, pilot?"

"Alvin Piper." He cleared his throat. "If you're going to make a complaint, lady, that's your privilege. But I got a wife and two kids in school—"

"I won't complain," I promised. "I was wondering, Mr. Piper, if you ever knew a pilot named Graf. Enic Graf."

"Graf? I don't think so—no, wait." He nodded fiercely. "I used to know a Graf who tested for the Stearman people. Had a broken nose, and a big scar on his hand."

"That's right," I agreed.

We suddenly sailed into a dim clearness. Moonlight washed the fogged windows.

"Weather's breaking up already," the pilot informed me with deep satisfaction. "That's Wichita up ahead, where the lights are. . . . But what's Enic Graf got to do with this business, lady? He died a year ago."

"Did he?" I asked, and in spite of myself I laughed shortly.

The pilot looked at me strangely, wonderingly, but I could not tell him why I doubted. I could not tell Swithin, or my brother Bill. I could not tell anyone.

I knew only that I must never fly again, lest Enic be waiting for me in the upper abyss. —✠—

HIS BROTHER'S KEEPER

CAPTAIN GEORGE FIELDING ELIOT

John Dangerfield was in love with his brother's fiancée—a position whose difficulties were somewhat ameliorated by the fact that from early childhood he had been accustomed to take away from his brother Horace any of Horace's possessions that he fancied; and oddly enough, he had always fancied what Horace cherished most.

Now he fancied Leslie Monroe—and that blond young lady was by no means unconscious of the fact. Nor was she unconscious of the difference between being the wife of a younger son, a mere pensioner, and being the wife to the heir of Cragmore.

She stood now by John's side in a dusty room on the third story of an old brick warehouse, listening to the chatter of a gray little man in a skull-cap. The room was filled with odds and ends of every description, over which the gray little man waxed eloquent.

"This armor is really remarkable," the gray little man was saying. "But if you aren't interested in that, Mr. Dangerfield, here's something that will strike your fancy. It's the queerest thing I've had here for many a day; I found it in Nuremberg, and I've had it restored and put in good order."

He had paused before an object that looked like an up-ended sarcophagus. It was a little taller than a full-grown man, and entirely of iron. On its front it bore a bas-relief of a female figure; it was perhaps three feet wide, and twice as deep.

"Looks like a deep coffin stood on end," John Dangerfield remarked.

"Right!" the dealer replied. "Look here!"

He swung the back of the thing out on heavy hinges, like a door. At the bottom of this door was a stout shelf of iron; above this was fitted an assortment of iron bands, hinged and provided with locks. The dealer flashed the ray of a pocket torch into the dark interior; protruding back from its forward wall Leslie and Dangerfield saw six long, tapering iron spikes, glittering and sharp.

"This," the gray little man gloated, "is a genuine Iron Maiden! It is four hundred years old—built especially to the order of Duke Otho of Franconia. That whole front is movable; moves back into the box at the rate of about a half-inch every ten minutes; propelled by steel springs of incredible power. You put your victim against this door, standing on the shelf, and fasten him tight with the iron bands. The man can't move a muscle when they're all locked. Then you swing the door shut—so—putting your victim facing the spikes; a touch on this lever releases the mechanism, and the spikes move toward him. They're over a foot away to start with; gives him plenty of time to think over his sins! Note the spikes—the two bottom ones are the longest, and are supposed to pierce the groin or lower abdomen; then when they are well embedded, the next two pierce the shoulders; finally the last two pierce the poor devil's eyes, reach his brain at last and put him out of his misery. I fancy the whole process takes about six hours, from the time the machinery commences to move until the victim is dead."

"What a horrible, dreadful thing, John!" Leslie Monroe exclaimed. "Please take me away—I can't bear to look at it."

"Just as you say, dear," John Dangerfield answered tenderly. "We'll be going now, Nathan; I may be back to see you later."

"Monday, if you please, Mr. Dangerfield," the little gray man answered. "It's Saturday afternoon, sir; I'm closing up."

He opened the door leading to the dark landing. The man who had been so patiently waiting there in the shadows struck one savage blow and lowered the limp body of the dealer gently to the floor.

"What's the matter, Nathan?" John Dangerfield asked, hearing the thud of the blow. There was no answer; John in his turn stepped out upon the landing, and again the watcher in the shadows struck. The blackjack did its work well; John Dangerfield collapsed in a crumpled heap beside the dealer. The man who had struck him down stepped over his body into the storeroom to confront Leslie Monroe.

"Why, Horace!" she cried. "What are you—"

Then the light from the window fell full upon his face—his eyes—and Leslie Monroe fainted.

Horace Dangerfield laughed; the cunning, triumphant laugh of a madman.

"I've waited long," he muttered. "Too long—nothing has been adequate before. But this—this will do. This will satisfy me."

When John Dangerfield came to himself, he was in dust-filled darkness. He could not move, something was choking him—

Something was an iron collar, locked tight about his neck—his forehead was held back by an iron band—his wrists and ankles were in manacles—there was a dreadful clanking sound somewhere in the gloom.

Warm against his breast he felt living flesh—he realized that Leslie Monroe was there, bound tightly to him by straps or ropes: he spoke her name, but she did not answer.

The truth leaped upon John Dangerfield like a pouncing tiger. He was locked in the Iron Maiden, with Leslie Monroe bound before him so that the spikes would reach her first! He raised his voice:

"Help! Help!"

The words reverberated mockingly in that iron tomb; even more mockingly a voice from without answered.

"Cry again, John! There is no one to hear—save the Iron Maiden! I was listening last night when you told Leslie you wanted to be with her even in death; you have your wish. Good-bye, John!"

"Horace, for the love of God—"

But only the sound of retreating feet and the slamming of a door answered. The machinery clanked again; and the first cruel touch of steel points revived the swooning Leslie.

The gloomy room rang with a woman's screams. ——

THE HUNCH

GENE LYLE III

John McCassey refused to admit, even to himself, that he was running away from anything so intangible as a hunch. He had to have a rest from the strain of work. This was his entirely legitimate excuse. But it was a rationalization too, because McCassey would not have left merely for a rest.

West, where the sun set, where nothing ever happened, was where John McCassey wanted to go. As usual he was in a hurry, and he started out in an airliner, but it got him no farther than Santa Fe. Landing at dusk at that ancient slumberous city, the flight was canceled due to the storm. So the agent got him a seat on the first train out, to which happened to be attached a special car bearing twenty or so congressmen on an inspection tour of naval equipment.

McCassey was a thin man, taut as a violin string, with sharp nose and restless eyes continually darting from one object to another. In the brightly lighted club car he tossed his dripping topcoat on the rack and plunked down beside a heavy-set fellow.

The warmth, the commotions of other passengers settling themselves, gave him a slight sense of peace. But deep within him the notion lingered that he was being fooled by it.

A hospital odor drew his attention to the man beside him. The fellow, dressed neatly in gray serge, was thick-lipped, broad-shouldered, middle-aged. He had stubby muscular hands and he might have been a prosperous farmer except that McCassey, thinking always in terms of headlines, detected a familiar crinkle about the eyes. McCassey recognized him as the most publicized surgeon in the land. He was gazing morosely out the rain-streaked window.

On an impulse McCassey introduced himself. "I'm managing editor of *The Chicago Call*," he said. "How'd you dodge the reporters while that Brandt case is still on page one?"

The surgeon frowned. His thick lips quivered. "The little Brandt boy will pull through," he said. "It was quite simple—we merely relieved the pressure on his brain. I don't think he'll have epilepsy any more."

"But that's revolutionary, isn't it?" the editor insisted.

"Possibly. It's been thought of before. All it required was the development of a technique. Look here," he said abruptly, "I'll tell you why I'm leaving town. I'm—well," his voice became a hoarse whisper, "I'm taking my daughter home to her mother in San Diego."

It sounded like domestic trouble and McCassey said no more about it. Besides, he distinctly felt a tightening at his throat. He had been half expecting this symptom, dreading it.

"You don't believe in premonitions, do you?" he asked.

Something in his voice made the surgeon look curiously at him. "Plenty of historical evidence," the surgeon said. "Witches, soothsayers, that sort."

"I mean living people," said McCassey.

"Such cases are reported. I wouldn't bet on one though."

"No, of course not," said McCassey. "I wouldn't either. But here's something funny. Whenever there's a major news break, hours before it happens I get to feeling tense."

The surgeon ruminated a moment. "Events leading up to a news break—movement of troops to a border for instance—could make you expect it before it happens, don't you think?"

"It's not that," said McCassey. "I never have any idea what it's going to be or where it's going to happen. That's the devil of it. I've come to rely on these hunches in spite of myself. They've never failed me. But each time the strain leaves me as limp as a wet rag."

McCassey grew more agitated as the journey progressed. Other passengers shot glances at him. The surgeon wondered if there was another seat where he could be by himself, but seeing none gave it up.

"I had one of those hunches when I left Chicago this morning," McCassey went on. "I'm afraid that's the real reason I left. Thought I could get away from it. But I can't—it's been growing stronger."

The harsh honk-honk of the engine whistle, sounding incongruously like an old-fashioned automobile horn, signaled for a crossing. Scattered lights of a mountain town flashed past outside, trees and frame buildings glistening in the rain. McCassey jerked back his sleeve and glanced at his watch.

"We're pulling into Albuquerque," he said breathlessly. "I'm going to send a wire."

He rang for the porter, demanded telegraph blanks, and when they came he frenziedly scribbled out a message. The surgeon watched the words appear:

HYLLIS GARDNER—CITY EDITOR THE CALL—
CHICAGO—KEEP WIRES OPEN HOLD STAFF
READY FOR EXTRA EDITION

That was all. McCassey's pencil ripped the yellow paper as he scratched his signature across the bottom.

"You'll have me believing it in a minute," the surgeon said.

Beads of sweat appeared on McCassey's thin forehead. "At times like this," he said, "something keeps driving me. I want to start organizing the story, getting the facts sifted, the leads written. But — but the story hasn't happened yet!"

The train eased into the station. McCassey hustled the porter off with his telegram. He fidgeted with his pencil during the few minutes halt. Then the train resumed its gentle vibration.

By now McCassey was powerless to fight off this sense of impending catastrophe. It had nothing to do with logic. It was maddeningly like a memory one tries to recall and can't. And like the memory of a thing that has happened, it was somehow irrevocable. It was the crashing drive of fate. He had to accept it as though it were fact and yet not completely fact either. Such thoughts have driven men crazy. Again he glanced at his watch.

"I sent that wire half an hour ago," he said aloud.

His voice startled the surgeon out of a deep revery. "Why, you're trembling like a leaf," the big man said.

"I've got to stop this train!" McCassey burst out. He started to rise, but the surgeon grasped his thin shoulder and eased him back.

"You need a sedative," the surgeon said. "You're on the verge of hysteria."

McCassey did not resist. Like a man in dread of the operating-table, he welcomed an anodyne to blank out his mind. The surgeon pulled down a grip and brought out a medicine-case. He brought a paper cup of water and handed McCassey a pill.

"Here," he said. "You'll feel better."

Greedily McCassey swallowed the pill.

The rhythm of the train pervaded McCassey as the drug touched and soothed his jagged nerves. The surgeon sighed, and slumped back in his chair as though exhausted. It struck McCassey as odd how phlegmatic this much-publicized man now seemed. For a short time McCassey remained aware of the imminence of disaster without much caring. And then even the awareness left him. A comfortable drowsiness crept over him.

He blinked, for he thought he saw a young woman bending over the back of his seat, talking to the surgeon. Possibly she was a deception of the eyes. He could not be sure. Still, he became aware of certain features. Lacking any make-up, with skin like ghostly blue marble, she had a sensuous, full-lipped beauty. Her voice came clear and bell-like. McCassey forced himself to concentration. He distinguished words.

"Daddy, daddy! Listen to me!" She seemed to be pleading. Strangely, the surgeon did not hear her. He was dozing, his head bowed over his thick chest. Yet the girl seemed frantic.

"Why don't you shake him?" McCassey asked.

Wildly, uncertainly, the girl looked about. She saw McCassey, and there was terror in her eyes. "I've tried," she said despairingly. "It doesn't do any good. But I've got to tell him something—I've got to! Maybe you—"

And then an odd realization came to McCassey. He was like a man in a dream who is restrained from doing certain ordinarily simple things. The surgeon was outside the realm of his dream.

"I guess I can't do it," McCassey said. "But wait—try this." He brought out his notebook and pencil and offered them to her. "Write down what you want."

She snatched the pencil and wrote frantically. "Oh, hurry—make him read this!"

As McCassey tore the sheet out of his notebook he saw what she had written.

"Stop the train," he read. "Bridge out. Alice."

He looked up, but the girl was not there. With a sudden chill the impending catastrophe flashed back to him. This was it, the thing the future had withheld! He tottered to his feet and ran stumblingly toward the vestibule. He found the emergency airbrake line and yanked it, hard.

Airbrakes screeched, couplings clashed. McCassey lurched to the floor. He felt the train shudder to a full stop. And then he wondered if he were mad, doing this thing. No longer did he have that feeling of imminent danger.

Excited passengers brushed past. McCassey pulled himself up, made his way through the vestibule and down the steps. People were running toward the engines, their feet grating in the wet gravel of the roadbed.

McCassey ran past the two locomotives, feeling the heat of their big driving-wheels. A crowd was gathering on the tracks in the headlights, not more than fifty feet ahead. He pushed his way through. He saw the approach to a trestle bridge. Twisted girders hung limp into the black chasm where the bridge had been. From far below came the rumble of torrential waters.

"There's the guy who stopped the train!" someone yelled. The voice sounded awed.

People crowded around McCassey. One man displayed a badge in his palm. He was a Secret Service man, and McCassey remembered the congressmen in their special car.

On the edge of the crowd McCassey saw the surgeon.

"It must have washed out only a few minutes ago," the Secret Service man said. "How'd you know?"

McCassey wiped the rain out of his eyebrows.

He called to the surgeon.

"Your daughter gave me a note," McCassey told the surgeon. "The note said the bridge was gone."

The big doctor stared at him, his thick lips gaping slightly. He seemed almost terrified. "What are you talking about?" he demanded.

"Her name was Alice," McCassey said. "Here—" he reached into his pocket, but his hand came out empty. "I must have lost that note," he said.

The blood had drained from the surgeon's face. It was gray.

"Alice was her name," he said. "Listen," he said, grasping McCassey's lapel, "she's—she's up in the baggage car!" ⭲

HYPNOS

H. P. LOVECRAFT

"Apropos of sleep, that sinister adventure of all our nights, we may say that men go to bed daily with an audacity that would be incomprehensible if we did not know that it is the result of ignorance of the danger."

—BAUDELAIRE

May the merciful Gods, if indeed there be such, guard those hours when no power of the will, or drug that the cunning of man devises, can keep me from the chasm of sleep. Death is merciful, for there is no return therefrom; but with him who has come back out of the nethermost chambers of night, haggard and knowing, peace rests nevermore. Fool that I was to plunge with such unsanctioned phrensy into mysteries no man was meant to penetrate; fool or god that he was—my only friend, who led me and went before me, and who in the end passed into terrors which may yet be mine.

We met, I recall, in a railway station, where he was the centre of a crowd of the vulgarly curious. He was unconscious, having fallen in a kind of convulsion which imparted to his slight black-clad body a strange rigidity. I think he was then approaching forty years of age, for there were deep lines in the face, wan and hollow-cheeked, but oval and actually beautiful; and touches of grey in the thick, waving hair and small full beard which had once been of the deepest raven black. His brow was white as the marble of Pentelicus, and of a height and breadth almost godlike. I said to myself, with all the ardour of a sculptor, that this man was a faun's statue out of antique Hellas, dug from a temple's ruins and brought somehow to life in our stifling age only to feel the chill and pressure of devastating years. And when he opened his immense, sunken, and wildly luminous black eyes I knew he would be thenceforth my only friend — the only friend of one who had never possessed a friend before — for I saw that such eyes must have looked fully upon the grandeur and the terror of realms beyond normal consciousness and reality; realms which I had cherished in fancy, but vainly sought. So as I drove the crowd away I told him he must come home with me and be my teacher and leader in unfathomed mysteries, and he assented without speaking a word. Afterward I found that his voice was music — the music of deep viols and of crystalline spheres. We talked often in the night, and in the day, when I chiselled busts of him and carved miniature heads in ivory to immortalise his different expressions.

Of our studies it is impossible to speak, since they held so slight a connexion with anything of the world as living men conceive it. They were of that vaster and more appalling universe of dim entity and consciousness which lies deeper than matter, time, and space, and whose existence we suspect only in certain forms of sleep — those rare dreams beyond dreams which come never to common men, and but once or twice in the lifetime of imaginative men. The cosmos of our waking knowledge, born from such an universe as a bubble is born from the pipe of a jester, touches it only as such a bubble may touch its sardonic source when sucked back by the jester's whim. Men of learning suspect it little, and ignore it mostly. Wise men have interpreted dreams, and the gods have laughed. One man with Oriental eyes has said that all time and space are relative, and men have laughed. But even that man with Oriental eyes has done no more than suspect. I had wished and tried to do more than suspect, and my friend had tried and partly succeeded. Then we both tried together, and with exotic drugs courted terrible and forbidden dreams in the tower studio chamber of the old manor-house in hoary Kent.

Among the agonies of these after days is that chief of torments — inarticulateness. What I learned and saw in those hours of impious exploration can never be told — for want of symbols or suggestions in any language. I say this because from first to last our discoveries partook only of the nature of sensations; sensations correlated with no impression which the nervous system of normal humanity is capable of receiving. They were sensations, yet within them lay unbelievable elements of time and space—things which at bottom possess no distinct and definite existence. Human utterance can best convey the general character of our experiences by calling them plungings or soarings; for in every period of revelation some part of our minds broke boldly away from all that is real and present, rushing aërially along shocking, unlighted, and fear-haunted abysses, and occasionally tearing through certain well-marked and typical obstacles describable only as viscous, uncouth clouds of vapours. In these black and bodiless flights we were sometimes alone and sometimes together. When we were together, my friend was always far ahead; I could comprehend his presence despite the absence of form by a species of pictorial memory whereby his face appeared to me, golden from a strange light and frightful with its weird beauty, its anomalously youthful cheeks, its burning eyes, its Olympian brow, and its shadowing hair and growth of beard.

Of the progress of time we kept no record, for time had become to us the merest illusion. I know only that there must have been something very singular involved, since we came at length to marvel why we did not grow old. Our discourse was unholy, and always hideously ambitious—no god or daemon could have aspired to discoveries and conquests like those which we planned in whispers. I shiver as I speak of them, and dare not be explicit; though I will say that my friend once wrote on paper a wish which he dared not utter with his tongue, and which made me burn the paper and look affrightedly out of the window at the spangled night sky. I will hint—only hint—that he had designs which involved the rulership of the visible universe and more; designs whereby the earth and the stars would move at his command, and the destinies of all living things be his. I affirm—I swear—that I had no share in these extreme aspirations. Anything my friend may have said or written to the contrary must be erroneous, for I am no man of strength to risk the unmentionable warfare in unmentionable spheres by which alone one might achieve success.

There was a night when winds from unknown spaces whirled us irresistibly into limitless vacua beyond all thought and entity. Perceptions of the most maddeningly untransmissible sort thronged upon us; perceptions of infinity which at the time convulsed us with joy, yet which are now partly lost to my memory and partly incapable of presentation to others. Viscous obstacles were clawed through in rapid succession, and at length I felt that we had been borne to realms of greater remoteness than any we had previously known.

My friend was vastly in advance as we plunged into this awesome ocean of virgin aether, and I could see the sinister exultation on his floating, luminous, too youthful memory-face. Suddenly that face became dim and quickly disappeared, and in a brief space I found myself projected against an obstacle which I could not penetrate. It was like the others, yet incalculably denser; a sticky, clammy mass, if such terms can be applied to analogous qualities in a non-material sphere.

I had, I felt, been halted by a barrier which my friend and leader had successfully passed. Struggling anew, I came to the end of the drug-dream and opened my physical eyes to the tower studio in whose opposite corner reclined the pallid and still unconscious form of my fellow-dreamer, weirdly haggard and wildly beautiful as the moon shed gold-green light on his marble features. Then, after a short interval, the form in the corner stirred; and may pitying heaven keep from my sight and sound another thing like that which took place before me. I cannot tell you how he shrieked, or what vistas of unvisitable hells gleamed for a second in black eyes crazed with fright. I can only say that I fainted, and did not stir till he himself recovered and shook me in his phrensy for someone to keep away the horror and desolation.

That was the end of our voluntary searchings in the caverns of dream. Awed, shaken, and portentous, my friend who had been beyond the barrier warned me that we must never venture within those realms again. What he had seen, he dared not tell me; but he said from his wisdom that we must sleep as little as possible, even if drugs were necessary to keep us awake. That he was right, I soon learned from the unutterable fear which engulfed me whenever consciousness lapsed. After each short and inevitable sleep I seemed older, whilst my friend aged with a rapidity almost shocking. It is hideous to see wrinkles form and hair whiten almost before one's eyes. Our mode of life was now totally altered. Heretofore a recluse so far as I know—his true name and origin never having passed his lips—my friend now became frantic in his fear of solitude. At night he would not be alone, nor would the company of a few persons calm him. His sole relief was obtained in revelry of the most general and boisterous sort; so that few assemblies of the young and gay were unknown to us. Our appearance and age seemed to excite in most cases a ridicule which I keenly resented, but which my friend considered a lesser evil than solitude. Especially was he afraid to be out of doors alone when the stars were shining, and if forced to this condition he would often glance furtively at the sky as if hunted by some monstrous thing therein. He did not always glance at the same place in the sky—it seemed to be a different place at different times.

On spring evenings it would be low in the northeast. In the summer it would be nearly overhead. In the autumn it would be in the northwest. In winter it would be in the east, but mostly if in the small hours of morning. Midwinter evenings seemed least dreadful to him. Only after two years did I connect this fear with anything in particular; but then I began to see that he must be looking at a special spot on the celestial vault whose position at different times corresponded to the direction of his glance—a spot roughly marked by the constellation Corona Borealis.

We now had a studio in London, never separating, but never discussing the days when we had sought to plumb the mysteries of the unreal world. We were aged and weak from our drugs, dissipations, and nervous overstrain, and the thinning hair and beard of my friend had become snow-white. Our freedom from long sleep was surprising, for seldom did we succumb more than an hour or two at a time to the shadow which had now grown so frightful a menace. Then came one January of fog and rain, when money ran low and drugs were hard to buy. My statues and ivory heads were all sold, and I had no means to purchase new materials, or energy to fashion them even had I possessed them. We suffered terribly, and on a certain night my friend sank into a deep-breathing sleep from which I could not awaken him. I can recall the scene now—the desolate, pitch-black garret studio under the eaves with the rain beating down; the ticking of our lone clock; the fancied ticking of our watches as they rested on the dressing-table; the creaking of some swaying shutter in a remote part of the house; certain distant city noises muffled by fog and space; and worst of all the deep, steady, sinister breathing of my friend on the couch—a rhythmical breathing which seemed to measure moments of supernal fear and agony for his spirit as it wandered in spheres forbidden, unimagined, and hideously remote.

The tension of my vigil became oppressive, and a wild train of trivial impressions and associations thronged through my almost unhinged mind. I heard a clock strike somewhere—not ours, for that was not a striking clock—and my morbid fancy found in this a new starting-point for idle wanderings. Clocks—time—space—infinity—and then my fancy reverted to the locale as I reflected that even now, beyond the roof and the fog and the rain and the atmosphere, Corona Borealis was rising in the northeast. Corona Borealis, which my friend had appeared to dread, and whose scintillant semicircle of stars must even now be glowing unseen through the measureless abysses of aether. All at once my feverishly sensitive ears seemed to detect a new and wholly distinct component in the soft medley of drug-magnified sounds—a low and damnably insistent whine from very far away; droning, clamouring, mocking, calling, *from the north-east*.

But it was not that distant whine which robbed me of my faculties and set upon my soul such a seal of fright as may never in life be removed; not that which drew the shrieks and excited the convulsions which caused lodgers and police to break down the door. It was not what I heard, but what I saw; for in that dark, locked, shuttered, and curtained room there appeared from the black north-east corner a shaft of horrible red-gold light—a shaft which bore with it no glow to disperse the darkness, but which streamed only upon the recumbent head of the troubled sleeper, bringing out in hideous duplication the luminous and strangely youthful memory-face as I had known it in dreams of abysmal space and unshackled time, when my friend had pushed behind the barrier to those secret, innermost, and forbidden caverns of nightmare.

And as I looked, I beheld the head rise, the black, liquid, and deep-sunken eyes open in terror, and the thin, shadowed lips part as if for a scream too frightful to be uttered. There dwelt in that ghastly and inflexible face, as it shone bodiless, luminous, and rejuvenated in the blackness, more of stark, teeming, brain-shattering fear than all the rest of heaven and earth has ever revealed to me. No word was spoken amidst the distant sound that grew nearer and nearer, but as I followed the memory-face's mad stare along that cursed shaft of light to its source, the source whence also the whining came, I too saw for an instant what it saw, and fell with ringing ears in that fit of shrieking and epilepsy which brought the lodgers and the police. Never could I tell, try as I might, what it actually was that I saw; nor could the still face tell, for although it must have seen more than I did, it will never speak again. But always I shall guard against the mocking and insatiate Hypnos, lord of sleep, against the night sky, and against the mad ambitions of knowledge and philosophy.

Just what happened is unknown, for not only was my own mind unseated by the strange and hideous thing, but others were tainted with a forgetfulness which can mean nothing if not madness. They have said, I know not for what reason, that I never had a friend; but that art, philosophy, and insanity had filled all my tragic life. The lodgers and police on that night soothed me, and the doctor administered something to quiet me, nor did anyone see what a nightmare event had taken place. My stricken friend moved them to no pity, but what they found on the couch in the studio made them give me a praise which sickened me, and now a fame which I spurn in despair as I sit for hours, bald, grey-bearded, shrivelled, palsied, drug-crazed, and broken, adoring and praying to the object they found.

For they deny that I sold the last of my statuary, and point with

ecstasy at the thing which the shining shaft of light left cold, petrified, and unvocal. It is all that remains of my friend; the friend who
led me on to madness and wreckage; a godlike head of such marble
as only old Hellas could yield, young with the youth that is outside
time, and with beauteous bearded face, curved, smiling lips, Olympian brow, and dense locks waving and poppy-crowned. They say
that that haunting memory-face is modelled from my own, as it was
at twenty-five; but upon the marble base is carven a single name in
the letters of Attica — HYPNOS. ——

I Can't Wear White

Suzanne Pickett

I didn't believe it of course. It COULDN'T be true. Nevertheless
—I glanced in the mirror. My dress was white and soft, as near
like the description Dereck had given me as I could make it.

He was honest at least. Better to have told me than for me to
go through life wondering—But things like that don't really happen.
It was a dream, a fixation. Dereck is the poetic type, one who
WOULD imagine something like that.

Well, *I* wasn't poetic and I didn't intend to let something he had
imagined spoil my whole life.

"She had the biggest, darkest eyes," he said when he first began
the story. I widened my own eyes. They were big and dark too. I
knew what they could do to a man, and this time I was playing for
keeps.

Dereck reached out and covered my eyes with his hand. "They
are like hers," he said. "Exactly." Then he kissed me gently and
began the story.

"I know you won't believe it," he said. "It's incredible even to me.
Nevertheless, it's true. You couldn't imagine a thing like that once a
year for five years could you?"

He had uncovered my eyes and I turned on all the voltage as I
looked at him, but his eyes were on his hands in his lap as he went
on. "I certainly wasn't thinking of anything like that," he said. "I
was coming home from a baseball game. It was Labor Day, had
been terrifically hot all day, but the night was cool, and I was as
sober as I have ever been in my life.

"There had been such a crowd at the ball park, it took me an hour
to get my car out and start home. It was just twelve as I came to the

lake. You know, the bridge is long and narrow. I didn't see a car at the other end, but I slowed down anyhow. Several people had been killed on that same bridge, so I wasn't taking any chances.

"Just as I started to pick up speed, a girl in a white dress stepped in front of the car. I swore softly and jammed on the brakes. 'What the—' I began. Then I saw her face. It was the sweetest thing. Little, like yours," his hand caressed my cheek. "With the clearest white skin, and big, dark eyes."

" 'I—' her voice had a soft, breathless quality. 'I'm—I've had an accident. I wonder if you could take me home.'

" 'Anyone with you?' I asked. 'Anyone hurt?'

" 'Oh no!' she said quickly. 'I'm alone. But I've GOT to get home. Daddy will have a fit.'

" 'Where do you live?' I asked. I had known her about two minutes, but already I would have tried to take her to the moon if she had wanted to go there.

"She gave me the address, I opened the door and she stepped into the car."

Dereck paused a minute and smiled. My fingers ached to slap that look out of his eyes, but I kept them quietly folded in my lap. "She was so—sweet, so beautiful," Dereck went on. "I knew before I had driven a mile that I loved her. There was a sort of luminous quality about her. She had on a soft, white dress that clung to her. Some kind of filmy material," he grinned. "I never did know much about such things."

"Her fingers were little and pink, like yours." He took one of my hands. I unclenched it and let it lie, little and soft and pink in his. He rubbed the fingers and continued his story.

I hadn't spoken since he began. I knew if I opened my mouth I might do anything from screaming to sniveling and begging. And whoever this girl was, she didn't sound as if SHE would do anything like that.

So I managed to listen quietly as Dereck went on. "I wanted to drive slowly. To never get home for that matter, but she was agitated, her face tense. 'Hurry!' she said over and over. 'Please hurry.' When I began to drive faster, she relaxed, lay back in the seat and smiled quietly.

"But she didn't have much to say and somehow, I couldn't think of anything either. But it didn't matter. She wasn't married, I learned that much. And I had the rest of my life to see her—to get acquainted."

Dereck paused, sighed and was silent awhile. "And then?" I managed to get past my lips without opening them too wide. My throat ached and my eyes filled as I tried to keep the tears from falling. This couldn't be Dereck sitting here and telling me there was another girl. It just COULDN'T be. Dereck loved ME. I knew he did. He hadn't looked at anyone else since we started going together. This COULDN'T happen to me.

But it WAS happening. I couldn't bear this, yet I must bear it. This sudden pain in my chest. This sickness that swooped over me; and I must sit silently, listen sympathetically while Dereck tore my life into shreds.

I swallowed, Dereck bit his lips, then opened them to continue. "We finally came to the address she had given me. It was a big, old white house set back among some ancient oaks. A light burned at the front, another dim light shone from the inside.

"I hadn't dared touch her though I wanted to. But she seemed always about to run away, and I held my hands on the steering wheel now, gripped them to keep them there as I said, 'I'll see you again?'

"She hesitated, gave me a queer look, then said in a low voice. 'Yes, you'll see me again if you, —"She didn't finish the sentence. We both sat a minute in silence, then the front door of the house opened.

"I hurried to open my own door, stepped out and around to the other side of the car. I certainly didn't want her father to have a 'fit' the first time I brought Opal home.

"I didn't know how she could have gotten out of the car so quietly, and without me seeing her; but when I opened the door on her side she wasn't there. I was a little vexed at her, then I smiled. She was afraid of course. She had seen that it was her father who was at the door and she had slipped out of the car.

"But the man still stood in the door and his face, in the dim light, had the saddest look I have ever seen. I started up the walk. At least I would speak with him, get his permission to call on Opal. I must have looked worried, for he tried to smile as I came up the steps. But the smile was worse than the other look.

"How are you, son?" he asked. I was eighteen then, and thought myself very much a man, so I didn't like the 'son,' but I smiled back as best I could. I certainly wanted to do everything I could to make him like me; especially as I expected to have him for a father in law some day.

"But his next words staggered me. 'I've been looking for you.' he said.

"What—' I began. 'I mean. I'm sorry but—'

"I know,' he said. 'I've never seen you before, and you don't know me.'

"That's right,' I admitted. And suddenly, I was afraid for him to go on. I didn't want to hear what he had to say, but I stood numbly, waiting for him to speak.

"You picked my daughter Opal up at the bridge and brought her home, didn't you?"

"How on earth could he know that? I thought as I nodded.

" 'When you opened the door for her, she was gone wasn't she?' His eyes were kind, yet with a haunted look.

"Yes," I said. "But how—"

"Opal was killed there on Labor Day night, five years ago," he said quietly.

"If he had exploded a bomb under my feet I couldn't have been more shocked. 'No!' I managed to say at last. 'No! It's impossible! She's as much alive as you or I.'

" 'I understand son,' he said and his voice choked. 'But I can't understand why—WHY. She's all that I had and she loved me. She never—' He caught himself, swayed against the door. 'She was hurrying to get home, she knew I'd be worried. Someone has brought her home every Labor Day night since then. Oh God!' he groaned then and put his hands to his face. 'Why can't she rest? Why must she keep trying to come home? Doesn't she know that I understand?'

"As I turned blindly and hurried back to the car I heard him pleading with her. 'Come in darling. Daddy isn't mad at you. Please come in, Opal.' "

Dereck paused again, then hurried on. "I don't know what I did the rest of the night. But the next day I managed to get home somehow. I was sick for two weeks. Mother told me I babbled and pleaded about some ghost that inhabited my dreams. She wanted to keep me at home that year. I had already made arrangements to enter the University; but I persuaded her that I was able to go.

"You know the rest; or most of it. I changed after that, was quieter, studied more and kept to myself. That's when I began writing; how I had time to write two novels and still keep ahead of my class in all of my studies.

"As you know, I never looked at another girl until I met you. Every year since then, I have met her again, taken her home—"

He took my hand and kissed it. "You are so like her," his voice was husky. "Sometimes I wonder if you are not a dream."

"I am no dream," I told him positively. "And I certainly don't intend to disappear."

"No," he smiled at me. "No, you're no dream except as a girl is everything a man can dream about. I love you Angela, YOU!" He kissed me fiercely. "And no girl who has been—" he hesitated, then went on, "has been dead for ten years can come between us. But," he stopped again. "I have to be sure—to see her once more or she might always be there—between us—and—You understand." He looked at me pleadingly.

"Yes, Dereck," I leaned my face against his. "Yes, darling, I understand."

That happened last night, Sunday night. Today is Labor Day.

Of course he imagined it all. After all, Dereck IS a writer; "The most imaginative writer of our era," critics say, so he has a right to imagine a dream girl if he wishes. Glad that he did. If he hadn't he might have married someone else before he met me. And I'm glad this dream girl looks like me. I don't believe it of course, but nevertheless—

My young brother Henry is a sweet kid. We've kept quite a few things from mother and dad in our day. I can always depend on him when I need him. So he didn't ask a single question when I wanted him to drive me to the lake and leave me about eleven o'clock on Labor Day night. I did tell him it was a joke, and that Dereck was to pick me up there.

I knew, too, that Dereck would be at the lake bridge at exactly twelve o'clock, so I wasn't taking any chances there either. I had slipped a quart of water in his gas tank. It should give him enough trouble to make him a few minutes late. If the girl DID show up, I'd get rid of her somehow; and I'd be the one Dereck carried home. I had a black raincoat around me so that other cars wouldn't see me and stop as I hid behind a post on the bridge.

I was glad I had on the coat. It made me feel sort of protected, and kept the chill which came out of the lake from making me too uncomfortable.

I huddled behind the post, shivered and wished that I was at home. I hadn't dreamed that I would be so scared. The night was dark, silent, oppressive. Mists rose from the lake in eerie wraiths, some in human, others in goblin like forms. It didn't take even a writer's imagination to people the bridge with ghosts. No wonder Dereck had been fooled.

But I DID wish he would hurry. This was a lonely road, and no other cars passed. If one had, I think I would have thumbed a ride home if the driver had stopped.

An owl hooted suddenly behind me; made me jump in terror. A night hawk swooped after an insect or something. Occasional plunking noises came from the lake as a frog or fish jumped in the murky depths. I had never been so lonely in my life. I seemed glued to the post, as if I would be there through eternity as if—

I think I must have fainted briefly.

I found myself lying on the planks babbling quietly that I hadn't really seen a girl in white step onto the bridge; that it was just another wraith from the lake, that I was as crazy as Dereck.

But I knew that I was lying. That I HAD seen the girl.

I opened my eyes, sat up and stared as I heard a car. But it wasn't Dereck's car. The sound of the motor told me that. "Thank God he's late," I whispered, and almost fainted again as I peered at the girl who stood in the headlights of the car.

She WAS the loveliest thing I had ever seen. No wonder Dereck couldn't forget her. If I were half as pretty as that to him—

The car stopped. "Opal!" a hoarse voice cried and a man leaped from the car to take the girl in his arms.

"Daddy!" she cried and ran to him. "Daddy, I've waited for you all of these years." I saw them enter the car, and I was choking. I couldn't breathe.

As the car backed up to turn around, I flung the black raincoat from me, tried to run from the bridge, but I was falling—falling—

It might have been thirty minutes later, Dereck said he was that late; that it was twelve-thirty, so it must have been that long—that I came to in his arms. He was crying and kissing me.

"Don't let it be Angela, God," he sobbed. "She's alive. She's GOT to be alive. Angela, speak to me."

"Dereck," I whispered and tried to raise my arms.

"Thank God!" he said. "You're not dead. Angela," he said fearfully. "I was afraid for a minute that you were Opal. I was afraid that I had dreamed YOU."

"Are you glad?" I asked. "Or do you wish that she had met you?"

"Glad!" he kissed me again. "When I found you and thought you were dead—"

Well, we went to Mississippi that night and were married. I called mother next day and told her, then asked for Henry.

He promised to hide all of the papers for the next week and save them for me.

Dereck and I bought clothes as we needed them, drove on to the coast and spent two wonderful weeks in California. We liked it so well that we moved out here a month later. We have only been home once since then. That was the last of August, almost a year later.

Dereck didn't want to do it at first, but I finally persuaded him to visit the bridge with me on Labor Day night. We took a blanket and huddled behind the post that had hidden me a year before. But I wasn't afraid this time. The night noises were friendly, and the mists, only beautiful vapors from which one might spin dreams.

We stayed until three o'clock. An occasional car passed, but no girl in white.

A little after three we drove home. "You'll never believe it," Dereck told me that night. "But Angela, I honestly did see the girl."

"You still think that she was real?" I asked.

"I don't THINK, I KNOW that she was real," he told me.

"Does it matter?" I asked.

"She hasn't really mattered since the first time I saw you." he said, and his kiss left no doubt of that.

"But I wonder," he said later. "I wonder why she quit coming."

I had the clipping with me. I had never been able to throw it away. I slipped it from the pages of my bank book and handed it to him. It read:

FATHER KEEPS RENDEZVOUS WITH DAUGHTER.

Car runs off bridge. Father of Opal Fenton drowns in same spot where his daughter was drowned ten years ago. Many think it was suicide. He had brooded over the death of Opal for years, talked of her to his neighbors as if she were still alive.

Others think it was an accident, but this reporter wonders. There seem to be too many coincidences. The accident happened at the same place, the lake bridge, the same night, Labor Day, and the same hour, midnight, according to the coroner's report.

Whatever it was, suicide or accident; it seems touching and fitting that these two; father and daughter, who, according to report, loved each other with more than ordinary love: are together at last.

Dereck was silent awhile after he read the clipping, then his voice was gentle as he turned to me. "You knew?" he said. "You knew?

"Yes," I whispered.

He took out his lighter, flicked it, held the clipping in the flame, then crushed it in an ash tray. "It's over now," he said. "Finished. Let's never think of it again."

I agreed. But sometimes I wonder. With my dark eyes and fair skin, white is my most becoming color, but Dereck will never let me wear it. I bought a white dress once.

And anyhow, I don't blame Dereck. You see—I can't forget her myself. ━━✦

In the Dark

Ronal Kayser

The watchman's flashlight printed a white circle on the frosted-glass, black-lettered door:

GREGG CHEMICAL CO., MFRS.
ASA GREGG, PRES.
PRIVATE

The watchman's hand closed on the knob, rattled the door in its frame. Queer, but tonight the sound had seemed to come from in there. . . . But that couldn't be. He knew that Mr. Gregg and Miss Carruthers carried the only keys to the office, so any intruder would have been forced to smash the lock.

Maybe the sound came from the storage room. The watchman clumped along the rubber-matted corridor, flung his weight against that door. It opened hard, being of ponderous metal fitted into a cork casing. The room was an air-tight, fire-proof vault, really. His shoes gritted on the concrete floor as he prowled among the big porcelain vats. The flashlight bored through bluish haze to the concrete walls. Acid fumes escaping under the vat lids made the haze and seared the man's throat.

He hurried out, coughing and wiping his eyes. It was damn funny. Every night lately he heard the same peculiar noise somewhere in this wing of the building. . . . Like a body groaning and turning in restless sleep, it was. It scared him. He didn't mention the mystery to anyone, though. He was an old man, and he didn't want Mr. Gregg to think he was getting too old for the job.

"Asa'd think I was crazy, if I told him about it," he mumbled.

Inside the office, Asa Gregg heard the muttered words plainly. He sat very still in the big, leather-cushioned chair, hardly breathing until the scrape of the watchman's feet had thinned away down the hall. There was no light in the room to betray him; only the cherry-colored tip of his cigar, which couldn't be visible through the frosted glass door. Anyway, it'd be an hour before the watchman's round brought him past the office again. Asa Gregg had that hour, if he could screw up his nerve to use it. . . .

He took the frayed end of the cigar from his mouth. His hand, which had wasted to mere skin and bone these past few months, groped through the darkness, slid over the polished coolness of the dictaphone hood, and snapped the switch. Machinery faintly whirred. His fingers found the tube, lifted it.

"Miss Carruthers!" he snapped. Then he hesitated. Surely, he could trust Mary Carruthers! He'd never wondered about her before. She'd been his secretary for a dozen years—lately, since he couldn't look after affairs himself as he used to, she had practically run the business. She was forty, sensible, unbeautiful, and tight-lipped. Hell, he had to trust her!

His voice plunged into the darkness.

"What I have to say now is intended for Mrs. Gregg's ears only. She will take the first boat home, of course. Meet that boat and bring her to the office. Since my wife knows nothing about a dictaphone, it will be necessary for you to set this record running. As soon as you have done so, leave her alone in the room. Make sure she's not interrupted for a half-hour. That's all."

He waited a decent interval. The invisible needle peeled its thread into the revolving wax cylinder.

"Jeannette," muttered Asa Gregg, and hesitated again. This wasn't going to be easy to say. He decided to begin matter-of-factly. "As you probably know, my will and the insurance policies are in the vault at the First National. I believe you will find all of my papers in excellent order. If any questions arise, consult Miss Carruthers. What I have to say to you now is purely personal—I feel, my dear, that I owe you an explanation—that is—"

God, it came harder than he had expected.

"Jeannette," he started in afresh, "you remember three years ago when I was in the hospital. You were in Palm Beach at the time, and I wired that there'd been an accident here at the plant. That wasn't strictly so. The fact is, I'd gotten mixed up with a girl—"

He paused, shivering. In the darkness a picture of Dot swam before him. The oval face, framed by gleaming swirls of lemon-tinted hair, had pouting scarlet lips, and eyes whose allure was intensified by violet make-up. The full-length picture of her included a streamlined, full-blossomed and yet delectably lithe body. A costly, enticing, Broadway-chorus orchid! As a matter of fact, that was where he'd found her.

"I won't make any excuses for myself," Asa Gregg said harshly. "I might point out that you were always in Florida or Bermuda or France, and that I was a lonely man. But it wasn't just loneliness, and I didn't seek companionship. I thought I was making a last bow to Romance. I was successful, sixty, and silly, and I did all the damn fool things—I even wrote letters to her. Popsy-wopsy letters." The dictaphone couldn't record the grimace that jerked his lips. "She saved them, of course, and by and by she put a price on them—ten thousand dollars. Dot claimed that one of those filthy tabloids had offered her that much for them—and what was a poor working-girl to do? She lied. I knew that.

"I told her to bring the letters to the office after business hours, and I'd take care of her. I took care of her, all right. I shot her, Jeannette!"

He mopped his face with a handkerchief that was already damp.

"Not on account of the money, you understand. It was the things she said, after she had tucked the bills into her purse . . . vile things, about the way she had earned it ten times over by enduring my beastly kisses. I'd really loved that girl, and I'd thought she'd cared for me a little. It was her hate that maddened me, and I got the gun out of my desk drawer—"

Asa Gregg reached through the darkness for the switch. He fumbled for the bottle which stood on the desk. His hand trembled, spilling some of the liquor onto his lap. He drank from the bottle. . . .

This part of the story he'd skip. It was too horrible, even to think about it. He didn't want to remember how the blood pooled inside Dot's fur coat, and how he'd managed to carry the body out of the office without leaking any of her blood onto the floor. He tried to forget the musky sweetness of the perfume on the dead girl, mingled with that other evil blood-smell. Especially he didn't want to remember the frightful time he'd had stripping the gold rings from her fingers, and the one gold tooth in her head. . . .

The horror of it coiled in the blackness about him. His own teeth rattled against the bottle when he gulped the second drink. He snapped the switch savagely, but when he spoke his voice cringed into the tube:

"I carried her into the storage room. I got the lid off one of the acid tanks. The vat contained an acid powerful enough to destroy anything—except gold. In fact, the vat itself had to be lined with gold-leaf. I knew that in twenty-four hours there wouldn't be a recognizable body left, and in a week there wouldn't be anything at all. No matter what the police suspected, they couldn't prove a murder charge without a *corpus delicti*. I had committed the perfect crime —except for one thing. I didn't realize that there'd be a *splash* when she went into the vat."

Gregg laughed, not pleasantly. His wife might think it'd been a sob, when she heard this record. "Now you understand why I went to the hospital," he jerked. "Possibly you'd call that poetic justice. Oh, God!"

His voice broke. Again he thumbed off the switch, and mopped his face with the damp linen.

The rest—how could he explain the rest of it?

He spent a long minute arranging his thoughts.

"You haven't any idea," he resumed, "no one has any idea, of how I've been punished for the thing I did. I don't mean the sheer physical agony—but the fear that I'd talk coming out of the ether at the hospital. The fear that she'd been traced to my office—I'd simply hidden her rings away, expecting to drop them into the river—or that she might have confided in her lover . . . yes, she had one. Or, suppose a whopping big order came through and that tank was emptied the very next day. And I couldn't ask any questions—I didn't even know what was in the papers.

"However, that part of it gradually cleared up. I quizzed Miss Carruthers, and learned that an unidentified female body had been fished out of the East River a few days after Dot disappeared. That's how the police 'solved' the case. I got rid of her rings. I ordered that vat left alone.

"The other thing began about six months ago."

A spasm contorted his face. His fingers ached their grip into the dictaphone tube.

"Jeannette, you remember when I began to object to the radio, how I'd shout at you to turn it off in the middle of a program? You thought I was ill, and worried about business. . . . You were wrong. The thing that got me was *hearing her voice*—"

He gripped the cold cigar, chewed it. "It's very strange that you didn't notice it. No matter what station we dialed to, always that same voice came stealing into the room! But perhaps you did notice? You said, once or twice, that all those blues singers sounded alike!

"And she was a blues singer. . . . It was she, all right, somewhere out in the ether, reminding me. . . .

"The next thing was—well, at first when I noticed it in the office I thought Miss Carruthers had suddenly taken up with young ideas. You see, I kept smelling perfume."

And he smelled it now. It was like a miasma in the dark.

"It isn't anything that Carruthers wears," he grated. "It comes from—yes, the storage room. I realized that about a month ago. Just after you sailed—one night I stayed late at the office, and I went in there. . . . It seemed to be strongest around the vat—*her* vat—and I lifted the lid.

"The sweet, sticky musk-smell hit me like a blow in the face.

"And that isn't all!"

Terror stalked in this room. Asa Gregg crouched in his chair, felt the weight of Fear on him like a submarine pressure. His cigar pitched to his knees, dropped to the floor.

"You won't believe this, Jeannette." He hammered the words like nails into the darkness in front of him. "You will say that it's impossible. I know that. It *is* impossible. It is a physiological absurdity—it contradicts the laws of natural science.

"But I saw something on the bottom of that vat!"

He groped for the bottle. His wife would hear a long gurgle, and then a coughing gasp. . . .

"The vat was nearly full of this transparent, oily acid," he went on. "What I saw was a lot of sediment on the golden floor. And there shouldn't have been any sediment! The stuff utterly dissolves animal tissue, bone, even the common ores—keeps them in suspension.

"It didn't look like sediment, either. It looked like a heap of mold . . . grave-mold!

"I replaced the lid. I spent a week convincing myself that it was all impossible, that I *couldn't* have seen anything of the sort. Then I went to the vat again—"

Silence hung in the darkness while he sucked wind into his lungs. And the words burst—separate, yammering shrieks:

"I looked, night after night! For hours at a time I've watched the change. . . . Did you ever see a body decompose? Of course not! Neither have I. But you must know in a general way what the process is. Well, this has been the exact opposite!

"First, I stared at the heap of grave-mold as it shaped itself into *bones*, a skeleton.

"I watched the coming of hair, a yellow tangle of it sprouting from the bare round skull, until—oh, God!—the flesh began making itself before my eyes! I couldn't bear any more. I stayed away— didn't come to the office for five days."

The tube slipped from his sweating, slick fingers. Panting, Asa Gregg fumbled in the dark until he found it.

Exhaustion, not self-control, flattened his voice to a deadly monotone. "I tried to think of a way out. If I could fish the corpse out of the tank! But I couldn't smuggle it out of the plant—alone. You know that, and so do I. Besides, what would be the use? If acid can't kill her, nothing can.

"That's why I can't have the lid cemented on. It wouldn't do any good, either! Until three days ago, she hadn't the least color, looked as white as a ghost in the vat. A naked ghost, because there's been no resurrection for her clothing. . . .

"I've watched her limbs grow rosy! Her lips are scarlet! Her eyes are bright—they opened yesterday—and her breasts were rising and falling—oh, almost imperceptibly—but that was last night.

"And tonight—I swear it—her lips moved! She muttered my name! She turned—she'd been lying on her side—over onto her back!"

The record would be badly blurred. His hand shook violently, bobbled the tube against his lips. Gregg braced his elbow against the desk.

"She isn't dead," he choked. "She's only asleep . . . not very soundly asleep. . . . She's waking up!"

The invisible needle quivered as it traced several noises. There was his tortured breathing, and the clawing of his fingernails rattling over the desk. The drawer clicked as it opened.

The loud click was the cocking of the revolver.

"Soon she's going to get out of that vat!" Gregg bleated. "Jeannette, forgive me—God, forgive me—but I will not—I cannot—I dare not stay here to see her then!"

The sound of the shot brought the watchman stumbling along the corridor. He crashed against the office door. It banged open in a shower of falling frosted glass. The watchman's flashlight severed the darkness, and printed its white circle on the face of Asa Gregg.

He had fallen back into the chair, a blackish gout of blood running from the hole in his temple. He stared sightlessly into the light with his eyes that were two gnarls of shrunken brown flesh, like knots in a pine board.

Asa Gregg was blind . . . had been, since that night three years past when the acid splashed. . . . ——

THE IRON HANDS OF KATZAVEERE

DAVID EYNON

près moi, le deluge,' said Hauptmann von Frolich pleasantly, puffing to start his Havana, "if you will permit me to quote a Frenchman—Louis XVI, *nicht wahr*?"

"Pardon, Mynheer Commandant?" said Burgomeister ten Brink, pulling his attention from the sound of the firing up the coast—guns that promised liberation to his village of fisherfolk. "You were saying?"

"In the morning," explained the German wearily, tired after three years of dealing with gross Dutch mentality, "when we leave your gemütlich little village—where, need I says, we have enjoyed our . . . 'Holiday'—the dike would be blown. I shall command the demolition squad personally."

Ten Brink stared at the German captain. The afternoon sun had faded now, the firelight licked at the German's crooked smile, brightened the decorations on his tunic.

"You would do *that*?" ten Brink asked hollowly. "Destroy the work of centuries, leave my people destitute and—"

"Oh, please," said von Frolich hastily, "it's nothing personal, you understand, my dear Herr Burgomeister." He settled his weight more comfortably in the large chair. "Purely a question of military expediency. I've grown quite fond of Katzaveere, actually. Perhaps, after the war, when my vacation permits . . ." The captain blew a ring of smoke towards the fireplace and mused.

"However," he drew himself back to the business at hand, "when the English arrive," he cocked his head and listened to the mumble of artillery for a second, "about noon tomorrow, I should imagine— you can express my regrets that I could not be here to receive them." He winked at ten Brink. "And also extend my apologies for the town's being under water," he added, showing a denture made by the best orthodontist in Hamburg.

"But my villagers," said ten Brink helplessly. "It means the end of everything for them!" he protested.

"Nothing actually ever begins or ends—does it really?" asked von Frolich. He had studied philosophy at Marburg. "And you can repair things, one day. Your town should be as good as new—in ten or twenty years!" he laughed, shaking until his chair groaned.

Ten Brink's mind flooded with desperation. He fought the urge to throttle the German as von Frolich sat laughing. That guaranteed immediate reprisal—a hundred fishermen shot, perhaps the whole village executed. His own death ten Brink could discount, but his people must survive somehow. If they lived, only, there always remained the hope of rebuilding.

Von Frolich's laughter ebbed into an amiable smile. He propped his boots on the grate, warming his toes against the evening dampness that seeped slowly into the stones of the Raadhuis floor.

"Oh, yes, Herr Burgomeister," said the Hauptmann familiarly, "before I take my leave, there is a point about which I have often meant to ask." He jutted his cigar towards the mantel. "Those hands," he said, indicating three black casts hanging by their wrists from hooks set in the stone, "iron, are they not? What brings them there?"

"Hands?" asked Ten Brink, wondering how the German, on the brink of disaster, could interest himself with trifles. "They are from the middle ages. It was then the custom to cut off a hand—as a punishment for great crimes. The hand was set in iron and hung in a public place as a warning to malefactors."

"Ach, so!" exclaimed von Frolich, bending forward with interest. He reached up and clasped the nearest hand, letting it clank back against the stone when he felt the coldness of the iron.

"And these hands," he asked, rubbing his fingers together, "to whom did they belong?"

"The two right hands belonged to a pair of traitors," said the Burgomeister pointedly. "They attempted to deliver our town to the Spanish, it was believed."

"Believed?" asked von Frolich. "There was no proof, then?"

"Perhaps in those days, barbarity was not so distinctly cut," said ten Brink acidly. "The third hand was a common murderer's."

"Wonderful!" said von Frolich, blandly ignoring ten Brink's barb. "Such a charming tale! Really, the things one encounters in out of the way spots!" He drew out a fresh cigar, struck a match on the nearest hand and lighted his smoke with deep drags.

As the Hauptmann savored his cigar the Burgomeister desperately made plans for the evacuation of his people. The two men sat in silence for several minutes, then the German spoke.

"You know, my dear ten Brink," he said jovially, "I have it! Those hands will make fine souvenirs—*wen wir nehmen Ubshied*. Just the memento I need of my pleasant sojourn in Katzaveere. May I?" he asked, cocking an eyebrow towards the mantel.

"Take them," said ten Brink softly.

"A thousand thanks, said von Frolich, tossing the burned match into the fireplace. "I'll wager, Herr Burgomeister," he said, winking slyly, "that you'd like to put my hands up there—as replacements— Nein?"

"If the Hauptmann will excuse me," said ten Brink bitterly, "I must see to the evacuation of my village."

"But of course, friend Burgomeister," said von Frolich politely, bowing from his chair. "Till morning, then."

Ten Brink nodded sharply and started toward the door.

"Oh, and also, Herr Burgomeister," called the Hauptmann as ten Brink reached the door, "thanks for the hands!"

The door slammed and von Frolich leaned over to poke up the coals in the grate. When they glowed to his satisfaction he loosened his belt, opened his collar and reached for a glass of brandy at his elbow. From the North the rising winds brought the sound of artillery stronger than before. Von Frolich listened to the barrage—mixed, he judged, listening to the muted whine of the lighter guns against the dull rumble of the 250's.

An orderly slipped into the room and closed the shutters against the night, leaving an oil lamp beside the captain, who sat staring at pictures in the fire. Von Frolich rolled the brandy slowly around his tongue and stared up curiously at the hands, etched against the old stone by the firelight. As he studied them in the flickering of the flames they seemed to pulse and clench with the slow, strong rhythm of the rising fire.

The North Sea wind moaned over the chimney, sucking the flames higher, and the hands seemed to dance from their hooks like tiny puppets, anxious for the show to begin. Von Frolich started as the iron fingers drummed on the stone—but no, it was only a flash of hail against the window panes outside.

The German broke his gaze from the mantel, gulped the rest of his brandy and stared determinedly into the fire.

"Odd," said Colonel Willoughby, lowering his binoculars. "They've *been* destroying the dikes all down the coast—you don't suppose they're planning to make a stand here, do you?' he asked a junior officer at his left.

"It's not very likely, is it, Sir?" said Lieutenant Downs. "Our patrols haven't drawn any fire—unless, of course, Jerry's planning some sort of trap."

The Colonel pulled a battered package of Players from his tunic pocket, offered one to Downs and tamped his own against a thumbnail. He continued tapping the cigarette absently, staring out across the dunes capped with tufts of grass swaying gently against a leaden sky. The cry of a gull drifted across the murmur of the waves and the Colonel turned unconsciously to accept a light from the lieutenant.

"Jerry isn't given to subtleties, as a rule," mused the Colonel, who was trying to reconcile his military logic with the fact that the situation didn't "feel" right. "Still, I expect you'd better go in for a look around."

"Of course, Sir," said the youngster.

"Take along anyone you like, Downs," the Colonel said as the boy started up over the embankment. "I'd suggest Sergeant Phillips."

"Quite, Sir," agreed Downs, motioning to an aging non-com in a scarred tin hat.

"Oh, and Downs," the Colonel added, glancing at his watch, "we'll follow you in at twelve-thirty—regardless."

"Just as you say, Sir," said the lieutenant, reaching the Sergeant a hand to the top of the dune.

The Colonel watched silently as the two figures moved off among the waving grass—Downs in the lead, Phillips moving warily on his flank with a submachine gun gripped at the ready. They disappeared down a slope, popped up briefly as first Downs, then the Sergeant, writhed over the top of the next dune, then were beyond the Colonel's view. He lowered his glasses, glanced again at his watch, then picked up the field telephone and asked for the artillery section.

The two Englishmen picked their way cautiously down a back street of Katzaveere, slipping quickly from doorway to doorway in the sinister silence of noon. Their hobnailed boots made brisk, urgent scrapes as they flicked across the cobbles beneath the gaunt windows of the narrow, leaning houses.

Downs twisted testily around a corner, into the street of the Ropemakers, and when he reached the next intersection motioned for Phillips to follow. The two men huddled together behind a coil of hawser, scanning the closed shutters along the street front. Directly ahead, looking down the street of the Never Ending Prayer, they could see the sparkle of the fountain in the main square. The sound of trickling water wandered merrily down the alley, chuckling to itself like an idiot in a graveyard.

As Downs turned to the Sergeant the clock in the Raadhuis tower started sonorously striking noon on a bell with the tone of a soul in chains.

"What do you make of it, Phillips?" whispered the boy.

"It's bloody quiet," said Phillips bitterly. "Probably a ruddy sniper behind every stinkin' window, Sir."

"I wonder," said Downs, doing his best to achieve the Colonel's tone. "Suppose we marched right up to their city hall and banged on the door—demanded that they surrender? They're caught, you know. They might be prepared to act reasonably."

"Well, Sir," said Phillips resignedly, "if they're still here, we're not goin' to get out anyway."

"Exactly," said Downs. "We could, of course, stay under cover until the Regiment moves in. However . . ."

"Look Lieutenant," said the Sergeant earnestly, "with all due allowances for our talents for sneakin' down back alleys, why we ain't hardly under cover, as I sees it. We didn't hardly come through the whole bloody town without anyone's noticin', Sir, and when the trouble starts . . ."

"Quite," said Downs. "Well, then," he sighed, straightening up from behind the coiled rope, "there's nothing else for it. Do try your best to look casual, Phillips. It makes all the difference, you know."

"Yes, Sir," said the Sergeant, who had a boy about Downs' age. "Casual, Sir."

Their boots rang loudly on the stones as they marched stiffly across the square, echoing back from the neat houses in the vacuum of silence. Together they passed the flashing fountain, tromped up the wide steps of the Raadhuis and pushed open the protesting iron studded door. For several seconds they waited in the entrance hall, tensed for a challenge, until their eyes adjusted to the shadows.

A door on their right stood open and they stepped simultaneously inside. Across the room, silhouetted against the dying embers of the fire, a German Captain in dress uniform sat facing them with a cracked smile on his bulging face.

A thin strip of light slanting through the shutters fell on the German's tunic, gilding his Iron Cross against his gray uniform. His booted feet lolled from the edge of the grate and relaxed in the ashes beneath. The Captain sat motionless, undisturbed by the sharp click as Phillips snapped off the safety catch of his weapon. The Sergeant leveled his automatic, but Downs stopped him.

"It's all right, Phillips," he said, stepping through the shadows to the German's elbow. "The Captain is quite dead."

The Sergeant moved rapidly to the door, swung it to and shot home the heavy bolt. He loosened his chin strap, tilted back his helmet and sidled to the window to peer through the slit in the shutters.

"Any activity, Phillips?" called the lieutenant from before the fireplace, where he stood staring curiously at Hauptmann von Frolich in the dim light. The Sergeant shook his head and tiptoted over beside Downs. Both men followed the Hauptmann's stare to the mantel, where a single hand hung beside two empty hooks.

Hauptmann von Frolich's body rolled slowly forward, expelling a thin stream of dead air from his cold lungs. He made a soft whistling noise as he bowed.

"Crikey!" gasped the Sergeant, swinging his gun butt around against von Frolich's head. It landed with a thud and knocked the Hauptmann's body to the flagstones. Phillips shot the safety on his gun and stood tensely over the German's sprawling legs.

"Just a last gasp, Phillips," explained Lieutenant Downs, reholstering his service revolver. "I expect we've had the final word from him—poor devil."

"How long has he been dead, Sir?" asked the Sergeant warily.

"Sometime last night, I should judge," said Downs, peering down at von Frolich's rigid smile. "About midnight, say."

"An extremely good guess, Lieutenant," said a voice with a thick accent. The two soldiers looked up sharply, faced a smiling, hoary headed figure in the doorway. Lieutenant Downs glanced at the silver chain of office across the old man's shoulders, then extended his hand cordially.

"Are you in authority here, Sir?" he inquired.

"It is you who are in authority, I think," smiled the old man. "However, I am the Burgomeister, yes. Are you here—" he groped for the proper English expression "—in force, Lieutenant?"

"The Regiment will be moving in soon," said Downs. "Unless they meet resistance?"

"Neen," said ten Brink. He beckoned to a priest who had appeared in the hallway.

"Fortunate," said the boy. "Oh, I'm Lieutenant Downs, Sir. And this is Sergeant Phillips. Leeds Rifles."

"I am Jonkheer ten Brink—and this is Father Vermue," said the old man. "Hauptmann von Frolich—whose acquaintance you seem to have made already—asked me to extend his apologies that he could not be here to receive you properly."

"He did his receivin' proper enough to suit me," said Phillips, running his sleeve across his forehead.

"Yes, your town has been rather full of surprises," said Downs. "We had quite expected the dike to be blown. It's been happening all down the coast, you know, Sir."

"So we imagined," nodded ten Brink.

"We have just come from the sea wall," said Father Vermue. "It is intact, *Gott sei dank!*"

"Did you manage to deactivate their explosive, or something?" asked Downs.

"Oh, no," smiled the Burgomeister. "We had quite another job at the sea wall. We were burying a pair of hands."

"From the fireplace," said Phillips.

"Yes, from the fireplace," nodded ten Brink, walking over to the empty hooks set in the stone mantel. "Father Vermue gave them his blessing and I—as the secular arm—hurled them into the sea."

"God willing," said the Priest, missing ten Brink's sally in his zeal, "perhaps they will find peace there, finally."

"I'm afraid I don't understand, Sir," said Downs. "About the dike's not being blown, I mean. Surely the Germans didn't plan to leave the town intact?"

"Not at all," said ten Brink grimly. "The Hauptmann, here was to give the order himself. At the last minute, when his troops had withdrawn, he was fortunately interrupted."

"Your underground, I imagine," said Downs, offering cigarettes.

"In a sense," smiled ten Brink. "Actually, two traitors who wished to redeem themselves." The old man walked to the window and slowly pushed out the shutters. A coffin shaped rectangle of light fell across von Frolich's body, making the Iron Cross sparkle as it hung askew on his chest. The Hauptmann was smiling, still, up into the darkened beams of the high ceilinged Raadhuis, as if he saw a familiar face among the shadows.

The click of hobnailed boots came through the window as advance parties of the Leeds Rifles moved cautiously into the streets of Katzaveere. The Burgomeister listened to the first shouts of recognition as his returning fisherfolk met the advancing British. He smiled wistfully, then turned back to the hearth where the Priest and the two soldiers stood silently over Hauptmann von Frolich.

"You will notice, Lieutenant," said ten Brink casually, "that the Herr Hauptmann has been strangled."

"Strangled indeed!" marveled Lieutenant Downs. "Why, the fingers must have snapped his spine!"

"Ya," said the Burgomeister. "The fingers of *two right hands.*"

THE JAPANESE TEA SET

FRANCIS J. O'NEIL

It was at that moment that he became sickeningly aware of his approaching madness. With a wrench of almost physical pain, he felt the last faint vestiges of his sanity tearing loose and fleeing in abject terror into the shifting shadows gathered at the back of his mind.

At that moment, Lieutenant Joshua Falter, United States Marines, felt the hand brush gently along his cheek, filling the whole of his quivering body with a strange and unearthly coldness.

A few minutes ago he'd been walking with swift intensity along the gray sidewalk of the *Ryokan Shimbashi,* completely unaware of the myriad piping cries of the Japanese vendors holding forth pewter and brass trinkets for his inspection. With a sort of desperate intensity he was recalling the address in his overcoat pocket. *Doctor*

Ato Taimai, 999 Ryokan Shimbashi, Tokyo, the damp scrap of paper had told him.

It was all that was left, that address—the last thin sliver of salvation thrust between himself and an inexorable dissolution into madness and, finally, death.

Ever since leaving the air force base at Haneda that morning, Joshua had been questing frantically through the maze of misty streets that splayed out in mud-spattered confusion from the macadam spine of the *Ginza.* Finally, long after nightfall, he'd found *Ryokan Shimashi,* and then the house 999, sitting back from the sidewalk, its thin walls and small windows showing in the saffron splash of a streetlamp.

Looking up at the delicately etched numerals above the stained, monkey-pod door, Joshua had felt that spasm of hysterical elation, and he had said aloud, "Now, Chicoro, you vicious, sloe-eyed imp, we'll see if I live or die!"

Walking up to the door, he'd knocked loudly and stepped back to wait. Then it happened.

In that little pool of lemon light, with the fog drifting in gauze tendrils around him, a hand reached out of nowhere and drew a soft, smooth caress across his cheek.

Joshua felt a snap behind the frontal bone of his forehead, felt a kind of draining, warm wetness, as though a fat grape had burst amid the convolutions of his brain. Gripping himself hard he spun about.

Then he knew the madness was coming upon him swiftly, for Chicoro, his sweet-faced girl-*san,* had died six months ago, a suicide in Osaka miles to the south. Yet the hand that just touched him was Chicoro's.

It *was* Chicoro's—of that there could be no mistake. There could be no mistaking the incredible softness of flesh, the long slender fingers, the singular scent of some musky Oriental perfume. Countless times, sitting at the tiny bar in the officer's club at Itami, Chicoro's hand had made that same caress. Looking up at him, the elfin face naive as a flower petal, Chicoro had said, "Ah, Josh, I love you, love you," and the words had been a whisper, almost a sigh of pain. Six months ago. . . .

There was a soft sound behind Joshua. He whirled around. The monkey-pod door had opened and, in the dim light issuing from within, stood an elderly Japanese wearing a black Occidental business suit.

"Hai?" he asked softly. "May I do something for you?" His voice

was a thin thread of sound. Controlling an impulse to look back over his shoulder, Joshua said, "You are Doctor Taimai?"

The old man nodded, his placid eyes, canted slightly in the fragile, brown face resting gently on Joshua. Surprisingly, he said, "A wise man once wrote that it is only fear itself of which we must be afraid, Lieutenant. Try to relax."

Doctor Taimai stepped back into the ante-way and made a gesture with his hand toward another door. Joshua entered and walked quickly across a deep-piled Oriental rug into a small room. He dropped into the lap of a leather chair beside a teakwood desk, and took his head in his hands as a sob shuddered up from deep inside him.

Closing the door, Doctor Taimai crossed to his chair and sat down in the cone of a single lamp that flooded the desk top. He watched Joshua weeping for a moment, then said, "You are gravely ill, my son. Even to the uninitiated that would be obvious."

"I had to come to you," Joshua said suddenly, leaning over to grasp the desk. "If you cannot help me I'm finished. I'll be doomed as surely as the Stateside wise-acres thought we were at Chosin Reservoir."

Joshua's palsied hand skittered across his forehead as he mopped at the sweat. "In fact, it was at Hungnam, after the withdrawal from Chosin, that I heard of you. We'd run a herd of Chinese prisoners down with us, and among them was this Major Tao, a tank commander. He'd been to UCLA; majored in psychology; knew about Freud, Adler, Jung.

"I got to talking to him, as a man sometimes will, and I told him a little of my trouble. Oddly enough, he was fascinated. He insisted I come see you. He said that you were without question the best psychiatrist in the East."

Joshua's reddened eyes stared across at Doctor Taimai. He hesitated, then said, "He also claimed that despite your knowledge of modern psychiatry, you have not completely abandoned a belief in the occult, or, at least, in things beyond the reach of academic pigeon-holing. In other words, Doctor, you haven't that damned, deadly smugness toward the outre and unexplainable that earmarks the medical world. If that's right, chances are you won't laugh at me."

Doctor Taimai's eyes flicked up at Joshua. "Laughter is too expensive," he said, "for me to indulge myself." Reaching into a drawer he took out a block of paper. "It is evident that you have experienced a severe fright, Lieutenant. Could you tell me of it now?"

"It's Chicoro," Joshua said and, though he fought it, a cold spasm ran through him.

"It's Chicoro," Doctor Taimai repeated. "Japanese girl?"

"Yes."

"So," Doctor Taimai said softly. "And this girl gave you such terror?"

"She's dead," Joshua said, his hands gripping hard at the desk. "She's dead, and she just touched me outside your door. Her hand came out of the fog, brushed across my cheek."

Doctor Taimai ran slender, sere fingers through his thinning hair, his lips pursed in thought.

Joshua took the look for one of disbelief. He said, "Yes, Doctor Taimai, I know. Such a statement relegates me to the ranks of the loony. No normal man wallows in conniption fits of this type.

Jumping up, Joshua paced the room. "You'd think I could laugh something as stupid and foolish as this right out of my mind. I'm a fairly rational man. I've seen it all from ouija boards to Haitian fetishes.

"But this thing is not to be shrugged off. There's the whole crux of this stinking business, the things that scare me: I can't stop thinking about what she said! I come awake at night and find my whole body sopping with sweat, my arms and legs trembling uncontrollably. I can't fight her any more; she's whipping me, pulling me down. Soon, very soon. . . ."

"Just a minute, Lieutenant," Doctor Taimai's soft voice cut in. "You are letting emotion become master. Let us be calm. Of what words do you speak? Where is the beginning of this thing?"

Joshua returned to his chair. He made a determined effort to control the chill spasms that chattered through him. "I met Chicoro at a dance in Osaka. She was unbelievably beautiful. Raven hair, clear skin, scarlet lips. She had a trick of tucking up her mouth in a way that got to you. I fell for her, hard."

Joshua rubbed his knees. "I had two months training before going into Korea, and I spent every spare minute with her. I was convinced I loved her."

Getting up, Joshua began to pace again. "And then, a week before I was to leave, something completely illogical happened. One of those things that make you shake your head. I ran into a nurse at the club, a tiny blonde kid from Indianapolis. I . . . I fell in love with her. Don't ask my why. Don't tell me about vacillation, about an unstable, immature mind. I was completely, irrevocably in love with Linda, and within the week we married."

"And Chicoro?" Doctor Taimai said.

"Yes, Chicoro." Joshua's smile was a leer of fear and pain. "After Linda came, I forgot all about Chicoro. It had been an infatuation — a blazing, peculiarly deep infatuation, I'll admit, but that was all. Unfortunately, it was more than that to Chicoro. Much more. She had fallen in love with me and had discarded all her old ties. I need not tell you about the social and moral dictum of the Orient. It is a strange thing to us Caucasians, but deadly serious to Easterners. Chicoro's intent to marry a white man had alienated her with her family, her friends. She'd become practically a pariah in Osaka."

Joshua paused in his pacing. "To sum up: I went to Chicoro when I finally realized how crudely I'd handled something very precious to her. When she learned of my abrupt marriage her senses seemed to leave her. If you have ever seen love and devotion change into bitter hatred, you will know what a frightening experience it is.

"Chicoro simply blew up. At first, she threatened to kill me. Later, she did away with herself, but before the suicide, just before I went to Pusan, she came to me once more. In a regular fury of passion she said that she would haunt me, that scalding searing hatred was far stronger than love, strong enough to fling aside the veil separating life from death. She would come back and stay right beside me, whisper thoughts down into my mind, little thoughts, drop by drop, that would wear away my patience, irritate me into self destruction as the only means of escaping her weird torture."

Joshua's voice rose, touching the edge of hysteria. "I thought at first it was the ranting of a demented woman, Doctor; just cheap prattle to goad me. But I was wrong. She's succeeding. Despite the gunfire on Korea, I could hear her tiny padding footsteps. In foxholes, on ridges, she was right there talking to me. I could hear her!"

"Wait. Wait." Doctor Taimai rose quickly from the chair, his eyes pinned on Joshua. "Easy, my son, please." He pulled a bell cord against the back wall. "We will have tea, Lieutenant. Tea is soothing." He turned as the door opened. A man, extremely old, but moving with the consummate grace of a dancer, came across the room.

"Naiko," the doctor said. "May we have tea. You'll use the Naratocki."

The old man frowned, then turned and left.

The doctor returned to his chair and smiled at Joshua. "Did you suspect, Lieutenant, that Naiko is blind? Completely. Yet he stumbles against nothing. Over the past thirty years he has developed a sort of animal sensitivity, a keen perception that is almost inhuman. Do you see how even the most terrifying tragedy can be turned into a triumph of courage?

"Why, Naiko is so well-adjusted, he even worries about such prosaic things as my Naratocki tea set. It is old china, long in my family, and the years have depleted it terribly. So few pieces left."

Doctor Taimai picked up the block of paper. "But, to return to you, Lieutenant, I believe you are suffering from a complex, a particularly severe and violent complex that is developing a realistic phobia in your mind. A complex is simply a group of ideas and feeling which have been wholly or partly repressed in the unconscious because of painful emotional associations. Just as a person, once burnt, fears fire, just as we unconsciously withdraw ourselves from painful stimuli of any kind, so does the mind attempt to withdraw its field of perception, or by deliberately opening avenues of escape, such as fantasies or daydreams.

"It is evident," Doctor Taimai went on, "that you are an intelligent, well-educated lad of good background. You are, too, sensitive, impressionable. Because of these, and because of an innate sense of decency, you have been unconsciously trying to repress your feeling of guilt concerning Chicoro. This attempt is rich soil in which grew a phobia. Your guilt has become a nebulous wraith shaped in the form of Chicoro. It is not Chicoro, but your own conscience that is haunting you, Lieutenant."

The door opened and Naiko came in. He placed a tray containing sandwiches and the gleaming, yellow pieces of a tea set on the desk. Doctor Taimai looked at the tray, then up at Naiko. He hesitated, then said, "*Aragato*. That will be all, Naiko."

Later, the tea finished and the block of paper scrawled with notes, Doctor Taimai took Joshua to the door. "If you will try to remember that this is something mental, Lieutenant, a fearful little quirk of your subconscious, I think that Chicoro will become less and less of a menace. Come back to see me on Sunday. I want time to look over these notes."

He opened the door and the fog swirled close. "Do not forget, my son, that this trouble is just a phobia, a figment of your imagination cruelly trying to be master."

Returning to his office, Doctor Taimai pulled the bell cord. Naiko entered quietly.

"And, why was it, Naiko," the doctor asked, "that you did not use my Naratocki? It is true the young man would not understand the gesture, but I wanted to show my appreciation for his presenting such an interesting case."

Naiko's smile was a silent apology. "I regret causing you displeasure. Doctor-*san*, but there were only three of the Naratocki tea cups left and, unhappily, I dropped and broke one of these. I was reluctant to affront the lieutenant or his young girl-*san* by bringing in only two of the Naratocki, and having to use an ordinary, uncomplimentary cup for the third. I hope you understand, sir."

"Girl-*san?*" queried Doctor Taimai. "How did you know of the young man's girl-*san?* You don't see, and she was so *quiet!*"

"When one is blind, Doctor-*san,*" replied the servitor, "other senses sharpen. So I hear what others fail to hear. The young man's girl-*san* sat much closer to him than we Japanese regard as proper, and was quite shameless in her profession of love. She kept saying, *"I love you and will never let you go! I love you and will never let you go!"* A Japanese girl should have pride. If the tea set had not broken I should still not have used the Naratocki, with all due respectful apologies, Doctor-*san.* This is understood?"

"It is understood, Naiko. Had I heard the young lady myself I should not have bidden you bring the Naratocki!"

Outside, Lieutenant Joshua Falter almost staggered, almost ran, from the doctor's office. Twice since leaving he had felt the hand of his late beloved, caressing his cheeks. Now something had been added that he could not understand, that made madness nearer, virtually upon him—a sound utterly *Japanese.* He heard it around every corner, from every open door; the tinkling small crash of breaking chinaware; as if exactly the same tea cup were being dropped countless times right behind him; as if the sound pursued him.

It did, with his knowledge of the Orient, indeed pursue him. A broken tea cup had a certain meaning: it was the symbol of a cast-off bride, of an unmarried girl no longer a maiden, of a suicide; it meant Chicoro.

The hands touched his cheeks, there were two of them now, and they slid slowly, caressingly, down to his throat, started to tighten. His neck, his face, swelled with fright and the heavy darkness closed in around him as the sound of the breaking chinaware multiplied, weaved together into a crashing crescendo. ——

THE JUSTICE OF THE CZAR

CAPTAIN GEORGE FIELDING ELIOT

Dimitri Minin, chief executioner of the prison of St. Peter and St. Paul, rose from his seat as an imperative knock clattered at the door of his quarters, high in the north tower.

"Be at ease, Tasia," he said to his wife, who had also started up. "I have many a summons lately, since this conspiracy against the holy person of His Majesty has been discovered. Doubtless it is but some wretched boyar to be put to the question."

He flung open the door. In the shadows of the stair-landing the light of a guard lantern gleamed on the accouterments of a sergeant of the Praeobajensky Regiment.

"To the lower dungeons, butcher!" snapped the soldier. "Quickly —you are wanted!"

"Dog!" retorted Minin. "Is it thus that you address an official of the Czar's household? Perhaps—you would like to feel the butcher's hands at work on you?"

He extended his long, powerful, sinewy hands toward the man, opening and closing the fingers suggestively.

"With the hot pincers, eh?" he added.

The soldier shuddered visibly. "No, no, good Dimitri!" he said. "I but spoke in haste. Yet come quickly, for it is the governor's own order!"

Dimitri nodded.

"I come," he said, and flinging a black cloak round his shoulders he stepped out on the landing.

"I think I shall not be long, Tasia," he said. "Have a bit of soup warm against my return—those dungeons are chill enough, all of them, but the lower dungeons especially!"

He closed the door behind him and followed the sergeant down the narrow, winding stair.

Down, down through the heart of the grim prison-fortress, past the guardroom, past the doors opening into the great hall, down to the cellars; then past a little iron door leading to the upper dungeons, and still the stair descended into black, dank chill—along a corridor, lit only by a single torch guttering in the cold air; then another iron door. Here Dimitri knocked, with a peculiar sequence; and instantly chains and bolts rattled within, the door was flung open, and Dimitri stepped into a vaulted chamber, lit by a dozen flaring lamps. A harsh voice—that of the prison governor—dismissed the sergeant.

The door clanged shut behind Dimitri as he bowed low to the governor.

The scene within was familiar enough to the executioner, and yet this night it had some novel features. There was the governor, and the slender, dark-clad figure of the prison physician. There, hanging from the ceiling of oft-used chains, was the naked figure of the victim: a slender white body, apparently that of a young man, his wrists high above his head in the grip of the iron bracelets, his ankles locked to the floor by the stocks provided for that purpose.

But—and this was strange to Dimitri—the victim's face and head were hooded and concealed by a black sack, drawn over the head and secured about the man's neck by a stout cord. It was the first time that Dimitri had ever seen this done, and he wondered.

One of his assistants silently glided forward from a corner and handed Dimitri a knout. Dimitri gripped the heavy oaken handle of the terrible whip in practised fingers—ran through his hands the long knotted thongs, with their cruel steel goads at the ends. He nodded.

"A good knout, Paul," he said, and turned expectantly toward the governor.

He was ready to begin.

But the governor was not looking at Dimitri. He was staring across the room—staring at a little group of men standing at the farther side, out of the direct glare of the lamps.

The governor's face was white beneath the brim of his fur hat; the eyes which had looked unmoved on so much torture and death were filled with a strange emotion.

Was it—fear? Dimitri, accustomed to reading the expressions in men's eyes, felt a sudden unaccountable dread clutch at his heart.

If his Excellency the Governor of St. Peter and St. Paul—known far and wide in Holy Russia as Black Nikolai—was *afraid:* Black Nikolai *afraid!*—ah, then common men might well look to themselves. God! what business was this?

Dimitri followed the governor's gaze.

There were five men at the far side of the dungeon—no, there were more; for in one corner were half a dozen Tartar troopers of one of the newly raised regiments of irregular horse, which the Czar had recruited in the south. Brutish, pig-eyed fellows these, short and squat and bowlegged: in stolid silence they watched the scene before them. A block stood there also, and a Tartar ax—and Dimitri thought he understood.

Here was quick release for the victim—after the knout had ripped his secrets from his quivering body! Dimitri had had experience of such methods.

But the silent group of five in the other corner—one in a long red cloak and hat drawn well down over his eyes, the others officers of the Imperial Guard in military cloaks, booted and spurred—why were they so silent? Were they witnesses—were they—? Again, unaccountably, Dimitri felt the icy grip of that strange fear.

The man in the red cloak suddenly inclined his head.

The governor bowed; turned to Dimitri. "Begin," he said in low tones.

Dimitri, in silence, stepped forward into the center of the floor, placing himself with practised deliberation at exactly the proper distance from his prey. He flung off his cloak, tossed it to his assistant; removed also his tunic, and stood bared to the waist, his tremendous muscles rippling under his hairy skin, his splendid torso like a figure of some pagan god, there in the flickering lamplight.

He swung the knout experimentally; the thongs whistled through the air; the naked man in chains shrank at the sound, as well he might. Dimitri, his strong hands gripping the handle of the awful knout, stepped back, poised for the first stroke—

"Wait!"

Surprized, Dimitri turned. It was the man in the red cloak who had spoken. Some great one, this, without a doubt; for instantly the governor confirmed with a sharp word the order given.

The red-cloaked one looked over the muffling edge of his cloak at the trembling victim.

"One last word, Alexis," said he. "The knout is ready—you have heard the whine of its thongs—will you speak? The names of your accomplices—of those who have led you into this conspiracy! The names! Speak—and a swift and merciful death shall be your reward!"

And then for the first time the masked one spoke. One word, muffled by the black hood. Yet firm, resolute, determined: "Never!"

The eyes of the man in the red cloak glared with a rage truly infernal. "By the bones of Saint Andrew!" he swore, grinding out the words between his teeth, "ere this night is over, you will speak, and gladly. Proceed, executioner!"

Again Dimitri took his stance; poised; swung back the knout. The thongs whizzed through the air and bit deep into the back of the naked man.

A scream rang out—a terrible scream, the scream of a man who has never before known physical pain; it echoed away through the arches of the vaulted roof, those grim old arches which had echoed so many screams of agony.

Across the white back of the victim were now seven red weals as the thongs fell away—weals dotted with larger spots of red, where the knots had torn little gouts of flesh from the quivering back as with practised hand Dimitri jerked them aside.

Again the knout swung back—forward—whined and struck home—again—again—and all the time the screams rang through the dungeon, till the Guard officers turned away their heads and even the stolid Tartars muttered in a vague distress which was as near to pity as they could come.

Twenty strokes of the knout had fallen; now the back of the naked man was one great mass of raw, pulsating flesh. No skin at all remained, save a few strips still hanging precariously here and there. And still the pitiless red whip rose and fell.

The screams were not so loud, now; they lost their piercing quality, sank into mere moans of unutterable agony. And at last even these were silent.

Dimitri paused in his dreadful task. "I think he has fainted, sir," he said to the physician.

"Revive him, and continue," grated the man in the red cloak, at the governor's inquiring—almost shuddering—glance.

The physician gave low-voiced instructions to the assistants; a bucket of water was flung over the poor bleeding body hanging there by its wrist-chains. It washed away some of the blood, some of the loose flesh; not only the back had suffered, for in front, on the stomach and chest, the flesh had been torn to ribbons by the steel tips of the thongs as they curved round the body at the conclusion of each stroke.

Another bucket of water; now the physician was forcing brandy between the clenched teeth of the victim—teeth which had at the last met and fixed themselves in the lower lip. There was a low moan—a choking sob; the torn body moved a little.

"Will you speak, Alexis?" demanded the inexorable voice of the man in the red cloak.

And again, from the depths of that black hood, faintly now but still with that ring of deathless resolution, came one word: "Never!"

The red-cloaked one snarled wordlessly; motioned with his arm; the governor spoke.

Again the knout rose and fell, rose and fell, rose and fell; now at every blow blood and flesh spurted forth, spattered the walls, reddened and soaked into the earthen floor beneath the victim, where no stones had been laid, so that there might be no need to remove the blood of countless poor wretches who suffered there.

The physician whispered to the governor.

"What is that?" snapped the red-cloaked one.

"He is saying, lord," replied the governor, "that a few more strokes will kill."

"So be it!" exclaimed the other, savagely. "Go on, executioner; finish your work!"

"To the death?" asked Dimitri, panting from his exertions, while the red thongs of the knout trailed their horror on the floor.

"To the death!"

The voice of the man in the red cloak seemed to break for a moment, but he spoke no more; the governor nodded, and the knout was at work again.

Swiftly now the strokes fell. Dimitri charged from one side to the other, shifting the knout from his right hand to his left. Long practise had made him equally dexterous with either hand, and the knout had been busy these past years.

The terrible shreds of what had been a strong and vigorous youth hung limply from the wrist-irons. No cries, no moans; not a sound save the whistle of the lash, the deep breathing of Dimitri, and the sodden thud of the blows.

Again the physician whispered to the governor.

"Enough!" said Black Nikolai.

Dimitri ceased his horrible exertions; stood aside, silent, waiting.

The physician stepped forward to the bloody thing that had once been human. A moment—then he bowed his head on his breast.

"It is done, lord," he said; and suddenly turned, sprang to the door, tore open the bolts and was gone. They could hear his footsteps clattering up the stone stair in mad haste.

An assistant executioner, at a sign from the governor, loosed the chains from their ring and lowered the body to the ground.

The man in the red cloak stepped forward to its side, moving slowly, almost wearily. Long he looked down at it in silence; then with a sudden motion tore the cloak from his shoulders and flung its ample scarlet folds over the horror on the floor, not less scarlet.

"Come!" he cried in a great voice to the Guard officers. "Come! Take up the body of His Imperial Highness, the Crown Prince Alexis Petrovitch Romanoff, and bear it with all fitting honors to the chapel of the fortress!"

He raised his head—his burning eyes seemed to shrivel Dimitri's very soul.

It was the Czar—Peter the Czar, surnamed the Great!

For a moment he stared at the executioner; then slowly his terrible eyes traveled downward to the hands which still gripped that bloody knout. There they rested for a long moment.

"Go, Nikolai, and see that all is done well!" said the Czar, choking on the words. Already the Guard officers were lifting, as gently and carefully as they could, the torn remnants of the Crown Prince of Russia. In silence they bore the body from the room; the governor followed.

"Dismiss your assistants," ordered the Czar; and Dimitri, still wondering, still with that chill of fear at his heart, obeyed.

The Czar took a step back.

It was over, thought Dimitri; his mind turned from the dreadful scene that had been to the hot soup that Tasia would have waiting for him in the tower. God! He would need a measure of brandy first, after this!

He glanced furtively at the lowering figure of the Czar; that burning gaze again was fixed on his hands—on the knout.

The Czar was trembling. Suddenly, with an indescribably violent movement—almost as though it required a terrific effort to tear his eyes from those blood-stained hands and that scarlet whip—the Czar turned away. His eyes fell on the silent Tartar troopers, on the block and ax that were to have been the instruments of his imperial mercy.

The Czar took a step forward—paused—

"Seize him!" he cried in a terrible voice, pointing at Dimitri.

The Tartars sprang forward in instant obedience; Dimitri, his blood congealing in his veins, felt their strong fingers grip his arms.

"To the block with him!" cried the Czar. "Strike off those hands —those hands that have torn the life from my son—ah, God! my son! my son!"

The Czar turned toward the stair; the last sound that came to Dimitri's ears as the Tartars dragged him toward the corner where waited the block and the ax was that despairing cry: "Ah, God! my son! my son!"

Then the door closed on the horror that remained. —✣—

THE LAST DRIVE

CARL JACOBI

It was a cold wind that whipped across the hills that November evening. There was snow in the air, and Jeb Waters in the cab of his jolting van shivered and drew the collar of his sheepskin higher about the throat. All day endless masses of white cumulus cloud had raced across a cheerless sky. They were gray now, those clouds, leaden gray, and so low-hanging they seemed to lie like a pall on the crest of each distant hillock. Off to the right, stern and majestic, like a great parade of H. G. Wells' Martian creatures, marched the towers of the Eastern States Power lines, the only evidence here of present-day civilization. A low humming whine rose from the taut wires now as the mounting wind twanged them in defiance.

Through the windshield Jeb Waters scanned the sky anxiously.

"It's going to be a cold trip back," he muttered to himself. "Looks mighty like a blizzard startin'."

He gave the engine a bit more gas and tightened his grasp on the wheel as a sharper curve loomed up suddenly before him. For a time he drove in silence, his mind fixed only on the barrenness of the hills on all sides. Marchester lay thirty miles ahead, thirty long, rolling miles. Littleton was just behind. If there were going to be a storm, perhaps it would be wise to return and wait until morning before making the trip. It would be bad to get stuck out here tonight, especially with the kind of load he was delivering. Enough to give one the creeps even in the daytime.

Marchester with its few hundred souls, hopelessly lost in the hills, too small or perhaps too lazy to incorporate itself, had been passed by without a glance when the railroad officials distributed spurs leading from the main line. As a result all freight had to be trucked thirty miles across the country from Littleton, the nearest town on trackage. But there wasn't much freight, as the officials had suspected, and although Jeb Waters drove the distance only twice a week, he rarely returned with more than a single package.

Today, however, the load had stunned him with its importance. In the van, back of him, separated by only the wooden wall of the cab, lay a coffin, and in that coffin was the body of Philip Carr, Marchester's most promising son. Philip Carr—Race Carr they had called him because he was such a driving fool—was the only man

289

who could have brought the town to fame. With his queer-looking Speed Empress, the racing-car which was a product of his own invention and three years' work, he had hoped to raise the automobile speed record on the sand track of Daytona Beach, Florida. He had clocked an unofficial 300 miles an hour in a practise attempt, and the world had sat up and taken notice.

On the fatal day, however, a tire had failed to stand the centrifugal force, and in a trice the car had twisted itself into a lump of steel. Philip Carr had been instantly killed. There was talk of burying him in Florida, but Marchester, his home town, had absolutely refused. And so the body had been shipped back to Littleton, the nearest point on rails, and Jeb Waters had been sent to bring it from there to Marchester.

Jeb hadn't liked the idea. There was nothing to be afraid of, he knew, but somehow when he was alone in these Rentharpian Hills, even though he had known no other home since a child, he always felt depressed and anxious for companionship. A coffin would hardly serve to ease his mind.

The wind was mounting steadily, and now the first swirls of snow began to appear. The cab of the van was anything but warm. A corner of the windshield was broken out, and the rags Jeb had stuffed in the hole failed to keep out the cold.

Premature darkness had swooped down under the lowering clouds, and Jeb turned on the lights. The van was a very old one, and the lights worked on the magneto. As the snow became thicker and thicker Jeb was forced to reduce his speed, and the lights, deprived of most of their current, dimmed to only a low dismal glow, illuminating but little of the road ahead.

Yet the miles rolled slowly by. The snow was piling in drifts now. It rolled across the hills, a great sweeping blanket of white, and swirled like powder through the crevices of the cab. And it was growing colder.

Frome's Hill, the steepest rise on the road, loomed up abruptly, and Jeb roared the rickety motor into a running start. The van lurched up the ascent, back wheels spinning in the soft snow, seeking traction. The engine hammered its protest. The transmission groaned as if in pain. Up, up climbed the truck until at length it reached the very top.

"Now it's clear sailing," said Jeb aloud.

But he had spoken too soon. With a sigh as if the feat had been too great, the motor lapsed into sudden silence. The lights blinked out, and there was only the gray darkness of the hills and the swishing of the snow on the sides of the cab.

For a full moment Jeb sat there motionless as the horror of the situation fell upon him. Snowbound with a corpse! Twenty miles from the nearest habitation and alone with a coffin! A cold sweat burst out on his forehead at the realization of the predicament.

But he was acting like a child. It was ridiculous to let his nerves run away with him like that. If he could only keep from freezing there would be no danger. In the morning when it was found he hadn't reached Marchester the people would send help. Probably Ethan would come. Old Ethan. He would come in that funny sleigh of his. And he would say:

"Well Jeb, howdja like spending the night with a dead 'un?"

And then they would both laugh and drive back to town. . . . But that was tomorrow. Tonight there was the storm—and the corpse.

He set the spark, got out, and cranked the engine. But he did it half-heartedly. He knew by the tone of the engine when it had stopped that it would be a long time before it would resume revolutions.

At length he resigned himself to his plight, returned to the cab and tried to keep warm. But the cab was old and badly built. The wind blew through chinks and holes in great drafts, and snow sifted down his neck. It suddenly occurred to him that the back part of the van, which had been repaired recently, would give better protection against the blizzard than the cab. There were robes back there too, robes used to keep packages from being broken. If only the coffin weren't there! One couldn't sleep next to a coffin.

Another thought followed. Why not put the coffin in the cab? There was nothing else in the van, and he would then have the back of it to himself. He could lie down too and with the robes manage to keep warm somehow.

In a moment his mind was made up, and he set about to accomplish his task. It was hard, slow work. The coffin was heavy, the cab small and the steering-post in the way. Finally by shoving it in end up he managed it successfully, and then going to the back of the van, he went in, closed the door, rolled up like a ball in the robes and lay down to sleep.

Sleep proved elusive. He stirred restlessly, listening to the sounds of the storm. Occasionally the truck trembled as a stronger gust of wind struck it. Occasionally he could hear the mournful Eolian whine of the power lines. Powdery snow rustled along the roof of the van. And the iron exhaust pipe cracked loudly as the heat left it. Minutes dragged by, slowly, interminably.

And then suddenly Jeb Waters sat bolt upright. Whether or not he had dozed off into a fitful sleep he did not know, but at any rate he was wide awake now.

The van was moving! He could hear the tires crunching in the snow, could feel the slight swaying as the car gained momentum. He leaped to his feet and pressed his eyes against the little window that connected the back of the van with the cab.

For a moment he saw nothing. A strip of black velvet seemed pasted before the glass. Then the darkness softened. A soft glow seemed to form in the cab, and vaguely he seemed to see the figure of a man hunched over the wheel in the driver's position.

The van was going faster now. It creaked and swayed, and the wheels rumbled hollowly. Yet strangely enough there was no sound of the engine. Jeb hammered on the little pane of glass.

"Hey!" he cried. "Get away from that wheel! Stop!"

The figure seemed not to hear. With his hands grasping the wheel tightly, elbows far out, shoulders hunched low, he appeared aware of nothing but the dark road ahead of him. Faster and faster sped the van.

Frantically Jeb rammed his clenched fist through the window. The glass broke into a thousand fragments.

"Do you hear?" he cried. "Stop, blast you! Stop!"

The man turned and leered at him. Even in the half-glow Jeb recognized the features—that deathly white face, the black, glassy eyes.

"Oh, my God," he screamed. *"It's Philip Carr!"* His voice rose to a hysterical laughing sob. His hands trembled as he clutched the careening walls, striving to keep his balance.

"Philip Carr," he shouted. "You're dead. You're dead, do you hear? You can't drive any more."

A horrible gurgling laugh came from the man at the wheel. The figure bent lower as if to urge the van to a greater speed. And the van answered as if to a magic touch. On it raced into the storm, rocking and swaying like a thing accursed. Snow swirled past in great white clouds. The wind howled in fanatical accompaniment.

Jeb plunged his arm through the broken window and clawed for the throat of the driver.

"Stop!" he screamed. And then he gurgled in horror as his hands touched the ice-cold skin.

Suddenly with a lurch the van left the road and leaped toward the blacker shadows of a gully. A giant tree, its branches gesticulating wildly in the wind, reared up just ahead.

There came a crash!

❄ ❄ ❄

"It's odd," said the coroner, and frowned.

Old Ethan scratched his chin.

"It 'pears," he said, "as if that danged van engine went and stopped right on the top of that hill. Then Jeb, he musta gone into the back of the van to keep warm, and durin' the night the wind started the thing a-rollin'. It come tearin' down the hill, jumped into this here gully and ran smash agin the tree. That's the way I figure it. Poor old Jeb!"

"Yes," replied the coroner, "but there doesn't seem to be the slightest injury on Jeb's body. Apparently he died of heart-failure. And the corpse of Philip Carr! . . . The crash might have ripped open the coffin. But that doesn't explain why the body although set in rigor mortis is in a sitting position. The way his arms are extended, it looks almost as though he were driving once more."

THE LAST INCANTATION

CLARK ASHTON SMITH

Malygris the magician sat in the topmost room of his tower that was built on a conical hill above the heart of Susran, capital of Poseidonis. Wrought of a dark stone mined from deep in the earth, perdurable and hard as the fabled adamant, this tower loomed above all others, and flung its shadow far on the roofs and domes of the city, even as the sinister power of Malygris had thrown its darkness on the minds of men.

Now Malygris was old, and all the baleful might of his enchantments, all the dreadful or curious demons under his control, all the fear that he had wrought in the hearts of kings and prelates, were no longer enough to assuage the black ennui of his days. In his chair that was fashioned from the ivory of mastodons, inset with terrible cryptic runes of red tourmalins and azure crystals, he stared moodily through the one lozenge-shaped window of fulvous glass. His white eyebrows were contracted to a single line on the umber parchment of his face, and beneath them his eyes were cold and green as the ice of ancient floes; his beard, half white, half of a black with glaucous gleams, fell nearly to his knees and hid many of the writhing serpentine characters inscribed in woven silver athwart the bosom of his violet robe. About him were scattered all the appurtenances of his art; the skulls of men and monsters; phials filled with black or amber liquids, whose sacrilegious use was known to none but himself; little drums of vulture-skin, and crotali made from the bones and teeth of the cockodrill, used as an accompaniment to certain incantations. The mosaic floor was partly covered with the skins of enormous black and silver apes; and above the door there hung the head of a unicorn in which dwelt the familiar demon of Malygris, in the form of a coral viper with pale green belly and ashen mottlings. Books were piled everywhere: ancient volumes bound in serpent-skin, with verdigris-eaten clasps, that held the frightful lore of Atlantis, the pentacles that have power upon the demons of the earth and the moon, the spells that transmute or disintegrate the elements; and runes from a lost language of Hyperborea, which, when uttered aloud, were more deadly than poison or more potent than any philtre.

But, though these things and the power they held or symbolized were the terror of the peoples and the envy of all rival magicians, the thoughts of Malygris were dark with immitigable melancholy, and weariness filled his heart as ashes fill the hearth where a great fire has died. Immovable he sat, implacable he mused, while the sun of afternoon, declining on the city and on the sea that was beyond the city, smote with autumnal rays through the window of greenish-yellow glass, and touched his shrunken hands with its phantom gold, and fired the balas-rubies of his rings till they burned like demonian eyes. But in his musings there was neither light nor fire; and turning from the grayness of the present, from the darkness that seemed to close in so imminently upon the future, he groped among the shadows of memory, even as a blind man who has lost the sun and seeks it everywhere in vain. And all the vistas of time that had been so full of gold and splendor, the days of triumph that were colored like a soaring flame, the crimson and purple of the rich imperial years of his prime, all these were chill and dim and strangely faded now, and the remembrance thereof was no more than the stirring of dead embers. Then Malygris groped backward to the years of his youth, to the misty, remote, incredible years, where, like an alien star, one memory still burned with unfailing luster—the memory of the girl Nylissa whom he had loved in days ere the lust of unpermitted knowledge and necromantic dominion had ever entered his soul. He had well-nigh forgotten her for decades, in the myriad preoccupations of a life so bizarrely diversified, so replete with occult happenings and powers, with supernatural victories and perils; but now, at the mere thought of this slender and innocent child, who had loved him so dearly when he too was young and slim and guileless, and who had died of a sudden mysterious fever on the very eve of their marriage-day, the mummy-like umber of his cheeks took on a phantom flush, and deep down in his icy orbs was a sparkle like the gleam of mortuary tapers. In his dreams arose the irretrievable suns of youth, and he saw the myrtle-shaded valley of Meros, and the stream Zemander, by whose ever-verdant marge he had walked at eventide with Nylissa, seeing the birth of summer stars in the heavens, the stream, and the eyes of his beloved.

Now, addressing the demonian viper that dwelt in the head of the unicorn, Malygris spoke, with the low monotonous intonation of one who thinks aloud:

"Viper, in the years before you came to dwell with me and to make your abode in the head of the unicorn, I knew a girl who was lovely and frail as the orchids of the jungle, and who died as the orchids die. . . . Viper, am I not Malygris, in whom is centered the mastery of all occult lore, all forbidden dominations, with dominion over the spirits of earth and sea and air, over the solar and lunar demons, over the living and the dead? If so I desire, can I not call the girl Nylissa, in the very semblance of all her youth and beauty, and bring her forth from the never-changing shadows of the cryptic tomb, to stand before me in this chamber, in the evening rays of this autumnal sun?"

"Yes, master," replied the viper, in a low but singularly penetrating hiss, "you are Malygris, and all sorcerous or necromantic power is yours, all incantations and spells and pentacles are known to you. It is possible, if you so desire, to summon the girl Nylissa from her abode among the dead, and to behold her again as she was ere her loveliness had known the ravening kiss of the worm."

"Viper, is it well, is it meet, that I should summon her thus? . . . Will there be nothing to lose, and nothing to regret?"

The viper seemed to hesitate. Then, in a more slow and measured hiss: "It is meet for Malygris to do as he would. Who, save Malygris, can decide if a thing be well or ill?"

"In other words, you will not advise me?" the query was as much a statement as a question, and the viper vouchsafed no further utterance.

Malygris brooded for awhile, with his chin on his knotted hands. Then he arose, with a long-unwonted celerity and sureness of movement that belied his wrinkles, and gathered together, from different coigns of the chamber, from ebony shelves, from caskets with locks of gold or brass or electrum, the sundry appurtenances that were needful for his magic. He drew on the floor the requisite circles, and standing within the center-most he lit the thuribles that contained the prescribed incense, and read aloud from a long narrow scroll of gray vellum the purple and vermilion runes of the ritual that summons the departed. The fumes of the censers, blue and white and violet, arose in thick clouds and speedily filled the room with ever-writhing interchanging columns, among which the sunlight disappeared and was succeeded by a wan unearthly glow, pale as the light of moons that ascend from Lethe. With preternatural slowness, with unhuman solemnity, the voice of the necromancer went on in a priest-like chant till the scroll was ended and the last echoes lessened and died out in hollow sepulchral vibrations. Then the colored vapors cleared away, as if the folds of a curtain had been drawn back. But the pale unearthly glow still filled the chamber, and between Malygris and the door where hung the unicorn's head there stood the apparition of Nylissa, even as she had stood in the perished years, bending a little like a wind-blown flower, and smiling with the unmindful poignancy of youth. Fragile, pallid, and simply gowned, with anemone blossoms in her black hair, with eyes that held the new-born azure of vernal heavens, she was all that Malygris had remembered, and his sluggish heart was quickened with an old delightful fever as he looked upon her.

"Are you Nylissa?" he asked—"the Nylissa whom I loved in the myrtle-shaded valley of Meros, in the golden-hearted days that have gone with all dead eons to the timeless gulf?"

"Yes, I am Nylissa." Her voice was the simple and rippling silver of the voice that had echoed so long in his memory. . . . But somehow, as he gazed and listened, there grew a tiny doubt—a doubt no less absurd than intolerable, but nevertheless insistent: was this altogether the same Nylissa he had known? Was there not some elusive change, too subtle to be named or defined, had time and the grave not taken something away—an innominable something that his magic had not wholly restored? Were the eyes as tender, was the black hair as lustrous, the form as slim and supple, as those of the girl he recalled? He could not be sure, and the growing doubt was succeeded by a leaden dismay, by a grim despondency that choked his heart as with ashes. His scrutiny became searching and exigent and cruel, and momently the phantom was less and less the perfect semblance of Nylissa, momently the lips and brow were less lovely, less subtle in their curves; the slender figure became thin, the tresses took on a common black and the neck an ordinary pallor. The soul of Malygris grew sick again with age and despair and the death of his evanescent hope. He could believe no longer in love or youth or beauty, and even the memory of these things was a dubitable mirage, a thing that might or might not have been. There was nothing left but shadow and grayness and dust, nothing but the empty dark and the cold, and a clutching weight of insufferable weariness, of immedicable anguish.

In accents that were thin and quavering, like the ghost of his former voice, he pronounced the incantation that serves to dismiss a summoned phantom. The form of Nylissa melted upon the air like smoke and the lunar gleam that had surrounded her was replaced by the last rays of the sun. Malygris turned to the viper and spoke in a tone of melancholy reproof:

"Why did you not warn me?"

"Would the warning have availed?" was the counter-question. "All knowledge was yours, Malygris, excepting this one thing; and in no other way could you have learned it."

"What thing?" queried the magician. "I have learned nothing except the vanity of wisdom, the impotence of magic, the nullity of love and the delusiveness of memory. . . . Tell me, why could I not recall to life the same Nylissa whom I knew, or thought I knew?"

"It was indeed Nylissa whom you summoned and saw," replied the viper. "Your necromancy was potent up to this point; but no necromantic spell could recall for you your own lost youth or the fervent and guileless heart that loved Nylissa, or the ardent eyes that beheld her then. This, my master, was the thing that you had to learn." ——†——

THE LAST MAN

SEABURY QUINN

One cup to the dead already—
Hurrah for the next that dies!
     —BARTHOLOMEW DOWLING: *The Revel*

Mycroft paused self-consciously before the little bronze plate marked simply TOUSSAINT above the doorbell of the big brownstone house in East One Hundred and Thirty-sixth Street. He felt extraordinarily foolish, like a costumed adult at a child's masquerade party, or as if he were about to rise and "speak a piece." People—his kind of people—simply didn't do this sort of thing.

Then his resolution hardened. "What can I lose?" he muttered cynically, and pressed the button.

A Negro butler, correct as a St. John's Wood functionary in silver-buttoned dress suit and striped waistcoat, answered his ring. "Mister — Monsieur Toussaint?" asked Mycroft tentatively.

"Who iss calling?" asked the butler with the merest trace of accent on his words.

"Uh — Mr. Smith — no, Jones," Mycroft replied, and the shadow of a sneer showed at the corners of the young Negro's mouth. "One minute, if you pleez," he returned, stepped back into the hall and closed the door. In a moment he was back and held the door open. "This way, if you pleez," he invited.

Mycroft was not quite certain what he would find; what he did find amazed him. Vaguely he had thought the place would reek with incense, possibly be hung with meretricious tapestries and papier-mâché weapons, perhaps display a crystal ball or two against cheap cotton-velvet table covers. He was almost awe-struck by the somber magnificence of the room into which he was ushered. Deep-piled rugs from Hamadan and Samarkand lay on the floor, the furniture was obviously French, dull matte-gold wood upholstered in olive-green brocade, on the walls were either Renoir and Picasso originals or imitations good enough to fool a connoisseur; somewhat incongruously, above the fireplace where logs blazed on polished andirons hung a square of rather crudely woven cotton stuff bordered in barbaric black and green. On second look the border proved to be a highly conventionalized but still disturbingly realistic serpent. More in character was the enormous black Persian cat that crouched upon a lustrous Bokhara prayer rug before the fire, paws tucked demurely under it, great plumy tail curled round it, and stared at him with yellow, sulphurous eyes.

"Good evening, Mr. Mycroft, you wished to see me?" Mycroft started as if he had been stung by a wasp. He had not heard the speaker enter, and certainly he was not prepared to be greeted by name.

At the entrance of the drawing room stood his host, smiling faintly at his discomfiture. He was a tall man of uncertain age, dressed with a beautiful attention to detail in faultless evening clothes. The studs of his immaculate white shirt were star sapphires, so were his cuff links, in his lapel showed the red ribbon of the Légion d'Honneur, and he was very black. But not comic, not "dressed up," not out of character. He wore his English-tailored dress clothes as one to the manner born, and there was distinction, almost a nobility, about his features that made Mycroft think of the head of an old Roman Emperor, or perhaps a statesman of the Golden Age of the Republic, carved in basalt.

He had planned his introduction, humorous, and a little patronizing, but as he stared at the other Mycroft felt stage fright. "I—" he began, then gulped and stumbled in his speech. "I—uh—I've heard about you, Mister—Monsieur Toussaint. Some friends of mine told me—"

"Yes?" prompted Toussaint as Mycroft's voice frayed out like a pulled woolen thread. "What is it that you want of me?"

"I've heard you're able to do remarkable things—" once more he halted, and a look of irritation crossed his host's calm features.

"Really, Mr. Mycroft—"

"I've heard that you have power to raise spirits!" Mycroft blurted confusedly. "I'm told you can bring spirits of the dead back—" Once again he halted, angry with himself for the fear he felt clawing at his throat. "Can it be done? Can you do it?"

"Of course," Toussaint replied, quite as if he had been asked if he could furnish musicians for a party. "Whose spirit is it that you want called? When—and how—did he die?"

Mycroft felt on surer ground now. There was no nonsense about this Toussaint, no hint of the charlatan. He was a businessman discussing business. "There are several of them—twenty-five or -six. They died in—er—different ways. You see, they served with me in—"

"Very well, Mr. Mycroft. Come here night after tomorrow at precisely ten minutes to twelve. Everything will be in readiness, and you must on no account be late. Leave your telephone and address with the butler, in case I have to get in touch with you."

"And the fee?"

"The fee will be five hundred dollars, payable after the séance, if you're satisfied. Otherwise there will be no charge. Good evening, Mr. Mycroft."

The impulse had come to him that evening as he walked across the Park from his apartment to his club in East Eighty-sixth Street. Spring had come to New York, delicately as a ballerina dancing *sur les pointes,* every tree was veiled in scarves of green chiffon, every park was jeweled with crocus-gold, but he had found no comfort in awakening nature, nor any joy in the sweet softness of the air. That morning as he unfurled his *Times* in the subway on his way downtown he had seen the notice of Roy Hardy's death. Roy had been the twenty-sixth. He was the last man.

More than fifty years ago they had marched down the Avenue, eager, bright-faced, colors flying, curbside crowds cheering. Off to Cuba, off to fight for Liberty. Remember the Maine!

> "When you hear that bell go ding-a-ling,
> And we all join in and sweetly we will
>   sing, my baby,
> When you hear that bell go ding-a-ling,
> There'll be a hot time in the old town
>   tonight!"

the band had blared. He could still hear the echo of Max Schultz's cornet as he triple-tongued the final note.

They didn't look too much like soldiers, those ribbon-counter clerks and bookkeepers and stock exchange messengers. The supercilious French and British correspondents and observers smiled tolerantly at their efforts to seem military; the Germans laughed outright, and the German-armed, German-trained Spanish veterans disdained them. But after El Caney and San Juan Hill the tune changed. Astounded and demoralized, the Spaniards surrendered in droves, the foreigners became polite, the Cubans took the valiant Americans to their collective hearts, and no one was more gracious in his hospitality than Don José Rosales y Montalvo, whose house in the Calle O'Brien became an informal headquarters for the officers and noncoms of the company.

Don José's table creaked and groaned beneath a load of delicacies such as those young New Yorkers had never seen or even heard of and his cellars seemed inexhaustible. Lads who had known only beer, or, in more reckless moments, gin and whiskey, were introduced to St. Estephe, Johannesburg and Nuites St. Georges. Madeira and Majorca flowed like water, champagne was common as soda pop at home.

But more intoxicating than the strongest, headiest vintage in Don José's caves was Doña Juanita Maria, his daughter. She was a *rubia*, a Spanish blonde, with hair as lustrous as the fine-drawn wires of the gold filigree cross at her throat. Little, almost tiny, she walked with a sort of lilting, questing eagerness, her every movement graceful as a grain-stalk in the wind. Her voice had that sweet, throaty, velvety quality found only in southern countries, and when she played the guitar and sang *canciónes* the songs were fraught with yearning sadness and passionate longing that made those hearing her catch their breath.

Every man-jack of them was in love with her, and not a one of them but polished up his Spanish to say, *"Yo te amo, Juanita* — Juanita, I love you!" And there was not a one of them who did not get a sweet, tender refusal and, by way of consolation, a chaste, sisterly kiss on the cheek.

❦   ❦   ❦

The night before their transport sailed Don José gave a party, a *celebración grande.* The patio of the house was almost bright as noon with moonlight, and in the narrow Saracenic arches between the pillars of the ambulatory Chinese lanterns hung glowing golden-yellow in the shadows. A long table clothed with fine Madeira drawnwork and shining silver and crystal was laid in the center of the courtyard, at its center was a great bouquet of red roses. Wreathed in roses a fat wine cask stood on wooden sawhorses near the table's head. "It is Pedro Ximenes, a full hundred years old," Don José explained pridefully. "I have kept it for some great occasion. Surely this is one. What greater honor could it have than to be served to Cuba's gallant liberators on the eve of their departure?"

After dinner toasts were drunk. To *Cuba Libré,* to Don José, to the lovely Noña Juanita. Then, blushing very prettily, but in nowise disconcerted, she consented to sing them a farewell.

> *"Pregúntale à las estrellas,*
> *Si no de noche me venilovar,*
> *Pregúntale si no busco,*
> *Para adorarte la soledad . . ."*

she sang,

> "O ask of the stars above you
> If I did not weep all the night,
> O ask if I do not love you,
> Who of you dreamt till the dawnlight . . ."

Sabers flashed in the moonlight, blades beat upon the table. "Juanita! Juanita!" they cried fervently. "We love you, Juanita!"

"And I love you—all of you—*señores amados,*" she called gaily back. "Each one of you I love so much I could not bear to give my heart to him for fear of hurting all the others. So"—her throaty, velvet voice was like a caress—"here is what I promise." Her tone sank to a soft ingratiating pizzacato and her words were delicately spaced, so that they shone like minted silver as she spoke them. "I shall belong to the last one of you. Surely one of you will outlive all the rest, and to him I shall give my heart, myself, all of me. I swear it!" She put both tiny hands against her lips and blew them a collective kiss.

And so, because they all were very young, and very much in love, and also slightly drunk, they formed the Last Man Club, and every

301

year upon the anniversary of that night they met, talked over old times, drank a little more than was good for them, and dispersed to meet again next year.

The years slipped by unnoticed as the current of a placid river. And time was good to them. Some of them made names for themselves in finance, the court rooms echoed to the oratory of others; the first World War brought rank and glory to some; more than one nationally advertised product bore the name of one of their number. But time took his fee, also. Each time there were more vacant chairs about the table when they met, and those who remained showed gray at the temples, thickening at the waist, or shining patches of bald scalp. Last year there had been only three of them: Mycroft, Rice and Hardy. Two months ago he and Hardy had acted as pall-bearers for Rice, now Hardy was gone.

He hardly knew what made him decide to consult Toussaint. The day before he'd met Dick Prior at luncheon at the India House and somehow talk had turned on mediums and spiritism. "I think they're all a lot of fakes," Mycroft had said, but Prior shook his head in disagreement.

"Some of 'em—most, probably—are, but there are some things hard to explain, Roger. Take this Negro, Toussaint. He *may* be a faker, but—"

"What about him?"

"Well, it seems he's a Haitian; there's a legend he's descended from Christophe, the Black Emperor. I wouldn't know about that, or whether what they say about his having been a *papaloi*—a voodoo priest, you know—has any basis. He's highly educated, graduate of Lima and the Sorbonne and all that—"

"What's he done?" Mycroft demanded testily. "You say he's done remarkable things—"

"He has. Remember Old Man Meson, Nobel Meson, and the way his first wife made a monkey out of her successor?"

Mycroft shook his head. "Not very well. I recall there was a will contest—"

"I'll say there was. Old Meson got bit by the love-bug sometime after sixty. Huh, love-bug me eye, it was that little gold digger Suzanne Langdon. The way she took him away from his wife was nothing less than petty larceny. He didn't last long after he divorced Dorothy and married Suzanne. Old men who marry young wives seldom do. When he finally pegged out everybody thought he was intestate, and that meant Mrs. Meson number two would take the jackpot, but just as she was all set to rake in the chips Dorothy came up with a last will and testament, signed, sealed, published and declared, and unassailable as Gibraltar. Seems the old goof got wise to himself, and, what was more to the point, to Suzanne, before he kicked the bucket, and made a will that disinherited her, leaving the whole works to Dorothy.

"They found it in the pocket of an old coat in his shooting cabin out on the island, and found the men who'd witnessed it, a Long Island clam-digger and a garage mechanic out at Smithtown."

"How?" asked Mycroft.

"Through this fellow Toussaint. Dorothy had heard of him somehow and went up to Harlem to consult him. She told my Aunt Matilda—Mrs. Truxton Sturdivant, you know—all about it. Seems Toussaint called old Meson's spook up—or maybe down, I wouldn't know—and it told them all about the will, gave 'em minute directions where to look for it, and told 'em who and where the witnesses were. He charged her a stiff fee, but he delivered. She's satisfied."

Mycroft had dismissed the story from his mind that afternoon, but next day when he read Roy Hardy's death notice it recurred to him. That evening as he walked across the Park he reached a decision. Of course, it was all nonsense. But Prior's story hung in his mind like a burr in a dog's fur.

Oh, well . . . he'd have a go at this Toussaint. If nothing more it would be amusing to see him go through his bag of tricks.

The furniture and rugs had been moved from the drawing room when he reached Toussaint's house ten minutes before twelve two nights later. Before the empty, cold fireplace a kind of altar had been set up, clothed with a faircloth and surmounted by a silver cross, like any chapel sanctuary. But there were other things on it. Before the cross there coiled a great black snake, whether stuffed or carved from black wood he could not determine, and each side of the coiling serpent was a gleaming human skull. Tall candles flickered at each end of the altar, giving off the only light in the room.

As his eyes became accustomed to the semi-darkness he saw that a hexangular design had been drawn on the bare floor in red chalk, enclosing the altar and a space some eight feet square each side, and in each of the six angles of the figure stood a little dish filled with black powder. Before the altar, at the very center of the hexagon, was placed a folding chair of the kind used in funeral parlors.

Annoyed, he looked about the room for some sign of Toussaint, and as the big clock in the hall struck the first stave of its hour-chime a footstep sounded at the door. Toussaint entered with an attendant at each elbow. All three wore cassocks of bright scarlet, and over these were surplices of white linen. In addition each wore a red, pointed cap like a miter on his head.

"Be seated," Toussaint whispered, pointing to the folding chair before the altar and speaking quickly, as if great haste were necessary. "On no account, no matter what you see or hear, are you to put so much as a finger past the confines of the Hexagon. If you do you are worse than a dead man—you are lost. You understand?"

Mycroft nodded, and Toussaint approached the altar with his attendants close beside him. They did not genuflect, merely bowed deeply, then Toussaint took two candles from beneath his surplice, lit them at the tapers burning on the altar and handed them to his attendants.

Fairly running from one point of the hexagon to another the acolytes set fire to the black powder in the little metal saucers with their candles, then rejoined Toussaint at the altar.

The big hall clock had just completed striking twelve as Toussaint called out sharply:

"Papa Legba, keeper of the gate, open for us!"

Like a congregation making the responses at a litany the acolytes repeated:

"Papa Legba, keeper of the gate, open for us!"

"Papa Legba, open wide the gate that they may pass!" intoned Toussaint, and once again his attendants repeated his invocation.

It might have been the rumble of a subway train, or one of those strange, inexplicable noises that the big city knows at night, but Mycroft could have sworn that he heard the rumble of distant thunder.

Again and again Toussaint repeated his petition that "the gate" be opened, and his attendants echoed it. This was getting to be tiresome. Mycroft shifted on his uncomfortable seat and looked across his shoulder. His heart contracted suddenly and the blood churned in his ears. About the chalk-marked hexagon there seemed to cluster in the smoke cast off by the censers a rank of dim, indistinct forms, forms not quite human, yet resembling nothing else. They did not move, they did not stir as fog stirs in a breath of wind, they simply hung there motionless in the still air.

> *"Papa Legba, open wide the gate that those this man would speak with may come through!"*

shouted Toussaint, and now the silent shadow-forms seemed taking on a kind of substance. Mycroft could distinguish features—Willis Dykes, he'd been the top kick, and Freddie Pyle, the shavetail, Curtis Sackett, Ernie Proust—one after another of his old comrades he saw in the silent circle as a man sees images upon a photographic negative when he holds it up to the light.

Now Toussaint's chant had changed. No longer was it a reiterated plea, but a great shout of victory. "Damballa Oueddo, Master of the Heavens! Damballa, thou art here! Open wide the dead ones' mouths, Damballa Oueddo. Give them breath to speak and answer questions; give this one his heart's desire!"

Turning from the altar he told Mycroft, "Say what you have to say quickly. The power will not last long!"

Mycroft shook himself like a dog emerging from the water. For an instant he saw in his mind's eye the courtyard of Don José's house, saw the eager, flush-faced youths grouped about the table, saw Juanita in the silver glow of moonlight, lovely as a fairy from Titania's court as she laughed at them, promising. . . .

"Juanita, where is Juanita?" he asked thickly. "She promised she would give herself to the last man—"

"Estoy aquí, querido!"

In fifty years and more he had not heard that voice, but he remembered it as if it had been yesterday—or ten minutes since—when he last heard it. "Juanita!" he breathed, and the breath choked in his throat as he pronounced her name.

She came toward him quickly, passing through the ranks of misty shades like one who walks through swirling whorls of silvery fog. Both her hands reached toward him in a pretty haste. All in white she was, from the great carved ivory comb in her golden hair to the little white sandals cross-strapped over her silken insteps. Her white mantilla had been drawn across her face coquettishly, but he could see it flutter with the breath of her impatience.

"Rog-ger," she spoke his name with the same hesitation between syllables he remembered so well. "Rog-ger, *querido*—belovèd!"

He leaped from the chair, stretched reaching hands to her out-stretched gloved fingers past the boundary of the chalk-drawn hexagon. "Juanita! Juanita, I have waited so long . . . so long. . . ."

Her mantilla fell back as his fingers almost touched hers. There was something wrong with her face. This was not the image he had carried in his heart for more than fifty years. Beneath the crown of gleaming golden hair, between the folds of the white lace mantilla a bare, fleshless skull looked at him. Empty eye-holes stared into his eyes, lipless teeth grinned at him.

He stumbled like a man hit with a blackjack, spun half-way round, then went down so quickly that the impact of his limpness on the polished floor made the candles on the altar flicker.

"Maître," one of the attendants plucked Toussaint's white surplice, *"Maître*, the man is dead." ——

THE LAST OF MRS. DEBRUGH

H. SIVIA

Letty," Mr. DeBrugh remarked between long puffs on his meer-schaum, "you've been a fine maid. You've served Mrs. DeBrugh and me for most of fifteen years. Now I haven't much more time in this life, and I want you to know that after Mrs. DeBrugh and I are gone, you will be well taken care of."

Letty stopped her dusting of the chairs in Mr. DeBrugh's oak-paneled study. She sighed and turned toward the man, who sat on a heavy sofa, puffing on his pipe and gazing across the room into nothingness.

"You mustn't talk that way, Mr. DeBrugh," she said. "You know you're a long time from the dark ways yet." She paused, and then went on dusting and talking again. "And me—humph—I've only done what any ordinary human would do to such a kind employer as you, sir. Especially after all you've done for me."

He didn't say anything, and she went on with her work. Of course she liked to work for him. She had adored the kindly old man since first she had met him in an agency fifteen years before. A person couldn't ask for a better master.

But there was the mistress, Mrs. DeBrugh! It was she who gave Letty cause for worry. What with her nagging tongue and her sharp rebukes, it was a wonder Letty had not quit long before.

She would have quit, too, but there had been the terrible sickness she had undergone and conquered with the aid of the ablest physicians Mr. DeBrugh could engage. She couldn't quit after that, no matter what misery Mrs. DeBrugh heaped on her. And so she went about her work at all hours, never tiring, always striving to please.

She left the study, closing the great door silently behind her, for old Mr. DeBrugh had sunk deeper into the sofa, into the realms of peaceful sleep, and she did not wish to disturb him.

"Letty!" came the shrill cry of Mrs. DeBrugh from down the hall. "Get these pictures and take them to the attic at once. And tell Mr. DeBrugh to come here."

Letty went for the pictures.

"Mr. DeBrugh is asleep," she said, explaining why she was not obeying the last command.

"Well, I'll soon fix that! Lazy old man! Sleeps all day with that smelly pipe between his teeth. If he had an ounce of pep about him, he'd get out and work the flowers. Sleeps too much anyway. Not good for him."

She stamped out of the room and down the hall, and Letty heard her open the door of the study and scream at her husband.

"Hector DeBrugh! Wake up!"

There was a silence, during which Letty wondered what was going on. Then she heard the noisy clop-clop of Mrs. DeBrugh's slippers on the hardwood floor of the study, and she knew the woman was going to shake the daylights out of Mr. DeBrugh and frighten him into wakefulness. She could even imagine she heard Mrs. DeBrugh grasp the lapels of her husband's coat and shake him back and forth against the chair.

Then she heard the scream. It came quite abruptly from Mrs. DeBrugh in the study, and it frightened Letty out of her wits momentarily. After that there was the thud of a falling body and the clatter of an upset piece of furniture.

Letty hurried out of the room into the hall and through the open door of the study. She saw Mrs. DeBrugh slumped on the floor in a faint, and beside her an upset ash-tray. But her eyes did not linger on the woman, nor the tray. Instead, they focussed on the still form of Mr. DeBrugh in the sofa.

He was slumped down, his head twisted to one side and his mouth hanging open from the shaking Mrs. DeBrugh had given him. The meerschaum had slipped from between his teeth, and the cold ashes were scattered on his trousers.

Even then, before the sea of tears began to flow from her eyes, Letty knew the old man was dead. She knew what he had meant by the speech he had said to her only a few minutes before.

"His heart," was the comment of the doctor who arrived a short time later and pronounced the old man dead. "He had to go. Today, tomorrow. Soon."

After that, he put Mrs. DeBrugh to bed and turned to Letty.

"Mrs. DeBrugh is merely suffering from a slight shock. There is nothing more that I can do. When she awakens, see that she stays in bed. For the rest of the day."

He left then, and Letty felt a strange coldness about the place, something that had not been there while Mr. DeBrugh was alive.

She went downstairs and made several telephone calls which she knew would be necessary. Later, when Mrs. DeBrugh was feeling better, other arrangements could be made.

She straightened the furniture in the study, pushing the familiar sofa back in place, from where Mr. DeBrugh invariably moved it. Then she knocked the ashes from the meerschaum, wiped it off, and placed it carefully in the little glass cabinet on the wall where he always kept it.

Times would be different now, she knew. She remembered what he had said. "You will be well taken care of." But there had been something else. "After *Mrs. DeBrugh* and I are gone."

Letty could no longer hold back the tears. She fell into a chair and they poured forth.

But time always passes, and with it goes a healing balm for most all sorrows. First there was the funeral. Then came other arrangements. And there was the will, which Mrs. DeBrugh never mentioned.

His things would have fallen into decay but for the hands of Letty. Always her dust-cloth made his study immaculate. Always the sofa was in place and the pipe, clean and shining, in the cabinet.

There was a different hardness about Mrs. DeBrugh. No longer was she content with driving Letty like a slave day in and day out. She became even more unbearable.

There were little things, like taking away her privilege of having Saturday afternoons off. And the occasional "forgetting" of Letty's weekly pay.

Once Letty thought of leaving during the night, of packing her few clothes and going for ever from the house. But that was foolish. There was no place to go, and she was getting too old for maid service.

Besides, hadn't Mr. DeBrugh said she would be taken care of. "After *Mrs. DeBrugh* and I are gone." Perhaps she would not live much longer.

And then one morning Mrs. DeBrugh called Letty in to talk with her. It was the hour Letty had been awaiting—and dreading.

There was a harsh, gloating tone in Mrs. DeBrugh's voice as she spoke. She was the master now. There was no Hector to think of.

"Letty," she said, "for some time now I have been considering closing the house. I'm lonely here. I intend to go to the city and live with my sister. So, you see, I shan't be needing you any longer. I'll be leaving within the next two days. I'm sorry."

Letty was speechless. She had expected something terrible, but not this. This wasn't so! Mrs. DeBrugh was lying! It was the will she was afraid of. Letty remembered Mr. DeBrugh's promise.

She did not complain, however. Her only words were, "I'll leave tomorrow."

That night she packed her things. She had no definite plans, but she hoped something would turn up.

❖ ❖ ❖

Sleep would not come easy, so Letty lay in bed and thought of old Mr. DeBrugh. She imagined he was before her in the room, reclining on the sofa, puffing long on the meerschaum. She even saw in fancy the curling wisps of gray smoke drifting upward, upward. . . .

It was sleep. Then, with a start, she was suddenly wide awake.

She had surely heard a scream. But no.

And then, as soft and as silent as the night wind, came the whisper: "Letty."

It drifted slowly off into silence, and a cool breeze crossed her brow. She suddenly felt wet with perspiration. She listened closely, but the whisper was not repeated.

Then, noiselessly, she got out of bed, stepped into slippers, and drew a robe about her. Just as silently she left her room and walked down the hall to Mrs. DeBrugh's bedroom.

She rapped softly on the door, fearing the wrath of the woman within at being awakened in the middle of the night. There was no answer, no sound from inside the room.

Letty hesitated, wondering what to do. And once more she felt that cool, deathlike breeze, and heard the faintest of whispers, fainter even than the sighing of the night wind: "Letty."

She opened the door and switched on the light. Mrs. DeBrugh lay in the bed as in sleep, but Letty knew, as she had known about Mr. DeBrugh, that it was more than sleep.

She quickly called the doctor, and sometime much later he arrived, his eyes heavy from lack of sleep.

"Dead," he remarked, after looking at the body. "Probably had a shock. Fright, nightmare, or something her heart couldn't stand. I always thought she would have died first."

Letty walked slowly from the room, down the stairs, still in her robe and slippers. The doctor followed and passed her, going through the door into the outside.

She walked, as though directed by some unseen force, into Mr. DeBrugh's study. She switched on a lamp beside the sofa on which he had always sat; and she noticed that it was moved slightly out of place.

There was something else about the room, some memory of old days. First she saw some sort of legal document on the table and wondered at its being there. The title said: *Last Will and Testament of Hector A. DeBrugh.* It was brief. She read it through and found that Mr. DeBrugh had spoken truthfully in his promise to her.

Beside the will on the table was another object, and she knew then what the "something else" in the room was.

The meerschaum! It lay there beside the document, and a thin spiral of grayish smoke rose upward from it toward the ceiling.

No longer did Letty wonder about anything. ⟶⊢

THE LATE MOURNER

JULIUS LONG

John Sloan awoke from a sound sleep. He sat up and peered through the gloom of his room at the faded face of his old clock. The hands pointed very nearly to two. He had not intended to nap so long. Two o'clock was the hour set for the funeral rites of his dearest friend. His failure to attend the services would be unpardonable. He would have to hurry.

He left his bed with an ease and agility that surprised him. He was very old, and at times it seemed that every muscle and joint of his body ached and pained him. He rang for Chester, his man. There was no answer, and he repeated the summons with vigor. The house remained silent. Sloan was annoyed by his desertion, but he had no time to investigate. He dressed himself hurriedly and fairly ran down the stairs. Somewhere in the house a clock struck two. The funeral services had probably begun.

He decided to walk to the mortuary, an outpost of the commercial invasion of his once aristocratic neighborhood. He quitted his deserted old house and entered the street. The autumn sun was warm and comforting. Brown and red leaves brushed playfully against his ankles. He was cheered and exhilarated by the October scene. It was many years since he had been able to enjoy the outdoors.

At the same time, he was saddened by the thought of his friend's death. Few of his cronies remained alive. Nearly all the world with which he was familiar had passed on. He had never married. There were not even relatives to dwell in his rambling old house.

His reflection was interrupted by the sight of Tom McGann, the policeman, who had walked the beat for fifteen years. He enjoyed seeing Tom, who was a good-natured and voluble fellow with a cheery greeting for all.

"Good afternoon, Tom," said Sloan, trying hard to equal the patrolman's usual smile.

Tom did not answer, but walked silently on, as if he had not seen him. Despite his lateness, Sloan paused and stared after the retreating figure. He was astonished and hurt by the snub. He could not account for such behavior. Had someone circulated a scandal about him? Why had Tom passed him by?

The sun lost its bright glow, and the air lost its soothing warmth. The leaves at his feet annoyed him, and October seemed a dismal and inimical month. A sensitive soul, he could not lightly pass off a slight from any human being. He trudged on to the mortuary, dejected and lonely.

Outside the funeral home there were parked a great many cars. His friend's death was deeply mourned. Sloan was a bit envious. When he died, he reflected sadly, there would be few to attend his funeral.

Two ushers loitered in the doorway. They did not deign to notice Sloan, as he climbed the several steps. He passed meekly between them and entered the building.

To the left was the entrance of the room in which the obsequies were under way. He waded through the thick carpets and stepped inside. No one in the crowded room seemed to notice his appearance. He discovered an empty seat in the rear. He made his way to it, not without treading on the toes of three persons who were sufficiently well bred to betray no notice of his clumsiness.

He settled himself in his chair and regarded the clergyman, who was concluding the obituary. Its details sounded familiar to his ears, and for the first time that afternoon, he tried to visualize the appearance of his departed friend. He discovered that he could not do so. He had quite forgotten the name and face of the man whom he had regarded as his most intimate companion.

The discovery stunned him. How could he excuse such a stupid lapse of memory? Was he so far gone in his dotage that the most important things in his life could escape his memory? He became frantic, like a schoolboy who has lost his place in his reader and trembles from fear that he will be the next to be called upon.

He tried to recall things that might lead to the recollection of his friend's identity. Where, when and how had he been apprised of his friend's death? How long had he been ill? He plied himself with many such questions, but could answer none of them.

He surveyed the people in the room. They were all known to him. Perhaps he could name his man by the simple process of elimination. One by one, he examined them, but his strategy availed him nothing. His bewilderment was increased by the unaccountable presence of his servants, among whom sat Chester. Why—devil take them!—had they rushed off without him?

He regarded the coffin, which was placed in a front corner of the room. The corpse was not visible. After the services, he would view it and enlighten himself with regard to its identity.

By this time the funeral sermon had been begun, but the minister's words gave no hint as to the name and situation of the departed. Sloan became impatient.

The obsequies dragged to a close. The proprietor of the establishment, with professional suavity, invited the late arrivals to favor the deceased with a last look. Sloan and several others rose and left their seats. Again he tramped on the toes of his neighbors, who took no notice of his second offense.

He came abreast of the coffin and looked down upon the countenance of the dead man. Enlightenment did not come. The pallid features were familiar, yet so very strange. Had death wrought such changes in his friend that, even now, he would be unable to recognize him?

Dazed, he continued to stare at the lifeless face. Then recognition came. He clutched the coffin for support. He did not attempt to struggle with his suspicions. He knew!

It was his own face that he saw. It was more withered and aged, bloodless and ghastly, yet indisputably his own. It was his body which lay there with its bony hands upon its chest.

With understanding came recollection of the scene which had been effaced from his mind. He lay in his bed. His doctor was authoritatively assuring him that his ailment was insignificant and could not possibly prove fatal. Chester, at his side, looked fearful and worried. Then something choked him. He gasped for breath. The faces of the doctor and Chester were lost in a blur. It must have been then that he had died.

Now he comprehended all. He knew why Tom McGann had not spoken to him, why the ushers had not noticed his arrival. All were oblivious to his presence, because he was without that ugly body which lay in its coffin. No longer would the desires and disappointments of the flesh pain him. Never again would its diseases rack him and try his soul. He was free of it.

It seemed that he was young again and strong and healthy. His thoughts were clear and lucid. Truly he was in the prime of life.

He was aroused from his revery by the sobbing of Chester and his old housekeeper. He would have made them understand that their tears were out of place, that he was alive and happy.

The mourners filed out slowly. Sloan regarded each appreciatively, but pityingly. The room became empty except for the attendants. The lid of the coffin was closed. Sloan was relieved when he saw the dead face disappear. He hoped that he would be able to forget it.

The coffin was wheeled away. He watched its removal with satisfaction. He lingered a moment in the vacant room, then stole silently out, to a new freedom. ——+——

THE MAN IN THE TAXI

LESLIE GORDON BARNARD

Enderby walked out of the barber shop with a sense that something must be done about it. Even Jake, the barber, had noticed.

"Not looking too chipper these days, sir. Kind of thought that trip you took would set you right. I'd sure see a doctor if I was you, Mr. Enderby. Why, I mind a chap I knew—"

Lugubrious fellow, Jake. Moreover, it was a beastly sort of day— fog and drizzle that was neither mist nor honest rain. No doubt Jake was right. Maybe he should see a doctor. "Physician of souls!" he thought, and was startled at the phrase.

He hailed a taxi. It loomed up in the fog, and came to a halt. Enderby seized the handle and, starting to get in, drew back.

"Sorry," he said. "I thought the cab was vacant."

The driver looked around sharply.

"Vacant? Why yes, sir, I'm free. Where to, sir?"

Enderby, considerably angered at himself, got in. He had been certain there was someone in possession of that back seat; yet obviously it was not so. He was alarmed at this hallucination. He must certainly see a doctor—or should it be an oculist?

"Doctor Coulter's, Crescent Terrace!" he told the driver.

Coulter was a material fellow, thought Enderby. Lungs, liver, heart, kidney and the rest—he knew all about those, but he didn't go much deeper. One of these nerve fellows might have probed. Suppose he should blurt the truth out—to Coulter or any other man —would they just stare or let him know, as gently as might be, that he was mad?

"Look here, Coulter," he might say, "I'll tell you what you're up against. You're dealing with a man who has committed the perfect, insoluble crime!"

Enderby shifted in his seat. The fog pressed thin fingers against the panes. It seemed to get right inside; and the driver on his seat ahead was wreathed and remote.

"On just such a day," thought Enderby, "I did the thing."

313

He remembered the quarrel with Anderson, his partner, a quarrel of such vehemence that it had ended in a disrupted partnership. But it wasn't Anderson who suffered. That was the irony. He recalled how he'd caught up his hat and coat, and the heavy cane he'd been carrying because of a wrenched ankle, and gone out into a fog so thick it was impossible to see two yards ahead. A man, coming along, bumped into him, and Enderby, reeling back from the contact, felt his ankle give again. It was the last straw. In one mad, distorted moment of anger he lifted the stick and struck. The man fell without so much as a groan. It was a blind, irrational impulse, over as soon as indulged. Enderby, frightened, sobered, incredulous at his act, disappeared painfully into the fog. He had struck down a perfect stranger! It was impossible to believe—until the newspapers featured it:

"Unknown Man Struck Down in Fog—Body Taken to Morgue."

No one came to identify him.

Enderby had committed the perfect crime—without motive—without witnesses—without clues. It was a nightmare thing. The closing up of the partnership saved his sanity; that and a long trip. But one could not outdistance conscience. He thought often of going to minister, or priest, or police. But he put it off, and each postponement made confession increasingly hard.

"It's frozen in there," said Enderby. "It'll never thaw now."

He suffered intensely. Even the face of Nature was against him; no former delight was open to him; he moved among familiar scenes, and people, and events, but without communication that mattered. People did not understand, of course. They only said: "Not looking so good, Enderby. Better consult a doctor!" Just like Jake, the barber! Well, to see him sitting in the reading-room at the Club, with a cigar between his lips and a magazine held in pretense before his eyes, or propped up in Jake's chair, face covered with lather—pursuing the comfortable routine of a man well fixed in the world's evaluation—would they ever guess that within him something was crying out, "Who shall deliver me from the body of this death?" Enderby had a sudden, disturbing idea that if one could peer in upon the souls of many men in clubs and barber chairs there might be disquieting revelations.

As for his own desperate case, if he could only bring himself to tell someone—Coulter, anybody! But there was the icicle within him, and it hung suspended in a region of perpetual winter. There were times when he would have welcomed the retribution of the law, but only he could take the initiative; and that moment was long since past.

Suddenly he was jerked forward in his seat, as the brakes screamed on. Steadying himself he saw another taxi bearing down, broadside on. In that split second he could see it coming; his mind actually framing words:

"This is the end. This is the end!"

The second taxi slewed. Enderby closed his eyes for the inevitable moment, but the shock, when it came, seemed chiefly an agony of laboring for breath; until he became aware that, by some miracle, he was still conscious and apparently unhurt, though he felt dizzy and queer, and as if his world, rather than two motor vehicles, had crashed.

Then the strange thing happened. He knew his previous feeling— that feeling he had had when first he stepped into this car—had been correct. *He was not alone in the taxi!*

Hallucination? Or was he having trouble with his eyes again? He was thinking that Coulter would have to see to this, when the stranger spoke.

"You look scared to death," he said.

His voice did something queer to Enderby, or else the shock had accomplished that. Without preamble, without reserve, out came tumbling all the frozen, pent-up tragedy of his guilt. What he had not been able to unburden to a living soul came from him now as easily as a spring flood.

"I do not know," he apologized at last, "why I should have told you all this—why I should have confessed to you, but that is my story!"

And now he looked at the man beside him in the cab; but the condition of Enderby was such that this stranger was not distinct, not clearly seen at all. Enderby could have endured this, but to hear some vague manifestation of humor was farthest from his expectation.

"You laugh!" cried Enderby. "My story amuses you? And I thought you so—so understanding."

"Who should understand it better than I?"

"But you laughed!" insisted Enderby.

"You must forgive me that," said the stranger. "You see—I am the man you killed!"

The second taxicab, slewing around, shot forward a little, and the scream of brakes became the shrillness of angry voices.

"Watch where you're going, you fool! An inch more and you'd have sideswiped me plenty."

"Well, keep your shirt on. There ain't so much as a scratch, is there?"

"No fault of yours," growled Enderby's driver. "You're enough to give a guy heart-failure, you are!"

It was only when, turning to look at his passenger, he saw Enderby's body, sagging and solitary, on the back seat, the face strangely composed and peaceful, that the driver discovered what truth lay behind these casual words. ———

THE MAN WHO WAS SAVED

B. W. SLINEY

Only I escaped." The man whom they had found adrift in the dory hung his head. "The others"—the listeners bent nearer to catch his throatily whispered words—"the others . . . it got them—that monstrous, cursed thing!" His eyes rolled back, showing bloodshot whites; his body tensed, and then he shook as with the ague. His attempt to say more resulted in stuttering failure.

"He had better be put to bed," the ship's doctor said. "His nerves are all gone. Heat and thirst and exposure, of course. Hallucinations. He'll come out of it in time."

So they put him in the hospital, where he raved for three days. And the things he said caused intense interest on board the freighter *Pacific Belle;* and among the crew lurking fear whispered that some of the things he said were true.

It was a week before he came into his right mind again, and then the fevers and fears which had beset him passed. He was able to talk to the captain, and to tell a coherent story.

"There were seven of us," he said with sad recollection, as he glanced at the ship's officers, who had gathered about him on the poop deck, "who set out in a two-topmaster—the *Scudder.* It belonged to Bob Henry, who was our captain. Just a sort of lark, you know—an idle cruise for the joy of the sea, and the freedom.

"I was mate, for next to Bob, I knew more about handling a ship than the others. And so we sailed along the coast, putting into whatever ports we fancied, and living an idle, ideal life. All of us had long been friends.

"Then we rashly decided to make it across the Pacific, depending on a season of few storms to aid us. We were successful. Honolulu was easy; and from there we headed southward, made the Marquesas, and then we sailed from island group to island group—you know them all—until we made the Philippines.

"There we turned homeward, pointing our course for Guam. But midway to Apia our luck failed, and we were becalmed for days. We had a small auxiliary motor, which we used for a time to make headway, but it got out of order, and we were forced to remain in virtually the same spot for nearly a week. We did not especially mind, for we were in no great hurry, except that it was somewhat monotonous with so very little to do.

"One evening during our becalmed period, just toward sunset, Hal Rooney pointed out a great disturbance of the water some little distance from us. It shot up in sprays, and eddied in a most inexplicable manner, and then it suddenly ceased. We wondered about it for a long while, but no thinking or imagining or deducing on our part could explain the phenomenon.

" 'Possibly,' Bob Henry said, 'it will appear again.'

"And, sure enough, it did. The next evening at the same hour we again noted that strange disturbance of the water. We knew that it could not possibly be a whale, nor any other large sea-creature of which we had ever heard, for the tumult was too vast; and the fact that none of us could offer an explanation of the mystery piqued our curiosity.

"The calm continued. The sea floated away from us endlessly, equally on all sides, caught at the edges of the sky, and became one with it. Once in a while a blackfish went blowing by, or an occasional whale. The waters teemed with life. At night the phosphor glow was almost livid, uncannily brilliant. And each evening that same disturbance of the water occurred somewhere in our neighborhood.

"It was with the third appearance that the thing became too much for us. We determined to put out in a dory and investigate the next time it appeared. It did not disappoint us. Again, at sunset, while the sky glowed extravagantly, flaunting an enormous batik at the parting day, the water almost dead ahead of our bows broke into a churning fury. We piled into the dory, which was ready alongside, and made for it, pulling as hard as we could. But before we were able to reach the spot, the maelstrom had ceased, and we gazed into the intense indigo of unruffled water that was nearly five miles deep.

"Following that attempt, we were more determined than ever to find out the nature of the thing. It was an amazingly large patch of sea that it churned, and, though the unbroken immensity of the space we were the center of gave us little for comparison, we judged the area to be approximately that of an acre—an unbelievably large expanse to show such agitation in the midst of so glassily calm a sea.

"The next afternoon, just as the sun fell into the sea, splashing all our horizons with myriad tints, a huge whale went lolling by, sounding and coming up with great jets of water cascading over it. I watched with the glasses as it drove powerfully through the water, peacefully taking its time. Suddenly, however, it changed. It displayed signs of confusion, of alarm. First it turned one way, then another, cutting about sharply—and then I very distinctly heard it give a groan of anguish. It was a heart-breaking sound—the cry of a great, helpless animal in mortal distress. Immediately afterward the water surrounding it broke into its daily wild disorder, and the leviathan seemed gripped by a force it could not escape. It struggled violently, throwing its huge bulk about with futile effort. Greater and greater the mêlée became, and then, suddenly, the whale was still.

"We looked at one another, fright in our eyes. It was tremendous, awful. And then, as we looked again out there, the whale lost all shape and the water became red with gore and blood as it was crushed to a pulp. In but a few minutes it was gone, utterly vanished from view—even the bloodiness of the water cleared—the whirling and splashing ceased, and the sun went down on a still sea. All of us were speechless. It was the most dreadful thing any of us had ever seen."

The speaker paused in his narrative, shaken by the memory of what he had related. The captain and his officers looked at one another with veiled skepticism. The doctor raised an eyebrow. There seemed no doubt of it; the man was insane.

Presently he went on with his wildly impossible yarn. His listeners were attentive, but secretly unbelieving. In time, it was hoped, he might regain his mental balance. In the meanwhile—

"To say that we were shaken would not be half expressing our state of mind. It was so inexplicable, so wildly preposterous! I was for getting away as soon as possible, and so were several of the others. But the rest were keen to learn what the thing was. And, to settle any argument, the calm held unbroken and the motor continued in disrepair, despite our efforts over it.

"For three days, then, the thing did not come to the surface. We had decided that it was some sort of deep-sea creature, some gargantuan monster that came out of the vast depths of the ocean to feed. But we had never heard of such a thing, save in stories of early navigators' superstitions. We hesitated to believe the thing we had seen—we were afraid to believe it!

"It was now that fear came to us. Hitherto we had been curious, idly speculative, and inclined to laugh. Now our thoughts were interrupted by premonitions of disaster. Flying fish, as they flashed from the surface and splashed into the water about us, startled; and porpoises blundering into our vicinity brought us all on deck. At night, a lost puff of breeze, slatting the rigging against the sails, startled us into alarmed awakening. And though the same subject of possible danger from the unknown out of the deep occupied the mind of each of us, it was never spoken of. But there was in the air a chilling presence of dread.

"I believe we would have left that place had we been able. For the memory of the fate of the whale was ever vivid in our minds. Following the death of the whale, the monster did not rise, however, for three days, as I have said. This gave us some sense of relief, but it was on that third day that the great tragedy occurred.

"I was occupied with fitting a new seat to the dory, which was swung up on deck, and the others were idling, making bets as to the quarter in which the creature would next appear, or if we should see it again.

"I was startled by a scream from one of the men, and immediately after followed the sound of churning water—a sound which sent the very essence of dread all through me and cowed my soul. Somehow I knew we were in the midst of the monster's rise to the surface. I stood and looked over the side. There was a horrible mass of pulsating green matter—a revolting substance that had no definite form, and yet was solid—a writhing, heaving island of the stuff.

"Even as I looked it surged up from the water and rolled over the side of the schooner, turning over on itself, slithering and cascading on the deck. Every one of us was frantic. Some rushed for the after cabin, but they were cut off by a slimy arm that slid across their path. It spread and lifted with terrorizing rapidity. Two of the men tried to climb a mast; Bob Henry raced toward the bow and fell. An instant later he was covered with the gruesome matter, even before he had a chance to cry out, and was hidden from sight. Hardly knowing what I did, I turned the dory over on myself, dragging Mark Whittmore, the nearest man to me, under with me. Fortunately I had removed all the seats, and there was just room for the two of us as we lay prone.

"Then came darkness and an inconceivably foul odor of decay as the monster mass pushed itself over the dory—a suffocating, interminable darkness, while we were cramped under that flat-bottomed boat, scarce daring to think, even, of the horror that crawled over us. When we thought our lungs would burst for the want of fresh air, light came under the dory once more, and gradually the slithering, churning, swishing of that thing which had boarded us ceased. For a long while, however, we were too frightened to move, but finally our concern for the fate of our companions compelled us to lift the dory.

"The sky glowed with the last rays of the setting sun, and the sea slept beneath it, undisturbed. But the decks of the *Scudder* were wet with a yellow-green, malodorous slime, and silence hung like a pall over the ship.

"We called. There was no answer—not even the mockery of an echo. With consternation seizing us we rushed into the afterhouse, but it was without a person in it. In a panic we ran to the forecastle, and it, too, was suggestively deserted. And nowhere on that ship did we find a soul. Every man, except ourselves, had disappeared. That thing"—his voice broke, and again into his face came that haunting pain—"that thing had got them all!"

For a while he paused, making strong effort to overcome his rising emotion, and the fear that memory brought him. The listeners looked away and were silent; and presently they heard his voice, firmly continuing the tale.

"You can not conceive of the terror which descended on us after that frightful discovery. Aimlessly, dazedly we searched the vessel through and through, but we were the only men aboard the *Scudder*. It was a fact that we had to face, but could not bring ourselves to believe.

"Night came quickly, and the moon and stars stared coldly down on us. We decided at length that to remain on the ship would be suicidal, for the calm still hung over the water like a dead thing, and the thought of the unspeakable thing that lived somewhere beneath us was appalling. So we fitted the dory with water and food, and rowed away in the night from that ill-fated ship.

"Then there came interminable days of torture under a malignant sun, and nights of terror of what might lurk in the waters around us. And one morning I awoke to find myself alone in the dory. The day before Mark had talked of insanity, and I believe that he could not face the possibility.

"Now I attained the utmost in despair. I was, I believe, too shocked to think clearly, or I, too, might have gone over the side. From the morning of that discovery, until you picked me up, I was in a coma. Of the passage of time I do not recall.

"And such is my story, gentlemen. You may find it hard to believe. I find it difficult, myself, and wonder, sometimes, if it is not an insane conception of diseased imagination. I wish it were. But I am tormented with the reality."

The *Pacific Belle* held her westward course for Manila. The story of the man who had been saved spread among the crew, where it was hotly debated, and quite generally accepted. The officers of the ship, however, avoided the subject, and particularly before the stranger it was never mentioned.

But one morning, just at dawn, a derelict schooner was sighted. The captain, awakened, ordered the *Pacific Belle* hove to while investigation was made. With closer inspection and increasing light it was made out to be the *Scudder*, of San Francisco. The man who had been saved was called.

"Yes!" he cried. "Yes! That's the boat—our schooner. But—"

He drooped, swayed. The mate caught him and called one of the crew.

"Take him to his cabin," he said, "and keep him there."

Investigation corroborated the statements the stranger had made. Furthermore, the *Scudder's* papers proved beyond doubt that the man they had aboard came from her. And since there was nothing to indicate that anything else could have possibly driven the men from the ship, their strange passenger's story assumed a verity that even the officers reluctantly admitted.

A short consultation decided the fate of the *Scudder*. Left as she was, derelict, she would have become a serious menace to shipping, and possible salvage value did not warrant the long tow into port. Dynamite was placed amidships and set off.

With a splintering crash the *Scudder* heaved upward and outward, and plunged into the deeps of the ocean. The *Pacific Belle* continued on her way.

Later in the day the captain studied his charts. "Do you think," he asked the mate, at length, "that there is really anything in the fellow's story?"

The mate shrugged. "Such things," he answered readily, "don't happen. He's off, that's all. All the men were gone from the *Scudder*, yes, but I'd hate to accept such an explanation for it."

"The water in this part of the ocean, mister," the captain slowly said, "is five miles deep—as deep as the tallest mountain is high. It's barely possible that there's a lot about things out here that we don't know, or even remotely suspect. However—"

That night, after the swollen moon went down, and after all slept, save the watches and the man who had come aboard from out of the ocean, the *Pacific Belle* plunged into stark, brief terror.

The stranger, affected by again seeing the *Scudder*, had been unable to sleep. After hours of restlessness, he had gone to the bows, where he stared dully across the water. As he stood there, slowly, almost imperceptibly, he felt himself to be afraid.

An odor had come to him, an odor which brought to his mind the horror of his last day aboard the *Scudder*—the sickening, decay-laden odor of the monster from the deep. Then he listened with super-intent ears, and above the vessel's vibration he caught a sound of churning, swirling water. He screamed with a loudness that awoke everyone on the *Pacific Belle* as he recognized these things—a scream that brought everyone to his feet, anticipating calamity.

He turned from the prow and ran in stumbling haste across the deck and up the ladder to the bridge. The mate was there, alarmed at the cry of horror.

"Mister," he gasped, his mouth dry with panic, "mister! The thing—the monster! Stop the ship! Reverse her, for God's sake!"

The mate laughed with relief as he recognized the man. He had been in dread of something terrible, and it was only another fit.

"Come, now, old boy!" he said in an effort to comfort. "Better quiet down a bit, don't—"

With another terrible scream the fellow was gone from the bridge. Jerking a preserver from the rail, he leaped free of the *Pacific Belle*.

"Man overboard!" The mate had seen him disappear and gave the alarm as he ran to the bridge controls. But before he reached them the speed of the *Pacific Belle* slackened abruptly, as though it had fouled the meshes of a gigantic net; and then it lost headway altogether. A bright, eery glow of phosphorescent green lighted the water in a vast area, suddenly bursting into a lurid brilliance which caught the vessel out of the night and revealed its helplessness to the stars.

The glowing green mass surged sweepingly toward the vessel, piled against it, rolled over it, clinging to its sides, flooding its decks. Men who had come out to investigate the shouting and confusion frantically rushed below deck, barricading ports and doors behind them. On his bridge the captain sent useless messages to the engine room. The ship could not move.

Then, slowly, inexorably, as the brilliance of the phosphorescent light lessened, the great mass which was its source began to sink. Gradually it settled, carrying the *Pacific Belle*, fair-sized steamer though she was, down with it. The waves closed over the ship's main deck, touched and submerged the bridge, poured down the funnels, sending clouds of steam hissing into the air, and finally even the tops of the masts disappeared. There had been no time for a wireless message, but a message would have been futile.

Again the waters calmed, but after a half-hour they were torn for a few minutes by a great rush of bubbles to the top, following the caving in, from depth pressure, of the *Pacific Belle's* bulkheads. But after that the surface was never more disturbed by the *Pacific Belle.*

Microcosmic in a terrifying vastness of water, a man floated on a preserver, in the path of a liner that later picked him up. And, as he slowly realized the irony of his second escape, he sobbed with futile pity for himself. —┼—

MASQUERADE

MEARLE PROUT

"May I cut in, please?"

It was as simple as that. Yet, for all the gay masquerade throng, Donald shivered at the voice. He looked at the intruder and was not reassured. Tall and gaunt, the man was clad in the long flowing robes of a priest of ancient Egypt. His eyes were shaded, nearly covered by the black hood of his mask, but as he looked into them Donald had the uncanny impression of looking across a great dark void. Below the line of the mask the face was thin and creased, yellowed like old parchment.

With the barest trace of a smile the intruder bowed and said again, "If you don't mind."

Donald hesitated. Strangely, he felt his partner would not object if he were to refuse the very usual request. But to refuse would be unthinkable. He released his partner, and in a moment the tall man had whirled her away. Yet Donald was aware of her gaze upon him as he threaded across the crowded floor.

Away from the dancers, he paused and looked for the first time at the card she had slipped into his hand.

"Leonora Starr."

The name was printed in simple pica type; beyond that, the card was blank.

He frowned at first, then smiled. She so obviously expected him to see her again. He recalled with pleasure her lithe surrender to his arms while they danced, the warmth with which she had pressed the small card into his hand.

Who was she? he wondered. The name, Leonora Starr, told him nothing. They had met less than five minutes before, and even then had spoken but little.

The music of the waltz rose to a higher, more exciting strain. Donald searched the crowd with his eyes until he found her, still dancing with the mysterious stranger. They were at the south end of the ballroom now, near the door that led into the garden. The tall man, Donald noted, danced gracefully but stiffly, as though he had once been an excellent dancer, but was now long out of practise.

Across the crowd Donald caught Leonora's eye, and something flashed between them. An appeal, he thought it was. His pulse raced while he stared across the intervening space, and then—his glance clashed with that of the giant. He was conscious of the same chilling sensation at the pit of his stomach, as though he were falling; felt the same prickling at the roots of his hair. . . . Then, in another whirl of the dance, the man had turned away.

A little group of people near by was not dancing. Donald strolled toward them, halted half-way and looked back across the floor. He felt a light touch at his elbow.

"That man who tagged you—who is he?" said Betty Cosgrove as he turned. She was obviously agitated.

"I've been wondering. Doesn't anyone know?"

"No—except that he wasn't invited."

"Are—you sure? It might be just the costume."

"No—none of the guests is so tall. Besides, he wasn't announced." She shuddered.

"He—he looks like a death's-head, or a mummy. If he asks me to dance, I'll faint."

Abruptly the music ceased, to be replaced by the hum of voices and scattered applause. Apprehensive now in spite of himself, Donald shouldered his way through the crowd in search of Leonora. She was not on the floor. Hurriedly he surveyed the guests again. The man too had disappeared. The garden, perhaps?

Quickly he stepped to the door. There was no moon, but the garden was dimly lighted by a single Japanese lantern hung near the center. Donald could see no one. Dense shrubbery bordered the walks, and in the far corner a thick grove of trees loomed black in the shadows. He drew a deep breath and walked swiftly toward it.

Behind him the music began again, a haunting Viennese melody in waltz time. He looked back at the lighted windows. People, in their brilliant costumes, were again taking the floor. No one else had come out after him; to all appearances he was alone in the garden. He hesitated, half minded to turn back. Fool's errand!

Suddenly, above the music, he heard a woman scream, a muffled scream that was not repeated. It came from the grove of trees. His heart leaping, he turned and ran toward it, searching his pockets for a weapon as he ran. There was none.

He reached the trees. It was not as dark there as it had seemed. The level rays of the Japanese lantern, though dim, shone redly through the shadows. Suddenly in his haste he stumbled over a creeper of vine, and, catching himself, stopped short at the sight before him.

At this spot the heavy growth of trees gave way to a circular clearing, and the ground was covered by a lush carpet of grass. The light of the Japanese lantern seemed to filter undiminished through the trees and become amplified at this spot, so that everything which occurred was as clear to the watcher as in the light of day. And at the very center of the circle, at the top of a small rise, was the horrifying tableau. Leonora was lying on her side, her face half buried in the grass; over her, his knee on her shoulder, his left hand covering her mouth, was the tall man in the priestly robe. In his right hand he held aloft a glittering knife with a long curved blade, which he held poised in a perpetual threat. He had not yet struck.

The man, disheveled by the struggle, could be seen better now. From the arm which held the knife aloft the robe had fallen away, revealing it to the shoulder; it was thin as bone, it had the appearance of bone stretched tightly over with yellow, parchment-like skin. His headdress was lost, revealing a smooth hairless head which seemed deathly white even in the red rays of the lantern. The mask, too, was gone, and his eyes—in the shadows they appeared like something which Donald, if he were to remain sane, dared not think about.

A cold perspiration beading his skin, Donald looked about him for a weapon, while the two before him held the same motionless pose. A stone, a broken limb of a tree, any weapon would suffice—if only the demon did not strike, if only Leonora could hold him back a moment longer! In his excitement he never wondered why he had not already done so, why, if he wished to kill, he had not killed and fled minutes before. Nor did he wonder how Leonora, facing death, could wait for it so passively. If he had stopped to think of those things, to realize their meaning, perhaps he might have noticed other, more obvious, circumstances: that the music, which had sounded so loudly in the garden a few seconds before, had died to nothing the moment he had entered the hellish grove; that the light breeze from out of the west no longer fanned his cheek, and now did not even rustle the leaves of the trees; that the very starlight seemed to drip unwillingly through the interlaced branches overhead. . . .

Twenty feet to the left, Donald saw a spade leaning against a tree.

He started for it, but at that moment a sudden burst of activity on the part of Leonora freed her mouth and she called weakly,

"Quickly—help!"

Being young, Donald could not resist that appeal. He left the spade untouched, and turned and ran to fling himself against the gaunt attacker.

With a single bound the other rose to meet his attack, the knife drawn to strike, the lips snarling. The girl too rose to her feet and stood.

"Back to the house, Leonora—run!" shouted Donald. He had halted, crouched ready to spring, ten feet from the towering skeleton before him.

But the girl stood still, apparently tense with excitement.

"You must kill him," she hissed, "or he'll kill me."

"Who is he?" Donald rasped.

"He's—a priest," she lied. "His name is Ozaman."

Donald knew that she was lying, though he could not tell how he knew it—nor why she was.

"Go to the house," he said again, "and send some men out; I'll keep him here."

A sardonic smile twisted the features of Ozaman.

"You—don't want me alone?" he taunted.

In that instant it happened. Leonora had crept up behind the priest; suddenly she charged him, grasped the hand that held the knife. The priest swung upon her, ready to crash a heavy fist upon her face. Donald rushed in.

He caught the blow in the chest. It staggered him. Then with all his power he flung himself forward and closed.

Donald was athletic. In college he had been a member of the wrestling team, had been rated fair at boxing. But he knew in a second that he had underrated his opponent. The arms of this fleshless skeleton were like bands of steel, the legs as firm as if rooted in the ground. Suddenly Ozaman laughed. He tossed the knife from him, picked Donald up bodily, whirled him through the air until he was dizzy, then threw him to the ground with stunning force. Then he dropped quickly upon him and pinned his arms to the ground.

Donald lay on his back in the grass, helpless, staring up at the twin caverns of the monster's eyes. A wave of revulsion shook him, left him weak and pale, his body wet with sweat. Those eyes again! Was he insane? But he knew that he was not. This was real. This was happening! Back there, behind those trees, was the ballroom, and a gay throng, and music, and laughter. And here—this!

His mind, stimulated by terror, worked fast. The knife! It had been lost in the struggle. Then, surely, Leonora—he twisted his head to look for her. She was standing on his left ten feet away, her eyes shining, her lips slightly parted.

He called to her. "Find the knife—and hurry!" he said.

She made no reply, but stood smiling, neutral. A gleam in the grass near her caught his eye.

"What's the matter? It's there at your feet. Help me!" he shouted.

As she made no move he realized that she would not—that what was to be done he must do for himself. A black rage gave new strength to his arms. She must be in league with the priest! She had confessed to knowing him. . . . He saw now that he had been lured into this unequal contest. But why?

The priest tightened his hold on Donald's arms again, so that Donald writhed with the pain.

"Why are you holding me? What do you want?" he cried at last.

"Only your body," said Ozaman softly.

His body! The man was insane!

If only he could reach the knife—if he could get an arm free!

He feigned a struggle, edging toward the knife as he fought. When he was again overcome, he was two feet nearer. He rested. Then another struggle, another two feet gained. He had a feeling the priest was playing with him as a cat plays with a mouse, encouraging him to escape and then dashing his hopes. Well, there might be a surprise! . . .

Two more pretended struggles, and the knife was within his reach. Now if an arm were free. . . .

Suddenly the priest bent his head low, so that his fetid breath seared the nostrils of the prostrate man.

"I'm going to kill you now," he said.

Simultaneously he loosed Donald's arms and clutched his neck with bony fingers. Donald felt the breath in his lungs pent up, fighting for escape while he flailed his left arm in search of the knife. He grasped the smooth handle, balanced it a moment in his hand. He focussed his staring eyes upon the figure leaning low over him, aimed his blow well. As he struck, the priest inclined his head to the left, leaving a clean path for the knife. It severed the veins in his neck.

At once Donald felt his body galvanized as from an electric shock. He was aware of a mighty force penetrating his brain. Red flashes seemed to shoot from the priest's eyes, to play into his own. Giddiness and nausea as in a violent earthquake racked his consciousness. And then, for a moment, he fainted away.

When he again opened his eyes the scene was, to all appearances, unchanged. Over him were the same trees, the same. . . . He raised his hand to a gutting pain in his throat, felt something warm spurt over it. He looked. Blood! But surely this was not his own hand—this was thin, and bony. The garment which covered the arm was not his own either, but white and flowing—the garment of a priest! The words of Ozaman resounded in his brain like a death-knell:

"I want your body!"

And now his dimming eyes beheld a scene which tore his soul with despair. A man, clad as he had been, with the same proud tilt of the head, the same athletic carriage, but with eyes which glittered strangely now in the pale light, stepped toward a beautiful girl.

"Come, Leonora," he said, in a voice which Donald recognized as his own. "It is time to go."

She looked at him with a slow smile.

"You really are very, very handsome, Ozaman," she answered.

And as the eyes of the prostrate figure slowly filmed in death the now perfectly matched pair looked back at him and laughed with wild abandon. ——▸

MR. BAUER AND THE ATOMS

FRITZ LEIBER

Dr. Jacobson beamed at him through the thick glasses. "I'm happy to tell you there is no sign whatever of cancer."

Mr. Bauer nodded thoughtfully. "Then I won't need any of those radium treatments?"

"Absolutely not." Dr. Jacobson removed his glasses, wiped them with a bit of rice paper, then mopped his forehead with a handkerchief. Mr. Bauer lingered.

He looked at the X-ray machine bolted down by the window. It still looked as solid and mysterious as when he had first glimpsed a corner of it from Myna's bedroom. He hadn't gotten any farther.

Dr. Jacobson replaced his glasses.

"It's funny, you know, but I've been thinking . . ." Mr. Bauer plunged.

"Yes?"

"I guess all this atomic stuff got me started, but I've been thinking about all the energy that's in the atoms of my body. When you start to figure it out on paper—well, two hundred million electron volts, they say, from just splitting one atom, and that's only a tiny part of it." He grinned. "Enough energy in my body, I guess, to blow up, maybe . . . the world."

Dr. Jacobson nodded. "Almost. But all safely locked up."

Mr. Bauer nodded. "They're finding out how to unlock it."

Dr. Jacobson smiled. "Only in the case of two rare radioactive elements."

Mr. Bauer agreed, then gathered all his courage. "I've been wondering about that too," he said. "Whether a person could somehow make himself . . . I mean, become . . . radioactive?"

Dr. Jacobson chuckled in the friendliest way. "See that box at your elbow?" He reached out and turned something on it. The box ticked. Mr. Bauer jerked.

"That's a Geiger-Müller counter," Dr. Jacobson explained. "Notice how the ticks come every second or so? Each tick indicates a high-frequency wave. If you were radioactive, it would tick a lot oftener."

Mr. Bauer laughed. "Interesting." He got up. "Well, thanks about the cancer."

Dr. Jacobson watched him fumble for his panama hat and duck out. So that was it. He'd sensed all along something peculiar about Bauer. He'd even felt it while looking over the X-ray and lab reports —something intangibly wrong. Though he hadn't thought until now of paranoia, or, for that matter, any other mental ailment, beyond the almost normal cancer-fear of a man in his fifties.

Frank Bauer hesitated at the corridor leading to Myna's apartment, then went on. His heart hammered enragedly. There he'd gone chicken again, when he knew very well that if he could ever bring himself to state his fear coldly and completely—that crazy fear that a man's thoughts could do to the atoms of his body what the scientists had managed to do with uranium 235 and that other element—why, he'd be rid of the fear in a minute.

But a man just didn't go around admitting childish things like that. A human bomb exploded by thought! It was too much like his wife Grace and her mysticism.

Going crazy wouldn't be so bad, he thought, if only it weren't so humiliating.

Frank Bauer lived in a world where everything had been exploded. He scented confidence games, hoaxes, faddish self-deception, and especially (for it was his province) advertising-copy-exaggerations behind every faintly unusual event and every intimation of the unknown. He had the American's nose for leg-pulling, the German's contempt for the non-factual. Mention of such topics as telepathy, hypnotism, or the occult—and his wife managed to mention them fairly often—sent him into a scoffing rage. The way he looked at it, a real man had three legitimate interests—business, bars, and blondes. Everything else was for cranks, artists, and women.

But now an explosion had occurred which made all other explosions, even of the greatest fakeries, seem like a snap of the fingers.

By the time he reached the street, he thought he was beginning to feel a bit better. After all, he had told the doctor practically everything, and the doctor had disposed of his fears with that little box. That was that.

He swabbed his neck and thought about a drink, but decided to go back to the office. Criminal to lose a minute these days, when everybody was fighting tooth and nail to get the jump. He'd be wanting money pretty soon, the bigger the better. All the things that Grace would be nagging for now, and something special for Myna— and then there was a chance he and Myna could get away together for a vacation, when he'd got those campaigns lined out.

The office was cool and dusky and pleasantly suggestive of a non-atomic solidity. Every bit of stalwart ugliness, every worn spot in the dark varnish, made him feel better. He even managed to get off a joke to ease Miss Minter's boredom. Then he went inside.

An hour later he rushed out. This time he had no joke for Miss Minter. As she looked after him, there was something in her expression that had been in Dr. Jacobson's.

It hadn't been so bad at first when he'd got out paper and black pencil. After all, any advertising copy had to make Atomic Age its keynote these days. But when you sat there, and thought and thought, and whatever you thought, you always found afterwards that you'd written:

INSIDE YOU . . . TRILLIONS OF VOLTS!

You wouldn't think, to look at them, that there was much resemblance between John Jones and the atom bomb. . . .

UNLOCKED!
THE WORLD IN YOUR HANDS
JUST A THOUGHT—

Frank Bauer looked around at the grimy street, the windows dusty or dazzlingly golden where the low sun struck, the people wilted a little by the baking pavement—and he saw walls turned to gray powder, their steel skeletons vaporized, the people became fumes, or, if they were far enough away, merely great single blisters. But they'd have to be very far away.

He *was* going crazy—and it was horribly humiliating. He hurried into the bar.

After his second bourbon and water he began to think about the scientists. They should have suppressed the thing, like that one fellow who wanted to. They shouldn't ever have told people. So long as people didn't know, maybe it would have been all right. . . . But once you'd been told. . . .

Thought was the most powerful force in the world. It had discovered the atom bomb. And yet nobody knew what thought was, how it worked inside your nerves, what it couldn't manage.

And you couldn't stop thinking. Whatever your thoughts decided to do, you couldn't stop them.

It was insanity, of course.

It had better be insanity!

The man beside him said. "He saw a lot of those Jap suicide flyers. CRAZY as loons. Human bombs."

Human bombs! Firecrackers. He put down his drink.

As he hurried through the thinning crowd, retracing the course he had taken early in the afternoon, he wondered why there should be so much deadly force locked up in such innocent-seeming, inert things. The whole universe was a booby trap. There must be a reason. Who had planned it that way, with the planets far enough apart so they wouldn't hurt each other when they popped?

He thought he began to feel sharp pains shooting through his nerves, as the radioactivity began, and after he had rushed up the steps the pains became so strong that he hesitated at the intersection of the corridors before he went on to Myna's.

He closed the door and leaned back against it, sweating. Myna was drinking and she had her hair down. There was a pint of bourbon on the table, and some ice. She jumped up, pulling at her dressing gown.

"What's wrong? Grace?"

He shook his head, kept staring at her, at her long curling hair, at her breasts, as if in that small hillocky, yellow entwined patch of reality lay his sole hope of salvation, his last refuge.

"But my God, what is it!"

He felt the pains mercifully begin to fade, the dangerous thoughts break ranks and retreat. He began to say to himself, "It must have hit a lot of people the same way it hit me. It's just so staggering. That must be it. That must be it."

Myna was tugging at him. "It's nothing," he told her. "I don't know. Maybe my heart. No, I don't need a doctor."

She wandered into the bedroom and came back with a large waffle-creased metal egg which she held out to him, as if it were a toy to cajole an ailing child.

"My cousin just landed in San Francisco," she told him. "Look at the souvenir he smuggled in for me."

He got up carefully and took it from her.

"Must be your dumb cousin, the one from downstate."

"Why?"

"Because, unless I'm very much mistaken, this is a live hand grenade. Look, you'd just have to pull this pin—"

"Give it to me!"

But he fended her off, grinning, holding the grenade in the air.

"Don't be frightened," he told her, "This is nothing. It's just a flash in the pan, a matchhead. Haven't you heard of the atom bomb? That's all that counts from now on."

He enjoyed her fear so much that he kept up his teasing for some time, but after a while he yielded and laid the grenade gingerly away in the back of the closet.

Afterwards he found he could talk to her more easily than ever before. He told her about the Atomic Age, how they'd be driving around in an airplane with a fuel-tank no bigger than a peanut, how they'd whisk to Europe and back on a glass of water. He even told her a little about his crazy fears. Finally he got philosophical.

"See, we always thought everything was so solid. Money, automobiles, mines, dirt. We thought they were so solid that we could handle them, hold on to them, do things with them. And now we find they're just a lot of little bits of deadly electricity, whirling around at God knows what speed, by some miracle frozen for a moment. But any time now—" He looked across at her and then reached for her. "Except you," he said. "There aren't any atoms in you."

"Look," he said, "there's enough energy inside you to blow up the world—well, maybe not inside you, but inside any other person. This whole city would go pouf!"

"Stop it."

"The only problem is, how to touch it off. Do you know how cancer works?"

"Oh shut up."

"The cells run wild. They grow any way they want to. Now suppose your thoughts should run wild, eh? Suppose they'd decide to go to work on your body, on the atoms of your body."

"For God's sake."

"They'd start on your nervous system first, of course, because that's where they are. They'd begin to split the atoms of your nervous system, make them, you know, radioactive. Then—"

"Frank!"

He glanced out of the window, noticed the light was still in Dr. Jacobson's office. He was feeling extraordinarily good, as if there were nothing he could not do. He felt an exciting rush of energy through him. He turned and reached for Myna.

Myna screamed.

He grabbed at her.

"What's the matter?"

She pulled away and screamed again.

He followed her. She huddled against the far wall, still screaming. Then he saw it.

Of course, it was too dark in the room to see anything plainly. Flesh was just a dim white smudge. But this thing beside Myna glowed greenishly. A blob of green about as high off the floor as his head. A green stalk coming down from it part way. Fainter greenish filaments going off from it, especially from near the top and bottom of the stalk.

It was his reflection in the mirror.

Then the pains began to come, horrible pains sweeping up and down his nerves, building a fire in his skull.

He ran out of the bedroom. Myna followed him, saw him come out of the closet, bending, holding something to his stomach. About seconds after he'd gotten through the hall door, the blast came.

Dr. Jacobson ran out of his office. The corridor was filled with acrid fumes. He saw a woman in a dressing gown trying to haul a naked man whose abdomen and legs were tattered and dripping red. Together they carried him into the office and laid him down.

Dr. Jacobson recognized his patient.

"He went crazy," the woman yelped at him. "He thought he was going to explode like an atom, and something horrible happened to him, and he killed himself."

Dr. Jacobson, seeing the other was beyond help, started to calm her.

Then he heard it.

His thick glasses, half dislodged during his exertions, fell off. His red-rimmed naked eyes looked purblind, terrified.

He could tell that she heard it too, although she didn't know its meaning. A sound like the rattle of a pygmy machine gun.

The Geiger-Müller counter was ticking like a clock gone mad.

Muggridge's Aunt

August W. Derleth

Mr. Leander Muggridge, having perceived the doctor's car at the curb, entered the house and stood waiting in the small vestibule until the medical man descended from his aunt's room. Muggridge was a methodical man, and his well-ordered mind was at this moment concerned with the thought of his aunt's always approaching but never imminent death. He stood, drawing off his gloves, having already placed his cane in the stand and hung his hat on the rack, and his thoughts were not kind.

It was useless to pretend any sort of sorrow over Aunt Edith. There had been no love lost between them, though it was probable that the old lady was not as conscious of it as he, since he could be pleasant, now that he was certain she must die. Then, too, there was the matter of having to support her and her old servant. True, it was not a large sum, considering his satisfactory income, but it was an annoying item to bother about. Besides that, her presence was an inconvenience in any number of ways. It was like her, he reflected, to take such a long time about dying.

Mr. Muggridge, despite the fact that he was very correctly attired in afternoon wear, was at heart intensely parsimonious, for which his aunt had frequently chidden him in those days when he had not taken the trouble to remind her of her dependence. In physical appearance, Muggridge was portly, with a fat, jovial face which thoroughly belied his small soul. He had fat, almost puffy hands, and his jowls were porcine. Add to that his sunken little eyes, and Muggridge emerged from the superficial aspect of a London gentleman to the status of a vulgar, moneyed poseur which he really was. Perhaps fortunately for Muggridge, few of his acquaintances ever realized his emergence, since they paid him scant attention, neither disliking him nor liking him.

The doctor came down the stairs just in time to stem Muggridge's rising impatience.

"Well, sir?" demanded Muggridge aggressively.

"She is sinking slowly, Mr. Muggridge," said the doctor, depositing his bag at his side while he shrugged into his topcoat and clapped his hat to his head. "She can not last longer than," and here he paused and cocked his head with his eyes fixed to a corner of the ceiling, "than tomorrow night, I should say."

"Is there anything to be done?" inquired Muggridge then, with surprizing civility.

"Nothing at all," replied the medical man, "unless it is to grant her anything she wishes, for she is certainly dying. She is, however, in no considerable pain; so rest easy on that score."

Muggridge smiled woodenly, reminded the doctor to send his bill promptly, and bade him good-afternoon. Then he ascended the stair slowly to his aunt's room, where he found the old lady deep in her bed, with her servant at one side of the bed, holding her hand with all the devotion of the old to the old.

"Good afternoon, Aunt Edith," he said with a false joviality which he never could have felt in the presence of the two old ladies.

Aunt Edith murmured his name weakly, but the servant said nothing. Then the sick old lady brought up once again a subject which he had forbidden her to speak about, the house in which she had lived and in which she now lay dying.

"It is, after all, my house," she said in a whisper.

"You forget that I took it up after your bankruptcy, Aunt," he said shortly.

"You had no right to change things the way you did," the old lady went on unheedingly. "You might have left things the way they were until I died."

"Really, Aunt Edith," he said firmly.

"Are you going to remind me that I've lived the last years of my life on your generosity, and am now dying on it?" And the old lady turned her head and looked at him with such dark hatred in her dimming eyes that even the self-contained Muggridge quailed under it and mumbled a reply into his collar.

There was an uncomfortable silence for a while after that, with Muggridge increasingly aware of the bond between the two women, and the mutual hatred with which they regarded him. Presently, however, he asserted himself once more and sought to stare them down.

"Is there anything you would like me to do, Aunt Edith?" he asked.

At this, the old lady made an unsuccessful attempt to nod, and whispered, "Yes."

"What is it?"

"I want you to let Elsie remain here until she dies."

He felt sick at that, and looked briefly at the aging white head bent now above the servant's hand, into which she was quietly sobbing. He stifled an impulse to deny this last request.

"Very well," he said. "I will promise to keep Elsie with me. After all, she is our next of kin, is she not, Aunt Edith?"

"A very distant cousin, yes," said the sick woman. "But all we have, since you never married, Leander." Then there was a slight pause, before the old lady added, "Never let me hear of you speaking to her as you have spoken to me—reminding her of your kindness in allowing her to live here. If you do—" But here she was seized with a fit of coughing which prevented her from finishing her sentence, and afterward she had forgotten.

In the night, the old lady died.

Muggridge's Aunt Edith had scarcely been buried before he was thinking of some way to rid himself of Elsie. This was all the more reprehensible of him because he was well able to afford the charwoman who did for him, and Elsie was not at all in the way, she being an unobtrusive little woman. But he could not get over the feeling that she hated him, and in this his impression was not in error. She had not witnessed his cruel mistreatment of Edith Muggridge without conceiving a lasting hatred for him, and she fostered this hatred now as the one thing that bound her eternally to the friend who now lay deep in the grave.

Muggridge presently convinced himself that he must harden his heart, which was a pleasant irony indeed, for his heart already had, figuratively speaking, a great many stony qualities, and force the old lady away through successive unkindnesses. Accordingly, that very evening Muggridge seized the first opportunity to remind Elsie that she was living here on his generosity. The old lady went off to her room in tears.

This result, while distasteful to him, nevertheless convinced Muggridge that his campaign against her would be entirely successful; he felt that Elsie would presently quit the house rather than endure such repeated reminders. He settled himself then to an evening with Compeers' *Legal Guide*, in the course of which he learned that in the event of sudden death and the absence of a will, the next of kin inherited the deceased's estate, subject, of course, to the usual tax for the Crown. This reminded him that he had not made a will, and he made a mental note to take care of that detail at his earliest convenience, since it seemed highly illogical to allow his estate to go to Elsie, presuming that by some accident his death should precede hers.

As he was going up the stairs that night he tripped and fell, and was able to avoid serious injury only because of the fortunate nearness of the banister, which he managed to seize and thus broke his fall. As it was, his shins were severely barked and one knee sustained a nasty bruise.

Having recovered momentarily, he thought that his accident was a curious one. There was nothing on the stairs to have upset his balance, and the rug was carefully tacked down. Upon mature reflection, it occurred to Leander Muggridge that his fall had been caused by his tripping over some object set in his way. But a search of the stairs and the hall below failed to reveal anything.

It was not until he was partly undressed for bed that it came to Muggridge how like an outstretched foot had been the thing that tripped him up. At the same time he remembered hearing an infinitesimally small sound just before he fell — like the rustling of skirts.

The emergence of these thoughts made him exceedingly angry, and, after a hasty whisky and soda, Muggridge went to bed. That night he dreamed that Aunt Edith was sitting upon his chest lecturing him the way she used to do when, as a small boy, he had accompanied her to the beach or down into the country. It was a most severe lecture indeed, and he awoke in a sweat, violently upset, so much so, indeed, that he could have sworn to having heard her voice very clearly saying, "This is my house, and you had no right to change it so!" He got to sleep again presently, feeling very unkindly toward the whisky and soda he had had.

In the morning he was inexpressibly rude to Elsie, but this time the old woman was vaguely defiant and did not burst into tears. This had the effect of upsetting Muggridge so much that he stamped off to the office leaving half his breakfast untouched, and convinced that he would have to be harsher than ever with Elsie. After he was gone, Elsie cried quite a bit, but of course Muggridge could not know that.

His return home that afternoon occasioned him a severe shock. He had not had the opportunity to enter his library in the morning, so that his entrance now was his first for that day. His shock was due to the fact that someone had ravaged his library. Some of his books had been torn in half and thrown into the grate, though a fire had not actually been lit. All his imported figurines had been smashed, and two pieces of rather modernistic furniture could never be used except as kindling from that time on.

He took in the details of the room seeing that almost everything smashable had been smashed, save for a few old chairs and an ormolu clock on the mantel, and then marched off in a cold rage to upbraid Elsie. Elsie, however, solemnly said that she had not been in his library, and claimed that the damage, if there was any, had certainly been done the preceding night, for what other explanation could there be for the crashings and bangings which had kept her awake well into the morning?

He stared at her in amazement.

If he would entertain young women at that hour of the night, she went on, it was not surprising what things could happen.

"Young women!" he exclaimed, almost beside himself with rage and disbelief.

"A woman, at least," she replied then, still defiant, though now less sure of herself. "I heard her screaming at you," she went on. "I heard some of her very words."

"What were they?" he demanded bluntly.

"She said, 'This is my house, and you had no right to change it so!' " Then, suddenly realizing when she had last heard those words, Elsie collapsed in tears and hurried from the room.

As for Muggridge, he was most disagreeably upset. He had heard those words, too. But in a dream. Or was it? He turned on his heel and hurried swiftly back into the library, as if to assure himself that the damage was not all the figment of a dream. Unfortunately, it was not. His parsimonious soul shuddered at sight of it. Then, with a catch in his throat, he considered the things that had not been destroyed.

It took him only a moment to discover that the ormolu clock and the few old chairs, together with the majority of the books which remained untouched, had been the property of his Aunt Edith before he had taken possession.

He salvaged what he could out of the wreckage, working all the time with an odd feeling of being watched. Once he could have sworn that someone tittered; it was a sound uneasily like his Aunt Edith's shrill laugh. Unnerved, he persuaded himself finally that rest was what he needed, and left the library for bed considerably earlier than usual.

He saved himself from falling when he tripped on the stairs that night only because he had gone up with extreme caution, as if he had expected that the thing he could not see would again obstruct his ascent. There was the sound of a skirt being drawn away, too; it was just like the sound made by the rustle of his Aunt Edith's old black silk dress.

Though Muggridge was not a nervous man, he locked his bedroom door that night. But never a lock can keep out dreams, and he dreamed again in the dark about his Aunt Edith, looking very harmless, indeed, but going at him like a vixen for what he had done to her garden after taking advantage of a poor old woman's financial need and imposing his false generosity upon her. He woke again in a cold sweat and distinctly heard her voice dying away into the far corners of the room—"Carnations indeed! When you can have lobelias!"

His attempts to go to sleep after that were unsuccessful. In the morning, he maneuvered the stairs with a gingerliness that bordered upon the ridiculous. In the middle of his breakfast, he happened to look out into his garden, in which he took a proper English pride, and abruptly lost his appetite.

Hastily shoving away from the table, he strode from the house. The garden was indeed an unlovely mass of foliage. Someone had torn out all his lovely carnations and all the Holland tulips. The lobelias, however, and some primroses had remained untouched.

This time he did not see Elsie, for fear of what she might say to him.

He felt rather sick, and not a little afraid. When he went down the hall on the way to the office, he had Lincoln's Inn on the telephone and made an appointment with his solicitor. He had an uncanny feeling that his unmade will would bear early attention.

He had a bad day at the office, and his return home late that afternoon was an uneasy one, for there was no telling what might have taken place during the day. Fortunately for his peace of mind, nothing had happened beyond the usual routine, and he settled down to a recent novel with somewhat more aplomb. At the supper table he managed to crush his uneasiness sufficiently to be unkind to Elsie, but she only sat and looked at him out of glittering eyes, so that he was conscious of the hatred in them. And for a few minutes he could have sworn that another pair of hate-filled eyes was regarding him alongside Elsie's, though he could see nothing to justify his impression.

Nevertheless, it was an uncomfortable thought. To his Aunt Edith's memory he made this concession: that, after all, the garden could feature lobelias, inasmuch as they had been her favorite flower. This, of course, was an easy enough concession to make, since almost everything else had been effectively destroyed, and it was too late to grow anything of great beauty in the ruins of his flower-beds.

It would have been reasonable to suppose that, in the light of these curiously suggestive happenings, Muggridge would have given up his campaign against Elsie. But Muggridge, being what he was, refused to back down in the slightest. He went to bed that night with the same caution that had characterized his descent of the treacherous stairs that morning. Once he could have taken oath that an attempt to trip him up had been made, and he came away from the stairs with a faint sense of triumph at having escaped.

That night again he dreamed. He saw himself playing cards with Aunt Edith, who held nothing but spade aces, half a dozen of them, with more in reserve. And Aunt Edith was saying with grim precision, "So now you have got to die, Leander. You were very unkind to me all the time—about the furniture and the lobelias and all. And I promised you that if you were unkind to Elsie you had got to die. And so you shall." All this time she played out those spade aces, which he knew very well were an absurd symbol of death for fortune-tellers, particularly gipsies. It was an unpleasant sort of dream, and how it might have gone on there is no knowing, for he was awakened out of his sleep by the conjuncture of the clock striking ten and the sharp skirling of the telephone bell.

The telephone sounded important, and, with the natural impulse of a trained business man, Leander Muggridge ran from his room and down the stairs. Half-way down, he tripped over something like an outflung foot and tumbled headlong. There was no mistaking the sound of Aunt Edith's tittering.

The telephone kept on ringing, and finally Elsie had to answer it. The call was from Muggridge's solicitor, who informed Elsie in an irate voice that Muggridge had failed to keep his appointment for that afternoon.

There was nothing, of course, that Elsie could do about that. For this time, because of the telephone, Muggridge had forgotten to be careful on the stairs, and had broken his neck.

Since there was no will, Elsie inherited Muggridge's estate fittingly enough. She was exceedingly cautious about little things, particularly about the lobelias. ——✝

MURDER MAN

EWEN WHYTE

The sun, like any April sun, made its way cautiously between showers, putting its early spring warmth here and there across the land in patchwork squares. In the country, greenness came out, the precious firstborn of a new season. In the city people came out, worn by the winter, used up and tired and stiffened by the chill blasts, out now blinking in the new, friendly light.

One of these people was Max Vollmer (Maximillian, his mother had named him in that strident burst of post-birth enthusiasm and hope that is as strong in a slum-district flat as a Florida estate).

Vollmer was a thinnish man in his late forties, probably indistinguishable from so many of the others who scurried across streets, down subway kiosks, up el stairs, to work and home to some drear hovel at night to gather strength for the next meaningless day.

There are millions of Vollmers, living their lives out with hardly an awareness even of the passage of time so intent are they on the tiny task or duty or urge of the moment.

Each, of course, as with all of mankind, thinks himself quite different, endowed with superior qualities than those of his fellow creatures who, in turn, feel the same way about him. It is man's inbred sense of individuality that enables him to survive — for mostly he does — the cogwheel, assembly-line, loud and ill-mannered absurdity that is present-day life.

But this Max Vollmer was different from the other millions of Vollmers, whatever their names might be, because of one greatly distinguishing feature.

This Max Vollmer was planning a killing, a killing that he would surely carry through and one which the police would not solve.

There are many humans walking the dusty, unsatisfying paths of life who think of murder, who, when you see them smile, are smiling at the delicious thought of destroying another human being. All the people you'd never suspect and some you would. But these people, most of them, keep their murderous hates against life and other humans to themselves, for they know with primitive instinct that to action the impulse means not only the end of someone else's life, which is fine, but also their own — not so good — while a fumbled attempt means an even more restricted incarceration than the four walls of their grubby little homes.

With Max Vollmer it was different. He had thought this proposition over for too long to be turned away from it. He had pondered it on his way to work and as he came home at night, one among the hurrying thousands upon thousands, but accompanying him this dread secret.

Strangely, the one who was to be killed was not much thought of. Vollmer, exercising the godlike privilege of the killer-to-be, was concerned only with the time, the method, and the tantalizing proposition of completely fooling the authorities. For this then was to be the one perfect thing in a lifetime of imperfection; the too-large family he'd been born into, the lack of money, of food, of care . . . all so imperfect. The public school growing up, the struggle, always the struggle, and then the best job — not at all good — that could be gotten and the day, week, month, year monotony of that.

To understand the whole dreadful scheme that would end in death, you would have to understand the whole tragedy of being a Max Vollmer—a medium size, less than average in all qualities including luck, unprepossessing in every way. A child, a boy and a man not once smiled on by fortune either in the endowment of natural characteristics or the good breaks which would serve to minimize the lack of these. Many Vollmers go wrong very quickly and therefore do not join the throngs that crowd the streets and paths of this community and that. A car "job," a quick snatch at a corner store, starting with clubs and knives, graduating to guns and plots more elaborate . . . these Vollmers are weeded out fast. They fill the gray, faceless tiers of penitentiaries across the world, and they themselves become faceless, with their identity whittled down to a number.

Others, of less physical or mental vigor, see less of life and are saved from some of life's burdens by the burden of their very own illnesses and they too travel the inexorable way across the stage of life—which after all, is a very poor figure, for life is no stage and nobody watches. That is it. Nobody cares as we slip in and out. Vollmers have cars and buy houses, woo girls and marry them and have children. But all the time they are pre-doomed to indistinguishment, and saved by their universal anesthesia from the dreadful knowledge of that fact.

But here one of them, Max Vollmer by name, was distinguished enough to know some of these things, to have a glimmering of them which made him unlike the rest and worthy of a story. Knowing in him did precisely what knowing does to most people . . . for, of course, if there is one thing sure it is that ignorance is bliss. Knowing made him naggingly unhappy. Unhappy, that is, until the perfect solution came to him. Until the strong emotions could be channeled into a new direction . . . into burning, overwhelming hatred as the alpha and omega of all of life and of the universe which, after all, was no bigger than he was. And the perfect solution was, quite simply, the perfect crime. He would commit it; the killing would right all wrongs.

This was what drove Max Vollmer on. What brought him through the noise-stained, dirt-stained nights of the city; what sent him on his way in the gray, diffused light of early morning to his stand-up breakfast. That took his thoughts from the awful faces of the crowd, in the subway, at work, everywhere. Those faces bobbing and ducking through the streets, carried along at incredibly eccentric paces by the peripatetic bodies that propelled them; tired faces, thin and fat, drawn, over-madeup, sagging, jouncing with the impact of heel on the infernal sidewalk; and the eyes—made him think of "the ayes have it"—the eyes, fish eyes, mackerel and cod, cold eyes and calculating eyes; occasionally the brown hurt puppy dog eyes of someone who hadn't been here very long. And wouldn't be. For you got like those others, or left, or perished.

The victim—Vollmer never thought of him by name—was a man of forty-seven. A good age for such an event as was about to befall him. A good age to write Finis to that life. The whole setup delighted Vollmer as though he had existed for this alone, for perhaps he had.

The monotony of life dropped away and began the supreme adventure of planning this creative effort of destruction. Max Vollmer became blessed with a peculiar sixth sense. A deep sensitivity developed, he thought, belied by his nondescript, one-like-millions face. It seemed now as though he were in league with forces beyond the ordinary ken. When he sat in a movie house, he thought he noticed the way people sitting near him would regard him with sudden but surreptitious interest; his next-door neighbor at the stand-up breakfast place; his co-worker at the office; the tired other sheep-people who lived in the old, creaking, smelling rooming house where he existed.

Max had the feeling that these people *knew, sensed* that he was different, different in ways they could not analyze. And that their knowing was a form of respect. But it pleased him to realize that they could not possibly guess his secret, as they said "Pass the mustard" to him and eyes held together for a flickering instant. He could root them to the spot by telling, cement them forever in that one place by revealing what he was going to do, but left it unsaid for each to go his own way into the maw of the city, to forget there in its throng and bustle all thoughts and dreams but the sheer, instinctive survival ones. But with Vollmer it was different. He never forgot.

The beauty was the way the police would be fooled. Those bumbling self-important idiots who were fit merely to stand on windswept street corners and misdirect traffic. The law, in a way, was symbolic of all the things that Max Vollmer detested. The police, in or out of uniform, represented man's hypocritical conscience, man's inbred distrust of himself. If there was, for instance, a church where one spoke of the freedom of the human heart and spirit, there would surely be a policeman on the corner of the street making sure there would be no freedom of heart of spirit.

For freedom was, after all, doing exactly what you wanted to do precisely when you wanted to do it, and isn't all of civilized life and its rules formulated against just that? So Max Vollmer was sure.

When a man kills, he is really free. And he is free in those quiet, whispering moments when the act belongs only to the killer and the victim — and is locked up forever as the last page of the snuffed-out life — and the silence of the night; before the deliciousness has been shared with the hungry hordes that live on the vicarious sensations of their tabloids, and with the minions of the law who are policemen because they lack the courage of the criminal yet still must be close to violence.

That is the exquisite moment that makes all the dullards worth the pain and insufferability. Even the dead, the victims legion, must know a kind of strange victory in this triumph over the usual, the mundane and the man-ordered ways of their lives which prescribe gallstones or cancer or an errant bus or atom bomb as being Good and quite moral but this as being Bad. This, then, was the final victory and the very horror of society, the smackings of their satisfaction over the thing, the agencies set in motion to catch the wayward human who had dared, yes, dared to do other than wait for the gallstones, the cancer, the misguided auto, the atom bomb . . . dared, and in so daring, freed both himself and the victim.

Max Vollmer had chosen as murder weapon a razor. Not the much-advertised safety kind with fancy streamlining rhapsodized by the subway posters, poor fang-drawn impotent device. Instead, he would use a fine, old-fashioned — weren't old things always the best despite commercials — straight-edged one, the kind still found in barber shops. Vollmer had thought over the possibilities of all lethal weapons and this appealed to him the most. And a razor was better than a knife; it had more subtlety; it was a flute as against a tuba; a rapier instead of a broadsword.

The sweet, clean pain of a razor cutting was a pure virtue. A razor slicing, cutting deep had the cleansing quality of fire; and Max had thought of fire for the victim, but that is improbable. How could a perfect crime be committed with the use of fire? Fire controlled was a beautiful thing, but it blossomed and mushroomed and soon lost its personalized intimacy.

No, it would be a razor. And the site was important. That too had been decided. A nighttime pier in the deserted dock district. A place left by the roustabouts and herky derricks and cursing after working hours, visited only by darkness, by fog and water-smell, and the eerie cries of river traffic moving their red and green and white lights up and down the great bosom of the ageless current out there beyond land's reach.

A razor could be dropped so easily into the deep water off the pier side, and nothing so small would ever be recovered. And the extra pair of shoes, they would go down too; heavy shoes they were and most important to the whole scheme.

Sundays daytime Max Vollmer had gone near the pier, by it, around it, not wanting to be seen or noticed by the Sabbath Day couples who love-strolled or the bums who lounged. The one chance in a million that if he walked boldly out on the rough wood planking, someone *might* say later, Yes, I remember this man. But there was not to be even the one chance in a million. So Vollmer noticed all the details he had to notice from the inconspicuousness of afar. And that was all that was necessary. It would be here that the final scene would be played; played in all its intensity with the dark and the sounds of the river as audience and the dark water as juror.

The blackest night came finally on the heels of unimportant days and other meaningless nights. After work—and how did those other fools know the importance of today as they worked beside him, with their crude jokes and talk about stupid things like women and poker and the fights—Vollmer took himself home to prepare. The extra pair of shoes had to be cunningly weighted; the razor was newly sharpened and secured in his thin, gray overcoat.

Nobody at the bedraggled rooming-house with its bedraggled people paid any mind to the comings and goings of the other inhabitants. Vollmer slipped out of the door unseen sometime before eleven. He took a subway downtown; at that hour it was not crowded, and when he reached his stop, he rose to street level alone. He stood for a moment in the little puddle of light from the kiosk, got his bearings and then plunged into the dark, deserted streets. These thoroughfares were unused at night. They were poor and squalid, dividing more desirable sections from the waterfront. Movie houses and bowling alleys and new construction had moved away from here. This part seemed to sleep in the memory of a long ago when the crumbling brick and masonry fronts had been new.

Vollmer went on more by instinct than sight, for it was very dark, but his feet told him the cobblestones were rougher and the smell of dark swirling water came strong to his nostrils. A street light bisected the gloom ahead and threw feeble yellow rays across the desolate street. Ahead the light faded into the nothingness of space. The river was there, unseen but waiting. And the pier.

Max Vollmer went on until, from his many previous visits here, he could sense the exact directions he needed. The mouth of the pier opened out on a concrete foundation. But beyond that, stretching out over the tide, the wood planking was dirty with disuse; footprints would show clearly from the moment one left the concrete. Vollmer stopped on the cement part and listened, but there was nothing but the swirl of the water and the river sounds. He made sure of the pair of shoes and the razor.

There were a few things he had to do; he'd thought them out; oh so carefully. And now there was the final screwing up of courage, and it was like squeezing a tube of paste. For a while you squeezed and nothing happened, and then suddenly out would pop the substance of determination and resolve.

Max Vollmer did what he had to do with the weighted shoes; then, standing just above where the tide lisped and murmured at the under-pier wood, there was another sound. The final rendezvous would be complete now in a moment or so more. It was impossible to see anything in the impenetrable gloom. Sounds there were, but remote, as of the darkness and the water and traffic borne along its surface, things belonging to the night and the river.

Soon now. Soon, so soon. Vollmer put his hand inside the pocket of the worn, gray overcoat and felt the reassuring handle of the murder weapon-to-be. His fingers on it tightened. He tensed at what could have been a sound of the wind—it would never do to have some blundering outsider stumble onto this scene now. His palm was sweat slick, and he forced his hand against the cloth side of the pocket to dry it.

Why was he nervous? It irked him ever so slightly. For this was the goal, the incentive that had guided him all these weeks and months. After planning this way, after holding his secret, after knowing his superiority over all the other poor fools, poor driven sheep that passed him by through the little moments of their lives, would he hesitate now? Not now.

The breathing, living thing was at his side now. In the impenetrable darkness where only the imagination could see and *know*. The other human was here. Vollmer's hand, with the razor in it, straightened against the night and task, slipped so easily out of the gray overcoat pocket. He struck then, with the frenzy of a man born for just this minute.

The razor touched cloth and parted it, caressed flesh and slitted it with thirst for the blood within. Vollmer himself felt every sweet, clean thrill of the slashing strokes.

He felt the solidity of an arm and struck at it; other solids came before the steel and were shredded, stroke by stroke, blow after blow until there remained in this weaving, drunken, monstrous hulk that had once been whole and human, only the supremely enticing and virginal area of the throat.

That too was fulfilled for ecstasy . . . a bubbling, gurgling ecstasy that slipped and slimed and then gaped so silently as the thing, once human, tottered and fell, no more than tree-like, to the kindred wood of the pier apron.

For Max Vollmer, this was the caress of a thousand beautiful women, the embrace of sublime delight, and only now at the very last moment before the end did he, with a tiny flip of his hand, send the razor—so coated with bright fulfillment even though unseen—into the night at pier side where the river water plopped it down to the depths to wash and forget the shining red deeds stained there. This, the final act of complete accomplishment.

And the wind that had been here and seen, the water that had flowed by and heard, these were gone far away after a time; away with the night.

With light and morning there was finally a person; then people and then the police. They came, sirens screaming with the impotence and noise of recriminators after-the-act. They swarmed to the pier and repaid the dear curious who had called them by pushing them back as though by denying them the pleasure of *looking*, the thing there at wharf's end would rise in all its grisly un-humanness and say hoarsely, "See, I'm all right again."

Patrolmen waved nightsticks, sergeants glowered and lieutenants-of-detectives thought. They noted the clear footprints, clear on the filth of the wood planking. The two pairs leading out to the end, the intermingling of prints, signs of scuffling there at the end, and the one set returning.

"Murder," the wise men of authority said positively and with distaste, for this was the kind of thing you don't solve.

"With a knife or razor," it was obvious.

And those in blue who had rolled him over and looked at the thing poorly hid by shredded clothes, the chest and arms and face and neck, they whistled and somebody who'd seen a lot of these said:

"Somebody sure must've hated this guy to do a carving job like this on him."

That was it, just a grudge, not robbery. Blind, terrible hatred.

For inside the worn, gray overcoat—what was left unshredded of it—was an equally worn wallet, two dollars in it and a card that said that this miserable, un-whole thing, to be bundled out of sight as soon as possible in the high, black morgue wagon, was once a human called Max Vollmer. ——

Murder Mask

Edgar Daniel Kramer

With conflicting emotions in his faded eyes, the stooped and wrinkled butler bowed Colletti into the sun-flooded drawing-room.

"I will tell the master and mistress you are here, sir," the old servitor's cracked voice quavered, as he backed away. "I would as soon meet the Devil!" he spat and crossed himself hastily as soon as he was out of the visitor's sight. "With his hypocrite's smile and his cruel, green eyes!" He shuddered. "Ugh!"

Colletti, tall, dark, slender, prematurely graying at the temples, set his hat, gloves and stick on the nearest chair and with the lithe, slinking movements of a velvet-footed jungle beast advanced to the center table. His inscrutable gaze fastened on the gardenia in his lapel, he drew a bit of silk from the inside pocket of his coat. For a clock-tick or two he scrutinized it. Then, sucking in his breath with a reptilian hiss, he let it slip from his tapering fingers to the sun-splashed table top. It lay like a clot of blood on the polished mahogany. From a vest pocket he thumbed a rectangle of pasteboard, dog-eared and time-yellowed, which bore the badly faded, delicately penned legend:

> *Who wears this mask*
> *Is doomed to slay*
> *Whom he loves best,*
> *Ere break of day!*

As Colletti stood, holding the worn card between his thumb and forefinger, a hideous change crept over him. The ghost of a smile playing about the corners of his thin-lipped mouth grew sardonic. His whole bearing became as deadly, as sinister, as a rattler ready to strike. Like a miasma lifting from a fen, he exuded an aura of evil that polluted the atmosphere around him and took the warmth from the sunlight.

His features grew wolfish and hardened into olive granite, while his eyes blazed feverishly, as he thought of his dead grandfather's will, that left all the eccentric importer's estate to his ward, Nita Tosca, in trust for her children, if she married either of his nephews, Antonio Colletti or Tomaso Romani, but divided the income equally among the trio if the girl remained single or married somebody else. In such a contingency, upon the demise of the last of the three, the principal was to be distributed to stipulated charities.

Nita had rejected Colletti's passionate suit and married Romani. Hiding his real feelings, Colletti had contrived to act as his cousin's best man. After the wedding, feeling cheated, nursing his wounded vanity, with hatred of the newly-weds festering in his veins, he fled to Europe. That was six months ago. Now he was back in his dead grandfather's house with a handful of silk, a frayed card, an all-consuming hate, an inexorable determination to get Nita and her husband out of the picture and—

"Tony!" A voice like the tinkling of silver bells roused Colletti from his devilish introspection.

Thrusting the card away, a quick smile driving the satanic expression from his face, he jerked around like an automaton, as a slip of a woman, blue-eyed, golden-haired, ivory-skinned, came fluttering toward him. Behind her, in the doorway, her husband paused. At first glance and to the superficial observer, he was strikingly like Colletti. Closer study of the cousins, however, brought out subtle differences. Whereas Colletti was soft, hinting of unclean, forbidden things, with the unhealthy pallor of a plant too long away from the sun, Romani was as hard as a shining rapier, as clean as the salt tang of the sea, as frank as the day itself.

"Nita!" Colletti's suave voice was a caress, as he seized the young woman's impulsively outstretched hands. "It *is* good to see you again. You are lovelier than ever."

She laughed musically.

"You're looking splendid, Tom." Colletti shook hands with his cousin.

"I've never felt better," Romani answered. "When did you get back?"

"Yesterday," Colletti told him. "On the *Normandie*."

"You'll be coming to our masque tonight, Tony?" Nita queried.

"Just try to keep me away!" Colletti chuckled. He didn't deem it necessary to explain that he had deliberately timed his return so that he would not miss the masque. "In fact," he went on, "I've just arranged for my costume. By the way," he turned back to the table, "here's a mask I thought one of you might want to wear tonight. I happened to find it, when I was unpacking this morning. It's unique, I think."

Nita caught up the mask and shook out its deep crimson, almost black, folds.

"I'd wear it myself," Colletti added hastily, "but I'm coming as Death and it wouldn't go very well with my costume."

"It's lovely!" Nita breathed, her eyes enigmatic. "So rich! So lustrous! So soft to the touch! Why, it's actually warm! Like living flesh!"

Colletti eyed her narrowly.

"It's been lying in the sunlight, my dear," her husband reminded her.

"I'd wear it, Tony," Nita spoke dreamily, "but I'm attending the masque as a Watteau shepherdess and I'm afraid it won't fit into the picture at all."

"I'll wear it." Romani relieved his wife of the mask. "As a Florentine dandy in the days of the Medici I couldn't ask for anything better. It's just the thing to go with my black outfit."

The late-afternoon sunlight vanished. The room became a place of whispering shadows. Nita shivered.

"What's the matter?" her husband asked anxiously.

"I'm getting jittery, I guess," she laughed nervously. "I've been going too fast a pace lately. I'll be glad when tonight's over. We won't unmask till we have breakfast at dawn." There was something akin to fear in her shifting glances. "After tonight I'll be taking a long rest."

Colletti unconsciously tautened.

"Where'd you get this, Tony?" Romani wanted to know, as his long fingers stroked the silk.

"In Padua," Colletti replied. "In a little cubbyhole of a shop off the beaten track. I figuratively fell into it." He chuckled at the recollection. "The mask struck my fancy as soon as I saw it." He fingered the card in his vest pocket. "I'll run along now. No need to ring for Benito. I'll see you tonight."

They were not hearing him. As though fascinated, hypnotized, metamorphosed into stone like those who looked upon the Gorgons, they appeared completely absorbed in the mask. Colletti gathered up his hat and gloves and stick and silently let himself out.

"After tonight," he chortled his satisfaction, as he strolled down Park Avenue, "the house and all the income from the old man's estate will be mine. I'll live like a lord and throw some parties that'll knock the town's eyes out." He gloated in anticipation. "The poor, blind fools! If the mask doesn't work, this will."

He brought a tiny vial to view and cuddled it in his palm.

"If the necessity arises, I will drop this into their wine. It is odorless, colorless, tasteless and leaves no traces. Nita and Tom will never see another dawn."

❊   ❊   ❊

"You're beautiful tonight, my dear!" Romani rapturously murmured his adoration. "Divinely lovely, Nita mine!"

"You're handsome yourself, Tom!" Her eyes glowed like summer stars.

"I'm mad about you, darling!"

She adjusted her domino. He caught her in his arms and clasped her close. Their lips met and clung.

"I couldn't," he muttered thickly, "I wouldn't live without you, dear!"

"Be careful!" She struggled for breath and reluctantly shoved him away. "You're crushing me, Tom! You're mussing me, too! Let me go now! Please!"

Unwillingly he released her. From below there floated up to them the dulcet strains of a stringed ensemble mingled with shrill feminine laughter, the hoarser mirth of men, the rustling of garments, the shuffling of feet. The air was heady with intoxicating perfumes.

"We must be going down!" she panted through Cupid-bow lips. "Are you ready?"

"Just about." He slipped on the mask Colletti had brought. "All set! Let's go!"

She started and gasped, while her tiny hands flew to her slender throat.

"What are you staring at?" he demanded, cold steel suddenly in his voice. "What's the matter, anyway?"

"Your eyes, Tom!" she choked. "They're—they're—they're—" She couldn't go on.

"You have a bad case of nerves!" he sneered, as he pulled the lower part of the mask away from his face. "This thing persists in pressing against my mouth. You'd think it was alive."

"Your eyes are wild!" she managed to gulp. "You never looked at me like this, Tom. Oh! Your eyes are hot and cruel! Like Tony's at times!"

"Like Tony's, eh?" he jeered in a voice that had lost all its tenderness. "I wish he had stayed on the other side," he continued vehemently. "I wish he had broken his neck, when he fell into that shop in Padua. If I never saw the beggar again, it would be too soon."

Blinking her amazement, she seemed on the point of saying something, changed her mind and turned to the door.

"Listen, lady!" He seized her arm and roughly yanked her back. "Don't be too nice to Tony. Don't encourage him. The rotter has a way with women."

"Tom!" She fought vainly to break his hold. "You're bruising my arm! Let me go! You're hurting me! Let me go! Please!"

"Not too many dances with Tony!" He glared at her. "Mind,

351

Nita! I don't like the way he looked at you this afternoon. Nor the way he held your hands. I felt like slamming him."

"What in the world has got into you, Tom?" she almost wailed, as she wriggled free. "You never—" Her strained voice broke. "Why— why," she stammered her bewilderment, "I actually believe you're jealous of Tony!"

"Jealous of Tony and every other man!" he confessed throatily. "I'd kill you, Nita, before I'd let Tony or anybody else have you." His hand dropped to the haft of the slender dagger at his waist. "I swear it!"

There was no doubting his sincerity. His eyes blazed at her challengingly through the thin slits in the mask.

"This thing seems to be blending with my skin." He tugged impatiently at the silk that rippled to his agitated breathing like a thing alive. "It seems to work convulsively against my mouth."

With a stifled cry, Nita staggered from the room like a stricken thing. For a split second her husband stood glowering after her, fighting for breath like a spent runner. Then he came to life and darted in her wake. He reached the top of the broad stairway, as his wife poised at the bottom like a bird on the point of trying out its wings.

The next instant, what appeared to be a skeleton, shrouded from head to foot in the habiliments of the grave and wearing a mask in the form of a grinning skull, detached itself from the swirling phantasmagoria of nymphs, priests, satyrs, ballet dancers, monks, pirates, harlequins, tramps, pierrettes, sailors, imps and other bizarre creatures, to bow over Nita's hand and whirl her away in a dreamy Strauss waltz.

"Dancing with him already!" Romani growled, as he leisurely descended the stairs. "They'd better not drive me too far!" All the while his fingers were fondling the hilt of his dagger. "They—" He broke off abruptly, while his angry gaze searched the hilarious throng for the dainty shepherdess and her gruesome partner.

On a flood of delirious revelry Nita catapulted through the heavy draperies into the dimly lit alcove. Her husband came bursting in after her. The curtains trembled into place and the sounds of the frenzied merrymaking came to them as though from far away.

"How dare you!" Nita expostulated furiously with a stamp of her foot. "How dare you, Tom!"

He stood glaring at her fixedly, breathing hard, his slim hands clenched until the knuckles showed like chalk. Her eyes were pools of fire. Her breasts heaved tumultuously.

"You have been hateful tonight, Tom!" She dabbed frantically at her eyes with a lacy handkerchief. "You have humiliated me terribly!"

He remained silent.

"You actually tore me out of Tony's arms just now!" she went on scathingly. "You actually flung me in here!"

Romani swallowed hard.

"You'll have to apologize to Tony."

He dismissed the suggestion with a shrug.

"You'll have to!" she insisted.

"You've been dancing with Tony all night!" he rasped savagely. "Every time I looked up, it seemed, he was holding you in his arms with his dirty eyes undressing you."

"Tom!"

"I asked you not to dance with him so often."

"You're being ridiculous!"

"You've been acting deliberately contrary to my wishes." He didn't hear her. "I pleaded with you but you persisted. It made my blood boil. I saw red, while Tony exulted. Finally, I commanded you to dance no more with him. After all, you are my wife, you know. You laughed in my face."

She tossed her head like a spoiled child.

"Hear it, Nita!" He eagerly took a step toward her. "The last dance! Shall we waltz it together?"

"No!" She meant to punish him for his show of jealousy.

Romani recoiled as though from a slap in the face.

"I shall dance it with Tony," she told him airily. "Let me pass!"

She started to brush past her husband, as the draperies parted and Colletti appeared.

"Nita," he began, "you—"

With a nerve-tearing snarl, Romani flashed his slender-bladed dagger and lunged.

"Oh!" Nita started to scream. "Tom, you—"

Her strangled shriek ended in a gurgling gasp, as the dagger sheathed itself to the hilt in her bosom. Blood gushed and bubbled around the buried blade. An expression of mingled bewilderment, surprize and incredulity flitted over her ghastly, painted face, as Romani caught his crumpling wife in his arms.

"Nita!" he croaked, his red rage dropping from him like a discarded cloak. "Speak to me, sweet! Nita! Nita! Nita! Good God! What have I done?"

"You've killed her, Tom!" Colletti could not keep the oily satisfaction from his voice. "You have murdered her!"

"Nita!" Romani was beside himself with grief. "Speak to me, dear! I wouldn't hurt you! I wouldn't! I'd die first!"

He covered her face with kisses.

"Nita! Nita! Nita!"

She hung limp in his embrace.

"Speak to me, darling!" He beseeched, as he tore off his mask and flung it across the shadowy alcove. "I love you! I love you! Speak to me, Nita!"

"It's no use, Tom!" Colletti mocked him. "She's dead!"

Romani seemed to become aware of the other man's presence.

"This means the electric chair for you, Tom," Colletti cruelly reminded his cousin. "You have murdered her."

For clock-ticks that seemed eternities. Romani stared hard at the speaker. Gently he lowered his dead wife to the thick-piled rug. Carefully he pulled the dagger from her breast. Tenderly he closed her eyes, crossed her hands on her bloody bosom and straightened her limbs.

"Thanks to the mask," Colletti pointed, "you have murdered your wife, Tom." He handed the anguished man the time-yellowed card. "Soon you'll be walking through that little green door."

"I can't live without you, Nita!" Romani declared brokenly, as he deciphered the faded legend. "I won't!"

"The state will attend to that, Tom," Colletti jeered. "You need have no worries on that score."

Romani retrieved the discarded mask and, whirling on Colletti, thrust it at him.

"Put it on!" he ordered bruskly and tickled his cousin's ribs with his blood-smeared dagger. "Put it on or I'll drive this steel into your devil's heart!"

Colletti paled and gulped and hesitated.

"Put it on!" Romani reiterated huskily, increasing the pressure of the dagger, while with his free hand he tore the death mask from his cousin's face. "Hurry!"

With trembling fingers Colletti adjusted the red silk mask over his twitching features.

"Who wears this mask!" Romani growled, as through the muted strains of the waltz the weary revelers chorused *Good-night, Ladies.* "It's your turn now, Tony! *Is doomed to slay!* Murder, Tony! *Whom he loves best!* That's yourself, Tony! You're going to kill yourself! *Ere break of day!* Which isn't far off! You'll have to hurry, Tony! You haven't much time!"

Like a man suffering the tortures of the damned, Colletti's whole body was writhing horribly. His palsied hands clawed at his throat. He appeared to be wrestling with an invisible antagonist.

"Whom he loves best!" Romani repeated hoarsely. "You're taking your own worthless life, Tony! Hurry!"

The crimson mask moving to his labored breathing, Colletti fumbled inside the hideous grave garments he was wearing. His groping hands brought a tiny vial to light.

"Is doomed to slay!" Romani hissed, stepping back, for the coercion of the dagger was no longer needed. *"Whom he loves best!"*

While Romani watched him balefully, Colletti slowly lifted the fluttering mask with his left hand, while with his right he tilted the bottle on his mouth. With a hollow gulp he drained its contents. His hands dropped like leaden plummets. For a split second he steadied. Then a tremor shook him from heels to crown. He swung half-way around, recovered, his knees buckled and he collapsed on his face. Romani rolled him over, nudged him callously with his foot, stooped and listened to his heart.

"Dead!" he mumbled and straightened. "Gone to the hell where he belongs!"

He sank on his knees beside his dead wife. Tenderly he kissed her cold eyes, her carmined lips, the little hollow at the base of her throat.

"Coming, Nita!" he spoke as though replying to an urgent summons and plunged the dagger into his own heart. "Com—"

He pitched forward over the dead woman. The music and the singing ceased. The gray dawning peered in at the window. ——

THE MURDERER

MURRAY LEINSTER

The murderer's hair lifted at the back of his neck. A crawling sensation spread down his spine. There was something moving in the room! It was pitch-dark, with vague rectangles of faint grayishness where windows opened upon the rainy night outside. The murderer had left this room half an hour before, maybe only twenty minutes before. He'd gone plunging away through the darkness, knowing that before dawn the rain would have washed away the tiretracks of his car. And then he'd remembered something. He'd come back to pick up a thing he'd left, the only thing that could possibly throw suspicion upon him. And there was something moving in the room!

His scalp crawled horribly. He had to clench his teeth to keep them from chattering audibly. . . . He heard the sound again! Something alive in the room. Something furtive and horrible and—and terribly playful! It was amused, that live thing in the room. It was diverted by the one gasp of pure terror he had given at the first sound it made.

The murderer stood teetering upon his toes, with his hand outstretched and touching the wall, fighting against an unnamable fear. He was in the right house, certainly. And in the right room. He could catch the faint acrid reek of burnt smokeless powder. His senses were uncannily acute. He could even distinguish the staling scent of the cigarette he had lighted when he was here before. . . . This was the room in which he had killed a man. Yonder, by the wide blotch of formless gray, there was a chair, and in that chair there was an old man, huddled up, with a bullet-wound in his throat and a spurt of deepening crimson overlaying his shirt-front. The murderer who stood by the wall, sick with fear, had killed him no more than half an hour before.

And there could not be anyone else in the house. The murderer listened, stifling his breathing to deepen the silence. Nothing but the shrill and senseless singing of a canary-bird that was one of the dead man's two pets. The bird stopped, began again drowsily, and was silent. In the utter stillness that followed, the vastly muffled purring of his own motor-car reached the murderer, and the slow, drizzling sound of rain, even the curious humming of the telephone wires that led away from the house.

But then he heard the noise again, such a sound as might have been made by a man drumming softly and meditatively upon a table with his fingertips. A tiny sound, an infinitely tiny sound, but the sound of something alive. The murderer stifled a gasp. It came from the chair where the dead man was sitting!

There was cold sweat upon the forehead of the man by the wall. It seemed, insanely, as if the dead figure, sitting upright in its chair, had opened its eyes to stare at him through the blackness, while the stiff fingers tapped upon the table-cloth as they had done in life.

A surge of despairing hatred came to the murderer, while icy-cold crawlings went down his spine. Those finger-tappings . . . those furtive, stingy fingers that were always so restless, always touching something, always fumbling desirously at something. . . . Why, he'd shot the old man when he was fumbling with his cigarette-case, avidly plucking out a cigarette to smoke in secret, being too miserly to buy even the cheapest of tobacco for himself.

The murderer felt some of his fear vanish. He'd shot the old man. Killed him. He was dead. He'd made only one mistake. He'd made sure the bullet went just where he intended, and then he'd fled, out to the car and plunged away. No need to stop and rob. The dead man was the murderer's uncle, and the state and the courts would deliver his wealth in time. Everything was all right, except for one mistake, and he'd come back to rectify that.

He deliberately fanned the hatred that he helped so much in the commission of his crime, and now was crowding out his terror. He had only to think of the old man to grow furious. Rich—and a miser. Old—and a skinflint. He wouldn't keep a servant, because servants cost money. He wouldn't keep a watch-dog, because watch-dogs had to be fed. It was typical of him that he kept two pets as an economical jest—a canary because it would eat bread-crumbs, and a cat because it would feed itself. The murderer by the wall had seen the old man chuckling at sight of the huge cat stalking a robin upon the lawn. . . .

The murderer moved forward confidently, now. He'd shot his uncle as the old man was fumbling cigarettes out of the nephew's case. He'd made sure that death had come, and he'd fled—but without the cigarette-case. Now he'd come back for it. It had been foolish of him to feel afraid. . . .

He heard the drumming of reflective finger-tips upon the table-top. Stark terror swept over him again, and he pressed on the button of his flashlight. . . . The old, unprepossessing figure was outlined in full. Grayed, unkempt hair, bushy eyebrows, head bent down, hand extended toward the cigarette-case on the table. . . . All was as it should have been. But the coat, the long, dingy coat that hung down from the extended arm—that was moving! Muscles in the sleeve had been flexing and unflexing. The coat was flapping back and forth. The man in the chair was alive!

With a snarl, the murderer sprang forward, his hands outstretched. An instant later he fell back with a rattle in his throat. The flesh he had touched was cold and already rigid.

He stood still, fighting down an impulse to scream. The man in the chair was dead. And then he heard that insane, deliberate tapping again. He could feel the dead eyes upon him, gazing up from a bent-forward head and looking through the bushy brows. A strange, malevolent joy was possessing the dead thing. It was gazing at him, tapping meditatively, while it debated a suitable revenge for its own death.

The murderer cursed hoarsely and groped for the table. He was livid with terror and a queer, helpless rage. He hated his victim, dead, as he had never hated him living. His fingers touched the cigarette-case—and it was jerked from beneath his touch.

The murderer choked. He had to have the cigarette-case. It was proof of his presence—proof against which his carefully prepared alibi would be of no use. He'd been seen to use it no more than an hour since, when he left the house in which he was a weekend guest to come hurtling across country for his murder. He had to have it!

And the tapping came again, insanely gleeful, diabolically reflective. The man in the chair was beyond reach. No more harm could come to him. And he could toy with the living man as a cat toys with a mouse.

Numb with unreasoning terror of the thing that was dead, and yet moved, that was not two yards away and yet was removed by all the gulf between the living and the dead, the murderer pressed the flashlight button again. He clenched his teeth as he seemed to sense the stoppage of a stealthy movement by the thing in the chair. His cigarette-case was gone, missing from the table.

The flashlight beam swept about the room in a last flare of common sense. It was empty. No one, nothing. . . . Nothing in the house except the dead man, to seize that one small article which would damn the murderer.

He remembered suddenly and switched off the light. There were neighbors. Not near neighbors, but people who would notice the glow of a flashlight if it met their eyes. They knew the old man for what he was, and probably whispered among themselves of buried treasure or hidden money. They would suspect a robber of like mind if they saw the flashlight going.

They might have noticed it then! He had to get the cigarette-case and go away quickly. . . .

Forcing his brain to function while he was stiff with a terror that he could not down, he masked the bulb with his fingers and let a little ray trickle over the table. The old, claw-like hand. It seemed to be nearer the telephone than it had been. The cloth table-top. No monogrammed case. It had been there. He had seen it not two minutes since. But it had vanished utterly.

The living man could have screamed with rage. He seemed to feel the thing in the chair shaking with silent laughter. The chair was shaking! God! It *was* shaking!

The murderer fled to the doorway upon caving knees, his whole soul writhing in panic. And then he heard the reassuring purring of his motorcar, waiting to carry him away. Outside was sanity. Only within was nightmarish horror. He could not go away and leave that case to hang him. . . .

He was grinding his teeth as he came back. He was doggedly desperate in his resolution. He got down on his hands and knees and let a little trickle of light slip between his fingers. Instinctively he kept out of reach of the dead fingers. Not yet had he come to think of danger there. The thing in the chair enraged him while it terrified him, because it mocked him. But he would get this one thing and go. . . .

The floor was bare. The case had not fallen from the table to the floor.

He let his light go out again, while his scalp crawled. But he could not go without the case. Leaving it, he left safety—perhaps life—behind. There was no single thing to connect him with this murder save that. His alibi was prepared, was perfect. But he had been seen to use that case an hour ago. Found here, it would damn him. If it were carried away, he would be unsuspected.

He had planned it perfectly. That was the only flaw in the whole plan, and he had only to pick up the monogrammed case of silver to be both safe and rich. Why, he'd even planned out the funeral! He would be dutifully grieved. Some of the neighbors would be there—some because it was the proper thing, but more from curiosity. The only person who would really regret the old man's death would be the telephone-girl. The old man paid her a small extra sum to give his line special attention. It was, he said, his burglar-protection. And every month, grudgingly, he paid her a small sum, with a deduction for each time he could claim to have been kept waiting for a number.

There was a scratching sound from the chair. The murderer sprang to his feet, his terror making his throat dry. The scratching came again, like a fingernail on rough-polished sheet metal. The telephone! The thing in the chair was reaching for the telephone!

The murderer acted without thought, in pure sweating fear. He sprang like a wildcat. The table toppled heavily to the floor and the telephone went spinning against the wall. He flung the extended wrist aside. . . .

It resisted his hand. And he jerked away and stood moaning softly, in an ecstasy of fear and desperation.

Once more the feeling as if the thing in the chair were laughing, shaking in silent, ghastly laughter. The one thing that held the murderer in the room was the cigarette-case that could hang him. And the thing was tormenting him and shaking in horrible mirth. . . .

Long past the power to reason, the murderer brought forth all his will-power. It was really a conflict between two fears, a panic-stricken horror of the dead thing before him, and terror of a noose that awaited him. He flashed his light despairingly—and saw the cigarette-case.

It was projecting invitingly from the pocket of the thing in the chair. It had been on the table. It had been filched from beneath his descending hand. It was in the dead man's pocket, as if tucked there by stiff and clumsy fingers—or as if left projecting to lure him to a snatch. And the extended hand, with its clawing fingers outstretched, quivered a little as if with eagerness for him to make an attempt to get it.

He whimpered. It was trying to get him to reach for the case, invitingly in sight. But if he reached, he would be within the length of its arms. And they would move stiffly but very swiftly to seize him. . . .

He whimpered. He dared not go without that case. He dared not reach in his hand to seize it. He sobbed a little with pure terror. Then, glassy-eyed with horror, he swung his foot in a sudden, nervous kick. If he could kick the case from its insecure position, he could retrieve it from the floor. . . .

He was quivering. The kick failed. The thing remained motionless, but it seemed to him that it was tensing itself for a sudden effort. . . . The murderer wrung his hands. He kicked again, and sheer icy fear flowed through his veins as he felt the soft resistance of the cloth against his foot. But he missed.

He heard a curious little chuckling sound that could not possibly have come from anything but a human throat. It was a human voice. It was syllables, divided to form words, but words in a strangled, distant, ghastly tone. . . .

Drenched in the sweat of undiluted horror, the murderer swung his foot a third time, desperately, with his eyes glassy and the breath whistling in his throat.

Then he screamed. . . .

The flashlight dropped to the floor. There was utter darkness. There was no noise for seconds save those chuckling sounds. They were louder, now. The murderer stood rigid, balanced upon one foot, his eyes terrible. He screamed again. Something had hold of his foot. Something grasped at his trouser-leg and tugged at it gently. Not strongly. Gently. But it was tugging. . . .

The murderer screamed and screamed, with his eyes the eyes of a man in the depths of hell. Not because his foot was caught, but because something was pulling him, weakly but inexorably, in furtive little tugs, toward the man in the chair—who was dead.

Then sharp nails sank in his flesh and the murderer broke away. He fell, and in falling his slipping foot crashed against the leg of the chair, and that turned over upon him. . . .

The telephone operator had been listening since the receiver was flung off its hook by the fall of the telephone. She had spoken several times, asking what was wanted, and the sound had issued from the receiver on the floor like—well—like the chuckle of a man amused in a horrible fashion. When she heard screaming, she sent men to investigate. And they found a dead man tumbled out of the chair in which he had died, and another man crawling about the room. The living man was crawling about on his hands and knees, his eyes wide and staring and terrified, while a huge pet cat made playful pounces at his trouser-leg, tugging at it, worrying it, pulling backward upon it. And whenever the cat pulled at the bit of cloth, the living man screamed in a sickly, terrified fashion.

They never did get at the rights of the matter, but the coroner was somewhat annoyed by the cat, during the inquest. He was sitting in the chair the dead man had sat in, beside the table on which the telephone stood. And the cat buffeted his coat-tails, hanging down, with playful pats of its paws. The sound was very much like that of a man drumming softly and meditatively upon a table.

But it was not that which annoyed the coroner. He liked cats. What did annoy him was the fact that he had put his lighted cigarette on the edge of the table for an instant, and the cat sank its claws in the table-cover. With the jerk, the cigarette fell from the table into the coroner's pocket, and burned a hole through to the skin.

"If that cigarette had been in its case, now," said the coroner, smiling at his own feeble joke, "it wouldn't have done any harm."

NIGHT AND SILENCE

MAURICE LEVEL

They were old, crippled, horrible. The woman hobbled about on two crutches; one of the men, blind, walked with his eyes shut, his hands outstretched, his fingers spread open; the other, a deaf-mute, followed with his head lowered, rarely raising the sad, restless eyes that were the only sign of life in his impassive face.

It was said that they were two brothers and a sister, and that they were united by a savage affection. One was never seen without the other; at the church doors they shrank back into the shadows, keeping away from those professional beggars who stand boldly in the full light so that passers-by may be ashamed to ignore their importunacy. They did not ask for anything. Their appearance alone was a prayer for help. As they moved silently through the narrow, gloomy streets, a mysterious trio, they seemed to personify Age, Night and Silence.

One evening, in their hovel near the gates of the city, the woman died peacefully in their arms, without a cry, with just one long look of distress which the deaf-mute saw, and one violent shudder which the blind man felt because her hand clasped his wrist. Without a sound she passed into eternal silence.

Next day, for the first time, the two men were seen without her. They dragged about all day without even stopping at the baker's shop where they usually received doles of bread. Toward dusk, when lights began to twinkle at the dark crossroads, when the reflection of lamps gave the houses the appearance of a smile, they bought with the few half-pence they had received two poor little candles, and they returned to the desolate hovel where the old sister lay on her pallet with no one to watch or pray for her.

They kissed the dead woman. The man came to put her in her coffin. The deal boards were fastened down and the coffin was placed on two wooden trestles; then, once more alone, the two brothers laid a sprig of boxwood on a plate, lighted their candles, and sat down for the last all-too-short vigil.

Outside, the cold wind played round the joints of the ill-fitting door. Inside, the small trembling flames barely broke the darkness with their yellow light. . . . Not a sound. . . .

For a long time they remained like this, praying, remembering, meditating. . . .

Tired out with weeping, at last they fell asleep.

When they woke it was still night. The lights of the candles still glimmered, but they were lower. The cold that is the precursor of dawn made them shiver. But there was something else—what was it? They leaned forward, the one trying to see, the other to hear. For some time they remained motionless; then, there being no repetition of what had roused them, they lay down again and began to pray.

Suddenly, for the second time, they sat up. Had either of them been alone, he would have thought himself the plaything of some fugitive hallucination. When one sees without hearing, or hears without seeing, illusion is easily created. But something abnormal was taking place; there could be no doubt about it since both were affected, since it appealed both to eyes and ears at the same time; they were fully conscious of this, but were unable to understand.

Between them they had the power of complete comprehension. Singly, each had but a partial, agonizing conception.

The deaf-mute got up and walked about. Forgetting his brother's infirmity, the blind man asked in a voice choked with fear:

"What is it? What's the matter? Why have you got up?"

He heard him moving, coming and going, stopping, starting off again, and again stopping; and having nothing but these sounds to guide his reason, his terror increased till his teeth began to chatter. He was on the point of speaking again, but remembered, and relapsed into a muttering:

"What can he see? What is it?"

The deaf-mute took a few more steps, rubbed his eyes, and presumably reassured, went back to his mattress and fell asleep.

The blind man heaved a sigh of relief, and silence fell once more, broken only by the prayers he mumbled in a monotonous undertone, his soul benumbed by grief as he waited till sleep should come and pour light into his darkness.

He was almost sleeping when the murmurs which had before made him tremble, wrenched him from an uneasy doze.

It sounded like a soft scratching mingled with light blows on a plank, curious rubbings, and stifled moans.

He leaped up. The deaf-mute had not moved. Feeling that the fear that culminates in panic was threatening him, he strove to reason with himself:

"Why should this noise terrify me? . . . The night is always full of sounds. . . . My brother is moving uneasily in his sleep . . . yes, that's it. . . . Just now I heard him walking up and down, and there was the same noise. . . . It must have been the wind. . . . But I know the sound of the wind, and it has never been like that. . . . it was a noise I had never heard. . . . What could it have been? No . . . it could not be. . . ."

He bit his fists. An awful suspicion had come to him.

"Suppose . . . no, it's not possible. . . . Suppose it was . . . there it is again! . . . Again . . . louder and louder . . . some one is scratching, scratching, knocking. . . . My God! A voice . . . her voice! She is calling! She is crying! Help, help!"

He threw himself out of bed and roared:

"François! . . . quick! . . . Help! . . . Look! . . ."

He was half mad with fear. He tore wildly at his hair, shouting:

"Look! . . . You've got eyes, you, you can see! . . ."

The moans became louder, the raps firmer. Feeling his way, stumbling against the walls, knocking against the packing-cases which served as furniture, tripping in the holes in the floor, he staggered about trying to find his sleeping brother.

He fell and got up again, bruised, covered with blood, sobbing:

"I have no eyes! I have no eyes!"

He had upset the plate on which lay the sprig of box, and the sound of the earthenware breaking on the floor gave the finishing touch to his panic.

363

"Help! What have I done? Help!"

The noises grew louder and more terrifying, and as an agonized cry sounded, his last doubts left him. Behind his empty eyes, he imagined he saw the horrible thing. . . .

He saw the old sister beating against the tightly-closed lid of her coffin. He saw her superhuman terror, her agony, a thousand times worse than that of any other death. . . . She was there, alive, yes alive, a few steps away from him . . . but where? She heard his steps, his voice, and he, blind, could do nothing to help her.

Where was his brother? Flinging his arms from right to left, he knocked over the candles: the wax flowed over his fingers, hot, like blood. The noise grew louder, more despairing; the voice was speaking, saying words that died away in smothered groans. . . .

"Courage!" he shrieked. "I'm here! I'm coming!"

He was now crawling along on his knees, and a sudden turn flung him against a bed; he thrust out his arms, felt a body, seized it by the shoulders and shook it with all the strength that remained in him.

Violently awakened, the deaf-mute sprang up uttering horrible cries and trying to see, but now that the candles were out, he, too, was plunged into night, the impenetrable darkness that held more terror for him than for the blind man. Stupefied with sleep, he groped about wildly with his hands, which closed in a vise-like grip on his brother's throat, stifling cries of:

"Look! Look!"

They rolled together on the floor, upsetting all that came in their way, knotted together, ferociously tearing each other with tooth and nail. In a very short time their hoarse breathing had died away. The voice, so distant and yet so near, was cut short by a spasm . . . there was a cracking noise . . . the imprisoned body was raising itself in one last supreme effort for freedom . . . a grinding noise . . . sobs . . . again the grinding noise . . . silence. . . .

Outside, the trees shuddered as they bowed in the gale; the rain beat against the walls. The late winter's dawn was still crouching on the edge of the horizon. Inside the walls of the hovel, not a sound, not a breath.

Night and Silence. ——

THE NIGHTMARE ROAD

FLORENCE CROW

The wind moaned dismally around the eaves of the hunting-lodge and the cold rain beat against the windows, making us all grateful for the cheer and warmth of the big, open fireplace.

There were five of us who had come up to J. P. Draper's lodge for a little holiday. Draper was a genial man in his middle thirties, well educated and widely traveled. He knew good liquors and told a story well—quite the ideal host. He was of distinguished appearance; with a broad streak of perfectly white hair drawn straight back from just above his right eyebrow to a little below the crown of his head in the back, where it became intermingled with the black and finally was lost. He had an odd mannerism of caressing the white streak when in deep thought, which, of course, drew attention to it.

We had all been in a reminiscent mood and telling some tall tales. Somehow our talk had turned to things occult and supernatural. I think the loneliness of the lodge and the dismal rain, with the tapping of the ends of the limb of a tree on the window-pane, like ghostly finger-tips, had something to do with it.

Finally some one asked J. P. to tell us some experience he might have had that was touched with the occult. J. P. was stroking his white streak in that absentminded way of his, but he looked up at the speaker and said,

"I shall tell you about something that happened a couple of years ago when I was in Germany.

"I was on a hiking tour through the Hartz Mountain district. As you know, the more elevated portions are rough and dreary and the soil is sterile, but the scenery is very interesting, with the rounded and graceful form of the Brocken towering above all the other mountains. The Rosstrappe, which stands near by in the same group, is not so tall but is far more rugged in aspect than the Brocken, and it was in this district that the events occurred which I shall relate.

"I had been enjoying it all immensely until the night of All Hallows Eve. The goal I had set for the evening was the town of Goslar, situated on the Gose at the base of the Rammelsberg. There are some public buildings there I wished to see which were erected in the Fifteenth Century: the imperial palace, in part a ruin, and the

Gothic church, the treasure of which is a number of Luther's manuscripts.

"The people of this town, and indeed of the whole district, are hard-working and God-fearing. The more ignorant are, however, very superstitious, believing in all sorts of witchcraft, charms and magic. Several friendly persons had mentioned that it was All Hallows Eve, that vampires, witches and other cohorts of the devil would be abroad that night and it were well that all good folk should be indoors with a holy cross on the door to protect them.

"I paid no attention to their talk, of course, and the day itself was uneventful except that toward evening, when I realized that it would be after dark before I could reach Goslar, I stopped for refreshments. The good woman who served me offered the hospitality of her home for the night and warned me against being abroad after sundown. I thanked her but said I would press on, as I would surely arrive in Goslar in time to secure lodging. She appeared troubled that I insisted on departing and at the moment of my departure thrust a crude, wooden cross into my hand, saying,

" 'All who are abroad tonight will be in great peril and will surely need the protection of the holy cross. Keep it with you. They will try to get it away from you, but don't let it go a minute. They will try all sorts of tricks, but don't let them have it. Don't let them fool you.'

"I felt foolish, but I thanked her for her kindness, and thrusting it into my pocket, forgot all about it until later.

"As the sun neared the horizon that evening an air of expectancy seemed to hover over the land, and the long shadows cast by the strange rock formations took on weird shapes. A queer, coppery glow covered the sky and the whole earth appeared to bask in the reflected glow from some vast devil's pit. The wind blew cold and chill and moaned as it rushed by, as though it fled in fear of something.

When the sun sank from sight I looked toward the west, and a long line of birds or bats was streaming across the sky. With that infernal glow behind them, it created a most uncanny effect. I could well understand how an ignorant and superstitious person might imagine them to be vampires, bats and witches flying to some unholy tryst.

"I was swinging along at an easy pace but still covering the ground in good time, when I heard a feeble hail. It came from a little distance from the road, and I stopped and listened. It came again from the direction of a mass of rocks, and I turned my steps toward them. As I neared the rocks I saw a poor, feeble old man lying in a twisted position as though in pain.

366

"'Are you hurt, my good man?' I asked as I bent to raise him from the ground.

"'Yes, but do not touch me, I am badly hurt. I think I am dying. All day I have lain here waiting for help, and now I fear it is too late. Before I die I should like to see the holy cross. Do you have one?'

"I remembered the one I had in my pocket and drew it forth and was about to place it in the old man's hand when he spoke in a voice astonishingly loud and strong for one dying,

"'No, no! Put it on the rock here beside me, so that it may be the last thing my eyes behold.'

"I was astonished at his vehemence and the look which crossed his face; almost one of terror, I should say. I was nonplussed for a moment and stood holding it rather uncertainly in my hand. Again the old fellow repeated his request in the weak and whining voice in which he had first spoken. I had stooped over to do as he asked when I happened to glance at his face again. Such a fierce look of exultation and triumph crossed it that I thought of what the old woman had said,

"'They will try all sorts of tricks.'

"Still it was not with real seriousness that I thought of it, but it occurred to me that he was probably fevered and did not quite know what he said. Therefore, I reasoned, I would place it to his lips, as would be pleasing to the pious man if his mind were clear.

"I made the move to do so and had almost touched him when a horrible shriek burst from the creature's lips and he leaped up and beyond my reach as though propelled by some mighty force stronger than human muscle and sinew. In an instant he was gone, but the sound of his shriek still trembled on the air.

"Hurrying back to the road, I started off rapidly toward Goslar, thinking to myself that he was probably a robber, but superstitious nevertheless about kissing the cross in the very act of committing a crime. Then I wondered why he had mentioned the cross in the first place. And again the words of the old woman rang in my ears,

"'They will try to get it away from you.'

"Just a coincidence, I decided; he was merely trying to throw me off guard by pretending to be dying, so that I should be unprepared for an attack. Still, highwaymen were not common in the district.

"At that moment a great night-bird swooped down with an unearthly scream. I almost jumped out of my shoes. Then I laughed as I thought how amusing it was that strange surroundings, loneliness and an unusual experience work on one's nerves till the cry of a harmless bird could throw one into a momentary panic.

"I had gone but a little way when something round and white rolled from behind a large rock. It had grown much darker, and the dim light seemed to play tricks with my sight, for it looked like a skull. I gave myself a mental shake for being such a fool. It couldn't possibly be anything but a rock that some small animal had loosened and it had rolled down an incline.

"I was about to move on when I heard a noise from behind the rocks. I thought of the highwayman and prepared for another attack. Sure enough, something was coming. I could hear someone running over the stones. Suddenly there burst from behind the rocks a skeleton—a hideous, headless human skeleton running after its own skull. The skull kept rolling while the skeleton ran after it and disappeared from sight.

"It was almost too much for me and I muttered aloud, 'I must be crazy, or else they are right and this is the devil's night.'

"There was nothing to do but go on and try to reach Goslar before my imagination should play any more grim jokes on me. I was still holding the wooden cross in my hand, and somehow, imagination or not, I was glad I had it.

"I had been hurrying and was somewhat breathless when I saw a light in the distance. It was a welcome sight, and I slowed my pace somewhat, as I did not wish to rush up like a small boy frightened of the dark. As I came nearer I noticed many figures milling about a big fire. Some travelers camping out, I thought; maybe gipsies, I decided, as wild shouts of laughter reached me and I noted that the figures were all moving about quickly in what was undoubtedly some sort of dance. However, I welcomed the thought of being among even so villainous-appearing a lot. I came to within a few hundred feet and halted to look them over before making my presence known.

"My eyes first fell on the bonfire, for so strange a one I had never seen. It burned with a strange, bluish light intermingled with bursts of crimson sparks. It was so remarkable that I scarcely saw the rest of the scene for a moment. Suddenly my fascinated gaze fixed on something moving in the fire. I rubbed my eyes and looked again. The fire was not burning ordinary sticks of wood, but snakes. Serpents, large and small, squirmed and twisted as though executing some devil's dance of their own as the flames mounted higher.

"A particularly bright flare occurred, lighting up the whole company, and I looked at the people. What people! Their eyes all glowed like the red stop-light on an auto, and their visages were demoniac. They shouted in wild bursts of laughter in which there was no mirth, only echoes of dead curses and groans.

"I tried to turn and slip away, but I could not. I seemed rooted to the spot. I raised my eyes and saw that grimmest of all structures—a gallows. At the end of the rope hanging from the scaffold dangled a human figure.

"My chest suddenly felt as though it were bursting from the horror and pity of beholding a hapless human so murdered by the fiends that made such terrible sport. Even as I watched, the hanged creature began to wave its arms and dance on the air. As it danced, shriller, wilder laughter rang out. Suddenly the rope parted and the creature floated to the ground and joined in the wild revelry.

"My senses were reeling. I thought I had surely gone mad and this was the hell of insanity. I don't know whether I laughed or began to pray . . . I think I tried to pray, and I must have made some noise which attracted the attention of that terrible host, for they all turned at the same instant and rushed toward me. Red light flashed from their fiendish eyes, and clawed hands stretched out to grab me. Instinctively I raised my hands, as one does in trying to ward off a blow, still holding the cross.

"They stopped as though transfixed at sight of what I held in my hands. Suddenly they set up a terrible howling and screeching as they danced and flew about me, but did not come any closer. I perceived that they would not touch me so long as I was thus protected by the cross, and so holding it extended before me I stepped forward. Those directly before me moved aside, leaving a gap, and I passed through.

"Numbers of the awful things followed me and I could hear their screams and wails and the sound of great wings thrashing the air. I stumbled on and on, feeling that I had been on this awful road for ever. I was breathing in great, sobbing gasps; grasping the cross with a strength that numbed my fingers, I tried to pray, but all I could say was, 'Oh God!'

"Far in the distance I again saw a light. I almost feared to approach it, but there was the chance that it was a house, a human habitation. There was ever a rustling behind me and I felt a cold wind on the back of my neck, like an icy blast from the lowest, frozen pit of hell.

"I stumbled along, and as I came closer to the light I could see that it was shining from the window of a house. Nevertheless, not to betray myself again into the presence of another such company as I had just escaped, I approached the window and looked within.

"There on his knees, I saw the dark-garbed figure of some saintly man of God, his white head bowed in prayer. I knocked on the door and heard the good priest move. I called aloud for admittance and he answered me, asking,

" 'Who is there?'

"I do not know what I answered, but the door was opened and I fell across the threshold, noting as I fell that the mat just within the entrance was made in the design of a cross.

"When I opened my eyes, the glorious mountain dawn had flooded the world with light and I was resting on the good man's own couch and he sat in a great chair close beside me. He smiled and placed his hand on my forehead, saying,

" 'You are less fevered now, my son. I think you will soon be all right.'

"I felt very grateful to the good priest, but my eyelids were heavy, and I slept.

"After a while the fever left and I was entirely recovered, but since that time this streak of white has marked my otherwise youthful head."

Our host smiled as he stroked the white streak across his head and looked at his guests. ——╁——

No Eye-Witnesses

Henry S. Whitehead

There were blood stains on Everard Simon's shoes. . . .

Simon's father had given up his country house in Rye when his wife died, and moved into an apartment in Flatbush among the rising apartment houses which were steadily replacing the original rural atmosphere of that residential section of swelling Brooklyn.

Blood stains—and forest mold—on his shoes!

The younger Simon—he was thirty-seven, his father getting on toward seventy—always spent his winters in the West Indies, returning in the spring, going back again in October. He was a popular writer of informative magazine articles. As soon as his various visits for week-ends and odd days were concluded, he would move his trunks into the Flatbush apartment and spend a week or two, sometimes longer, with his father. There was a room for him in the apartment, and this he would occupy until it was time for him to leave for his summer camp in the Adirondacks. Early in September he would repeat the process, always ending his autumn stay in the United States with his father until it was time to sail back to St. Thomas or Martinique or wherever he imagined he could write best for that particular winter.

There was only one drawback in this arrangement. This was the long ride in the subway necessitated by his dropping in to his New York club every day. The club was his real American headquarters. There he received his mail. There he usually lunched and often dined as well. It was at the club that he received his visitors and his telephone calls. The club was on Forty-Fourth Street, and to get there from the apartment he walked to the Church Avenue subway station, changed at De Kalb Avenue, and then took a Times Square express train over the Manhattan Bridge. The time consumed between the door of the apartment and the door of the club was exactly three-quarters of an hour, barring delays. For the older man the arrangement was ideal. He could be in his office, he boasted, in twenty minutes.

To avoid the annoyances of rush hours in the subway, Mr. Simon senior commonly left home quite early in the morning, about seven o'clock. He was a methodical person, always leaving before seven in the morning, and getting his breakfast in a downtown restaurant near the office. Everard Simon rarely left the apartment until after nine, thus avoiding the morning rush-hour at its other end. During the five or six weeks every year that they lived together the two men really saw little of each other, although strong bonds of understanding, affection, and respect bound them together. Sometimes the older man would awaken his son early in the morning for a brief conversation. Occasionally the two would have a meal together, evenings, or on Sundays; now and then an evening would be spent in each other's company. They had little to converse about. During the day they would sometimes call each other up and speak together briefly on the telephone from club to office or office to club. On the day when Everard Simon sailed south, his father and he always took a farewell luncheon together somewhere downtown. On the day of his return seven months later, his father always made it a point to meet him at the dock. These arrangements had prevailed for eleven years. He must get that blood wiped off. Blood! How—?

During that period, the neighborhood of the apartment had changed out of all recognition. Open lots, community tennis-courts, and many of the older one-family houses had disappeared, to be replaced by the ubiquitous apartment houses. In 1928 the neighborhood which had been almost rural when the older Simon had taken up his abode "twenty minutes from his Wall Street office" was solidly built up except for an occasional, and now incongruous, frame house standing lonely and dwarfed in its own grounds among the towering apartment houses, like a lost child in a preoccupied crowd of adults whose business caused them to look over the child's head.

*   *   *

One evening, not long before the end of his autumn sojourn in Flatbush, Everard Simon, having dined alone in his club, started for the Times Square subway station about a quarter before nine. Doubled together lengthwise, and pressing the pocket of his coat out of shape, was a magazine, out that day, which contained one of his articles. He stepped on board a waiting Sea Beach express train, in the rearmost car, sat down, and opened the magazine, looking down the table of contents to find his article. The train started after the ringing of the warning bell and the automatic closing of the side doors, while he was putting on his reading-spectacles. He began on the article.

He was dimly conscious of the slight bustle of incoming passengers at Broadway and Canal Street, and again when the train ran out on the Manhattan Bridge because of the change in the light, but his closing of the magazine with a page-corner turned down, and the replacing of the spectacles in his inside pocket when the train drew in to De Kalb Avenue, were almost entirely mechanical. He could make that change almost without thought. He had to cross the platform here at De Kalb Avenue, get into a Brighton Beach local train. The Brighton Beach expresses ran only in rush hours and he almost never travelled during those periods.

He got into his train, found a seat, and resumed his reading. He paid no attention to the stations—Atlantic and Seventh Avenues. The next stop after that, Prospect Park, would give him one of his mechanical signals, like coming out on the bridge. The train emerged from its tunnel at Prospect Park, only to re-enter it again at Parkside Avenue, the next following station. After that came Church Avenue, where he got out every evening.

As the train drew in to that station, he repeated the mechanics of turning down a page in the magazine, replacing his spectacles in their case, and putting the case in his inside pocket. His mind entirely on the article, he got up, left the train, walked back toward the Caton Avenue exit, started to mount the stairs.

A few moments later he was walking, his mind still entirely occupied with his article, in the long-familiar direction of his father's apartment.

The first matter which reminded him of his surroundings was the contrast in his breathing after the somewhat stuffy air of the subway train. Consciously he drew in a deep breath of the fresh, sweet outdoor air. There was a spicy odor of wet leaves about it somehow. It seemed, as he noticed his environment with the edge of his mind, darker than usual. The crossing of Church and Caton Avenues was a brightly lighted corner. Possibly something was temporarily wrong with the lighting system. He looked up. Great trees nodded above his head. He could see the stars twinkling above their lofty tops. The sickle edge of a moon cut sharply against black branches moving gently in a fresh wind from the sea.

He walked on several steps before he paused, slackened his gait, then stopped dead, his mind responding in a note of quiet wonderment.

Great trees stood all about him. From some distance ahead a joyous song in a manly bass, slightly muffled by the wood of the thick trees, came to his ears. It was a song new to him. He found himself listening to it eagerly. The song was entirely strange to him, the words unfamiliar. He listened intently. The singer came nearer. He caught various words, English words. He distinguished "merry," and "heart," and "repine."

It seemed entirely natural to be here, and yet, as he glanced down at his brown clothes, his highly polished shoes, felt the magazine bulging his pocket, the edge of his mind caught a note of incongruity. He remembered with a smile that strange drawing of Aubrey Beardsley's, of a lady playing an upright cottage pianoforte in the midst of a field of daisies! He stood, he perceived, in a kind of rough path worn by long usage. The ground was damp underfoot. Already his polished shoes were soiled with mold.

The singer came nearer and nearer. Obviously, as the fresh voice indicated, it was a young man. Just as the voice presaged that before many seconds the singer must come out of the screening array of tree boles, Everard Simon was startled by a crashing, quite near by, at his right. The singer paused in the middle of a note, and for an instant there was a primeval silence undisturbed by the rustle of a single leaf.

Then a huge timber wolf burst through the underbrush to the right, paused, crouched, and sprang, in a direction diagonal to that in which Everard Simon was facing, toward the singer.

Startled into a frigid immobility, Simon stood as though petrified. He heard an exclamation, in the singer's voice, a quick "heh"; then the sound of a struggle. The great wolf, apparently, had failed to knock down his quarry. Then without warning, the two figures, man and wolf, came into plain sight; the singer, for so Simon thought of him, a tall, robust fellow, in fringed deerskin, slashing desperately with a hunting-knife, the beast crouching now, snapping with a tearing motion of a great punishing jaw. Short-breathed "heh's" came from the man, as he parried dexterously the lashing snaps of the wicked jaws.

The two, revolving about each other, came very close. Everard Simon watched the struggle, fascinated, motionless. Suddenly the animal shifted its tactics. It backed away stealthily, preparing for another spring. The young woodsman abruptly dropped his knife, reached for the great pistol which depended from his belt in a rough leather holster. There was a blinding flash, and the wolf slithered down, its legs giving under it. A great cloud of acrid smoke drifted about Everard Simon, cutting off his vision; choking smoke which made him cough.

But through it, he saw the look of horrified wonderment on the face of the young woodsman; saw the pistol drop on the damp ground as the knife had dropped; followed with his eyes, through the dimming medium of the hanging smoke, the fascinated, round-eyed stare of the man who had fired the pistol.

There, a few feet away from him, he saw an eldritch change passing over the beast, shivering now in its death-struggle. He saw the hair of the great paws dissolve, the jaws shorten and shrink, the lithe body buckle and heave strangely. He closed his eyes, and when he opened them, he saw the figure in deerskins standing mutely over the body of a man, lying prone across tree-roots, a pool of blood spreading, spreading, from the concealed face, mingling with the damp earth under the tree-roots.

Then the strange spell of quiescence which had held him in its weird thrall was dissolved, and, moved by a nameless terror, he ran, wildly, straight down the narrow path between the trees. . . .

It seemed to him that he had been running only a short distance when something, the moon above the trees, perhaps, began to increase in size, to give a more brilliant light. He slackened his pace. The ground now felt firm underfoot, no longer damp, slippery. Other lights joined that of the moon. Things became brighter all about him, and as this brilliance increased, the great trees all about him turned dim and pale. The ground was now quite hard underfoot. He looked up. A brick wall faced him. It was pierced with windows. He looked down. He stood on pavement. Overhead a streetlight swung lightly in the late September breeze. A faint smell of wet leaves was in the air, mingled now with the fresh wind from the sea. The magazine was clutched tightly in his left hand. He had, it appeared, drawn it from his pocket. He looked at it curiously, put it back into the pocket.

He stepped along over familiar pavement, past well-known façades. The entrance to his father's apartment loomed before him. Mechanically he thrust his left hand into his trousers pocket. He took out his key, opened the door, traversed the familiar hallway with its rugs and marble walls and bracket side-wall light-clusters.

He mounted the stairs, one flight, turned the corner, reached the door of the apartment, let himself in with his key.

It was half-past nine and his father had already retired. They talked through the old man's bedroom door, monosyllabically. The conversation ended with the request from his father that he close the bedroom door. He did so, after wishing the old man good-night.

He sat down in an armchair in the living-room, passed a hand over his forehead, bemused. He sat for fifteen minutes. Then he reached into his pocket for a cigarette. They were all gone. Then he remembered that he had meant to buy a fresh supply on his way to the apartment. He had meant to get the cigarettes from the drug-store between the Church Avenue subway station and the apartment! He looked about the room for one. His father's supply, too, seemed depleted.

He rose, walked into the entry, put on his hat, stepped out again into the hallway, descended the one flight, went out into the street. He walked into an unwonted atmosphere of excitement. People were conversing as they passed, in excited tones; about the drug-store entrance a crowd was gathered. Slightly puzzled, he walked toward it, paused, blocked, on the outer edge.

"What's happened?" he inquired of a young man whom he found standing just beside him, a little to the fore.

"It's a shooting of some kind," the young man explained. "I only just got here myself. The fellow that got bumped off is inside the drug-store,—what's left of him. Some gang-war stuff, I guess."

He walked away, skirting the rounded edge of the clustering crowd of curiosity-mongers, proceeded down the street, procured the cigarettes elsewhere. He passed the now enlarged crowd on the other side of the street on his way back, returned to the apartment, where he sat, smoking and thinking, until eleven, when he retired. Curious—a man shot; just at the time, or about the time, he had let that imagination of his get the better of him—those trees!

His father awakened him about five minutes before seven. The old man held a newspaper in his hand. He pointed to a scare-head on the front page.

"This must have happened about the time you came in," remarked Mr. Simon.

"Yes—the crowd was around the drugstore when I went out to get some cigarettes," replied Everard Simon, stretching and yawning.

When his father was gone and he had finished with his bath, he sat down, in a bathrobe, to glance over the newspaper account. A phrase arrested him:

". . . the body was identified as that of 'Jerry the Wolf,' a notorious gangster with a long prison record." Then, lower down, when he had resumed his reading:

". . . a large-caliber bullet which, entering the lower jaw, penetrated the base of the brain. . . . no eye-witnesses. . . ."

Everard Simon sat for a long time after he had finished the account, the newspaper on the floor by his chair. "No eye-witnesses!" He must, really, keep that imagination of his within bounds, within his control.

Slowly and reflectively, this good resolution uppermost, he went back to the bathroom and prepared for his morning shave.

Putting on his shoes, in his room, he observed something amiss. He picked up a shoe, examined it carefully. The soles of the shoes were caked with black mold, precisely like the mold from the wood-paths about his Adirondack camp. Little withered leaves and dried pine-needles clung to the mold. And on the side of the right shoe were brownish stains, exactly like freshly dried bloodstains. He shuddered as he carried the shoes into the bathroom, wiped them clean with a damp towel, then rinsed out the towel. He put them on, and shortly afterward, before he entered the subway to go over to the club for the day, he had them polished.

The bootblack spoke of the killing on that corner the night before. The boot-black noticed nothing amiss with the shoes, and when he had finished, there was no trace of any stains.

Simon did not change at De Kalb Avenue that morning. An idea had occurred to him between Church Avenue and De Kalb, and he stayed on the Brighton local, secured a seat after the emptying process which took place at De Kalb, and went on through the East River tunnel.

He sent in his name to Forrest, a college acquaintance, now in the district attorney's office, and Forrest received him after a brief delay.

"I wanted to ask a detail about this gangster who was killed in Flatbush last night," said Simon. "I suppose you have his record, haven't you?"

"Yes, we know pretty well all about him. What particular thing did you want to know?"

"About his name," replied Simon. "Why was he called 'Jerry the Wolf'—that is, why 'The Wolf' particularly?"

"That's a very queer thing, Simon. Such a name is not, really, uncommon. There was that fellow, Goddard, you remember. They called him 'The Wolf of Wall Street.' There was the fiction criminal known as 'The Lone Wolf.' There have been plenty of 'wolves' among criminal 'monikers.' But this fellow, Jerry Goraffsky, was a Hungarian, really. He was called 'The Wolf,' queerly enough, because there were those in his gang who believed he was one of those birds who could change himself into a wolf! It's a queer combination, isn't it?—for a New York gangster?"

"Yes," said Everard Simon, "it is, very queer, when you come to think of it. I'm much obliged to you for telling me. I was curious about it somehow."

"That isn't the only queer aspect of this case, however," resumed Forrest, a light frown suddenly showing on his keen face. "In fact that wolf-thing isn't a part of the case—doesn't concern us, of course, here in the district attorney's office. That's nothing but blah. Gangsters are as superstitious as sailors; more so, in fact!

"No. The real mystery in this affair is—the bullet, Simon. Want to see it?"

"Why—yes; of course—if you like, Forrest. What's wrong with the bullet?"

Forrest stepped out of the room, returned at once, laid a large, round ball on his desk. Both men bent over it curiously.

"Notice that diameter, Simon," said Forrest. "It's a hand-molded round ball—belongs in a collection of curios, not in any gangster's gat! Why, man, it's like the slugs they used to hunt the bison before the old Sharps rifle was invented. It's the kind of a ball Fenimore Cooper's people used—'Deerslayer!' It would take a young cannon to throw that thing. Smashed in the whole front of Jerry's ugly mug. The inside works of his head were spilled all over the sidewalk! It's what the newspapers always call a 'clue.' Who do you suppose resurrected the horse-pistol—or the ship's blunderbuss—to do that job on Jerry? Clever, in a way. Hooked it out of some dime museum, perhaps. There are still a few of those old 'pitches' still operating, you know, at the old stand—along East Fourteenth Street."

"A flintlock, single-shot horse-pistol, I'd imagine," said Everard Simon, laying the ounce lead ball back on the mahogany desk. He knew something of weapons, new and old. As a writer of informational articles that was part of his permanent equipment.

"Very likely," mused the assistant district attorney. "Glad you came in, old man."

And Everard Simon went on uptown to his club. ——|——

Nude with a Dagger

John Flanders

Old Gryde was a money-lender, and a hard one. In the course of his career, five thousand clients owed him money, he was the occasion of one hundred and twelve suicides, of nine sensational murders, of assignments, bankruptcies and financial disasters without number.

A hundred thousand maledictions were called down on his head, and he laughed at all of them. But the hundred thousand and first malediction killed him, in the strangest and most frightful fashion.

I owed him two hundred pounds, he ground out of me the most abominable interest payments every month, and yet he had made me his intimate friend. As a matter of fact, this was only a way he had of torturing me, for I was forced to submit to every sort of cruelty and malice at his hands, to echo his boisterous laughter as his victims begged, entreated, and even died at his hands.

He scrupulously recorded all this suffering and blood in his day-book and his ledger, as his ill-gotten fortune grew day after day.

But today I do not regret the pain he caused me, because I was allowed at last to witness his death-agony. And I wish all his dear colleagues a like fate.

One morning I found him in his office engaged in an argument with a client, a very pale and very handsome young man.

The young man was speaking:

"It is impossible for me to pay you, Mr. Gryde, but I implore you not to sell me out. Take this painting. It is the one good piece of work I have done. I have worked it over a hundred times; I have put my heart's blood into it. Even now I realize that it isn't quite finished. There is something lacking still—I can't tell exactly what it is—but I know I shall find out in time, and then I will finish it.

"Take it for this debt which is killing me—and is killing my poor mother!"

Gryde sneered. When he noticed me, he called my attention to a moderately large painting which stood against his bookcase. When I caught sight of it, I started with surprise and admiration. It seemed to me that I had never seen anything so perfect.

It was a life-size nude, a man as handsome as a god, standing out against a vague, cloudy background, a background of tempest, night and flame.

"I don't know yet what I shall call it," said the artist in a voice filled with pain. "That figure you see there—I have been dreaming of it ever since I was a child; it came to me in a dream just as certain melodies came from heaven in the night to Mozart and Haydn."

"You owe me three hundred pounds, Mr. Warton," said Gryde.

The young man clasped his hands together.

"And my painting, Mr. Gryde! It is worth twice that, three times that, ten times that!"

"In a hundred years," assented Gryde. "I shan't live long enough to get the good of it."

But as he spoke I seemed to catch in his face a sort of vacillating glimmer which was different from the steel-hard gaze I had always seen there before. Was it admiration of an artistic masterpiece, or was it the prospect of fabulous profit?

Then Gryde went on:

"I am sorry for you," he said, "and away down in my heart I have a weakness for artists. I will take it and credit you with a hundred pounds on your debt."

The artist opened his mouth to reply. The usurer cut him off.

"You owe me three hundred pounds, payable at the rate of ten pounds a month. I will sign a receipt for ten months. Don't forget to be prompt in your payment eleven months from today, Mr. Warton!"

Warton had covered his face with his beautiful hands.

"Ten months! You are giving me ten months free from worry, ten months of relief for Mother—Mother is sadly nervous and ill, Mr. Gryde—and I can work hard in these ten months—"

He took the receipt.

"But," added Gryde, "you admit yourself that there is something still lacking to the picture. You must put the finishing touch to it, and you must find a name for it by the time the ten months are up."

The artist promised all this, and the picture was hung on the wall above old Gryde's desk.

Eleven months went by, and Warton was unable to pay his installment of ten pounds. He begged and implored Gryde to allow him more time, but to no avail. The usurer secured an order for the sale of the poor boy's effects. When the officers came, they found mother and son sleeping the sleep of death in a room filled with asphyxiating fumes from a brazier of live coals.

On the table, there was a letter for Gryde.

"I agreed to furnish you a name for my picture," the artist had written him. "You may call it *Vengeance*. And as for my promise to finish the picture, I will keep that promise, too."

Gryde was very much annoyed.

"The name," he argued "doesn't fit the picture at all. And how can a dead man come back and finish a picture?"

But his challenge to the other world was answered.

One morning I found Gryde terribly worried and excited.

"Look at the painting!" he cried, the moment I entered the room. "Don't you see something strange about it?"

I studied the painting, but I could discover no change in it. My assurance seemed to relieve him greatly.

"Do you know—" he began. He passed his hand over his forehead, and I could see drops of perspiration standing out on his brow.

"It was last night, sometime after midnight. I had gone to bed; then all at once I remembered that I had left some very important papers lying on my desk.

"I got up at once to see that they were put away safely. I never have any trouble in finding my way about in the dark in this house, for I know every corner and crevice of it. I came into my office here without taking the trouble to turn on a light. There was really no need for one, for the moonlight fell square on my desk. As I leaned over my papers, I had a feeling that something was moving between the window and me—

"Look at the picture! Look at the picture!" Gryde cried out suddenly in abject terror.

Then, in a moment, he murmured: "I must be imagining things. I have heard of hallucinations but I can't remember ever having had one—I thought I saw the man in the picture move again.

"Well, when I came in here last night, it seemed to me I saw—no, I swear I *did* see that man in the painting reach out his arm to seize me!"

"You're going crazy," said I.

"I wish I could explain it so," said Gryde; "that would be better than—"

"Well, why don't you destroy the painting, if you think all this isn't just imagination?"

Gryde's face brightened.

"That hadn't occurred to me," he said; "I suppose because it was too simple."

He opened a drawer and took out a long-bladed dagger with a delicately chiseled handle.

He walked toward the picture with the dagger in his hand. Then, suddenly, he seemed to change his mind.

"No!" he said. "I'm not going to fling a hundred pounds into the fire just because I had a bad dream. You're the one that's crazy, young friend."

And he flung the weapon angrily down on his desk.

When I went back the next day, I did not find the same Gryde. In his stead was a broken old man with the eyes of a tracked beast, shaking with insane terror.

"No," he howled, "I'm not crazy, I'm not an imbecile! I know what I'm talking about. I got up again last night, and came in here to see if the other thing had been a dream. And I tell you—I tell you—*he* came out of the picture," Gryde bellowed, twisting his hands around each other, "and—and—look at the picture, you damned fool! He took my dagger away from me!"

I put my hands up to my head. I felt myself turning as crazy as old Gryde was. The thing was impossible, but it was true. The nude figure in the painting held in his hand a dagger which had not been there the day before, a dagger that I recognized by the artistic carving on the handle. It was the weapon which Gryde had flung down on the desk when I was here last!

I begged Gryde, by all he held sacred, to destroy the painting. But mad with terror though he was, he could not bring himself to wreck an object that had money value.

He still did not believe that Warton would keep his promise!

Gryde is dead.

We found him in his armchair, his body emptied of blood, his throat cut clear across. The murderous steel had slashed into the leather of the chair.

And when I looked at the painting, I saw that the blade of the dagger was red to the hilt. ⟶╪

THE OCEAN OGRE

DANA CARROLL

June 2.—Our stiff canvas, faded and gray, hangs lifeless from the yardarms. We are stilled in one of the great calms. There is slowly rising water in the well, and our food is nearly gone. We heave on the greasy, heavy water, foul and green. The fog hides all from view. I confess that I am afraid. What an expressive word is despair! Luckily a flying-fish came scudding over the rails this morning.

June 3. — The fog has lifted a bit, but there is no relief in sight. The seven of us worked all last night on the pipes, until our backs ached and our hands were raw. The crew seems gruff and surly, but I haven't the heart to assert my authority at a time like this. They don't realize how near death they are. I write for record only, for who knows what may happen in the next few days? We are at present in the open sea a thousand miles from land. A fine situation for the skipper of the *Jolly Waterman!* Three months ago I had a full crew and a lucky boat, but now—scurvy isn't pleasant. No, sir, not pleasant at all.

June 4. — Hope! I have given up even entertaining the word. By working desperately we are able to keep the water in the well down, but our hardtack is nearly gone. We have pumped and sweated on empty stomachs for twelve hours. Losier collapsed. He folded like the others, but thank God he died quietly. No reproachful blasphemies heaped on my head. Just a tired fading, glad it was all over.

June 5. — It was funny. Another flying-fish came aboard today, and Herbie Tastrum made a dive for it. He looked like a maniac as he slid along the deck, filling his belly with splinters. He caught it between his two hands and bit into it, and finally disposed of it, bones and all. I was a bit put out. He could have divided it. I could shred a donkey's carcass in my present state. Yet, I write it was funny.

June 6. — Our case is desperate. No two ways about it, something has to happen, and soon. There isn't a breath of air stirring, and Hanson is below, unable to raise a limb. The five of us are able to keep the water down, but we are tired—dog-tired.

June 7. — We have one thing to be thankful for, the water hasn't risen much in the last twelve hours. Not that we would pump it out if it did. We are too tired to pump. We lie on the decks and curse, and make faces at the sky. I lost my temper many times today, but I am suffering acutely. Why do I continue to write futilely in this log book which no one will ever read?

June 8. — We are saved! What glorious good luck! A boatload of provisions and a jolly companion to cheer us up. He says he is the sole survivor of the *King William.* You have probably heard of the *King.* A finer brig never put out from Marseilles. A hurricane and a leak did for her. Six or seven pulled away in the longboat, but my friend (what else could you call your savior?) threw them overboard. They died first, of course. They died from fright, or from drinking salt water. My friend didn't elaborate on details, but not liking the unsociable company of corpses, he naturally disposed of them. That's his story, and I accepted it at its face value. I am not a man to go poking about and asking questions. It's enough that he brought us a boatload of provisions and his own buoying companionship. He has actually injected spirit. We were growing to loathe each other, we five. He calls himself Alain Gervais.

June 11.—Gervais (he insisted we call him that) has been with us now for three days. He has the run of the ship, and I have turned the mate's cabin over to him. The mate has no further need for a cabin—he spends his nights rolling on the ocean floor. Gervais is tall and emaciated. His face is oyster-colored, drawn and haggard. His eyes are set deeply in dark caverns and actually seem to consume you. There is something devastating about those eyes; sometimes they seem a hundred years old. His forehead is high and as yellow and dry as parchment, and his nose is shaped like a simitar. With long, gangling arms and thick wrists he presents an awesome picture. A very peculiar fellow now that I get to know him better. But he is one of us.

June 12.—Gervais has kept more to himself. He remained locked in his cabin all morning, and answered my anxious questions curtly, through the closed door. But I was too busy to investigate; there is a chill in the air that encourages hope for a wind in the near future. Some of the crew seem too tired to work. They came across a bottle of rum in Losier's locker, and by mixing it with salt water they concocted an elixir to alleviate their suffering. Who am I to assert my authority, but I hope for the first breeze, as it will surely bolster the ship's morale. At that time I plan to regain my old power of discipline.

June 13.—A breeze is surely coming. It is eerily still, all around us, except for a sharp report every now and then, as another deck plank snaps under the direct rays of a broiling sun. I am working frantically on a miserable substitute of a rudder. I am stripped to the waist, and the sweat rolls down into my eyes, almost blinding me. I have been over the side twice this afternoon for relief, but there is very little in the brackish water.

June 14.—Gervais slept on the planks with the crew last night, and this morning he looks ten years younger. His face is flushed and full, and the greenish hollows have disappeared from beneath his eyes. But Hanson isn't well. He complains of pains in his chest, and once or twice he spat a mixture of blood and rum. His big face seems sandpapered by age, and he is abnormally pale.

June 15.—No breeze. Hanson is surely stricken. Death hovers over him like an impatient doorman. He lies in his cabin and groans, and I can do nothing for him. His pallor is genuinely alarming. Even his lips are bloodless. He complains of his nose, and noises in his ears. And Gervais has shown his first glints of ill-nature. His eyes smolder when he speaks, and for the first time I discern a hard cruelty in the man. He is an alarming personality.

June 16. — Hanson died this morning. A horrible, racking death. It seemed as though he wanted to tell us something. I laid my ear on his broken, watery lips, but was unable to make out anything intelligible from his forced moaning. Gervais actually gloated over his death. What can it mean? Why such a metamorphosis in the man we befriended? He owes everything to our generosity. Human beings are utterly despicable, and I have lost faith in them. He gloats over the misfortunes of others. He actually smiled as we dropped poor Hanson into the sea. Imagine it!

June 17. — There is still no wind. There is something unnatural about this floating hulk. Even the cook has noticed it.

"It ain't natural," he said, "for a ship to smell like this, and that Gervais fellow's cabin, phew! It not only stunk, but—"

I clouted him behind the ear. "You're a fool!" I shouted. "He's all right."

You have a feeling that he knows more than ten ordinary men whenever he opens his mouth to tell one of his amazing yarns. And that tale of the French fleet he told yesterday was so real, so vivid! But it set me to thinking. I must confess the smell of Gervais' cabin did horrify me. I entered it while Gervais was on deck, and the stench nearly laid me out. The place smelt like a charnel house. The odor of decaying shell-fish mingled with a peculiarly offensive and acrid smell that in some way suggested newly shed blood. Tonight I shall finish the rum. Oh, I will get gloriously drunk, but what does it matter?

June 18. — Gervais has grown currish and cynical. He has assumed the authority to curse my men, and refuses to speak to me. This morning Harry Knudson went below to lie down. He was as white as a squid's belly. All I could do was to perform a cursory examination. I told him to strip, and examined his entire body. He was pitifully lean and bloodless. Something had bitten him in the chest. A round discoloration showed plainly on the center of his chest, and in the very middle were two sharp incisions, from which blood and pus trickled ominously. I didn't like the looks of it and told him so. Harry smiled grimly and turned over in his bunk.

June 19. — Gervais seems to have appointed himself king of the ship. He does whatever he pleases. This morning he cut a strip of sail down and improvised a novel marquee for himself on the poop-deck. All during the late afternoon he reclined under the canvas, smoking his briar and gazing reflectively out to sea. None of the men approached him; they want as little as possible to do with so temperamental a person. We were all occupied forward when we heard a triumphant shout from Gervais. He was jumping around under his marquee and pointing over the side. It was Hanson's body, floating face upward, not ten feet from the ship. His nose was gone, and his cheekbones protruding through the wasted skin. The water was so still he seemed to hang there, leering up at the ship. When we buried him yesterday, we sewed his body in canvas and weighted it. Evidently the stitching had loosened, and the suddenly released, air-filled body had popped to the top like a cork.

June 20.—An unaccountable incident occurred on deck today. I am obliged to believe that Gervais is insane. Roland Perresson was working on the braces, and his hand accidentally slipped. He cut himself badly. The blood gushed down his arm, and we all feared he had severed an artery. His under lip trembled, but he didn't complain or cry out. He simply walked with unsteady steps toward the fo'castle. Gervais was on the poop-deck, in his throne room, as we have begun to call it. The sight of Perresson's uncertain steps somehow excited him. He made for Perresson. Perresson saw him coming, and stopped, a little puzzled, a little hopeful. In a moment Gervais had seized upon the injured arm. He gripped it forcefully and stuck it under his shirt. Gervais was sweating and acting like one possessed. I feared for Perresson. The situation was unhealthy. I stepped forward to interfere. But when I reached them they were free of each other. Perresson held his arm and groaned.

"There's no blood on it," he bellowed, "and it's as cold as ice."

I could only stand and stare. Is Gervais mad, or has he mastered some monstrous system of healing?

June 21.—Roland Perresson is dead. I disposed of the body this morning. It was white and rigid, and I noticed an extraordinary discoloration above the wound on his wrist. From the elbow down, his arm was a bright green. I cannot explain it. Blood-poisoning, perhaps; but I will stand little more from Gervais. His presence has become odious to me.

Something walked again tonight. It bent above my bed and I heard it gulp. We have become so few, we are mentally drawn together for protection against an alien evil. We are not certain what it is, but we must do something.

June 22.—This morning after a half-hearted gesture at making my rounds I retired to the ship's library. It was fairly cool there and I thought I could get away from myself for a bit, although there is no breaking from this ship and sea and sky. But now I wish I hadn't. I picked up an old water-stained parchment volume, called *The Islands of France,* a ridiculous miscellany of witchcraft and spirits. I chuckled to myself as I indolently flicked the pages until my interest was finally arrested by the childish awe and belief in the following:

"There lies a beautiful island called Gautier off the southwest tip of France. You may walk from heavy 'Druid' depths of the forest to the brilliant blue glare of the ocean, where the fishermen spread out their nets of bright blue cord to dry, and fisherwomen make out at low tide to gather mussels, sold in the shell for two cents a quart. If you ask them what is the next land they reply, *'L'Amerique est là-bas'* —America is over there. They are a naïve folk, few of them ever having been away from the island. They will gladly tell you about the old legends of the island, and what's more, believe them. There was the unfortunate Suzanne, the young girl, cruel or unfaithful to her lover, who was changed into a big black dog or female wolf. Unless she repented or a miracle restored her to her natural shape, she was doomed to lope, howling through the black naked woods, longing for death, until killed. Only a special bullet, properly blessed, could kill her, which made it difficult.

"There were also the beak-faced hunchbacks, that lived in the sea. These deformed people made periodical raids on the good villagers. If they were displeased they had the unpleasant habit of dragging corpses through the streets with loud cries. And it didn't take much to displease them, although no one could remember their ever having perpetrated bodily harm.

"There were the 'slacks' or noisy drones. Spirits of those that had met a violent death, they wandered through the night, repeating the cries of agony with which they had died, often from age to age. The old fisherwomen even yet hear them howling on long winter nights.

"There were, and according to the belief of many still are, sorcerers and sorceresses; they are looked upon as outsiders, feared, hated and never touched. It is a form of our ancient and respectable belief in witchcraft. If you meet one in your path, to avoid destruction you must immediately make the sign of the cross, seize a piece of earth, and hold it above your head, because between two pieces of earth, the ground under your feet and the piece held in a quivering hand above your head, no evil spirit can harm you.

"It is a dangerous sign on this island when those little corpse-dragging dwarfs ring a bell as they go along, for that means another death; a bad sign also if a church bell rings without any hand touching it.

"Those are still living who have seen the *dames blanches*—white ladies—howling in the night at church doors, seeking salvation and relief.

"Alain Gervais, the villagers relate, was swimming with other youths of his age in the St. Jacques basin; of a frolicsome and adventurous nature, he swam some distance from shore. According to another youth who was making his way to Alain at all possible speed, he took what seemed an intentional surface dive, and did not appear again. Many hours were spent fruitlessly diving for his body. A few years later, one of the boys, now grown into a man, was stationed at the watch of a fishing-boat, when he saw the rough caricature of a man, diving and breaking for air a short distance from his craft. He insisted he recognized Gervais."

A few lame conjectures followed, on the ability of a man being enabled to live at the bottom of the sea.

I remember flinging the book from me as if it were some abhorrent dead thing, and rising weakly, I made my way on deck with a troubled mind.

June 23. — I buttonholed Peter Bunce this morning forward of the lee scuppers. I told him in ragged, forceful exclamations just what I had read. He ponderously turned my story over in his numbed brain. His eyes rolled crazily and his mouth sagged. His face turned yellow, but he caught himself with determination.

"We must act at once," he said.

June 24. — Our plans have been worked out. Peter and I are to bunk together tonight. We have my revolver and a razor-sharp, double-edged knife. Peter contends that the knife will be necessary. He insistently babbles of vampires and other blood-sucking demons. His obsession took an active form this noon. He jumped up and stepped around deftly, brandishing his knife in dark corners, and lunging wildly in offensive alacrity, cutting an imaginary victim to bits. I smiled rather wanly. Finally, exhausted, he slumped down on a stool, his head between his hands. My smile faded as I contemplated his abject dejection. Frankly, we don't know what to expect.

June 25. — It is over — poor Peter is gone — but Gervais will trouble us no more. I am stunned, horrified, but I owe it to Peter to write it all out.

I lay awake in my bunk, flat on my back, and the gnawed beams above me twitched like raw tendons. I had that tight, sick feeling of excitement twisting my stomach. We distinctly heard the door creak on its hinges. Something poised itself in the doorway. The door closed and it slid snake-like into the room. We could hear the thing gulp. Peter gripped my arm. I made ready to strike a match. I stiffened until its soft, slimy approach became unbearable; then I waited until it swayed at the foot of my bunk, until its green, glassy eyes were vaguely discernible in the almost total blackness. It was watching me, and I realized it could see in the dark.

I clawed at the match, lit it, and with a frantically shaking hand carried it to the tallow wick, and then—it sprang. But it didn't spring at me. It went higher and got Peter by the neck. I could hear him choke and gasp. In passing me the thing had knocked the match from my hand, plunging the room once more into total darkness. I was paralyzed, unable to move or think. I sat on the edge of my bunk, deathly sick, and my heart seemed to come up in my throat. The small room careened drunkenly. I finally became conscious of two dark objects struggling on the floor. I heard a gulping and a low moaning, and then the still night was rent with Peter's forced screams of horror. "Oh Lord, where are the rest?"

He shrieked and shrieked, and between the screams he vomited a torrent of jumbled words. "Green—eyes! Ugh! Ooze! Mouth! Wet!"

His last throttled shriek lashed at me like a whip. I finally managed another match and lit it. I kept my eyes averted, and carried the match quickly to the candle-wick. I knew that if I looked at the thing on the floor I would drop the match. I waited until the sickly glow flared, and then—I looked. Something was on top of Peter. It covered him and seemed about to absorb him. In its evil, distorted features I recognized a caricature of Gervais, but the evil in the man had sprouted. It had turned him into a jellyish, fishy monstrosity. His middle was festooned with soft flesh. His legs and arms actually gave. But worst of all, the body of the creature was covered with greenish scales, and it had pulsating pink suckers on its chest. These were lustily at work on Peter.

I thought of the revolver on my bunk, found it, and gripped the butt and leveled it. I aimed it at Peter and the thing on the floor. I fired at the two of them, for I honestly had no intention of sparing Peter. I knew that Peter would not want it, and the mute appeal in his eyes was unmistakable. Again objects refused to retain their identity in my sight. I cracked mentally.

I have a vague recollection of bringing two bodies on deck. I remember one was light, brittle and hollow like an empty matchbox. The other, wet and strangely heavy, silvered its path with slime as I laboriously dragged it up the companionway. In the dim halfglow of the ship's watchlights, I bent over the bodies. Peter was done for, there was no doubt about it. My merciful shot at short range had found its mark, and one temple was singed with powder. I stooped and lifted him tenderly; then with a sob I lowered him gently into the ocean. I stood for a moment looking over the side, thinking of the finality of it all, and watching the ever widening ripples on the surface of the oily water.

Finally I turned to regard what was Gervais. With a mingling of loathing and interest I unhooked a lantern and set it near his head. The sickly glow jumped and played on the cruel, twisted features. To my surprize I perceived a slit deep in the folds of his neck, very much like the breathing-organs of a fish. The gill was rigid and distended now, revealing a dark inner lining of red. The body exuded an oily scum, malodorous even in the clean salt air. I hunched closer over the body, and to my amazement a look of ineffable happiness and gratitude had suffused Gervais' face. Was it the weird light, the softening touch of death, or final liberation? No one will ever know. But I do not think it requires an answer. I am ready to be finished with the entire matter, just as Gervais is finished. I later went down into Gervais' cabin and breathed deeply of the fresh, clean air that blew through it.

June 26.—We are saved. There is a breeze this morning. The heavy canvas is bellying, and all hands are busy forward. The gray sky above us is sagging like a wet blanket filled with spring rains. Our casks are on deck waiting for the downpour. I thank God that we are safely headed toward France. —━┼

OFF THE MAP

REX DOLPHIN

Excuse my shivers, but it's good to sit down over a cigarette and recover my wits, and talk to someone who can perhaps persuade me that it never happened.

I often knock around about the countryside, looking out unusual and picturesque places, and one of my pleasures in an old English town is to haunt the second-hand bookshops in search of local lore.

See this? Yes, it's an old map—seventeenth century to be exact—and I found it in a musty old shop in a part of the country I'd better not mention. No, this has nothing to do with buried treasure, though to be truthful it does concern some golden guineas; guineas that no one will touch. Give you the chance? Maybe, but there's something you should know first.

Here on the map are three villages. Let's call them Burgholme, Wychburne and Ervington. Burgholme and Ervington you can still find on modern maps; you'll look in vain for Wychburne. Where has it gone, you ask? That's the whole point. . . .

As you see, Wychburne lay between the other two villages, but today's large-scale map will show you nothing but wild and waste land, moor, hill and bog. Intrigued by this, I searched encyclopedias and guide-books old and new, but not a word about Wychburne. There seemed to be a conspiracy of silence wrapped about the place, and I began to wonder if it had ever existed except in the old map-maker's imagination; or, due to the primitive cartographic methods of that day, it had been placed many miles from its true site and now bore a different name.

That disastrous curiosity made me take a train to the nearest town and hike six miles to Burgholme. This place was little more than a hamlet, with no church, chapel or pub. The weather that late summer afternoon was Novemberish, damp with a swirling mist, and the sun giving up his efforts in disgust.

After the long walk the sudden ending of exercise made me chilly, and the need for refreshment was evident. I searched the dismal village for the usual battered and ill-written TEAS sign without which no English village however small is complete. There wasn't one in Burgholme.

So it would have to be a cottage. They all looked equally unfriendly. I picked one, and knocked at the door.

It was opened by a thin-faced middle-aged woman, who said: "Well?"

A ragged staring little girl appeared beside her, and in the background, a brawny farm-laborer.

"Excuse me, but can you provide me with a tea?" I said politely.

She didn't answer. Instead, the man came nearer, and said, in a pointedly unfriendly manner:

"What are you doing in Burgholme, anyway, mister? Nobody ever comes here."

Since I never dress in conventional hiker's kit, perhaps the question was understandable.

"Just hiking," I replied. "And I've got hungry and thirsty."

"Ha!" said the man. And they all looked at me as if I were a being from another world.

"I'll pay you well."

That turned the trick. "All right. Come in."

"Thanks."

It was a silent meal. All attempts at conversation failed. As I ate they sat and watched every movement of my face and hands; and though to be fair, the food was good and plentiful, it was the most uncomfortable meal I've ever had.

At the end I made one more attempt.

"What is the quickest way to Ervington?"

The inevitable answer: "Why d'you want to go to Ervington, Mister?"

"I'm just walking for pleasure—seeing the countryside. Can't you understand that?"

"No." But he gave me the route to Ervington all the same. It was a roundabout way and entailed going backward to get forward.

"Can't I get there across country, then?" I asked.

"Not if you don't want to get lost."

"Surely there must be some sort of a footpath?" I asked. And then came what I had been leading up to: "After all, long ago there used to be a village—probably in ruins now—between here and Ervington. . . ."

A look, queer, as of suppressed horror, came to the faces of the man and woman.

". . . a place called Wychburne. . . ."

The woman went dead white. The man made the Sign of the Cross and said in an unnatural voice:

"There are some places it don't do to talk about, mister. Better go."

"What's the matter with Wychburne?" I persisted.

The man got up, stood between me and his family.

"Go," he said, and almost pushed me through the doorway.

As I walked away I saw their terrified faces watching me from behind the curtain.

The air seemed to get grayer and colder as I passed the last few huddled cottages that marked the end of the village—the end that according to the old map led past the entrance to the Wychburne road. There was a sound now, that of shuffling and of sticks tapping on the pebbled road.

It came towards me. It came out of the swirling mist, a bent old man making wearily for home. He must have been eighty, to judge by his folded and lined face and deepset rheumy eyes which he turned questingly in my direction. His tattered black coat hung loosely on his body.

I stopped. So did his shuffling.

"Should there be," I said loudly, for I imagined he would certainly be deaf, "be a road leading to Wychburne somewhere along here?"

Dead silence for a few seconds, the silence of utter shock.

Then he dropped his sticks and ran—yes, this old man ran—

towards the village. Hoppity-hop, like a crippled crow, his coat flapping about him.

My first feeling was to laugh, both at the idea and the spectacle. Then I checked myself. What, other than intense fear, could have given those withered legs wings? What was there about the mere name of Wychburne that inspired terror?

I shrugged my shoulders to myself, and persuaded myself that country superstitions—whatever they were in this case—were sheer nonsense. Well clear of the village now, I seemed to be in a deserted land. Getting out my maps, I checked my position. Yes, just around here, perhaps fifty yards along on the left, should be the road or track to Wychburne.

Then the mist closed about me like a blanket dropped over my head. This is where, if I hadn't been dead stupid or hungry with curiosity, I should have turned back to the comparative civilization of Burgholme. Instead, I searched around and found what seemed to be a rough track. I got out my compass, set a course, and went into the fog.

What I had struck I don't know, but I stumbled over rocks, tore my trousers in thorn bushes, sank up to my ankles in squelch, tripped over what the folk in those parts call pot-holes, and fell flat on my face more than once. And all these hazards were invisible. Sweat poured off me from sheer pig-headedness and exhaustion.

How long this lasted I could not judge, but just as I said to myself, "Stop it, you fool, you're all in!" I seemed to come to the end of the difficulties and found beneath my feet a level although still stony track. All my strength flowed back.

Then, from far ahead in the mist, came the thin flowing notes of a fiddle, playing some kind of an old country jig. And, faintly, the ebb and flow of voices raised in revelry, as if Merrie England were here again.

The road led steeply down into the valley, but still nothing could be seen. The sounds of merriment got nearer and nearer, and finally I felt, "I'm here!"

Very gradually, the mist cleared, and there it was—Wychburne! A compact little village, nestling under the surrounding steep cliff-like hills, almost as if a giant had scooped out a spoonful of the earth's surface and dropped the village neatly into the cavity. The houses were grouped around a neat village green on which the fiddlers were playing and a merry crowd dancing. Girls and men, all dressed in the colorful clothes of Restoration days.

There wasn't a thing modern in the place, from the rose-covered timber-and-white cottages to the horse-wagons "parked" in the inn-yard. What could there be about this place to inspire terror? Wychburne was charming!

But what was its secret? Was it a "lost village"—a place that was unknown to outsiders, that had resisted the inroads of modern progress, had become cut off and was so completely self-contained as to be capable of carrying on an independent existence? It was inaccessible enough, and its approaches certainly didn't invite visitors, let alone motor traffic. Surveyors, map-makers, census-takers, county planners—how could all these have overlooked its existence? Yet the fact remained that it didn't exist in present-day records!

The mist—perhaps that explained it. If Wychburne was permanently hidden from view both from land and air, all these things were conceivable.

I moved towards the inn-yard, stood looking at the scene, now close-up, and a strange feeling of timelessness and of not being myself came over me. Everything now was larger than life, over-intimate, and as I threaded among the people I saw their faces close to mine, felt the push of their bodies, and the air was full of their rich voices and laughter and snatches of song and music. There was, too, an indefinable odor—a thing one notices only among people of a different race.

Suddenly a face turned towards me, and eyes looked straight into mine. It was a heavy, countryman's face, but full of dignity and independence, and the wide-brimmed tall feathered hat added to its stature.

"What do ye here, stranger?" the man asked, in accents I'd never heard before.

"Travelling," I answered. "What goes on here, a carnival?"

"And whence come ye, stranger?"

"From London."

"From London!" he echoed, and there was a gasp in his voice. Then he shouted to the crowd, "The stranger comes from London!"

The crowd took up the words in a kind of prolonged echo: "From London! From London!"

The words hummed around for some seconds, then the music stopped. The laughter stopped. The voices stopped.

From a window above the inn a low wailing shriek started, gathering strength and building up to a horrible scream that ended abruptly in a choking sob. I looked, and saw that it had been uttered by a girl whose beautiful face now expressed final hopelessness.

A hundred faces seemed to turn in my direction, seemingly all accusing me of some awful crime. And indeed there was a feeling of guilt on me, but guilt of just what I didn't know, although I felt I should have knowledge.

The people now seemed to peel away from me, until I was left isolated on the green. The man who had spoken to me had vanished; now he suddenly reappeared, at the head of a small group of purposeful-looking men.

They all bore long staves, and the foremost—my man—lunged at me with his, catching me a painful blow under the heart.

"What means this?" I gasped in anger. Fear was to come later.

"Begone, bringer of evil!" he roared.

Then they all set about me with the staves, not one man coming near enough to touch me with his hands. Argument was futile. I turned and ran—ran while I still had brains in my head and whole bones in my legs.

Crash, crash, they hit me with their sticks as they pursued. I stumbled over rocks and tree-roots as I made the rough ascent out of the village in the opposite direction to that from which I had entered. I fell, was beaten all over, rose, ran, fell again—a deadly, killing repetition. In the middle of all this the mist closed about me again. And still those fiends hounded me. I must have run miles.

I fell for the last time. I was finished. I tried to rise. It was useless. A savage flurry of blows rained on my head. Then—blackout.

When I regained my senses I was lying flat, face down on the hard rock, soaked to the skin with mist and bruised all over. A few inches from my eyes, lying on the stony ground, was what I took at first to be a much-weathered halfpenny. I reached out for it painfully—I suppose it's a human instinct to pick up a coin however valueless—scraped it and rubbed it clean on my tattered sleeve.

I sat up sharply, my distress forgotten. It was a Charles II golden guinea! And there was another, and another! Five altogether I found, and the remnants of metal buckles, which seemed to argue a whole leather bagful of coins. The others were no doubt scattered around or buried. I told myself I would come back here later and search properly. Meantime my exhaustion had returned, and I had to get to shelter if I wasn't to die of exposure.

There was some sort of a track here, and I followed it as best I could. Presently, still with thick mist hiding everything, I felt my feet touch tarmac, and I pushed on, miles it seemed, till a glimmer ahead showed another village. This, I knew, must be Ervington, last of the three villages on the map.

A hanging sign, unreadable in the mist, appeared ahead, and below it the welcome warmth of lights; and soon I heard the friendly undertone of casual inn-conversation. I walked in, feeling like a second-hand scarecrow that the crows have defeated.

The conversation stopped. The few customers, all seated, stared at me. The landlord, a shrewd-looking, puckered-faced short man, stopped polishing a glass. His look was enough question.

"Wychburne," I muttered. "What is Wychburne? Can anyone tell me? I've just got back. . . ."

The drinkers all stood up, as if drilled, edged their way round me one by one, and dashed out into the road. I gazed after them. When I looked back to the bar, the landlord had laid a double-barrelled shotgun meaningly across it, the snouts in my direction.

"Stay," he rasped. "Don't move an inch nearer my bar."

"Look," I said desperately, "I'm sick of these riddles. Everything that's happened since I arrived in these parts has been inexplicable. Do *you* know the answer?"

He twisted a grin. "I'm no oracle, mister. But though I'm not as dumb as the local population, being a bit of a travelled man and partly educated, I still respect their superstitions. Let's see . . . somehow you heard of Wychburne? You tried to find it? You're a Londoner? You found Wychburne and they drove you out, nearly killing you in the process?"

I answered each question with a nod.

"Yes," he mused, "I suppose it was bound to happen one day."

"You've not quite finished," I pointed out.

"How, mister?"

I fished in my pocket. "Where I fell I found the remains of a leather bag, and these." I held up the gold pieces.

"My God, that as well? *So it isn't just a legend!*" The last words were muttered almost to himself.

He was scared.

"Yes—and now the explanation, man!" I pressed. "What is Wychburne?"

"There's no such place," he said. He lifted the bar-flap, picked up the gun, and grunted: "Go through that door and out into the back-yard, quick!"

In no condition to argue with a shotgun, I obeyed.

"How can you say there's no such place?" I demanded. "After what I've just been through? And what's the meaning of this panto-mime?"

"There was such a place. Not now. Get undressed."

"*What?*"

"Get undressed. Jump into that old butt. Don't argue, man. It's the best I can do for you. Good. Stay there a minute."

He went across the cobbled yard to the back door; returned quickly carrying a can of liquid. He found a long stick, pushed my clothes, still containing the guineas, well away from me as I stood shivering in the empty barrel, and poured the fluid over them. It was kerosene, from the oily stench. A match, a sheet of smoky flame, and my clothes were ashes.

What was he going to do to *me?* So far I had believed him—he was by far the most rational being I'd met since arriving in the neighborhood—but now, was I dealing with a maniac?

Back into the house he went, coming out this time with a large jug, and a long hose which was still attached to something inside the house. He pointed the hose at me. . . . Something sprayed out. . . .

It was nothing more than water, but almost unbearably hot. "Soap coming over!" he called. "Catch!"

Then he poured the contents of the jug over me into the butt. A very powerful disinfectant, by the smell.

"Now wash!" he ordered. "As thoroughly as you can."

"All right," I spluttered. "You seem to know what you're doing, though it still beats me. Now you tell me all about Wychburne."

"Nearly three hundred years ago," he said slowly, "a traveller set out from London on a horse, carrying all his gold in a leather bag. He was escaping from something, and looking for an isolated country hide-out where he could stay till the trouble was over.

"Yes, he found Wychburne. He stayed at the inn there. The first to die was the innkeeper's daughter. They knew he was the cause. They chased him out of the village and beat him to death with the staves. The gold stayed with him. Nobody would touch it.

"In less than a week there wasn't a life left in Wychburne. The men of Ervington and Burgholme pitched oil, straw, and everything inflammable they could find into Wychburne from the steep hills around it, and set fire to the whole village. Then they rolled boulders into it, and filled up the little valley with rocks and earth till not a sign of the village remained. That's the story, and it's known to every soul in the two villages—and until today by nobody else."

"But what happened to me?" I cried, shivering.

"That's anybody's guess, mister."

"And what—?" I began, but he'd vanished into the house again.

This time he came back with a rough outfit of clothes, shoes, an old towel, half a bottle of brandy and some sandwiches.

"When you're dressed, get yourself to a doctor, and don't use any transport. You might be all right, but there's no telling."

"You mean I'm to walk?" I gasped.

"Sorry, mister. Yes."

"No chance of staying the night?"

"Ugh. Not likely. You see, these things happened in 1665—the year of the Great Plague."

Don't go, my friend. . . . Don't look at me like that . . . for God's sake. . . . ——+——

On Top

RALPH ALLEN LANG

Swingle's excuse for the shooting of Shorty Baker was exceedingly flimsy, even when the character of the town and the position of the killer were considered. Shorty was sitting in a game of draw across the table from a bull-necked mule-skinner who had hit town early in the afternoon; and Shorty, in a rare streak of luck, was dragging in pot after pot. It was on the square, all right enough; but bad luck and bad whisky, both in excessive quantities, had soured the big fellow's mood; and as his chips continued to dwindle, his growing sullenness was measured by the deepening purple of a jagged scar across his right temple.

It happened just as Swingle, badge glittering on his vest front, stepped through the door. With an oath, the mule-skinner ripped out the old "cold deck" squawk and threw his cards in Shorty's face, getting a stinging backhand slap in payment.

It might have gone no farther than fists if somebody at the end of the table had not sent it careening as he leaped away. In the straining necessity of maintaining balance and protecting themselves at the same time, both men went for their guns. The big fellow took it in the flesh of his left shoulder. Shorty was drilled cleanly through the heart, but the mule-skinner's bullet had never touched him. He had been dropped by a shot from behind; and Swingle, the marshal, was ready with words to back up his action.

"That's giving notice that quick-trigger days are over in Red Dog," he said coolly. "Any gunman who don't savvy that can run, not walk, to the nearest exit—said exit being either by horseflesh or Boot Hill, as they prefer."

He turned a level look upon Steve Craig, Shorty's partner, who had risen from a table in the back of the room. Steve's eyes met the marshal's for a long moment, and it seemed that he was about to speak. Then he turned abruptly and walked to the crumpled form of his dead partner.

The burying hour at Red Dog was nine A.M., and Steve rose early for the job he had to do, setting out for Boot Hill with a shovel and his thoughts for company. A sleepless night had failed to suggest any other reason for Swingle's action than the one that had leaped into his mind as he faced the marshal across the barroom. The diggings around Red Dog were comparatively worked out, and with a single exception the days of rich pay dirt were over. The single exception was the claim belonging to Shorty and Steve, in which a rich vein had cropped out a week back. Evidently, Swingle wanted that claim, and what he wanted he was accustomed to take by the gun. It had been his means of livelihood through a notorious past, at first on the outer fringe of the law, and later, for a year past, as the official lawman of the hitherto lawless mining town of Red Dog.

Certain things were crystal-clear in Steve's mind as he heaved the yellow clay out of the deepening grave. One was that Swingle had him marked for the same play that had cleared Shorty out of his way. With both partners dead, the claim would be open to whoever could file on it first—and claims could be filed only through the marshal's office. It was nicely cut and dried for the marshal, and nothing could prevent its successful working except the second item fixed in Steve's mind. This was that he must kill Swingle first, a proposition that presented rather stiff difficulties, considering the fact that the marshal had added to this same Boot Hill a large section containing the remains of some of the best gun-slinging talent in the hills. The chances in an equal fight were not so good; in fact, not much better than the chance Shorty had had with his back turned. Aside from this, the killing of a lawman backed by influential interests in the town might force him out of the country. And the claim was too good to leave. The contemplation of this classic problem was interrupted by the appearance of the marshal himself. Swingle eyed the hole with simulated interest.

"You're crowding six good feet there, Steve," he ejaculated. "Aiming to plant him so he'll stay planted, I suppose. I'll admit Shorty had a way with him of generally coming out on top, but I reckon that ought to hold him down." He indicated with his foot the high-piled mass of yellow clay.

Steve scooped out another shovel of loose gravel before he answered, held silent for a time by a tremendous idea the marshal's words had sparked in his mind. He gazed down the deserted hillside, and along the equally deserted single street of the town. The miners were at their diggings by now, and the store and saloon keepers were not yet astir. It was strange that the marshal had appeared so early, nearly an hour before the time of the funeral. Perhaps he meant to finish the work started the previous night, claiming self-defense in the total absence of witnesses. He was squatting on his heels by the edge of the hole now, evidently planning no action for the immediate present. Grasping his pick-handle near the head, Steve leaned his weight easily upon it as he replied.

"Shorty did have a way of coming out on top," he said slowly, "in nearly everything. I partnered with him for six years, and he's pulled me, as well as himself, out of more than one tight hole. You downed him last night, Marshal, and this is one hole he'll never pull out of. But at that—this sounds queer, I guess—the notion just struck me that he'll still manage to wind up on top."

Swingle's eyes narrowed ever so slightly as he laughed.

"Every dog has his day," he replied, "but once he's been whipped to his kennel—"

With a short swishing movement the pick swung out and down, punctuating the unfinished sentence with a convulsive gasp. Steve recoiled against the side of the trench as the sprawling form fell heavily forward, pressing backward to allow it to slump at full length on the bottom. Then he began the awkward task of moving the body from side to side while he scooped out another foot and a half of earth. When he started back to town the seven-and-a-half-foot grave he had dug was only five feet deep. And the bottom, packed down hard with the shovel, covered even the handle of the buried pick by an inch.

Red Dog turned out for the funeral at nine o'clock, standing silently with Steve as the last shovelful of earth was mounded over his dead. The marshal had failed to appear at a funeral of his own causing for the first time, and on the way to the hill there had been comment.

"Oh, he'll be there all right," Steve said. They thought it was bitterness.

Now, as they turned away from the new grave, expressions of sympathy were forthcoming. Steve smiled wanly.

"He was a good partner," he said simply. "I've seen old Shorty in many a tight scrape, and he never failed to wind up on top." ———

ONE CHANCE

ETHEL HELENE COEN

t was the terrible summer of 1720. The plague hung darkly over shuddering New Orleans. Its black wings beat at every door, and there were few that had not opened to its dread presence. Paul had seen his mother, father, sisters and friends swept down by its mowing sickle. Only Marie remained for him—beautiful Marie with her love for him that he knew was stronger than any plague—the one thing in all the world that was left to sustain him.

"Let us fly from this accursed place," he pleaded. "Let us try to find happiness elsewhere. Neither of us has a tie to bind us here—is not your sister to be buried this very day? Ah, Saint Louis has seen many such scenes in this last month—we will fly to Canada and begin all over."

"But, my darling," she protested, "you forget the quarantine: no one is allowed to enter or leave the city; your plan is hopeless."

"No—no—I have a plan—such a terrible one that I shudder to think of it. Here it is—"

While he rapidly sketched their one desperate chance Marie's face blanched, but when he finished, she agreed.

The daughter of the mayor had died that morning. A special dispensation had been secured to ship her body to Charleston for burial. The body rested in its casket in Saint Louis Cathedral and was to be shipped by boat that night.

At six o'clock that evening the cathedral was empty save for its silent occupants awaiting burial. The tall wax tapers glimmered fitfully over the scene of desolation. Paul and Marie crept in and went to the casket of the mayor's daughter. Paul rapidly unscrewed the wooden top, removed the slight body, put it into a large sack; and Marie, nearly swooning from terror, got into the coffin.

"Here is a flask of water," Paul whispered, "and remember—not a sound, no matter what happens. I shall sneak aboard the boat before it sails at nine. After we are out for half an hour I will let you out of this. It is our only chance."

"Yes, I know," Marie whispered chokingly. "I shall make no sound . . . now go . . . the priests will soon be back, so one last kiss, until we are on the boat."

He kissed her passionately, then loosely screwed the top on the casket.

Stealing with his awful burden to the yard in the back of the cathedral he remembered a deep, dried-up well in one corner of the yard. Just the place to dispose of the body.

"God rest the poor girl's soul," he thought; "she, wherever she is, will understand that I meant no sacrilege to her remains, but this is my one chance of happiness . . . my only chance."

His task ended, he climbed the iron wall and walked rapidly up Pirates Alley and wandered over the Vieux Carré until eight-thirty. Thank God—it was time to try the success of their daring venture. His head whirled and his heart beat like a trip-hammer as he slipped onto the boat unobserved by any but the dock hands, who probably considered him one of their number. He secreted himself in a dark corner and waited. After centuries had passed, or so it seemed to him, the boat started moving. It would not be long now. He did not stop to think what would happen when they were caught—that would take care of itself.

Ah—voices, coming nearer and nearer. From his corner Paul could distinctly see the silhouettes of the two men who were approaching.

"Yes," said one, "it is sad. The mayor is broken-hearted—we were going to take her body to Charleston—but the mayor had her buried from Saint Louis just after the sun went down." ——✠——

THE OTHER SANTA

THORP McCLUSKY

This story really begins weeks ago, one autumn afternoon when two bright boys in a New York advertising agency thought up a super-special Christmas Eve radio stunt for one of their clients. The idea was to broadcast a miracle; oh, not the kind that happened in the Bible, of course, but the next thing to it. Have something unexpected, wonderful, and impossible happen to someone and put the whole thing on the air. Corny, but effective.

The gimmick was simply this: find a little girl who needed a major operation but whose parents were too poor to afford it. On Christmas Eve, have Santa Claus come right into her home, give her some presents, and, for a punch finish, hand her a great big check drawn on that bank in Santa Claus, Indiana. The check is signed *Santa Claus*; it's perfectly good; and obviously it's to pay for the operation. There's a microphone hidden in a vase of flowers on a table right beside the little girl's wheelchair, and a couple of others concealed around the living room. Everything completely extemporaneous.

The idea was terrific, all right. Sure fire. Couldn't miss. More punch than Lionel Barrymore playing Scrooge in Dickens' *A Christmas Carol.* Not even a word of commercial—just let the public go around asking, "Say, did you hear that program *The Spirit of Christmas* on the radio Christmas Eve? Who put it on, anyway; the network, or some sponsor smart enough not to plug his product for once?"

And, of course, the news would leak out ultimately who'd footed the bills. Get the sweet, beautiful, lovely indirection of it all?

Well, we scouted around and found a suitable little girl in a tiny New England village. She was six, going on seven, pretty as a doll and sweet, really sweet. A year before she'd had a fall and injured her spine. She was paralyzed from the waist down, and only one of those big-shot specialists could fix her up. Her parents were made-to-order, too—both kids in their twenties, presentable, loving each other and their daughter, honest, hard-working, poor as church mice and worried to death. Get the poignancy of the set-up?

We gave the parents microphone tests and their voices projected fine; we wouldn't even have to use actors to double for them. In the afternoon of December 24 we installed and tested the equipment while the little girl was taking her nap. We stuck a portable, sound-proof control-room in the dining room and cut narrows slits through the living room wall so we could see that was going on in there. There was a little red light behind where the little girl's wheelchair would be so the parents could tell when they were on the air. We had a record-player and telephone connections; and we'd gone to the trouble of having a delivery truck painted bright red with a big, jolly looking portrait of Santa Claus on the side. You see, Santa Claus would have to drive out from the village—and we wanted the little girl's reaction to be realistic when she got her first glimpse of Old Whiskers from the living room window. We even hired Tim Donovan to play the part of Santa; you know Tim, how big he is and what a magnificent voice he's got and how he can ad-lib better than any other actor in radio.

We went on the air right on the dot, coast-to-coast, with a recording of *Silent Night, Holy Night,* fading behind Jim Allen and that butter-wouldn't-melt-in-my-mouth narrative voice of his. "Good evening, all, and a very Merry Christmas to everyone, everywhere," Jim drooled. "During the next half hour . . . blah, blah, blah . . . a program so unique, so unusual, so heart-warming . . . blah, blah, blah"—putting the radio audience wise. It was a prepared introduction, and it was beautiful prose; Abe Lincoln couldn't have written any better. But it made me sick, just the same. What difference did it make if we kept the name of the family and the village out of the broadcast?—the whole country would find out soon enough. I didn't like any part of what we were doing—except the check we would give the kid.

Well, as soon as Allen finished reading the phone rang, and Santa Claus Donovan announced from the village that he would start in just so many minutes. Then the little red bulb lit up and we brought in the family, all singing *Jingle Bells* as prearranged—very Christmasy and gay. When the song was finished the father coughed, very nervous, and said, "Your back, Jane. How does it feel?"

You could tell the little girl was surprised. She piped right back, "It doesn't hurt at all, Daddy. Why should it? It never hurts much anymore."

I grinned all over when she said that.

"Well," the father persisted, forcing the point as per instructions, "I just wondered if it might be hurting." Then he switched hurriedly to, "Hmmm! I wouldn't be surprised, Jane, if Santa Claus will be along any minute now."

Jane was skeptical. "Why are you so sure I'll see Santa Claus this year, Daddy?" she wanted to know. "Every other year you always said he wouldn't come until after I was asleep."

The father started to muff that one, but the mother jumped right in with gentle assurance, "This year, Jane, Santa is making his rounds in a big, shiny, new red automobile. He can travel a lot faster than by reindeer, so he'll be around much earlier."

Trust a woman to think faster than a man in a pinch every time.

Well, the family chatter went on for a minute or so longer, then Jim Allen cut in again, pompous as usual, "Santa Claus, driving the big red delivery truck, has now left the village and is on his way to Jane's house. In just thirty seconds Jane will see him coming over the crest of the hill."

And in just thirty seconds Jane's father, who was watching out the window, tipped her off. 'Look, Jane! Here he comes now! Santa Claus!"

I never heard a child squeal or clap her hands so much. "Ooooh! It's Santa Claus! It's Santa Claus! It's Santa Claus!" Jane babbled, over and over again in that high, choked voice of pure happiness, and the family chimed in, too. It really got me for an instant. Jim Allen—than whom nobody on earth and maybe in Heaven too loves the sound of his own voice better—almost ruined the whole effect with his big trap by pontificating, "Ah, now Santa Claus is approaching so fast you'd almost think he was flying. We're even excited ourselves, here in the control room, as we watch that big red truck zoom over the hill and down the snowy road! Now it's turning into the yard. It's a thrilling sight, really thrilling."

You'd have thought he was reporting a sports event. But he couldn't steal the show no matter how much he loused it up; there was too much honest-to-goodness drama going on in that living room. You could hear everything—the door opening, the whistle of the storm—and boy, it was really a blizzard! You could almost feel the cold rush in before the door closed.

"Merry Christmas, everybody!" Santa Claus boomed—and I mean boomed. Jane promptly burst out crying. And the father and mother both said, "Merry Christmas, Santa Claus," while the mother added, so softly that few listeners caught it, "God bless you!"

I can't understand it, but for once Jim Allen decided to keep his yap shut. He didn't utter a word while Santa spoke to Jane, "Don't cry, Jane. This is no time to be sad; this is the happiest night in the year. Dry your tears and look at the wonderful presents I've brought you. A doll—a beautiful, beautiful doll . . ."

"I wasn't crying because I'm sad but because I'm glad," Jane protested, as her sniffles quickly ceased. "Ooooh!—what a beautiful doll . . . !"

Well, Jim had to horn in again. "The doll is very lifelike," he gloated. "Its eyes open and shut and it has two expressions—a great big smile and a sad, sad frown."

He should have been an auctioneer.

"And here's some pretty nighties for you," Santa Claus continued. "Pink, and white, and lavendar—and trimmed with lace and ribbons. And a pair of lovely red slippers, and a royal blue robe. . . ."

That set Jane off crying again worse than ever, and even Jim Allen, who seldom recognizes drama unless it's spelled out to him in capital letters, knew enough to keep still. "Nighties," Jane was sobbing. "Slippers. Robe. They're just what I want, Santa Claus, because I'm in bed almost all the time. I can't walk, Santa Claus. I can't walk again ever."

All I could think of just then was that the ghouls who had thought up this show must really be having a swell time for themselves, listening.

Santa Claus cut right in with the punch announcement. "Oh, yes you can walk again, Jane! And very soon, too. Next week your father and mother are going to take you to the hospital and a very nice man is going to do something to your back that will make you all well again. And here is a piece of paper—Santa's own personal check (you know what a check is, don't you, Jane?) — that will pay for everything. So there's no reason to cry any more at all, is there, Jane?"

And of course Jim Allen had to flap his tonsils some more and explain about the check and the Santa Claus, Indiana, bank. Jane was still sobbing, but it was the happy kind, all mixed up with incoherent words of gratitude. The father said soberly, "We can't thank you enough for this, Santa Claus. It means everything in the world to Jane." And once again the mother whispered, "God bless you."

They were a wonderful couple.

Then Santa started to leave. He was very businesslike about it, too; no dawdling or mushiness of the sort I expected from Donovan. Without hurrying, but also like a man with plenty of other business to attend to and not any too much time, he said briskly, "Well, Jane, I have lots of other boys and girls to visit tonight; I must be getting along. So goodby — and the best of everything in life for you, for many, many happy years — for as long as God wills that you live."

It sounded screwy to me — not the sort of thing Donovan would say. Jane seemed to sense a strange finality in that farewell, too, for she pleaded, almost panic-stricken, "Won't I see you again next year, Santa? Aren't you coming back again, ever?"

Santa Claus only said, very gently, "Well, Jane, I don't know. If you need me enough, and if you have enough faith. . . ." And he smiled reassuringly.

It was completely screwy. None of that mawkish tripe about being a good little girl — none of that rigmarole at all. Just need, and faith. I thought Donovan must have decided to commit professional suicide — but good!

The door opened, letting in the sound of the storm again, and closed. Santa was gone. Everybody in the living room started talking at once, and the talk and gasps and sobs and laughter coming over were really heartwarming, at that. Then Jim Allen cut in, still unctuous but urgent. "Something's gone wrong here," he announced portentously. "Santa Claus' watch must have been running ahead of ours. The schedule called for him to remain another three minutes, but, as we all know, he's already left. His explanation should be interesting. Probably he'll phone in from the village any minute now. In the meantime, we'll just go on listening to happy Jane and her family, in the living-room."

Well, we listened another fifteen seconds, maybe, while Jane's folks were putting her presents over under the tree — and then we got the surprise of our lives. Another red truck rolled into the driveway, and a second Santa walked into that living room.

It was a ticklish situation. Who was this guy, anyway? What would he say? Did he even know we were on the air?

The mother's nerves, strained to the limit by the ordeal she'd already undergone, just let go; she went off into hysterical laughter mingled with racking sobs. The father whispered to her fiercely, "Get hold of yourself! We're still on the radio, do you understand? I don't know who this fellow is, but he could be Art Phelps. He's about Art's size."

And Jim Allen, of course, licked his chops and orated, "Well! Well! Well! What have we here? A second Santa has showed up, no doubt someone from the village. Here's drama nobody expected. Who is he? As soon as we find out, we'll let you know. Ah, this would warm the heart of old Scrooge himself!"

Santa Claus Two was a showman all right. "Ho! Ho! Ho!" he bellowed jovially. "If it isn't good little Jane herself! Here's Santa Claus with lots of wonderful presents for you Jane, because you've been such a good little girl all year!"

There was an instant's silence, then Jane said defiantly, "You're not the real Santa Claus; you're just a great big fake. That's just an old false face you've got on; I can see the string behind your ears."

"Ho! Ho! Ho!" Santa Two boomed. "Don't you worry about string behind my ears! I'm the real Santa Claus all right!" And Jim Allen was sounding off hurriedly, "Aha, the mystery is solved, folks! This Santa Claus who just came in is *our* Santa; he just held up a card on which he'd printed DELAYED; SKIDDED INTO DITCH. So the other Santa was the man from town; is that clear? Ah, isn't it wonderful that the neighbors, too, remembered Jane; even sent their Santa here ahead of ours. What an inspiration! What a coincidence!"

Santa Two was working fast, because the half-hour had almost run out. He yanked from his pack a huge doll, some frilly and costly nighties, a robe, pretty little slippers, and a big check signed *Santa Claus* and drawn on that bank in Santa Claus, Indiana. . . .

Now, get this straight. I am not a superstitious man. But, as I watched and listened to these goings-on, the weirdest chill ran up my spine. You know how you feel when you're in the presence of something you can't understand? Well, that's the way I felt. For, present for present, our Santa was giving Jane the exact duplicates of each and every gift she had just received from the unknown stranger. The very lifelike doll, with its eyes that opened and shut and its two expressions—the great big smile and the sad, sad frown. The pink and white and lavender nighties, trimmed with lace and ribbons. The lovely red slippers, the royal blue robe.

And the check. It was the exact duplicate of the other—down to the tiniest detail of color and design of the paper and the highly individual flourishes in the hand-inscribed signature. Remember, our check had been "made to order." No even remotely similar check had ever existed before.

Every gift was not only similar; it was identical. But that was impossible. Coincidence—or deliberate intention either—just couldn't stretch that far.

My gaze swiveled toward the resplendent tree in the corner of the living room. And I swear the short hairs on the back of my neck rose. . . .

I watched the rest of the show mechanically. It was completely disrupted; anything might happen. Jane was the most self-possessed of all; she just sat looking down quietly at all the lovely things Donovan had piled in her arms and saying gently, "Thank you, Mr. Santa Claus. But you should take back all these nice things and give them to some other little girl who needs them, because I don't need them now. The real Santa Claus just gave me the very same presents, not two minutes ago."

I liked the way she emphasized, "the *real* Santa Claus!"

Jim Allen's majestic baritone was in there pitching too: "What a surprise! What a marvelous surprise! Two Santas instead of one; isn't that terrific? We've just been reliably informed that the first Santa was a local personage named Art Phelps and that his gifts represent the combined contributions of all the residents of this little village, young and old, rich and poor alike. It's wonderful, just wonderful."

Well, it was getting into the final minute, so Jim added hurriedly, "And now our time is running short, so I'll just signal everybody in the living room to join in singing *Hark, the Herald Angels Sing,* and we'll put on a record and just let's everybody sing along with it—in 20 million homes all over America and everywhere this program is being heard! All join in, everybody, and the happiest Merry Christmas to Jane and her family and to both Santas and to you all!"

So the engineer started the recording and everybody sang, and it was all very confused and loud and joyous and inspiring right up until the program went off the air. I never heard so much real happiness packed into the punch finish of a radio broadcast in my life.

But after it was over there were some things that needed explaining. The first Santa's gifts had disappeared, vanished completely, without leaving a trace. That's what had given me the shock as I'd looked over under the tree for them—they just weren't there anymore. We milled around that living room for awhile looking for them, but I think everybody knew in his heart then that they wouldn't be found. Then we went out on the porch and down into the driveway, where we clustered around the red truck.

"Holy Mother of Mercy!" Donovan whispered. "D'ya notice that there's only the tracks of my truck and my footprints—nobody else's?"

After a minute, his breath white in the bitter cold, Jim Allen asked querulously, "Well, you met this other guy on your way up here, didn't you Donovan?"

Donovan shook his head. "I met nobody. There wasn't a car on the road, all the way out."

"You had to pass him," Allen insisted doggedly. "There's no other road."

Donovan merely pointed to the road, with its blanket of fresh snow unbroken save for the marks of his truck.

No one spoke as we went back into the house. Jane was asleep in her wheelchair, a smile crinkling the corners of her mouth, the doll cradled in her chubby arms. She didn't awaken as her father wheeled her out into the hall, her mother trailing silently after. They both smiled wistful apology as they went out, and we nodded understandingly.

"Well," Jim Allen said grimly as the door closed behind them, "there's an awful lot about this broadcast we'll always have to keep our traps shut about. I, for one, don't want to land in Bellevue psychopathic ward. Was it a hoax, or what?"

We were all surprised when the engineer spoke, for he was ordinarily such a silent man.

A saturnine, lean-jawed Scotsman with deep-sunk, brooding eyes, he was a type you'd know believed in nothing except the evidence of his own senses and the analysis of his own reason.

Yet this practiced man said quietly, "Somehow it reminds me of those visions of St. George, fighting at the head of phantom armies. Thousands of soldiers saw them because—through some sort of mass faith—they expected to see them. Something like that must have happened here tonight. Twenty million people including all of us here now—expected Santa Claus to come riding over that hill in a red truck at an exact split-minute. And so he came—the wish-fulfillment of all of us."

He paused reflectively, then went on. "It struck us as incredible that the presents were exactly like those Donovan brought later. But —didn't they have to be? Remember, we all knew just what presents Donovan would bring.

"And, of course, after Donovan arrived and we began to wonder the presents vanished. The spell was broken. Yet, who knows if they would not have remained real had we kept our faith?"

"Good grief!" Jim Allen exclaimed incredulously. "You believe that?"

The Scotsman looked him square in the eye. "I believe that," he said simply. "And I also believe that—if Jane ever again needs Santa enough, and has faith enough—the same Santa who was here tonight will come back to her—as real and true as anything that exists in the universe. You see, Allen, he was the real Santa Claus. He was a creation of the mind and of the spirit—the only reality there is, and the only attribute we have in common with God."

And that, I think, is the only satisfactory explanation we shall ever have of the other Santa . . . ———

A Pair of Swords

Carl Jacobi

We had lingered and passed through the Egyptian Room, the Jade Room, and the chambers of the French and Italian Renaissance. Before that there had been many others, hundreds of others, it seemed, on either side of the long statue-lined halls with their floors of polished parquet. Curious how easily one forgets. Curious, rather, what the mind chooses to remember. A mummy or two, a necklace more delicate than the others, a wine cabinet which I childishly fancied and longed to have in my study, and a rare old candle chandelier, said to have illumined the table of the Spanish Philip II.

The drone of the guide's voice, low-pitched and endless, seemed to emerge from somewhere behind the Flemish hangings that covered the walls. It went on and on without the slightest inflection, and I caught myself wondering whether he talked the same when the day was over and he had left the gallery.

"One of the early works of Jean Baptiste Monnoyer, late Seventeenth Century. Formerly of the Fielding collection. Note the peculiar shadow-work in the background. . . . That will be all in this room, ladies and gentlemen. Next we have the weapon gallery, said to be the most complete in all Europe. This way, please."

I was the last of the group to pass through the intervening doorway, noting with some relief that we had reached the final point of tour. It was five o'clock, and I must hurry if I wished to make that appointment with Luella.

An interesting chamber, this. It looked like the armor room of a mediæval castle. The art of killing a person has certainly developed. I munched another orange lozenge and moved across to where the guide was standing.

"This is the last executioner's sword used in France before the introduction of the guillotine. The blade is thirty-three inches long. All the blades on this wall are either Spanish or Spanish-owned. The carved saber on the right was presented by the Duke of Savoy to Philip III in 1603. Observe the graceful hilt. The smaller one next to it is a Persian sword, Sixteenth Century, probably brought from Tunis by Charles V."

Pistols next, from the earliest handcannon down, and the guide continued his litany like the hum of a lazy fly.

"A pair of holster pistols, Lazarino Cominazzo, mounts in chiselled steel. Probably the most perfect arms ever fashioned by the hand of man. An early Italian snaphance, a Kuchenreuter duelingpistol with double leaf sight. Here we have an early Seventeenth Century arquebus, lock engraved with hunting-scene. . . ."

Some one had tapped me on the shoulder, and I turned abruptly. For a moment I stared, chewed hard on my lozenge, then restrained a smile. Two men stood just beyond the last of the curious gallery crowd, two men dressed in a most unusual manner.

Rich blue velvet doublets, white and black satin knee-breeches, flowing lace cuffs, swords at their sides, and large hats with flowing plumes. I smiled again. Silly idea this, masquerading the gallery guards as old French musketeers.

"Pardon, *M'sieu,* but would you be kind enough to step into the next room and help two gentlemen of France settle an affair of honor?"

"Would I–?" I surveyed them coldly as refusal rose to my lips. But the words died without being spoken. For some queer reason the room with its glinting array of yatagans, colichemardes and historic blades seemed to reach far out into the background and blend with the two curiously arrayed figures before me. As I stood there, the guide's voice continuing its monotonous drone, the atmosphere slightly touched with dust pressing close at my nostrils, my first start of surprise gradually passed away, and I received the man's question as if it had not been unusual at all.

No other word was spoken. The two men, taking my silence for consent, led the way through a little doorway on the right and into a larger chamber, unfurnished save for an enormous painting of Cardinal Richelieu on the farther side.

The light from the two arched windows was better here, and I studied with interest the features of the two outlandishly dressed strangers. One, slightly the taller, was fair as a young girl, with a blond waxed mustache and blue pleasant eyes. The other, older and more at ease, was dark, smooth-shaven and thin-lipped. Both strode forward with a haughty fearless air.

"Sir," said the blond man to me, "you must be second for both of us. Should my opponent be fortunate enough to dispatch me, you will please give proper notice of my death. I am—"

"Zounds!" cried the other. "What matter who you are? Once you are dead, you are dead, and that is the end. For rest assured I am going to teach you a lesson, and when I do there will be none to despoil my claim to the hand of Lady Constance. Sir, on guard!"

There was a ring of steel, and two swords glistened in the slanting sunlight. I stepped back and stared at the two as they parried, thrust, and sought to pierce each other's guard. Back and forth, in and out, they moved, blades gyrating with the skill of masters.

"You fight well, sir," muttered the darker man through his teeth. " 'Twill be a shame to take such a blade from the king."

"Love inspires strength," breathed the other. "I fight for the most beautiful woman in the world, one whom your hands shall never touch."

The dark man curled his lip in a sneer. "Fool!" he said. "She loves me, not you. Did she not hang this locket round my neck to keep with me always, a token of her love? You are but a boy and her plaything. Behind your back she laughs at you. Look at this locket, I say. See the seal of her house upon it? You are a twice-born fool!"

Slowly the face of the blond youth paled. "She gave you that?" he cried.

"Even now she laughs at the thought of you," taunted the dark man. "Put up your sword, fellow, and I will let you live and forget."

The blue eyes were glinting like agate now, the blond hair trembling in the double shaft of sunlight.

"Then you shall wear it to your death, *M'sieu*," he said. "Do you hear? That seal shall lock your lips for ever."

It happened then in the wink of an eyelash. The blond youth feinted, dropped back, and shot his rapier straight for the throat of his opponent where the golden disk hung suspended from a silken chain. Too late the dark man strove to parry. The blade struck the locket, pierced its center and passed through the man's throat. With a gurgling cry he sank upon one knee and fell to the floor.

Perhaps I closed my eyes for an instant after that as a wave of vertigo rushed through my head. Perhaps a cloud momentarily shut off the golden sunlight that streamed through the windows. But when once again I looked out before me, the scene had changed. I was standing back in the weapon gallery with the queer arms on all sides. The last of the curious crowd was passing through the exit, and the guide was following them a few steps behind.

"One moment," I said as he was about to step across the sill. "One moment, please. What are these two swords mounted here on this wall? Is there a history attached to them?"

The guide frowned. "Weren't you listening, sir?" he asked. "I explained that only a moment before. Those blades are the least interesting in the entire room. They are here only because they represent a type. Musketeers' swords. Once owned by guardsmen of Louis III. Why do you ask?"

Before the man could stop me, I had reached up and lifted the right-hand sword from the wall.

The guide suddenly hissed an exclamation over my shoulder, then snatched away the blade and scrutinized it closely. When he spoke there was a tone of anger in his voice.

"Damme, if some one hasn't had the nerve to take a locket from Tray Six in the Jewelry Room and stick it here on the blade!" he bemoaned. "Say, won't the superintendent be furious! Utterly ruined the thing, and for no reason at all. That locket was valuable too. Belonged to an old French noble family once. Look, sir, you can see the coat of arms just where the blade passed through." ——

THE PALE MAN

JULIUS LONG

I have not yet met the man in No. 212. I do not even know his name. He never patronizes the hotel restaurant, and he does not use the lobby. On the three occasions when we passed each other by, we did not speak, although we nodded in a semi-cordial, non-committal way. I should like very much to make his acquaintance. It is lonesome in this dreary place. With the exception of the aged lady down the corridor, the only permanent guests are the man in No. 212

and myself. However, I should not complain, for this utter quiet is precisely what the doctor prescribed.

I wonder if the man in No. 212, too, has come here for a rest. He is so very pale. Yet I can not believe that he is ill, for his paleness is not of a sickly cast, but rather wholesome in its ivory clarity. His carriage is that of a man enjoying the best of health. He is tall and straight. He walks erectly and with a brisk, athletic stride. His pallor is no doubt congenital, else he would quickly tan under this burning, summer sun.

He must have traveled here by auto, for he certainly was not a passenger on the train that brought me, and he checked in only a short time after my arrival. I had briefly rested in my room and was walking down the stairs when I encountered him ascending with his bag. It is odd that our venerable bell-boy did not show him to his room.

It is odd, too, that, with so many vacant rooms in the hotel, he should have chosen No. 212 at the extreme rear. The building is a long, narrow affair three stories high. The rooms are all on the east side, as the west wall is flush with a decrepit business building. The corridor is long and drab, and its stiff, bloated paper exudes a musty, unpleasant odor. The feeble electric bulbs that light it shine dimly as from a tomb. Revolted by this corridor, I insisted vigorously upon being given No. 201, which is at the front and blessed with southern exposure. The room clerk, a disagreeable fellow with a Hitler mustache, was very reluctant to let me have it, as it is ordinarily reserved for his more profitable transient trade. I fear my stubborn insistence has made him an enemy.

If only I had been as self-assertive thirty years ago! I should now be a full-fledged professor instead of a broken-down assistant. I still smart from the cavalier manner in which the president of the university summarily recommended my vacation. No doubt he acted for my best interests. The people who have dominated my poor life invariably have.

Oh, well, the summer's rest will probably do me considerable good. It is pleasant to be away from the university. There is something positively gratifying about the absence of the graduate student face.

If only it were not so lonely! I must devise a way of meeting the pale man in No. 212. Perhaps the room clerk can arrange matters.

I have been here exactly a week, and if there is a friendly soul in this miserable little town, he has escaped my notice. Although the tradespeople accept my money with flattering eagerness, they studiously avoid even the most casual conversation. I am afraid I can never cultivate their society unless I can arrange to have my ancestors recognized as local residents for the last hundred and fifty years.

Despite the coolness of my reception, I have been frequently venturing abroad. In the back of my mind I have cherished hopes that I might encounter the pale man in No. 211. Incidentally, I wonder why he has moved from No. 212. There is certainly little advantage in coming only one room nearer to the front. I noticed the change yesterday when I saw him coming out of his new room.

We nodded again, and this time I thought I detected a certain malign satisfaction in his somber, black eyes. He must know that I am eager to make his acquaintance, yet his manner forbids overtures. If he wants to make me go all the way, he can go to the devil. I am not the sort to run after anybody. Indeed, the surly diffidence of the room clerk has been enough to prevent me from questioning him about his mysterious guest.

I wonder where the pale man takes his meals. I have been absenting myself from the hotel restaurant and patronizing the restaurants outside. At each I have ventured inquiries about the man in No. 210. No one at any restaurant remembered his having been there. Perhaps he has entrée into the Brahmin homes of this town. And again, he may have found a boarding-house. I shall have to learn if there be one.

The pale man must be difficult to please, for he has again changed his room. I am baffled by his conduct. If he is so desirous of locating himself more conveniently in the hotel, why does he not move to No. 202, which is the nearest available room to the front?

Perhaps I can make his inability to locate himself permanently an excuse for starting a conversation. "I see we are closer neighbors now," I might casually say. But that is too banal. I must await a better opportunity.

He has done it again! He is now occupying No. 209. I am intrigued by his little game. I waste hours trying to fathom its point. What possible motive could he have? I should think he would get on the hotel people's nerves. I wonder what our combination bellhop-chambermaid thinks of having to prepare four rooms for a single guest. If he were not stone-deaf, I would ask him. At present I feel too exhausted to attempt such an enervating conversation.

I am tremendously interested in the pale man's next move. He must either skip a room or remain where he is, for a permanent guest, a very old lady, occupies No. 208. She has not budged from her room since I have been here, and I imagine that she does not intend to.

I wonder what the pale man will do. I await his decision with the nervous excitement of a devotee of the track on the eve of a big race. After all, I have so little diversion.

Well, the mysterious guest was not forced to remain where he was, nor did he have to skip a room. The lady in No. 208 simplified matters by conveniently dying. No one knows the cause of her death, but it is generally attributed to old age. She was buried this morning. I was among the curious few who attended her funeral. When I returned home from the mortuary, I was in time to see the pale man leaving her room. Already he has moved in.

He favored me with a smile whose meaning I have tried in vain to decipher. I can not but believe that he meant it to have some significance. He acted as if there were between us some secret that I failed to appreciate. But, then, perhaps his smile was meaningless after all and only ambiguous by chance, like that of the Mona Lisa.

My man of mystery now resides in No. 207, and I am not the least surprised. I would have been astonished if he had not made his scheduled move. I have almost given up trying to understand his eccentric conduct. I do not know a single thing more about him than I knew the day he arrived. I wonder whence he came. There is something indefinably foreign about his manner. I am curious to hear his voice. I like to imagine that he speaks the exotic tongue of some far-away country. If only I could somehow inveigle him into conversation! I wish that I were possessed of the glib assurance of a college boy, who can address himself to the most distinguished celebrity without batting an eye. It is no wonder that I am only an assistant professor.

I am worried. This morning I awoke to find myself lying prone upon the floor. I was fully clothed. I must have fallen exhausted there after I returned to my room last night.

I wonder if my condition is more serious than I had suspected. Until now I have been inclined to discount the fears of those who have pulled a long face about me. For the first time I recall the prolonged hand-clasp of the president when he bade me good-bye from the university. Obviously he never expected to see me alive again.

Of course I am not that unwell. Nevertheless, I must be more careful. Thank heaven I have no dependents to worry about. I have not even a wife, for I was never willing to exchange the loneliness of a bachelor for the loneliness of a husband.

I can say in all sincerity that the prospect of death does not frighten me. Speculation about life beyond the grave has always bored me. Whatever it is, or is not, I'll try to get along.

I have been so preoccupied about the sudden turn of my own affairs that I have neglected to make note of a most extraordinary incident. The pale man has done an astounding thing. He has skipped three rooms and moved all the way to No. 203. We are now very close neighbors. We shall meet oftener, and my chances for making his acquaintance are now greater.

I have confined myself to my bed during the last few days and have had my food brought to me. I even called a local doctor, whom I suspect to be a quack. He looked me over with professional indifference and told me not to leave my room. For some reason he does not want me to climb stairs. For this bit of information he received a ten-dollar bill which, as I directed him, he fished out of my coat pocket. A pickpocket could not have done it better.

He had not been gone long when I was visited by the room clerk. That worthy suggested with a great show of kindly concern that I use the facilities of the local hospital. It was so modern and all that. With more firmness than I have been able to muster in a long time, I gave him to understand that I intended to remain where I am. Frowning sullenly, he stiffly retired. The doctor must have paused long enough downstairs to tell him a pretty story. It is obvious that he is afraid I shall die in his best room.

The pale man is up to his old tricks. Last night, when I tottered down the hall, the door of No. 202 was ajar. Without thinking, I looked inside. The pale man sat in a rocking-chair idly smoking a cigarette. He looked up into my eyes and smiled that peculiar, ambiguous smile that has so deeply puzzled me. I moved on down the corridor, not so much mystified as annoyed. The whole mystery of the man's conduct is beginning to irk me. It is all so inane, so utterly lacking in motive.

I feel that I shall never meet the pale man. But, at least, I am going to learn his identity. Tomorrow I shall ask for the room clerk and deliberately interrogate him.

I know now. I know the identity of the pale man, and I know the meaning of his smile.

Early this afternoon I summoned the room clerk to my bedside. "Please tell me," I asked abruptly, "who is the man in No. 202?" The clerk stared wearily and uncomprehendingly.

"You must be mistaken. That room is unoccupied."

"Oh, but it is," I snapped in irritation. "I myself saw the man there only two nights ago. He is a tall, handsome fellow with dark eyes and hair. He is unusually pale. He checked in the day that I arrived."

The hotel man regarded me dubiously, as if I were trying to impose upon him.

"But I assure you there is no such person in the house. As for his checking in when you did, you were the only guest we registered that day."

"What? Why, I've seen him twenty times! First he had No. 212 at the end of the corridor. Then he kept moving toward the front. Now he's next door in No. 202."

The room clerk threw up his hands.

"You're crazy!" he exclaimed, and I saw that he meant what he said.

I shut up at once and dismissed him. After he had gone, I heard him rattling the knob of the pale man's door. There is no doubt that he believes the room to be empty.

Thus it is that I can now understand the events of the past few weeks. I now comprehend the significance of the death in No. 207. I even feel partly responsible for the old lady's passing. After all, I brought the pale man with me. But it was not I who fixed his path. Why he chose to approach me room after room through the length of this dreary hotel, why his path crossed the threshold of the woman in No. 207, those mysteries I can not explain.

I suppose I should have guessed his identity when he skipped the three rooms the night I fell unconscious upon the floor. In a single night of triumph he advanced until he was almost to my door.

He will be coming by and by to inhabit this room, his ultimate goal. When he comes, I shall at least be able to return his smile of grim recognition.

Meanwhile, I have only to wait beyond my bolted door.

The door swings slowly open. . . . ———

Parthenope

Manly Wade Wellman

To his brine-deadened ears came soft, clear music. Had he been able to think after swimming so long, with salt water dashing into his sagging mouth, with his arms turned to dull stone, he might have pondered that this was the singing of death, a prelude to sleep under the waves of the Mediterranean.

But next instant he stirred, as though by another will, to a final effort. His hands, that had all but ceased flailing, framed once more a stroke-rhythm. His feet fluttered and kicked. His head came up out of the water, so that he saw what he had despaired of—a white beach with a face of dark rock behind, and at the blue water's edge a tall, waiting figure. The music rang its way into him, coursing through his blood like an elixir violently infused. He dared to bob upright, and solid bottom met his downward-groping toes. A few struggling, strides, a scramble in foamy shallows, and he sprawled in the sand at the feet of the singer.

It was blessed to lie there, then it was painful. He made shift to gasp and pant, then to moan. Gentle laughter slid down from above, and a questing pressure came upon his sodden shoulder. With the last of his strength, he turned over upon his back.

She must have bent to touch him, but now she stood straight again. She towered, almost as tall as himself, with a figure both full and fine. Her garment was a plain dark drapery, so caught around her as to line out her strongly smooth curves from chin to ankle, leaving bare one round shoulder and one smooth, slender arm. Above this tilted her brown face, framed between winglike sweeps of black hair, with bright inky eyes under wise lids, a regally chiselled nose and full red lips that smiled but did not part. She'd be lovely, he thought, if he were in any condition to appreciate loveliness.

"I was almost food for fishes," he muttered in Italian.

"No, you're too soaked in salt," she replied, and her speech was as musical as her song had been. "Not even a crab would eat you."

"Who are you?" he croaked, and sat up. "A siren?"

"*Seiren,*" she repeated after him, in the Greek manner, as though to cheer him by falling in with the feeble pleasantry. And the rescued swimmer had recovered enough to look up at her with admiration. This was beauty, classic but living, and only a mannerless clod would sprawl at its feet.

He tried to rise, swaying, and she caught his arm to steady him. The quick grasp of her fingers was as strong as steel, and her nails dug into his water-sodden skin. He smiled thanks, trying to brush the drenched blond hair from his young face. He knew what a sorry sight he must be—naked except for his dripping white trousers, pallid and shrunken from his long immersion. But she smiled her slight smile—like the Mona Lisa, like the Empress Josephine—and asked his name and country.

"George Colby," he supplied. "I'm an American student. This morning I was out in a fishing boat with some friends from Sicily. The boat sprang a leak, went down under us. Maybe they drowned. I just swam—kept swimming—got here—"

His head began to ring and whirl and, for all his efforts, he crumpled down to sit on the sand.

"You're weak," she said above his head. "Weak and famished. Wait."

He waited, in a sort of dreamy blur. Then an arm slid around his shoulders. She knelt to support him, and held to his mouth a sort of big plum.

"Eat," she urged him.

He nibbled at the pulpy thing. The first bite refreshed him enormously, the sweet juice cleared his head like wine. "Eat," she said again, turning the fruit against his hungry mouth, as a mother feeds a child.

After a moment, he could stand again. His shadow was long on the sand. The sun was sinking—he had been swimming most of the day.

"I don't know how to reward you," he said.

"I will be rewarded when I see you well and strong," she made the gravest of answers.

"You're being good," he half babbled. "Now, may I impose further? May I go to a house, will you help me there to spend the night? Tomorrow—"

"My house?" she echoed, as though the word and idea came strangely. "You mean, a place where men live. There is none on this beach."

George Colby was far too weary and grateful to digest this amazing information. He only gazed into her steady black eyes.

"You may sleep on the sand," she told him. "It's soft and warm. I'll keep watch."

"Don't bother," he began to say, but she smiled compellingly. She put one hand on his shoulder, and with the other offered him a bunch of grapes.

"I don't want to eat up your fruit," he protested.

"I do not care for them. Eat."

He did so, thankfully, sitting on the sand. She watched with a sort of happy relish as he devoured the grapes.

"Now sleep," she directed as he cast away the stem. "Grow strong. Let the bitter salt seawater flow from your body."

There was nothing he wanted to do more. He let her hands apply pressure, he stretched out on the sand. "Sleep," she said. "Sleep." Her musical voice was hypnosis.

He wakened once, shivering under a high-prowling moon. At once she was there, moving to sit beside him. Taking him in her arms, she held him close to her. She handled his considerable weight as easily and gently as though he were a baby. Colby mumbled a sleepy protest, but she began to croon a song, a soft memory of the music that had seemed to draw him out of the sea. Now it comforted him, it weighed upon his eyelids. His face drooped against her soft, warm bosom, and he slept again.

He wakened to daylight, and a sensation as of stroking. Starting violently, he looked up into her serene black eyes. She was washing his body with palmfuls of fresh water. Her tight lips smiled.

"I did not want to clean away the salt when it was dark and cold," she said. "But now you are better. Your flesh was ridged by the brine, and I have washed it away. Are you hungry?"

He was, and got up. He moved easily after the night's rest. His rescuer offered him a new fruit, that had a thick, thorny rind.

"Aren't you going to have breakfast?" he asked her.

"Later," she said, and watched while he peeled the fruit. Its flesh was firm, like a yam, but more delicate in texture. As he bit into it, she offered a great fluted sea shell, full of fresh water.

Now the sun had risen, and Colby could be aware, for the first time, of the place where he had come to land.

It was not an island, really; rather a reef or a bar, with a tall central spire of rock, like a monolithic dolman reared with determined toil by some ancient cult. The sandy beach that surrounded this fragment was no larger than a ballroom floor, and almost as smooth and flat. Several small trees grew, in a scrubby clump, at one side of the stone pillar, and there were a few wisps of grass. Colby could see no house, nor any trees or vines that might have produced the fruit he had eaten.

"Don't tell me you live here alone," he cried protestingly.

"I've always lived here," she assured him. "Always." And her eyes looked at him critically. "Do you feel well? Healthy?"

"Perfect, thank you." He walked toward the foot of the rocky pillar. It towered above him like a gigantic domino set on end. Colby studied its substance. It defied what little he knew of geology—smooth and gray as whetstone, with dark veins that looked metallic. And there were cracks—no, carved lines, an inscription. Slowly he pondered the letters in his head, translating them in his classroom Greek. They spelled a word. Yes.

Parthenope.

"It is my name," murmured her voice at his shoulder.

"I've heard it before," said Colby, without turning. "It's lovely—strange. Wait, I remember. Wasn't it the name of somebody in the Odyssey? Didn't Odysseus say—"

"Oh," she said gently, "Odysseus lied about so much. He said that, when he escaped me, I jumped into the sea and was drowned."

"Parthenope," Colby said again. "She was one of the three sisters, the—"

"My sisters perished, long ago. But I have stayed."

He turned and stared, wondering what joke she made. But she did not smile. She stood straight and tense inside her loose robe.

Her right arm crept toward him, the fingers crooked like talons.

"My song drew you," she said. "Odysseus got away, but you came. You were too ill and faint when you reached the shore. But now the salt is drained out of your flesh and blood, and it is sweet."

Colby drew back against the rock as she closed in on him.

"Who are you?" he screamed.

Her lips parted in a smile, and at last he saw her teeth, narrow and keen and widely spaced, the teeth of a flesh-eater.

"I am a *seiren*," she told him again. ——✦

THE PHANTOM BUS

W. ELWYN BACKUS

I

Out of the vagueness of the half-dawn a dark bulk loomed to the accompaniment of a dull rumble. To Arthur Strite, waiting for his regular bus—the big, orange six-forty-five to the city—this nondescript contraption which usually preceded it by a minute or two seemed more like a ghostly coffin than a public conveyance. Its sweating black sides glistened oilily in the gray light as it passed him. A single dim incandescent lamp seen through the windows silhouetted stiffly nodding heads against the background of a dingy interior. Then the black bus was gone, swallowed up in the swirling December mist and fog.

As always, a feeling of odd disquiet possessed Strite with the passing of this conveyance—a fleeting impression of mystery, strangely repellent and defying description; of ill omen. What manner of passengers it carried or whence and whither it traveled, he did not know—and cared less. Yet, queerly enough, the affair had increasingly irritated and disturbed him ever since his moving to Emerymont three weeks before.

"Just an old junk-heap that loops out through Norwood and back over this direction," a fellow commuter said in answer to his question. Until this morning Strite had refrained from what he deemed the weakness of a query about this thing. For he had hesitated to give definite shape to his senseless disquiet by admitting any curiosity, even to himself. "I believe a couple of death-traps like that one comprise the company's entire rolling-stock," his informant finished.

"Oh," said Strite, mentally categorying the bus line with several that operated a sort of cross-country service between outlying sections of Cincinnati. Of course, he reflected, *some* concern had to serve this need. But he was conscious of a feeling of relief that he did not have to use that service.

Arthur Strite was boarding in Emerymont with the Ransons, not because of any liking for the make-believes, the rabble of bourgeoisie and scandalmongers that peopled the little suburb, but because he did enjoy the shrubbery and lawns and the quaintly designed houses, despite the crazy butting of garbage-can-studded back yards against living-room windows of adjoining homes. He minded his own business, displaying no curiosity in the neighbors or affairs of the place—which was one of the reasons why he had not discovered sooner the purpose of the bus line mentioned.

The night of the same day he had asked about the bus, he found himself pondering, with some intentness in the midst of an absent-minded perusal of the evening comic sheet, on the dingy conveyance that passed him each morning. Why should that silly bus thus intrude itself into his mind? He smiled self-indulgently and turned over to the sports page. The thing actually was becoming a nuisance! And for no logical reason. What should it matter to him how uninviting, how disagreeable a box on wheels those people rode in every morning?

Nevertheless, he dropped off to sleep thinking about the ghostly bus.

The same thing began to be the rule on the nights that followed. Always that ridiculous feeling of indefinable dread would come over him, would cling tenaciously to his thoughts from the moment he happened to think of having seen the shadowy bus that morning. He had half a notion to hail the confounded contraption some morning and see where it took him, just to dispel all this absurd air of mystery about it which had so unaccountably fastened upon him. Though perhaps there was some reason for his strange obsession after all. Not quite one year before, his fiancée, Doris Tway, had been killed in a terrible bus crash. He remembered the crumpled remains of the fatal bus, which he had seen afterward, vividly. It, too, had been black and shabby. An odd girl—she had always said that if she left first, she would return for him. Her idea of a joke, of course, but unusual.

In spite of his notion about hailing the other bus, Strite did not ride it—not for several weeks anyway, although its daily rumbling and jangling approach, made more eery by the shortening of the days, had driven that impression of weird mystery deeper than ever into his waking thoughts. Waking, because, so far, the dark bus had troubled him only during the evenings before he retired.

However, there came a night when he dreamed that he obeyed an impulse and boarded the strange bus!

He was conscious of a sickly odor as he entered the rickety door, which had slid back with a softness in strange contrast to the outward clatter of the conveyance. The vizor of the operator's cap was pulled well down over his face as he leaned over his levers. Strite felt the bus begin to move. Oddly, there was no vibration, none of the jarring rattle and bang he had expected. He might have been on a river barge, for all the motion he could feel. Startled more by this unnatural quiet than he could have been by the loudest of banging or jolting, he raised his eyes toward the occupants of the bus. Perhaps it was the strange effort this act seemed to impose upon him; at any rate, he awoke in that instant, seized by unreasoning, incomprehensible terror!

It was an hour before his taut nerves had relaxed enough to let him drop off to sleep—and not before he had vowed to ride that bus in fact the next morning.

2

Strite did not ride the black bus the next morning. It was nearly seven o'clock when he opened his eyes from a troubled sleep. This meant that he would be late to the office where he worked, on the other side of the city. Of course he missed his regular bus, and, with it, the other. Too, the daylight put a different aspect upon things. It would have been ridiculous, after all, to board a bus bound for another part of the city merely to humor a crazy impulse.

Yet, when that night came, Strite hesitated to go to bed. He told himself that he was hopeless, a fool and a coward. Then he undressed and resolutely turned out the light.

His hesitancy had not been unfounded. Again he found himself boarding the mysterious, sweating conveyance with its leaning operator and strange, illusive odor. And again a sudden, agonized awakening.

But this time he saw the other occupants before he awoke. They all—there were six of them—had their eyes closed as they sat nodding slightly with the almost imperceptible swaying of the bus. There was a repellent something about those faces, other than their closed eyelids, that struck a chill into Strite's heart. He wondered whether they were just weary, like him, or—

A cold finger touched his wrist. He managed to turn and face the operator. The latter, his face still hidden, was pointing to the fare box. Of course, these ill-built, ill-kept buses *would* reverse things by demanding their fare when one entered. He reached into his pocket for a dime, and in that moment caught sight of a seventh passenger, seated in front on the other side. The operator's head and shoulders had partly hidden her from him before, despite her slender tallness.

As his fingers found and automatically brought forth a dime, he observed that this passenger's eyes were not closed like the rest—that they were pale gray and staring at him. They were like—oh, God, it couldn't be—Doris! But it was—it was! How could he have failed to recognize her sooner, despite her position on the other side of the operator? Now he could understand why this bus had drawn him so strangely, irresistibly.

As he stared back at her, speechless with amazement, her eyes left his face, turned toward the windshield. Her pale lips twitched oddly, as if, mute with fear at what she saw there, she sought vainly to scream.

Then abruptly the spell was broken. She leaped to her feet, throwing one arm across her face in a gesture of one warding off some fearful harm. A shrill, hysterical scream pierced the quiet of that closed space like the stab of a knife!

That cry jarred Strite back to consciousness with a suddenness that jerked him upright in bed.

As he sat there trembling with the realism of his dream and that agonized scream, he became aware that he held something tightly in one closed hand. A fresh chill passed through his body at the familiar feel of that something. He needed no light to tell him that it was a dime he clutched—the dime he had been ready to drop in the fare box of his dream!

3

Of course he found that the coin evidently had fallen out of his vest when he sat on the bed while undressing. In fact, he usually kept some change in his vest pocket so as to have it handy for tips, newspapers, and such. Perhaps the accidental finding and touching of that coin in his slumbers had even started the train of thought that had made him dream of the fare box—and the other things. But there was no more sleep for Strite. After tossing about for the rest of the night, he got up about five o'clock.

This morning he was determined upon one thing. He would ride the black bus—"the phantom bus," as he had come to term it privately—this morning, and kill for once and all this persistent subconscious illusion that had taken root in his mind from the seed of his first absurd impression of the rickety conveyance in the eery light of half-dawn.

Once more his intention was to be defeated, however. The black bus failed to appear before the six-forty-five, though he had arrived at its stop more than a quarter-hour before it was due. He even waited for it ten minutes after his regular bus had gone—only to learn later that the other line finally had been discontinued.

His first reaction to this information was an overwhelming relief. No longer would he be reminded by this shadowy, rumbling hulk each morning, of things he wanted to forget.

But on the heels of this thought came the realization that the very discontinuance of the line had removed all chance of his ever killing the illusion if the latter continued to trouble him.

That day at noon as he walked along a downtown street a peculiar odor halted him. There was an illusive, dread familiarity about it. He was before a florist's open shop, and a great bowl of tuberoses, those once choice flowers for all those departed, was set out in front. He knew now where he had smelled their scent before—on the phantom bus of his dream.

4

Once again Strite was in the phantom bus—in his subconscious mind. This time he knew exactly what was coming. He seemed powerless to change a single detail of it all. The pause just inside the doorway as he forced his gaze up to where the six passengers sat in plain view, their eyes closed, in death-like weariness or worse. The icy touch of a finger on his wrist, the reaching for a coin, and the discovery of the slender, tall girl up front. Doris!

At this point the sequence of events suddenly galvanized him into a feverish alertness for the next thing. As Doris' hysterical scream rang in his ears, he was abruptly released from the grip of immobility. He turned quickly and looked out of the front of the bus.

What he saw there made him throw up his hands in an involuntary gesture similar to her own instinctive gesture of terror. He heard the brakes squealing shrilly—felt the bus skid on the sleet-covered road even as he caught a side glimpse of the operator's face —saw with sudden added horror that half the face was missing. Beyond that fleeting glimpse, he had time for no further examination; for just ahead a heavily loaded truck was emerging from a narrow bridge-end, blocking their way. Then a terrific, rending crash. . . .

5

The six-forty-five bus was four minutes late on account of the icy condition of the roads; they had been that way for two days. A little group of commuters on the roadside were talking in subdued tones, for once unmindful of the delay as they waited.

"Personally," a pompous, red-faced man was saying, "I believe Ranson killed and—mauled—him for attentions to Mrs. Ranson."

"But Strite didn't appear to be that type," objected a young member of the group. "Nor is Mrs. Ranson the sort who would encourage him. Besides, consider the condition of the body. Why, Ranson or no one else could have so mangled another—to say nothing of leaving it in bed and persistently claiming that he didn't know how it happened, except that he and his wife were awakened in the middle of the night by a frightful cry—and found him that way! No, I say there is some deeper mystery about the affair, the nature of which we haven't suspected."

The big, orange-colored bus hove into view at this juncture, interrupting the discussion for the time. Presently they all had boarded it and found seats at various vantage-points. A little distance along the road one of them pointed out to his neighbor a twisted and splintered mass of wreckage at the foot of an embankment of the narrow bridge they were just then crossing.

"Lucky it jumped off when it struck—didn't even delay us yesterday when we followed a few minutes after it was discovered."

"Queer thing about how it got there," said the other. "Nobody witnessed the accident, and the defunct bus company's officials swear that the last they saw of their 'death trap' was when it was locked away in an old garage on the other side of Norwood. Can you imagine any one swiping a can like that for a ride? But the present-day young coke-head will grab anything for a joy-ride."

"No queerer than that—that mess inside the wreck—as if some one had been crushed like—well, like poor Strite, for instance. Yet they could find no trace of a body!" ——

Rendezvous

Richard H. Hart

"Tell Marcel I said to hang on—that if he lets go I'll kick the daylights out of him! I'll be there as soon as possible."

Doctor Dumont spoke earnestly, although his words were light; they were meant to encourage the sufferer, to stiffen the will-power which alone could whip on the flagging heart until his arrival.

The doctor hung up the receiver with fingers slightly trembling and snatched his medicine case from a chair. He opened the little bag and glanced within it to make sure that his needle-set and a plentiful supply of digitalis were in their places. Then he seized his hat and rushed from the house; a moment's delay might mean victory for his ancient enemy, Death.

A plan of action—the only plan that might succeed—had popped into his head at old Etienne's first words. Etienne had said: "Mist' Favret is tak' bad, Mist' Doct'! T'ink pro*babl*' you bette' come quick!" Etienne was only an unschooled Cajun, who "cou'n' read one w'd, if he's big as box-ca'"—but he loved Marcel Favret even as Doctor Dumont loved him, and there had been an agony of fear in his voice. The doctor had decided instantly that he must catch the westbound train.

The difficulty was that the train had already left New Orleans. It was at that very moment aboard the huge iron ferry-barge being shoved across the Mississippi by a puffing tug. Doctor Dumont would have to catch it, if at all, somewhere along the opposite bank.

As ill-luck would have it, he had chosen that particular week to have his car overhauled. He could telephone for a taxi, of course, but at that evening rush-hour too many precious minutes might elapse before it arrived. The street-cars were reasonably fast and dependable, and he knew that he could afford to run no risks. He would take one.

An up-river Magazine car rumbled to a stop just as he reached the corner, and he swung thankfully aboard. The decision as to which ferry to choose had been made for him; he would cross the river at Walnut Street, and try to catch the train at Westwego.

Unconsciously, he seated himself at the extreme front of the car, as if to be that much closer to his goal. Marcel Favret was his life-long companion and dearest friend, and his patient only incidentally. Favret, suffering an unexpected relapse, needed the administration of digitalis most acutely, and only Doctor Dumont might ascertain from his symptoms the exact dosage which would save him.

There was not the slightest use in looking at his watch, but the doctor found himself doing so constantly. At each single tap of the conductor's bell, demanding a stop, he ground his teeth impatiently. Each double tap, signaling renewed progress, caused him a sigh of relief. He must—he *must*—arrive in time.

Then, only five minutes' ride from Walnut Street, Disaster showed its ugly face. The street-car's bell emitted a shower of angry *clangs;* the motorman whirled back the controller and threw on the brakes. The car ground to a stop.

Doctor Dumont was on his feet instantly, trying to beat down a great surge of despair.

There was no need to ask questions. Squarely across the track sprawled a huge tank-truck with one wheel missing and a rear axle gouged into the pavement. The street-car was effectively blocked.

Acting without volition, the doctor leaped down from the car and started walking rapidly along the street. The outraged passengers behind him might expostulate with motorman and truck-driver until they were tired; it would do them no good. As for him, he must catch the west-bound train across the river.

He had covered nearly two blocks at a furious pace when he realized the futility of his course. He couldn't walk to Walnut Street in less than twenty minutes, and he knew that his old legs would carry him less than half the distance if he attempted to run. He must find some other way.

At the corner, he turned abruptly to the left and made his way toward the Mississippi. He would have to find a boatman to ferry him across; surely there were motorboats in plenty along the levee. A motorboat he must have, for the river was high and its rushing current would carry a skiff too far downstream in the crossing. Even now, he could hear in the still night air the whistle of the train as it left Gretna. And he must catch that train.

The thought galvanized his tired legs; he crossed Water Street at a trot. He dashed between rows of mean shanties and found himself upon a crumbling wharf. As he paused for breath, his gaze automatically wandered out across the swirling water.

Abruptly, he dashed a hand across his eyes as if to brush away an impossible sight. He had exerted himself too much, he thought. Otherwise how could he be seeing a steam ferry-boat at this point? Surely he wasn't as ignorant of New Orleans as all that!

But the sight remained, and to his ears came the confirmatory *pow-pow-pow* of the stern-wheeler. In eager amazement he heard the jangling of the pilot's bell and watched the boat glide smoothly up to the landing-stage. A moment more and he had sprung aboard.

The ferry-boat remained at the landing-stage for a minute or so, its huge paddle-wheel turning over at half speed. But no other passenger came aboard, and presently the bell jangled again and the boat swung out into the current. The paddle-wheel churned with an accelerating rhythm as the black water swirled past and the crumbling wharf fell farther and farther back into the darkness.

As suspense and excitement subsided within him, Doctor Dumont realized that the air off the river was something more than chilly. He turned up his coat-collar and stepped through the door of the engine-room in search of warmth. He recognized the possibility that this was against the rules, but the fact that there were no other passengers aboard emboldened him. The little infraction would surely be overlooked.

"Pretty cool, tonight," he remarked to the engineer.

The engineer nodded without speaking. He was a big-framed man with an immense red nose. One of his legs had been cut off just below the knee and the missing portion had been replaced with an old-fashioned, hand-carved wooden peg. It struck the deck with a dull thump whenever he moved about.

Doctor Dumont's feeling of relief impelled him to be sociable. He drew out his emergency flask.

"Prescription liquor—twelve years old," he said. "Have a drink with me."

He was wholly unprepared for the change which came suddenly over the engineer. The fellow's eyes opened wide, his nostrils dilated, and his lips drew back from yellow teeth in a grimace of frightful rage. He took two steps forward and raised a ham-like fist. Doctor Dumont backed prudently through the door without stopping to argue; he had seen madness often enough to recognize the gleam from those wild eyes.

At that moment came a fortunate diversion. The bell overhead clattered loudly, and the engineer sullenly allowed his arm to fall, then went back to his levers. Doctor Dumont replaced his flask and hastened around to the opposite side of the deck. The crossing was at an end.

A narrow lane bordered with tall weeds diverged from the levee, and the doctor made his way along it at a brisk walk. A hundred yards farther along, he found himself at the highway. Roaring up the pavement came a westbound bus; frantically the doctor flagged it down. Only when he was safely aboard did he realize that he had not paid his ferry-fee: in his haste he must somehow have missed the ticket office. He made a mental note to drop by sometime and pay the delinquent fare; notwithstanding the mad engineer, that had been one trip which was certainly worth the money.

He caught the train at Westwego with only seconds to spare. An hour later he was descending from it at the little town where he had practised for so many years, and where his patient awaited him. He hoped fervently that he would be in time.

Etienne met him at the station with a little automobile; it seemed to the doctor that the wheezy motor quivered with impatience.

"How's Marcel?" he demanded as he climbed in.

"Wo'se," said Etienne. "I promise *le bon Saint* can'le long's my a'm if he's get bette'—but he's wo'se." He fed more gasoline to the now roaring motor.

The little car shot forward along the dark road and began a nerve-torturing race. It turned unbanked curves on slithering tires and missed trees, fenceposts and culverts by inches. At last Etienne threw his weight on the brakes and racked it to a stop.

Both men were out of the car before it had ceased to vibrate, and Etienne led the way into the house. They found Marcel Favret unconscious, and the old Cajun went down on his knees beside the bed as the doctor fumbled with the latch of his medicine case.

"I'm just in time," the doctor muttered, fitting needle to syringe with practised speed. "Thirty minutes more—perhaps even fifteen—and Marcel would have been done for. That ferry-boat came like a dispensation."

It was a long, tense fight, and although Doctor Dumont prided himself on his freedom from superstition he more than once seemed to feel the air about him stirred by unseen wings as he labored and watched over his patient. There was an acrid taste in his mouth, and it was as if restraining hands tugged at his every muscle. Never had his enemy appeared so loth to relinquish a victim.

But skill and devotion triumphed at last, and the presence of Death was no longer felt in the room. The patient was breathing quietly and regularly when Doctor Dumont signed to Etienne to accompany him from the bedchamber.

"He needs nothing but sleep, now," said the doctor as he closed the door behind them. "And, while he's getting it, maybe you could scrape me up a sandwich. I've eaten nothing since noon."

"You bet," Etienne said, his brown old face aglow with gratitude and admiration. "I fix you somet'ing bette'. I fix you nice om'lette an' drip you pot *café*. Good *souper* fo' good doct'."

They went out into the kitchen, and while he skilfully cracked eggs and dropped them from their shells into an earthenware bowl Etienne asked the doctor how he had managed to catch the train. Doctor Dumont settled himself comfortably at the table, then recounted his difficulties and told of how they had been overcome.

Etienne shredded a clove of garlic and added it to the eggs. "You say you catch de *ferie* somew'ere aroun' State Street o' Jeffe'son Av'nue?" he asked. "You *certain* it not Napole*on* o' Walnut?"

"Absolutely," the doctor assured him. "I didn't notice the name of the street, but there was a box-factory alongside the wharf where I caught the boat, and there's no such factory at either Walnut Street or Napoleon Avenue. I know that much about the city."

"Hoh—de box-fact'ry f*erie*!" exclaimed Etienne. He thoughtfully added salt, pepper, tabasco and fresh basil leaves to the mixture in the bowl. "You say de enginee' had a wooden leg?"

"Yes. And, if you ask me, the old devil's crazy as a bat."

"Hmmm. Maybe. Hmmm." Etienne whisked the omelette to a creamy froth, then turned it into a skillet under which a low fire burned. "You want I should tell you 'bout one-leg' enginee' which wo'k on box-fact'ry f*erie*?"

"Go ahead," said Doctor Dumont, his eyes on the omelette.

Etienne chuckled. "A hom'lette mus' cook slow," he said.

He put a lid on the skillet and took up a small coffee-pot.

"It all happen' w'ile I living in Nyawlins," he began. "I living on Magazine Street, an' wo'king ove' at *sirop* fact'ry. I have to cross rive' two time eve'y day on box-fact'ry fe*rie*. Enginee' on boat name' Leblanc. Big man wit' red head."

"The engineer on the boat tonight had red hair," put in Doctor Dumont, looking up momentarily.

"Yeah?" The old Cajun poured boiling water over the dark-roasted coffee and chicory and set the pot on the back of the stove to drip. He resumed:

"Enginee' Leblanc like w'isky too much. All time he have bottle in's pocket. Drink, drink, drink; all day long. Not get so ve'y dronk, but drink too much. One day he's not pay 'tention to pilot's bell, an' not reverse hengine quick 'nough—bump landing float ha'd. Ca*bam!* Leblanc' own brothe' is was standing on float, waiting fo' fe*rie;* bump make him fall off an' drown."

"You mean that he caused his own brother to drown?" demanded the doctor.

"Yeah. He's brothe' is can swim, but bump head on piling, is knock out. Neve' come up. Dey is not find him fo' two hou's."

"Did that stop the engineer's drinking?"

"Non!" snorted Etienne. "Not'ing is stop him drinking. Two week afte' he's brothe' drown, he drinking some mo' an' put's foot unde' connecting-rod. *Bam!* Mash foot *comme ça!"* He crushed one of the egg-shells in his brown fist.

"I see," said the doctor. "Gangrene—and amputation. That is how he acquired his wooden leg. What happened then?"

"One night w'ile he's in *l'hôpital* he's brothe' come to him an' tell him—"

"You mean another brother?" interrupted the doctor.

Etienne folded the omelette dexterously and transferred it to a platter. He poured out a cup of coffee and set platter and cup before the doctor before he spoke.

"Non. Same brothe'. Brothe' tell him if he's not stop drinking so much w'isky he's going to be sorry. Going be sorry long's he's live—an' lots longe'."

"Wait a minute!" exclaimed the doctor, pausing in the act of putting his fork into the savory omelette. "You're getting all mixed up. First you say his brother was drowned, and then you say his brother came to him while he was in the hospital. I don't understand what you mean."

"Maybe you un'e'stan' mo' bette' w'en I'm finish'," Etienne returned. "W'en Leblanc get out of *l'hôpital,* wit' he's wooden leg, de *ferie* comp'ny is not want him to wo'k fo' dem some mo'. But he's tell 'em he's going get lawye'—bigges' lawye' in Nyawlins—an' sue 'em fo' big *dommage* fo' lose's leg in acci*dent*. Den *ferie* comp'ny is say he can go back to wo'k if he's not sue 'em.

"He's not drink much fo' one-two week afte' he's go back to wo'k. Den one day he's got he's bottle again, an' a big crowd of people is going ove' rive' to ball-game. Mus' be dey is hund'ed men an' women on *ferie*-boat. Leblanc is drink too much, an' not watch he's wate'-gage. Steam-gage go all way round. Den Leblanc is tu'n mo' wate' into boile'—an' she's blow up. Ca-*bam!* People dat's not kill' is drown'. Eve'y one. Leblanc too."

"Another kind of drunken driver," commented Doctor Dumont, turning from Etienne and attacking the omelette with vast appetite. "It was a good story, all right, but you got mixed up about the brother who was drowned coming to the hospital. The way you told it, it seemed as if he came to the hospital after he was drowned."

"He *did* come afte' he's drown'."

The doctor swallowed a huge draft of the black Louisiana coffee, wiped his mouth, and set down the cup with an air of satisfaction. Then he said reproachfully:

"I'm surprised at you, Etienne: telling me a story like that. What did I ever do to deserve it?"

"Do?" echoed the old Cajun, shrilly. "W'at you do? You tell me you cross de rive' tonight on box-fact'ry *ferie*, between Walnut an' Napole*on*—di'n't you? It's twenty-fi' yea's, dis ve'y mont', dat En-ginee' Leblanc is blow up boat wit' hund'ed people on him—an' dey ain' been no steam-*ferie* on dat pa't of de rive' since!" ——

THE RING

J. M. FRY

I looked up. The man who had interrupted my gastronomic enjoy-ment was a tall individual, a little stooped, with a face as long as the prohibitionists' in the cartoons. He had dark hollow places under his eyes. He might have been a Canova statue for all his expression, but his features displayed deep lines as if life had given him more to worry about than most.

"You are —— ?" he said, and mentioned my name.

I told him I was. I arose and accepted his card. Arvid Hedon. It stirred a faint recollection.

"Have a chair?"

"Thank you," he murmured. I didn't invite him to such close intimacy, but he drew the chair from the opposite side of the table and sat down at the corner next my elbow. He didn't seem to want the people seated nearest us to hear whatever he was going to say.

He leaned over to me and spoke in low tones.

"I take it you're interested in antiques," he said.

I told him I wasn't.

"But," he insisted, "you bought a rare ring at the Felbinger auction not two hours ago."

I told him I had. "What about it?"

"Well—" He hesitated, studying the table-cloth. Then he apparently changed his mind and switched off on a new line.

"Will you sell it to me?" he inquired.

I reminded him that I had just bought it.

"I'll give you any amount you ask; a thousand, ten thousand, a hundred thou—"

I said no, feeling very stubborn.

"But think!" he kept on. "It isn't worth very much—a thousand dollars is a big price for it and I'm offering you a fortune!"

"No," I said, "I won't sell it." I told him I already had more money than was good for me but that I had never had such an unusual ring. I told him that I always had a weakness for unusual rings and now that I had one I was going to keep it.

He hung his head for a moment. When he looked at me again the pockets under his eyes seemed to have grown a shade darker. He caught hold of my arm.

"Listen," he said. "I feel—or rather I *know* it's my duty to warn you. If you persist in wearing that"—he tapped the ring on my finger—"you die within twenty-four hours!"

I looked at him in astonishment. "You mean to threaten?"

"No, no! You misunderstand me. I mean that the ring is fatal—it brings death to whoever wears it."

I laughed. "Then to frighten—"

"Don't be a fool!"

"That's what I'm trying not to be," I said a little hotly.

"Oh—bother!" he expostulated. "See here. You've heard of such things before—"

"Of course," I cut in. "Simply myths or coincidences."

He spread his hands deploringly. "That's just it; that's why I hesitated about telling you this. It isn't the characteristic of educated people to be superstitious. Too bad!"

"I think it's common sense. Have a cigar?"

"No, thanks. Listen! Do you remember the Arvid Hedon Archeological Expedition that made several discoveries in the lower Nile valley a few years ago?"

I thought back and told him I guessed I did.

"Well, I led that party—it bore my name. We made some remarkable findings, among them the tomb of a noble in the court of Rameses II. In his sarcophagus we found that ring. . . . That ring, yes sir! It's over three thousand years old! Look at it."

I was looking at it. Three thousand years old! Well, well. I shouldn't have thought it and told him as much.

"No, I don't suppose you would've," he remarked a little dryly. Then he paradoxically added, "It's never been worn very much— although plenty have worn it."

It made me curious. "How's that?" I asked.

"Well-l . . . I'll tell you," he said. "The ring caught my eye, and I—just kept it. That's a confession. I should have turned it over to the British Museum, which supervised the expedition, but its curious design and the little history I found concerning it made it valuable as a keepsake. So I kept it.

"Perhaps I ought to tell you that history. It was written in the ancient sacred hieroglyphics—on a papyrus roll I found in the sarcophagus. It wasn't long, though most ironic. This man had wished to do away with his twin brother, so he made the ring and had a curse put on it by the High Priest of Ammon-Re. But then he wanted to make sure it would fit his twin brother's finger when he gave it to him, so he tried it on himself. As he did so a bolt struck him down from the clear sky—from Ammon, the sun, as the history stated.

"Of course I put no stock in this story. It was too fantastic, too mythical; I was a skeptic as you are.

"I brought the ring home with me. I never wore it because it was too small, but I gave it to my sister—"

He stopped to wipe a tear from the corner of his eye.

"She wanted it," he continued, "so I gave it to her, and—that same afternoon I looked upon her dead body. She had been run down when crossing the street."

There was another pause while he threw back his stooped shoulders as if to strengthen himself; then, seeming to sag a little more in his chair, he went on:

"I had the ring again in my possession. I couldn't bear to see it every day—it sent chills over me—so I hid it away in a secret drawer in my desk.

"My brother wanted it and I refused to give it to him. How he ever got it I don't know, because on the morning of that fatal day I had looked in the drawer to make sure it was still there. I think he must have seen me do that. He was a cocky young devil and only laughed at what he called my 'whim' in keeping it hidden.

"He was a zealous yachtsman—on this day an adverse wind switched his boom around and tossed him overboard, and when we dragged his body from the Thames almost the first thing I noticed was this ring on his finger.

"They laid him on one of the docks and worked on him with a pulmotor for over an hour. It was no use. In my frenzy I forgot about the ring. When later I came to look for it, it was gone. There had been quite a crowd around and someone must have stolen it.

"I spent days after that, searching every pawnshop in London. I finally found one in Whitechapel where they had bought such a ring, but had sold it again.

"I kept my eyes on the daily papers. I investigated every violent death I found chronicled. Oh, the weary, nerve-racking chase that ring has given me! I have done some marvelous pieces of detective work. It has led me all over Europe, and I've found in its wake only death—violent deaths ranging from accidents to suicides and murders!

"Man, listen to me! Only once since it was stolen off my dead brother's finger have I got as close to it as I am now. That was at Lavenue's, in Paris. A young artist was wearing it. I tried to warn him as I am warning you—but he was very rude, would not listen. He had me ejected from the place. I waited for him and when he came out I tried to collar him again. He avoided me, ran for a moving cab. He slipped and fell under the wheels. They rushed him away before I could crowd through the jam to get near him.

"It wasn't until the next day that I managed to find out where he lived. I arrived there in time to learn that his relatives had sold the ring to help pay his funeral expenses.

"You can imagine that it has eluded me many times. There have been months when I have lost all trace of it, only to pick up a clue from some tragedy that came to my notice.

"I was in Ostend when I got a hint that it had preceded me to New York. I arrived here only yesterday and frantically renewed my search. This afternoon an article in the paper caught my attention; it mentioned that a certain Felbinger had fallen from his bedroom window and become impaled on a spike fence that ran close to his house. It also stated that his heirs were selling off his goods at auction.

"I followed what you would call my hunch and went down there —only to find that I was too late. You were ahead of me.

"I got your name, and your address at the Devereux Club. There they told me that you were probably dining here—so here I am."

He leaned closer to me and grasped my arm again.

"Oh, I ask you, I beseech you, not to wear that ring. Carry it in your pocket, hide it away, but don't wear it! I know what I'm talking about. It has driven me almost mad. I was the means of giving it to the world and it's up to me to get rid of it again. If you are wise you'll destroy it—or if you don't wish to do that, sell it to me for any price you want and I'll destroy it. I won't toss it in the sea or hide it, but I'll grind it to powder and cast it to the wind—utterly destroy it!"

I casually blew a smoke. ring and watched its vortical action. I thanked him for his consideration in warning me. I told him that if I decided to destroy the ring I would give him the satisfaction of doing it; and in the meantime I would be very careful.

He sighed heavily and arose. "Yes," he said, "I should like to have that satisfaction. I've certainly earned it! You have my transient address. Good-bye."

He was gone, then, and presently I followed.

It was dark and cold outside. A drizzle was coming down, freezing as it hit the pavement. It was so slippery one could hardly walk.

I hailed a taxi and directed it to the Devereux Club. As I settled back in my seat I held up my hand to look at the ring by the passing lights. It was certainly curious; I didn't doubt but that Hedin's tale was simply the fabrication of an ingenious brain and that he had become a little cracked over his Egyptian exploits and the story about the ring which he had read. At least I believed the explanation would run somewhere along that line.

I can't tell you just how it happened. I had been engrossed in my thoughts when suddenly I was aware of the tire chains grinding on the ice, then the sensation of spinning in a tub.

Instantly Arvid Hedin's warning flashed into my mind. I grasped hold of the door-handle and hung on in a panic. I think that was what saved my life, for otherwise when the crash came I should surely have been thrown to the opposite side of the taxi—and that side was battered in by a street-light standard.

There were plenty of helping hands to extricate me from the wreckage. I waited there a moment to see if I was needed, but the driver wasn't hurt, and after shaking my clothes into shape and recovering my hat, I proceeded to negotiate my way on foot.

I hadn't gone far when I was passing a skyscraper that was being erected—they work on these buildings day and night. I heard a deafening crash overhead and ducked out into the street just as a load of bricks broke through some faulty scaffolding and landed upon the sidewalk.

I skated back to the curb in time to miss narrowly being struck by an oncoming car.

You may suppose that my faith in our practical beliefs was just a little shaken by this time; and can you blame me for what I did? Even if you do not blame me, I blush to admit it. I took the ring off my finger and dropped it in my pocket.

I felt somewhat safer as I walked on.

But in another block I was calling myself names for my superstitious cowardice. Was I to be frightened by a man's freakish fancy and a few narrow squeaks that seemed to corroborate it? Of course I wasn't! I was simply making a fool of myself in doubting Plato's philosophy.

I pulled the ring out of my pocket and jammed it on my finger.

Just then a car sped by, followed closely by another with siren going full blast. I heard the barking of automatics and instinctively ducked. It was lucky that I did, for a stray bullet bored a neat hole through the crown of my hat.

With jaws tightly set, I hurried my pace. The Devereux Club was just ahead of me, and within its portals I knew I should be safe. Nothing ever happened there.

Now to me the Devereux Club was an institution embodying all the comforts a respectable loafer could wish for. Its old-fashioned architecture appealed to me and in spite of its exclusive atmosphere it was very home-like. It was there that I kept my bachelor quarters.

I heaved a great sigh of relief as the doorman let me in. It was my haven—I felt like a mariner just getting into port after a stormy voyage. Safety was all around me. I stood for a moment in the foyer intoxicated with it, glorying in it, drinking in the homely reek of tobacco smoke with deep breaths and listening to the loving kisses of the billiard balls.

Never shall I forget what a wonderful sense of freedom and security I had at that moment. It was an elixir for the most fatalistic constitution. I was thrilled to the marrow.

With my head held high I buoyantly took a step, tripped over a Persian rug and sprawled headlong.

My foot struck the jamb of a knight's suit of armor standing inside the door. A halberd was loosened from the mailed fist, and I rolled out of the way as it cut a gash in the floor where my neck had been.

I scrambled to my feet. I think that I was very red of face, and I know that I was swearing. I coarsely told the porter who rushed to my assistance that he'd better see that such menaces to life and property were banished from the Devereux Club. "Y-yes, sah," he said, he would. I told him that knights never carried such things anyway, so a halberd was particularly incongruous with that suit of armor.

I brushed past him and made for the stairs. I hesitated only long enough to remove the ring from my finger, figuring that the plaster might fall off the ceiling.

Has someone said that one's bedroom is one's fortress? It was in mine that at last I was able to breathe air untainted with mystery and danger; for, I ask you, what could ever happen to me now? Nothing—absolutely nothing! I locked the door and sat down in my lounge chair to think matters over in a rational mood.

I drew the ring from my pocket. Now that I was safe from all harm my thoughts had dropped into a more tranquil groove and the idea that a mere ring, however curiously wrought and old, could bear a fatal curse again struck me as being beyond reason. A ring bring death? Absurd! It was inconsistent with common sense. It was all right for the ancient people of darkest Egypt, but not today.

I laughed aloud.

Besides, a new and pleasant suspicion dawned upon me. Perhaps after all the ring was a good-luck charm! Of course, that was it. Why hadn't I thought of that before? Just look at the close calls I had had—and here I was alive and uninjured!

I joyously slipped it on my finger. I recalled that our civilization sometimes permitted us to believe in good-luck charms, for such a superstition is not nearly so bad as a belief in curses.

I twisted it round and round on my finger, reveling in the sensation of protection its influence ensured me.

I read for perhaps an hour; then, feeling a little drowsy after my eventful evening, I repaired early to bed.

Thinking seems to be more adapted to a reclining position and a darkened room. It was now that I began to attribute a psychological significance to my misadventures—a significance based on suggestion. Arvid Hedon had given me the suggestion; in spite of myself it had leaked into my subconscious mind, and though my conscious mind had not believed, my subconscious had. It was a logical hypothesis, as any psychologist will tell you. I had simply unwittingly led myself into danger through Arvid Hedon's deep-planted suggestion.

Strange, it hadn't occurred to me before.

Then I thought that perhaps I had not yet meditated sufficiently on the suggestion of good luck to implant it on my subconscious mind, and to inhibit the evil suggestion that had been or was already there. This brought a cold sweat upon my brow. I decided to use Coué's formula to pierce the subconscious at the moment of lapsing into sleep.

But what if I shouldn't succeed? It's so much easier to believe in bad luck than in good!

My imagination began to prove annoying. I thought of a dozen things that might happen, the likeliest of these being the possibility of a meteorite dropping through the roof. But, pshaw! Imagination is the stuff that cowards are made of.

I rolled over and concentrated on sleep.

My window rattled. I leaped out of bed. It was only the wind; but what if there should be a cyclone? There are precedents even in New York.

I quickly tore the ring from my finger and laid it on my dresser; and the next day I gave Arvid Hedon the satisfaction of destroying it.

Was I foolish? Possibly I was—but let me finish before you judge too harshly.

I said the Devereux Club was an old-fashioned affair; it still clung to combination chandeliers even in the bedrooms. As I turned back from the dresser I smelled a familiar, pungent odor. I instantly turned on the lights and investigated. How it happened, I don't know.

The gas jet was turned on. ——+——

THE SEALED CASKET

RICHARD F. SEARIGHT

For nearly an hour Wesson Clark had been studying the sealed casket, his shrewd black eyes feasting avidly on its crudely carved metal contours. It lay before him in the pool of light from the desk lamp; the light which illumined his classic, calculating features with a pallid glow, while making a shadowy obscurity of the cavernous, book-lined study. Outside, the high March wind shrilled, and plucked with icy fingers at the cornices and gables of the old house. It gave Clark a pleasing, luxurious sense of security to relax in the overheated gloom of the upstairs study and listen to the rising moan without. Careless, slipshod old Simpkins had gone for the night, after stoking the ancient furnace to capacity; and Clark was alone in the house, as he had wished to be for this occasion.

He smiled slightly and hummed a snatch from the latest Gershwin hit, as his gaze returned to his prize. The casket was small and compact, perhaps sixteen inches long by six or seven wide, and formed of a dull, age-tarnished metal that defied casual identification. The crude, writhing images carved into its surface offered no aid to classification; Clark failed to assign them to any known period of early art.

A gratifying legacy to a connoisseur of antiques was this ancient box. Old Martucci had never suspected, then. There had been times when Clark had wondered—and feared—as he carried on his surreptitious affair with Martucci's youthful wife. Not that it mattered now—the sinister old scientist, with his perverted sense of humor, was dead; and Nonna, though filled as ever with Latin fire, seemed much less fascinating, now that legal barriers were removed. Also, she was growing a bit proprietary, a little too assured. Clark knew the signs. He smiled ironically as he studied the casket. While Martucci lived, Clark had cultivated his friendship and enjoyed the conquest of Nonna at stealthy assignations, employing the greatest caution. But now there was nothing to fear. For the moment, at least, he was surfeited with Nonna's charms; and he felt free to discard her as he saw fit, without the haunting dread of discovery and vengeance by the suspicious old archeologist. Besides, he needed freedom to reel in his new catch; one more alluring than the Italian girl had ever been, and endowed with a fortune that ran into almost mythical figures. His intentions were very serious here.

His smile deepened as he recalled the peculiar clause that formed a part of the codicil to the last testament of Martucci—the clause which was the instrument conveying the casket:

"And I do hereby bequeath to my one-time friend, Wesson Clark, the ancient coffer of Alû-Tor; and urge him only to leave the leaden seal thereon intact, as I have done for thirty years."

Clark chuckled softly. Martucci had been a naïve fool in spite of his dubious reputation in scientific circles, where certain ruthless and unethical practises attributed to him were frowned on heavily. He had kept the seal intact, had he? And no guessing what rare treasures of antiquity might be hidden inside! He had spent his life delving in the earth and incidentally acquiring the meager fortune (now almost dissipated) with which he had retired, while, quite possibly, real wealth waited in the casket. But then, the Italian had been a strange character—one of those rare, incomprehensible creatures who appear to place little importance on the mere possession of money. The aggrandizement of his name in scientific discoveries, the search for the forbidden in hidden occult lore, the cynical study of human nature, had seemed to mean much more to him. Certainly he had never opened the casket, for the splotch of melted lead that sealed it was black with age and bore no signs of having been tampered with.

With all the leisurely indolence of his sybaritic nature, Clark lay back and gloated over his acquisition. He scrutinized more closely the cryptic, wavering symbols, vague and spidery, which had been impressed at some remote time on the leaden seal, no doubt while the metal was still hot. They were quite unfamiliar in that they resembled nothing he could recall having seen before; but there was something indefinably disturbing in their almost sentient lines. They brought to mind some utterly impossible *living* thing. He laughed at the absurdity of the impression.

But whatever they represented, the symbols were very old. Their primitive crudeness suggested an antiquity antedating the Phenician alphabet, or even the Mayan inscriptions. Clark regretted his scanty knowledge of such things; for here, he half suspected, might lie a specimen of the very first primal writing; the groping pictorial attempt to transcribe thought, from which had developed the earliest known written characters. He would preserve the seal intact and have it examined by an authority. Possibly it possessed a definite intrinsic value of its own. Martucci must have known: his knowledge of epigraphy had been profound, and it was whispered that all his developments in that field had not been turned over to science. It was even possible that he had deciphered the inscription, if inscription it were. But in the meantime Clark intended to open the thing.

Certainly he was going to open it. It was quite characteristic of Martucci that, because of some squeamish eccentricity or other, he had refrained from doing so himself. But had he really thought the new owner would use such illogical restraint? Clark chuckled again.

Still, it was odd that the Italian had never spoken of the casket, especially as he must have decided on its disposal some months before. The date of the codicil showed that. No doubt a little surprize for the "one-time friend"—but odd, just the same, for it was an object over which the failing scientist, with his wide knowledge of antiquities, and Clark with his dilettante love for them, might have had many of the discussions the archeologist had so seemed to enjoy.

And that was a strange wording—"one-time." It almost suggested that Martucci had suspected when he dictated the sentence. But that was impossible. The very assignment of such a rare relic was proof in itself of complete trust and good feeling. After all, the import of the words, intended for reading after the writer's death, was plain enough.

Well, there was no need for further delay. He had gloated long enough. His black eyes sparkled greedily as he picked up the heavy brass paper-knife from his desk and dug tentatively at the seal. The leaden smear was surprizingly hard; perhaps it was some strange alloy. He pried harder, finally succeeding in inserting the knife-point between the seal and the age-blackened metal of the box itself. The lead refused to bend further; it clung tenaciously to its age-old moorings. At length Clark left it to rummage about the house for tools. He returned with a hammer, and carefully relocked the study's only door before he sat down.

He used the knife as a wedge, and at the first blow the lead peeled neatly away, disclosing a patch of dully shimmering metal beneath. He had not expected to find that the seal covered a keyhole, and nothing of the sort was visible. Evidently the box was far too ancient for that contrivance.

His heart was pounding. He drew an anticipatory breath, and pried the knifepoint under the lid. A little leverage and it was done. The cover came up. The casket was empty.

Clark was genuinely surprised. Strange that the box should be so tightly sealed when it held no contents to be guarded. This lacked plausibility.

As he stared in puzzled bewilderment at the burnished inner surface, he became aware of a faint, fetid odor creeping into his nostrils. He sniffed, his nose wrinkling in distaste. Slight though it was, the smell suggested vaguely the charnel emanation from some long-closed tomb.

Then came the cold draft.

Through the close air of the study, which was gradually becoming oppressively hot, it breathed against his face in a single icy gust, laden with a sudden augmentation of the nauseating odor of putrescence. Then it was gone, and the heated air had closed about him as if nothing had disturbed it.

Clark started up, then sank back in the chair. He frowned, staring hard at door and windows half hidden in the shadowy gloom beyond the circle of lamplight. He knew them to be locked securely, and an uneasy disquiet stirred in his breast as his probing eyes verified the fact.

His attention was drawn back to the subtle odor of corruption which had gradually grown stronger. It permeated the room now—a dank, mephitic fetor, grotesquely out of place in the quiet study. He rose slowly to his feet, alarm spreading over his features. And as he did so, the icy, noisome chill puffed again upon his face like a breeze from some glacial sepulcher. His head jerked back, and fear dawned in his eyes. Here, in a locked room on the top floor of the old house he had lived in for years, something utterly uncanny, something entirely beyond the realms of sanity, was taking place. Clark started slowly across the study toward the door, then stopped abruptly.

A faint sound had come from the shadows at the far side of the room where the heavy Sarouk rug stopped short a foot from the wall. It was an insidious, barely audible, rustling noise—such a noise as might be made by a great snake writhing along the uncarpeted strip. And it came from *between* him and the door!

Clark had prided himself, in the past, on his cold-blooded imperturbability; but his breath came quickly now, and the wild, unreasoning fear of a trapped animal flooded his mind. Whatever the nature of the Thing in the room with him—could he doubt its presence?—it was intelligently cutting off his escape. It must be watching his every movement with malignant, brooding eyes. A shudder of stark horror convulsed him at the realization.

He stood very still in the center of the study, his mind racing in frenzied, terror-driven circles. A sense of the crowding presence of some bestial, primordial depravity, of overwhelming defilement, surged with paralyzing certainty through his brain. Thoughts of escape were crowded out—the imminence of the danger routed reasoning power. And yet, through the waves of terror that beat through his consciousness, he realized that his life—yes, his very soul—was menaced by an unspeakable cosmic malevolence.

With a tremendous effort he checked the rising, smothering hysteria and succeeded in regaining a partial control of his thoughts. His eyes pierced the gloom ahead and about him. Nothing stirred. What hideously ancient entity had been imprisoned in the casket? He could not guess, nor did he wish to know. But Martucci had known—Martucci, the authority on ancient writings; the delver in hidden lore! Martucci had known everything. He had schemed—oh, so cunningly!—for revenge, and this was the result. If the dead could know, how the old man must be gloating to see his crafty trap closing about his victim!

Now Clark felt cold vibrations beating upon him; vibrations of inhuman, impersonal evil. His nerves crawled and shrank as from a loathsome physical contact. He shifted uneasily, and there came the sound of a stealthy, slithering movement toward him across the rug. He backed away, until his shoulders bumped against the wall behind him. Still the soft noises continued, slowly drawing near. They detoured to one side, then to the other; then they were back in front of him, and much closer. His eyes searched the shadows desperately. Empty, formless, mysterious, they were; but nothing moved that his physical sight could detect. The lurking menace, its presence proclaimed by every taut nerve in his body, was still invisible. If he could trust his eyes, he was alone in the room. But he felt the close proximity of something cold and yet alive; something which was a definite physical presence, manifesting itself to him through pre-human senses, semi-atrophied by eons of disuse. Whatever it was, it was absorbing the suffocating heat of the room, actually lowering the temperature, and at a rapid rate.

Quite suddenly, the utter horror of the impossible, incredible situation broke through the dam of desperate resistance his mind had built up. Something snapped, and he laughed—a high-pitched cachinnation of rising hysteria that echoed wildly from lips drawn back in a grinning frenzy of terror. He cringed, flinging up his arms in an abject surrender to fear. A torrent of gibbering incoherency pushed the terrible laughter from his lips. The dusky room swam about him and he did not know that his knees had buckled and that he had plumped forward on them, his arms rigid before his face to ward off the approaching danger.

Again came the icy breath, rank with primeval filth, terrifying in its nearness. It passed lightly over his face, making him retch with its overpowering fetor. Then he shrieked once in paralyzed despair, as slender, groping tentacles, cold as outer space, caressed his throat and body, their deathly chill striking through his clothing as if he had been naked. A vast, flabby, amorphous coldness enveloped him. Repulsively soft and bulky it was, but as he struggled it gripped him with the resistless strength of chilled steel. He could feel the regularly spaced vibrations of some utterly alien, incomprehensible life— a life so frightful that he shrieked again and again as its purpose became apparent.

Then the murky room whirled about him—he had been whisked up, was staring with starting eyes at the ceiling, through which little flames were eating, while the fetid horror gradually compressed its icy folds.

He was falling down, down, through endless shafts of icy blackness into a bottomless quagmire of primordial slime. A vast roaring filled his ears. Monstrous fantasms leered through the bursts of flame that punctuated the rushing descent. Then all was silence and blackness and oblivion.

Fanned by the high wind, the flames had gutted the old house when firemen arrived. Little remained to aid the coroner in his investigation. Naturally, he discounted heavily the fantastic testimony of certain early arrivals regarding a high-pitched, agonized whistling sound which they claimed had proceeded from the upper part of the building, and the belching clouds of foul-smelling smoke which had

445

found an exit after the upper floors collapsed and the whistling stopped. Simpkins' admission that he had neglected to close the drafts of the furnace cleared up the cause of the fire; but, privately, the coroner was exceedingly puzzled by certain peculiarities that the post-mortem disclosed in the charred and blackened corpse, identified by a dentist as Wesson Clark's. It was surely a matter of wonder that virtually every bone in this body had been broken, as if in the embrace of some gigantic snake of the constrictor species; and it was an insoluble mystery how the veins and organs had been *drained of every drop of blood!* ───╫───

The Seeds from Outside

Edmond Hamilton

Standifer found the seeds the morning after the meteor fell on the hill above his cottage. On that night he had been sitting in the scented darkness of his little garden when he had glimpsed the vertical flash of light and heard the whiz and crash of that falling visitor from outer space. And all that night he had lain awake, eager for morning and the chance to find and examine the meteor.

Standifer knew little of meteors, for he was not a scientist. He was a painter whose canvases hung in many impressive halls in great cities, and were appropriately admired and denounced and gabbled about by those who liked such things. Standifer had grown weary of such people and of their cities, and had come to this lonely little cottage in the hills to paint and dream.

For it was not cities or people that Standifer wished to paint, but the green growing life of earth that he loved so deeply. There was no growing thing in wood or field that he did not know. The slim white sycamores that whispered together along the streams, and the sturdy little sumacs that were like small, jovial plant-gnomes, and the innocent wild roses that bloomed and swiftly died in their shady cover — he had toiled to transfix and preserve their subtle beauty for ever in his oils and colors and cloths.

The spring had murmured by in a drifting dream as Standifer had lived and worked alone. And now suddenly into the hushed quiet of his green, blossoming world had rudely crashed this visitant from distant realms. It strangely stirred Standifer's imagination, so that through the night he lay wondering, and gazing up through his casement at the white stars from which the meteor had come.

It was hardly dawn, and a chill and drenching dew silvered the grass and bent the poplar leaves, when Standifer excitedly climbed the hill in search of the meteor. The thing was not hard to find. It had smashed savagely into the spring-green woods, and had torn a great raw gouge out of the earth as it had crashed and shattered.

For the meteor had shattered into chunks of jagged, dark metal that lay all about that new, gaping hole. Those ragged lumps were still faintly warm to the touch, and Standifer went from one to another, turning them over and examining them with marveling curiosity. It was when he was about to leave the place, that he glimpsed amid this meteoric debris the little square tan case.

It lay half imbedded still in one of the jagged metal chunks. The case was no more than two inches square, and was made of some kind of stiff tan fiber that was very tough and apparently impervious to heat. It was quite evident that the case had been inside the heart of the shattered meteor, and that it was the product of intelligence.

Standifer was vastly excited. He dug the tiny case out of the meteoric fragment, and then tried to tear it open. But neither his fingers nor sharp stones could make any impression on the tough fiber. So he hurried back down to his cottage with the case clutched in his hand, his head suddenly filled with ideas of messages sent from other worlds or stars.

But at the cottage, he was amazed to find that neither steel knives nor drills nor chisels could make the slightest impression upon this astounding material. It seemed to the eye to be just stiff tan fiber, yet he knew that it was a far different kind of material, as refractory as diamond and as flexibly tough as steel.

It was several hours before he thought of pouring water upon the enigmatic little container. When he did so, the fiber-like stuff instantly softened. It was evident that the material had been designed to withstand the tremendous heat and shock of alighting on another world, but to soften up and open when it fell upon a moist, warm world.

Standifer carefully cut open the softened case. Then he stared, puzzled, at its contents, a frown upon his sensitive face. There was nothing inside the case but two withered-looking brown seeds, each of them about an inch long.

He was disappointed, at first. He had expected writing of some kind, perhaps even a tiny model or machine. But after a while his interest rose again, for it occurred to him that these could be no ordinary seeds which the people of some far planet had tried to sow broadcast upon other worlds.

So he planted the two seeds in a carefully weeded corner of his

447

flower garden, about ten feet apart. And in the days that followed, he scrupulously watered and watched them, and waited eagerly to see what kind of strange plants might spring from them.

His interest was so great, indeed, that he forgot all about his unfinished canvases, the work that had brought him to the seclusion of these quiet hills. Yet he did not tell anyone of his strange find, for he felt that if he did, excited scientists would come and take the seeds away to study and dissect, and he did not want that.

In two weeks he was vastly excited to see the first little shoots of dark green come up through the soil at the places where he had planted the two seeds. They were like stiff little green rods and they did not look very unusual to Standifer. Yet he continued to water them carefully, and to wait tensely for their development.

The two shoots came up fast, after that. Within a month they had become green pillars almost six feet tall, each of them covered with a tight-wrapped sheath of green sepals. They were a little thicker at the middle than at the top or bottom, and one of them was a little slenderer than the other, and its color a lighter green. Altogether, they looked like no plants ever before seen on earth.

Standifer saw that the sheathing sepals were now beginning to unfold, to curl back from the tops of the plants. He waited almost breathlessly for their further development, and every night before he retired he looked last at the plants, and every morning when he awoke they were his first thought.

Then early one June morning he found that the sepals had curled back enough from the tips to let him see the tops of the true plants inside. And he stood for many minutes there, staring in strange wonder at that which the unfolding of the sepals was beginning to reveal.

For where they had curled back at the tips, they disclosed what looked strangely like the tops of two human heads. It was as though two people were enclosed in those sheathing sepals, two people the hair of whose heads was becoming visible as masses of fine green threads, more animal than plant in appearance.

One looked very much like the top of a girl's head, a mass of fluffy, light-green hair only the upper part of which was visible. The other head was of shorter, coarser and darker green hair, as though it was that of a man.

Standifer went through that day in a stupefied daze. He was almost tempted to unfold the sepals further by force, so intense was his curiosity, but he restrained himself and waited. And the next few days brought him further confirmation of his astounding suspicion.

The sepals of both plants had by then unfolded almost completely. And inside one was a green man-plant—and in the other a girl! Their bodies were strangely human in shape, living, breathing bodies of weird, soft, green plant-flesh, with tendril-like arms and tendril limbs too that were still rooted and hidden down in the calyxes. Their heads and faces were very human indeed, with green-pupiled eyes through which they could see.

Standifer stared and stared at the plant girl, for she was beautiful beyond the artist's dreams, her slim green body rising proudly straight from the cup of her calyx. Her shining, green-pupiled eyes saw him as he stood by her, and she raised a tendril-like arm and softly touched him. And her tendrils stirred with a soft rustling that was like a voice speaking to him.

Then Standifer heard a deeper, angry rustling behind him, and turned. It was the man-plant, his big tendril arms reaching furiously to grasp the artist, jealousy and rage in his eyes. Hastily the painter stepped away from him.

In the days that followed, Standifer was like one living in a dream. For he had fallen in love with the shining slim plant girl, and he spent almost all his waking hours sitting in his garden looking into her eyes, listening to the strange rustling that was her speech.

It seemed to his artist's soul that the beauty of no animal-descended earth woman could match the slender grace of this plant girl. He would stand beside her and wish passionately that he could understand her rustling whisper, as her tendrils softly touched and caressed him.

The man-plant hated him, he knew, and would try to strike at him. And the man hated the girl too, in time. He would reach raging tendrils out toward her to clutch her, but was too far separated from her ever to reach her.

Standifer saw that these two strange creatures were still developing, and that their feet would soon come free of their roots. He knew that these were beings of a kind of life utterly unlike anything terrestrial, that they began their life-cycle as seeds and rooted plants, and that they developed then into free and moving plant-people such as were unknown on this world.

He knew too that on whatever far world was their home, creatures like these must have reached a great degree of civilization and science, to send out broadcast into space the seeds that would sow their race upon other planets. But of their distant origin he thought little, as he waited impatiently for the day when his shining plant-girl would be free of her roots.

He felt that that day was very near, and he did not like to leave the garden even for a minute, now. But on one morning Standifer had to leave, to go to the village for necessary supplies; since for two days there had been no food in the cottage and he felt himself grow-ing weak with hunger.

It hurt him to part from the plant girl even for those few hours, and he stood for minutes caressing her fluffy green hair and listen-ing to her happy rustling before he took himself off.

When he returned, he heard as soon as he entered his garden a sound that chilled the blood in his veins. It was the plant girl's voice —a mere agonized whisper that spoke dreadful things. He rushed wildly into the garden and stood a moment aghast at what he saw.

The final development had taken place in his absence. Both crea-tures had come free of their roots—and the man-plant had in his jealousy and hate broken and torn the shining green body of the girl. She lay, her tendrils stirring feebly, while the other looked down at her in satisfied hate.

Standifer madly seized a scythe and ran across the garden. In two terrific strokes, he cut down the man-plant into a dead thing oozing dark green blood. Then he dropped the weapon and wildly stooped over his dying plant girl.

She looked up at him through pain-filled, wide eyes as her life oozed away. A green tendril arm lifted slowly to touch his face, and he heard a last rustling whisper from this creature whom he had loved and who had loved him across the vast gulf of world-differing species. Then he knew that she was dead.

That was long ago, and the garden by the little cottage is weed-grown now and holds no memory of those two strange creatures from the great outside who grew and lived and died there. Standifer does not dwell there any more, but lives far away in the burning, barren Arizona desert. For never, since then, can he bear the sight of green growing things. —+—

THE SIXTH GARGOYLE

DAVID EYNON

The tiny town of Veere sits snugly on the coast of Zeeland, huddled against the dunes which protect it from the harsh Nordzee winds. On the land side thick, serrated walls hide all but its rooftops and the tower of the Raddhuis which leans, ever so little, to the North, as if it had been bucking the gales for centuries.

A sea wall edging the harbor stands staunchly against the waves which come roaring in and, when halted by the huge gray stones, throw furious clouds of spray against the tiny houses that peep out over the quay. Stubby fishing smacks bob anxiously up and down and cluster together with squeals and groans, their nets blowing frantically from their masts.

The cathedral roosts on the hill, casting a benevolent eye over the village. It soars into the gray sky and sings minor liturgies to itself as the wind flies through its spires. Flying buttresses, crumbling with age, hang at its sides like town lace. In the cemetery sheltered under the south side of the cathedral are five graves, new, without headstones. Four of the graves are filled and show fresh mounds of earth. The fifth grave is waiting, open and expectant, for its occupant.

The fifth would be filled by morning, of that much Inspector Ter Horst was certain. Who it would be he could not say for sure, but the choice fell between two men—the murderer of the preceding four villagers, or the fifth of the murderer's victims. When the last gray light of evening dwindled and darkness and the north sea wind took possession of the village streets the choice would be made.

"It was a matter of practicality," said the gray haired Burgomeister, "to have five graves dug instead of only four." The old man leaned back in his carved chair and pulled thoughtfully at his chin. The smoke from the bowl of his churchwarden pipe trailed upwards towards the ceiling and lost itself among the blackened beams of the ancient city hall. Jonkheer van Berendonk looked as quaint—and as timeworn—as a Rembrandt study. His silver chain of office, worn by ten generations of Burgomeisters of Veere, shone softly against the background of his black velvet cloak. Inspector Ter Horst waited patiently until the old man spoke again.

"It is true," the Burgomeister went on, "that we have only four dead at present. Still, if your theory is correct, by morning we will have five. It is cheaper, then, that all the graves be dug at once, and so did I arrange it."

"Yes," said Ter Horst, "Mynheer is right. By morning we will undoubtedly need another grave. What would I not give to know who it is that will lie in it!" Ter Horst spoke vehemently, irritated with his own failure to catch the murderer and apprehensive about the possibilities of a fifth crime. An idea crossed his mind and he spoke again to the Burgomeister.

"Pardon, Mynheer," he said, "but what if both the murderer and the victim both die this night? Then there will not be enough graves to go around."

"No," the Burgomeister admitted, "but in that case, the murderer would have to be buried elsewhere than the churchyard—in unhallowed ground—so it was still cheaper to arrange the matter of the graves as I have." The old man, pleased with his logic, smiled as he bent over to light the two candles on his desk. The clock in the city hall tower struck five and both men listened intently until the last sonorous note died out.

"Then, if the schedule is adhered to," said the Burgomeister refilling his pipe, "the architect should be murdered next?"

Inspector Ter Horst nodded. The schedule, he thought, would not be kept. It could not be kept. After all, wasn't he going to be at the architect's cottage, armed, on guard? And besides, he thought, it was impossible that any man could hope to complete a series of five murders, each a week apart, each but the first fully expected by the police.

Four killings perhaps. Certainly the killer had had luck so far. But five murders, never. This time the criminal would fail and, in failing, become the occupant of the fifth grave. Inspector Ter Horst turned to the Burgomeister and, more to clear his own thoughts than to be enlightening, reviewed the details of the case.

"It is unthinkable," he said, "that this madman could strike once again.

"Imagine, Mynheer, even the shrewdest madman—for we certainly deal with a madman—being able to kill five persons in accordance with a set plan and still escape capture. Especially when his identity is known."

The Burgomeister raised his eyebrows. "You know who the man is?" he asked.

"In a sense, we do," said Ter Horst. "His name, of course, not. But we know he is mad—and that is something. Then, we know he is of a family that has been here since the cathedral was built. He is agile, enough so to baptize each of the succeeding stone figures with blood after he has destroyed their human counterparts. He is not, therefore, an old man."

The Burgomeister's wrinkled face arranged itself into a slight smile. He was amused at the way this policeman built up theories on nothing—houses of cards, he thought, that stood but a short time in the wind of reality.

Ter Horst continued talking, not noticing the old man's amusement. "A man of some education, I should say. Enough, at least to have made use of the records in the cathedral crypt. He must have traced records far enough to determine that each of his victims is a direct descendant of someone who helped construct the church. Our man knows Latin, at least."

The Inspector paused to light his cigar, which had gone out as he waved it about to illustrate his points. The Burgomeister got up for a moment to secure a shutter that had blown loose and was banging against the window frame.

"But this schedule," the Burgomeister asked, "on what is it based? How do you ascertain that the architect is next in his thoughts?"

"Ah," the Inspector chuckled. "A lucky accident, that. Pure chance that we noticed a spot of blood on the forehead of the first gargoyle. Just in searching the cathedral for a possible fugitive did we see it. Then, of course, certain facts fell into place and forced a conclusion.

"Imagine, six gargoyles straddling a flying buttress. Six little stone figures climbing toward the spires of the church. An artist, an engineer, a stonemason, a bricklayer and an architect."

The Inspector stopped and lighted a fresh cigar with one of the candles. He spoke between puffs.

"One by one each is murdered."

"Except the architect," the Burgomeister inserted.

"Except the architect," Ter Horst nodded. "But each of the others has been murdered, and in the order of his position on the buttress. Each man a direct descendant of, and in the same profession as, his ancestor who is represented in stone by the gargoyles.

"Imagine the uniqueness of the motive behind such a crime—if madness can be called a motive."

The Burgomeister leaned forward in his chair. "How," he asked, "do you know that the sixth gargoyle is the criminal? Why not, for instance, the fifth gargoyle?" With this he smiled laconically at the short, fat Inspector.

Ter Horst was not impressed by the idea. He deprecated it with a wave of his hand and, noticing that his cigar was out again, leaned towards the candles.

"It is," he said between puffs, "the sixth gargoyle because he is the only one who cannot be located. The first five are easily traceable. From the church records we know exactly who the first five men must be. And the subsequent deaths of the first five men must be. And the subsequent deaths of the first four hold exactly with our findings. Of the sixth gargoyle there is not a trace of information."

The Burgomeister settled back in his chair and mused to himself for several minutes. The crackling of the fire was almost drowned out by the wind's moan as it writhed around the tower of the Raddhuis. The Burgomeister looked up sharply at Ter Horst.

"This sixth stone figure," he asked, "what does it represent? What sort of figure is it?"

Ter Horst gently stamped out his cigar butt on the tiles of the hearth. "The sixth gargoyle," he said quietly, "is the figure of a man committing suicide."

"So," said the Burgomeister. His tone showed a heightened interest. "Then we *are* perhaps dealing with a madman." The old man's huge dog lumbered up from the hearth. He stretched himself laboriously and then stalked over to be petted. The old man rubbed the dog's neck gently and the animal groaned in appreciation.

"And just what do you do now?" the Burgomeister asked. "Is it necessary to wait until the architect is murdered to discover this madman's identity? Or do you wait until he kills himself, as he must, if your theory is correct."

"Two things I plan," Ter Horst said earnestly. "First, in the crypt below the cathedral, my men are pouring over the records to find any clue that remains which will point to our criminal."

"And if he has removed such records," smiled the Burgomeister, "when he made his own investigation?"

"Then," said Ter Horst, "there is a grave on the left side of the church, in unhallowed ground. Perhaps it may hold a clue, since it is, in all probability, the resting place of our original suicide."

"You would open the grave?" asked the Burgomeister. "There won't be much after four centuries."

"No," said Ter Horst, "but it is worth trying. If Mynheer would give his permission for such an act?"

The Burgomeister rubbed his leonine head, fingering the silver chain with his other hand. "I don't know," he said slowly. "It is an unusual request—and rather futile to search in any case, I fear. I would have to think it over. Besides, it is time for dinner," he said, noticing that his dog was nervously scratching at the door. "I will let you know in the morning."

"Of course, Mynheer," Ter Horst said, rising as the old man left the room and moved slowly down the stairs.

Ter Horst left the city hall and made his way over the slippery cobblestones to the architect's small cottage, just inside the city gates. The Inspector knocked and was admitted by the tall, thin architect who knew the stubby policeman from the past weeks of investigation.

The host seated Ter Horst before the fire and took his coat. In a few minutes the policeman was nursing a glass of fiery Dutch "Geneva" and posting the architect on the latest developments of the case.

"As soon as we have the permission of the old Burgomeister," said Ter Horst, "we will open that grave. The Burgomeister is rather old-fashioned, you understand. He feels that it should be permitted only as a last resort, and we have to humor him."

"It is easy for old Berendonk to be conservative," the architect said with a smile, "where my life is concerned. Still, I don't think you would gain much in any case." He got up and went to a closet in the corner of the room. Opening the door, he drew out a raincoat and turned to Ter Horst.

"Since it is the night appointed for my demise," he said, "I feel guilty about wasting it in inactivity. Perhaps if we go to the cathedral I, as an architect, can help you in locating some information."

"If you're not nervous about going out," said Ter Horst.

"I will be less nervous if I am busy," said the architect.

On the slippery cobblestone road up the hill to the cathedral Ter Horst explained the circumstances of the crimes. He spoke loudly to be heard above the wind. Occasionally he had to repeat as he skipped along to keep up with the lanky architect.

"They were bludgeoned," he shouted as they reached the cathedral steps.

"What?"

"Bludgeoned, heads bashed in," Ter Horst said. They had stepped within the doors by now and his voice soared up into the roof of the darkened church. A policeman, on guard in the shadows, flashed his light on them. Seeing Ter Horst, he saluted.

"We're going down to the crypts," Ter Horst said.

The officer nodded and stepped back into the shadows.

As the two men descended the stone steps to the underground section of the church their feet rang on the stairs. At the first doorway they were met by a young lieutenant.

"Ah, it's you, sir," he said, "I think we've got something."

Ter Horst introduced the architect. The young policeman showed obvious admiration for the man's nerve. "I can imagine you can make more sense from these documents than I can," the lieutenant said, handing the papers to the architect.

The architect took the sheaf of yellowed parchments and leafed through them slowly. At intervals he bent closer to scrutinize a poorly written phrase. Occasionally he muttered to himself. At the last page he chuckled and looked up at Ter Horst.

"You were indeed right, Inspector," the architect said. "Our madman has a unique motive indeed. It would appear that he, just as his victims, has followed the calling of his family—though how long this madness has lain dormant in his line no one knows."

"What do you find?" Ter Horst asked anxiously.

"This," said the architect, rustling the sheaf of parchment, "is the record of an unfortunate incident. It occurred during the construction of the cathedral, as you guessed.

"It seems that one of the casters—the men who made and installed the bells—went mad. Perhaps from the constant vibrations. In any case he jumped from the tower one day. Not necessarily a suicide, you understand—it could have been an accident. However the priest was doubtful. He called in the witnesses—an artist, an engineer, a stonemason, a bricklayer and an architect. On the basis of their testimony he decided that the man was a suicide. Of course, he could not then be buried in holy ground."

Ter Horst thought for a minute. "You mean, our murderer now takes revenge for an ancestor who was buried without grace? Five murders for a madman of the sixteenth century?"

"So it would appear," said the architect.

And even as he handed the parchments back to the lieutenant a stone, dropped from the ceiling high above, fell directly on his head and crushed his skull. The lieutenant had taken the sheaf of papers from a dead hand and before he realized what had occurred the architect was slumped on the floor with a widening pool of blood around his head.

The two policemen instinctively jumped back and then, seeing that the architect was beyond aid, rushed up the long stairway to the floor level.

The ground floor of the church was empty. No one could have passed out the door. Ter Horst ordered it locked and then beckoned the lieutenant and his men to follow him up the stairway into the spire.

The exposed steps were mouldy with age and slippery with rain. The wind's strength made going difficult. As they approached the level where the still intact buttresses leaned against the church wall, Ter Horst stopped.

Across the stairway was a rod about six feet long. At one end it had a knob. On the other was a bunch of feathers. The feathers were stiff and dark with dried blood.

"So," thought Ter Horst, "we are not dealing with such an agile man after all. He has baptized the gargoyles with a tipstaff's rod."

He handed the rod to an officer at his side and walked over to the edge where he could see the six figures on the buttress. The moon went behind the clouds at intervals. As he leaned over the edge it appeared again. In the pale light he looked down the row of figures to the sixth gargoyle. Standing on the buttress was a huge dark figure that looked like an oversized bat with its wings flung out.

As the moonlight came to full strength Ter Horst could see the white haired old Burgomeister clearly. His silver chain of office hung around his neck, over the black velvet robe. The Burgomeister caught sight of Ter Horst and laughed loudly. His laugh got more and more intense until it shook his whole body. Ter Horst was about to call out when the Burgomeister lost his footing on the slippery stonework and tottered.

He fell a few feet and then his body was snapped up sharply. Ter Horst saw that his chain of office had caught around the stone figure of the sixth gargoyle. As the moon went behind the clouds once more Ter Horst could see the figure of the Burgomeister swinging back and forth in the wind, his cloak flapping out behind him like the wings of a bat. ⸙

Soul-Catcher

Robert S. Carr

Around the hospital, folks said that John Dorsey was a nice old man—kind of puttery, but still a mighty good all-round M. D. He was small and mild and chubby and had soft white hair—the sort of kindly old gentleman you see telling stories to the kiddies in the park.

Old John had his ways, too; peculiar, maybe, but harmless. He was unobtrusive and fitted well into the general scheme of things around the hospital; unobtrusive, that is, except when the emergency cases came in. Old John was an emergency specialist. The ambulance boys would bring 'em in, screaming, moaning, or sometimes huddled up in a silent, blood-stained heap under the stretcher coverings and rush them into Old John's "emergency parlors," as one of the young college interns used to term it.

The ambulance boys would sometimes call me in from the orderly room to help them with some poor devil who had gotten more than his share of hard luck at a grade crossing smash. At these times I noticed that Old John wasn't the same as he generally appeared to be. He would flash into action as quickly as any first aid man in the front line trenches ever did. Old John had his own operating room, and as he didn't have much else to do, he always kept things in readiness for the emergency cases. The water in the sterilizing basin was always gently simmering over the sharp, wicked-looking things with which he did his wonder-work; the bandages, the antiseptics and the sponges were always laid out in readiness on a long table which he kept close at his side while operating.

Here is where Old John's peculiarity cropped out—he would not use an assistant or have another person in the room. The moment he heard the ambulance siren—and he always heard it before any of the rest of us did—he would hurry to his room, and by the time we had the howling unfortunate stripped and laid out and under the ether, Old John would know what the trouble was and be ready and waiting to begin.

"Clear out of here," he'd say good-naturedly, "but stay close around outside the door where I can call you if I need you."

Only, he never seemed to need any help.

But after all, there wasn't so much use for an assistant in the kind of emergencies we handled. The very messy cases often died in the ambulance boys' arms, much to their disgust, and the poison cases were taken care of with a stomach pump on the way to the hospital. The majority of Old John's patients required only to have a shut-off jammed on a squirting artery or a splintered bone yanked out of some vital organ in a hurry.

"Seems like with just me and the patient in there by ourselves, with no fool girl to get pale and shiver and act heroic, and everything right where I can reach it without having to ask for it or fall over somebody, I can do my best for a patient in the least time—and that's what counts." So spake Old John and no one disagreed.

One time McCarty said something kind of queer about Old John. McCarty's the slim young doctor who wears the thick horn-rimmed glasses and smokes so many cigarettes. It was when some Italian window-washer did an eleven-story nose-dive to the pavement and smashed himself all up. He didn't look very bad, though, so the ambulance boys rushed him in to Old John. Anybody with any sense at all would have known the wop would cash in inside of five minutes, but as an M. D.'s business seems to be taking nothing for granted, Old John ran everybody out of the room as usual and went to work. Pretty soon—according to McCarty—Old John came to the door shaking his head kind of sorrowful-like and said "too late, boys," the way he always does.

"Humph!" said McCarty, with a queer sideways look through those big glasses of his, "it does seem as if it took Dorsey a long time to find out that man was dead. And listen, Jack"—he looked up and down the hall before he spoke—"Old John didn't put his rubber gloves on all the while he was in there! Must not have even examined the man!"

Not being as smart as some, I didn't see anything special about that to bowl anybody over, but I kept still. I wasn't there when it happened, being busy at the time on the fifth floor sitting on the chest of some looney fever-case who thought he needed an airing out on the fire escape. After the little blond nurse in Ward 10 gave him a shot in the arm and got him quiet, she said to me, "Gee, but you're strong," and I kind of grinned and—

But as I was saying, Old John sure did do some wonderful things there by himself in that room. One time he took a bullet out of a fellow's head—I forget the long names the M. D.'s called the operation—but it made the other doctors sit up and take notice. Of course, a lot of the emergency cases died—but that's why they're emergency cases—because they're dying. None of the deaths were Old John's fault.

Well, things went on as usual for a while; the interns and me bribing the drug room man to give us our little drinks of prescription whisky; the nurses smoking their cigarettes up in the roof-garden; and the ambulance boys charging the hospital double for every tire they bought.

One day along in the spring, when the auto-wreck cases began to pile in, Old John asked me to go down to the supply room and get him a new pair of surgeon's gloves. I said I would, and while I was down there rummaging around, I heard the ambulance siren, but didn't think anything about it. I came back upstairs with the gloves and went to Old John's room. The door was closed and nobody was around. I suppose if I'd stopped to think I would have guessed that Old John had an emergency case in there, but I didn't—I went right on in. Now working around a hospital just naturally gets you to be mighty light-footed, and with the noiseless door and soft floor-pad, I guess I must not have made a sound. Old John had his back turned and didn't hear me come in. For a moment I looked, then sank back against the wall and stared while my eyes popped out and I began to sweat.

There was one of the usual busted-up fellows, all bloody and out-of-joint, lying on the operating table under the strong light. Over him bent Old John, holding in his hands a light rectangular frame about six feet long and two feet wide. Inside the frame was stretched the queerest, webbiest fine net-work I ever saw. The netting wasn't wire and it wasn't thread—I don't know what it was. A big, black wire ran all the way around this frame, under the handle by which Old John was holding it and into a round glass jar. The whole thing kind of reminded me of an old-fashioned indoor radio aerial. As I stood and looked I could see that the patient was pretty far gone, but that didn't seem to worry Old John. He stood very quiet, very tense—and waited. Soon the figure on the operating table quivered a little, then sighed and went limp all over, the way they do.

Right then is when the hair started to rise up on the back of my neck, for just a second after that fellow had passed out, the thin, delicate netting in the big frame began to flutter as if something had got tangled up in it—something you couldn't see. Then the glass jar that was hooked up with the big black wire began to fill up just as if someone was blowing cigarette smoke into it, only this stuff was thicker and gray-colored—not bluish like cigarette smoke. Pretty soon the net quit quivering and the jar was full of this smoky stuff. Old John laid down the frame on the dead man, unhooked the wire and held the jar up to the light.

"Got him, all right!" he chuckled to himself.

I guess I must have moaned or made some kind of a noise about then, for Old John wheeled quick as a cat, and when he saw me his eyes blazed up like a bad brain-fever case's. I don't know how long we stood like a couple of stone statues staring at each other—all I know is that I felt numb and sick and paralyzed all over, the same as I did the day I got hold of the wrong bottle down in the drug room.

Then little by little the glare died out of his eyes, till at last he set the jar down and smiled.

"Here's your rubber gloves," I said kind of shakily, and turned to go.

"Wait a minute," he said in his kindly soft voice, just as if nothing had happened.

I stopped. The gray vapor in the jar seemed to be restless, moving. . . .

"You saw everything?" he asked.

I nodded.

He smiled the same sad way he does when he says, "Too late, boys."

"Sit down," he said, "I want to talk to you."

I sat down.

"I get all the bad cases in here," he began, "and I do all I can for them. I work mighty hard to keep them from dying and I often do it, don't I?"

Again I nodded.

"And listen," he said, leaning toward me, "if I can't save their bodies I—*save their souls!*"

Seeing the look on my face, he arose and led me to a tall black cabinet in one corner of the room. Lifting out a dummy shelf of books, he pointed with pride at row after row of glass jars, all filled with a thick, grayish vapor.

The instant he uncovered those things I nearly keeled over. It's a

460

hard thing to explain, but I'll try to do it. Before I got this job, I worked behind the scenes in a big theater. Sometimes, when the stage was dark, I'd slip out to fix a set for the next scene, and from the very first I noticed a queer sensation caused by suddenly stepping into the gaze of so many eyes. I could *feel* the eyes of the audience out there in the dark even though I couldn't see them. And so it was with the jars in Old John's cabinet—*I* immediately felt that I was the target for a great many eyes. There was nothing I could see except those little jars full of something gaseous and gray, but—

Old John closed the cabinet and it was the same as stepping off the dark stage. The feeling of eyes was gone.

"I may need an assistant some time," he began again, "and since my secret had to be found out, I'm glad it was you and not one of those know-it-all young interns. I can depend on you to keep still about this, can't I?"

There was nothing for me to do but say yes. Suddenly the ambulance siren screamed in the distance, then screamed again, coming closer.

"Another case," he breathed. "Here—get behind this screen until after they have gone."

I hid, and in a few moments the ambulance boys had brought in another limp, sprawling bundle and turned it over to Old John. As they carried the other one out I heard him say his customary "too late, boys" and add something about "this one's going to take a lot of time." After he had locked the door I came out of hiding.

He motioned me to be still, so I stood quietly and watched him.

The case on the operating table was a big, beefy, middle-aged man, his throat and shoulders horribly crushed and bloody. I marveled at Old John's magic rubber-gloved fingers as they twinkled over the mangled area. He bent forward, quivering in his intensity of purpose, snatching up or flinging down an instrument like lightning; probing here; or with a fairylike lightness of touch tying up a severed artery. Truly Old John needed no assistant. Presently, after a most painstaking final examination, he stood back and sighed, shaking his head sorrowfully. I saw his lips silently form the words, "Too late, boys." Then suddenly another light came into his eyes, a different expression gripped his face. The transformation somehow reminded me of a story I had read about a Collie dog that tenderly guarded a flock of sheep by day, only to slip out and murder them by night.

Old John took the big net from its place of concealment. He motioned for me to help him, and together we lifted the dying man and laid him on a long pair of hospital scales. As Old John felt his pulse, he pointed at the register hand, which stood at 173 pounds and

6 ounces. He made ready his soul-trapping apparatus and held the net close over the body. In a moment that indescribable yet definite change took place which marks the death of an unconscious person. Old John directed my eyes to the scale hand and I watched carefully. The hand held its mark steadily; then, precisely as the delicate web before me began to flutter, *the hand quickly dropped back four ounces!*

I sat dumbly as Old John completed the capture of the soul and stowed the jar away with the others. I had heard—had even read in the Sunday supplements—that the weight of a body decreases sharply at death, but never had I expected to have it proved to me in such an awful manner. I became dimly conscious that Old John was speaking.

"You see, there *is* something definite which escapes from the body at death. That something I have in my jars, ha, ha! But the weight of the something is quickly replaced by air, exactly on the same principal as when you submerge an uncorked bottle in water—the air bubbles out and the water rushes in. . . . Look at the hand."

I looked, and saw that the body had regained the lost four ounces, the four ounces of gray nebulosity now imprisoned in the glass jar. . . .

Later, as I fled unsteadily down the corridor, I heard Old John announcing sadly that it was "too late, boys."

Next day I came upon Old John stretched on a couch in his room, oblivious of everything. I shook him gently, but as he did not wake, I left him to sleep on.

An hour afterward he called me in, shut the door, and went to some lengths explaining that he had been "astralizing" himself. The whole story didn't sound very plausible to me, this thing of leaving your body for a jaunt in spirit form. Still, I told myself, if anyone should know about that kind of things, it would be Old John.

To a rough, practical mind like my own, this astralizing process would seem more realistic and believable if a hypodermic syringe and a bottle of morphine went with it. But even so—there's nothing left on earth that's ungodly and spooky enough to surprise me any more. . . .

When they told me Old John was dead I was almost afraid to go and look at him, but I went.

He hadn't been dead very long—hadn't been disturbed. He was stretched out on his old couch the same as if he were astralizing himself. But what made my knees start to give in like soft rubber was the sight of the janitor before the tall black cabinet, sweeping up the fragments of a great many small glass jars.

"Wha—what happened there?" I asked one of the nurses weakly.

"Why, when the elevator motor tore loose up in the attic it shook the whole building. Broke several vases in my ward and it must have jarred those glasses out of that rickety old cabinet. What on earth Old John was saving them for beats me."

I had been away from the hospital all day. The more I looked at those broken jars the queerer I felt. Pretty soon I stepped over to see Old John. The M. D.'s had his face covered up and were arguing loudly about apoplexy. I pulled the cloth down and looked at him.

Ugh! I'll never forget it! It was awful. He looked as if—oh, I can't half describe it!—looked as if he had been torn to pieces from the inside. Just as a light sack would break if there were a dozen big cats all trying to get out in different directions. Oh, his body was all together, it wasn't mangled, but—well, you could see that was the way he had died.

It took me quite a while to figure it out, but when I had, believe me, I didn't feel any better. I guess it must have happened like this:

Old John had astralized himself, and his body was lying there without any astral, or soul, or spirit, or whatever you want to call it. This must leave a sort of empty space, as near as I can understand. Then when all those jars full of captured souls, or astrals, were broken and released those things inside, then *they*—I guess you'd say "they"—saw Old John's body lying there empty—and they must have had it in for him keeping them canned up like that— maybe they all saw it was a chance to get a body and live again. . . . They must have all crowded inside and taken possession of his body at once. . . . Wonder what his astral did?

Maybe they fought. . . .

Anyhow, they couldn't all occupy one body, and so. . . .

This thought is driving me crazy.

The ambulance boys say I'm getting jumpy.

This hospital gives me the creeps.

Guess I'll see if I can't get another job. —✦—

THE STATUE

JAMES CAUSEY

Jerome Winters pursed his lips.

"Young man," he said coldly, "a bargain is a bargain."

"But can't you give me just a little more time!" The young man's eyes were dark and pleading against the pallor of his face. "Another two months. Another month! I could surely find some way—"

His voice trailed off. Winters was shaking his head from side to side, staring at him with his frosty blue eyes.

"Three months you were given," he said curtly. "Seventy-five dollars. You've had time enough, my good man. Plenty of time. Seventy-five dollars, with interest. And—you don't have it, do you?" His voice was faintly mocking.

The young sculptor buried his face in his hands. "No," he said hoarsely. "I haven't. But I could surely scrape up the money some way—if only—"

Winters looked queerly at him. He stood up. He was a short, slight man, small and withered as an old persimmon, his blue eyes wearing a perpetually frosty gaze.

In the little town of Hammondville, Winters was by far the wealthiest—as well as the most hated. His loans bordered upon usury—and those who could not pay were given no mercy. He had caused more than one suicide, and a very appreciable amount of misery and suffering. A wizened, dried-up little spider he was, who spun his web carefully, showing not the slightest pity to those unfortunate enough to fall into it.

Just now, contrary to his usual satisfaction when foreclosing a mortgage, he felt curiously frustrated. Perhaps—he had not made enough profit this time.

"Young man," his voice was thin and sharp, "three months ago you came to me with a desperate plea for money—on my terms. As security, I was given a small bit of sculpture, unfinished at that." His voice hardened. "It is not my usual policy to be so generous—"

"Generous!" The young sculptor's face twisted. His voice was bitter. "You speak of generosity! The Dawn Child—my statue. Seventy-five dollars! Finished, I could very easily sell that statue for—"

"For some considerable sum, I suppose?" Winters' words dripped

464

cold. "Remember. The statue is incomplete. I may have a hard time disposing of it, for that very reason."

He frowned petulantly.

The young man stared at Winters as if seeing him for the first time. Slowly Winters flushed, and his eyes fell under that penetrating gaze.

"So," De Roults said softly. "I might have known."

He straightened, drew a deep breath, and looked at Winters again. "It is absolutely useless to ask for more time, I see."

"Absolutely," Winters said, some of his poise returning to him.

"Then—" Two spots of color appeared in the young man's cheeks. "Then, sir, may I see the statue? May I? Just once, since it is for the last time."

There was no harm in letting him see it. Winters shrugged. "Why not?"

He made his way toward the back of the study, where he opened the door to a closet. De Roults followed him slowly. In one corner of the closet stood a shapeless something on a pedestal, draped in a sheet.

"Your statue, young man." Winters turned sideways, and lifted the sheet. In spite of himself, a small glint of appreciation came to his eyes as he looked at the statue.

It was the nude figure of a child. Exquisitely carved, it was, in pink marble, life size. The statue stood on tiptoe, a smile on its rosy face—a childish, contented smile, both arms stretching skyward, as to greet the sun.

But the hands—they were unfinished. The fingers were crudely blocked out—rough, like marble mittens. Evidently, some work was needed before the whole was completed.

But even as it was, the statue was beautiful. Winters, in spite of himself, had to admit that. Unconsciously, his fingers caressed the marble in a possessive gesture. He turned to look at the young man.

De Roults was standing there, leaning against the door jamb, gazing at the statue intently. There was an odd expression on his face—a strained, rapt expression.

"But it is unfinished," he breathed. "It is unfinished."

"Eh?" said Winters sharply.

De Roults started. He turned slowly, and looked at Winters. He looked then, at the statue, caressing it with his eyes.

"I put my soul into that statue," he murmured softly. "I labored to produce a masterpiece, a work of art that would endure—" He broke off.

"Winters," he said, his face strangely white, his voice suddenly

465

hoarse. "Could I—finish the Dawn Child. Her hands—they are incomplete. She—would not like that. It is hard to reach for the sun, when ones hands are—ugly. Would it be possible? Even though the statue is yours now. I could do the work in this room here. With chisel and hammer—" His eyes held the quality of a prayer, his voice trembled.

"Could I—finish it, sir?"

Winters looked at him. A faint streak of perversity—which, incidentally, was to cost him his life, rose in his brain.

"I see no reason why I should," he snapped. "You have looked at the statue. It was enough that I should let you do so. Quite enough. I expect to have the statue disposed of by the end of this week, unfinished as it is. Of course, the profit will be negligible, but—" He spread his hands, indicative of his disinterest in the matter.

"Good-day, sir."

De Roults turned slowly ashen.

"Then—then you will not allow me to finish—" he said, almost childlike.

"Precisely."

The young sculptor walked slowly toward the door, his head bowed. At the threshold, he turned, and looked first at Winters, then at the Dawn Child. There was an enigmatic expression on his face.

"Nevertheless," he whispered, "the Dawn Child shall be finished. Soon. I asked you for but a week more, Winters. *I give you a week, now.*"

He turned and walked stiffly out.

Winters raised his eyebrows.

It was, perhaps, thirty seconds later that he heard the crash. He hurried out of the house, his pale blue eyes curious behind the glasses. There was a rather large crowd clustered in the middle of the street, muttering excitedly. The truck stood by, its fender rather badly dented, with a splotch of red. The truck driver was standing by, addressing empty air for the most part, and telling how, "He just walked right out in the street, front of my truck. Wasn't *my* fault. Can't help it if a man walks out'n the street in front of a truck, and doesn't even look where he's going. He walked out—"

Winters pursed his thin lips, then he turned back into his study, where he made certain entries in a large black ledger. On impulse, he checked up upon De Roults. The young sculptor had lived alone in a garret in the poorer section of town, and from what Winters could ascertain—seemed passionately devoted to his work. He was poor—very. Indeed, Winters wondered how he had ever managed to keep body and soul together.

It certainly was not *his* fault, if De Roults paid no attention to where he was walking, while crossing the street. The remainder of the day Winters spent in his usual pleasant fashion—that of figuring how to dispossess certain hapless clients.

It was late that night, around eleven-thirty, when Winters awoke suddenly, with the conviction that someone, or something was making strange sounds downstairs. He lay awake for some minutes, staring into the blackness, and suddenly he sat bolt upright in bed. The sound was repeated. It was an odd scraping, and scratching noise.

Muttering to himself, Winters got out of bed, put on his robe and slippers, and shuffled out into the hall. As near as he could determine, the sounds were coming from downstairs—in the general direction of his study. He shuffled downstairs, and into his study, where he turned on the light.

The glare of the light exploded whitely, throwing everything in the room into harsh relief. Black ugly shadows. Dark corners illuminated.

There was nothing in the room.

Winters grunted, and reached again for the light switch. He froze. The sound had recommenced; it was distinctly audible, and it seemed to come from the closet.

Winters went over and opened the closet door. Probably rats, he thought, peering through the darkness of the closet.

No rats.

Winters frowned and looked more carefully. There was no corner where a rat might hide. Winters looked at the statue, standing there in the corner, and his breath hissed softly between his teeth. He distinctly remembered having draped a sheet over it, before going to bed.

But now the sheet lay on the floor.

Well, then.

Rats could drag down sheets.

Large rats.

Frowning, Winters picked up the sheet and stood staring at the statue, before covering it. The general appearance of the statue had changed; it was not quite right somehow.

Winters shook his head angrily, and went back to his room. Rats, no doubt. He was not the sort of man to be bothered by such occurrences. Perhaps half an hour after going to bed, he was roused again.

The same sounds. Grating, rasping, scratching noises. Oddly muffled they were. Coming from downstairs. Winters swore softly and tried to sleep.

The next day Winters examined the statue critically. There was, he observed, a peculiar quality to the Dawn Child's smile—an oddly unpleasant quality—and the arms of the statue did not look quite right.

And the hands, Winters could see—were changed. As if someone had been working on them. With a sculptor's chisel!

He did not bother to puzzle the matter out. Methodical and precise as ever, he cleaned up the shards of marble, and went about his business for the day.

Possibly some prankster—or his imagination. Or it might be the rats. Gnawing. No matter. He would make sure.

A substantial remainder of the morning, he spent in setting rat traps in likely spots throughout the house. Later, he would see about selling the statue.

That afternoon, Winters called several dealers in antiques, and *objets d'art.* There was, it seemed, little or no demand, of unfinished statues. No, he could find no buyer anywhere. After the dozenth call, Winters hung up, disgusted, and sat meditatively staring into space for several seconds. His thoughts were not pleasant. It was probably the first time in his life he had failed to come out a winner in a business transaction.

The remainder of the afternoon, he brooded over it. Mentally he kicked himself a dozen times for having failed to take advantage of the young sculptor's offer. He should have let De Roults finish—

Winters' brows furrowed. Had not De Roults said something about—*about finishing the statue!*

But—De Roults was dead.

Mentally Winters kicked himself again.

That night, before going to bed, Winters investigated the entire study thoroughly. Everything was in perfect order. The statue was covered, the closet was locked, the windows and the doors were all barred.

Winters grunted in satisfaction and then went to bed.

Three hours later he was roused suddenly. He could hear nothing now, save the faint echo of a somehow familiar sound, seeming to echo in his ears. Possibly one of the rat traps going off, he decided in some satisfaction, and so deciding, turned over again on his side.

Abruptly he raised himself on one elbow and glared through the darkness toward the hall. The sound had been repeated. He could hear it now—the same *chipping* sound. Winters cursed silently, and got up, taking care not to creak the bedsprings.

Very stealthily, he tiptoed downstairs. He opened the study door silently, and quite suddenly snapped on the light and stood on the threshold blinking.

There was no one in the room.

Winters looked around. The closet door was still locked. Muttering querulously to himself, he opened it, and looked inside. For an instant he wondered if his eyes were beginning to play tricks on him.

Then he took a step backwards.

The statue's hands were beginning to take definite form. Moreover, the arms had moved. Moved a good three inches.

Winters rubbed his chin doubtfully, and wondered how he could have ever thought the face of the statue beautiful. The lips were not smiling at all, and the whole face seemed to have a definitely unpleasant cast.

"Humph," said Winters.

He retrieved the sheet and placed it upon the statue. He looked around the study carefully, and into each corner of the closet, more than once narrowly escaping the sticking of his foot into a rat trap.

Before going back to bed, he eyed the tiny pile of marble chips around the pedestal of the statue, and though his lips moved queerly, he said nothing.

Jerome Winters got very little sleep that night. He heard the chipping, scraping sounds from downstairs quite audibly, no matter how hard he tried to bury his head underneath the covers.

Next day, business did not go well at all. Every little thing seemed to go wrong, his papers were not where they should be, and he forgot several important matters relating to interest payments and debts.

But he would not admit, even to himself, that he was worried. Toward noon, Winters received an unexpected telegram. He scowled at it, and pursed his lips.

This was decidedly unfortunate. He had planned to get rid of that statue today. To take it to some antique dealer, and—and give it away if he had to.

What was he thinking of! Give something away that had cost him seventy-five dollars. And for that matter—two sleepless nights. But after all—De Roults had said that the statue would be finished within a week. And the look on the face of the statue last night—possibly there was something to the young sculptor's threat, after all.

Winters dismissed the thought.

At any rate, he would be out of town for the next four days on business. A piece of property he had acquired from some poor debtor must be appraised. Well, he could get rid of the statue in the city. At some small profit, of course. It would be comparatively simple, since the statue was almost finished.

So it was that while away from Hammondville, Winters saw and interviewed the manager of a certain prominent antique shop, one Sir Arthur Manwell, in regard to coming out to Hammondville to see a very valuable statue he possessed.

Yes, the statue was easily worth five hundred dollars. Exquisitely carved, it was. By a young sculptor named De Roults. What? Oh no. The young man had met with a very tragic accident. Yes. Too bad.

And he would come out to Hammondville today, to appraise the statue? What? Not until tomorrow. But the week would be up then. What? Oh nothing. Nothing at all. Tomorrow then.

Winters arrived home that afternoon with a curious feeling of mingled relief and apprehension. The very first thing he did was to open the closet door. There was absolutely no doubt about it this time. The arms of the statue had moved downward to an almost horizontal position. The hands—they were nearly completed! But they had changed. The fingers were bent as if to grasp something— they looked like small pink claws.

The marble dust, Winters saw, was thick about the base of the statue. One foot was poised, with knee lifted high *as though the statue were about to step off the pedestal!*

Winters slowly raised his eyes and looked at the face. It was twisted in a rather frightful leer. Winters shut the closet door and leaned weakly against it. He locked it carefully and walked out of the study, mopping his damp face with a handkerchief. His mouth was strangely dry, and his face was pale.

Tomorrow would be the seventh day.

Late that night, he heard the now familiar chipping of stone. The noise this time, was fast and furious, almost—eager. Winters did not get out of bed. He knew it would be no use. After a little while, the sounds ceased. The statue, then, was finished.

Winters did not venture downstairs next morning until almost noon. When he did, he stayed as far away as possible from his study. In an agony of dread and apprehension he waited for the arrival of Sir Arthur, from the city.

Sir Arthur did not come.

By mid-afternoon, Winters was almost frantic.

Finally, he tiptoed into his study. There was a telephone on his desk.

Swiftly he dialed the operator, and staring fixedly at the closet door, waited for his call to be put through.

Sir Arthur Manwell, dealer in antiques and *objets d'art* answered. Yes, he was sorry, he was desolated, but he had not been able to keep the appointment. No, he would not be able to come down to make the appraisal until tomorrow. Sometime in the morning— What? What was the matter?

But it was impossible. An important matter had come up—he had to remain at the shop—and—

"I don't care!" Winters shrieked into the mouthpiece, suddenly panic-stricken.

"You've got to come down! Today, you hear? I've got the damned thing locked up in the closet, but the week's up, I tell you. The week's up!"

Sir Arthur informed him politely—and frigidly, that he would arrive tomorrow morning.

"But the statue!" shrilled Winters. *"The statue!"*

There was the audible click of the man hanging up.

"Operator, operator!" Winters dialed frantically.

Abruptly he froze.

Behind him. The sound of a splintering wood. A door smashing open . . .

The *closet door . . . ?*

Involuntarily, Winters dropped the receiver on its hook, and trembling, stared straight ahead.

A soft thud of something striking the carpet. Then the quick pattering of footsteps across the floor.

Winters worked his mouth convulsively, but before he could scream, he was seized by the throat.

Like Winters, Sir Arthur Manwell was a very punctillious man. So it was that he arrived in Hammondville early the next day to see Winters on the matter of the statue. It so happened that when he arrived, there was a rather large crowd of people clustered about Winters' house. Managing to get in, he saw the police and the coroner probing about Winters' study.

Winters had been found in his overturned chair, and the studio in his immediate vicinity was somewhat messy. His head had been almost torn from his body. Indeed, the coroner was quite puzzled.

"Strangled," he murmured gravely. "Um—handprints like those of a small ape. Or possibly those—of a child."

Manwell was extremely shocked.

"Yes," he explained. "I came out here to see the poor chap about a statue he intended to sell. Any idea how it happened?"

The coroner had no idea.

As he turned to leave, Manwell caught sight of the closet door at the back of the room. The lock was ripped away, and the door hung loose on its hinges. Manwell frowned, puzzled.

"Winters mentioned the closet," he murmured under his breath. On sudden impulse, Manwell looked around to see if he were being observed. Everyone's interest was focused upon what lay in the center of the room. Manwell went slowly to the closet door. He opened it. He drew a slow deep breath of awe.

"Superb," he breathed.

The Dawn Child stood on tiptoe, both arms stretching high, its face smiling in contentment. Manwell looked at it for a long minute. Quite suddenly he stiffened. He glanced back toward where Winters lay.

He looked again at the statue.

Then, his face very white, and his hands shaking, he shut the closet door softly. His lips were a jagged thin line, as he strode slowly outside. He recalled again, the words of the coroner.

"Very tiny handprints. . . ."

He remembered Winters' frantic shrieking over the phone.

And on the soft pink of the statue's hands, he had seen a deeper, more ominous stain of red. ———

THE STRANGER FROM KURDISTAN

E. HOFFMAN PRICE

You claim that demonolatry went out of existence at the end of the Middle Ages, that devil-worship is extinct? . . . No, I do not speak of the Yezidis of Kurdistan, who claim that the Evil One is as worthy of worship as God, since, by virtue of the duality of all things, good could not exist without its antithesis, evil; I speak rather of a devil-worship that exists today, in this Twentieth Century, in civilized, Christian Europe; secret, hidden, yet nevertheless quite real; a worship based upon a sacrilegious perversion of the ritual of the church. . . . How do I know? That is aside from the question; suffice it to say that I know that which I know."

So high was the tower of Semaxii that it seemed to caress the very stars; so deep-seated were its foundations that there was more of its great bulk beneath the ground than there was above. Bathed in moonlight was its crest; swathed in sevenfold veils of darkness was its ponderous base. Old as the pyramids was this great pile of granite which took its name from the ruined city, of equal antiquity, sprawled at its base.

A dark form approached, advancing swiftly through the gloom-drenched ruins, a darkness among the shadows, a phantom that moved with sinister certitude.

Suddenly the shadow halted, and its immobility became a part of the surrounding darkness. Other and lesser forms passed, slinking silently to the cavernous entrance of Semaxii, there vanishing in its obscure depths. And all were unaware of the form that had regarded them from its vantage-point.

A cloud parted. A ray of moonlight fought its way through the Cimmerian shadows, dissolving all save one, the darkest; and this darkest one it revealed as the tall form of a man wrapped in a black cape, and wearing a high silk hat.

Another rift in the clouds; more light, which now disclosed the features as well as the form of the shadowy stranger; haughty features with a nose like the beak of a bird of prey; the cold, pitiless eye of an Aztec idol; thin lips drooping in the shadow of a cynical smile; a man relentless and magnificent in defeat.

"The fools have all assembled to pay tribute to their folly; seventy-seven of them who will tonight adore their lord and master . . . and with what rites? . . . It is long since I have witnessed . . ."

He paused in his reflections to count the strokes of a bell whose sound crept softly across the wastelands.

"Little of my last night remains; however, let me waste it well."

So saying, he gathered his cape about him, and swiftly strode to the entrance of the tower.

"Halt!" snapped a voice from the gateway.

The ray of an electric torch bit the darkness and fell full upon the stranger's face.

"Halt, and give the sign."

"Who am I to give, or you to receive?" answered the stranger, as if intoning an incantation or reciting a fixed formula.

"Pass on."

And thus the stranger passed the outer guard of the shrine of demonolatry, the holy of holies where Satan received the homage of his vassals. Past the outer guard was the stranger, but far from the sanctuary wherein the Black Mass was celebrated, wherein the Lord of the World was worshipt with blasphemous rites.

A thousand steps of icy granite, winding in endless succession like the coils of a vast earthworm, led to the foundations of the tower. And at intervals, sheeted and hooded warders halted the stranger and demanded sign and password; and each in turn, as he received a sign, shrank and dropped his gaze before the hard, inscrutable eye of the stranger.

Down, down to the very basements of the earth; and then he found himself before a door guarded by two masked figures garbed in vermilion. Again there was an exchange of signs, after which the two vermilion figures bowed low as the door opened to admit him to the vaulted sanctuary where the Devil was that night to be invoked.

The stranger doffed his high hat, then, after a courtly bow to the assemblage, strode up the aisle and seated himself on one of the brazen stools that were placed, row after row, like the pews of a chapel. Once seated, he gazed about him, taking stock of his surroundings.

The black altar before him, with its crucifix bearing a hideously caricatured Christ, received but a passing glance; nor was any more attention accorded to the walls and vaulted ceiling whose grotesquely obscene carvings leered at him through the acrid, smoke-laden air like the distorted fancies of a perverted brain. Nor yet, apparently, did he note the acolyte who was trimming the black candles at the altar, nor did he seem to wonder that the floor beneath his feet was sprinkled with powdered saffron. It was the company itself that he studied, observing with interest the old roués and young sybarites, male and female, the seventy-seven who had assembled to adore Satan, their lord and master.

In the main, the seventy-seven were persons of wealth and distinction, who, having tried and found wanting every field of human endeavor and achievement, had sought thrills in the foulness and degradation of the mediæval rites of devil-worship; rakes whose jaded appetites sought satiation in the orgies that followed the celebration of the Black Mass; atheists who, deeming passive atheism an inadequate form of rebellion, found expression in a ritual whose sacrilege satisfied their iconoclastic desires.

Attendants bearing trays made their way among the seventy-seven, offering them glasses of wine and small amber-colored pastils. These last the worshipers either swallowed or else dissolved in their wine and drank.

The stranger turned to the initiate who occupied the stool at his side.

"Tell me, brother, the nature of the rites to be celebrated here tonight."

The initiate eyed him narrowly as he sipped his wine.

"What do you mean?"

"Why," began the stranger blandly, "I am a foreigner, and I fancied that the ritual here may be different from what it is in my native land. I must confess," he continued, "that I am puzzled to see an altar and a crucifix in this shrine devoted to the worship of the Evil One."

The initiate stared at him in amazement.

"It must be a curious rite that you witnessed. Do you not know that we have a priest who celebrates the mass, and then—"

"A priest?" interrupted the stranger. "The mass? Why—"

"Surely; if not a priest, if not a mass, how could the arch-enemy become incarnate in the bread which we, the worshipers of Satan, defile and pollute as a tribute to our lord and master? Surely you must be a foreigner from some heathen land not to know that only an ordained priest of the church can cause the miracle of transubstantiation to take place. But tell me, who are you?"

"You would be amazed," replied the stranger, smiling enigmatically, "if you knew who I am."

Then, before the initiate could continue his queries, a gong sounded, thinly, rather as the hiss of a serpent than as the clang of bronze; a panel of the vault opened, admitting the vermilion-robed, misshapen bulk of the priest. Following him were nine acolytes, likewise robed in vermilion, and bearing censers fuming with an overpoweringly heavy incense. As they marched slowly down the aisle, they raised their voices in a shrill chant. The seventy-seven sank to their knees, heads bowed.

The high priest halted before the altar, bowed solemnly, then, with the customary gestures and phrases, went through the ritual of the mass, the kneeling acolytes making the responses in Latin. He then descended to the bottom step of the altar and began his invocation to Satan.

"Oriflamme of Iniquity, thou who guidest our steps and givest us strength to endure and courage to resist, receive our petitions and accept our praise; Lord of the World, hear the prayers of thy servants; Father of Pride, defend us against the hypocrisies of the favorites of God! Master, thy faithful servants implore thee to bless their iniquities which destroy soul and conscience alike; power, glory and riches they beg of thee, King of the Disinherited, Son who battles with the inexorable Father: all this we ask of thee, and more, Master of Deceptions, Rewarder of Crime, Lord of Luxurious Vice and Monumental Sin, Satan, thee whom we adore, just and logical god!"

The high priest rose, faced the altar and crucifix bearing its life-sized mockery of a caricatured Christ, and in shrill, malignant accents cried out his blasphemies: "And thou, thou in my office as priest I compel to descend into this host, to become incarnate in this bread, Jesus, filcher of homage, thief of affection! Harken! From the day that the virgin gave thee birth thou hast failed in thy promises; the ages have wept in awaiting thee, mute and fugitive god! Thou wert to redeem mankind, and thou hast failed; thou wert to appear in glory, and thou liest asleep; thou who wert to intercede for us with the Father, hast failed in thy mission, lest thy eternal slumber be disturbed! Thou has forgotten the poor to whom thou hast preached! Thou who hast dared punish by virtue of unheard-of laws, we would hammer upon thy nails, bear down upon thy crown of thorns, draw blood anew from thy dry wounds! And this we can do, and this we *will* do, in violating the repose of thy body, profaner of magnificent vice, glutton enamored of gluttony, accursed Nazarene, idle king, sluggish god!"

"Amen," came the hoarse response of the seventy-seven through the stifling, incense-laden air.

The priest, having once more ascended the altar steps, turned and with his left hand blessed the worshipers of Satan. Then, facing the Crucified One, in a solemn but mocking tone he pronounced, *"Hoc est enim corpus meum."*

At these words the seventy-seven, crazed as much by the drugged wine and amber-hued pastils as by the sacrilegious madness of the ceremony, groveled upon the saffron-sprinkled floor, howling and moaning, overcome by a demoniac frenzy. The priest seized the consecrated bread, spat upon it, subjected it to unmentionable indignities, tore it to pieces which he offered to the worshipers of Satan, who crept forward to receive this mockery of a communion.

The first of that mad group of devil-worshipers rose to his knees and was about to receive his portion when there came a startling interruption.

"Fools, cease this mockery!"

It was the stranger's voice, a voice whose arrogant note of command, ringing through that vaulted chapel like the clear, cold peal of destruction, silenced the frenzied devotees, so that not a breath was audible. The acolytes stood transfixed at the altar. The high priest alone retained command of himself; but even he was momentarily abashed, shrinking before the flaming, fierce eye of the stranger.

Yet the priest quickly recovered himself.

"Who are you," he snarled, "to interrupt the sacrifice?"

The seventy-seven, though still speechless, had recovered from the complete paralysis that their faculties had suffered. They saw the stranger confronting the high priest on the altar steps; they heard his voice, in reply, rich, sonorous, majestic:

"You, the high priest of Satan, and ask me who I am? I am Ahriman, whom the Persians feared; I am Malik Taûs, the white peacock whom men worship in far-off Kurdistan; I am Lucifer, the morning star; I am that Satan whom you invoked. Behold, I have returned in mortal form to meet and defy my adversary."

He pointed to the crucifix, then continued, "And a worthy adversary he is. Nor think that yonder simulacrum is the Christ I have sworn to overthrow. Fools! Besotted beasts, think you that it is serving me to deride a foe who has held me at bay these countless ages? Think you to serve me by this mummery? This very mass which you have celebrated, though in derision and in defiance of him, acknowledges his divinity; and though in mockery, you have nevertheless accepted him in taking this bread as his body. Is this serving me, your lord and master?"

"Impostor!" shrieked the high priest, his face distorted with rage; "imposter, you claim to be Satan?"

That high-pitched scream stirred the seventy-seven from their inertia, aroused them again to their frenzy. Gibbering and howling, they leapt to their feet and closed in on the stranger.

But at that instant a cloak of elemental fire, the red, blinding flame of a thousand suns, enshrouded Satan's form, and from it rang that same clear, cold voice, "Fools! Madmen! I disown and utterly deny you!"

Once again in the ruins at the foot of the Tower of Semaxii was the dark stranger, Satan as he had revealed himself to his followers. He seemed to be alone, yet he was speaking, as if with someone facing him.

"Nazarene," he said, "on that day wherein I challenged you to meet me with weapons and on ground of your own choosing to do battle for the empery of the world, I was foolish and knew not whereof I spoke."

He paused, lowered his eyes for a moment, as if to rest them from the strain of gazing at an awful and intolerable radiance, then continued: "You they crucified; me they would have torn in pieces, their Lord and master; both of us they have denied. I wonder whose folly is the greater, yours in seeking to redeem mankind, or mine in striving to make it my own."

And with these words Satan turned, his haughty head bowed, and turning, disappeared among the ruins. ━┿━

Swamp Horror

Will Smith and R. J. Robbins

Mayhap it was the influence of the moon's rays playing on my recumbent form—or was it a subtle stealing of that eerie sound into the innermost recesses of my subconscious mind? I had suddenly awakened from a profound slumber, every nerve atingle with the premonition of evil. It was as if a ghostly touch on my brow had called me from the enshrouding incubus of sleep and brought me up all standing with fright! The whole atmosphere seemed surcharged with an electric something that still lingers in my memory. Cursing myself for a timid fool, I crossed to the window, through which the moonlight streamed in sickly fashion. And now, as I gazed out upon the vista of grey field and ink-black wood I became conscious of a strange stillness, a complete silencing of all the familiar sounds of nature, becoming with each moment more oppressive. Hark! What was that? Reverberating over the distances, horribly loud, came a frenzied, screeching cry!

As I stood at the open window, wildly straining my ears, it came again. This time the cry had almost a human quality, but there had also crept into it a suggestion of eeriness that made my flesh tingle all over, and a tremor ran over my spine.

Now, I am not a coward, and since early childhood I have never feared the dark nor anything which might lurk under its cover. Still, to an essentially city-bred man such an occurrence as this was bound to have a fear-inspiring flavour. I had always, indeed, detested anything rural, even before I suffered the frightful experience I am about to relate; had always entertained for the woods and swamps a nameless, unreasoning fear. It was in response to that same fear that I had migrated from the ancestral residence at the tender age of sixteen, getting a job as errand-boy in the near-by city. After this I had held down several minor jobs until I had finally found my métier in telegraphy. It was the latter occupation that was earning me my living when the awful horror of the swamp took place.

That morning Sam Falton, operator and general factotum at my home-town station, had started the ball rolling by engaging me in some small-talk on the wire. Both being desirous of learning the Phillips press code, we had, for practice, been couching every possible word of our conversation in that language. Apparently he had decided to sign off for the time being when he gave a signal for me to hold the wire a moment. His next words gave me a severe jolt.

Literally, they were, "ML MAN JS CA IN SES U BTR CM SES TRS SMG MYX AB IT UR DAD BN MSG NRY A WK." These words, unintelligible to the reader, were sufficient to cause me to demand leave of absence for an indefinite period. Translated, they are: "Mail man just came in. Says you better come. Says there's something mysterious about it; your dad been missing nearly a week!"

I had about decided to go back to bed when I heard the sound repeated again and again. It was nearer this time, and sounded like the wail of some creature in a frenzy of torture. At times it would end in a long-drawn-out, strangling, rattling howl that made my blood run cold.

Could this have anything to do with my father's disappearance? The sounds might have been made by madman or beast, or by something altogether unearthly. My mind, ever used to quick decisions, was instantly made up. I resolved to see.

The night was hot and humid, and in the hollows a heavy ground-fog was beginning to manifest itself, and I suspected that before sun-up the air would be pretty chilly. Plainly, time was short, so I contented myself with a pair of trousers, a sleeveless jersey, and a pair of tennis-shoes which lay at hand. Snatching a hastily lighted lantern, I dashed out into the pulsing night.

The sounds had evidently issued from a stretch of forest about a quarter-mile to the rear of the house, and towards this I made my way. The ground-fog had by this time become quite thick, so that at times I had to grope my way through it. Nature had resumed all her various discordant notes. As I entered the forest the odour of decayed vegetation and mould smote my nostrils. The lantern, a relic of bygone days, cast a feeble circle of light which but served to intensify the surrounding gloom. My thoughts, as I struggled through the underbrush and thickets, were anything but cheerful.

At times fantastically formed roots took on the appearance of serpents ever waiting to drag me down. That I did not fall on more than one occasion was more a result of good luck than of agility on my part. I must have proceeded into the depths of the woods for at least a mile when suddenly the fearful cry came again, now in a direction more to my left and somewhat nearer. I shivered and grasped the lantern more tightly, meantime cursing the folly that had sent me on this wild quest unarmed. Then again the cry — fearsomely close!

At this juncture, grown careless of the terrain beneath my feet, I suddenly stumbled violently over a rotting log lying directly in my path. I remember taking a desperate grip on the lantern, which barely prevented it from flying from my hand, when—a most unearthly scream resounded in the bushes not ten feet away, and a huge body dashed against me, brushing me flat and extinguishing the lantern. Before it died the flame flared up into momentary brilliancy, giving me a passing glimpse of a great, wolf-like creature with blood-slavering jaws and terrible glistening fangs!

I struck my head as I fell, and my senses reeled.

I have no distinct recollection of my return to the house, I must have lain unconscious in the forest for some time, for it was nearly dawn when I finally got up and somehow made my way out. Once in bed, I dropped again into oblivion, and did not awake until some hours later.

Since my father had had no hired man, and mother had died long years before, there was no one to call me or prepare the meals. When I finally found the ambition to rise and dress, my first act was to get together a meal, for I intended to cover a lot of ground during the day, and felt that my stomach should be well fortified. Had I known what lay ahead of me I doubt if I could have eaten anything!

I had about finished my bacon and coffee when I was aroused from a momentary abstraction by a sound from the outside. A quick glance around the premises revealing nothing, I was about to give up the search, when I heard it again; but this time it was a low moan, and of a character which I recognized. Hurrying to the back shed, I threw open the door. There, brilliantly limned in the shaft of sunlight that streamed in, lay the still form of a huge wolf-hound!

I started back aghast. Could this gaunt creature be our good old Fang, the pet with whom father and I had used to spend so many happy hours, and who had greeted me with such rough joy only yesterday? Yes, it was indeed he, for at my call the faithful fellow struggled feebly to his feet, and, swaying drunkenly, wagged a heroic tail.

But to what a terrible state the animal had been reduced! His whole form was wasted to a painful thinness. The skin, hairless in patches, was nearly white, colourless. The poor creature seemed to be suffering from what I could attribute to no other cause than such a weakness as is caused by a heavy loss of blood. And yet, minutely examining every inch of the slackened skin, I could find not a scratch, *no visible wound whatever!*

I lost no time in feeding the dog, and did my poor best at doctoring him. My efforts, aided no doubt by the vitality of his ancient wild ancestry, were sufficiently successful to enable the animal after a while to recover enough strength to walk without difficulty, and even to run and fetch sticks. But I knew well that it would be many days before he could regain the robust sturdiness of the day before.

What, I kept wondering, could have been the agency that had brought Fang to this pitiful condition? What could have drained his veins so completely without leaving a single mark? Where had he been the night before, and what frightful thing could have reduced him to the state of abject fear that caused him to dash so madly through the forest uttering those agonized, strangled screams? For I was convinced that the creature I had encountered last night under such terrifying circumstances was none other than Fang, his really monstrous size enlarged in my terror-stricken eyes to gigantic proportions.

But I could swear to the blood I had seen dripping from the beast's jaws. Whence had that come?

The horrible answer to all these questions was vouchsafed me that very day.

It being by now early afternoon, I realized that if I were to search for my father today I should have to start at once. As I locked up the house preparatory to setting out I tried to recall to mind the general topography of the region.

The farm, which has been in the possession of our family more than a century, is of considerable extent, and is made up mostly of timberland and swamp, there being only a few acres of open land. Directly to the rear of the house is a large forest tract, some parts of which have not been penetrated by men for years. Beyond this is an almost unexplored waste known as Marvin's Swamp.

Legend has it that Old Man Marvin, who owned the farm before it came into my family, died in this vicinity under mysterious circumstances, and it is thought that his bones found their last resting-place at the bottom of the morass. The only clue to his fate was furnished by his ancient shotgun and a few blood-stains found near a stagnant pool in the depths of the marsh. I shudder as I recall the terrible solution I myself was enabled to furnish to this mystery of long ago!

In starting on the search my footsteps followed almost without deviation the course I had pursued the previous night, but this time I was not alone. The great wolf-hound was now my guide, and I soon discovered he was following a scent. Indeed, I had considerable difficulty at times in keeping up with him, so great was his evident desire to lead me to a definite spot.

This forest tract is in itself extensive, and is pretty wild. My father had never allowed anyone to hunt here except members of the family, and as a result the place abounded with partridges, squirrels, rabbits, and other small game. Occasionally, even, I would get a glimpse of a deer or a fox as it leapt away at my approach. Everywhere was the odour of pine, hemlock, and decaying vegetation. The silence of the place was so profound that the smallest sound was immediately noticeable, and even the snapping of twigs underfoot and the breaking of dead branches as I made my way through the thickets served to keep my nerves continually on edge. At length we had penetrated to the other side of the forest, and I found myself at the edge of Marvin's Swamp. Somehow, call it premonition or what you will, a cold shiver passed up my spine as I gazed upon this dreary stretch, and I glanced around apprehensively.

Nothing appeared within my field of vision which could possibly be alarming, so after a brief hesitation I followed the big wolf-hound on the trail. Within a few minutes I could see that we were heading towards the vilest part of the great morass, and again that strange presentiment of evil came over me. The ground was getting softer now, and small sinkholes became more and more numerous. For an hour we pushed on, the way becoming more difficult every minute. The vegetation grew here very rankly, and had become almost entirely aquatic. Cat-o'-nine-tails were now in evidence everywhere, especially about the spot where the dog now impatiently awaited me. This spot was at what marked the centre of Marvin's Swamp—a small stream of almost stagnant water known as Dead River.

The name is rather a dignity, for Dead River is in reality little more than an arm of the main pool of the swamp. Its course had once been traced back and found to extend through the worst part of the region for about a mile and thence into the hills, where its only source was found to be a series of small springs. At the bank of this repulsive waterway I stopped and began to examine the locality closely. Finally I found what I had been looking for, namely a multitude of foot-prints in the soft mud. A glance at these was enough to convince me as to who had made the tracks, but such evidence was nothing to that which now met my eye. For a little to the right of the trail, half hidden in a tuft of rank grass into which it had evidently been unwittingly dropped, lay Father's familiar old hunting-knife! I bowed my head; all hope had left me.

But I had little time to stand here sadly musing, for the strange behaviour of the dog now claimed my attention. He stood a little way ahead of me along the bank, trembling from head to drooping tail; first whining beseechingly back at me, then snarling with a sort of frightened ferocity as he gazed ahead to where the trail led into a dark, evil-looking glade. Absently dropping the knife into a trousers pocket, I hastened to follow his fear-halted lead; and my quest came to an abrupt end!

* * *

The glade—what a hideous spot it was! The river at this point was but a desolation of cat-o'-nine-tails, rank growths, and green, slimy water. Little green lizards basked dreamily on rotting logs and swam lazily about in the stagnant pool. Brilliant-coloured dragon-flies poised for a breathless instant over foul, exotic lilies, only to dart away into black, hot aisles of the swamp. Leeches were every-where, and now and again a water-snake came zig-zagging among the lily-pads in search of prey. More noisome still, the bottom of the pool and its filthy banks were littered with all kinds of dead crea-tures—all sizes of bodies, from those of tiny squirrels up to the carcasses of bob-cats and even deer. Not one of them bore a visible wound, and every one was almost colourless. Those soaking in the murky water were bloated into gross exaggerations of their proper sizes, but those on the banks were dry, shrivelled, shrunken things! All this I noted as in a wondering dream, the while I gazed on the body of my father.

It lay on the bank with one leg dangling in the water, the limbs weirdly contorted, as though the man had succumbed only after a terrific struggle. Nearly demoralized, I flew frantically at the body, seizing it by the shoulders and yanking it clear of the horrible pool. A hasty examination sufficed to show that Father had met the same mysterious fate that had taken toll of so many lives in this hateful place.

I had barely made the discovery when I was completely undone by a distant, long-drawn-out howl—the frightened bay of the wolf-hound. His mission accomplished, he had promptly deserted, leav-ing me alone with my dead.

I was not long to wonder why!

What was the terrible fate that could strike down a man in the sanguine glow of physical strength and activity and leave this shriv-elled, white, bloodless death? And that, too, without leaving a single mark on the husk of a body! To be sure, the clothing was covered with dried blood-stains, but whence had the blood come? Was there not some tiny wound which I in my first frantic pawing of the corpse had overlooked—perhaps the two little purple holes which I shudderingly remembered were supposed to be the mark of venom-ous snake-bites? I stooped again, and, clenching my jaws to still my chattering teeth, began a careful search of the drained thing that had been my father. And as the fruitless quest went on there came again that hush, that awed stilling of the myriad sounds of this rank nature about me.

I became conscious of each noise, as it were, when it had ceased to beat its note on my ears. The shrilling of the frogs first dropped out of nature's discordant symphony, to be followed by the chirp of the crickets, the various low bird-twitterings and rustlings, and other sounds, most of them to me fearsomely unidentified. Now all that remained was the droning of bees, punctuated at longish intervals by the mournful *sol ∂o-∂o-∂o-∂o-lo ∂o-o-o* of a far-away swamp robin.

Now, after one dismally long-drawn-out call, the bird became silent, and the only sound left in the steamy, fetid swamp world was that bee-hum. This now seemed slowly to increase in volume until finally the very air became charged and volatile with its menace. At last I could endure the deafening sound no longer, and, ear-drums bursting with the throbbing, zooming waves—smothered in them, overwhelmed, I toppled over in a black faint.

I was destined soon to bless that fainting-fall, for I was to realize it had saved me from a fate worthy of the ingenuity of a thousand fiends—the same ravaged death that had claimed my father.

Of course, I could not have lain unconscious more than a minute or two, but at the time it seemed ages before I opened my eyes— opened them to a sun-drenched, somehow less fearful world—to find myself sprawled on my back, evidently in a little depression. Of this hollow, the bottom seemed covered with some wet, sticky substance, which to my not over-critical bones made a rather pleasant couch.

Nature had resumed her normal note, and I became gratefully conscious that the horrible droning of bees was no longer in evidence. As I again closed my eyes in response to a certain feeling of lassitude that bound me I wondered if it had been a sound from the outside world or if it had come from within me. Dreamily revolving the affair in my mind, I was inclined to believe the whole thing—the hush, the drumming in my ears, and the fainting—had been caused by the gradual weakening of my faculties. But then how to account for that weakening?

The mystery was getting too deep for me, and I almost decided to give it all up and flee from this hellish swamp, sending someone in after Father's body. At any rate, I could not lie long dreaming in this soft bed. Lazily I opened my eyes; wearily I stretched out an arm; limply I let it fall at my side; and then, screeching with all my poor strength, I leapt to my feet. My outflung arm had dropped with a syrupy splash in what was revealed to my popping eyes as thickening, dark-red blood!

And now began the horror—ugh! an experience so incredibly,

grotesquely horrid that recollection of its lewd details now halts my pen and imbues me with stark nausea. If I had disliked and distrusted the woods and waste places before, my feeling was nothing compared to the seething, loathing hate that grips me now at the mention of that dread word "swamp."

Reeling giddily, my unmanning utterly completed by the sickening realization that I had been lolling so softly in a bed of blood, I had time only to clutch at a low-hanging vine for support before the things—oh, those fat, slime-sweating, crawling *things*—came on! There seemed to be hundreds of them—snail-shaped things as large as dogs—hemming me in on every side. With a slow, irresistible purpose they advanced in a horrible silence. As they closed in, their silence became broken by a nasty greasy sound as of molasses being lazily lifted and stirred with a million sticks. Now they were upon me, and I ran amuck!

I leapt on the nearest and tried to scuff them into the earth; I beat them foolishly with my fists; I sought to hug them off my heaving chest; I rolled over and over them; I tore at their filthy bodies with my teeth; the while I uttered one tortured shriek after another. But in my unarmed state I was no match for the horde, and the things continued in their deadly purpose, bearing me down and beginning to fasten themselves on to every part of me. At last my frenzied yells were stilled by a clammy body laid across the whole lower half of my face; and now my eyes, rolling in dumb agony, encountered the foullest scene of all, and I understood.

The blood-filled hollow in which I had been lying! Crowding around all sides of it like pigs at a trough were a dozen of the monsters, greedily and with many blubbery swilling sounds absorbing the clotting gore!

Now I knew the fate that had befallen Father, had taken old Marvin years before, had claimed the deer and other animals, had dragged at Fang when he had searched out Father's body, and now bade fair to add me to those other letted *cadavres*. Yes, I could see it all now, could understand anything in this rank world of evil growths.

Bloodsuckers! That's what they were! Great, fat, overgrown leeches; spawned of the filth and grown here to this morbid size by centuries of breeding and interbreeding in the lushness. Oh, the horror that swept me!

It was when the obscene feast drew to a close that I thanked God for the fall I had taken a few minutes before when I had fainted, for there was now revealed in the bottom of the depression the empty, sack-like body of one of the gigantic leeches. Evidently the scout of the main herd, it had stolen and fastened itself to my back as I stooped over the remains of my father. Its slow sapping of my life's blood had caused the humming in my ears and finally the deathly faint which had saved my life and been the thing's undoing. For in falling I had landed on my back on a jagged bit of stone, which had pierced and emptied the creature, filling my resting-place with blood.

The sharp tip of the rock now protruded through the flattened carcass and became my inspiration. What did it suggest to me? I was fast sinking into a soft, black oblivion and could not think—did not care to, particularly. Now another slimy body drew along my head and settled itself in such a way as to cover my eyes, shutting out the scene completely. Still the memory of that rock sliver persisted and disturbed me vaguely. What did it remind me of, anyway? Well, I didn't know—never mind. But, yes, I *did* know! Now I had it—a knife! Father's knife, in my pocket!

Gone in a breath was that deathly languor. I became imbued with the strength of desperation. I heaved, I threshed—one hand came clear. Lifting the arm, almost unmindful of the weight of a monster still clinging to it, I worked my hand between two foul bodies into my pocket. And now I drew it out, clutching that blessed knife!

Butchery! Blood!

My first kill was the bloated thing that lay across my scalp and eyes. But what a flood of gore now cascaded over me, filling hair, ears, and eyes! Blinking an eye, I plunged the knife into the stinking monster that blocked my mouth—and was again soaked in a green-streaked red deluge. My mouth free, I found strength once more to yell, but now a note of battle and triumph in the cry!

Slashing and hacking, I gained my feet. Now I seemed to swim in a sea of blood as, sinking the knife to the hilt again and again, I finally freed my legs. And even as I had used my mouth the instant I had cleared it, so now I used my legs. Stumbling, groping, crying, laughing, I ran. ———

Take the Z Train

Allison V. Harding

The seer had said—all things of certain wisdom and uncertain origin would derive so well from seers—"At the end, the old look back to relive and see again the pattern of their lives. But the young, peculiarly favored by a destiny which otherwise seems to have neglected them, look searchingly forward, and for this brief instant of eternity see truly what would have been ahead—before the light snuffs out."

It was a few minutes past five when Henry Abernathy left the office. It was always a few minutes past five when Henry Abernathy left the office. By that time he had taken care of the overflow of work which somehow always found its way to his desk toward the end of the working day and had put away his seersucker coat in the General Employees' Locker.

Longer ago than it would do to remember, Henry had been pleased by the title of Junior Assistant Supervisor of Transportation. He was Assistant all right—to everybody in the office—Supervisor of nothing, and Junior—that was a laugh, with the gray in his hair and the stooped shoulders!

As usual, Henry walked three blocks directly south from the office to the subway station, stopping only for the evening paper at the corner stand. It was all quite as usual. But he had been telling himself all day that this was an important day. He was going to break clean from the old life.

From the earliest, a phrase had been running through his head. It ran in well-worn channels for he had thought this thought before, he knew, though its authorship was obscure. The seer had said . . . and the quotation, for that it must be, fascinated him, he knew not why, he'd never known why. Henry Abernathy had believed before in the clean break from his meaningless routine, from the same old faces at the office, the same stupid tasks, the same fear that lashed him with its thongs of insecurity to his humble position.

Thinking this way took him down the metal-tipped subway stairs, through the turnstile and onto the lower level where he waited for his train as he had, it seemed thousands of times before.

He was suddenly struck with this dim, twinkle-lit cavern way beneath the perimeter of the earth's surface. The people around him, the steel girders holding the rest of the world from tumbling in upon him, the gum machines, the penny scales . . . all these seemed to go out of focus with his concentration on his inner thinkings.

Through instinct he watched the black hole to his left at the end of the platform. He watched more closely, narrowly, as first the noise and then the flickering something away in the tunnel came closer, still closer. He looked up, he knew not why for it was a completely irrelevant act, at the ceiling of the underground station. It seemed, in the subterranean gloom, as far away as the top of the universe.

He was tired, he supposed. Supposed? He *knew*. Life does that to you, doesn't it? To everyone. Abernathy wondered if those around him were as miserable as he was, or if their misery was an unrecognized, locked-up something deep inside. For this underground tomb was a place for reflection, although conversely, in its bustle and noisome urgency, humans could take holiday from their consciences, and pushing, wriggling, hurrying off and on these mechanized moles that bore them to and from their tasks, forget, and in the forgetting be complacent.

Times before beyond counting when Henry Abernathy had waited here like this for his A or B train, he'd thought that people must age faster in such an alien environment—the so-hard, yieldless platform, the dank air, the farness away from things that counted like sky and sun and wind. He wondered if people like himself didn't surely age more rapidly in a subway tomb like this where neither hope nor anything else could grow or flourish.

The dull metal thing slid into the station, its caterpillar length bucking with shrill, rasping protests, its garish-lit cars beckoning. The doors slid open and Henry Abernathy walked automatically forward, glancing as he always did—for he was a meticulous man— at the square in the window that gave the alphabetical letter of the train. There were only two that came to this platform—the A, which was an express and the B, a local. Both would get him home.

He was aboard with the doors slid silently closed behind him and the train jerking, jumping to life again; he was sitting on the uncomfortable cane seats when what he had just automatically glanced at in the identification square on the outside window took form in his mind. So strongly that he got up and walked over to the window and looked at the letter in reverse. It glowed smally against the moving black background of tunnel, for they were out of the station now. It said plainly, so there could be no mistake, Z train.

The subway shook with its gathering speed, and Henry went back to his seat. It was most peculiar. Never before had any but an

A or a B train run on this track. He'd never heard of a Z train! Why . . . he didn't even know where he was going!

He sat with his hands clasped in his lap and felt on the other side of the wonder a relief that maybe this was the beginning of his adventure. The train lurched and zoomed on, and as the moments ticked away ominously, he realized that the underground monster fled headless and heedless without the reprieve of those occasional lighted oases in the dreadful night of the subway. Surely they would have come to another station by now! Then . . . wait a moment more. Certainly by *now!* This, then, was his adventure! This was the difference that would, despite himself and his own weakness to effect the change, *any* change, alter the course for him. That part he gloated over—no more boss, no more regular hours. . . .

The train was going faster. It has been a monotonous life, Henry Abernathy, he told himself. Monotonous and quite terrible. He could confess to himself now something that he would never do in the sunshine or on the street that was somewhere miles above him and this rushing thing that bore him on. He would confess that he had thought of self-destruction.

A clamminess came over him. The air from the tunnel was dank as it whistled in an open window at the other end of the car. It was a very long way between stations, and at this speed, that wasn't right!

He sought out other faces for reassurance. Somehow, quite suddenly, there seemed to be so few of them, and with those, the eyes were averted or hidden behind bundles or papers. Abernathy cleared his throat to test his voice. He would say to someone—the nearest person—"Beg pardon, but what train am I on?" Now wasn't that a silly question! He was sitting nearly directly across from the window whereon the identification plate was set, and that plate said so clearly—Z train.

He sat more stiffly against the seat back, tension taking hold of him and ramrodding his body. It was his imagination that said that the train plunged forward eagerly into the ever-greater darkness of the unfolding tunnel, for a train doesn't plunge eagerly—not even a Z train! A poetic liberty, a figment of the imagination!

Henry fixed his eyes on the nearest person to him—a very young man with books and sweater, obviously just from school, an eager young man, so eager. With dreams, Henry Abernathy thought with a kind of sadness. The young man was looking at nothing particularly, and Abernathy thought, Ah, soon he will look at me. I shall catch his eye and say, leaning forward so I don't have to advertise it to the whole rest of the car, "Young man, I seem to have gotten on the wrong train"—a small smile at my own stupidity—"but just *where* are we going?"

But the young man in the sweater would not look this way. He tapped his books with his fingertips, tapped his foot on the floor, whistled through his teeth and looked out the window or up and down the car, casually, swiftly.

Abernathy got up to speak to him directly then thought better of it. He passed by close enough to see that the youngster was cleaner than most. He rather imagined *he* had looked something like that on his way home from school years ago, but that was far from here in both time and space.

There was a girl, a pretty girl, he noticed—for he was not too old to miss those things—wide-set eyes, a good chin, nice mouth, well-dressed. He would ask her, but of course one didn't do that. With other men in the car, it would look . . . well, *forward* if he directed his inquiries to a pretty young girl.

There were several other men, heavy set, semi-successful or better, watch chains over their paunches, briefcases—the business type. Bosses. They reminded him so. . . .

Then nearly at the door that opened between the cars there was another man, youngish, in an ill-fitting tuxedo, probably going to a party. It was a rented tuxedo, Henry Abernathy thought to himself with some satisfaction. He knew what *that* was, all right! Why, when he'd been just about that age, he'd once rented a tuxedo and it probably had looked no better on him than it did on this fellow.

Abernathy reached the door and clutched at the reddish-yellow brass knob. It had the reassuring feel of all of life, of reality, with the stickiness from scores of hands; people opening and closing it, walking forward, walking back, touching it with their hands.

He went forward then, adding his steps to the speed of the train in that direction. Was it one, two, or three cars, he wasn't sure, nor was he of the other passengers. He staggered a little to the rocking of the subway beneath him. He yearned suddenly to be rid of this thing—this scene, this place. All those figures, those persons he'd sat with in the first car took on a strange, nightmarish familiarity in his mind.

It was the drudgery, the overwork, and the hopelessness of his life that made him this way he excused, like other people say, "Something I ate."

That was what made him *know* that the young boy with the sweater was Henry Abernathy, and so too perhaps, was the slightly older man in the rented tuxedo. The girl was the *she* who had said no. That was long ago too. And those men, those out-of-shape pudgy, expensive cigar-smoking men, were the bosses he'd worked for and others he hadn't worked for, who had given him a glance and dismissal with a look as being beneath them and unworthy of their attention.

The fullness of horror overtook Henry Abernathy as he reached the front of the first car. He leaned against the motorman's compartment and looked ahead at the tunnel rushing onto them and around them. The tunnel curved away, curved away always turning, it seemed, as though they were going in a circle.

Henry stood and watched fascinated. He could go no further. He could not go back. He looked curiously into the motorman's cubicle. That place was dark, the shade drawn nearly to the bottom of the window.

But there was a man in there with a motorman's cap, and a gloved hand rested on the throttle pulled full open . . . a man who swayed with the motion of the train he drove. A motorman.

The years came back to Henry like leaves falling in sequence, and those people back there behind him were all parts of it, of himself and of others he had known. This train then was what? His life from beginning to end and his destiny?

He stood hypnotized by his thoughts, drawn by the dark fascination of the tunnel ahead, the little yellow lights that flashed by, marking with their feebleness both space and speed. It was an eternity that Henry Abernathy stood there . . . or it was one second. It mattered neither.

But ahead, finally, he saw something. It was not exactly a station, but there was a light, a small flickering light set in the side of the tunnel, and they seemed now instead of rushing towards it, to float towards it.

The screeching, groaning, complaining shrieks of the subway at high speed died away so they must be slowing down. The light came nearer. There was a sign, a very big sign. He'd seen them before on the occasion when a crowded train at rush hour stops between stations in the darkness of the tunnel and the sign, perhaps pointing or indicating a nearby stairway that leads to the above—the sign says "Exit."

There was a sign here under the light. But look, there was more. Across the tracks there was something. He watched intently during the hours it seemed that it took their train to roll closer. It mattered not which he saw first, in what order he perceived these things—the sign, the thing on the tracks; the thing on the tracks, the sign.

It was a body on the tracks, lying face upward fully across them like a sack of something. The face was strangely luminous in the tunnel's darkness, and that face was as terribly familiar as those others behind him in the train. And it was so *right* and so *of course* that the sign under the flickering, yellow light simply read "Z."

They were close now, within a couple of rapid pulse beats; the body nearly under the metal monster; the sign, the Z of it growing larger and larger.

And then there was a blinding flash—all the brightness of all the world, of all time exploding in the tunnel, across the so-familiar face and body and Z sign into the train, into him and his head, touching chords and notes that came out like music—that's what it was—music, easy to hear as it played around and around.

It was the sound of the carousel, the calliope, and as the little series of whistles, played by keys like an organ, popped and hooted, Henry Abernathy went around and around in the sea of remembering on the gaily painted horse—a horse that fed and brightened itself on his tears of joy and pleasure.

This was an important train day for Henry. He was going to break clean from the old life, and perhaps the old life started—or the only part of it that counted started—on the floor at home with the cream-colored walls that seemed so tall at the age of seven.

And though he was much beyond it, there were blocks on the floor. He was to spell something out with them, and Mother was persistent. It was a word, a meaningless word, that matters not among the thousands in our language. He was perverse, and there was one letter he would not add, but Mother was so persistent.

"Think!" she said. "Think!"

And he remembered the deepening color of her face, remembered it as he remembered now all these other things, past and future.

"Think!" she repeated. "Think!"

One letter he had to add to make the word perfect, to fill it out for her adult mind to correctness.

"Think!" she said again. *"It's an unusual letter!"*

He knew the letter so well. He had but to push it into place with his foot or his hand. But revolt stayed him.

And then Mother said darkly: "Think, Henry! Do it or you don't go to the fair!"

And with that the roulette wheel completed its final spin and stopped, marking its choice, and he, petulantly and still unwilling but broken down by the knowledge that he would lose something greater, kicked the letter into place.

And she smiled with the victory and said, "Of course! Z! You knew it all the time, Henry!"

It was later, then, that he had gone to the carnival almost exploding with his small-child excitement. Was there enough time for all the things that had to be done and seen, touched and played with? Was there enough of him to smell and eat all the things to be smelled and eaten?

And at the end, the best of all—the merry-go-round, on the horses that went *up* and down, *up* and down, round and round, with the strange, strange wonderful music of the calliope—he would travel miles on his green and yellow horse even as Mother stood outside the world of his racetrack and gestured and seemed to stamp her foot, wanting him to stop and making motioning noises.

It was then—sometime during his umpteenth ride on the bucking green and yellow merry-go-round horse—then so that his seven-year-old mind knew well the whistling sounds of the calliope organ, then that something had come out of another world, it seemed—a thing of crashing noise and blinding light; a thing prefaced only by a little wetness and Mother's anger as she stood, no longer controlling him, already completely outside of his world, under a hastily raised umbrella, stamping her foot and calling to him.

Henry was caught up then in that instant by his friend, who took him in this time of greatest joy bursting like the nod of a flower. It was for that moment that the seer had spoken . . . that the calliope played . . . that Z was remembered.

It was that moment that showed him how it would have been in times yet unborn, to be forgotten forever in time never to be. . . .

THE TEAKWOOD BOX

JOHNS HARRINGTON

Better pay the cash," snarled sallow San Pedro Joe into the telephone mouthpiece. The speaker jerked his head to one side and glanced from the cramped phone booth into the almost-deserted drug store, checking to see whether his conversation had been heard. It was late afternoon—a sultry and stuffy summer day.

"That teakwood box don't mean much to me," Joe continued in a hoarse tone. "And if you want it pretty bad, I'll sell it—otherwise the thing gets chucked out, see?"

Mrs. Floyd Wright's tiny, ill-painted cottage in a smelly Los Angeles suburb had been ransacked a few days previously, leaving bedding overturned, furniture stuffings tumbling everywhere. The teakwood box, to the fidgety old woman, far overshadowed in importance the amount of cash and the few pieces of silver which had also been stolen. Oddly carved and strangely arresting, the prize had been a gift to Mrs. Wright from her husband, recently killed in a factory explosion where he had been night watchman. He had purchased the box during a vagabond trip to China in his boyhood days.

The teakwood container had never been opened by either Mrs. Wright or her husband. "Betty," he used to say while dozing in the parlor and studying the box, "that thing is jinxed, just like I was told. It's dangerous, leave it alone. There is a dreadful native curse on it.

"I got the box from a streetpeddler in Shanghai, who told me he bought it from a priest; he said there was a dire curse to anyone who opened the box, but that it would bring power and good luck to the owner as long as he did not try to do so. I always have said that the box was most likely stolen from a temple by the peddler, or by some other member of the street-scum parade," Wright would conclude.

It would have been difficult to open the box, even if someone did want to pry into it, because its lid was apparently operated by a complex series of springs and pivoting levers. The singularity of the object, its weirdness and strange delicacy, gave it a curious value. When it had been made and by whom—what exotic sights the container had witnessed—were unanswered queries which added to the living personality of the teakwood box. An evil power, dull and half asleep, yet again glowing, awakening, seemed inclosed within the meticulously decorated teakwood. Though the Wrights had been almost afraid of the box from the start, they had nevertheless believed that the spirit which might lie within it would not hurt them if they did not molest it, for they had lived good lives.

Some day, the spirit would awaken and strike, but it would not be at a time when they were about. Death, red, grinning, and yellow-fanged, was a part of the exotic treasure; it was not the death of God-fearing men and women, but the bloody, merciless deity of those who belonged in the realm of evil. The little wooden ghouls which stuck forth from the sides appeared to be tireless, unearthly sentinels, waiting, watching for a suitable offering for their drooling master within.

The stick-bodied widow, shut off in a little corner impervious to the noisy streets around her, had prized the six-inch-high box much more than anything else she owned, because of the eccentric affection her husband had placed on it when he was alive. Though he always feared the box, he would sit and watch it for hours, without uttering more than a phrase. One time when his wife had returned from shopping, she found him standing in the little yard, blanched and trembling.

"Never, never, can we sell or dispose of that box!" he cried. "The devil inside told me so; if we did, he would do something horrible!"

Mrs. Wright wondered whether her husband had concentrated for so long on the object that his imagination had given him that message, but because of the frightened look in his eyes she accepted what he said and did not question him about it. Wright never spoke about the teakwood box after that, but he sat with it oftener than before; his face, rather than appearing curious, had a grim, hypnotized look as he gazed in silence upon the treasure.

Carefully dusted several times a week, and kept glistening with polish, the curio had rested in a place of honor on the living-room mantelpiece, where it sometimes glowed a mysterious, uncanny luster when a few stray rays of the sun penetrated to it from the curtained windows.

But Mrs. Wright could not comply with the ransom demands of the thief who had snatched it and realized the esteem placed on the box by its owner, because of the obvious care with which it was kept. The old woman was sniffling softly into a tiny, lace handkerchief which she clutched in thin, ivory-colored hands.

"One hundred and fifty bucks or nothin'!" sneered San Pedro Joe. These old people got on his nerves. They were so damned irritating and slow.

"But I can't—can't get that much money," trembled Mrs. Wright, her fingers tightening around the phone receiver.

"You're out of luck then, old woman," deridingly returned the thief, and hung up. Ordinarily, he would have dickered to get the best price possible for the stolen object, even though it was lower than he first demanded. But in this case, it gave him a feeling of satisfaction to crush brutally the faltering woman's happiness. San Pedro Joe slowly stepped out of the phone booth, and quickened his pace as he neared the store entrance. He spat at the curbing.

His pasty, selfish face was set off by thin, twisting lips. The black suit he wore was ill-kept, bulging in the wrong places. It was young Joe's habit to drum his fingers on any surface convenient when he was uneasy, and that was most of the time. His watery, cold blue eyes were continually shifting, weighing people he encountered. Joe specialized in robbing ill-kept, run-down homes; there was nearly always something worth his troubles, and then his victims seldom could afford to have much investigation concerning their losses. He was like a cunning spider feeding on bewildered, fluttering moths caught in his net.

In half an hour Joe arrived at his apartment, located in a battered, two-story stucco in the southwest part of Los Angeles. A brief stretch of yellow, dry grass ran between the sidewalk and the plaster-chipped structure. Light from the disappearing sun was shining on the cheerless front windows. Leaving his poorly-kept coupé at the curb, he stepped quickly across the withered lawn and up the cement steps of the building to his rooms.

After a snack of cold beans and white bread, gulped with some warmed-over coffee, Joe brought the teakwood box out from the place where he had hidden it under the messy sink. Darkness had come and the moon had not yet risen. Billows of black, angry clouds were scattered in the sky. Putting the box on the kitchen table, he stood back and regarded the thing. It appeared ominous and resentful on the scarred table-top under the white ceiling light. Joe thought he sensed a feeling of unearthly life in the booty before him. Someone down the hall was coughing hoarsely, and the thief felt chilled.

Suddenly, Joe returned to himself and became intensely curious about that box. He considered what he had found out about it from Mrs. Wright, who, in her desire to get her treasure back, had breathlessly poured out the whole story when questioned. Maybe Mrs. Wright's old man had cached some precious stones or money in the container, conjectured Joe, and had fabricated the yarn about the curse in order to keep people from trying to open the box. The thief, flamed by his greed, decided the teakwood curio deserved an investigation before he discarded it.

At first, he picked up a hammer which was kept in one of the dish-closet drawers, but after a moment's consideration, he determined to try and open the box by its mechanism. Perhaps he could sell it to an antique-dealer after examining what might be inside. Yet had that been the real reason for his decision to use care? Joe wished that fool down the hall would keep quiet; for the first time in his life he felt uncertain, confused.

San Pedro Joe was proud of his ability to do a neat job on breaking into houses, opening strong-boxes, and his conceit prompted him again to forget his forebodings and test his skill by attempting to discover the combination of the box; otherwise, being increasingly nervous, he probably would not have taken the pains which he did to open it so carefully. His fingers trembled—he licked dry, swollen lips. After working for some minutes, he roughly pushed the box from him. Joe imagined the curse, the words of evil, an idol guardian might have incanted on the one who pried into the sacred

496

box, for perhaps it contained some treasured jewels or a temple secret, rather than being simply a hiding-place for Wright's pennies.

The investigator eagerly, impatiently, bent over the shining teakwood again, as though suddenly possessed, and continued his manipulation of the curio's carved knobs and queer levers. For a moment, he thought he detected a slight, shrill cry, followed by a tiny, penetrating whistle. Sweat broke out on Joe's brow as he doggedly kept at his task, fascinated, now unable to pause. Shortly he pressed an unobtrusive bump which had been revealed by sliding a ghoulish little figure ornamenting the container's front to one side. The lid slowly raised upward, as though controlled by a hidden spring. The crook nervously pressed harder on the button he had discovered, in order to hasten the opening of the lid. He was waiting for something—his finger seemed frozen to the box, his whole body was stiffened. Sweat was trickling down his back, yet he was somehow cold.

Suddenly, a sharp, biting flame burned in his thumb, as though he had put it in a fire of hot coals. A strange numbness ran through his arm. He stared down at the table to see a neatly-concealed needle, probably hollow, slowly retreating into the side of the box; in the same glance he saw that the teakwood curio was empty, contained nothing.

Blood was on his thumb, dripping from under the finger-nail, where seemed to be an inflamed, tiny wound. He heard a peculiar, spine-stiffening cackle, on the same penetrating high key as the whistle. First it came spasmodically, but broke down into a low gurgle, a sucking sound. The thief's heart seemed to bloat and swell, yet tried to beat faster; Joe clutched at his hot brow with clammy, weak hands.

Young San Pedro Joe, a short time ago successful light-finger man, fell dead on the kitchen floor. The white light shone on his ill-proportioned, slight body. For a moment, there seemed a slight rustling. A dirty, filth-incrusted window banged open. But all was quiet outside in the hot, choking night air. ——

THESE DOTH THE LORD HATE

MANLY WADE WELLMAN

Before me lies open E. A. Ashwin's translation of *Compendium Maleficarum,* just as three hundred years ago the original lay open before judges and preachers, a notable source of warning against, and indictment of, witchcraft. And from its pages have risen three folk long dead.

The magic that gives them life is that of imagination, concerning which power Brother Francesco-Maria Guazzo writes with sober learning in the very first chapter of the *Compendium.* Their simple embalming was a lone paragraph, barely a hundred and fifty words in length—one of Guazzo's "various and ample examples, with the sole purpose that men, considering the cunning of witches, might study to live piously and devoutly in the Lord."

Guazzo has written shortly and with reserve, though never dryly; and in 1608, when the *Compendium* was first printed under patronage of Cardinal Orazio Maffei, his style was adequate. James I of England still shuddered over the memory of Dr. Fian's conspiracy with Satan to destroy him. In Bredbur, near Cologne, lived a dozen or more aging men who horrifiedly had seen a captured wolf turn back into their neighbor, the damnable Peter Stumpf. Gilles Grenier, prisoned in a Franciscan friary at Bordeaux, would cheerfully tell any visitor his adventures as a devil-gifted warlock, shape-shifter and cannibal. But times and beliefs have changed. Since Guazzo himself foresaw that his book might provoke "the idle jests of the censorious," let his shade not vex me if I embroider his brief, plain citation.

The phenomenon occurred near Treves, upon the goodly river Moselle, immediately east of the present Franco-German border. Some know Treves, ancient and pleasant, with the cathedral where is preserved a coat of Jesus Christ to call forth the world's wonder and worship. Around the town, now as in Guazzo's time, are pleasant fields and gardens. The scene we are to consider, though unfolding upon land properly German, is more than a trifle French.

In the district of Treves, writes Guazzo and translates Ashwin, *a peasant was planting cabbages with his eight-year-old daughter. . . .*

Frenchmen hold cabbages in notable esteem and affection—a favorite love-name, throughout the provinces and environs of France, is "cabbage." Without good store of this vegetable, no Moselle farm

498

would be perfect, and certainly no Moselle stew. The peasant was planting, and so it was spring, a fair day with the sky clear and bright, as we shall observe. Our man of the soil comes readily to life before us, stooping and delving at the fresh, good-smelling furrow. He seems a sturdy fellow, sharp-featured like a Gaul, blond-bearded like a Teuton. His widely spread feet are encased in wooden shoes, he wears a loose, drab frock and a shapeless cap. For all the distance of years, he is amazingly like a peasant cabbage-grower of today.

And beside him, as we have read, works his daughter. Eight years old—is that not young to be a gardener? Yet she is vigorous and intelligent and willing beyond her years. The trowel and seedbag seem to do their own duty in her small, quick hands. Her father is deeply impressed. He, continues the commentator: . . . *praised the girl highly for the work. The young maid, whose sex and age combined to make her talkative, boasted that she could do more wonderful things than that; and then her father asked what they were.*

It is well worth another full stop to consider that complete picture —one of rustic endeavor, not too heavy or too distasteful, especially when the gardeners are so bound together in mutual understanding and affection. Seed-sowers of today can understand Father's pride in his industrious daughter. "How well you dig, my little cabbage!" And his eyes crinkle up in his good-natured brown face as he enjoys his own play upon words. He doubts honestly if there was ever such a good child. She is a true daughter of her mother, and here he turns to glance over his shoulder at the house above the garden—small but snug and well repaired, with an ample gush of smoke from the chimney hole.

His wife is evidently concocting the noonday meal. Something more than bread and soup, he warrants—he is mystified at the plenty of good things she provides, as if she got it by enchantment.

I will grant that the picture is too bright, too cheerful; were it fiction, we might borrow from Edgar Allan Poe the device of a black cloud dimming the sky. But perhaps the contrast will be the greater with things as they are.

The excellent child finds the more savor in Father's commendation because she knows that well she deserves it. Nor is she backward in telling him that planting cabbages is not her lone virtue and study. Other of her talents may please and benefit him.

Again Guazzo: . . . *she said, "Go away a little, and I will quickly make it rain on whatever part of the garden you wish."*

And Father? It takes no further effort of the mind's eye to see that peasant visage broaden and the beard stir in a great grin. This daughter of his never fails to warm his heart. Surely she must have heard him say that rain would be welcome in this planting season. As she grows older, she will hear from the priest that only God almighty can send rain. But her pretense is innocent—today let her have her fun, play a game to make them both laugh. Guazzo calls the good man astonished, but more probably he achieves an elaborate burlesque of surprises as he says: *"Come, then, I will go a little away."*

Jovially he tramps off, fifty paces or so, taking care not to tread on the freshly seeded cabbage-rows. He and his daughter have gone far ahead of their intentions this morning; there can be a minute or two of rest and sport. He pauses and turns.

Now, for the first time, perhaps he scowls.

The child has caught up a gnarled stick and is beating up a froth of mud in a shallow trench. She is speaking, too, or saying a litany. He can catch only the rhythmic sound of her voice, no words.

. . . and behold there fell from the clouds a sudden rain upon the said place.

"From the clouds"—whence came those clouds so suddenly? And now this deluge; from his point apart, the cabbage-farmer stares. His shoulders hunch in his loose smock, as though they supported a sudden heavy weight. His sabots dig into the earth. One square-fingered hand steals upward to sign the cross upon his thick chest.

And over yonder falls a rain such as no Christian cares to see, heavy and narrow. It is a shimmery, drenching column of down-darting water, no thicker than a round tower of the baron's castle at Treves, but tall as infinity. He can hear it, too, a drumming rattle on the thirsty clods, like the patterned dance-gambols of many light impious hoofs.

He crossed himself again, and the rain is over, as abruptly and completely as it began. Now is the time for him to inquire in his heart if indeed he saw and heard rightly.

He knows that he did. The rain is gone, but there remains a circular patch of earth all churned to mud; and here comes trotting his daughter, smiling and triumphant, and her garments are drenched. Her eyes sparkle; so sparkled the eyes of her mother, no later than last Sunday, when a roast of pig came to the rough table, as if from nowhere. The hungry husband did not ask about it then; now the question burns him—whence came that meat?

All this detail is romance, a careless padding of Guazzo's narrative, which is much shorter and balder:

The astounded father asked: "Who taught you to do this?" She answered: "My mother did; and she is very clever at this and other things like it."

We may assure ourselves that there will be no more cabbage-planting this day. The peasant nods dumbly, and plucks at the hem of his smock. Then he clears his throat and says that the sun is high, and that the midday meal is undoubtedly ready.

Together they go to the hut above the garden—the man's sabots thudding heavily and lifelessly, the child's bare feet skipping and dancing. A hearty, rosy-cheeked woman greets them loudly at the door. To be sure, dinner is ready; but he who suggested a stoppage of work to eat, he finds himself unable to swallow a crumb.

Finally he rises, lurches rather than walks from the door. Near by is a secluded spot; we can readily visualize it as a clump of bushy young trees beside a narrow creek. Into that hiding plunges the peasant. Screened by the trunks and branches, he sinks wretchedly to his knees. He feels that this is not enough of humility. His face droops, his shoulders go slack, and a moment later he lies prostrate upon the shadowed mold of last year's leaves.

There he prays, for an hour and an hour. Sometimes he finds words to say, oftener he achieves only moans and unaccustomed tears.

Can he not be forgiven for having merciful doubts as to his duty in this case? Even the Savior once pleaded that a bitter cup be withheld from His lips. But the peasant makes shift to rise at last. His face is set as firmly as the carven granite of a saint on the cathedral's doorway, yonder in Treves. True, his hands tremble a little, as Abraham's hands must have trembled as they lifted to sacrifice Isaac at God's command; but the final answer has come into his heart, and he knows what to do.

Here is that answer, as Guazzo gives it:

The peasant nobly faced his right and plain duty; so a few days later, on the pretense that he had been invited to a wedding, he took his wife and daughter dressed in festal wedding robes to the neighboring town, where he handed them over to the Judge to be punished for the crime of witchcraft.

It is hard to imagine how the man lived during those intervening "few days." It is impossible to divine what were his arts and powers that he kept a smiling face and calm manner while his heart smoldered like a coal from the smithy.

And the plan of betrayal, that was a shrewd one and worthy of the greatest witchfinder, let alone a peasant. Yet I doubt if he congratulated himself upon it.

They go to the fair town of Treves, all three in holiday gear. Sometimes, on that journey, the little rain-maker must have been weary, and rode perforce on Father's shoulder. Was his arm tighter than usual around her little body?

Did his voice quiver as he answered some question she prattled?

I make no doubt of that; but from Guazzo we know what the end of the jaunt turned out to be.

Of a sudden the mother and daughter are in the hands of the judge, under guard of his men-at-arms.

With what fierce scorn does the witch-woman deny the charges — until, after hours of questioning and perhaps a touch of the lash or thumbscrew, she makes confession. True, she is a sorceress. She has signed the Devil's book, attended the Sabbat, sworn the oath of evil. She has schooled her daughter to the like infamy.

Look elsewhere in Guazzo's absorbing *Compendium* for what must have been the rest of the story. Death by fire, he says confidently, is the only right punishment for the dreadful sin of witchcraft. A stake, therefore, is set upright in the market-place of Treves, and heaped about with faggots. To this the witch and her fledgling are borne, high upon the armored shoulders of the law's servants. With the last of her tears, the older culprit pleads and prays that she be allowed to walk. Sternly the judge refuses this request; is it not a commonplace that a witch, going to execution, need but touch toe to earth for her bonds to dissolve and her executioners to fall as if struck by lightning?

That double witch-burning is a rare treat and curiosity in Treves, and it receives the attention it merits. Not a soul in all the district, from the baron of the castle to the beggars whose home and heritage is the gutter, but must draw near to see.

No, that is not strictly true. Not every soul in the district is present at the burning; for a solitary man trudges away, to his empty home by the cabbage garden. His big hands are locked behind him, his chin weighs like lead upon his breast, the lines of his face teem with tears. He dares to utter the supplication refused by the priest at the cathedral — a timid prayer that two spirits even now taking flight, shall not be utterly consumed in hell; O Lord, let them win at last through long punishment and sincere repentance to some measure of comfort in a most humble corner of heaven.

Not all agonies are of the fire. ⬦

THINKER

MALCOLM KENNETH MURCHIE

The building sat on cliff haunches looking west across the rolling river. Its gray-whiteness was appropriate for a hospital; its columns and arches a part of the imposing something that men try to build up in the face of things they do not understand and therefore fear. Like death—which always hovers over hospitals. And things worse than death—which hover over the psychiatric divisions of such institutions.

In these small worlds that encompass so much pain and suffering of mind and body, there are men whose detachment is called "scientific attitude" and whose smugness passes for "position" and "prestige." They are the cataloguers, the book-learned who feel that they need but walk down the aisle of a clinic to pick and diagnose the poor human wrecks who fringe their tour of duty.

Dr. Larabie Warren, head of the psychiatric division of Metropolitan State, was a man of unquestioned ability. And he showed none of the conceit and contempt which often characterized the attitudes of his friends. Not that he was so different. But his practice as consultant had brought him some of the most talented people of the day; he had learned to hide well the feeling that nearly every doctor, consciously or unconsciously has. The feeling of contempt for and superiority over the patient.

From where he sat in a richly leathered chair behind his wide maplewood desk, he could see the river flowing by and beyond, as it curved against the grand silhouette of the city. This scene stimulated him; the plumes of smoke against the blue sky, the plane flights that regularly dotted the distant horizon from nearby Central airport, the fussy tugs and rusty freighters on the water below; the excursion boats in summer. It was a thought that pleased him that he would only confess to himself, but he wondered how many people here in this great metropolis knew him and his work. Perhaps not many, judged by the standards of a radio or movie star, but he, Larabie Warren, was known in most of the circles that counted. He was, beyond even a detractor's doubt, an outstanding success in his line.

His desk buzzer sounded discreetly. Warren frowned at the interruption, glanced automatically at the folding clock. It was three. Oh yes, he was to see somebody of Machlen's, a disturbed ward case, penniless and therefore charity. Warren had a mind good at filing things, even unimportant ones like these. This particular patient was to be granted a visit with the "Chief" for a very special reason. As Warren remembered the details, the man had been picked up in the squalid Tri-State Bridge district. The policeman who had helped the oldster aboard the Metropolitan ambulance raised his eyebrows at the interne and tapped his temple significantly.

The complaints hoisted first upon the law and then relayed faithfully by the patrolman to the cynical ears of the interne were of a not untypical nature. The very old man, the stories went, "frightened" children, "cast spells," "stopped" people and made dire predictions. All these accusations poured forth in a variety of excited tongues and languages. The old man confirmed his "craziness" by not having a name and shaking inquiries about it off, although from reports he seemed most articulate about all other matters. He was registered at the disturbed ward of the psychiatric division merely as a case number.

But the special reason that was to enable what the entrance doctor mentally catalogued as an old, dirty lunatic to enter the inner medical sanctum, that would grant him a few most precious moments with none other than Larabie Warren himself, was a simple report handed in by the ambulance physician. It might be added that the interne doubted the whole thing himself—but he'd heard it —and passed it on. On his ride uptown from the ramshackle tenement district which had been so glad to see him incarcerated in the white-painted ambulance and borne away from them by this red-eyed, shrieking monster, the oldster had turned to the interne and said, oh clearly, so there could be no mistake, "So now I shall see Machlen and Warren."

It was wholly incredible that this ancient flop bum had mentioned the chief of psychiatry at the hospital, plus one of his assistants (who would probably get this case). But even more unbelievably, the old man seemed then concerned with the attendant's discomfort and said gently, "Don't be surprised, Greenwald."

The interne, Greenwald, who'd never laid eyes on his charge before this call, had reported this to Machlen, whose case in Disturbed Ward it turned out, sure enough, to be. Greenwald added his own and unasked for comment: "There's something creepy about the guy, Doctor Machlen!"

Machlen who had scoffed away this irrelevant comment as being the "impressionism" of the young, had come, through the days, to take a different view. The old man who had no name "knew" things he *couldn't* have known. Of course he was quite insane, but. . . .

"I'd suggest you see him for a moment, or two," Machlen relayed to Warren. "Chief, it's weird how much that man knows about the damndest things! He's uncanny, with that sharpness of mind you see in some types of mental unbalancement. Why, just the other night when I was making rounds, I stopped at his bedside—there's been some trouble in the ward again about the food—and this old codger started to talk about the hospital budget and," Machlen's voice lowered discreetly, "your administration of it! It's all uncanny, I tell you! You'll see."

So Dr. Larabie Warren, head of the psychiatric division, saw for himself. At precisely three P.M., when his desk buzzer rang and he remembered who was waiting to see him, he was much of the opinion that this demented man had won himself this prized interview with a series of "guesses" and "coincidences" which had foolishly rattled attendants and physicians alike downstairs. Totally aside from a certain grudging curiosity about the man, Warren knew it looked well for him, every now and again, to see one of these "hardship" cases.

Warren signalled his secretary, and the door of his office opened to let in one of the oldest men the head psychiatrist had ever seen. As the ancient came into the room, Larabie purposefuly ignored the meaningful look directed at him by his subordinate from the disturbed ward who'd accompanied the case to this floor.

"That'll be all, Machlen," Warren murmured, reaching for the case chart and gesturing the patient to a chair before him. The other doctor withdrew.

"Now then, you haven't given us a name so I hardly know what to call you."

The old man inclined his head as though he had no quarrel with that. His face was lined and wrinkled; his hands veined and long-fingered.

"Tell me, tell me how you knew my name was Warren and that you would also be under a Dr. Machlen and ride in the ambulance with an interne named Greenwald?"

The ancient smiled, and though the expression was a gentle one, it irritated Warren. He, not the patient, was the one who did the smiling. . . .

"I know many things, Doctor Warren. Some of which I speak, others . . . I do not."

Grudgingly, Warren admitted the man spoke well. Too well for one of his decrepit appearance and appalling background. It was probably a case of one who had fallen on evil times from a higher plane.

"You have made some other statements," Warren said softly. The room was quite soundproof, but these things were better whispered or not said at all. "Some remarks about the money affairs of my division here at the hospital: Critical remarks. Pray, old man, what is your meaning on this?"

Larabie Warren fixed the patient with his cold, blue eyes, but his gaze was met steadily and squarely. The silence was most uncomfortable until it wore itself out. The elderly man spoke.

"If you refer to certain remarks I have made about the management of your division of the hospital. . . ."

"And I do. What do *you* know of it?" The psychiatrist's meaning was plain. What did the old man know about *anything!*

There was another of the uneasy silences.

Then softly, so softly that Warren found himself straining to hear, the old man replied: "I know a great deal about a great many things, Doctor. You see, one's creator usually understands one, or at least recognizes if not understands, for the way of life is strange. . . ." His voice trailed.

Warren rustled some papers on his desk and felt with discomfort and anger that he was not in as much control of the situation as he would wish. He took the offensive, lightening the usually resonant timbre of his voice only so that no whisper should go beyond these walls.

"I have a report here, Doctor Machlen's, in which, replying to questions about how you knew the identity of certain persons who certainly had never crossed your path before, you said, and I read . . ." Dr. Warren did . . . " 'I created them, therefore of course, I know them.' "

Warren looked up, and the ancient met the physician's smirk with a nod.

"That is so. I said it. It is so."

"You mean to sit there, old man, and tell me that *you* created Greenwald, Machlen, *and* myself?"

"And a great deal more, Doctor. You see, all things are thoughts before they are realities. I can explain this by reminding you that a bridge, for instance, is first a dream, an idea; then it is created on a drawing board. Only after that does it take substance and shape men call reality."

The ancient spoke all the while in a soft and gentle manner, but Warren's rising anger with this decrepit old man, who managed an air of dignity despite his drab hospital attire, knew no bounds.

"By some freak of coincidence, you have been able to impress guileless and poor minds with your abilities, your so-called powers!"

The old man nodded. "Naturally, Doctor."

Despite his studied control, Warren burst forth. "What do you mean, man, 'naturally?'"

"I mean, naturally you would say just that, and as a product of my own thought processes, nothing you could do would really surprise me."

This moulding, decaying old folk, with the big words he had no right to, with knowledge he must have partially guessed or gleaned through some weird quirk of fate, was the exasperation of all the ages!

Larabie Warren forced himself to study some laboratory reports on his desk. This man's greatest danger was his nuisance value to other rational human begins. And that would soon be over and done with.

But the old man was talking again, this time without prompting or urging, softly, without rancor and despite himself, Warren was listening, almost as though he would hear something he should know.

"You see, my dear Doctor Warren, one creates in the mind. Not in the biology laboratory. Not the science of the genes, the atom, but of the mental. And yet, alas, so many things turn out in unusual patterns, quite unforeseen, quite unavoidable. It is for one to create but not direct."

The man had a god complex. Every psychiatric hospital is familiar with the species. Their fanaticism knows no bounds; and why may it not on occasion be accompanied by coincidence to lend dignity to the ravings? For that was precisely what had happened here.

Warren's main reason for seeing this patient was to plug any possible loophole. And, as admitted, curiosity. The old man had said some extraordinary things about methods and other matters at the hospital. Things the papers, the mayor and perhaps the board of governors would like to know . . . and not like to hear. But who would take the ravings of an insane man? Still. . . .

The ancient's voice was droning on, but Warren had been busy for a few minutes with his own thoughts. He was impatient now to bring this "charity" interview to a speedy close.

He glanced again at the medical and laboratory reports on his desk. Here was the factor that made everything else all right. This was, of course, his final trump. In fact, it was a distinct pleasure to play it. He opened his mouth to speak.

But the ancient said the words, said them first, taking the sting and impact and cheating the doctor of his moment.

"I am going to die. You were about to tell me that, Doctor Warren? I know it, and it must be so for there are many powers greater than mine. This is a small thing, Doctor Warren, in the eternity of the mental. An instant, you and I, and all our surroundings. Meaningless, tiny grains in the limitless sands of forever."

Warren puffed with annoyance at the linking of identities. "You have guessed what I was going to say. Nothing super-natural; a premed student would arrive at the same conclusion. Is it unfortunate that you place such a low valuation on yourself? Although in that, you are quite probably right. I am, of course, different."

He bit his lip. Why did he allow himself to be maneuvered into this position of the explaining defensive?

"You are dying. Nothing can save you . . . although I realize that in your mental condition my words mean very little as tangible symbols." Warren rose, signifying the meeting was at an end.

"I quite understand, Doctor. It is precisely what I knew."

"I suppose," Warren sneered, "that you also created my desk clock, the river outside here, the sun and the sky!"

The elder inclined his head even as he rose to his feet. Dr. Warren's nurse, Miss Benstead, ushered the old man out of the chamber afterward. Warren smiled at her in his most charming manner. "Really, one of the most advanced and amazing cases of mental aberration I've seen in a long time!"

The nurse sniffed disdainfully in agreement and as though the air itself might be polluted by the old man's visit.

It was in mid morning four days later that Dr. Warren's intercom buzzed. It was Machlen downstairs. About the old man. He was bad, very bad. And sinking. Maybe an hour or so, but possibly at any minute. He couldn't last the morning.

Warren listened dispassionately. It was allowable and at the discretion of the chief to have so seriously ill a patient taken out of the psychiatric ward and put, for the time it took to die, in semi-private or private. Also, it was quite possible that the chief might wish to have someone else called in from the regular hospital. They were, after all, psychiatrists.

"Shall I get someone else from Medical, Chief?" Machlen asked.

It afforded Warren considerable pleasure to snap back, "No!"

An hour later Machlen called again. His voice, Warren thought, was unduly dismal as he relayed the news. "He's dying!"

Larabie Warren snapped sharply, "Well, what of it! Don't bother me again about this, Machlen! You'd think he was somebody important the way you're going on!" And Warren slammed up the intercom.

The desk clock said eleven-thirty and it was stuffy in the room. The chief crossed to his French windows overlooking the water and threw them open. He liked to watch the river flow by, the great, oily swells and eddies. The nearly noon sky was bright over the city, and the May sun touched his face warmly as he looked south.

He stood there for a few minutes, long enough for the cloud that hadn't been there before to creep up on the horizon. He studied it even as the finger of sun on his face lost its warmth. To the south, following the sweep of the river, the city's skyscrapers looked stark and naked in the new light.

Dr. Warren turned his eyes to the river again. He knew nothing of the tides, but it must be getting to the flood, the turn, for the swirling currents had abated. The wind plucked at the window and was suddenly cold. He started to close it, but something made him stay his hand.

It was a peculiar sky. Streaked and mottled, it was, and rapidly darkening . . . such a pity on a lovely spring day . . . black, but not like a thunderstorm . . . the sun had gone. . . .

Larabie Warren felt some of the clouds in himself. He turned abruptly from the window, lit the room lights automatically and sat down in his leatherette office chair. Been working too hard lately . . . let's see, he had an appointment at noon.

He looked at the desk clock. Studied it and suspected it. Miss Benstead hadn't wound it . . . but yes, on holding it to his ear there was a faintly discernible tick. Irregular, slower in tempo than rightfully.

He rose then again, not knowing just why. The window drew him. And the sky and sun and river outside. The city stood unhealthily white around him, the buildings praying to a sky that was thunderous, but blacker now than thunderhead . . . he hadn't noticed with the room lights on . . . there was no sun, no trace, ray or hint . . . but as though gone or never been . . . and the river . . . the river . . . was . . . not . . . right . . . either.

Warren staggered from the window. The inertia of the river, the blackness of the sky and the deadness of the sun already in him. With both hands he grabbed the desk clock and held it to his head. The beats were slower, slower . . . more and more irregular . . . slower, slowing the ticks as though numbered . . . and the square that was the window, opening now not out onto sky but neuter, neutral *nothingness* . . . still holding the clock in one hand. Listening to the measured tick . . . the accompanying pound in his head and heart . . . irregular and slowing. . . .

Dr. Larabie Warren reached the master key of his intercom with an effort . . . with an effort he keyed the downstairs number.

The river, the sky, the sun and the desk clock all in his head, all in his being . . . the number . . . the number. There, that clock . . . connection.

"Machlen," he croaked with a stranger's voice. "Machlen! That old man. Machlen, get Medical! Right away, understand. I want everything done! *Everything! That man must not die!*"

But Machlen did not hear. Of course it was too late. ———

THRESHOLD OF ENDURANCE

BETSY EMMONS

This morning she struggled awake slowly, with the feeling that her dreams had been unpleasant, though she could not remember what they were.

She looked at the clock, raised herself on her elbow, and called sharply "Time to get up!" But her husband's rumpled bed was empty.

She went to the head of the stairs and called him in a voice that sounded hollow in the quiet house. There was no reply. He must have wakened early, dressed, and gone to the office. She felt annoyed, as she was always annoyed at a break in the routine she had established for her husband and herself.

Now she set to work. It was impossible for her to leave a room until she had tidied it, though she felt unlike herself this morning. Her movements seemed to have the strange lightness of fever, and she could not shake off the oppression of the forgotten dream.

First she made her husband's bed, for the sight of an unmade bed was not endurable, and there was something particularly unpleasant about an unmade bed where her husband had been sleeping. Next she went to his closet, conscientiously overcoming the repulsion she always felt at the faint male smell which somehow could not be banished, though he no longer smoked tobacco even at the office. His pajamas were on the floor, not placed neatly on a hook as she had taught him.

A book lay on the night-table beside his bed, one of the odd old things he liked to read. It opened at a bookmarked page, where an underscored paragraph caught her eye. "There is a Threshold of Endurance with the Soul as well as with the Body, and one who has Long Endur'd may of a sudden break the Bounds of Reason, hurling himself 'gainst the oppressor with a Vigor the greater for his Long Control."

510

She removed the bookmark. Her husband, she decided, ought to stop reading at night. She took the book with her when she went downstairs, wondering as she descended why the house seemed queer this morning. She was not an imaginative or nervous woman. Surely she must be sick.

Downstairs the living-room was cool and orderly, with the window shades drawn as she left them the evening before. She raised each shade and went into the kitchen. On the sink stood an empty glass filmed with milk and a plate with sandwich crumbs. Her husband had come downstairs last night to find something to eat and had left his dishes unwashed. There was nothing she disliked so much as dirty dishes. She washed and dried them before she made her coffee.

She was drinking the coffee when the back doorbell rang. Looking through the kitchen window, she saw an old tramp.

"I'm sorry," she called, "but I have nothing for you." He stood as if he had not heard, and she impatiently turned away. She washed her breakfast dishes, brought the morning paper in from the front porch, and was dusting the living-room when she heard a noise in the kitchen. She went to see. The kitchen window was open and the old tramp was rummaging in the icebox. "I am going to call the police," she said.

He did not seem to hear. As if unaware of her presence, he closed the icebox, tucked the stolen food under his arm, unlatched the back door, and walked out. She watched with helpless anger, for he had not even seemed frightened. She moved to the telephone to call the police, then stopped, putting a hand to her forehead as memory nagged vaguely.

Last night at midnight she had awakened and heard her husband in the kitchen. She had put on her neat wrapper, gone downstairs, stood in the kitchen doorway, and said, "This is a bad habit. It is unnecessary and wasteful, and bad for your stomach." She had gone. upstairs without waiting for his answer, and he had followed without washing his dishes. And then something else had happened. What was it? Or was she merely haunted by that dream?

Glancing toward the sink, she saw that his milk-filmed glass and plate with sandwich crumbs stood there unwashed, just as they had stood when she first came into the kitchen that morning. But she had washed them. Surely she had washed them. She frowned, not understanding, trying to remember what had happened after her husband followed her upstairs.

She went into the living-room. The shades were down, drawn for the night, as if she had never touched them. Through the window she saw the morning paper lying on the porch, exactly as it had lain there earlier.

But it was impossible. Frightened now, she ran upstairs to the bedroom. On the night-table, was the book her husband had been reading, with the bookmark still in place, though she knew she had taken the book downstairs. The words she had read thrummed in her brain: "One who has Long Endur'd may of a sudden break the Bounds of Reason, hurling himself 'gainst the oppressor. . . ."

Her husband's bed was unmade, exactly as it had been when she awoke. Everything was as it had been. And remembering suddenly what had happened when her husband followed her upstairs the night before, she understood why she felt strange and bodiless, why the house remained untouched by her hands. She looked toward her own bed for the first time that morning, knowing already what she would find there. Knowing that her own body, which would never again control the external world, lay sprawled and lifeless, with a red gash across its throat. ——§——

TOP OF THE WORLD

TARLETON COLLIER

It happened in Miami, in Flagler Street. With the idea of asking somebody where he could find the transient bureau, Jones paused in front of one of those curio-souvenir shops with its glitter of gaudy wares fashioned from shells, its jewelry of coral, imitation jade, lapis lazuli; small bottles of orange blossom perfumery; horses, elephants, Scotties carved in bone; colored post-cards, ashtrays shaped like skulls, like dice, like cartoon characters; aquarium turtles with painted backs and all the other catch-penny plunder that is displayed for tourists. Next to the door sat a dark-haired girl, beside a cage in which sprawled striped reptiles and which bore a sign: "Baby Alligators, $1 — We Ship Anywhere." Jones asked the girl.

Without a sound or any other stir she fluttered olive fingers in a gesture that directed him to the interior of the shop, then continued to stare heavy-lidded past him into the bright sunlight of the street. Jones paused a moment, his face sharpened with irritation. His feet ached. He would have shuffled along the sidewalk, but some movement amid the clutter of the shop attracted him and he went inside.

An old man stood awaiting him behind a counter which held a

row of grotesque masks carved in the fibrous husks of coconuts. He might have been himself one of the effigies conjured into life, so brown and wizened he appeared, his eyes as bright as the glistening counterfeits in the carven faces.

"Is there anything you want?" he inquired in a voice of deep music.

"I couldn't buy a stamp," said Jones. "I want to know where is the transient bureau."

The amazing voice seemed to melt in a chuckle, to savor a pleasant dissent. "Ah! That is no wish at all. Your real desire lies in your reason for wanting to know. Why?"

"I want something to eat," said Jones. "I'm hungry. I want a bed. I'm tired."

The unction of that voice was broken by a kind of scornful laughter. "Is that all?"

"Ain't that enough?" asked Jones. "But since you ask me, I'd like to have two dollars to buy a ticket on Racketeer in the fifth race at Arlington Downs tomorrow."

The other's voice rose in a startling thunder. "What about your soul, man?"

"What about my belly?" asked Jones.

"You are a fool," said the curio merchant.

"If you wasn't so old," said Jones, "I'd smack you one."

"Ah!" The music dwindled in a sighing fall, as if by stratagem of softness to beguile an evil mood. "I may be your friend."

"I haven't got a friend," said Jones. "I don't want a friend."

The booming of the old man's voice may have been triumph, yet there was in it a vague bantering mockery. "Behold! The simple existence that should lead to contentment! Your wants are few, you have no burdens because you love nobody."

"I love my kid," said Jones with an odd passion, "and don't you forget it. I'd die for him."

"Live for him," said the old man. He peered past Jones with a sort of blind look. "Go back to him. He needs you."

Jones laughed bitterly. "You're telling me? Well, tell me how I can go, old-timer. If the transient bureau —"

The little brown man leaned toward him with a quick eagerness. He raised a skinny finger. His voice was bated, and now a discord of excitement had entered to mar its melody. "I have something for you and your boy." He strained farther forward. His eyes were bright, and narrowed as by some shrewd intent. "Not our best, but sufficient for one with your simple requirements."

From the little finger of his left hand, the old man drew a ring of bronze. His hands were clammy, but there was strength of steel in their clutch upon Jones as he slipped the ring on the finger of the younger man. It was a strange thing, but the band which had come from his bony talon fitted snugly upon the stout hand of the other.

Jones looked at it with a sour eye, turning his hand. The ring was worn and grimy, with a sort of dim hieroglyph on its back. Not worth a cent.

"What's the gag?" asked Jones.

"It is yours now," said the old man with a deep sigh. He seemed to shrink, to lose life. "Its power is yours. Will it profit you to possess a sight of the future? You have it now—with that ring—one day ahead."

"Hooey," said Jones.

The old man smiled wearily. "Only one day. Tomorrow. But that is eternity. I have seen that I shall die tomorrow."

"Nuts," said Jones, and began pulling the ring from his finger.

The old man's gesture stopped him. "What do you want to know? It will be only what you ask to know. Not everything. Nor can you change anything."

Jones paused, seemed to droop expectantly. A blindish look came into his eyes. Then he gave a cry you could have heard from the street.

"God Almighty!" he said. "It's Rose Marie in the fifth race!"

He turned, lunging, toward the door; turned back so sharply that he staggered.

"Thanks, pal," he said, then was gone, trailed by the ghost of a chuckle.

Jones strode along Flagler Street to the hive of Second Avenue. He knew a place to make a bet, but when he reached it, he stopped short outside and cursed as his hands clapped his empty pockets. He stood brooding at the corner while the lights changed many times, red and green, then darted heedlessly into a red light and kept walking. It was pitch-dark when he paused in a quiet street, blinked away his daze in the incandescence of a shop window and sidled into a doorway at the tap of footsteps. A man approached, immaculate in light trousers and belted sport coat.

"I've got to have two dollars," said Jones, stepping in front of him.

The man made a gesture of impatience. "Get out of—"

Jones smashed his fist upon the words and the man went down. His head struck the metal base of the plate glass and he fell in the inert loose sprawl of a dummy. For Jones, it was the matter of less than four seconds to lift his bill-fold.

Downtown, the book-maker was mildly sardonic on the point of

Rose Marie, but took Jones' two dollars and gave him a ticket. There was still seven dollars in the bill-fold, and Jones found a late barber shop and asked for the works. Afterward he ate, paid for a dollar room in a hotel, and sent a telegram to a town in West Virginia:

"TELL GRANDMA TO GET YOU READY FOR TRIP. BE GOOD. DADDY."

Rose Marie paid $109.60 at the track, but Jones collected only the bookie's fifteen-dollar limit. He left six dollars on a parlay in the next day's races, looked at the sport clothes in the windows along Flagler Street, bought a shirt and a three-dollar necktie.

When he collected the next day, he bought shoes and a pearl-gray hat; the day after, a suit of clothes.

The sky was blue and the crowds thickened day by day . . . Yale to beat Princeton . . . Fisherman's Luck at Tia Juana . . . Machine Gun at Pimlico . . . Alabama and fifteen points . . . The daily double . . . The right dog on the nose . . . U.S. Steel to buy . . . Nice over Ritchie . . .

The boy came down early in December, and Jones, in splendor, met him and the grandmother at the station. Jones sobbed happily as the kid leaped into his arms.

"You little mutt! We're sitting pretty! On top of the world, pal!"

The six-year-old treble was ecstasy. "Daddy! I hardly knew you!"

"How do you like the old man's layout, you bozo? Look at the car! Wait till you see our shack!"

The ocean was green, with white lace as a fringe . . . October cotton for three-point rise . . . Sweetheart Mine at Epsom Downs . . . Guffey to beat Reed in Pennsylvania . . . Insull to be acquitted . . . Navy over Army . . . General Motors to sell . . . General Motors to buy . . . Londos five to one . . . Buy wheat . . . Notre Dame . . .

Jones swung the car southward from Coral Gables, swung across the canal into the twisting road to Tahiti Beach.

"You been here a month, bimbo. How'd you like to go to Monte Carlo?"

The kid squirmed cozily under his arm. "If you go too, daddy."

Jones laughed, deep-throated and content. On top of the world.

Sparkling, the bay came upon them around a bend.

"Tomorrow—" Jones began. He slowed the car. He leaned forward, seemed to peer, his thumb stroking the ring upon his little finger. Suddenly he screamed, jammed his foot upon the brake so sharply that the car quivered and the steering-wheel smashed into his chest.

"Daddy!"

"Bimbo! Kid!"

The mangroves moaned in the wind. The kid whimpered in fright and pain from Jones' savage clutch.

"Don't leave your old man, bimbo!"

"No, daddy. You hurt!"

The automobile careened, roaring, as Jones turned it around with a single wild sweep of the wheel. It rocked crazily as he drove it at eighty miles with one hand, the other holding the kid.

At the house in the oleanders he thrust the boy into the arms of the old woman, the grandmother.

"If you let him out of your sight—you let him in the street—I'll kill you!" he panted.

He dashed away in the car. Sunlight and shadows were blurs. Time was a blur. The gift shop in Flagler Street was gone, a fruit-juice booth was in its place. A woman there, edging nervously away from Jones, said she had heard the shop was closed when somebody died.

Jones wailed, then collapsed, sobbing.

"Died!" he babbled. "Died! I can't do nothing! I can't do nothing for my kid!"

Suddenly snarling, he tore the ring from his finger and flung it into the street. He shouted: "Damn you, devil!"

Lurching into his automobile, he fumbled for the handle of the door, to close it, and his hand struck the pocket in its side. His fingers jerked, stiffened, upon the harsh outlines of the object it contained.

"Bimbo!" he cried wildly.

The woman in the tropical fruit booth, who had been watching him, called out as he raised the pistol to his head, but above everything was the sound of the shot. In an instant people were running along the street to peer into the bright new car, that splendid car, at the limp huddle of the man who for a little while had been on top of the world, where no man may stay. ——

THE TREE OF LIFE

PAUL ERNST

It was cold. God, it was cold! Outside the cabin a blanket of February snow showed leaden white under the heavy, midafternoon clouds. A keening wind growled through the bare-limbed trees. It rattled the dry boughs like the fingers of skeletons; and stole between the slats of the crude window to twitch at the shroud of the thing beneath.

It was from that sheeted, stark figure on the long bench that the greatest cold seemed to emanate. Nothing can be colder than a corpse. Nothing! A corpse seems to radiate a deathly chill that numbs the heart of whoever is near it.

Because of the shrouded body more than because of the actual temperature, I was chilled to the bone in spite of my inches of heavy clothing. I got to my feet and walked up and down the one room of the cabin, averting my eyes from the figure on the bench.

Then, in an effort to conquer fear with familiarity, I crossed the room and lifted the shroud from the hatchet face beneath.

An old woman, looking far older than her years because of her lifetime of toil and disappointments! The hair was scant and yellow-gray. The eyes, open and staring, were like gray stones. The nose seemed to have projected even farther in death than in life. It jutted out like the point of a wedge. There was nothing lovely in *this* pilgrim, set out for the farther shore. There was nothing reposeful here.

It was Mrs. Whilom, wife of Ab Whilom, our nearest farm neighbor. The old couple had been swindled out of their modest Ohio farm five years before. In their old age they had been forced to come to upper Michigan, bare-handed, to wrest a living from the unfamiliar soil. And now—this!

That noon my father and I had hitched up for the twelve-mile drive over laborious roads to town. (This was before the day of teeming autos and cement highways.) In front of the Whilom cabin my father had pulled up the horses and stopped.

Standing before us was Ab—a spare, gnarled man in whom age had curdled like milk in a thunderstorm.

"Jest a minute," he called, coming to the side of the wagon. "I need help."

"Anything we can do—" my father began amiably. He stopped at the look in Ab's eyes.

"My old woman's jest died," he said. The words were as perfunctory as though he had just announced that his hogs had cholera. But his eyes spoke for him. They were dazed, hollowed out with sense of loss.

"Somebody'd ought to stay with her while I go to town for the undertaker," continued Ab. "She couldn't never bide being alone. I'd hate to leave her alone now."

My father turned to me, doubtfully, speculatively.

"Think you can keep her company, son?"

My look must have showed how repulsive I found the idea of a lonely vigil in the squalid cabin with a dead woman, for he hastened on.

"Never mind. I'll do it. You're pretty young. . . ."

Now the youth of youth is a sore point. His reminding me of my sixteen years was sufficient to make me insist on staying there while he drove Ab on into town.

So here I was, shivering in the mean little hut beside the dead Mrs. Whilom, blue with a cold that did not come entirely from the winter wind but that emanated straight from the shrouded thing on the bench under the window.

I replaced the sheet over the hawk features, and sat down before the fireplace. That psychic cold that struck through jacket and mackinaw, knee-high boots and heavy socks! I huddled closer to the fire, resolutely turning my eyes to the leaping flames. I did not want to look toward the dead woman.

I wondered if the body, in life, housed a deathless spirit, as most people claim it does. I wondered where this woman's spirit was. I fancied I knew what other spirit it was with at the moment.

Just before the land deal that had cheated the Whiloms out of their little farm, Ab's daughter had died. The daughter was an unfortunate creature, born blind and dull-witted and ugly. Her whole life had been filled by Mrs. Whilom. And the old lady, to hear Ab tell it, had concentrated all her frustrated hopes and ambitions in a ferocious maternal flame of love for her unfortunate child.

The two had talked without words, Ab had once said. The girl's soul, he said, was twisted around the mother's like a creeper around a tree.

Now was the daughter rejoined in death by the only person that had ever meant anything to her—the only light that had shone in her warped, blind world—her mother? Was the daughter's spirit hovering somewhere near, come to escort the spirit of her beloved parent?

I thought of these things as I huddled miserably over a fire that could not warm me, and prayed the time would not be too long in passing till my father and Ab got back with the undertaker.

I turned to the wood-box, which was full to overflowing, and dumped a big armful of split branches into the fire. This awful cold!

The fire roared higher as I fed it more wood. In an effort to counteract that chilling cold I built a blaze that threatened the safety of the cabin.

The first keen edge of my formless terror gradually wore off, as all keen edges do in time. The psychic chill was less numbing. Or, possibly, it was more numbing. I don't know. Perhaps my fear was now so great that my nerves refused to twitch to its stimulus any more. At any rate, calm, of a sort, came over me. And with this unnatural, stunned calm there came a relief from the coldness.

In spite of the open window, covered only by the few meager slats, in spite of the low temperature outside, I began to feel suffocated. I was dressed to be comfortable at zero. It must have been nearly 60° now in the low, small room.

I took off my mackinaw and loosened my collar. Then, as my feet felt the heat, my boots began to bother me. They were new—and stiff as only new knee-high boots can be. I took them off, too, and padded about in my heavy socks. I opened the door for a foot or so and propped it with a piece of firewood.

Trying to make my mind a blank, I sat down, a good way from the scorching fire. Another two hours would be needed before the trip to town and back could be concluded. Two hours. Two centuries!

I sat there, keeping my eyes on the partly opened door so that I would not see the way the drafts twitched like ghostly fingers at the edge of the shroud.

There was a faint scratching on the bare-swept step outside. A small, tapered head, in which were set two beady eyes, was poked inquisitively around the edge of the door. A wood-rat. And an astonishingly bold one! Driven past fear, no doubt, by the attraction of the warmth and the smell of food in the cupboard.

Cautiously, with many a spasmodic retreat, it came into the cabin. It kept its hard little eyes warily on me. I stayed motionless, glad of any distraction.

After perhaps five minutes of maneuvering, it reached the center of the room and crouched, staring impudently up at me. I reached slowly down beside me for one of my boots. Slowly—

The wood-rat jerked toward the door, but stopped as my descending hand was stayed. It came back. And now my fingers were around the boot-top.

My hand snapped back and up. The rat raced for the door, but a foot away from it the flung boot chanced to catch it squarely. It kicked a little, and lay still, with a fleck of red dabbling its spiky, repulsive whiskers.

I started up to throw the dead rat out of the cabin, when another scratching sound on the step outside came to my ears.

It was a second wood-rat. And this one was either entirely fearless or lost to caution in its discovery of its fellow's fate.

Without even a glance at me, it streaked from the door to the furry body lying beside my boot. It sniffed around the dead rat with inquisitive nose, and stared at it with beady eyes. Then, almost before I could follow its movements, it had streaked for the door again, and was gone.

Almost at once it was back again. And in its mouth was a green leaf, about the size and shape of an oak leaf.

A green leaf! *Green!* In the middle of February in a region where winter is unrelenting and iron-bound!

My face must have been a mask of stupidity as I stared at that leaf. Where in the name of all that was miraculous could the rodent have found it? There were no green trees in the countryside at that time of year! I knew there were none. Yet—here was this leaf!

The rat was less quick this time, less bold. It crept slowly toward the stiffening body of its mate. As it advanced it kept its glittering little eyes directed—not toward me, curiously enough, but toward the corpse.

There followed a most astounding spectacle.

The rat began to scurry aimlessly around the room as though something were chasing it. Carefully holding the amazing leaf clear of the floor, it dodged wildly from one wall to the other, always keeping its eyes fixed on thin air in front of it. I was as completely disregarded as though I had not been there.

Toward the improvised bier the rat scurried, only to double spasmodically away from it and run under my very chair. Had the thing gone mad? I began to fumble for my other boot, fear of a bite overcoming my curiosity to see the outcome of this inexplicable play.

The rat approached its dead mate again, keeping its eyes on a spot on the wall over the body—as if there were something there that was invisible to my eyes.

With a quick move it placed the green leaf squarely on the little stark body. And behold—a miracle!

The rat that was dead was no longer dead! Under my very gaze it quivered and came to life. The legs jerked once or twice. The body twitched. The creature rose, limping and stiff, and followed its mate out the door!

My mind whirled in a blind chaos. That impossible green leaf— its contact with the dead rat—the resurrection of the little pest!

As had everyone else who lived in that part of the state, I had heard tales of a fabulous Tree of Life. Somewhere in the region there was said to be a tree that could raise the dead at a mere touch. The myth had been handed down to the old-timers by the Indians. My father had heard the yarn from his father, and had told it to me when I was a youngster and begged for a fairy-story.

It was a myth. Of course it was a myth! There could be no truth in such a thing! But—that wood-rat had surely been dead. And now it was alive!

I stared at the leaf, still lying on the floor. Like an oak leaf, it was, but of a softer texture and a lighter green. A leaf from the Tree—

My gaze went, fascinated, from the leaf to the body under the window.

A dead rat had come to life. Why could not a dead human being? Both were flesh. Both were made of the same stuff. And here, to my hand, was this incredible green leaf.

I left my chair and picked it up. It seemed to curl about my fingers with a life of its own. It was soft as the softest silk, and warm —like no other leaf I'd ever touched. The feel of it went through me like wine. I seemed to expand, to grow larger than my own self.

Clutching the leaf, I started toward the corpse. As I went the numbing chill that had paralyzed me before, laid hold of me again. And suddenly, as though the touch of the leaf had given my eyes new power, I thought I saw something wavering protectively over the dead body. I say "thought" because by now it was early dusk, and the misty shape I seemed to see was so intermingled with the gathering shadows that I could not be sure. Also, when I blinked my eyes to test their veracity, the vision disappeared.

I lifted up the shroud, and started to touch the leaf to the dead woman's face—

Icy fingers seemed to catch at my wrist! My hand was torn away! "Will!"

It was like a shower of ice-cold water, that whip-like crack of my name sounding behind me. I gasped with the suddenness of it, combined as it was with the sheer terror that had crept through me at the fancied touch of those unseen fingers.

My hand opened convulsively. As though caught up by some invisible force, the leaf whirled out the window and was gone.

"Has anything happened to upset you?" asked my father, putting his hand anxiously on my shoulder.

"No," I mumbled. "No. Nothing at all has happened."

"I thought I saw something blow out of the window," he persisted. I made no answer.

Ab, meanwhile, was taking a last look at the woman who had helped and cared for him for so long.

"She's happier now, I reckon," he muttered. "She's with Patty, prob'ly, with our poor blind daughter. . . ."

I never told them what had happened in that cabin. A kid of sixteen doesn't tell such things. He's too sure he'll be laughed at. It's only now, when I am well along in years, that I dare to relate the affair and speculate about it.

Was the rat really dead? Possibly not; I am in no position to prove it. Did I merely imagine that wavering thing by the corpse, and the touch of those cold fingers? Perhaps; one's imagination is apt to work overtime during such a vigil. Could the spirit of the dead daughter have really been in that room, and did it first chase the rat and then clutch at my wrist in an effort to keep the mother from being resurrected? It sounds unbelievable.

The only fact that I can reiterate is that the leaf—in the midst of winter—was green. I saw it, held it in my hand. What would have happened had I touched it to the corpse? I don't *know*, of course, but I think . . . I think. . . . ———

THE TRYST IN THE TOMB

M. J. CAIN

The Signora Beatrice lay dead, perfumed and enshrouded, in the Junetime of her life; and the proud old Neapolitan, who had been her husband, sat near, dumb with the love of his young bride.

Silent forms passed in and out. They made no attempt at speech with the master of the palazzo; his look and attitude forbade it. Even the entrance of Carmina and the Countess Valeria, who had been very dear to the dead, drew from him no sign of recognition. They passed over to the bier and hung shaken with sobs above the beautiful form. Carmina, a tiny, passionate creature, stooped and touched the darkly fringed lids.

"Oh, I know, *carina*, these glorious eyes could not go on longer, smiling a lie; so you closed them forever. You were forced to give up Don Orlino for the wealth you despised. Now, all we have of you is this." Again she bent, and passionately kissed the cold, still face. "Why did you do it, darling, why, why?"

The countess tenderly slipped an arm about the hysterical girl and gently drew her from the death-chamber.

By some magnetic current, some miracle, an echo of the words reached the grief-stricken husband, hitherto deaf to all around him, and, had they two glanced back, they would have seen a changed man. His form stiffened into a sudden erectness and flames leaped to his olive cheeks.

Don Orlino! Don Orlino! The name rang on his emptiness a deeper knell.

Ignoring her love for another, he had won through the pressure of her parents and claimed the hand of the radiantly beautiful Beatrice. He never dreamed, in his vanity and self-complacency, that the heart of his bride would yearn, in the midst of the splendors he could provide, for the summer hours spent with her forsaken love. He took pride in her beauty, grace, and intellect. Rapidly and gloriously, for him, the days flew by. In his fevered happiness, he could not see the decline in his wife that was visible to all. The shock of her death froze his heart, and he, too, had been as one dead from that first dark instant, until the words of Carmina touched him like a flame from hell.

He strode across the room and gazed fiercely down on the lifeless eyes. All the blood in his body seemed striving for outlet at temples and throat.

"Say they so? Say they so?" His voice sounded strangely thin and sharp like the cut of a lash. "That Don Orlino had thus effectively snatched my heaven from me? If I believed it true, I would kill him —yes, kill him miserably." The words trailed away to a husky whisper.

After that, he no longer sat unnoticing. He eagerly scanned everyone who approached the lovely dead. But no soldier form with martial bearing entered to offer itself to a jealous husband's vengeance; and finally they laid the Signora Beatrice in the family vault without Don Orlino having looked on her dead face.

Daily Sardinossa wended his way to her resting-place and put fresh flowers on her satin shroud. This duty he reserved for himself alone; no other hand was allowed to touch the adored form. Agonizingly he waited for the first sign of the deadly decay. Those who served him feared for his reason, when it should make its appearance. But it tarried long, and, every day, new-blown flowers were necessary to match the surpassing loveliness of the dead woman's face.

Finally the strange truth was evident to all, and, with overwhelming joy, was borne in on the doting husband. She was petrifying. Petrifying! He cried the word aloud and asked in wild-eyed exultation, of those about him, if they realized that the ravaging worm had been held at bay; that the cycling stars could record no destruction of her beauty; that the face of his Beatrice would be his to look on, as long as life was allowed him. The vault became for him a shrine, and many trancelike hours were spent within its silent precincts.

One evil day the rumor reached him that the shrine had a rival devotee, that one came often during the reign of the full moon, who feasted long on the beauty of the dead bride's face. A horrible suspicion thrilled through him like the touch of a live wire, and mad passions, unleashed in his heart, rendered him deaf and dumb and blind.

That night the moon would be full. In a fever, he waited the waning of the day. He seemed hours within the moon-drenched tomb when, at last, a quick step without made him hastily regain his place of concealment behind a fluted column.

A key grated in the lock, and the stalwart young form of Don Orlino stood silhouetted in the entrance. Evidently he knew the exact moment to come, the moment when the moon would serve him, when no artificial light would be necessary, that might betray his tryst with the dead.

The moonbeams had just crept through the barred window and softly outlined the marble form. In its light the white shroud shimmered and the still face shone wondrously, hauntingly beautiful.

Only the dawning of a ghastly, hideous determination kept the bereft husband from springing upon Don Orlino and choking him to death, as he watched him rain kisses on the beloved eyes and lips and hair. A fury of fiendish hate shook his heart almost audibly, as the minutes of the strange love-tryst waned, and there was a mad hilarity in his eyes as he watched the reluctant departure of Don Orlino.

He crept from the shadows and leaned, ghastly pale, above the shrouded corpse. All the love, all the worship, were gone from his eyes. Only a searing, withering hate for her, too, shone in them.

"So you went to him through death, as they said." The tremulous quavering of his tone manifested the descent of a sudden insanity. "Well, by the most terrible God, through death he shall go to you!"

The following day, and two thereafter, workmen were busy within the tomb, at a task over which they greatly wondered. What did the grand *signor* want with the carefully hewn-out niche in the vaulted wall and the heavy iron gate that enclosed it from ceiling to floor! Did he intend to place the gentle Signora Beatrice erect within it, after the fashion of the ancient Egyptians? Two shook their heads gravely over the contemplated desecration, but the third shrugged his shoulders indifferently and went on with his work, arguing that there was no accounting for the vagaries of the rich and powerful.

When their work was completed, Sardinossa came to look it over, and astounded the three with the munificence of his reward. A diabolical exultation swept over him as he tested the working of the iron gate. It swung to, swiftly, easily, with a click that spoke for the security of its fastenings. Then, consumed with a malignant eagerness, he watched the daylight die.

It is inconceivable with what satisfaction he dwelt on the carrying out of the horrible purpose that possessed him. He had a task before him, a diabolical task, which must be performed. His soul was on fire to accomplish it speedily and well.

Moonrise found Sardinossa in the region of the tomb, and a smile, or rather, a hideous grimace, wrinkled his countenance, as Don Orlino's shadow fell long on the silvered grass. He allowed time for the caresses that maddened him, then moved in the direction of the tomb.

At the sound of his footstep, Don Orlino, surprized and startled, stood erect and faced the entrance. The two men stared at each other for a full half-minute.

Sardinossa was the first to break the silence. "Rather a tardy visit, this, Don Orlino. You never honored us so during the lady's lifetime." His voice was steady and betrayed no sign of the black purpose hidden in his soul.

"That it was impossible will always be counted my greatest regret," replied Don Orlino.

"One can readily believe that, who sees you take this time and this place to recompense yourself for impossible or neglected visits."

The biting sarcasm of his tone sent the hot blood to Don Orlino's face and warm words to his lips.

"Sardinossa, Beatrice was, as you know, once the dream of my life. If she ever was of yours, then you knew the ecstasy of its realization. This"—he pointed dramatically to the moon-bathed figure—"was its nearest fulfilment for me. Of course, I do not expect you to approve—"

"On the contrary," interrupted Sardinossa, "strange as it may seem, you will find that I shall expend special effort in assisting you to a fuller realization of your dream. Do not think I shall forbid you the place. Indeed, you may consider it yours from tonight forth."

The tenseness of the voice, the cold light in the eye, like the flash of steel on steel, the ominous calm before the storm—all were lost on Don Orlino in the joy of the privilege granted. His cherished love, with its mingled grief and pain, made him, the soldier and strategist, like an unsuspecting child in the hands of this finished master of cunning.

"They tell me you come always at night, when the moon is full." Sardinossa's cold, even voice again woke the echoes of the tomb.

Don Orlino started. Sardinossa had been aware, then, of the stolen vigils. For the first time, Don Orlino, somewhat distrustful of the apparent calm, searched Sardinossa's face for a sign of suppressed passion, but it was bland, smiling.

"I thought, perhaps," the almost sarcastic tones went on, "the moon might enhance charms already more than heart-breaking, so I came to see."

"That were impossible," Don Orlino returned passionately. "Beatrice was, and remains, beautiful in all lights, at all times. I come at night because she gave you the right to come in the daylight, to love, to adore before men. For me, she left only this tryst in the tomb, these stolen moments. Can you not understand? Can you not pity?"

The old eyes flamed with a horrid mirth. "Yes, I can understand, I can pity. You will not long be without an evidence of the fact." A short, hard laugh finished the remark. Evidently the laugh was involuntary and instantly regretted, for he went on with an undue haste and overdone affability. "Of one thing I have assured myself: that the cold, damp atmosphere of the vault at night is not for the old. It has stiffened my knees painfully." He stooped and pressed them in a helpless manner. "My stick, I left it there." He pointed toward the newly made niche at the foot of the casket.

Don Orlino sprang in the direction indicated and felt about for the stick. Unable to find it, he moved closer to the wall and felt about more carefully.

Like a flash, the old form unbent, and, with the speed of a tiger in action, Sardinossa had crossed the little space and swung shut the gate on his victim.

Startled, Don Orlino struggled about in the narrow enclosure and faced a fiend incarnate. Blue lightnings leaped from Sardinossa's gloating eyes, and his voice was like the taunt of a demon.

"Now realize to the full your dream—look your fill." Sardinossa spat out the words. "You see I have placed you conveniently at her feet, and when the extremity of hunger and thirst begins to burn and torture, curse her, curse love, curse God, and die."

He darted a final glance of undying hate at Don Orlino, who stood, magnificently defiant, like an American Indian at the torture. Going out, he locked the tomb and turned his back on it forever.

Years after, when the body of Sardinossa was brought home from a foreign land for burial, those who entered the tomb with the remains shrank back in terror. There were sharp cries. With a thud that echoed dismally, the coffin slipped from their trembling hands; and, powerless to withdraw their eyes, they gazed with unutterable horror on the ghastly monument Sardinossa had raised to the green-eyed monster.

Behind the bars of the gate, gleaming white and ghostly, and hung with tatters of moldering garments, was the skeleton of Don Orlino.

His cavernous eyes were fixed on the statuesque dead, and dangling down against the protruding ribs, just where the noble heart once beat, was an ivory miniature of the laughing girl-face of the lady of his worship. —✠—

UNDER THE EAVES

HELEN M. REID

Thump—thump—thump.

Spasmodically, above the wailing of the wind and the dismal battering of the rain against the windows, the ominous sound was repeated.

Thump—thump—thump.

Something was hitting against the side of the house—something heavy. Hannah rose uneasily and laid down her sewing. Susan would be coming for the dress in the morning, but she could not keep her mind on the stitches.

She thought resentfully of Judy. The ingrate! That was the thanks you got for twenty years of slaving. To be left alone with nothing to listen to but the wind and the rain and that hideous thumping.

For perhaps the twentieth time that night she pulled the shade back from one of the windows and stared out into the darkness. Thump—thump. The sound was close now, but beyond the window was an abyss of blackness in which she could see nothing. Shivering, she sat down once more in front of the grate, where a fire struggled fitfully against the fury of the storm without and the semi-darkness of the room within. In its wavering circle of light she sat erect and defiant, the flames outlining her sharp features and thin knot of graying hair.

It wasn't because she was getting old, she told herself sternly. A night like this would get on anybody's nerves. If Nate hadn't cleared out as he did— She frowned impatiently.

"Where'd they a been without me, I'd like to know," she muttered. "And now they don't care what becomes o' me. Neither one o' them."

Anyway, thank goodness, the thumping had stopped. But what was that? Someone knocking? Who on earth would be venturing out in such a storm? But the knocking was repeated.

Resolutely she threw the door open. A rush of rain and wind blurred her vision for an instant, and in that instant a man pushed past her, a tall man, thin and somewhat stooped, with straggling gray hair that hung dripping about his seamed face; for in spite of the roughness of the night he wore no hat.

Hannah turned to face him; then abruptly she slammed the door shut and locked it.

"So you've come back to the old woman, have you?" She confronted him scornfully. "Found out nobody else would put up with you, I suppose."

He made no reply but settled himself in his favorite chair by the grate.

"That's right," she went on bitingly. "Make yourself comfortable. How you've got nerve to come back after walking out on me like you did I don't know."

"Seems to me you told me to walk out." His words were pleasant but disturbingly sarcastic. She noticed that his usual docility of manner was entirely gone.

"Better get on some dry clothes," she snapped. "You'll catch your death of cold."

A faintly sarcastic smile was his only reply. He made no movement, and for once she was at a loss what to say. She felt baffled and confused.

"You told me to go," he repeated, "and I went. Why do you blame me?"

She felt her face growing hot at the quiet rebuff.

"Blame you?" she retorted. "I blame you for being a shiftless, good-for-nothing fool, that's what. Look at Clem Hanks. You don't find him dilly-dallying his time away, and what's the result? He makes more money in a day than you'll ever make in a month. And if there's anything more useless than a man that can't make a decent living, I don't know what it is."

"You convinced me of that."

Something in his voice made her look at him intently. "Nate," she said slowly, "you know I don't mean things half as bad as I say them. If I'd a thought you had spunk enough to get out I'd a never told you to and that's God's truth."

She pointed to the sewing that lay where she had left it. "If it wasn't for the work Susan Hanks gives me to do I don't know how I'd keep body and soul together. Now you're back, maybe—"

"Won't Judy help?"

She fidgeted under the gaze of his steady eyes. "That girl—" She checked herself.

"Well?"

"She left after you did."

"Because—"

"Because she turned against her own mother, that's why. Didn't I do everything for her with my own hands? and now she takes sides with you. I'm sure I don't know why."

"Maybe I *was* of some use," he suggested.

"Land knows I'm glad enough you came back. I don't know what's come over me, but what with you gone and Judy gone, this place is like a tomb."

Thump—thump—thump. There it was again!

"I wish you'd see what that is," she said. "It gave me quite a turn when I was alone, but now you're here—"

The fire had burned low. Nate's chair seemed to have drawn back into the shadows.

"You won't mind, will you?" She was not in the habit of asking that question, but tonight seemed different.

Thump—thump—thump.

"Nate!"

A sudden flare from the dying fire illumined the room. Nate's chair was empty!

"Nate! Nate!" she called wildly.

The wind shrieked around the house in a paroxysm of fury. The rain lashed against the windows. There was no other answer.

Thump—thump.

A cold trembling seized her. She ran to the window and threw it open. Thump—thump. The thing was almost close enough for her to touch. She reached out. Her hand closed on a sodden sleeve, a man's arm. She screamed. The next instant she had swayed and fallen.

529

When she opened her eyes she was stretched out in bed with Susan Hanks bending over her.

"Clem heard you scream and came and got me to look after you," she explained.

"Is he—dead?"

Susan looked away. "Yes," she said.

"Can't they do—something?" There was a note of pleading in Hannah's harsh voice. "He was in here," she said. "I was talkin' to him just before I found him—out there."

Susan left the room quickly. Hannah heard her speaking to someone in a low voice. Then the words of Clem's reply came to her distinctly.

"Better send for Judy," he said. "She is delirious. Nate was hanging from those eaves all evening. The doctor says he's been dead for hours." ——+——

The Unveiling

Alfred I. Tooke

Ravenoff's studio," Parker told the cabman. "Sorry I kept you waiting, people."

"Don't apologize," Buchanan said. "I don't think any of us are in a hurry to view Ravenoff's latest."

"But please, I am!" Patricia Clark protested. "I'm really anxious to see one of what Ted calls Ravenoff's 'diabolical' paintings."

"Ted should be shot at sunrise for bringing you," Parker growled.

"I tried to dissuade her, but—" Ted shrugged expressive shoulders.

"I can't believe Ravenoff's paintings are really so terrible," Pat continued. "When I met him, he seemed such a pet rabbit of a man."

Parker chuckled delightedly. "Ravenoff is an enigma. There's Ravenoff the man; frail-looking, soft-spoken, kind, gentle, considerate. His wife and youngsters adore him. His friends swear by him. But Ravenoff the painter? He's a madman! He seizes a brush, and *voilà*—he's possessed of a devil! He slaps pigments on with wild, slathering strokes and vicious jabs. He doesn't harmonize colors; he clashes them. He doesn't paint human beings; he strips civilization and convention away and paints emotions, the base, cruel, terrible emotions. He paints stark fear and sheer terror and grisly horror and bestial cruelty only as one who has lived through them can paint them."

"As one who has lived through them?" prompted Pat.

"Ravenoff was the child of aristocrats when the Russian revolution broke. They let *him* live. To kill him would have been too easy, too kind. But his pitiful, starved body and cringing soul absorbed the fear and terror, the horror and cruelty, and survived. Now he paints those things with such vivid reality and intensity that pigment and canvas cannot hold them imprisoned. They leap out at you to fill your bloodstream and inflame your brain. You grind your teeth with rage or hate; you break out in a cold sweat of fear; or overpowering greed or cruelty possesses your soul—or should I say dispossesses it?" He turned to Buchanan. "Did you see his first great picture, *Beelzebub?*"

Buchanan shuddered. "And had nightmares for weeks And *Greed* was even more repulsive. The bestial expressions on the faces of the rabble, the utter cruelty of their grasping, claw-like hands—ugh! Thank Heaven I was too late to see *Hate.*"

"I think nobody regretted the fate of that picture," Parker said, then answered the question in Pat's eyes. "A local millionaire bought it and presented it to the Public Museum. People would go and stare at it until hate burned in their eyes and distorted their features. Two people went away and committed murder under its influence before an attendant was stationed beside it to keep people moving. For three days he performed that duty. The fourth day he didn't show up."

"Why?" Pat asked.

"Your fiancé covered the case for the paper."

"And may I never cover another like it!" Ted breathed. "He was a likable old chap, but his domestic life had evidently been anything but happy. He brought home the money. His wife and two grownup daughters squandered it for him, nagging constantly because there was not more. After three days with that picture he murdered the lot of them in the most brutal fashion imaginable. Next day someone slashed the painting to ribbons. Ravenoff's next picture was *War*, but it was sold privately to a collector and has never been publicly exhibited."

"What ghastly titles!" Pat said. *"Beelzebub! Greed! Hate! War!"*

"And now *Death.*"

Patricia shuddered. "I'd think Ravenoff would want to forget such things, or keep them hidden in his mind instead of perpetuating them on canvas."

Buchanan shook his head. "To forget them he must first work them out of his system. People who bottle up things in their minds brood over them and go mad. The pressure becomes too great and the bottle bursts; then *all* their mind, instead of just part, is affected. Psychiatrists bring such things into the open to be dispelled, just as matter from a festering sore is got rid of so the injured part can heal cleanly. Perhaps when Ravenoff has rid his mind of the unpleasant emotions, his kinder, gentler self may gain dominance over his brush, and he may give us—but here we are."

Alighting, Parker eyed the cars parked solidly on both sides of the street. "Not a very exclusive unveiling, I'm afraid," he apologized. "Even model-T Fords!"

"Sure! Didn't you hear what the old geezer who bought the picture done yesterday?" the driver asked. "Chartered a cab for the afternoon." He indicated Parker's invitation, taken from his wallet with the fare. "He had a stack of them things. Yeah, he filled 'em in that way, too: Admit So-and-so and friends, and he told 'em no limit to the number of friends, 'cause he wanted everyone to see this picture."

"To whom did he give the invitations?"

"Cripes, everybody, Mr. Parker! Workmen on buildings, folks in stores, truck drivers, shoppers, folks in the West End and the East End and the Ghetto and Chinatown, on the docks and—well, he covered the city. While I unloaded a gent here at two o'clock, along come a Kosher butcher I know, with forty-three relatives. I counted 'em! And a little Eyetalian boot-black brought all his relatives from his great-grandmothers down to the latest flock of bambinos. And three Chinese in tails and toppers—say, they've had to let folks in in relays. Thank you, sir. Thanks!"

Parker joined his guests. "Up this driveway," he said.

"Look!" Patricia gestured. "The people coming out!"

"A motley crowd, certainly!" Parker said. "I understand Neville Walker went into the highways and byways to invite all and sundry, not to mention their friends and relatives. Rather perverted sense of humor, if you could call—"

"No, no! I mean their expressions. Look at that woman's face."

Parker did. His gaze followed the woman after she had passed.

"They're all like that," Patricia said. "They don't notice us. They all look as if they were seeing a vision."

They followed Parker to the barn-like studio behind the house. Ravenoff's secretary received them in an ante-room where a dozen people already waited.

"Monsieur Ravenoff was suddenly called away," he said. "He left a note asking me to express his regret that he could not greet you personally and show you his painting." He waved toward the studio door. "The others are nearly all out now."

And presently the last of the others emerged, and the secretary ushered the latest comers in. The only lighting in the studio was at the far end before a great drape that entirely hid the end wall.

"Monsieur Ravenoff wishes you to look at the painting as long as you wish," the secretary said, "but he does not wish you to advance beyond the rail. The painting is so large, he says, that only from back here can you get the proper perspective."

He vanished. Something whirred. The drapes slid aside and there was the painting. One or two gasped; then there was silence, utter and complete.

On the great canvas, as wide and as high as the studio wall itself, not one in that silent audience saw what had been expected. Only at one end did colors clash. There one saw the trenches and shattered buildings, the shell-torn trees and wrecked bridges of a battlefield, and people, infinitely weary people, coming away, staggering, stumbling, some with improvised crutches, some crawling, some without arms or legs, some without sight.

And there was a great city of factories and foundries, docks and railroad yards, store and office buildings and traffic-congested streets. At a railroad crossing was a wrecked train and school bus. On a mountainside a great airplane had crashed. On a rocky coast a ship was pounding to pieces. Beyond, a village was being devastated by an earthquake. Everywhere, in some form or other, was Death, and people coming, some crippled, some whole, some with hopeless defeat in their bearing, some with a look of great questioning, but all converging toward the path leading up the storm-swept hill, to meet and mingle and toil onward and upward.

And presently they passed out of the storm clouds to sunshine and flowers and singing birds, and then they did not look so tired or so defeated, but their eyes were alight with hope. And reaching the top of the hill none were crippled or deformed, for no longer did the discarded mortal body encumber them; and on each face was infinite peace and joy as they scattered, the children to play in flower-strewn fields, the elders to wander by twos and threes into the sunlit vistas beyond.

And the gaze of those in the studio came back, from time to time, to the words lettered along the bottom of the great canvas: "Death is not fearsome or terrible. Death is a beautiful, shining adventure."

It was Buchanan who broke the silence at last. "Wonderful! Magnificent!" he said. "But Ravenoff slipped up on one tiny detail."

"What might that be?" Ted asked.

"The shadows cast by that figure down in the corner of the battle-field. See it, right down in the lower left-hand corner of the canvas; the figure of a man with the bullethole in his forehead and the blood running down his face onto the revolver clutched in his hand. The shadows are on the wrong side."

"Merciful heaven!" There was horror in Ted's voice. He leaped the rail and raced forward. He stooped. When he straightened, his face was a mask of horror. He moved between the figure and the canvas.

"It—it's Ravenoff!" he said. ——+——

THE VIOLET DEATH

GUSTAV MEYRINK

A day or two before Pompejus Jaburek died in the hospital in Lucknow, he called the head nurse, entrusted to her a bulky envelope which he had been keeping under his pillow, and urged her, after his death, to see that its contents were given as wide publicity as possible. She might turn it over to the Government, to the press—she would know better than he how it could be made widely known. He had no doubt that the information contained in it was profoundly important—at least it was extremely strange and curious—and the only reason why he had not told his whole story when he had first got back to civilization and safety was that he was afraid of being tempted to betray a secret which might do the world incalculable harm. Well—she would understand what he meant when she had read his story, and after all, the delay was not important, since he was growing so much weaker that he knew he could not live a great deal longer. And when he died, carrying the secret with him, the danger would be over, at least the danger of any harm for which he should be responsible, and only the strange and perhaps valuable information would remain.

Pompejus Jaburek was a nondescript southeast European who had been a servant of the British explorer Sir Roger Thornton. The most remarkable thing about him was that he was as deaf as a post —he had told the nurse once that he had gone stone-deaf as a child and had never heard a sound since—but that he was so expert at lip-reading that in a good light he could talk to you for hours, so easily and intelligently that you would have had no suspicion of his deaf-ness if it had not been for the careful, singsong tone that all deaf persons acquire, like the extraordinarily cautious step of a blind man. Aside from this, his English was perfect.

He had been brought to the hospital from somewhere off to the north, two or three months before, in a very dilapidated condition, with a bad wound in his foot, and apparently with his mind clean gone. He had recovered his faculties in time, and had grown so much better that he was able to sit up in bed and write, industriously, for hours—hence the manuscript which he was bequeathing to the hospital—but although he talked intelligently and sometimes rather freely, his eyes glittered with terror when anything was said about his relations with Sir Roger, and he would cut the discussion short with a curt declaration that he was sure the English explorer would never be seen again. And since no one was sure that Pompejus Jaburek was entirely sane, no one pressed him for an explanation. He wasted away from what seemed to be the effects of a slow poison, and one morning he did not awaken.

His manuscript, written in spite of great weakness and distress of mind, was almost impossible to decipher and was full of gaps and inconsistencies. But its drift was approximately as follows:

Somewhere up on the Tibetan frontier, Sir Roger Thornton had been visited by a Tibetan "Sannyasin" or penitential pilgrim, on his way to Benares. Sir Roger had a profound respect for the Sannyasin. He knew that they are pretty sure to be intelligent, and that they are filled with an earnestness that makes them entirely honest. He did not know why the Sannyasin told him the story of the strange Tibetan colony in the isolated valley, but he had seen and heard so many mysterious things in his contacts with this strange race that nothing he heard about them surprized him. He knew that they hate the Europeans and that they cherish magic secrets with which they hope some day to destroy them. But Sir Hannibal Roger Thornton was one of the bravest men who ever lived, and he determined at once to see with his own eyes whether this colony possessed the magical powers which the Sannyasin imputed to them.

Sir Roger had a group of Asiatic guides and servants with him, but he knew that they were superstitious and cowardly, and that they would be entirely useless on such an expedition as this. So he touched his deaf Balkan lieutenant with his stick, and he told him in detail all that he had learned from the Tibetan ascetic.

Some twenty days' journey from their camp, in a side valley of the Himavat, which had been so carefully described to him that he could go directly to it, it appeared that there was a very curious bit of territory. It was a tiny valley, and on three sides of it the mountains rose almost perpendicularly, so that there was no entrance or egress except from the fourth side, and the fourth side was very strangely cut off by gaseous exhalations which rose constantly from the spongy earth, and which were so deadly poisonous that any living being which tried to cross would be almost certain to be suffocated and never reach the other side. In the ravine itself, which was reported to be in dimensions perhaps half a dozen miles each way, lived a little tribe, in the midst of the most luxuriant vegetation, a tribe belonging to the Tibetan race, wearing a characteristic pointed red cap, and worshipping a Satanic being in the form of a peacock. This devilish being, in the course of the centuries, had taught the tribe a potent black magic, and had transmitted secrets to them which were capable, in time, of changing the face of the earth. Thus, they had perfected a kind of melody, which if properly executed would destroy the strongest man in an instant. . . .

Pompejus grinned sarcastically.

Sir Roger explained to him that he had thought out a way of passing the poison-gas region with the help of diving-helmets and reservoirs of compressed air, and that he was sure there would be no serious difficulty about reaching the valley in this way. Pompejus Jaburek nodded approval, and rubbed his dirty hands together delightedly.

The Tibetan pilgrim had told the exact truth. The two Europeans reached a spot where the strange ravine was plainly visible, with its marvelous vegetation; and between it and them stretched a yellow-brown, desert-like girdle of loose, friable earth, not more than a mile wide, and cutting the marvelous valley completely off from the rest of the world.

The exhalations which rose incessantly from the girdle of desert were pure carbonic acid gas. Sir Roger Thornton climbed a little hill and studied the situation very carefully. Then he decided to cross the poisonous belt the next morning. The diving-outfits which he had ordered from Bombay worked perfectly.

Pompejus carried two repeating rifles and various other articles which his chief deemed necessary.

An intrepid Afghan adventurer who had first thought of accompanying the two had flatly refused to go along when he had learned that the black art was involved. He had remarked that he was perfectly willing to crawl into a tiger's den, but that he declined to embark on an enterprise which might imperil his immortal soul. So Sir Roger and Jaburek constituted the expeditionary force.

The copper helmets glittered in the sun. The poison-gas crept out of the spongy soil in numberless tiny bubbles. Sir Roger had set out at a rapid, swinging gait, so that there would be no danger that the supply of air would be exhausted before the gas-zone was passed. The mountain-backed valley in front of the two floated and swayed before the eyes of the invaders like the bed of a moving brook. The sunlight had a ghostly green tinge and colored the distant glaciers — the "Roof of the World" — with its gigantic profile, like a wonderful landscape of death.

Sir Roger and Pompejus had passed the arid belt, had stepped out on the beautiful green turf, and with the help of a match or two had convinced themselves that good oxygen was present at every distance from the ground. Then the two removed their diving-outfits.

Behind them the wall of gas wavered like a strangely tenuous stream. The air was filled with a heady perfume, like the odor of amberia blossoms. Gleaming, party-colored butterflies as big as your hand, with markings these white men had never seen before, sat on the silent flowers with their wings spread wide, like open conjurers' books.

The two, several steps apart, moved toward the little wood which cut off their view of the main part of the valley. . . .

Sir Roger gave his deaf servant a sign — he was sure he had heard a noise. Pompejus lifted the trigger of his gun. . . .

They skirted the little forest, and came out on a broad meadow. A quarter of a mile from the wood, they saw perhaps a hundred men, evidently Tibetans, all topped with pointed red caps, and drawn up in a semicircle. They must have had wind of their visitors' coming, and they were ready to receive them. Sir Roger and his servant walked intrepidly, abreast of each other, but several feet apart, toward the waiting phalanx.

These Tibetans were dressed in the sheepskin coats which are the usual garb of the race; but as the Europeans came nearer to them they were startled by the unearthly ugliness of all the faces, which were naturally hideous and were moreover distorted by expressions of violent loathing, hatred and malice. They allowed the two to come very near them; then all at once, in perfect unison like one man, at a signal from a leader they all raised their hands and held them tight against their ears. Then they all shouted something at the top of their voices.

Pompejus Jaburek looked toward his master for instructions, and brought his gun into position, for the strange maneuver of the group seemed to presage some hostile intention. But what he saw as he glanced at Sir Roger drove every drop of his blood from his heart.

About the Englishman a trembling, floating garment of gas had formed, like that which the two had traversed a short time before.

Sir Roger's form began to lose its contours, as if it had been attacked by the gas and were disintegrating under its influence. The head seemed to grow pointed; then the whole mass began to sink into itself as if it were dissolving, and on the spot where a few moments before the big, athletic Englishman had stood, nothing was visible any longer but a clear violet cone like a great lump of colored sugar. . . .

Deaf Pompejus was seized with an impulse of mad rage. The Tibetans continued to scream, and with his uncanny skill at lipreading, he noticed that they were uttering the same word or phrase again and again. His anger seemed to have given him a clairvoyant clearness of intelligence, and his lips began to form the sound which he saw on all those ugly lips in front of him. . . .

Suddenly their leader sprang out before them, and they all stopped yelling and took their hands away from their ears. Like panthers they all rushed at Pompejus. The deaf man began to fire into the mob like a madman with his repeating rifle. This stopped them for a moment.

Then, obeying some mysterious impulse, he began to bawl at the company the syllables which he had learned from their lips. He had caught the thing perfectly, and he bellowed it with his mighty lungs like a whole army shouting a war-cry.

He grew dizzy, everything went dim and dark before him. The earth began to sway under his feet, and he came near falling. But the feeling of dizziness lasted only a few seconds, and his mind and his senses cleared again.

The Tibetans had disappeared—disappeared exactly as his master had done—and in their place he saw a great number of the little violet cones.

Their leader was still alive. His legs were already transformed into a bluish paste, and the upper part of his body was shrinking away. It seemed as if his substance were being digested in a great transparent or invisible stomach. This man did not wear a red cap like the others, but an elaborate head-dress like a bishop's miter, in which yellow, living eyes could be seen moving to and fro. . . .

Jaburek stepped up to the creature and struck him on the head with the butt of his rifle, but his enemy still had the strength to hurl a sickle-shaped weapon at him and wound him in the foot. . . .

The victor stood and looked about him. No living thing was visible anywhere on the plain. . . .

The odor of amberia blossoms had grown so intense that it was almost suffocating. It seemed to be given out by the violet cones, which Pompejus now examined with some care. They were almost entirely uniform, and all consisted of the same clear violet gelatinous slime. Since the Tibetans had moved forward to surround him, Pompejus could not distinguish the remains of Sir Roger from the other violet pyramids.

Mad with rage, Pompejus crushed the pitiful substance of the half-dissolved leader under his heavy heels; then he made his way back to the edge of the green island. The copper helmets lay shining in the sun. . . . He pumped one of the reservoirs full of air and started back across the gas-zone. He struggled on over the strip of desert, his head buzzing with confusion, grief and horror. The ice-topped giants of the Himalayas towered toward heaven—what cared they for the pain and perplexity of a poor deaf vagabond who had lost his best friend and who would have gone to eternity in the same moment with him if it had not been for the accident of his deafness? . . .

"The knife the fellow threw was poisoned," Pompejus had traced painfully at the end of his manuscript, "but I think I might have worked the poison out of my system if I hadn't grieved so at the death of Sir Roger, and especially if I had not been tormented all the time by the fear that I should blurt out the awful word some time or other and exterminate a whole roomful, or a hallful, or a streetful, of innocent victims. The crazy thing rings in my head all the time and I can't forget it. But I am so near the end now that I think the world is safe from me. And when I die, the danger will be past. The word will die with me—" ——

A VISITOR FROM FAR AWAY

LORETTA BURROUGH

The wind was scooping great whining hollows in the air, whirling the snow against windowpanes and frosted roof of Laurel House, piling it deep upon projecting cornices, rolling it into sift white drifts on the unprinted path to the front door. It was very still within the house; the hinges of a loose shutter squealed, groaned, worked up to a terrific bang against the wooden walls, squealed again.

It was so silent that to the woman lying quiet and nervous in the bed, the page she was turning seemed to shout hoarsely as it slipped back against its fellows, although she knew it had only whispered beneath her thumb. She was reading a book on astronomy, but as time passed she found it harder and harder to think about stars, harder to remember that they were shining somewhere beyond this blizzard in all the veiled brightness of their galaxies.

It was the knowledge that she was alone in the house, completely solitary, that frightened her. There were too many rooms beyond whose empty lighted windows (lighted by her as darkness fell, to cheat that dark) the pale white storm dipped and swayed. Ever since the Occurrence—that was how she phrased it to herself, as though it had been an eclipse, or an earthquake—she had taken good care not to be without a friend or servant in her house at night. Solitude was an invitation to those dreadful and oppressive thoughts that would sometimes descend upon her like a dark hawk even in the midst of a crowd's gaiety; but more apt to happen—oh much more!—in solitude. And although the source of those thoughts lay twenty years back, and Mrs. Bowen at forty-five did not look in any way like Mrs. Bowen at twenty-five, they were one and the same and therefore subject to bad dreams and a strange horror of being left alone.

Mrs. Bowen closed her book and threw it aside, lay there a moment listening to the high-pitched voice of the storm, and then turned to look at the pink enameled face of the French clock on her dresser. Since she had last looked, time had crept on, turning the soft ticking into minutes, into half an hour; the small fragile hands pointed to a quarter of twelve. Her heart seemed to sink with depression. What was the matter with those intolerable servants! They knew the way she felt about being left alone. "Sure, ma'am," Nora had said, the rosy Irish brogue thick in her voice, "we'll be back quick as ever. If 'tweren't Mother was so sick—" And she had taken her sister in tow behind her, repeating, "We'll be back by ten-thirty, sure." An hour and fifteen minutes late, and not one word from them!

The doctor said this fright of hers, this horror of being alone, was all nonsense. Well, perhaps so, but it was not toward the doctor that Roger's reptilian head had turned that day in the dark shining courtroom, with the rain falling in thunderous torrents outside the windows. It was not to the doctor that Roger had said, in the moment of silence after the judge's voice sentencing him to life imprisonment for killing his wife's lover had ended, "I'll get even with you. I'll never stop thinking of how to do it. I'll never forget you—or forgive you." No; it had been to her, his wife, that Roger had pointed his long hand that always made her think of a spider, and spoken his ugly words.

Her dark brows contracting, Mrs. Bowen, forgetting now that it was all over long ago, put her hands to her throat with a curious look of terror. She was thinking of Roger and *that* night, months before his trial, when, the smoking empty gun flung away from him, he came at her, his fingers crooked for her throat, filthy names pouring from his lips.

And then, exhaling a deep relaxing sigh, she got out of bed and went to the window. She had been near, that time twenty years back! It had been touch and go for days after their man-servant had broken in and pulled Roger's fingers from her neck. She had testified at the trial gladly, eager to weave a thick strong rope for Roger's death. But they had only given him life imprisonment.

The curtains pulled behind her, she looked out at the blizzard. The snow seemed very deep, swirling into queer high shapes along the roof edge, like punch-bowls and cardinals' hats. In the light from the windows downstairs the flakes shone like sugar, rising and dipping; she had an oppressive feeling of the vastness of this billowing frozen movement that filled the night. Could it possibly—she sucked in her breath at the thought—be bad enough to keep the servants in the village? And even as she wondered, one hand pressed against the cold pane, the telephone rang in the room behind her.

The sound of the bell was like a gleam of light brightening her dreary thoughts; it suddenly made her again the middle-aged Mrs. Bowen whom everybody imagined a respectable widow, retired, occasionally taking a quiet part in the life of the near-by town, of whom nobody would have believed a connection with murder. Her steps quick across the thick rug, she hastened to answer.

"Ma'am?" That was Nora, her rich Irish voice coming faintly across the crackling wires; the connection was poor. "I'm terribly sorry, ma'am, but we can't get out tonight. The snow's that deep! I tried the garage and Haley's taxi stand, everywhere—nobody'd take us—they said 'twas suicide."

Mrs. Bowen was silent for a dark moment before she burst out, "But you girls can't, *can't* leave me alone here all night. It'd be different if George was home." George was her chauffeur, away on a two-weeks' vacation; it would be days before George even bought the return ticket that would bring him ultimately to Laurel House again.

Behind her back, she felt the empty place listening as though it were sardonically amused, the wind drawing away and returning to batter at the walls with a vigorous shout of renewal, the shutter at its unending cycle of squeal and bang. From the corner of her eye, she could see the white face of the snow peering in at her.

"You've got to come," she said, her voice rising. "You've got to come! Walk, if it's necessary."

"Ma'am!" Nora's voice was exasperated beneath its coating of servility. "We couldn't get two feet, ma'am. If you'll just look out the winder—the drifts is terrible. There ain't a car on the roads. Sure God himself couldn't walk it! Maybe tomorrow morning—we'll try hard then."

"Oh, Nora—" she said, despising herself for pleading, yet unable to stop. She had never been alone all night since *it* had happened twenty years ago; deep in her was this fixation, black with pain—not to be alone with the darkness and the unforgotten past. "Nora," she stumbled on, "I'll double your wages, if you start now and get out here!"

"Ma'am, we couldn't. We couldn't for a million dollars." The voice at the other end sounded protesting and cold. "Nobody can get out of town tonight, ma'am. Why don't you just turn on the radio nice and loud, fix up a little snack to eat, and then go to bed?"

"Oh!" said Mrs. Bowen, dropping the receiver back on the hook with a choked groan. It seemed to her that in the few moments she had been talking, the storm had grown worse. The wild sleety rattle of the snow against the windows sounded like unhappy voices complaining of something strange and terrible, beginning to speak of it far away in the white hills, and coming closer and closer until they shouted it against the shingled walls of Laurel House.

"Now," she suddenly said aloud, standing in the middle of the room with her fingers pressed against her forehead, "I'm not going to be an idiot. There's nothing to harm me here; certainly *he* can't harm me here, and that's all I'm afraid of, isn't it?" Disliking the foolish sound of her voice speaking in the emptiness, she stopped. What had Nora said? Turn on the radio, fix herself something to eat, go to bed. But—

The lights flickered; for a moment, the small glowing filaments in the bulbs failed and faded before they burned brightly again; somewhere, distant in the storm, a line had gone down, there had been some trouble.

Mrs. Bowen looked, her mouth quivering, at the room now bright again. That wouldn't do, would it? It wouldn't be very nice if the lights, all the lights, should go out; that would leave her alone in the dark. But there was, she was sure, a candle wrapped in the lower drawer of her dresser. She had it out in a moment, a bright yellow candle, set it in a holder on her dresser and lighted it. *Now* if the current went off— She saw that her hands trembled.

I'm a fool, she thought, looking at herself in the mirror; it showed a middle-aged woman with a fair, quiet face. It was all because Roger was not, somehow, an ordinary man. The threats of an ordinary man you could meet with laughter, but Roger's threats—his narrow gray eyes, with the look one moment so drowsy, the next so intense, the sharp cruel curving lines of his mouth, the long narrow hands that had always reminded her, because they were dark, crooked, brown and covered with hair, of two spiders crawling—all of Roger made it seem too sure that he had the power to make *his* threats come true.

It gave her pain to remember his face or his words or anything about him; memory of him was like a hand at her throat. She picked up the small French clock from her dresser and began to wind its delicate key, telling herself that when the hands touched twelve again it would be tomorrow and the sun would be shining.

And just as the slight little clicking sounds ceased within the mechanism and she set the clock back in its place, she heard a door open, and close, in the house.

For a moment she stood there, an imperceptible flash of time while her heart did not beat or air move in her lungs, and then she said suddenly, very loud, "Who's that? Is that you, Nora? Katie?" But of course it could not be Nora or Katie because she had been speaking to Nora only a few minutes ago, and she had said they could not come out. Besides, they could not have reached here from the village in so short a time; even on a fair night in an automobile they could not have made it. Nevertheless—her fingernails dug sharply into her palms, and her head turned slowly, listening—she was no longer alone in the house.

It had not been the wind that had opened and shut that door; although she was hungry to believe it, she knew it had not been the wind. The house was too sound, too solid. No, there was someone else within these walls and she must be sure at once whether it was friend or enemy. Her mouth was a little open; she could hear her breath coming between her lips with a small whistling sound—she could not help thinking that in the intervals when the wind outside sprang up blasting snow against the ringing windows, someone, anyone, could be coming slowly nearer and nearer to her while she could not hear him.

Spasms of cold seemed to sweep over her body as she moved to the dresser, jerked open the top drawer and took up the small revolver she always kept there. With it in her hand, she went to the bedroom door and paused with her fingers on the knob. Suddenly, a feeling of relief came hot and strong into her heart. Of course, of *course!* That was it. In the letter she had received from her chauffeur this morning, he had said he would be back Thursday, and this was only Monday—but he must have changed his plans. This was good sensible George who had come in downstairs, probably half numb with the bitter cold. She would give him the key to the cellaret in the library, and tell him to take some whisky to prevent his getting a chill. She twisted the door-knob.

Puzzled, she stared at the complete darkness beyond the door. Why had he turned out all the lights that she had left so brightly burning downstairs? The sound of sleety snow rattling on the long windows of the hall landing came up to her out of the blackness; an apprehension, formless and vague, seized her heart.

"Is that you, George?" she called. "Did you just come in a moment ago? Answer me, please!"

She waited, breathing quickly, listening to the noise of the storm and the silence of the dark lower house that seemed to be listening too, and then slammed the door shut and locked it quickly. She had just realized that if there were no cars on the road, no foot travelers, because of the blizzard. neither could there have been a George. A few words turned slowly in her mind as she looked at the blank panels: *But it was not the wind! There is someone here; yes, there is someone here.*

And there was nowhere to look for help. Outside the house was nothing but the whirling wastes of drifted snow and the wind that came rushing from the hills. Her eyes, turning here, there, and back again, touched the telephone. The police! They would surely try to come, to one in need.

She hurried across the room, the pearl-handled revolver clutched in her fingers, her ears intent, listening behind her. As she stooped to pick up the instrument, it rang with a sharp jangle beneath her hand.

"Hello, hello!" she cried into the mouthpiece. "Please, will you get the police for me? I want the police—I am all alone in my house and someone has broken in. This is Mrs. Bowen, Mrs. Bowen—Laurel House—please—"

A small voice, distinct and cool, came back. "I'm sorry, the connection is very bad—they are having trouble with the line. I cannot hear you. I want Mrs. Bowen, I have a telegram for her. Is this Mrs. Bowen? Will you speak louder, please?"

"Yes, yes," she groaned. "But please, I want—"

"I will read your telegram now," the voice went on. " 'Mrs. Roger Bowen, Laurel House, Galeville, Connecticut. Regret to inform you Roger Bowen died suddenly here today. Please wire disposition of body.' Signed Henry Adams, Warden San Marco Penitentiary. This connection is so poor, I'm afraid—there it goes!"

A series of sharp, sputtering clicks and the line went dead, as though it had suddenly frozen under the long piling weight of the snow. And almost as the telephone connection went, the electric lights faded, brightened, dimmed out at last to dark bulbs, and slowly the lighted candle on her dresser seemed to grow stronger in the dimness.

But Mrs. Roger Bowen was not aware of the telephone or the lights. She was watching the candle from the corners of her eyes. It seemed to her that two thin crooked brown hands were slowly descending out of the darkness toward the flaring flame.

The hands made her think—yes, they made her think of two spiders. ——

WARNING WINGS

ARLTON EADIE

Steady, sir! Please don't do that."

Quietly as the words were uttered, their tone of urgent entreaty was such that I stopped dead and allowed my hand—already raised to crush the moth which had for the past half-hour been blindly dashing itself against the bulb of the electric tablelamp—to fall limply to my side. Surprised at the unexpected exclamation, and secretly somewhat amused at his evident concern for the life of the fluttering insect, I turned and faced the speaker.

He was a fresh arrival at the hotel, for his face was unfamiliar to me. Tall and broad-shouldered, with a neatly trimmed, pointed gray beard, his features tanned to that warm, even tone which only the sea can give—one does not need to spend many hours in the neighborhood of the Southampton water-front before becoming accustomed to the type to which he belonged. Evidently he was an officer of one of the ocean liners which are to be counted by the score in the docks near by. There was a flicker of amusement in his keen gray eyes as he stepped forward in answer to my look of surprize.

"Seemingly this little wanderer of the night has incurred your displeasure," he observed, pointing to the moth which had now renewed its frantic dashes against the brightly lit globe.

"It seemed so determined to beat its life out that I thought it only kindness to end its misery," I shrugged.

The stranger shook his head slightly. "There is another way."

He stepped toward the lamp and after several attempts managed to catch the little creature between his cupped hands. Then, holding it with infinite tenderness, he crossed to the open window and al-

545

lowed it to flutter away into the summer night. As he turned, after shutting the window, I saw that he was regarding me with a queer little half smile.

"You may think it strange that I should take the trouble to preserve the life of an insect that another man would crush without a second thought," he said. "But I have a fondness for moths, especially of that particular kind. Oh, you mustn't run away with the idea that I'm a learned entomologist," he went on with a laugh. "As a matter of fact, I do not know the scientific name of the species, although its common designation is, I believe, the 'Ghost Moth.' No, sir, my action just now was purely sentimental. The sight of those tiny fluttering wings brought back the memory of a strange adventure which I had in mid-Atlantic, many years ago."

A far-away expression had crept into his eyes, only to vanish the next moment as he turned again to me and resumed briskly:

"If I tell you the story, it may serve for both explanation and excuse for my unwarrantable intrusion just now."

I hastened to assure him that no excuse was necessary; but at the same time I hinted rather strongly that I should be glad to hear the account of what had happened. To confess the truth, I was not a little curious to know why such a strong bond of sympathy existed between this clear-eyed matter-of-fact man of the world and the little white moth. Sailors' yarns are seldom uninteresting to a landsman, and occasionally they are true as well. Whether this one comes in the latter category I am unable to guarantee; but I can vouch for the fact that the teller of it did not look like a man who would gain any satisfaction from "twisting the ankle" of a casual stranger. As I listened to the story being told in his deep, earnest voice, glancing occasionally into the speaker's frank, bronzed face, I know that I believed every word of it.

"At the present time I am in command of the R. M. S. S."—he mentioned the name of a famous Atlantic flyer which had arrived at Southampton the previous day—"but at the time of which I am about to speak, some twenty years since, I was in charge of a smaller vessel belonging to the same line. I was a youngish man then—as liner-captains go—and she was my first command. But you must not imagine that I was nervous on that account, for I'd been in the ferrying trade ever since I'd taken my third-mate's ticket, and I flattered myself that I knew the 'lane' blindfold.

"I suppose it sounds strange to you when I speak of a 'lane' across the Western Ocean. If you talk about the sea to the average landsman, he conjures up a vision of 'the trackless deep,' a phrase which he has learnt from story-writers who have more poetical imagination than actual sea-going experience. True, there was a time when the shipmaster was left free to set this course by the most direct route from port to port, and especially was this so in the days when the competition between the different shipping companies led their captains to strain every nerve to secure the speed-record for their particular ships. But all that is changed now. With the furnaces of a modern liner eating up a ton of coal every one-and-a-half minutes—to say nothing of the food and wages bills mounting up—it is essential for the captain to maintain speed, and the man who takes a 43,000-tonner at twenty-five knots through the zone of drifting icebergs, and the fogs which lay over the Grand Banks in summer, is simply asking for trouble. Consequently two 'lanes' are marked out on his chart; the 'northern' and most direct sea-passage, to be followed when the icebergs are bound up by the Greenland winter and the fog zone off the Grand Banks is of smaller area; and the 'southern,' which is calculated to pass outside the limit to which the bergs drift before melting, and to avoid the larger fog area over the Banks. For the Southampton boats the course is set from the Lizard; those coming from Liverpool set theirs when they drop the Fastnet Light, off the southwest coast of Ireland; while those coming 'north about' through the Pentland Firth steer from a spot well to the nor'rad of the rocky islet of Rockall. And once the course is set, the helm is not shifted unless it is in response to a signal of distress.

"It is necessary for me to make these details quite clear in order for you to appreciate the position of difficulty in which I found myself during the particular voyage I am about to describe.

"It was June when we sailed from this port, so we were due to take the southern route. We stood down Channel until the Bishop Light was winking away on our starboard beam—it stands on an outlying reef of the Scilly Isles, and is the last beacon you pass sailing west—then the course was set 'West, three-quarters South,' which brought the ship into the usual summer route. A little over three days' steaming brought us into the neighborhood of thirty-five degrees of longitude west of Greenwich. At this point our track met the track of the Liverpool and Queenstown boats, and, according to schedule, our bows were pointed farther south, which made our course 'West-South-West.' You must understand that I'm describing the track we followed twenty years ago. Since the *Titanic* disaster in 1912 the route has been altered, so that it now swings more to the southward until it reaches the same latitude as the Azores, after which it curves north again to New York.

"Well, we shifted our helm, as I have said, about one bell in the first watch (8:30 P.M. shore time), and shortly afterward I came off the bridge to turn in. I took a last look round before going below. It was one of those perfect nights which make passengers think that a sailor's life is all beer and skittles. The ship was threshing her way over the gentle swell with scarce a tilt showing on her long lines of decks; the stars shone bright in the cloudless sky; the slight following breeze was hardly strong enough to lift the drooping folds of the ensign at our stern. It seemed that on such a night the most nervous of new-fledged captains might sleep in peace. Certainly no thought of sudden and unexpected disaster was in my mind when I threw myself down on my cot to sleep.

"But for some unaccountable reason sleep would not come to me. I tossed restlessly from side to side; got up and opened the ports of my cabin; closed them again; tried the old trick of counting the steady beats of the throbbing propeller. But all in vain. In spite of my effort to overcome it, the sense of expectant wakefulness seemed to increase rather than diminish. At last I gave up the struggle, and, switching on the light, took a book from the rack and settled myself to read. It was then that I noticed for the first time a vague sound mingling with the familiar noises of the ship.

"At first it seemed nothing more than a soft intermittent tapping, but as I continued to listen I noticed that the same number of taps was repeated again and again. Subconsciously at first, but soon with awakened interest, I realized that the sounds fitted into certain letters of the Morse code. I laid the book aside and sat up, listening.

"*Tap-tap-tap—Tap . . . tap . . . tap—Tap-tap-tap.*

"I raised my eyes to the spot whence the sound proceeded and at once saw what was causing it. Attracted by the light a tiny white moth had entered the porthole and was now fluttering frantically against the illuminated dial of the telltale compass that was fixed in the ceiling above my bed. The soft tapping had been caused by the creature dashing itself against the glass in its effort to reach the light within. I smiled to myself as I saw the commonplace explanation of the sounds which had so puzzled me; but at the same time I could not help being struck by the fact that the noise it was making was strangely like the Morse code.

"But I was in no mood to be kept awake by so trivial a thing. Picking the towel from the rack, I mounted on the cot and raised my hand to sweep the little creature out of existence, even as you were about to crush that other moth in this room a few minutes since. But just as I was about to strike, the moth's flutterings began afresh.

"*Tap-tap-tap—Tap . . . tap . . . tap—Tap-tap-tap.*

"I stood like a man turned to stone as the real meaning of this chance spelt signal rushed upon me. It was 'SOS'—the sailors' call for help!

"Nor was this all. I had already noticed that the creature had come to rest in the same position every time it had finished the ninth stroke, but now I saw that its head was resting on the compass at almost exactly the same point where our present course lay. The difference was only a quarter of a point to the southward; that is to say, we were heading 'West-South-West,' whereas the course indicated by the moth was 'West-South-West, *quarter South.*'

"Even as I stood staring the signal was repeated. The light feathery wings beat the air once more; again came the three rapid taps, the pause, the three slower taps, another pause, and then the three final taps in quick succession. Again the creature alighted on the glass with its head resting on the same quarter-point of the compass.

"Now, I'm not naturally a superstitious man, but I don't mind admitting that I felt a very curious feeling stealing over me as I stood alone in that cabin and watched that little grayish-white insect spell out the signal which is never sent out unless a vessel be in dire straits, and then come to rest pointing so unerringly to a course so near our own. It was useless for me to try to persuade myself that it was pure coincidence; that the three fluttering taps might be the natural movements of the moth; that there might be something on the covering-glass of the compass which would account for the thing always seeking the same spot. Try as I might, I could not get it out of my head that the little moth was trying to tell me to shift my helm a quarter of a point to the south.

"Still, one does not act on impulse when in charge of an ocean liner, nor does one depart from the specified track without good cause. First of all I must make sure that my imagination was not playing a trick on me. I slipped on my uniform and quietly made my way aft to the First Officer's berth. McAndrew was a hard-headed and eminently practical Scot in whose sound common sense I felt I could trust in such a case as this. He was asleep, but his eyes snapped open the instant I laid my hand on his shoulder.

" 'Anything wrong, sir?' he cried as he recognized me.

" 'Not exactly,' I answered. 'But I want your advice on a little matter that's been troubling me a bit.'

"Mac looked a little surprised, but he was a good deal more so when I led the way to my cabin and pointed to the compass.

" 'Why, it's naething but a wee bit moth,' he cried. 'They call them "ghaistie-flutters" up where I was born, them being white, ye see—'

"I interrupted him by holding up my hand.

" 'Watch—and listen,' I said, purposely refraining from telling him what to expect in case it should unconsciously influence his judgment.

"As I spoke a slight movement began to agitate the soft, downy wings, and presently:

"*Tap-tap-tap—Tap . . . tap . . . tap—Tap-tap-tap.*

"McAndrew glanced round at me when the wings had become still.

" 'If I'd ha' heard that on a wireless receiver I'd have thought I was listening to an "SOS," ' he said slowly.

" 'It's been rapping out the same three letters for the past half-hour,' I told him. 'And every time it has come to rest over the same point of the compass.'

"He craned his neck upward and I saw him start.

" 'Guid preserve us!' he jerked out. 'The wee beastie is heading within a quarter of a point of our ain course!'

"I nodded silently, for the moth was again repeating its strange message.

" 'West-South-West, quarter South,' I read as the frail wings ceased quivering. 'And I'm very much tempted to follow the new course.'

"He gave me a long, searching look before replying.

" 'Yon is a matter about which nae mon can advise another, sir,' he said at length. 'It's something clean beyond the rules of seamanship and navigation. But speaking for myself, sir, if I were in command of this packet I'd shift my helm to the quarter where yon puir beastie seems trying to guide us.'

"I stood for a long while in thought after he had finished speaking. A young master mariner can make or mar his reputation on his first trip. I had been given the command over the heads of older and more experienced men, and I well knew that my conduct would be closely and jealously watched, and, if needs be, criticized. If I were to veer out of the usual track and ill came of it, I would be a marked man for the rest of my life—and I'd seen too many out-of-work shipmasters kicking their heels round the agents' offices not to know what *that* meant. On the other hand, there was the little white moth fluttering out the message that no sailor worth his salt can listen to unmoved, and pointing persistently to the south. I was not a man who loved taking chances, but—for good or ill—I determined to take one then.

"I turned briskly.

" 'Pass the word to the quartermaster, Mr. McAndrew,' I ordered. 'The course is "West-South-West, *quarter South*"!'

" 'Quarter South it is, sir,' the old Scotsman returned, with glistening eyes. Then he raised his hand and touched his cap reverently. 'May the good Lord reward ye if ye're doing right—and may He help ye if ye're not!'

"He went out on the bridge, and a few seconds after I saw the 'lubberline,' which coincides with the head of the ship, veer round until it came abreast of the spot where the moth was resting, showing that we had swung on to the new course.

"Almost at the same moment, as though it knew that its mission had been accomplished, the little moth fell to the deck, quivered for an instant, and then was still for ever. I gently lifted the little dead messenger, placed it in an empty matchbox, and stowed it away in my locker. I have it still, and sometimes, when things go wrong and the world seems to be just a huge ant-hill of humanity ruled by blind chance and brute instincts, I take out that matchbox and look upon the tiny white moth that came to me in mid-Atlantic . . . and my faith is restored.

"For, thirty-six hours after changing course, we sighted the old *Rangoon*, outward-bound and crowded, and blazing from bridge to stern. Over a thousand souls lived to bless the change of course indicated by that little winged messenger, and among them was the lady who is now my wife. . . .

"And that's why I have a tender spot in my heart for the little light-blinded creatures which flutter in out of the night." ⟶╂

WHAT WAITS IN DARKNESS

LORETTA BURROUGH

With a thick, choking sob, Christy Tenniel woke in the silvery coolness of early morning. The pigeons that the Jones boys kept on the roof were airing their flute throats in the dawn as Roger lumbered out of sleep beside her, making startled sounds.

"What is it, Chris? What's the matter?" He circled her shaking body roughly with his soft, fat arm. "That damn dream?"

Its trembling bloody mists began to float away from her; their commonplace room came clear, with the picture of Roger's mother smiling dimly from the opposite wall.

"Again. I can't stand it much longer." Night after night, in the thickets of darkness, it waited for her. For months now she had fought sleep until she was haggard and thin.

He reached for a package of cigarettes on the bedside table. She could imagine the angry bewilderment in his eyes; he did not like his wife to be in any way abnormal. And she saw it as the match flared, lighting puckers of annoyance about his mouth.

"That nerve specialist didn't help much," he said. " 'Some hidden fear, or hatred.' Expensive bunk, that's all. You've got no fears or hatreds." He snorted, and sucked on the cigarette so hard that bright red sparks flew.

Roger's talk was all very well, but Doctor Wilks had said softly, watching her from opaque brown eyes—"Do you love your husband, Mrs. Tenniel?"

She had answered, "Of course."

Then Wilks had frowned, glowering at his clean fingernails. "You must tell me the truth, not lie. Otherwise I can not help you."

She had stared dumbly at his desk, shining with wax, and then suddenly the words had pushed their burning way out of her. "No, I do not love him. I loved another man, my husband's best friend. He was killed in an accident, a week before he was to marry me."

Duncan, light-hearted, quick, warm, like the old song—"Duncan, Duncan, tender and true." She could have spared the lumbering dull Roger so much more easily. And then, two years after Duncan had died, she had married Roger, since he was always around, since she could talk of Duncan with him. A wrong sort of marriage, all wrong.

Doctor Wilks had thought so too. "Better for you to separate," he had suggested.

"But how could not loving Roger make me have this dream?" She had looked at Doctor Wilks' face with numb bewilderment in her own. "Why should I always dream"—she had repeated it again— "that I am standing in a drafty hall. There is a night-light burning in a little crystal bowl, and rain pouring down a black window-pane. I am in a night-dress—there is blood on my bare feet, down the side of my gown, and dripping from the end of a knife I hold in my right hand." She had stumbled then, and hidden her eyes with her gloved fingers.

And if she separated from Roger, who would wake and hold her when she started up trembling and crying? Doctor Wilks believed she would no longer have the dream, if they were apart. But how did he know?

"Here, I've got an idea!" Roger had been smoking cigarettes furiously beside her, while she sat and shivered. "My vacation's coming next week. What say we go up to my aunt's place in Maine, where we had our honeymoon? She's not using it this year. She's bought new things, fixed it up nicely, and that sun and air'll cure you in a hurry."

"No, not there!" Every nerve in her body had shuddered at the suggestion. It had been such a dreadful honeymoon, with Roger never suspecting that it was a dead man she desired at her side.

"Why not?" Placidly, he squashed the cigarette. "It's quiet, but it'll be good just for that reason. Better than a noisy hotel. I'll phone Auntie tomorrow. We *will* go there."

Impossible to turn as an avalanche when he had fastened to an idea—she knew that they would go.

"Cozy, huh?" Roger thumped down the bags and shook his big shoulders. He went about thumbing the light switches, and the little oblong room suddenly blinked back at them, as though surprized. The wife of a near-by farmer had cleaned it and left a fire laid; Roger stooped above the long logs and touched a match to kindling.

"My aunt's changed it a lot, hasn't she? Nifty. What say?" He looked at her.

"Very nice, Roger," she answered mechanically, spreading her palms to the warmth that began to trickle from the fire. Even on the train she had dreamed, and wakened suffocating, in the coffinlike berth. "Shall we get the bags upstairs?"

He pounded up before her, making the small house shake. "Same room we had—I told the woman in my letter. Looking out on the bay."

Wearily, she made the twin beds and set the new cottage furniture to rights. Down in the kitchen, with unusual good humor and a great clatter, Roger was getting supper ready. She unpacked the bags and hung their clothes in a closet that smelled of salt air and mice, then went to the window and looked out. Night was curving like a gentle hood over everything; stars shone, tiny candles in a great dark room. But nothing had seemed beautiful to her since Duncan died; it was a curiously empty world.

"Come and get it!" Roger called, and she walked out into the quiet, still hall. She stopped instantly, while her heart thudded in bad, false beats, and the air turned to lead within her lungs.

It was a narrow passage, paneled in ugly dark wood, with a big dormer-window at the end of it. Because of the dormer it had a queer effect of closing in; it was like a tunnel ending in the black panes sprinkled with starlight. On a small table to the side was a night-light in a crystal bowl, and beneath her feet a rough, thick carpet splotched with roses like pink blisters. She had seen it all many times. She stared a moment longer, and she felt as though the darkness outside the window were entering her brain. Then she ran down the stairs.

He was setting a little table in the living-room, with food they had bought in the village as they passed through.

"Roger!" she cried. "Roger!"

He stared at her, startled. "What's the matter now?" he asked, with a peevish undertone to the words.

"Roger"—she slipped into a chair at the table; life was beginning to flow in her again—"we must leave here. Right away. That hall upstairs, the hall—"

He put a hand on her shoulder, shaking her a little. "Talk sense, Christy," he said irritably. "Why must we leave here? And what about the hall?"

With a spasmodic effort, she controlled herself. "Roger, that hall is the one I see in my dream. Always. I did not notice it when we carried up the bags, but I saw, just now. The one I see in my dream," she repeated. "The same dark panels, the same dormer-window, the same carpet on the floor."

"Is *that* all?" He sat down opposite her, picked a bit of pink ham from the plate and chewed the edge of it reflectively. "You'll go nuts if you don't watch out. It's nothing but a dream, and to let yourself get in such a stew about it—"

"But you see that of course we must leave here?" Leave the place where the dream's setting had become real. Leave it before—before what? In silence, she pleaded with the stubborn blue eyes across the table.

"Of course nothing." He wiped his greasy fingers on the edge of a napkin. "Pull up your chair and have a go at this. The ham's good."

"Roger!"

He laid a slice of meat on her plate, and heaped salad beside it, his thick mouth drawing close in determined lines. "If you think I've paid those walloping train fares for nothing, just to give in to a silly woman's whim! . . . We're here, and here to stay until my vacation's over."

He ate a forkful of potato with a look of deep relish.

"Roger—"

She stared at him; she felt cold and frightened.

Queerly enough, although she expected it that night, although she went to bed with her mind darkly open to receive it, the dream did not come. And clear night after clear night dropped with its stars into day and never did she wake trembling, the sweat of fear freezing on her.

"You see," said Roger complacently, the evening before they were to leave; almost two weeks had slipped by, smooth, happy enough—"What did I tell you?" He was standing by the small table in the dining-room, sharpening a knife with quick, hard strokes of his hand, downward and upward. "All you needed was to get away from the city. Fresh air, exercise, sun, they cure anything. Look at this knife—isn't it a beaut? Going to take it home with me—Auntie'll never miss it."

"Where did you find it—let's see," she said absently, thinking: "Perhaps he's right. I was overwrought—I needed rest."

"In the attic." He turned toward her; the smooth gleaming blade came into view and the handsome carved handle. "It was all rusted, but it's a peach now. Good steel."

Her eyes straining at it, aching beneath the delicate skin of her lids; her breath rushed from her lungs in a gasp. Beneath her, knees went to boneless putty.

"Roger," she moaned, "I've seen that before."

She leaned against the wall for support, her stare still held to the long, curving line of metal; all the light in the room seemed to stream toward her from the shining steel.

He dropped the blade, snatched a glass of water from the table and held it to her mouth. "What's the matter?" His heavy features sharpened with bewilderment.

She sipped the water, cold and flat, then pushed the glass away. "Oh, take me seriously," she begged, clasping one hand on his arm. "*That* knife—it is the one I see in my dream. Just like that, except—" Except that blood ran down the thin sharp steel, dripping from the tip to the floor, spreading in a small still pool on the patterned rose carpet.

She was aware as she watched him, terror freezing in her fingers, in her breast, that rain was beginning outside in the darkness; the first drops touched the panes like soft wet feathers.

"We must get away, now," she said, "tonight," and saw his eyes grow bright with anger. He took up the small whetstone and the knife; the blade made a weak, shrill sound, faster and faster as the speed of his strokes increased.

"We will not." His hard face concentrated on the whetting. "You little fool, to give a second thought to a dream!"

She was a wave beating against rock, and knew it. "Duncan would have listened to me. Duncan would have been patient, kind, not like you. . . ." She slipped into a chair and dropped her face into her cold hands. Where was Duncan? Gone beyond reach and touch, lost in a lightless world.

She heard her husband's footsteps coming dimly toward her; her eyes as she lifted her head rested again on the knife that he still held in his blunt fingers.

"I'm going to tell you something," he said sharply. A bleak malice shrilled a little in his words—he was angry. "You're still thinking of him, aren't you? Still loving him. I was only the second best. Duncan would have been the perfect lover, 'patient, kind,' not like me." He sent the knife spinning across the table with a fling of his wrist. "I'll tell you what he said to me, a few days before he was killed."

She waited, her heart drained of everything but a trembling apprehension. He could not touch her memory of Duncan, he could not hurt it, could he?

"He said—" He leaned toward her, face blind with jealousy of a dead man. "He was very intimate with me, you know. He said that he wished to God he could get out of his engagement to you; he said he was tired of you."

She got up clumsily. She had forgotten the dream; she had forgotten everything but his words. But was it the truth? Often had Roger lied to her. But if it were *not* a lie? Always now, between her and Duncan, would be this dull veil of doubt. She stood there, beginning to see herself as a loving fool, discarded by Duncan. Within her skull, a sharp little pain flickered and went and came again.

Into the trembling, nervous silence of the room Roger's conciliating laugh plunged. "Let's forget it all," he said, "dreams—and Duncan. He's dead; it's done with. Now we'll eat, and then we'll go to bed early and get a good night's sleep. A good sleep," he said again.

Down the back window of the hall, the rain was pouring with a wild, gushing sound. Into the dark regions of unconsciousness the noise flooded, together with the buffeting screech of wind. Her eyes, although they had been staring dully before her for many minutes, began really to see; she raised her head and looked about her, with a strange heavy feeling of pain and suffering.

First she saw the window; it seemed to move slightly under the press of rain streaming beyond it. "I have known all this before," she thought, and then her cold stupefied glare fell to the nightlight, flickering a little in its small crystal bowl.

Within the house was a thick, petrified stillness that troubled her ears. "Where is Roger?" she wondered, touching her left hand to her head where it lingered upon the shooting ache beneath damp sweaty curls. Always in the night his hoarse, asthmatic breathing had been somewhere near her. "Where am I now?" she puzzled wearily.

Just under the fringe of blankness that veiled her mind was a dreadful meaning; it was like the wind about the house—now it came nearer with a leap, now it whirled away into the distance.

Something touched her bare foot, a soft, cool drop, and another. "The roof is leaking," she thought dully, and looked down at her naked ankle, her long white foot. Not quite white now, for on it were spreading little red circles, dripping from the knife she held clumsily in her hand.

She could feel the skin crawling on her skull, her mouth widened in silence, as her eyes crept to the knife. The blade no longer gleamed; it was slippery, wet—the bright red stain went on, past her wrist; down her night-dress, over her thigh, was a dark clinging splash.

She fell to her knees; she could hear the wind and the rain. Within her head was the breaking down of all thought. She was alone with the silent house. The dream come true. ——✦——

WHEN THE SEA GIVES UP ITS DEAD

ROBERT PEERY

With slow strokes I pushed my tiny craft among the dead brown grasses of the creek that wound its way over the flatlands of southern Carolina toward the distant sea. About me, as far as my eye would see, there stretched a level waste of melancholy sands topped with sparse dead grasses. Now and then a low-flying beach bird trailed its legs in dejection and uttered its long wailing cry, wending a dispirited way toward the quagmires of the swamp lands in search of food. In the east, black clouds were banking toward the zenith; jagged lightning darted eerily, blue and white and yellow, before the ominous ascension of the cloud masses. The wind was rising; the grasses flowed down to the water, as if accomplishing some ritual to a gray, forbidding god. And now and then, breaking the depressing silence, the slow mutter of a thousand drums in the distance—the guttural complaint of the god of thunder—rolled up to me like waves of the sea, and receded again into a fearful silence.

Loneliness! It is more than a word to one in a small boat upon the meandering stream that will carry one to the beaches of Carolina. Melancholy! The word, upon that depressing shoreland, drips with the ooze of despair, when one's lips roundly utter its syllables.

For many days I had found myself becoming more and more depressed at being away from my family. Perhaps this depression, this saddened condition of my spirits, accounted for my being on that creek in my boat that late afternoon in September. I had not returned to the government camp with my fellow workers, but had turned my boat seaward and had by the time the storm broke gone miles farther than any of us had been before. It was not a pleasant work in which we were engaged—this discouraging search for the breeding-place of an insect that was destroying millions of dollars' worth of crops annually—but someone had to do it, and the bureau had selected me to head the investigation.

My first intimation of the nearness of the storm came with a crash of thunder that followed hard upon the most tremendous lightning stroke I ever saw. The very heavens seemed to split asunder and the echo of the thunder rolled almost endlessly against the gray, forbidding horizon. Then came the rain, a typical South Carolina coast rain—the beating sheets of gray water of those dreary savannahs.

I turned my boat about and began poling furiously upstream. Somewhere, I remembered, along the creek was a shack that had been pointed out to me as the habitation of an old beachcomber and odd-job man of the neighboring town. I searched the landscape as I moved sluggishly up the stream. It was difficult to see any great distance through the gray avalanche of rain. But at last I espied the shack set back about fifty yards from the marshy bank of the creek. I shunted the boat into the bank, tied it to a clump of small willows, and raced up the path toward the shelter of the shack.

When I entered—the door was not locked, and I pushed it open without ceremony—the old man was kneeling before the open hearth lighting a fire of grasses and driftwood. He turned his face when I entered and said—with a note of petulance, I thought—"The hospitality of necessity."

"I shall not trouble you long—only until the storm is over," I told him. "It is not pleasant punting along in the pouring rain. And then, the lightning, you know."

"Oh, you're welcome, as far as that goes," he said, in that whining, creaking voice that is so often an affectation of the aged. "Nobody can ever say that Sailor Jack ever turned a needy man from his door."

He motioned me to take one of the two chairs with which the room was furnished, but I stood for a moment or so in the doorway under a small sheltering awning of planks so that I might not wet the floor more than I could help.

"Don't mind the water," he said. "Come on in and dry yourself by the fire."

I complied, and when I was seated I looked about the room. I had heard many tales of Sailor Jack—tales the town folk didn't believe —old sailor myths he'd strewn through the district. People wondered how he managed to live on the little work he got to do.

In the room were two bunks, one above the other, sailor fashion, and in a corner an old chest of black, carved wood. In a room at the back I could see a skillet hanging from a nail and a small iron stove in which a fire was already lighted. A coffee-pot was bubbling and the faint aroma of good strong coffee came to my nostrils. A cup of coffee, I decided, would be just the thing to take the sudden chill from my body.

Evidently Sailor Jack thought so, too, because I saw him go into the kitchen and pour a cup from the pot. He was very old, was Sailor Jack. His face was wrinkled like old parchment, and his beard and hair were streaked with a yellowish tinge. The beard was splashed with brown stains from the lips to the tip of the white straggly growth. His eyes were "hollows of madness." Upon his head was a curiously shaped blue cap, something similar to the cocky little hats that French sailors wear in port. He was terribly thin, and stooped, and old.

He returned with a cup of coffee, which I drank without sugar or cream. It warmed me deliciously, and I forgot the raging wind and the rain for a moment or so. Sailor Jack seated himself in the other chair and lighted his knotty black pipe.

"Bloody night," he said between puffs. English, was Sailor Jack.

"Bad storm," I said.

"They don't last, though," he said, staring into the fire. "Be all over betimes the dance goes on."

I stared at him rigidly. "The dance?" I queried.

There was within the cabin only the puffy sound of his thin old lips over the stem of the black pipe and the licking whir of the flames on the logs of the hearth. Sailor Jack gazed abstractedly into the brightness of the fire and spoke as if he were not talking to me but only reiterating some thought that haunted him and must have utterance. It had grown quite dark outside; the lightning threw the windows into shimmering, dazzling flame at each forked bolt.

"The dance," said Sailor Jack. "The dance of the dead of the bark *Greta*. You must be a stranger to Pineville, else you would have heard ere now about how the men who perished when the *Greta* foundered offshore near here more than fifty years ago come back each dark of the moon to dance and drink above the grave. Always at the hour of 9 at night they come whimpering out of their sea graves to dance upon the grave of Naika. Always at 9 because that was the hour at which we buried her; 9 o' the night when the moon was dark."

A heavy blast of the wind tore the door from its fastenings and the rain swept into the room. Sailor Jack got to his unsteady feet and together we shut the door and tied the leather thong more securely.

"Tonight is the night for them. Be a wild night, but what do the dead care? Aye, what do they care? It is the living who suffer."

"Is there a story?" I asked.

"Aye, lad, well you ask if there is a story! A story of goblins and the sea-dead. A body never rests beneath the waves. All will tell you that. The earth is a man's proper burial ground, and the poor spirits of the dead doomed to a watery grave are never at rest. I hear 'em coming up across the savannahs, to dance their monthly rituals. Always at Naika's grave, too. I know where she was buried; I helped cover her wasted body."

"When—where—" I began, drawing my chair closer to the fire.

"Of course," he said. "You're wantin' to hear, an' it's me as would be tellin' yo' about the night we buried the poor brown body of the dead Naika. She's never at rest, and the ship's crew, it never rests.

"This all happened, lad, more than fifty years ago when I was a strapping lad myself, and mate o' the bark *Greta*, keeled at Bedford by Derwood who was one o' the best o' the builders in those old days. A sweet ship, she was, as easy to handle with dry sticks up above as when she was all plain sail with heavy jib and spanker. Sweet to the helm as a brood mare. A bird of a ship, lad. She'd never ha' foundered off the savannahs if three-fourths o' the crew had not been down with the fever—the tropic fever as Naika give 'em.

"But you don't know about Naika, do ye? Naika was mine in the beginning. I found her at the wharf at Pameti an' she begged me to bring her home with me. I did, or I started with her. I smuggled her aboard at night and she kept herself stowed away for three days after we pulled anchor from the harbor. She was a beauty, lad— brown, seductive, limbs and a face as any man might ha' fancied. The cap'n—Beideman, his name was—the dirty lying dog—he took her away from me an' we fought for her, an' he won! I was near wild, I tells ye, lad. For I loved her, an' he—he only wanted her for his evil purposes!

"Well, we was coming home under a good wind with all sail aloft, whipping it in easy after touching Montevideo on the coast of South America. Bedford was our next point of call. An' at Bedford—I had figgered it out—was where I'd leave the ship. With Naika, yo' understand. But I reckoned without consulting that fate that follows the sailor. Naika took down with a fever. She died, an' never once did that beast of a Beideman let me see her. We anchored off shore here."

Sailor Jack pointed to the east and resumed his tale.

"The cap'n detailed the five o' us to bury Naika on the beach. She'd made him promise her he'd give her a decent burial on land an' he meant to keep the promise. She knew the dead at sea never rested. For Naika was wise with the wisdom of women. They shrouded her body in a sheet and lowered it away into the bumboat and we pulled to shore. It was at 9 o'clock that we digged the grave. Before we buried her I swept back her shroud to see her face for the last time. I touched her eyelids and said a little prayer for the peace of her soul. I touched her little brown hands. I saw the ring on her finger. I drew back in surprize! The last link of her spirit with me, who really loved her, was gone! The ring I had given her was gone and in its stead was a ruby set about with green stones, the whole set in a gold band. I knew it was Beideman's ring. I wanted to snatch that ring from the finger but something held me back. The men of the crew, who watched me at my prayer, warned me of the dreadful penalty that follows the robbing of the dead. So it was that we buried Naika, the beautiful, the beloved, on the sands of the beach behind a rotting hull of a ship's boat."

The storm was decreasing now. I had leaned forward under the strange spell of the old man's words. His eyes were beginning to fill with tears. His breath became more labored.

"But she was never allowed a moment's rest from that night to this. Her soul, that she wanted buried in decent Christian ground, is desecrated by the terrible carousals of the crew of the brig *Greta*. For the *Greta* foundered that night, trying to draw off the shore. The crew was short on account of the fever Naika had spread among them and she went down before a single boat could be lowered. I was strong and I swam ashore, and was saved."

He grew silent then, and I feared to question him. It was so evident that his mind was filled with the memory of the burial of his beloved Naika. It was an almost unbelievable tale; I cast about in my own mind for reasons to doubt his story, but the crowding memories were so plain in his dim old eyes that I could do naught but believe.

"They will not let her spirit rest," cried Sailor Jack. He sprang to his feet and cast his arms upward and raised his head to stare at the ceiling. "They dance their fiendish dances over her grave at every dark of the moon. They drink their rum and sing their braggart songs above her grave and her spirit is never still! Beideman leads their drunken revels!"

I stepped to his side and helped him back to his chair.

"Forgive me," he said softly, his head bowed into his hands. "I forget myself when I think of Naika's soul that never rests."

I looked at my watch. It was after 8 o'clock.

"I think I'll try it back," I said to him. "The rain has stopped."

He rose and confronted me. "No," he answered, "you must go

with me tonight to watch the dance of the dead at Naika's grave. It is not too far across the marsh. Come and I will show you that I am telling the truth. Come and you will hear the creaking of the sails of the *Greta;* you will hear the lowering boats, and the landing; you will hear all I have said you would hear, but you will see nothing! No man is privileged to see save me! I alone must bear the horror of the sight."

I made feeble protest but he only stared into my eyes and placed his hands on my shoulders in entreaty.

"I will go," I said at last.

He went then into the kitchen and prepared a supper of bacon and milk with a hard bread he had made of cornmeal. We washed this coarse fare down with great cups of hot coffee. When we had finished he went into a cupboard and fetched an old ship's lantern, lighted it and set it down near the door. He delved into the trunk, or chest of black wood, and brought forth a silk scarf of blue and an old curved simitar.

"We will go now," he said.

He led the way along a path that curved around the house toward the sea. For an hour I walked behind him. We passed no word between us. The lightning had passed around us, and now made futile yellow glares in the southwest. The wind still swept in gusts over the wet brown grass of the savannah. I began to suspect something of the foolishness of the night's affair. Why should I be here with this crazed old man? What would my friends at the camp four miles up the stream think of my absence? They perhaps might set out to search for me. I was just on the point of stopping the old sailor when he turned off the path and sat down in the sand behind a clump of willows. I could hear the rushing of the waves along the beach that could not be very far away. His hand touched my shoulder. He extinguished the lantern.

"There is the place. You can see the ribs of the old boat half-buried in the sand of the beach. It is beneath the bow of that rotting old boat that Naika is buried. The stream enters the bay just there— the stream you came down this afternoon. Our way was shorter, that is all."

I settled myself into the sand beside him and waited.

"What is the time?" he asked.

"Almost 9 o'clock," I replied.

"I will know when 9 comes," he said. "I will hear the flapping of the sails of the *Greta* as they pull her inshore."

I will make no effort here to say what I heard that night; I can only say what I, under the recurring monotone of his voice, thought he made me hear. The space before us was possibly fifty yards wide, running to the right into a dark clump of willows and large grasses; to our left the same. Between were the lapping wavelets of the sea and the sand of the beach, in the center of which I could just distinguish the black ribs of a ship's boat buried quite more than half its depth in the sand. The willows nodded and shifted in the wind. Complete silence pervaded this deserted strip of beach, except for the heavy wheezy breathing of Sailor Jack; that was the only sound.

I did not hear the first sound, but I knew that Sailor Jack did. His skinny, clawlike hand almost cut into my flesh with the tenacity and the fear with which he gripped my arm. He sat half erect.

"The sails! The *Greta* is pulling inshore!"

I listened intently. The sound was of bellying sails, booming low, but quite audible, down the wind. There was then a clanking, a creaking, a sound so tiny that I feared for an instant that I was only imagining I heard. Sailor Jack had not released his grip upon my arm.

"The boat is going over. There will be two of them lowered. You will hear; I have heard every month for fifty years. They are coming to dance their terrible rituals of sacrilege over the grave of Naika so that her soul can have no rest!"

The flesh of my body tightened perceptibly. The sounds were real! I could no longer doubt their reality, try as hard as I might! I heard the splash of lifted oars, the scraping of a boat upon the sand! And nowhere the sight of any moving thing or human figure. Had I seen any tangible substance, a wraith, a moving ghostly figure, it would not have been so terrifying to my spirits, my nerves. But there was nothing except the rattle of phantom chains and the splash of shadowy oars in the surf. It seemed to me that the waves grew larger at the point where I had heard the scraping of a boat's keel along the sand.

"They will roll their casks of rum along the sand," said Sailor Jack.

His voice startled me. I looked at his face. Every muscle was drawn in horror.

"They will stamp their feet upon Naika's grave in a ghost dance. They hate Naika! Naika, whom I loved with all my soul and my heart! Naika comes to my cabin at night and lays her woes at my feet. Her lips touch mine in a kiss that is of her hungry, searching soul!"

His voice grew louder in his wild, demoniacal denunciation of the despoilers of his sweetheart's grave. My mind grew weary with the dreadful thoughts that thronged its avenues. The dance began — smothered voices, the clinking of mugs, the low, shrill laughter of drunken men! Sounds without bodies capable of producing them! It is indescribable!

"Come," said Sailor Jack. "It is time to avenge her desecration! I shall slay the spirit of Beideman, who leads these ghastly revels!"

He sprang with a loud cry from his hiding-place behind the willows and ran, crouching, toward the hull of the boat. The sounds died away! There was none except the soft murmur of the wind in the willows. I sprang behind him, quite confident now that he had gone mad. He was brandishing the simitar at an unseen adversary close to the rotting hull of the boat.

"Die! Ah, die, grave-wreckers! Destroyers of the peace of souls!"

Suddenly he stumbled back into my arms. It was almost as if some tremendous blow had been delivered upon his head. His simitar—rusted, useless thing that it was—fell from his grasp. Sailor Jack was dead.

I bent over him, not daring to move, cold with a sudden fear! The sounds had begun again. I dared not look. The rattling of boathooks, the creaking of windlasses, the bellying, and the popping of sails—I heard them all and I dared not raise my head. I knelt there in the sand above the grave of Naika and held the poor old body of Sailor Jack in my arms.

I tried later to bring him back to his cabin, but the burden was too great. I set off alone in the darkness then, found my boat, and went to the camp for help. We brought Sailor Jack to Pineville and left his body with the local undertaker. I told no one of the night's affair, except that I was on the beach with the old man when he died. The local doctor pronounced it heart-failure.

The next afternoon I went alone to the beach where the rotting hull still stood half buried in the sand. I found Sailor Jack's simitar and the blue silk sash. I had brought a spade along with me and I began excavating the sand upon the spot where the old man had engaged his ghostly enemy in combat.

I had not to dig long. I came at length upon a sort of white earth, the crumbled remains of human bones, and a little to one side I found a ring—a ruby set about with green stones in a gold band.

THE WITCH-BAITER

R. ANTHONY

Mynheer Van Ragevoort did not like the dark! There were things he could not see in the dark, but which he knew were there. But there were also things that he knew did not exist, which the darkness nevertheless conjured before his eyes. Faces! Spectral figures that floated and threatened and mocked! Many faces, many figures! And those of women chiefly, and girls. Of course, they had been witches, and he had condemned them to the torture, to the stake, to the rope. But why should they trouble him, dance about him, beckon him? He had not executed them; he had merely been their judge, the administrator of the Law! The Law forced him, and he was helpless! Still they bothered. Sometimes they seemed so real! . . .

Emphatically, Mynheer van Ragevoort, the Justice of Hegemonde, did not like the dark! Worse, noises often came from the night, noises that were mysterious and unaccountable. Sounds like the voices of people, especially sounds of women in pain, shrieking in torture, gasping brokenly!

There! The Justice started. He seemed to recognize a voice—yes, he heard it distinctly! It sounded like—ah, now he remembered— the voice of Melisande zer Honde, a slight girl, pale and pretty, a child of scarcely twelve. How she had screamed when the rack drew out her joints and stretched her muscles and ripped the ligaments! Yet she had confessed! He had been amazed that so young a child should be a witch! But witnesses had stated so, and under the torture she had admitted it. So he was forced to sentence her—to burning at the stake! How she had pleaded for life! How she had shrieked when the flames enveloped her! And then that appalling stillness, broken only by the crackling of faggots and the rush of flames!

And there was the sweet, innocent face of Gertrudis Bourdelaide. No, he doubted her accusers. He had known the girl since her birth in fact, he had lifted the child over the baptismal font as her godfather! Terrible she had been accused—*and had confessed!* They had to carry her away from the torture. He remembered how her crushed legs had quivered in agony, the white bloodless features, the maimed hands. She had endured much, but she had confessed! The rope and

565

quartering! But those moans, long-drawn, haunting, unending! Never a shriek, never a cry, only moans! Would he ever forget?

The Justice shook himself. He flung his cloak around his head and moved down the road, carrying in his hand a small lantern, from which a candle shone weakly. "Not much good in this thick gloom," he muttered. There was a fog in the air, which scarcely stirred with his movements. Yet the stillness, the lack of motion made him feel unsafe, restless. What was behind the gloom?

Hurriedly he trod the road towards his castle, his home. This stood somewhat apart from the city, as became the overlord and Justice. Not for him to live among gossips and smaller tradesmen! Besides, it was the home of his fathers.

A faint rustling sound made him pause. He peered around intently, but perceived nothing. Even his candle seemed unable to pierce the fog beyond his arm's reach. Silence around him! Well, he must move on, towards home, towards rest—perhaps. At least he would see his daughter. . . .

Something huge and light fluttered from the fog and fell over his head, covering him with soft folds. In fright he dropped his lantern and gurgled a shriek. He fought back the folds, but they enveloped him tighter and tighter, drawing around him till his arms were helpless.

And then hands seized him, on the right and the left, and a voice whispered: "Come! But say naught!"

"What—what . . ." he began. But an insistent prod of some pointed weapon made him move forward.

Forward! But where? Where were they taking him? And for what purpose? The cloth covering his eyes made little difference; he had been unable to see anything without it. They left the road, moved across ditches, over the veldt. Stops when he was lifted over some obstacle—a hedge or boundary mark, he thought. More veldt. And around him the faint thuds of numerous feet, slithering noises of mantles brushing against each other, muffled clinks of metal. God! What was in store for him?

The Justice stumbled through a ditch. Then hard and rounded bumps under his feet—ah, he was back in Hegemonde, in the city—among people! If he called—!

A sharp point pressed his side and a warning hiss apprised him of what would happen. So he was silent.

Some steps up which he stumbled, then a chamber. He felt himself led to a seat. How familiar that seat felt! With his feet he cautiously felt about himself. Yes, there were the legs of the table, and there his own footstool. It was his own: he was in the Court of Justice, his own court!

"Your own court! Your own dais!" came in deadened tones beside him. "We are here to try the witch of witches, to try her under the Law! But she must not know us lest sorrow come to all of us. So speak not above a whisper!"

Routine! But why in the night? And who was the woman they called the witch of witches?

"Begin!" the dull command was given.

Routine! Well, he would go through with it! "In the name of the Lord on High," he intoned in a penetrating whisper, "and in the name of His Majesty, the King of Spain and the Netherlands! There stands before us a—a—"

"A maiden!" prompted the voice.

"—maiden accused of having sold her immortal soul to the foul fiend in unholy conspiracy and of having exercised her black power in wanton sorcery and witchcraft to the detriment of man, woman, and child, upon their property, their goods and possessions, and upon their produce." A pause, then: "Woman, do you confess?"

Silence.

"Who witnesseth against her?" he continued.

"We all do witness against her," whispered someone in front of him.

"Aye! Aye! It is true!" whispered many voices.

"We vow she hath bewitched us or those of our families and contributed to our loss, even the death of our loved ones," said the accuser.

"Aye, she hath! We so vow it!" chorused the others.

"Doth the witch confess?" asked Mynheer the Justice.

Silence.

"Then to the rack with her—till she confesses!"

A scream of terror, quickly muffled, a sardonic cackle whose uvular tone seemed familiar, then the shuffle of many feet.

The Justice remained seated. No need for him to enter the torture chamber. Besides, he would not be able to see. In fact, he did not care to see. He had seen too many, too many! And they always confessed!

Through the open door he heard the spinning of rolls, the weak clatter of winding drums. A hush replete with indefinite sounds—they were fastening loops around the ankles and wrists of the witch. Then the squeak of turning handles, a pause, another squeak, a moan, a stifled shriek! A wait, then the splash of water! Another squeak of the drums. . . .

In accustomed routine the Justice leaned to one side of the great chair. Another twist of the rack, then would come the familiar sounds, and then—confession! He listened inattentively. For there was a bigger, a personal question. What were they intending to do to him? And why this secret trial? If they would only talk in loud voices, and not in those awful whispers! It was unreal—unreal!

Again the splash of water, then another squeak, followed by faint clicks and tears, joints giving way and flesh ripping! A ghastly shriek! "God, I confess!" in a pain-shocked voice. "A-a-h-h!" and silence.

Yes, that was the usual result, sometimes a little slower in coming, but not often. There! That quiet cackle! He knew it! No wonder— the skilled hands of the executioner were in charge!

The shuffle of feet once more and then a voice: "Your Worthiness, she hath confessed her guilt! Your sentence?"

Mynheer van Ragevoort roused himself. Sentence! Very well! "To be hanged by the neck until death do claim her! At once!" This would be sufficient, and few preparations necessary! A rope and . . .

He must be short, he wanted to be away! Let them hurry and free him!

For a long time he sat there and waited—waited silently, for around him all noise had ceased. There had been a little shuffling of men entering the prison enclosure—to see the witch hung, of course —but nothing more. So he sat and pondered. He felt stifled. The cloth over his head impeded his breath, and drowsiness overcame him.

The tramp of feet aroused him. A moment later the fetters were removed from his arms and the cloth lifted from his head and shoulders.

He blinked in the sudden light of torches. Before him he saw a number of hooded figures, all with voluminous cloaks, faces hidden behind black veils. Were these the same men? he wondered.

"So it is here we find you, Sir Justice!" said the leader.

Mynheer did not recognize the voice.

"We looked for you in the castle. You were not there!"

Him. So they looked for him. What did it mean? Why should they look for him when they had him already? And why no longer the whispers? At least he was thankful for that!

"Arise, sir, and take your place. You are to be tried!" said the leader.

Nine men in all, noted Mynheer. Two of them pushed him from the chair and led him down to the bench before the dais.

The tall leader at once occupied the chair of justice.

"Sir Justice, note what I say! You have been tried in secret trial and found guilty! We came tonight to execute sentence! We went to your home and waited for you. You did not come. Later we searched and found you absent. So at length we thought to look here. And here you are!" with sudden humour.

Mynheer van Ragevoort said nothing, only gazed bewildered at the mummer.

"Sir Justice, we are the *Vehmgericht!* In secret we met and considered you and the justice meted out by you. Sir, you have been an unjust judge. You have been a plague to this land. Like a wild beast you have persecuted the innocent and condemned them to death. Nothing has held you back—not friendship, not pity, not justice, not even the ties of blood! You lusted only to kill!"

He paused and seemed to wait for an objection. Mynheer found the words. "They were witches all. They confessed! The Law gave me—"

"The Law!" scorned the leader in stinging tones. "Your wild superstition was the Law. Not the written Law! With you an accusation was the equal of proof! You never gave fair trial!"

"They confessed!" the Justice muttered.

The leader stood up and pointed an accusing finger at him. "They confessed—under insane torture. They confessed—to escape further torture! They confessed—what you wished them to confess! Confession, indeed! So would you confess! Can an innocent child of ten —for such was Gertrudis Bourdelaide—know anything of wickedness, of sorcery, of witchcraft? Yet you forced her by the vilest tortures to say she was guilty. Did Melisande zer Honde know of witchcraft? She confessed to it—after you tore her on the rack. Did Roberta Deswaarters ever perpetrate any wickedness—she, a patient little saint, who spent most of her young life in pain? Yet you forced her to admit unholy practices—by means of the rack, the stocks! Did Margaret Van Voelker, or Pieta der Groote—oh, why name them all, the dozens of decent folk you put to death! For years you have sown terror in the land, you have revolted minds with your unheard-of cruelties. You were the scourge of the people until they wearied of it!

"Men came together and in secret protest asked the *Vehmgericht* for justice. When the Law is in unjust hands, man may—and must take the Law from those hands and punish them! That is what the *Vehmgericht* has decided. Sir Justice, stand and hear your sentence."

Mynheer van Ragevoort arose stiffly. It was all like a dream and still terribly real. For some reason he could not muster his thoughts to utter a protest. Pictures of trials, of tortured women, of executions, raced through his mind. It was true, terribly true, what the leader had said. But he had not meant to be unjust. He, too, had suffered because of his duty. He had wanted to rid the land of the plague of witches, he had wished to make his land free of sorcery and witchery for all time to come. Many times he had wavered when friends, and even relatives, proved guilty, but resolutely, without fear or favour, he had administered the Law.

The leader was speaking. "You were sentenced to torture and death!" he said in sombre tones. "Such was the sentence decided on!"

A pause—Mynheer twisted his hands, his face suddenly pale and beaded with cold drops.

Again the leader spoke, solemnly, impressively, and the eyes that gleamed blackly through the veil held something of pity. "Torture and death! Such was the sentence. But—this sentence will not be carried out—not completely! You shall not die through our hands! For there is worse than death that has struck you! Perhaps it is the Hand of God! We assembled tonight to carry out the sentence on you. But we found that others had been at work! We found that they had seized you—grief-stricken fathers they were, men fully as crazed with fear of witches as you—they had captured the witch of witches, as they thought—had tried her before your court, tortured her and hung her. Their venegeance is gruesome!"

What did it all mean? Mynheer van Ragevoort seemed paralysed. His eyes were wide, his mouth open, all his features expressed complete lack of understanding.

"You know not," continued the leader, "who the witch of witches was? Nor will I tell you. They blinded you, Sir Justice, and blind was your judgment. But a taste of the torture shall be yours, and then you will be freed. Perhaps—perhaps you will be more forbearing hereafter. To work, men!"

Strong hands seized Mynheer van Ragevoort and quickly stripped him of his clothes. In a trice, so it seemed, they bore him to the torture chamber and looped the ropes around his wrists and ankles.

A spin of the drums, the ropes tautened and squeaked, pain unbearable shot through his limbs and scorched his joints.

"Another turn!" commanded the leader.

Agonized sweat rolled over the Justice's body, his mouth sagged and a croak came from his throat. "I—I—confess!" he moaned.

"Confess!" exclaimed the leader in chill tones. "Confess—what?"

The taut body could not even writhe—could only quiver. "I—I know not!" Mynheer gasped.

"Nor we!" the leader made a gesture, the drums swung back a half-turn and tightened with a jerk.

Suffering indescribable tore into him—the Justice fainted. Water, splashed over his head, awoke him. God! Now he knew that crazing agony! He had sometimes wondered why the accused gave in so readily after a few whirls of the drums! He had been inclined to despise them as weaklings. Guilt alone could not endure, innocence certainly must! But now he knew! Oh, to escape this torment! Anything—anything—even death! But to escape!

A searing pain at his sides, yet he knew not whether it was hot or cold metal that touched him! And then the ropes became slack. What they did with him he scarcely knew—his whole body ached with tearing pains! And his head! It pounded and pounded and pounded.

A raw pang on his forefinger seemed to swell and swell until his arm—no, his body—grew large with the torment. What were they doing? He saw it—a pincer was plucking at a finger-nail—slowly pulling it from its foundation. God! What could he do to get away from such torture? Waves of pain welled forth from the finger, greater than his body could endure!

Something else! They had bound his wrists behind him; his ankles also were bound and heavy weights attached. Why this? Why didn't they simply kill him and be done with it?

A hook slipped under his fettered wrists, there was a pull, and suddenly he soared, his weighted body suspended by the wrists. And then he dropped. Again they drew him aloft and dropped him. Shoulders twisted and cracked and ached, his body seemed an immense pain. He fainted.

A rocking motion aroused him. He was dressed and covered with a cloth; they were carrying him! He felt strangely numb, conscious of ever-present but subdued pain. And so weary, so weak, so exhausted!

At last the motion changed. They had entered some dwelling, and now they laid him down. Steps moved away, and then someone spoke—the leader!

"The sentence has been executed, Sir Justice! May it teach you to be more merciful hereafter! We leave you now—with your victim!"

Half-conscious, he wondered. "My victim?" he asked, his voice muffled by the enveloping cloth.

"Look and see!" in a chilling whisper. There were quick steps, the slam of a door, and then silence.

Mynheer van Ragevoort scrambled painfully to his feet, weakened hands tore at the enshrouding folds. There, he saw light—the cloth fell away! But he knew that room—those paintings—that table, the chairs—why, he was in his own home! So they had carried him to his house, his castle!

He was thankful for even that. But why this strange, oppressive silence in the house? Where were the servants? And his—

His roving eyes caught sight of something. Over there, on the great divan, lay something very limp and still, covered with a white drape. That—that—his victim, the leader had said! But in this house —was it—everything was so silent—was it his . . . ? No, no, it must not be!

He crept weakly to the divan and tore the sheet from the still figure. "God! Anne-Marie! My daughter!"

He stared at her, unbelieving, uncomprehending. His victim? Oh no! Not that, not that! But it was his daughter that lay there, lifeless, features frozen in an eternal mask.

Slowly he inspected her. Quivering fingers felt the soft flesh, not yet rigored in death. He saw raw welts around her wrists and bare ankles. Around her neck an irregular stripe—they had hanged her!

His victim! It was she—Anne-Marie, his daughter—that had been tried as the witch of witches that night! They had tortured her and—and—he had ordered the torture! *"And she confessed!"* he groaned. "I—I ordered—her execution—*as a witch!* God!"

The room reeled and he crashed to the floor. ——╬——

THE WITCH-BALL

E. F. BENSON

It was quite impossible to determine which of us had seen it first, where it gleamed, blue and resplendent, in spite of the grime which covered it, behind the dingy panes of that obscure little shop. It reposed on a rusty steel fender, in the middle of frayed rugs, Britannia-metal teapots, wine-glasses, cracked plates, billiard-balls, stamp-albums, glass beads, pewter mugs, odd volumes of obsolete fiction and history primers at twopence each, false teeth with coral-colored gums, all the depressing miscellany of an unprosperous curiosity shop. . . . Simultaneously and without a word we stepped off the pavement and hurried across the street.

"But is it to be yours or mine?" I said to Margery. "Who saw it first?"

Margery's good sense is always admirable. "Oh, what does that matter at present?" she said. "The only important thing just now is that it should be ours. We'll settle the other point when we've got it!"

She opened the door of the shop, setting a bell jangling, and, after an anxious pause made hideous to us both by the frightful thought that before we had secured it, somebody else might come in on the same quest, a slow step creaked down the stairs within, and the proprietor, eyeing us suspiciously, entered.

"I should like to look at that glass ball in your window," said Margery quite calmly. "How much is it?"

Ten shillings were all that he asked for it, and though Margery dearly loves a little genteel chaffering, she made no attempt to get it cheapened or to examine it closely for cracks, for it must be securely ours without delay: so a minute later we emerged again with the witch-ball wrapped up in a greasy leaf of antique newspaper. Though our intention had been to go for a stroll through the streets of Tillingham till lunch-time on this hot May morning, there was no thought of that now, and we went straight back to my house a few hundred yards distant with our treasure.

"I shall go and wash it at once," she said, "and then we'll settle whose it is."

She hurried upstairs, while I went on into the bookroom where, but a few minutes before, we had left her husband, Hugh Kingwood.

"Back again?" he asked. "I expected you would be. Far too hot to walk on such a morning."

"Oh, that's not why we're back," said I. "We found something in a shop which we had to buy and bring straight home. A witch-ball, the most wonderful ever seen: Margery's washing it. And then we've got to settle whose it is, for we saw it absolutely at the same moment."

Presently she came downstairs with it. Even when it had been covered with dust and dirt it had gleamed like blue fire veiled beneath a scum of ashes, but now that she had washed it, it burned with a far intenser splendor. It was of uncommon size, more than a foot in diameter, and of soft sapphire blue, and it reflected, gorgeously steeped in its own color, the rounded image of the room. Fireplace and bookcases, ceiling and floor, sofa and piano all appeared there with that magical distortion which convex reflection gives, and all was dyed deep in that superb hue. And the window was there with curved sashes, and where at the top of it was a blink of sky, that was of some luminous turquoise tint such as shines in dreams or in fairyland. And yet though these pictures were only a matter of a reflecting surface, it was like looking into fathomless depths of blue: the vision seemed to sink into that shining globe, and dive further and further into gulfs of azure. Witch-balls have always had for me some mysterious charm, born perhaps of the memories of twinkling Christmas trees in childhood, but here there was something more: something of intrinsic lure. . . .

There arose the agonizing question of ownership: Margery, as a matter of fact, had actually paid for it, but, being one of the few women I know who is a thorough gentleman, she spurned so feminine an argument, merely calling attention to her nobility.

"I can't think what's to be done," she said. "I shall go into a decline unless I have it, but then no doubt you will, too. And as far as I can judge we saw it on the same tick of time. Hughie, what's the fair thing?"

Hugh did not answer, and I saw he was looking stedfastly into the witch-ball with some sort of rapt detachment. Then, as if with an effort, he shook himself free of it.

"What a marvelous piece!" he said. "But I don't like it, Margery: there's something uncanny about it. Let Dick have it."

"If that's all you've got to suggest," she remarked severely, "you might as well not have said anything."

She turned from him with scorn.

"I can only see one way of settling it," she said to me, "and that's by the foolish device of tossing up. If I believed that you saw it a fraction of a second before me, I promise you that I should let you have it. But by chance we saw it absolutely together: so let's go to chance again."

I could think of nothing better, so I spun a shilling and Margery called "Heads." I opened my hand, and the witch-ball was hers.

"Rapture!" she said. "Oh, Dick, how I sympathize with you!"

"I don't," said Hugh. "I congratulate you. There's something queer about it."

The two of them, Margery a first cousin of mine, and Hugh one of my oldest friends, were staying with me in this small Sussex town, for a week or ten days. There was a spell of blazing weather, and though golf had been an intended diversion, it was really impossible to play in this smiting and windless heat. The sky was as brass above and the ground as brass beneath, and instead we often motored down to the shore for a bathe in the afternoon, with some subsequent expedition vaguely in view such as a visit to Bodiam or Dungeness, or merely drove about the lanes and by-ways of the Romney Marsh and the wooded inland. We did not very much care whether we got anywhere in particular, for the hedgerows were brimming with pink rose-blossom and the woods still milky-green with the foliage of the spring. We lighted on adorable little villages nestling in folds of the downs, on hammer-ponds fringed with cotton-rush, from the edge of which mallards got up with a clangor of wings, or on the wide levels of the marsh we came to antique and solitary farmhouses of timber and rough-cast with glowing gardens set in red-brick walls, and Margery would declare that life was but a tinkling cymbal when lived in such a place within sound of the sea and within sight of Rye.

It was the pearl of them all that we passed that afternoon on our ramble; a plot of garden rather wild and overgrown fronted the road, and on the tall iron gate in the wall was affixed a board to announce that it was to be sold or let unfurnished. Margery, of course, insisted on our stopping, the gate ground on rusty hinges, and we went up the paved garden-walk to the house. But the door was locked, and no knockings or ringings produced any response, and we had to get an idea of the interior by peering through the unblinded windows. The rooms were absolutely empty, but the paint and papering looked fairly fresh, and it was clear that the house had not been untenanted for long. The flower-garden through which we had passed and the kitchen-garden at the back afforded similar evidence, for neither had been neglected for long: vegetables, for instance, peas and beans, had been sown in the spring though not staked. The kitchen garden was unwalled, and had only a wooden paling between it and the marsh-meadows, and along a side of it ran one of the drainage dikes that intersect the marsh. Along the raised edge of it had been planted, evidently not more than a year or two ago, a row of young willows: these had prospered, and now formed a screen for the garden against the prevailing southwesterly winds. At one end of them was a tool-shed, the roof of which was beginning to sag, at the other a couple of derelict beehives. It certainly was an entrancing retreat for any who cared to live the solitary life, and it was sad to see a house and garden full of such charm and tranquillity beginning to suffer from want of care.

"Oh, how I long for it!" said Margery. "Hughie, how happy we should be here! You would start very early every morning to go up to town, driving into Rye, not more than four miles I should think, and then a mere two hours and a half in the train. What's five hours every day in the train with a nice drive at each end?"

"Delicious!" said Hugh, "especially on a winter evening with a south-westerly gale blowing. And I don't like the feel of the place. There's something sinister."

"Darling, you're rather hard to please," said Margery. "You didn't like my witch-ball, and now you don't like my adorable house. How blissful I should be living here with my witch-ball!"

He shook his head. "No, you wouldn't," he said. "There's something here: you would feel it before long."

"Don't be spooky," said Margery.

She could not tear herself away without another look through the ground-floor windows of the house, and meantime Hugh and I strolled down to the gate where we had left the motor. In spite of his almost savagely practical mind in matters of business, he has always had some queer clairvoyant power of perception, which every now and then pushes its way to the surface of his mind. He sees odd scenes which prove to be actual, if he looks in a crystal, whenever he will consent to try the experiment, but his conscious mind fights shy of this gift, and he will not often attempt to exercise it. Another queer thing is that if I look into the crystal at which he is gazing, I see there what he sees, though I might crystal-gaze day and night by myself without seeing any tremor or shadow appear there. But we have tested this odd joint phenomenon many times and always successfully, so that it seems proved that he can establish some telepathic communication with me though I have no independent power myself, and that this conjunction of my mind with his helps his own power. It occurred to me now, when he said that there was "something here," that some blink of this psychic perception had come to him. I asked him whether it was so.

"Yes, there is something here," he said, "which I don't like a bit. There's a wicked unquiet atmosphere in the kitchen garden particularly; it's steeped in horror of some sort. And the queer thing is that Margery's witch-ball gives me the same feeling: no, I don't mean a similar feeling, but the same. I think you and I will have to gaze, and see if we can get at anything."

It so happened that Margery went early to bed that night, and as soon as she had gone, Hugh and I moved in from the garden where we had been sitting after dinner for the sake of coolness into the bookroom, where stood the witch-ball. His notion was to make it his crystal, and see if by gazing into it any manifestation appeared. We turned out all the lights but one so that the reflection should not be distracting, and now in the dimmer illumination the witch-ball lost its sapphire hue, precisely as the stone itself does by artificial light, and seemed black. Just one point of radiance gleamed in it in the middle of this pool of clear, deep darkness.

We must have sat there long before anything came through to Hugh's vision, for the house had grown quiet, and the church clock had twice chimed a quarter-hour before he spoke.

"Look: something is coming," he said in that dreamy monotonous voice, which always betokens that he is in that state of half-trance which precedes vision. "Tell me what you see."

There was something seething far down in the dark pool of the ball: it was as if clear black water was beginning to boil from below and break into bubbles. These bubbles bursting on the surface were slightly luminous, and as they multiplied the darkness cleared as if with the approach of dawn on night. It grew rapidly brighter.

"There's a line of house-roofs against the sky," I said, "and in front of the house there's a garden. There's a row of trees on the left, young trees, and they're blowing about in a wind. And there's the figure of a woman . . . I can't make it out: she seems to be lying under the trees—among their roots, I mean, not on the ground beside them. And there's a tool-shed close by—"

Suddenly, with a gasp of my breath, I recognized the scene. It was the kitchen garden of the house in the marsh which we had visited that afternoon. In the shock which came with this recognition my attention was jerked away from its quiet scrutiny, and in the instant the vision had vanished. I was staring into a black witch-ball with one point of light in it.

Hugh was still gazing into it with wide eyes.

"Yes, yes," he said. "I see all that. But she's moving now: she's standing upright: and now she's gone. Ah, the whole thing has vanished. Yes, of course it was the place we saw. But who was the woman? We didn't see her this afternoon. And where has she gone?"

He raised his head, and peered out, as if trying to focus something, through the open door into the garden, and though following his eyes I saw nothing but the deep dusk there, I knew that there was some presence, which had come out of the witch-ball, and was hovering there watching us.

"Hugh, what are you looking at?" I said sharply.

It was with an evident effort that he detached his gaze, and turned it back into the room.

"I don't know," he said. "But there was someone there, though I saw nothing. We won't try it again tonight, because I've got the jumps, but tomorrow we must sit again. Don't tell Margery anything about it."

I came down next morning after an uneasy night, during which again and again I thought I heard some stir of movement in the house, to find that Margery had already breakfasted and gone out. Presently she came back in a state of high heat and excitement.

"I have been clever," she said. "I've found all about the adorable house. A certain Mr. Woolaby is the owner of it, and two years ago his wife disappeared and was never traced. He lived on there alone till this spring, when he made up his mind to sell the house, and had an auction of all its contents."

"Where did you learn all this?" I asked.

"From the house agent whose name and address was on the board there. He lives just down the street. And the name of the house is Beetles. Just Beetles! Did you ever hear of anything so attractive!"

"Beetles would smell as sweet—" I began.

"No, it wouldn't. And then I was cleverer still, and you'll never guess where I went next. It was an inspiration."

"Do you want me to have an inspiration, too?" I asked. "Or say that I've no idea?"

"No: have an inspiration if you can," said Margery.

"You went to the shop where we bought the witch-ball yesterday, and found that it came from the sale at Beetles."

"Heavens! We're both inspired," said Margery. "Quite right. But how did you think of that?"

"Well, you mentioned an auction."

"Very brilliant," she said. "And now, as I know you hate talking at breakfast, I shall go away and look at my witch-ball. Isn't it odd that I said I should be so happy living at Beetles with it, and that now I find that it came from there?"

Though I was late this morning, Hugh was later, and it was not for some minutes after Margery had gone that he appeared. He helped himself to food, and propped up a daily paper in front of his place, but after staring at it in silence, whisked it away again.

"There are odd things happening," he said. "Something, or some-body, came out of the witch-ball last night—at least that's how I felt it—and stood at the open door of the bookroom. I saw nothing any more than you did, but it was there. And it's been here ever since; it was moving about the house all last night, and it wants something of us."

"I felt it was here, too," I said.

"Well, we've got to give it a chance," he said. "We must sit again, and now that it has established some sort of communication it will probably manifest itself more clearly. I believe that the figure we first saw lying underneath the trees is what is wanting us. So we must sit again, and there's no use in waiting till the evening. Let's have a gaze at the ball this morning when Margery's occupied else-where. I fancy there's something horrible behind it all, and I don't want her to know about it."

That was easily arranged, for Margery soon announced her intention of sketching in one of the old streets of the town, and as soon as she had gone, we went into the bookroom again. There on a table near the door into the garden stood the witch-ball, a huge blazing sapphire, and once more we prepared to gaze. There were disturbing cross-lights, and we drew the curtains over all the windows, so that the illumination came only from the open garden-door. . . . But though it was daylight now we had hardly begun to concentrate when the color faded from the ball, and presently I was gazing into thick clear darkness, depth upon depth, in which, as last night, there seethed the luminous bubbles, and there emerged again the house we had seen, and the kitchen garden, and the row of willows. But now there was no figure of a woman lying there beneath them, and I wondered where she had gone. I told Hugh what I was seeing, and he nodded without speaking. . . .

And then with some cold shuddering and sinking of the spirit, I knew that there was someone else here besides us, and a dimming of the light which came in from the garden-door made me look up. Just outside, in the hot bright sunshine there stood the figure of a woman. She was dressed in some sort of cloak, mold-stained and rent and decaying, and snails and fibers of root clung to it. One hand was wrapped in it, holding it to her, but the other with the arm up to the elbow was visible: here and there the bone showed; here and there lumps of rotting flesh dangled from it. Above, thick rusty-colored hair drooped on each side of what had been a face. But now the flesh had fallen away from the mouth, exposing the rows of discolored teeth; the nose was an earth-stained stump of cartilage; and the eye-sockets were empty. The decay and horror of it all were vividly illuminated by the sunlight.

Something froze within me: I could only look. And then the specter advanced to the open door as if it was about to step into the room. At that my panic-stricken nerves broke through their paralysis of terror, and I screamed out. . . . And, behold, there was nothing there but the wash of hot summer sun over the garden, and the breeze that stirred in the myrtle-bush by the door.

Now the inspector of police at Tillingham is a friend of mine, and ten minutes later Hugh and I were closeted with him.

"Not burglary or anything of that sort, I hope," he said genially, as we sat down.

"No, nothing of the kind," I said. "But there were just a couple of questions my friend and I wanted to ask you. I fancy that about two years ago Mrs. Woolaby disappeared from her husband's house down in the marsh."

"That's correct," he said. "And her husband continued living there till the spring of this year, when he had an auction of his furniture, and put the house up for sale."

"And has anything ever been heard of Mrs. Woolaby?" I asked.

"Never a word: not a trace has been seen of her since she disappeared. Most mysterious thing. Has either of you gentlemen got anything to tell me about her?"

"Was search made for her in the neighborhood of the house?" asked Hugh.

"Certainly, sir. The dikes were dragged in case she had fallen into one, for there was foggy weather, and if she had lost her memory and gone wandering, she might have slipped in and been drowned. But there wasn't much else to search, for it's a bare bit of land, with no woods anywhere near."

"We were there yesterday," I said. "There's a kitchen garden adjoining the house and on one side of it a row of young willows, planted evidently not very long ago. My friend and I both believe that if you dig under them at the end which adjoins the tool-house, you may learn something about Mrs. Woolaby's disappearance."

The inspector stared at us a moment in silence.

"Can you give me any reason for your believing that?" he asked.

"Nothing that would carry any weight with you," said Hugh. "But we're both fearfully serious about it. You hardly imagine, I suppose, that we're trying a hoax on you."

He sat there a moment longer, looking from one to the other of us, and then got up.

"I should like to know more," he said, "but if you don't mean to tell me, there it is. I'm bound to look into any information given me. I expect what you gentlemen mean is that her body will be found there, though I can't tell why you think so. Below the willows along the kitchen garden, and at the end by the tool-shed, I think you said. I'll let you know at once if anything is discovered."

A few hours later I was called to the telephone. The inspector wished to tell me that the body of a woman had been found at the place indicated. A couple of days later an inquest was held, and her identity established.

For several days, and more than once a day, Hugh and I gazed into the witch-ball. But never again did we see that black boiling-up of something within it, which presently disclosed the row of willows and what had lain beneath, nor did any apparition again manifest itself. It had been used, I think we must suppose, by some occult and mysterious agency to perform a certain office, and had now given forth the perilous stuff with which it was charged. It hangs still, a blue and radiant splendor, in Margery's sitting-room, and sometimes she almost makes up her mind to give it me, but has never yet quite scaled those heights of altruism. The sequel of the discovery of the body of Mrs. Woolaby I need not recount, for I am sure it is familiar to all those who take an interest in murder trials.